CRISSY'S FAMILY

CRISSY'S FAMILY

Malcolm Ross

PIATKUS

Copyright © 1995 Malcolm Ross-Macdonald

First published in Great Britain in 1995 by
Judy Piatkus (Publishers) Ltd of
5 Windmill Street, London W1P 1HF

The moral right of the author has been asserted

*A catalogue record for this book is available
from the British Library*

ISBN 0 – 7499 – 0303-1

Typeset by the author using Spellbinder™ DTP
Glyphix™ Times fonts and a
Hewlett-Packard™ Laserjet 4Mplus printer

Printed and bound in Great Britain by
Mackays of Chatham PLC, Chatham, Kent

for

Brian and Elyse Thompson

Ζεῖ χύτρα, ξῆ φιλία.

Part One

Camborne

The World all in Pieces

When a mother dies she takes the heart out of the family and carries it with her into her grave. Even as I watched my mother's box (it was too mean to dignify with the name of coffin) being lowered into her grave on that chill March afternoon in Helston churchyard, I knew our family had died with her. My father, whose drunkenness had done so much to hasten her end, could not even stay sober for that most solemn sabbath in our family's life. As the gravediggers lowered the box into its final place of rest, he fell over, knocking poor little Teresa to the ground with him. It was her birthday, too, I remember. What a present for a little maid of five!

She began to cry at the pain from her crippled hip, caused by that same consumption which carried our mother off. My father, no doubt thinking in his fuddled way to lighten the situation, giggled and tried to tickle her to make her laugh. Meanwhile the curate and the gravediggers looked on in disgust and we six children stared at the two of them, sprawled in the snow, and burned with our shame.

Marian picked up Teresa and hugged her tight. I reached out and stroked her curls with the backs of my fingers. Our father stayed where he was, coughing and panting heavily. No one cared to help him and he fell asleep before the burial was over. We stood around the grave — Marian, still holding Teresa, me, Gerald, Tom, and Arthur — and watched while they filled in the hole, all the way to the top. We could not think what else to do. When they finished, each man gave the mound of soil a little pat with his shovel, as if for comfort, and one of them said to us, "That's over and done with now."

We looked forlornly at each other and then at our snoring father. I took a few reluctant paces toward him, intending to shake him back to life, but Marian said, quite sharply, "No!" Just that. She didn't say to leave him to sleep it off ... or some such explanation to soften that one harsh word. Just *No!* And she is usually the gayest and most light-hearted maid.

We left him there and never saw him alive again.

I felt someone should say something personal about our mother. The curate had been engaged by the Poor Law Infirmary where she had died. He hadn't known her personally, so his words, though adequate, had been rather general. I said, "She was one of the noblest of women, but only we are left to remember her. We must try not to forget what a wonderful mother she was to us, not ever." Then a lump filled my throat and I could not continue.

Tom giggled and then looked away because his eyes, too, had filled with tears. Gerald and Arthur just stared at the mound and nodded. Marian hefted Teresa onto her other hip and said, "I suppose I shall have to carry you, little pig." We were all taking care to speak very properly, out of deference to our mother, who was 'high-quarter' by birth and hated to hear us speak in slovenly dialect.

We had no money for the bus back to Porthleven so we set out to walk the two-and-a-bit miles home. Teresa's hip hurt her sorely and she was very fretful, even though Marian was carrying her. Half-way up the hill I saw my sister was exhausted, so I took the child piggyback until she said it gave her 'wonders in her legs' — that is, pins-and-needles. Then Mr Chigwidden of Sunset Farm came past with an empty wagon (it being Sunday) and took pity on us for once, and so we got a good ride almost all the way home. We were scrupulous to thank him, especially after what Gerald and Arthur had done to his haymowie.

Our little cottage was perched upon the cliff top in the part of Porthleven called Gravesend, just below Sunset Farm. As we set off down the last bit of the lane I turned round to see why Chigwidden wasn't moving, for I could not hear his cartwheels. He was just sitting there, staring after us with the saddest expression. I've often wondered since if he was thinking of adopting us, for he and his wife were not blessed with children — and what a different tale I'd have to tell if he'd done so. There is no legal adoption in England, of course. We aren't like the French, who want the law to control everything. But plenty of it goes on with the blessing of the Poor Law guardians, and to the torment of any private citizen who tries to oppose them.

Seeing Chigwidden sitting there, looking so sad, rekindled a feeling I'd had in the churchyard — that we were doomed as a family. Because of our mother's illness the Poor Law Guardians were now aware of us. There was a shiver in my backbone as I trotted to catch up with my brothers and sisters. It was as if I could feel those invisible forces of institutional charity gathering in our wake and preparing to visit us with their cold good intentions. Something told me these were our last days together and I must cherish and treasure each moment.

That night, when I should have prayed for the repose of our dear mother's soul, I could think of no other blessing to ask of Almighty God than to let the six of us go on living together somehow. Surely nothing could have given her soul greater repose than that? And it should have been possible. We worked it out that evening after the younger ones had gone to bed, Marian, me, and Tom, though he was little help. Men may end up wiser than women (though even that I doubt) but at twelve they are no match.

Marian was seventeen — would turn eighteen in September. I had just turned sixteen, though I looked almost as old as Marian. And Tom would be thirteen in August. He could leave school now if he liked — in fact, whether he liked it or not, he'd have to. Our mother had given us a far better education than most other poor children could hope for. We were well-spoken. We wrote with passable hands, spelled correctly, could keep simple accounts. Marian and I could sew neatly. We knew the ways of high-quarter folk even if we had not the means to follow them in our own lives. And we were scrupulous in person and clothing. All in all, then, we decided, we three older ones should be able to find work enough to bring in a pound a week between us. If we ate one meal a day at our place of employment, we should be able to get by. And if we took home some kind of outwork — needlework, copying, writing envelopes, bunching flowers for market, and so on — we should be able also to cope with the disasters of life, too, like children growing out of their clothes, and boots whose uppers and soles part company after only a couple of dozen patchings.

Not one of us even mentioned our father — as if the simple act of speaking his name would conjure him up. He was a blight on our life. We, the three eldest, were the breadwinners now.

I was teaching at the Dame school then for five shillings a week, so I'd have to seek better wages than that — or five shillings plus board and lodging. Marian had helped our mother with the washing she took in, but, without her, that would not pay. So none of us had been in really worthwhile employment before.

We therefore determined that I should try my luck in Helston while Marian and Tom took turns to go into Porthleven — so there'd always be one of them at home with the children. They thought me very noble, volunteering to do that long walk up and down two steep hills, especially as I'd have to do it twice every day if I gained a place in the town. I said nothing as to my real purpose, which was to visit our mother's grave and tell her of our decision. The curate had said she was beyond pain but I didn't think that meant the same as beyond caring.

The snow had melted overnight but the damp wind made that Monday morning seem even colder and I was thankful for our stout Cornish 'hedges,' which are, in fact stone walls, mortared with earth and greenery. I shivered as I entered the churchyard — a premonition, though I thought it was just the chill. So the sight of our father's body, lying where he had fallen in his stupor yesterday, hardly surprised me. If it stirred any feelings within me, I no longer recall them. I think I must have been numbed beyond grief by then, for I did not go to him at all. I knelt at the graveside and prayed, and spoke to my mother, as if he were not lying there, a mere dozen paces away. She must know he was there, anyway. She knew everything now.

As I rose to leave — intending to start my search at the domestics' agency in Meneage Street — I heard her voice say quite distinctly inside my head: "Go to your grandparents, Cristobel." She never called me Crissy, like everyone else. "Mister and Mrs William Trevarton, Fenton Lodge, Swanpool, Falmouth." That proves it was my mother speaking, because, although I knew her parents lived in Falmouth, I had no idea of their exact directions. Clever people scoff at me for believing this. They tell me I must have heard it at some time and forgotten it. I don't argue. People are free to believe what they want, and I believe I heard my mother's voice telling me to call on her parents somewhere. It wasn't anything spooky, like her voice coming from a great cavern or anything like that. It was just her ordinary, everyday voice talking in normal, measured tones and inside my head, as I said. I found it very comforting and my spirit was uplifted — except that Falmouth was about fifteen miles away and I had no money for the bus fare.

I was leaving by the churchyard gate when I remembered my father's body still lying there. I recall it with shame — except that it is a measure of the poverty and desperation into which his drunkenness and indolence had plunged us — but my only thought then was to return and go through his pockets for any money he might have left over from his last binge. I did so, and found three shillings, which fed us well that evening. But I should have done better to find a shovel somewhere and open my mother's grave and put him into it, too. For it was the discovery of his corpse that led to all our troubles. Indeed, if we had been more worldly-wise, we should have dragged him home with us the previous day and kept him alive by whatever means. For while a father lived, no matter how drunken or wretched, the Guardians would leave his family alone. And our little family was all we had left in the world that was good.

I returned home to find Marian in a strange sort of mood. I asked her if she'd had any luck, as I hadn't. Even then she didn't ask where I'd got the three shillings. She said she'd tell me all about it after we'd got the young ones to bed. Tom had found evening work as pot boy at the Harbour Hôtel, where they would also feed him. Really, for the three of us to get given one good meal a day each was worth seven shillings a week, so it was a fine start. Anyway, it meant he was out of the house till midnight.

When the three young ones were asleep Marian and I stepped out and walked up and down between the cottage and the cliff edge, which was then a good dozen paces away but shrinking every year. Our mother had made our father build a bath house anenst the back wall, which gave our neighbours some amusement. But we'd always had a bath in our better days, when we had a house in St John's, in Helston. I recall once when we couldn't use *that* bath for six weeks and had to bathe in the Cober because the tub was full of wine from a wreck on Loe Bar. That was the start of our father's decline into a state of almost permanent inebriation. Anyway, Marian and I walked up and down and talked. It was half-past seven and the sun was just setting, with a waning crescent moon on its heels. First I told my sister what I had done that afternoon in Helston — everything except about hearing our mother's voice and the idea of going to Falmouth. She'd only suspect me of fibbing about it, thinking it was really just my whim to visit our grandparents and I was trying to cloak it in our mother's moral authority. Also I was fearful she might scold me for neglecting our father's corpse but she passed no remark on that at all and was only interested in the money I had found on him.

There was always a fatalistic streak in Marian. If disaster was about to befall, she'd be as anxious as anyone else. Like the time Mrs Kernick's baby fell in the middle harbour and Marian ran along the sea wall screaming her head off. But when they brought the tiny body ashore, she was all calm and collected again. "Poor little mite!" was all she said. She could accept things calmly once Fate had struck. It did not do her much good but she was like a rock to the rest of us in those dark days.

On that particular evening she was in a strange in-between condition, anxious and fatalistic at once. She said she'd called on Harry Angell, our landlord, that afternoon. "I thought if he was worried about how the rent would be paid, he might help out with some employment — or know someone who'd give me a position."

"And?" I asked eagerly, thinking what a resourceful maid she was, for a thing like that would never occur to me — my instinct would have been to run at the very sight of a landlord.

"It's my own fault," she said ruefully. Or half-ruefully. Opposites always thrived in Marian's breast. She was rueful, but with a twinkle in her eye, too. "I didn't put it quite as clearly as I ought. I can see that now. I said something vague about working off the rent 'in kind' — meaning anything from scrubbing floors to writing up his ledgers for him, but I didn't put it like that. Or I didn't get time. Because as soon as I uttered those words — 'in kind' — I saw a certain glint in his eye and I knew *exactly* what *he* had in mind!"

And so did I. The children of the poor were not shielded from that side of life. Poverty may have gone hand in hand with ignorance, but not with *that* sort of ignorance.

"You didn't ... hit him?" I asked. It was what any heroine in *Peg's Weekly — Moral Reading for Servant Girls* would have done.

Marian just laughed. "No. That's the dreadful thing, Crissy. I didn't say anything — not yes, nor no, nor maybe. I just felt faint — no, not faint. Unreal. Everything swimming slightly, like just after you bump your head. And I walked away."

"You wouldn't, though — would you?"

Her big brown eyes were still full of amusement. "I don't know," she said guardedly. "It would solve a lot of problems for us."

"The Guardians would break up the family before you could draw so much as one breath."

She was crestfallen. I could see she hadn't considered that possibility. She'd pictured herself as some kind of heroine — though not the *Peg's Weekly* kind! — nobly sacrificing her honour and virtue for the sake of her family. *And* not having to work too hard, either. Face it — we've all thought of it, especially half-way through scrubbing an acre of quarry tiles with ice-cold water at six o'clock on a winter's morn. Who wouldn't think of lying in a nice warm bed, planning how to spend the money, while the man does what he has to.

I told her then of hearing our mother's voice, and about going to seek help from her parents in Falmouth. She didn't question my truthfulness or sanity or anything like that, bless her. She just said it was a desperate thing to contemplate and our mother must be at her wits' end to suggest it. We knew nothing of our grandparents beyond what she'd told us — except what the whole of Cornwall knew, anyway, for we all saw their carts and steam lorries passing by with the name TREVARTON'S MILLS in big green letters along their sides, and they also had bakeries in Penzance, Redruth, Falmouth, and Truro. You know those fairy stories in which children live outside some place surrounded by great high walls and they wonder about the unknown life going on inside that enclosure? But all they ever hear is second-hand accounts? Well, the name Trevarton on all those lorries and flour sacks and shops was like that for us — a conspicuous public barrier to an unimaginable way of life, which I heard at second-hand from our mother.

Sometimes she spoke of her upbringing with contempt, sometimes as of a dream from which she'd been rudely awakened. In my earliest memories, in the days when our father had started a good little carrying business, her tone had almost always been contemptuous, as if we Moores were the future and the Trevartons the past. But after he took to drink she became regretful and nostalgic. We used to love to huddle up in bed, with our knees to our chins for the warmth, and listen to her memories of the great balls and the grand garden parties she once had known. She made a merry mock of the rituals — like how the gentlemen would bring their hats and canes into the drawing room for an At Home if they did not intend to stay long, or the way ladies would turn down the corners of cards to include an unmarried daughter in a visit, or there was that deep, implacable division between the Mifs and the Mils (milk-in-first or milk-in-last!), which rent the whole of polite society into two warring camps. But for all her scornful tone, she nursed a nostalgia for those days until her dying breath.

Marian, who did most of the nursing through her final illness, had written a letter to Mr and Mrs Trevarton, begging them to come and visit her before it was too late, but they sent it back marked *Not accepted.* So she had better reason than most for her pessimism as to the reception I should receive at Fenton Lodge, grandparents or no.

However, she agreed I should try. Perhaps, now that our mother was liberated in time and space, she might work some invisible mellowing in those steely hearts. Marian also suggested that I should use some of the money I found on our father for the bus to Falmouth, for it would be a goodly walk each way, even if I took the byroads through Treloquithick and Treverva.

Dan Nicholls had a bus leaving Helston for Falmouth at eight each morning, so I was up well before dawn to dress in my Sunday best — which, of course, was my only best — and to shine up my best boots. Though my dress was black, I also wore the black crape armband our mother had worn when each of her younger sisters had died. I ate a bread-and-dripping breakfast on the road, drinking water from the brook at the bottom of Penrose Hill, at Lower Lanner. I arrived with so much time in hand that I went on to the churchyard to visit our mother and tell her of Tom's bit of luck at the hôtel. Also in some trepidation that *he* might still be lying there cold. But someone had obviously found him and carried him to the mortuary. So, I reckoned, PC Hoad would probably be calling on Marian sometime that day. The greatest surprise was to find fresh flowers on the grave — and not just celandines and things you might find in the hedges, which any of her friends could have picked and laid there — these were big, pink carnations, such as would only grow in a hothouse at that time of year. I broke one off and trimmed my bonnet with it as a sort of talisman — a bit of our mother to go with me into the lion's den.

As I went back up Church Street to catch the Nicholls bus outside the Angel Hôtel, I fell to thinking that perhaps our mother had had a secret admirer somewhere in Helston, a man of wealth with a hothouse full of flowers. This implausible but pleasant reverie was interrupted by a cry of, "Young maid!" from a little way down the hill behind me, just before the Methodist Chapel.

I turned and saw a heavy-laden steam lorry grinding its way up the hill toward me, with the driver leaning out of his window. "Can I get onto the Falmouth road that way?" he asked urgently, pointing to the lane just uphill from the chapel.

Taking a chance I skipped back down the road and leaped onto the running board. "I'll guide you," I said, as if it were a bit of a maze ahead.

In fact, it was one sharp-left turn — the one he'd pointed at — then straight up the hill, with a quick right and left at the top. But by then I had cajoled him into carrying me all the way to Penryn, just three miles short of Swanpool — or even less if I could tramp along the railway line without being stopped. The driver, a man from Hayle called Bert Eddy, was in his forties, married and with four children. He took pity on me, though at the time I felt sure it was my smile and my sparkling eyes that persuaded him. That was the first time I remember consciously using my femininity to win a man over. I felt grand and grown-up as I settled in the seat beside him with my bus fare intact and the Falmouth road slipping effortlessly beneath us.

I did not realize how widely the scandal of our mother's elopement was known until I gave him my name and added — with an intriguing air of mystery, I hoped — that it was a fitting coincidence for me to be travelling to Falmouth in a Trevarton lorry.

"Oh, so you're one of *those* Moores," he replied at once. Then, seeing a new significance in my crape armband, his face fell and he asked hesitantly after my mother.

When I told him what had happened and what my intentions were that day, his attitude changed at once. Until then he had been slightly flirtatious — in the way that ancient, elderly men often are with little maids. (To me, at sixteen, forty was dotage, of course.) But now he turned solicitous, paternal.

Wise employees in family businesses paid close heed to their employers' characters, whims, histories, vagaries ... everything and anything that touched on the continued survival and prosperity of the firm. So the story of our mother's elopement with Barry Moore, the handsome coachman, in the April of 1872, was well known among all who worked for Trevarton's. Mr Eddy asked me what I knew of the family and was shocked to discover the extent of my ignorance.

It struck me then that his attempt to find a new short-cut through Helston on that particular morning had been no accident. Perhaps our mother's spirit, still hovering near, had played a part — sending him to me, both to afford me the ride and to tell me something of the Trevartons. Anyway, we passed most of the journey to Penryn with him talking about my grandparents and me listening — and thanking *whatever* power had directed our paths to this brief conjunction.

Mr Eddy had worked for Trevarton's for more than twenty years, so there was little he could not tell me. Of course, I already knew bits of it, in a disjointed fashion. I'd heard it in dribs and drabs, mostly as little asides in our mother's reminiscences. For instance, I knew she had a brother called Archie, but I had no idea what he did, what he looked like, nor even whether he was older or younger than her.

In fact, I now learned, he was older by just over twelve months. So he'd be thirty-seven this year. He was short, fat, already bald, and rather pompous, I gathered — though Mr Eddy did not say as much, not in so many words. He spoke with a nod and a wink, so you could understand things without the actual words.

My Uncle Archie was, naturally, being groomed to take over the business from his father, Bill Trevarton, who was now sixty. He, too, was portly and bald — but then at his age he had a right to it. The men had great respect for 'Old Mister Bill' but were full of doubts about his eldest son. He was married to a Welsh woman called Megan, the daughter of some big landowner up beyond Truro. "Up beyond Truro" was clearly beyond the rim of the known universe for Mr Eddy. There were four children — my cousins.

"Your mother, Selina, was next," he said. It was odd to hear her named so, just like any other person. "The apple of your father's eye, she were. He give I a cigar at her fifteenth birthday party, when I druv them all in one of the big wagons up Pendennis Castle to see the fireworks. Then come Catherine. Lovely maid, she was. She died falling off of her horse, they do say. Twenty year ago. Bit older'n you, she'd have been." He sucked a tooth at the sadness of it all.

"Then Chloë. She never lived more'n a fortnight — died of the purple fever, they said. And Mrs Trevarton, she near died of it, too. Then come Walter. He'd be what — thirty, now? Thereabouts, anyroad. He's a solicitor over Redruth — Trevarton and Jacko. He's married to his partner's sister — you've surely heard of him?"

I had, of course, but only as a boy, for he had been no more than twelve when my mother eloped. "There was also a boy called Mark, I think?" I said.

He chuckled. "He's what they do call a Johnny-come-late. He'd be your age now — seventeen, I reckon."

I was not surprised to be given an extra year. People are always doing it. "And there were other girls?" I asked.

"None reared," he replied gloomily. "There was Sarah. She was born dead backalong in 'sixty-three, poor wisht little cooze. But they got her baptized — and planted in hallowed ground — which you can do if your name's Trevarton, I s'pose."

"They had little luck with maids," I remarked. "Wasn't there one called Monica, too?" I remembered her because she had died after the elopement, when I was about a year old, and Marian and I were vying to recall our earliest memories once with our mother and she fished out the crape armband and asked if we could remember seeing her wear it. Marian could, of course, or claimed she could. I couldn't, being only a year old when Mother had worn that band, but that's how I came to know its history — and about Monica's death.

Mr Eddy nodded. "When she were ten. She catched the dip-theria. I carried her in her box. She never weighed no more'n a rasher of wind." He shook his head sadly. "Four little maids tooken from them by death — and the eldest carried off by the coachman!"

I darted a glance to see if he were joking. The seeming comparison between our father and Death, the universal leveller, was too huge not to be comical. He saw — and understood — my surprise, for he said, "To Old Mister Bill that one loss was as great as the other four. Your mother saw him grieve at the deaths of the other three and yet she ran off with that Barry Moore, knowing it was as good as another death — another daughter's death — to him."

"I suppose he never forgave her?" I surmised.

"He did," he assured me — and then repeated the words with a different emphasis: *"He* did. He's a forgiving sort of man. But not she. Forgive is one thing she never could."

"Our mother?"

"No. *Her* mother. Mrs Trevarton. She gave it out that the name of Selina was never again to be spoken in her presence. And it never has been, neither. If you'm seeking assistance from that quarter, maid, my advice is to steer well clear of your old grandmother."

I was so dismayed at this news I did not realize what he was really suggesting — or trying to prompt me into suggesting. I suppose that in his eyes I was already a Trevarton — to however small a degree — so he could not simply tell me what he thought I should do.

I can see it now. What I should have done is I should have gone to the Penryn depôt with him and bearded 'Old Mister Bill' in his den. Instead, being young and innocent, still, and trusting in the ties of blood and the innate decency of our family, I walked onward to Swanpool, there to throw myself on my grandmother's mercy.

Swanpool is a tear-shaped lake of fresh water densely fringed with reeds. A wide bar of sand — rather stony sand — separates it from the salt sea of Falmouth Bay. The bar is higher than the highest tide, which is just as well, since it also carries the road from Falmouth south toward the Helford River. The lake is over half a mile long and about a third as wide. Fenton Lodge stood on the western shore, where it bulges out into the lake. Thus it commanded a fine view of the water on three sides. Also, as you'd guess from the name (for *fenton* or *venton* means a spring in Cornish), a pretty little stream bubbled up in its garden, about half the way up the hillside, and ran down to a broad, marshy area on the shore.

Its only view of the sea was slantwise, down the lake and over the sand bar. The opposite shore was dominated by a tall headland, Swanpool Point, which was all part of Whitethorn Farm. The skyline of that headland was wooded, which is uncommon in Cornwall, where most hills are round and smooth and rolling.

There were two entrances. One was marked *Tradesmen Only* and the other *No Hawkers, Salesmen, or Circulars*. I don't know why this should have taken me by surprise, but it did. Many humbler dwellings also had 'trade' and 'respectable' entrances. I hesitated before them, knowing full well I ought to go in by the tradesmen's entrance, for what it really meant was *Persons of the Humble Classes*. But a stubborn sort of logic urged me to go in by the 'respectable' gate. After all, I was neither a hawker, nor a salesman, nor a circular. And so that is what I did.

My courage deserted me halfway up the path but it was too late to turn back. I could sense that someone in the house had already spotted me and that my every move was being studied. There was little in the garden to distract me. A few snowdrops, a pretty crop of daffodils and paper-whites, and the last show of winter jasmine, trailing over a pergola that spanned the path. The breeze rattled drily in a thicket of bamboos and sent a shiver of apprehension through me. I returned my gaze to the house and tried reminding myself that it was the home of my grandparents. But that was no more than a legal truth. Real grandparents are there to spoil the children, to hug them, and to say things like, 'Try to understand your mummy and daddy. Life isn't easy for them at the moment, either.' We never had real grandparents like that. The cold, hard granite façade of Fenton Lodge suggested the sort of welcome I might expect.

Nor was I misled. The door opened while the harsh jangle of the bell was still ringing through the house — so my approach had, indeed, been observed. A maidservant of about seventeen ran her eye swiftly from my boots to my bonnet, an appraisal that left me feeling naked and despicable. Then she settled a cold stare upon my face. "Yes?" she said sharply, realizing that no courtesy was due. She had a round face and piercing eyes. Her long, fair hair was tightly curled and plaited in two flat discs over her ears. I think I never felt uglier than at that moment.

My gloves were soiled from the lorry and my dress dusty from my walk. The maid's smart livery of dark green, with a starched white apron and cap, made me feel like a tramping maid.

"If you please," I stammered in a trembly, fluttering voice I hardly recognized, "may I ... that is, I have a message for Mrs Trevarton."

"You may give it to me," she responded curtly, holding out her hand.

I tried to swallow the lump in my throat but it would not budge. My words just squeezed out around it. "Not that sort of message. Something ... I've something to tell her."

"Concerning?"

"Death. A death. Someone she ... a death that touches her."

The maid showed the first signs of hesitation. She glanced at the carnation in my bonnet. If my sombre clothes were the weeds of mourning, the flower was a contradiction. She licked her lips and sort of half-looked behind her. When her eyes met mine again the hostility was gone. No warmth replaced it, just a kind of guarded sympathy. She lowered her voice and asked, "Is it about Miss Selina?"

I nodded and fought hard not to cry. "Could I have a drink of water, please?" I managed to say.

The maid gave the briefest smile and told me to go round to the back door. She'd meet me there.

The path led through a narrowing funnel between the house and banks of viburnum and Portugal laurel, evergreens designed to keep the world of the kitchen yard and stables ever-hidden from respectable people. The breeze whipped and howled in that dark strait. Like a cold hand it thrust me back there where I truly belonged — out of sight of respectable people. But there in the back yard the maid could at last dare to smile at me. "What's your name, young 'un?" she inquired as she handed me an enamel mug. "Are you the one they call Cristobel?"

She swam before me. I might have burst into floods of tears if I had not been so surprised to find the mug empty. She nudged me toward the pump in the middle of the yard, saying, "That's much better water than what's in the tank." She had a London accent, saying *van* for *than* and *whoss* for *what's*. "I'm Susan, by the way," she added.

She turned the pump wheel with strong, sinewy arms while I steadied my trembling hand and the mug against the spout. The water was crystal clear and icy. It turned me as cold inside as I was out but it steadied my nerve and I felt more ready to face her, and Mrs T, and the whole world, when I'd drained it to the last drop.

"More?" Susan asked, now in much gentler tones.

I smiled gratefully and shook my head.

Her expression became concerned. "You're not hoping for too much, are you, gel?" She tilted her head toward the house.

I shrugged. "Just some assistance to keep the family together. Why?"

"How many are you?"

"Six. But three of us ..."

"Lumme — six!"

"But three of us can work. We can *almost* get by without help."

She smiled at me as if she thought I was pulling her leg.

"Truly," I assured her.

"Troo-lee!" She parroted my 'posh' accent and giggled. "Is that the way you all speak? What a lark!"

Before she could explain herself we were interrupted by the screech of a sash window up on the first floor. The dark, open square framed a tall, angular woman with pinched features and a forbidding presence. "Callaghan!" she rapped out. "Who is that young person? And what are you doing out there when you're set to answer single knocks?"

"Coming, Mrs Bourdeaux." Susan sounded crestfallen and submissive, but she winked at me as she took back the mug and turned to the house.

She was gone so long I thought they must have forgotten me. I had no idea of the consternation, not to say panic, my unexpected arrival had caused in that most clockwork of households. At last Mrs Bourdeaux herself opened the back door and said, "Come on then!" quite sharply.

By that time I had endured so many imaginary terrors I had lost the capacity to be overwhelmed, so it was as well for me that Susan had intercepted me and brought me round the back. But as soon as we were indoors I got another fright when Mrs Bourdeaux turned on me, flourishing a brush. For a moment I thought she was going to bend me over and tan me with it, but instead she brushed my dress down with a vigour that hurt, especially my bosom, which was developing rapidly and so was particularly tender.

"Impertinence!" she murmured, but more to herself than me, so I felt unable to respond.

I tried smiling at her but she looked away and tutted impatiently. Then, grabbing me fiercely by the arm, she drew me up the passage, through the proverbial 'green baize door' — which was actually a rich mahogany — and across a marble-tiled hall to the drawing-room door. I had a fleeting impression, as we sped across that chilly space, of a house full of trophies. Not hunting trophies, though there were several of them, too, but trophies of innumerable shopping expeditions, foreign tours, and friendly mementoes.

The drawing room, whose door Mrs Bourdeaux pushed open without ceremony, was even more of a clutter, so much so that I did not immediately see Mrs Trevarton — my grandmother — sitting like a statue by the fireside. She was just another decorative object in a sea of pictures, feathers, fans, glass domes, wax fruit, china dogs, brass bric-a-brac, ivory screens, whatnots, rugs, cushions, drapes, antimacassars, tumpties ... to say nothing of palms, aspidistras, and spider plants.

"Well?" she snapped, forcing me to locate her at last. She was quite beautiful, especially for a woman in her late-fifties, though it was not the sort of beauty one warms to. I have never known another person, man or woman, with such a capacity for stillness. But it was not the repose of peace, it was the menacing silence that presages a storm. "Thank you, Mrs Bourdeaux," she added in a tone so neutral it was far more dismissive than if she had simply told her to get out.

When the housekeeper had closed the door behind her I said, "If it please you, Mrs Trevarton, I fear it is now my melancholy duty to convey to you ..."

"Duty?" she echoed quietly. "You have come here to tell me about duty, have you?"

"*My* duty," I said. I knew she'd expect me to call her 'ma'am' — which many a granddaughter would have done for a grandmother she loved. But my stubbornness prevented me.

"You have no duty in *this* house, let me assure you." Her words were made doubly menacing by the fact that she spoke them so quietly, so matter-of-factly. "What is that in your bonnet?"

I raised a hand and touched it. "A carnation, ma'am." The word slipped out and I regretted it. I think she saw my regret, too, for she gave a tiny smirk of triumph, as if I had conceded the first, minor point of a long contest.

"I realize it is a carnation," she said witheringly. "What I meant was — do you think it an altogether appropriate thing for a maid to wear when her mother is hardly cold in her grave?"

I wanted to say I thought it as appropriate as was a cream-coloured velvet dress, embroidered with parma violets, on a *mother* whose *daughter* was hardly cold in her grave. But I did not trust myself with so long a sentence, not in my fragile mood. Besides, it would not aid my purpose there. She saw my eyes rake over her dress, though, and she knew very well what I was thinking. We were, after all, grandmother and granddaughter, and I guess there was a kind of rapport between us that neither could suppress. Looking back on it now I even think it unnerved her a little to realize I was within an ace of giving back as good as I got — and that I'd have right on my side in such an exchange. But such thoughts were then beyond my inexperienced years. All I saw was that my own silence and my rather obvious glance at her dress had said all that I might have uttered with my tongue — and that she was not going to flare up at me for it. And that degree of rapport between us frightened me rather.

"Where did you get it?" she asked in a deceptively neutral tone. (I say 'neutral' because I did not then realize the significance of the origin of that bunch of carnations on our mother's grave. Mrs T did, though.)

"I see it is no news to you that your daughter — my mother — is dead, Mrs Trevarton," I responded.

She dipped her head in acknowledgement and then repeated her question: "Where did you get that carnation? You didn't pick it from the vase in the hall, I hope?"

I was no match for such cleverness — accusing me of petty theft just to make me answer. It stung me into telling her where I got it. A smile of grim satisfaction briefly stretched her prim little Cupid's-bow mouth, and I knew I had let something slip.

I remember thinking that if she played such a trick again I must try to smile as if *I* were the one who'd tricked *her* into believing something. It may seem an astonishing thought to have run through the mind of a sixteen-year-old maid. But it just shows what a fine teacher adversity can be — and how people who are ruthless with us can also sharpen our wits and make us more self-reliant. I think I learned more self-reliance in that brief interview with my grandmother than in any other half-hour in my entire life.

"If you merely came to inform us of your mother's death," she pointed out, "you now understand that your journey was wasted. And if you had any further purpose with us, I'm afraid you will make the identical discovery about that, too."

"May I sit down, please?" I asked. "It has been a long, tiring walk."

"No," she said. "You may go out to the kitchen, where Mrs Gordon will give you a cut of cold pie ... and she'll wrap up some cake for your journey home. We have no further business, you and I."

I should have heeded that cold light in her eye. I should have realized what an adamantine will was there, and what an implacable hostility she felt for our mother — even for her memory. Perhaps I did. Perhaps I saw I had absolutely nothing to hope for from this woman, my grandmother. I stood my ground and said, "She was your daughter, Mrs Trevarton. We are of your blood."

"*Our* blood?" Her tone was amused. She would not even pay me the compliment of outrage. "She *was* our daughter, once upon a time — until the April of 'seventy-two. Not a day longer. *Your* blood is that of a drunken ne'er-do-well called Barry Moore. Seek help from him, not us." Under her breath, but intended for my hearing, she added, "Much good may it do you!"

So news of his death had yet to reach this house. "We cannot," I said. "He is also dead."

It shook her. She had clearly been relishing the thought that the 'drunken ne'er-do-well' who had stolen away her daughter would now have six hungry mouths to feed, all on his own — and serve him right! "How?" she asked, then, realizing she did not know how thin the ice might be beneath her feet, she immediately added, "Never mind. It's of no significance how he met his end. It changes nothing. You are orphans and that's that. You may not now look to us for assistance. Your mother — our *former* daughter — carried you beyond our ken eighteen years ago. There is no way of putting the clock back."

Knowing I had nothing to lose, I spoke as if her words had simply glanced off me. I wanted her to hear the names of these she dismissed as 'orphans' — or hear them again, for the fact that Susan had asked me if I were Cristobel, proved we were known, if rarely talked about, in this house. "Marian and Tom and I can find work, you see. Between us, we can earn a pound a week, perhaps a little more. We can keep Gerald and Arthur and little Teresa — and ourselves, too — on those earnings. Gerald is nine and can mind them at home — and tend the vegetables, for we have three roods of garden and the potatoes don't mind the salt spray off the sea."

She held up a hand to ward off my words, but she said nothing. I realized that my picture of our simple life held some odd kind of fascination for her. So then I got in my main point: "All we need is to be sure of the rent, d'you see? Five pounds would settle Harry Angell and secure us there for the year. We'd not need to trouble you further, Mrs Trevarton."

She was tempted. But pride got the better of her. She must have said too many bitter things to too many close friends to take back her words now. Also, from what I later came to know of this woman, I realize she was a quick thinker — one of the quickest I ever met — and my picture of our little family, living on in Porthleven, was enough to disturb her. Perhaps she sensed that, together, we possessed a strength we could never have as individuals.

Or was it something much simpler and more commonplace than that? Something very English middle-class? When Mrs Bourdeaux had come to tell her of my sudden arrival at the back door, my grandmother probably expected a dialect-speaking ragamuffin. To find my speech as genteel as hers must have been unsettling. She would then have realized she could not simply fob me off and turn me away.

Whatever the reason, and whatever she had planned for me in the few minutes between Mrs Bourdeaux's announcement and my appearance in that drawing room, she brushed it all aside and made a new plan on the spot. She did not tell me of it but I could see the calculations going on and I knew when they had arrived at a happy conclusion.

Happy for her, that is.

Mrs Gordon, a short, stout, loud-voiced woman, gave me the promised slice of cold pie — and a very generous cut it was, too — laced with pickles and cold potato. She also wrapped a big slice of fruit cake for me to carry home. She, too, did not know what to make of me. I was dressed like a ragamuffin in fifth-hand clothes cut down from a much larger original. But I spoke like the sort of lady to whom she would naturally defer. So she blustered politely and ordered me about with the odd jocular diffidence nannies use on children who have almost outgrown them.

I did not see Susan again that afternoon.

Mrs Bourdeaux, the housekeeper, was not nearly so pleasant to me. Besides, I had seen her mildly humiliated by the mistress of the house so I had to be put firmly in my place. She escorted me to the back door, as if she thought I might steal something if let go on my own, and she told me to be sure to leave the premises by the tradesmen's entrance. Thank heavens I obeyed, for otherwise I should have missed an encounter even more important (and fateful) than the one just past.

He turned his gig into the tradesmen's drive, which was also the drive to the stable yard, only moments after I had started along it from the other end. I soon realized it could only be my grandfather — not just from his generally proprietorial bearing but from the carnation he wore in his buttonhole. His coat was trimmed with a broad astrakhan collar against which it showed up particularly well. Almost in that same instant I realized why Mrs Trevarton had shown such interest in the flower in my bonnet. Carnations in the hall, a carnation in his buttonhole, a fresh bunch of carnations on our mother's grave — it did not take a Sherlock Holmes to put them all together and understand why she had given that grim little smile.

He had the advantage of me, as his opening words revealed. "I'm not too late!" he called out as soon as he was within hailing distance. "I set off as soon as Bert Eddy told me." When he, or the horse, rather, reached me he reined to a halt and, smiling broadly, said, "Take his head, maid, and turn him back up the way I came."

It was a big horse, made more for riding than drawing a gig, but I grasped both reins and turned him almost in his own length. "Well done," my grandfather said, slipping across to one side of the driver's bench. "Now jump up here beside me." I did as he bade, carefully placing the bag of cake underneath the seat for fear of crushing it.

"Ah," he said, arranging his rug around my knees, too. "You weren't sent away completely empty-handed, then." He looked me up and down admiringly, undoing all the hurt Susan's first survey of me had caused, and said, "Cristobel, eh! I'd know you by your smile, if nothing else." He looked as if he were about to say more, but then thought better of it. "Well, well, well!" was all he added. "Let's go for a little drive, eh? D'you know Falmouth at all?"

I told him my mother had brought Marian and me here once — not to Swanpool but down to the Moor (which, despite the name, is actually the centre of the town) to buy us new dresses. The only bran-new clothes we'd ever had.

"And did she show you Fenton Lodge then?" he asked.

I shook my head. "She said what's past is past."

We turned toward Swanpool Beach. "But it's not, is it?" he replied sadly. "It's ever present. And it's caught up with all of us this last week."

I thought it an odd remark.

He saw my bewilderment and went on, "I had intended calling on your mother this week. Whether or not I'd actually have done so is another matter. I've intended it many times in the past and never managed it. But, or so I now assure myself, I think I really might have done so this time."

He stared at me closely, to see if I were about to cry. I realized he wanted me to cry. He did not want everything between us to be mere words. He wanted something richer. I did not then know what a lonely and bitter man he was. All I knew was that he wanted me to cry — and it was not very difficult to oblige.

The actual moment that prompted my tears may have been a little contrived — that is, I did it to oblige him because he smiled and was kind and said things that spoke directly to my heart without much need to think about them. But the moment the floods started, the artificiality was gone. I wept as I had not wept before, not even when Marian brought the dreadful news from the infirmary and Teresa and Arthur clung to me like limpets, howling their hearts out. Not even then.

My grandfather dropped the reins and the horse halted at once — in the middle of the road over the sand bar. Then he half turned, put his arms about me, and hugged me to him. A moment later I became aware that he, too, was crying. He kept saying, "My dear child … my dear little Crissy!" and the words kept jolting to his sobs. What a picture we must have made, if there had been anyone there to see us! Actually, I've often wondered if Mrs Trevarton wasn't watching us through binoculars; I cannot believe that his loud arrival, and equally loud about-turn, had gone entirely unnoticed from *that* house of eyes and ears!

Anyway, such thoughts were far from us as we wallowed in (I would not go so far as to say luxuriated in) our common misery. It did us both a lot of good, him especially, for he turned almost jovial after we had dabbed our eyes and sniffed back nostrils filled with salt. "I should be used to it by now," he remarked ruefully. "You know, I suppose, that all your mother's sisters are dead, too? She was the last survivor."

Remembering Bert Eddy's words I said, "Aunt Catherine, Aunt Chloë, Aunt Sarah, and Aunt Monica."

"Bless my soul!" he murmured softly and stared at me in admiration.

I felt like the most awful hypocrite, for until that day I would have had difficulty recalling any of their names.

"Well!" he clucked the horse to a brisk trot. "I suppose you had a word with Mrs Trevarton? Or she had a word with you, more likely!"

"She didn't know our father had died, too," I told him — I don't know why. Perhaps because it was the one bit of news that had surprised her and I didn't want her to use it in some way to surprise him in his turn.

I certainly wasn't trying to test him, though, from the sly look he gave me, I could see he thought I was. *"I'm* the one who found him there," he said. "I told the police."

I nodded. "Mrs Trevarton noticed my carnation," I went on. My tone alerted him to the fact that there was more to it than that. I continued: "She asked me if I picked it out of the vase in the hall."

He chuckled, though with little mirth. "And so you told her."

"I'm sorry, Mister Trevarton ..."

"Grandad, please!"

I took his arm. "Sorry, Grandad, I should've thought before I spoke."

"I'd have been horrified if you'd done so. A young lady your age who could harbour such suspicions — fully justified though they might be — would be some kind of monster, I believe."

If he'd been a little less protective of my innocence, I should have been spared much heartache in the months that followed.

We were bowling along the foot of Swanpool Hill now. We could hardly see the lake because of the tall reeds but we were in view of the house all the way to where the road winds up to Whitethorn Farm.

"What brought you here today, may I ask?" he went on.

"Your lorry," I answered in surprise.

He chuckled. "No — I mean what impulse? What was your purpose? To tell us the bad news?"

I nodded. "How did you know about it, anyway? You must have put the flowers on her grave yesterday afternoon."

"The whole of Cornwall is one big parish, really," he answered. "West of Truro, anyway. And we have lorries going here, there, and everywhere. Tell me all about yourself — and your brothers and sisters. We have so much to catch up on! Let me see if I can do as well as you. There's Marian — the oldest — am I right? She'd be, what? Seventeen?"

"Going on eighteen."

"Ah. Then you — going on seventeen? Then Tom ... twelve?"

I simply nodded at each correct guess, if that is what they were.

"Then Gerald, who's nine, and Arthur — seven or eight?"

"Soon be eight."

"And finally but not forlornly, as my father used to say, Teresa — four or five?"

"Five."

"Not bad, eh?" he commented.

I felt worse than ever about my own false pretences, and because of that I was probably too effusive in describing his unknown grandchildren to him, presenting them rather obviously in the best light. He was, after all, a businessman and used to flannel and soft soap from people who wanted things from him. Still, he put up in his good-humoured way with my sentimentally rosy picture of our simple life in a clifftop cottage just outside Porthleven.

"Well," he said when I'd finished, "you may tell me about the warts another time."

I did not know then about Oliver Cromwell telling some artist to paint him 'warts and all.' I was just amazed he seemed to know so much about us, for both Arthur and I had recently had our warts charmed away by Mrs Bennett in Helston. Half the potato she had used was still sewn into the hem of my everyday dress at home!

"What I wanted to ask," I said anxiously, "was whether you could possibly assist us in staying together, as a family, I mean, by contributing toward the rent of our cottage?" I was so eager for him to understand our plight and say yes of course he would that I repeated everything I'd said to his wife about how Marian, Tom, and I could earn enough to keep ourselves and the other three — but what a great weight it would be off our minds if we knew we had the cottage secure for a year ahead.

"Is that all?" he asked when I had finished.

I could see — and hear — my mother in him when he said those words, except that she used to say them sarcastically, more often than not. "Oh, is that *all* you want, young lady!" ... and so on. I thought he, too, was being sarcastic, so I said, "Half would do — fifty shillings a year. I know it's a lot to ask but ..."

"Oh child!" His eyes were filled with tears again and he flung his arms around me and hugged me even tighter than before.

There were few about on the streets in that cold wind, but I saw two servant girls nudge each other and point to us, so I knew the tale would soon start coursing through the town, especially about a man of my grandfather's prominence. Even if the girls themselves didn't know me from Eve, someone would soon twig what must have happened.

I don't suppose I went on to think it consciously but somewhere lurking in the background must have been the realization that my grandmother wouldn't tolerate such goings-on. But — not knowing the woman then — I had no idea of the desperate lengths to which she'd go in order to prevent them.

I think it was the happiest day of my life up until then, or one of them. My dear grandfather approved of my plan to secure the cottage for a year in advance. He hinted strongly that he had his own plans to look after us in the months to come but that he would have to 'win others around' to his point of view. No names were mentioned, but I had no doubt as to whom he meant. By way of a beginning, he sent me home that evening with a five-pound note, which, innocent that I was, I took directly to Harry Angell, handing it over with a triumphant flourish.

His eyes almost popped out of his head, but Reenie, his wife, was all suspicion. "Where did 'ee come by all that money?" she asked sharply.

My grandfather had made me promise to say nothing about his gift for the moment. Of course, I realize now that he probably didn't mean I was to say nothing to our landlord — just not to blurt it out all over the town. If he'd worked it out, he'd have realized what suspicions would start flying if I suddenly turned up with more money than I'd ever had in my life before. But I took my promise both literally and seriously and just said it had been given to me.

"A likely story!" she said and, snatching the note from her husband's hand, stuffed it down her bosom. "Us'll take this to PC Hoad, maid. Leave he look into it."

"But it's the rent," I protested, tears springing in my eyes. "A year in advance. You must take it — please! That's what it's for."

"Not lest we know where you got it from."

Angell chimed in: "Tell us who you got it off of."

I mastered my weeping fit before it got truly started, but only by fanning my anger. "You've no right to keep that money if you're not going to accept it as rent. If you call in the constable, I shall prove I came by it lawfully and honourably." I added that about 'honourably' because I knew very well what was going through Harry Angell's mind, what with his improper advances to Marian still so fresh in my memory. "Then I shall tell him you took it from me."

He held up a finger and chuckled harshly. "We never took nothing, maid. You handed it over, didn't she, missiz?" He turned to his wife. "You seen 'er, didn't 'ee — as you'm my witness." He chuckled at what he imagined was his supreme cunning.

"I handed it over as rent-in-advance," I reminded them. "If you accept it as rent, that's a different matter. But if you just take it and keep it, that's plain stealing."

He licked his lips nervously and looked at her. Really, he was keen to get his hands on that much money. He wouldn't have cared if I *had* stolen it. Also, I could tell by the glint in his eye that he was sure I'd earned it in the only way a dirty-minded man like him could think of, and he was eager to get me on my own and make a proposal along those same lines.

She hesitated, too, because she saw the force of my argument. "If we give her the note back," she objected, "and then tell PC Hoad, she'll deny she ever had it."

"No I shan't," I said.

"You will," she responded stoutly.

I was so angry by then that I just flounced out of the house, shouting over my shoulder that I'd go and fetch PC Hoad myself and we'd sort it out here and now.

It was almost half a mile to the constable's place, which gave me time to cool down and think.

Porthleven harbour is set in a natural inlet, or cove, almost half a mile deep and curved like a crescent moon, with the bulge facing east. In fact, it is three harbours, all built out of huge blocks of ochre-coloured granite. The innermost one is the largest, being several hundred yards broad and long. At low tide it is almost all mud, and in stormy weather, when a south cone is hoisted on the flagpole by the Porthleven Institute, they lower huge, square-cut timber logs — called the 'bock' — across the narrow mouth, so keeping the fury of the storm at bay from the inner harbour. The middle harbour is always navigable, so the fishermen may land their catches on its quays at any state of the tide. The outer harbour is just the mouth of the cove, protected by a granite jetty, about a furlong in length.

The Angells lived at the end of a terrace overlooking the stub of a breakwater that marked the division between the middle and outer harbours. It was close on eight in the evening by the time I stormed out in search of the constable. The sun had set more than an hour earlier and the harbour was visible only by a higgledy-piggledy of oil lamps, some on the quays, others on the fishing boats — on mastheads, in wheelhouses, and on deck. The tide was in, the bock was lifted, and they were preparing for a night's trawling. One of the clifftop lookouts must have spotted good shoals of mackerel or herring, for almost every vessel in the village fleet was being readied and one or two were already under sail.

What a curious world those tiny pools of light revealed. In one I could see a lobster pot — I could even count the ribs — though a foot or so beyond it the darkness was total. Another, in a wheelhouse, gleamed on a gaudy biscuit tin — a midnight feast for some frozen skipper. Another showed an apparently disembodied head and hands climbing aboard — the navy-blue trousers, pullover, and jacket being as dark as the surrounding night. The waters of the harbour seemed to be alive with dozens of squiggly glow-worms, reflections of the lamps in its choppy surface. The fishermen got about the harbour in little rowboats, though they did not actually row them. Instead, they put a single oar into a notch in the stern and they sculled it from side to side, which both impelled them forward and let them steer among the hulls and anchor lines with amazing dexterity. Even in the dark they found their way unerringly through the labyrinth. The broken water behind these little boats was a living kaleidoscope of fractured light. And then came the smell of hot lamp oil — and tar, salt, and fish — wafted toward me on the breeze. It was all so heady and exciting, and I wanted to live in Porthleven with my brothers and sisters for ever and ever. It was *our* place and there was nowhere else like it in all the world.

My anger had turned quite cold, not dead but cold, by the time I reached the Hoads' house, which overlooked the farther corner of the inner harbour. I knew the constable would be every bit as suspicious as the Angells had been about the source of my windfall wealth, and I worked out a way to set his mind at rest without actually breaking my word to my grandfather.

Mrs Hoad answered my knock and said her husband was busy filling in the boar register, so she hoped I could come back another time. Two or three farmers in the district kept boars and were supposed to let him know whose sows they had served and when. Of course, they were always hopelessly behind, which put Hoad into arrears, too. She said he wasn't in a very good humour.

I told her I wanted to report that Harry Angell and his wife had taken five pounds off me and wouldn't accept it as rent and wouldn't give it back — and I hoped that was important enough for him to leave his boar register for half an hour.

"Are you reporting this as a theft?" she asked.

Had my anger still been hot, I should have said yes. But, being somewhat more composed now, though no less aggravated, I said that was for the constable to decide when he'd spoken to the parties.

She went off muttering that she hoped the day would never come when the police would have to keep a register of the *human* boars and bulls of the parish. It wasn't strictly relevant to the present business but it was her favourite smutty remark, which she liked to come out with on the smallest pretext. She probably thought I was too young to be so favoured, so she only muttered it over her departing shoulder.

"What's all this, then, maid?" PC Hoad came from the back parlour, shrugging himself into his jacket. "Five pound? Where'd you get five pound to?"

"Please, sir," I replied, "the man who gave it me made me promise to say nothing of his generosity for the moment. He says he has certain arrangements to make. But I can tell you this much — I went over to Falmouth today, to visit my grandparents, my mother's people — you know who I mean?"

He nodded. "Are 'ee saying Mister William Trevarton hisself did give 'ee this 'ere old five-pound note?"

I shook my head. "I'm not at liberty to say that, sir. Not yet, anyway."

He smiled and patted my bonnet. "You got a head under there, maid. I'll say that much."

"If so, I wish I'd used it half an hour ago! Can you come to the Angells with me now and tell them they've either got to accept my fiver as rent, which is its purpose, or let me have it back? They've got no right to keep it, just because they *think* I stole it."

My anger was heating up all over again. My whole frame was shivering and it congested my chest so that I found it hard to both speak and breathe. He saw it and gave my arm a reassuring squeeze. "All in good time, maid," he replied. "Sit 'ee down and have a bit chat awhile." I was about to protest that the business was urgent when he added, "I got word 'bout you Moore children today."

"Word?" I sat down warily.

Kindly Mrs Hoad put a cup of sweet, well-stewed tea and a slice of fuggan in my hand. She kept a pot warm on the back of the stove most of the day.

"The workhouse beadle in Helston Union, Harvey Knight, he's asking how you're going on, the six of 'ee. I was coming up your place tonight, so you've saved me the walk."

"Half the walk," I said — for the Angells, in Harbour Terrace, were about half way to our cottage.

"What do I tell they in Helston? Shall I say your mother's people are taking care of 'ee?"

"Not yet, please!" I said in alarm. "Nothing is arranged, but I'm sure it will be."

"How didn't Marian go over to Falmouth? She's the oldest."

"Because our mother told me to go," I replied with sinking heart.

"Afore she died?" he put in — and then gave a single brief laugh as he realized what a silly thing it was to ask.

I just smiled and let the question fade. "You can tell Mister Knight that our rent is paid up till Lady Day next year, and we've enough to get by on for now. And that Marian, Tom, and I are seeking employment. Also that Gerald is old enough to tend house and take himself and the two little ones to school and back, and ..." I spread my hands in a what-more-could-they-want? gesture. "We needn't come on the Union for a penny piece."

"Good!" he said.

I was filled with a great sense of relief. Until then I hadn't realized how close the Union had come to breaking us up — all while I was blissfully imagining that my grandfather would see us provided for.

"Will you come with me back to the Angells, sir?" I asked.

He glanced at his wife, gave her a resigned sort of smile, and, picking up his helmet, said, "Come-us on, then! Best be done with it, I s'pose."

Together we walked back along the quays, with me prattling happily on about Fenton Lodge and my drive round Falmouth with my grandfather. It never occurred to me that he was testing my story about having been over there that day. When he was satisfied I was telling the truth, he switched his questioning (which to me still seemed like 'a bit chat,' as he called it) to the subject of our father's death. Had it surprised us? How did we hear about it? When had we seen him last? And so on.

I said nothing about finding his body there the day after the funeral, just that he'd fallen in a stupor and we hadn't been able to wake him — which had happened often enough before. Even so, if the constable had not known what a drunken bully the old man had been, he might have thought our abandoning him to the cold like that was rather callous. He passed no remark of that sort, though, and shortly afterwards we arrived at the Angells. My heart suddenly started beating fit to leap right out of my body and I thought I should bring up the tea and fuggan I had just put down me.

They'd had the best part of an hour to decide what to do — and they had chosen to brazen it out.

" 'Ello, my lover," Reenie said to me, all warmth and sympathy. "Come to pay the rent, 'ave 'ee? 'E's due next week if I'm not mistaken. Lady Day?" She turned her simpering smile on the constable as if asking him to confirm her calendar.

"Why, you ... but I ... not an hour ago ..." I sputtered incoherent fragments in my rage — and fear. For I suddenly thought, *What proof have I that this fiver ever existed?* I had not thought to ask for a receipt, nor to make sure someone witnessed my passing over the money. This chilling thought dried even my rambling outpourings in my mouth and I was ready to cry in my despair.

"The maid says she did give 'ee a fiver," Hoad told them. "She says she paid 'ee up to Lady Day twelvemonth."

"A fiver!" Angell laughed richly.

His wife joined him. "A likely tale! Where'd the like of 'er lay hands to a fiver!"

They were not even showing anger, as most other people would have done if I were lying. They were treating it as a juvenile prank, not worth getting hot under the collar over. They were even implying it was something I was rather apt to do, as if they were used to it by now and wouldn't dream of taking offence.

I could bear it no longer. I rushed at Reenie and thrust my hand down between her big-jellied breasts to get the note back. She was alarmed when she thought I was attacking her, but when she realized my true purpose, she relaxed and smiled triumphantly. Then I knew how foolish I was to have imagined they wouldn't have hidden it well — if this was to be their game.

"But you did! You snatched the note and put it there. I saw you!" I turned to the constable. "She did!"

Angell spoke next. "You be careful, maid, what you do say — accusing respectable folk of stealing and that. You'll only go and get yourself in trouble."

I'm ashamed to say I burst into tears at that. All my hopes dashed! My grandfather's generosity scattered to the winds. The year of security in our darling little cottage ... vanished. How could I go back to him and confess what folly I had committed? I buried my face in the rough blue

serge of Hoad's tunic and howled. "She did ... she did ... I saw her ..."
was all I could say.

He let me cry briefly and then gave my shoulder a surreptitious
squeeze. "Your grandfather, now," he said. "Mister William Trevarton."

He knew it would shock me to silence — which it did — a silence he
then put to most dramatic effect. Very quietly, almost as if he were
talking to me alone and did not want the Angells to overhear (except
that he made jolly sure they did!) he went on: "He's a *careful* man, I
expect?" He gave me another squeeze, pushing me a few inches away
from him.

"Yes," I agreed, knowing I must take my cue from him now.

"He's not the sort of man who'd part with a fiver without first writing
down its *number,* would you say?"

I understood his drift then, though the actual words to express it were
still only half forming in my mind. All I could do was shake my head in
agreement, though I was feeling more calm and hopeful with every
passing moment.

"He'd have that number written down somewhere *safe,* I'm sure?"
Hoad said, making a little question of it and forcing me to speak: "Yes,
I'm sure he will."

The constable drew in a deep breath of satisfaction and smiled all
round. The Angells were beginning to look rather crestfallen. "Well
then," he said, "our troubles are over. If anyone feloniously spends that
fiver, its number will be like a golden thread leading us back to the
culprit — or," he added significantly, "culprits — as sure as the vixen's
scent do bring on the hounds. All we need do is get that number off of
him ... and wait."

He nodded a cheery goodbye and ushered me toward the door.
Almost as an afterthought he added — again as if speaking to me:
"'Course, if Mister and Mistress Angell here was to take pity on 'ee,
orphans that you be, and if they was to *waive* the rent for a twelvemonth
... well, I s'pose that'd be every bit as good as finding this lost fiver, eh?"

I nodded, mesmerized by his cunning and his worldly wisdom. "I
suppose so," I murmured.

"So!" He pushed me out by the door. "One way or another you'll get
the value of that note."

The moment we were outside he hurried me off along the terrace and
down the steps to the Institute, which stands at the very end of the
outer-harbour wall, where the big stone jetty thrusts its protective arm

out into the bay. All his breezy good-humour was gone. His manner was urgent once more.

"They're a cunning and deceitful pair, they two," he warned me. "You was some little fool to hand over a fiver without witness or receipt. Still, you won't never do such a thing again, I shouldn't think, so that's enough said about that. You're to go back to your grandfather without fail tomorrow and get the number of that fiver. If he haven't got it, you bring back a empty envelope addressed to me in his hand, and ask 'n to write in the corner, *Re stolen five-pound note.* Got that?"

"Re stolen five-pound note," I echoed. "Addressed to you."

"That's it. And come back by bus with it lying flat and plain to read on top of your basket. Never mind how many people do read it — the more the merrier. The word of it going round will be like the baying of hounds in *their* ears."

We parted at Gravesend. I felt much happier then about going home and confessing my folly to Marian.

She was annoyed with me, of course, but that fatalistic streak I mentioned earlier soon overcame her anger and she joined me in pinning our hopes on our grandfather's carefulness in noting the numbers on fivers — which was a thing many people did. After all, five pounds would pay a living-in scullery maid's wages for a year.

In any case she and the others were all eager to hear about Fenton Lodge and its beautiful gardens and splendid setting and the grand way of life people enjoyed there. In all of which I was happy to indulge them.

I was up betimes next morning and stood an hour in Wendron Street, waiting for Bert Eddy's lorry — or any lorry from Trevarton's — to come by. I was just beginning to wonder if the mills had gone on strike when at last I saw the lorry labouring up Coinagehall Street on white skirts of steam. He slowed down to let me jump on the running board and open the door, which I did most nimbly.

"I thought you weren't coming today," I complained as I settled gratefully into the warmth of the cab.

He did not smile. He gave me only the briefest glance and looked away, biting his lip.

"What's the matter?" I asked.

"You haven't heard, then. I thought 'twas all over Cornwall by now."

"What?"

"Why — your old grandfather, he lay down and died yesterday evening — that's what."

The events that followed Bert Eddy's dreadful announcement are doubly hard for me to record. Not only were they painful — even more so than the death of our mother, perhaps, because that, at least, had been long foreshadowed — they were also confused. Things happen at random, but the human mind can't seem to tolerate that. Something inside us makes us look for patterns, even if they aren't really there — like seeing faces in clouds or pictures in old, rough plaster. And people are complicated. They do things for three or four reasons at the same time, some of them contradictory. But that doesn't satisfy us. It seems untidy. We try to boil it down to a single explanation.

So, with the best will in the world, I know that my account is probably quite different from what the Recording Angel has written in his great book. However, this is my honest memory of these awful days and my best explanation of it all.

My first impulse, of course, was to leap down from the lorry and race back home to let Marian and the others know. Then I recalled PC Hoad's advice that I had to come back from Fenton Lodge with *something*, some bit of paper to frighten the Angells. So I just sat there, dumbstruck, while Bert Eddy told me what little he knew. He said the rumour was there'd been a family argument and that poor old Mr Trevarton had fallen down in a fainting fit from which he had never recovered.

Since I could very well imagine what the subject of that argument was, you can guess how bright that made me feel! My urge to turn about and go back home was almost overpowering, but I told myself that the best thing to do if you know a horse is going to kick you is to get as close to the offending leg as possible. Mind you, I've never had the misfortune to try the advice out myself, but I can see the logic of it. I knew I'd never be at peace until I'd gone to Fenton Lodge and paid my respects to that dear old man who had been so kind to me at our one brief meeting.

Again the lorry stopped at the Penryn depôt. The yard was filled with them — steam and horse-drawn — and all were being painted black for the funeral, which was clearly going to bring the whole of Falmouth to a halt. Walking briskly, I covered the final two miles in about forty minutes, arriving at Swanpool just before noon. Once again, my courage began to flag over the last few hundred yards. If the fatal argument had been about us Moores, I could just imagine the sort of reception I'd get.

However, the front door was open and people were coming and going in a steady trickle, for it was the custom to call and view the body — and pray beside it, of course — and even to say absurd things like how *healthy* it looked! I've heard such things said without a trace of unease. So I waited for a carriage containing about half a dozen people to draw up and I slipped indoors in their midst.

But alas, the sight of my dear grandfather lying there ... the memory of his great affection for me ... and the thought that our companionship, which had flourished even on so brief an acquaintance, was never more to be — all overcame me and I fell upon his body, hugging myself tight against him and bawling my lungs out.

Of course that fetched my grandmother in from the next room and she recognized me at once, though all she could see was the back of my head and my dress.

Actually, that was *not* all she could see — which was why she let rip a bellow of outrage that terrified me into silence. How was I to know that rich people are buried in clothes that aren't really clothes at all? Our mother was buried in her Sunday best, even though we could ill afford such extravagance. It could have been put by and would have fitted me or Marian in a couple of years. But the morning coat in which Mr Trevarton had apparently been laid out was, in fact, only the façade of a suit, just tucked in loosely all round and held underneath him with little ribbons. My impetuous action had disarranged it all so that now you could see his puckered flesh, which did not spring back where I had dented it, and his long woollen combinations, and, of course, the rumpled pretend-suit, which now looked very tawdry, indeed. I just stood there, aghast.

Mrs Trevarton grabbed the nearest weapon to hand — a three-foot candle, which was fortunately unlit — and began beating me wildly with it about the shoulders and back, me doing my best to fend her off. In her passion she broke it into so many pieces, all held on the stout wick, that it soon resembled a human backbone of the kind you see hanging in doctors' surgeries.

Bourdeaux, the butler, restrained her as tactfully as he could while his wife gripped me firmly by the scruff of the neck and hauled me from the room. Nor did she stop until she had lugged me to the attics, where she bundled me in among the water tanks and bric-a-brac. "Now you may just stay there until we can deal with you," she said ominously, and turned the key in the door behind her.

I cried until I fell asleep. Then I awoke and cried again, this time without the balm of oblivion. I wept for my mother, for the family she had forsaken, and the long, bitter path she had trod without hope of betterment or content. I wept for my grandfather, whose smile my own would never again answer. And for myself and our melancholy family, whose hope of staying together now seemed vested in miracles alone ... I wept until I had no more tears to give — and no more feelings to provoke them, either.

Then, as the light of day was fading, I heard someone approaching the door. It was too furtive, I thought, to be either Mrs Trevarton or the housekeeper — an impression that was heightened by the hesitant scratching of the key in the lock — in fact, of a succession of keys. Someone had found a spare set and was trying them out, one by one.

"Who's there?" I whispered urgently.

"Shh!" was the peremptory response. Then, quietly, "It's Susan."

God bless her! Never was a friend in need more welcome. After several attempts she found a key that worked. "Here!" she said, thrusting a handkerchief bundle into my hand. It contained a handful of scraps for me to eat. "I didn't dare risk carrying water."

"It's all right," I told her. "I'm not thirsty at all. I've been drinking out of the tanks. Actually, it's water at the other end that's my problem now. I'm just waiting for it to get dark so I can poke my b-t-m out of the window."

We both giggled. It was the first light moment I'd known in that dreary day, the longest and saddest of my life. I almost had hysterics. Only the fear of giving Susan away prevented it.

"Listen, I can't stop long, gel," she said, "but there's things you ought to know."

"About the argument they had last night?" I suggested, hoping to make it easier for her.

"Oh, you heard about that?"

"Yes. It's all over the county — or, at least, among Trevarton's workers, anyway. They were arguing about us, weren't they, me and my brothers and sisters?"

"Not half! One minute they was going at it hammer and tongs, next minute the poor old man ups and drops down dead. But listen — what you should know is this. It all started when he wrote a coddy-something ... like an extra bit to his will?"

"Codicil?"

"That's it! He wrote a codicil and he got the Bourdeauxs to witness it, which they was very unwilling to do, I may assure you. But they had no choice, see?"

"What was in it?" I asked, munching greedily at the cold chicken and beef and other funeral meats she had brought. Crying, I discovered, works up a powerful appetite.

"Dunno," she replied. "But it must have concerned you Moores because when he read it out to her — Missus T, that is — that's when the fur began to fly. And the argument *was* all about you — no doubting it. Anyway, the minute he died — before they even sent for Doctor Mayer — she took it out of his pocket and threw it on the fire! *I* saw her do it — though she doesn't know I did, so for gawd's sake don't let on, not while I'm still here, eh?"

"Of course not," I promised. I don't know what made me add, "Did the Bourdeauxs see her do it?" Perhaps it was just the way she stressed that *she* had witnessed the deed.

She shook her head. "They wasn't there. Maybe she's told them, mind. But I wouldn't think so. They're not too thick. She likes to keep them at a distance. She'd not tell them 'less she felt she had to. Anyway, I thought you should know."

I thanked her, though I didn't see that the information was of much practical use to me. However, I appreciated what a risk she'd taken, for she hardly knew me and certainly owed me no favour. Before she went she said, "You can widdle out of *that* window now, if you like. There's only the laundry yard down there and there's no one around at this hour of the evening."

I took her advice and the relief was enormous. My weeping fit had stilled my sorrow, for the moment, anyway — leaving only 'that grief which doth lie too deep for tears.' I passed the next half hour or so in examining the lumber about me and imagining the life that had gone with them. There was a lady's saddle with a broken tree. And an officer's dress uniform, laden with dust. Books galore, of course, mostly ex-nursery and covered with childish scribbles. I tried reading one, about a child called 'Child,' who had an insatiable curiosity and asked questions like, 'Pray tell me, dearest Mamma, what holds the stars and planets in their appointed places?' and then sat quiet and contented through two or three pages of fluent explanation from 'dearest Mamma' before immediately leaping onward to: 'And why does our wonderful blue sky turn orange and red at the setting of the sun?' I'd have throttled Child by page nine. Also, I never did learn why skies change colour at sunset because, somewhere above me, and above the clouds, on that chill March evening, the Cornish sky was doing just that, and the light filtering in at the small panes grew too dim for my eyes.

I played with a musical box for a while — a selection of Viennese waltzes — but it kept sticking, which is presumably why it was sent up to the attic. There were broken croquet mallets, punctured tennis balls, racquets with torn strings. There was a set of Ping-Pong, the first I'd ever seen, and there it was, already broken and discarded. And there were trunks and trunks full of things, all locked. It was quite a contrast with our own little cottage, where there was nothing that was not of immediate and almost daily use. Our most 'luxury' item was a cobbler's last, which we used only a few times a year — for hammering steel brads into soles and heels or blunting nails that worked through to the inside and tore holes in our stockings.

I had never seen so much useful or half-useful stuff just put aside to rot and gather dust. It was a fascinating half hour, just poking around and marvelling at it all, and I think it sowed the seed of my later addiction to junk shops and flea markets.

My good cheer annoyed Mrs Bourdeaux when, shortly after sunset, she came to release me. I'm sure she expected to find me chastened, bedraggled, starving, and desperate to go. Since I was none of these things, I must have seemed almost superhuman to her.

However, Mrs Trevarton soon wiped the smile off me — and off my spirit. I was brought back to the drawing room where she had interviewed me the previous day and made to stand before her like a prisoner — which I was, I suppose. It was like that picture, *When Did You Last See Your Father?* except that there was only one of her, but the atmosphere was the same. I fixed my gaze on her chin. I was determined not to stare at my boots, which is like pleading guilty I always think, but also I didn't want to give the impression I was set on staring her out.

"I suppose you're pleased with what you've done to this household?" she said. She spoke with a sort of ultra-refinement, even more genteel than her tone of yesterday.

Grand ladies use grand English to intimidate people of the lower orders. Like the soldier on 'jankers,' the hapless servant was just supposed to stand there, downcast and guilt-laden, mumbling the civvie equivalent of 'I have nothing to say, sir!' But, thanks to our mother's rearing and our absolute addiction to good books (I mean, I'd read a lot of Macaulay, Carlisle, Ruskin, and all the poets, of course, and Dickens and ... well, enough said) — thanks to all that, I was able to answer in kind.

"I cannot think, Mrs Trevarton, that you truly suspect me of planning anything so perfidious."

A little too much, I agree, but it set her back on her heels. All she could think of to say was, "Hoity-toity!" — which wasn't very crushing. Nor particularly original, either.

Her eyes reassessed me. Also I fancy I saw a hint of guilt there, too. Was it because of the codicil she had burned? Or because she knew her opening remarks had been unnecessarily harsh? It could have been both, of course, which is what I mean about people doing things for many reasons at the same time.

"Sit down," she said.

I took my time about it, though not so long as to become provocative. She stared at me a long while and I resumed my observation of her chin and neck. She was even more beautiful all in black. I think she knew it, too, for her dress had been chosen and tailored with some care — not just in a great rush since last night.

"What's to be done?" she said at last, more to herself than to me.

I folded my hands in my lap and waited.

"Why did you come back here today?" she asked.

I began to explain: "Because Grandad gave me ..."

"You are *not* to call him that!" she interrupted.

"He told me to."

"Yes, well, he's not ... that is, *I'm* telling you not to."

I started again: "Yesterday Mister Trevarton gave me the money to pay a year's rent in advance, and ..."

"And how much was that, pray?"

I think she was expecting a figure up around the fifties for she prepared an expression of shock and outraged dismay. She can have had no idea how humbly we lived. It was dismay of a different kind she showed when I told her it was five pounds. "Oh," she said, disappointed.

"And the landlord and his wife just snatched the money out of my hand and refused to give a receipt."

"And you had no witness?"

I bit my lip and shook my head. "So I thought that Grand ... that is, Mister Trevarton must surely have taken the number of the note, so the police could set a trap for them if they ever tried to spend it."

"It is obviously a precaution *you* neglected to take," she said. "To make a note of the number."

"For the first and last time in my life," I replied. "From now on no note shall leave my hands until I have its number."

She thought that over quite a while. I was beginning to get the feeling she enjoyed being answered back, in an odd sort of way. Mind you, she'd also have enjoyed it if I'd just sat there meekly and let her berate me to her heart's content, for she was undoubtedly a bully. But, unlike many bullies, she also had a liking for a fight. She'd never have encouraged it openly but she trod a careful path between an outrage strong enough to shut my lips and a zest that would have spurred me on to a right old ding-dong row with her.

Her next words took my breath away. "I thought you might have been seeking a position with Trevarton's," she said.

Looking back I think it strange that such a notion had never entered my mind — especially since the question of finding employment *somewhere* was very much on my mind. And many an heir to a family business has started in the humblest way, down on the shop floor. But, of course, none of us Moores was an heir in that sense — in which case, a decent man like Mr Trevarton would have been ashamed to offer his own flesh and blood a lowly position from which they had no particular hope of rising. Especially a female.

So my honest answer to my grandmother was that I had never thought of such a thing.

"Will you think of it now?" she asked.

Bless my innocence but I began thinking of a commercial position in the Penryn depôt, or in the smaller yard at their mills in Helston, and I was wondering what on earth they could find for a maid of sixteen to do. But Mrs T cut across all that. "I cannot and will not recognize you as full members of this family," she said. "Yet nor can I ignore you entirely. It would look very bad and people would talk. So let us come to an agreement, you and I — a commercial agreement, you understand. A purely business arrangement. Mister Trevarton told me last night that your elder sister — Marian, is it? — that she has found employment in Porthleven and so has your brother Thomas. But it appeared that you had not yet been so lucky. That is why I thought you might have come looking here. What sort of trade have you in mind?"

I shrugged awkwardly. "Anything. I'm quick to learn, though I say so myself, and I'm ...'"

She shook her head. "Believe me, you would not stick at just *anything*. There is too much fight in you. Don't smirk! It will cause you a great deal of grief before you learn to direct it properly. What I wish to propose is that you should take a position in *this* household."

I sat bolt upright at that and I'm sure my jaw dropped in a most inelegant manner.

"I know," she went on. "I can see madness in it, too. It will be very unsettling. Everyone will know who you are and no one will be sure how to treat you. So understand this — I shall make it perfectly plain from the very start that you are not to be treated nor addressed nor even thought of, in any way, as a member of our family. It so happens that I detect in you the makings of a first-class lady's maid. Properly trained, you would be welcomed in the grandest home — indeed, the grandest *palace* — in the kingdom. I will undertake your training. I shall turn the other cheek upon the injury your mother did to me. This shall be my act of charity to the brood she spawned in despite of us."

Words of anger rose to my lips at this but, to my shame, I was so intrigued by this monstrous proposal that I held them in check. May my mother's spirit forgive me!

Mrs T had tried to provoke such an outburst, of course. When none came, she smiled and said, "Yes, I believe you will prove quite tractable in the end. So think it over. It will take several years to teach you all you need to know. By the time it is over you will be able to recite Madge backwards." (Madge was the pen-name of Mrs Humphry Ward who wrote the bible of etiquette in instalments in her column in *Truth*. Later they were published in *Manners for Men … Manners for Ladies …* and so on.) She went on: "You'll be able to sew as fine a silk as any little spider. Also to ply a gophering iron, curl straight hair, straighten frizzy locks, apply cosmetic colours that none can detect, carry letters discreetly, and cause duchesses to say they cannot imagine the world continuing on its course without you. Don't answer me now. Think it over and come back this day week."

"The wages, ma'am," I said at once, unconsciously slipping in the word that revealed what my answer would be.

"Very little," she replied with equal speed.

"I want little for myself but it would have to be enough to send home five shillings a week for the support of my brothers and sisters."

She dipped her head solemnly and said, "I think charity can stretch that far."

harity! The word jars as a description of my grandmother's antics, and yet, when she actually spoke it, I cannot remember thinking it at all odd. Most of her contemporaries — the Foxes of Rosehill, the Dicks, the Stantons, the Allens of Killiganoon — thought she was being foolishly soft-hearted. The sins of the parents were to be visited on the children, even unto the seventh generation. It said so in the Bible. We Moores should be left to sink or swim — preferably to sink — as an example to would-be wayward daughters everywhere. Daughters of the commercial classes were an important part of the commercial system. They couldn't *do* much in the way of anything useful — certainly not earn their own livings, most of them — but they could cement profitable alliances and keep the wealth moving around within the charmed circle. I have heard people say it was a genteel form of prostitution and, though I'd not go so far as to agree with that, I must own there were a lot of loveless and unhappy marriages around because of it. And certainly the spite and venom they directed against girls like my mother, who married for love, is hard to explain if money wasn't part of it all.

Anyway, as I say, Mrs Trevarton was considered foolishly liberal in taking even one of us Moores into her household, no matter how menial the position. And, of course, lady's maid was the least menial of all. In theory, the housekeeper outranked her but only as a subaltern outranks the regimental sergeant major; God help the subaltern rash enough to *use* his theoretically superior position! The things a lady's maid could say about a housekeeper while running a soothing brush through her mistress's hair and bringing the blessed relief of untying her corset strings were just not worth risking.

PC Hoad was right about my grandfather — he had indeed been the sort of man to take a note of the fivers that passed through his own private wallet — and my grandmother was able to furnish me with the requisite letter to frighten the Angells. Hoad was right, too, about the curiosity of my fellow bus passengers on my return journey home that day. The sight of an envelope with the words *Re stolen £5-note* writ large across it was a better conversation opener than a holiday hat saying *Kiss me quick!* Before the day was out, half of Helston and Porthleven must have known of my loss (though I never mentioned the Angells by name) and what folly it would be if some person tried to pass the note anywhere locally.

The following morning the constable handed a slip of paper with the number on it to the Angells, 'just in case it should turn up somehow'!

I talked over Mrs Trevarton's offer with Marian, who was all for my accepting it. The funny thing about Marian and me is that, although she was older by eighteen months, we had always treated each other as equals, even when very young. And lately I had come to be like the *older* sister, or the one who made the important decisions. Marian, apart from having that fatalistic streak, which helped her to accept the most dreadful strokes of ill fortune, was also dangerously impetuous. If she liked the sound of something, or even just thought it'd be a bit of a lark, she'd be skipping on the spot to get started. Darling Marian! She had such spirit and a heart big enough to take on the world.

Of course, it made me 'worse' (her word for it) than I would naturally have been. By that she meant I was always saying, 'Hold back — let's look before we leap' — and other negative things of that sort. By the time we both entered our teens, she was the source of all invention in the family, but the sensible, solid decisions came from me.

"Can't you see *anything* wrong with the idea?" I asked her, concerning our grandmother's proposal. It wasn't that I couldn't see for myself what Mrs T had called 'madness' in it, I just wanted Marian to stop and think for once. If I was going to be away except for my one day off every fortnight, I wanted her to start thinking soberly about things for herself — and not to go saying an enthusiastic yes to one and all, as she had almost said to Harry Angell and his scandalous proposition.

"What?" she asked, genuinely puzzled.

"I'll be putting myself in that woman's power. It's not as if I could walk out at any time. She could deny me a character, or give me one so lukewarm I'd never find work this side of Plymouth — and not much on the other side, either." (Not being brought up in the servant class, I did not realize how easy it is to buy good characters and what a farce the whole thing is.)

"Yes, you're right." Marian's hopes now plunged as low as they had been high, only seconds earlier.

"And she's nobody's fool," I went on. "She'd know I was in her power. She could make my life a living hell."

"Yes ... yes." She nodded gravely. "You can't possibly put your head in the lion's mouth like that."

"Oh, Marian!" I gripped her by the shoulders and shook her angrily. "Stop it!"

"Stop what?" She searched my face with her big, trusting eyes, desperate to please me, eager to win my approval.

"Stop bouncing between one extreme and the next. It's not a simple yes-or-no situation where the answer's obvious for all to see. I must put all the benefits in one pan of the scales and all the drawbacks in the other and see how it balances. It's what Mother always said — look at both sides of everything and go in with your eyes open." (Mind you, I didn't add that she spoke that advice with regret that she had not acted on it herself in her own life; if she had, things would have turned out very differently. But Marian and our mother were very alike.)

"Yes," Marian said earnestly, still keen to please. *"Weigh* everything up — that's the *way!"* She laughed at her own 'joke.'

I did not tell her that her happy, feckless manner was among the heavier items in the drawbacks pan. Our mother had been feckless enough but at least she was of age and had her innate breeding (as it was called) to buoy her up. The thought of leaving Gerald, Arthur, and Teresa in Marian's care for thirteen days out of every fourteen was not one that brought peace of mind.

Before I went back to Fenton Lodge to tell Mrs Trevarton that I accepted her 'charitable' offer I tried to make Tom see the dangers in these arrangements and so shoulder some of the responsibility, too. I took a pasty down to the hôtel for his croust, and the pair of us went for a walk along the inner harbour quay. A collier was in port, sitting on the mud of low tide. They could only come in and out on the high spring tides and the men were working furiously to get her unloaded before the next high water. It was impossible for anyone to hang out any washing in the village during those hours — and even at the cottage if the wind was in the wrong direction. We moved quickly away from the dust clouds, down toward the relative cleanliness of the timber yard at the innermost end of the harbour.

Seagulls were quick to spot the half-eaten pasty in Tom's hand. They sidled with us, before and behind — the ones behind being boldest. I made a sort of parable out of it for him, saying how the world was full of cunning, sharp-eyed, and rapacious people who were only waiting to snatch what little we had and leave us really destitute. We couldn't afford to ease our vigilance for a second. I tried to distract him to the point where he'd drop his guard and one of the gulls would make a successful snatch of the remnant of his pasty. But they had fed too well off that morning's catch and were not sufficiently interested in gobbling a little more.

"You know what Marian's like," I went on. "She's a lovely maid with a smile ready for all the world. She doesn't see the harm that's in people, not the way you and I do, Tom. You're the man of the family now. You must do your best to curb that heedless streak in her. I'll do what I can, too, but I may only come back once a fortnight. So in between I want you to write to me and tell me everything that's going on here. After church on Sunday, yes? Like all the good little boys in the posh boarding schools, you'll sit down and write a duty letter to me, without fail, every Sunday after church."

Poor Tom! I can't really blame him. In the first place the only man he'd ever had to take pattern from was our father. Enough said. And in the second place, he was just launching himself into the manly world of work, that world where men gang up on us women, make jokes about us, convince each other they don't need us really, that we just fuss-fuss-fuss and make their lives a misery. He was learning to say yes to our faces and shrug us off the moment we were gone.

Also, there was a lot of hatred and anger and general nastiness in society, at all levels. Poverty was so awful and so many people lived just poised on the brink of it that they behaved like any crowd would behave when the ship is sinking and there aren't enough lifeboats for all on board. You'd have needed to be a saint to stand out against that tide. And Tom was a good lad but not a saint. So, as I say, I can't blame him.

If I did, I'd have to blame myself even more. I was the one who was dishing out the advice about trusting no one and looking every gift horse in the mouth. But when Harry Angell came to us, just before I returned to Fenton Lodge, and said that, although they hadn't found the fiver I *claimed* to have lost in their parlour, he and Mrs Angell had decided to waive the rent for a year — as an act of charity to a young family made double orphans within the space of a few days — well, I took him at his word and even thought a little better of him for it.

I cringe with shame inside and wish I could go back and live that one day of my life over again. I thought I was the clever one to make them put it in writing this time — which they did with an eagerness that ought, by itself, to have pricked my suspicions. They even made two copies, which we both signed. And I walked away singing, convinced I had snatched a wonderful victory from the depths of my own folly.

I got off to a poor start at Fenton Lodge. I said, "Good morning, madam!" to my grandmother. She at once told me, very severely, that I was never to speak unless spoken to, except to convey information from others or give warnings and things of that nature. She went on to add that I was never to initiate any conversation, never to wear a bonnet indoors (as if I were a daughter of the house), and never to remain seated in her presence unless some task on which I was engaged (such as needlework) required it. All this with scarcely a pause for breath. And such was my induction into the duties of my new station in life. But I was so happy with the general upward turn in our family's fortunes that I took it all in good spirit and with a smile. That, too, did not please Mrs T.

I was happy because everything was now secure for us. The rent was settled for a whole twelvemonth. Tom and I had work and I was better paid than I had any right to expect — fifteen pounds a year, which was three times the wages of a scullery maid, and almost unheard of for a maid of sixteen whose only skills were that I could sew deftly and write with a good hand. And it could not be long before Marian, too, gained some employment. Then our little orphaned household would be better off — financially, that is — than at any time since our haulage business went smash. In the space of less than a month our prospects had turned from the bleakest to the most promising.

So, looking more chastened than I felt, I followed Mrs Bourdeaux upstairs to my attic room — actually, *our* attic room, for I was to share it with Susan, the upper housemaid who had befriended me that day of my first visit.

We had candlewick counterpanes with a lozenge-shaped pattern. Susan had not pulled hers quite straight and the housekeeper tut-tutted and pointed out her indolence to me, saying I was not to take my pattern from such slothful behaviour. She looked hard for other signs of delinquency — bits of fluff on the carpet, dust on the chest of drawers, and so forth — and, finding none, was most disappointed.

I had imagined that life below stairs was a matter of *Us* and *Them*. And when *They* were out of sight and hearing, *We* would be comrades together in adversity. But not a bit of it. I soon learned there was more backbiting, more snobbery, more clique-forming, more bullying, and more petty cruelty among servants than ever took place across that almost unbridgeable divide between servants and masters.

Not that we were *all* at one another's throats, mind. Susan and I were the greatest of friends all the while we were together in that house. She was the only one who thought my grandmother's behaviour in making me her servant a scandal. Like me, she had a powerful sense of what 'family' means. Unlike me she was entirely free from snobbery, or as free as anyone could have been at that time. I wasn't. Our mother had been what I call a *practical* snob. She had no time for artificial distinctions whose only purpose was to divide people from one another, but the 'snobbery' that had given us a good education, good speech, and an appreciation of good books was quite another matter. Maybe I shouldn't call it snobbery. It was just a matter of wishing to better oneself.

To my surprise I discovered that no one was more eager to better herself than my new mistress. By her airs you'd think she was born with the proverbial silver spoon in her mouth — not to say the whole silver canteen — but still her ambition was to climb higher and ever higher. I made this discovery on my very first night, when Susan and I retired to our beds. (And thank heavens we had a bed each. Betty Coath, the fat little under housemaid, and Clarrie Benjamin, our all-skin-and-bone scullery maid, had to share a bed and were at each other's throats like Kilkenny cats all the time.)

Susan was the upper housemaid, seventeen years old — younger than Marian but much more mature. She was very friendly but not without her cunning side. She asked me if I wanted to practise on her hair, saying it was quite like Mrs T's. Actually, the only thing they had in common was that they were both fine and straight. But Susan's was lustrous and pale honey-coloured while my mistress's was silver and getting sparse, she being fifty-six years of age. But I didn't mind. I enjoyed combing out her hair and making her look 'fit to break a heart or two,' as she put it.

That first evening, while so engaged, I remarked that it seemed odd to me that Mrs T was to train me herself. I had expected her present lady's maid — who was perhaps about to retire or move on to another position — would at least start me off.

Susan just laughed. *"What* 'present lady's maid'?" she asked. "The mistress never had such a thing in her life. Me and Mrs Bourdeaux's been managing her between us. And she dresses herself mostly. Or has done up until now. She's only needed us to pull her corsets tight."

While I was absorbing this surprising news she went on, "You know what all this is about, don't you — *she's* got the purse-strings now! She was always on at him to have a maid-in-attendance. Not just a lady's maid, mark you! A 'maid in attendance'!" She parodied a genteel accent and laughed. "That's what she'll make of *you* before she's done. You mark my words."

I was still hazy about the differences between upper and under housemaids, so this fresh distinction made no sense to me. Susan had to explain that a lady's maid was really just an upper housemaid with special responsibility for her mistress's bedroom, dressing room, clothing, and personal needs. But a maid-in-attendance had the duties of a private secretary as well, and even, to some extent, of a companion. She dealt with milliners, haberdashers, tailors, and the like (and usually received little *bonnes-bouches* from them at Christmas to keep her custom). She had her own budget and account books. She travelled with her mistress whenever she went visiting, and stayed where she stayed. And she was expected to read all the fashion magazines and be ready to advise her mistress on what was in and what was out.

"That's what she wants to turn you into, my gel!" Susan concluded. "A maid-in-attendance."

She spoke as if it was an unpleasant fate — something she herself was lucky to have avoided, because, as she then added: "If you hadn't come along just when you did, she'd be trying to make a silk purse out of *me* by now. She must have thought the angels sent you, that day you turned up — with the master lying in his box and all."

"And the first thing I did was to pull his clothes off!" I said.

We collapsed in a fit of giggles, which only came to a halt when one of the Bourdeaux tapped with a stick on their ceiling below.

We blew out the candle and sank gratefully between our sheets. I asked Susan if my grandparents had often quarrelled.

"All the time," she replied. "They was worse than what Betty and Clarrie are."

"What about?" I asked.

"Everything. If he said it was a lovely day, she'd say it was going to rain later. If she said they must get a new carriage, he'd say there was nothing wrong with the old one. She never wanted him to go down the depôt. She said he always come back smelling of *trade*. She couldn't never bear *trade*, as she called it. Find a little bit of bran in his turnups and she'd go beside herself. 'Why can't we be like the Stantons?' she'd ask. 'You never see Willy Stanton with sawdust in his cuffs.' But he'd always tell her that when people in trade turned their backs on the business and left it all to managers, it was the shortcut to ruin. She couldn't bear it when he spoke like that — 'people in trade'!"

I told her that my first sight of him had been coming in by the tradesmen's entrance. She said Mrs T would never go in that way. Even if it was raining spikes and nails, she'd get down from the carriage and walk up the garden path.

I was to learn a great deal more from Susan during the months that followed. I think masters and mistresses have a special blindness which permits them to imagine that a servant sees little of what goes on 'above stairs' and forgets it all within days. In fact, as I'd already learned from Bert Eddy, no one watches them more closely and discusses them more keenly than those whose bread and butter depends on it.

The following morning I was up at six to prepare for my day — or, rather, my mistress's day, for it can be truthfully said that a maidservant has no time to call her own. It was all written down for me. My mistress must have had a wonderful time planning my utter exhaustion. I wish I'd kept the bit of paper because you could read a sort of grim malice in every line. Mind you, I have no difficulty remembering the duties it set forth. They did not vary throughout my time with her.

My first duty, once I had done my own ablutions and dressed, was to go minutely over the clothes she had worn the previous day and remove all trace of mud. It was hard at that time because they were all black — and mourning for a spouse lasted a full six months, followed by another six of half-mourning. The black tweed dress she wore before luncheon was easy. I just stretched it on a table and brushed the specks away. You can hardly damage tweed. But the twill she wore in the afternoon and the silk for the evening — both of which also had specks of mud, I don't know how, though I was sure it was just to test me — were too fine for brushing and I had to flap at them for ages with a yellow duster. In fact, for the evening gown I found another scrap of silk of the same colour, without which I should have been in trouble.

And it wasn't only mud. There were also little scuffs and runs in the material of her clothes. These had to be repaired at once, on the principle of 'a stitch in time saves nine.' At once meant literally before breakfast if my mistress was to wear the item that day. Otherwise it meant before sundown and certainly before the item was next laundered. (Except stockings. They were always laundered before mending.)

Fortunately on that first morning, although *Running Repairs* was written in her list, there were none needed, so I was able to get on with my next task, which was to sprinkle damp tea leaves over the dressing-room floor, rugs and all, and sweep them up into a pile beside the door. Meanwhile, Betty Coath, the under housemaid — or plain Coath as I had to call her — cleaned out the grate, relaid the fire, and lit it. Then she took the ashes away, together with my heap of dusty tea leaves by the door, which she reused downstairs. The whole house was like a piece of clockwork, really.

As soon as the fire was bright I had to lay out all my mistress's clothes for the day, spreading the chemises and petticoats over chair backs before the fire to warm and air them. Then to lay out her toiletries and things according to her programme for the morning. If she was paying calls or shopping, there could be a couple of dozen items to lay out, from bands and black feathers to pomatums, bandolines, and combs. No artificial flowers or jewelry, of course, except jet. Also a selection of suitable gloves. (No true lady wore jewelry by day, anyway.) It was common for her to wear half a dozen different pairs of gloves each day.

By then *my* day was two and a half hours old and she was still fast asleep! I had but ten minutes to make her a pot of tea and take it up together with two marie biscuits, the first post, and a flower from the hothouse, which Tony Pascoe, the under gardener, brought to the kitchen when he came to take the orders for that day's vegetables from Mrs Gordon. On his way to deliver this order to Charley Dexter, the head gardener, he would give the water pump a hundred cranks, which would start to fill the water tank up in the attic — where I had been imprisoned on the day after my grandfather's death. He gave it a further hundred cranks every hour of the morning or until the overflow came splattering down all round him.

While my mistress read her post and munched her biscuits I had the delightful task of emptying out her night slops. Very few houses had water closets, but there was an earth closet at the end of the second-floor landing. We servants were forbidden to use it, of course, no matter how desperate. We had to go out across the back yard and use a bucket privy, even on a stormy night in the depths of winter. And even when we were ill. The earth closet was only for the family and their visitors. It looked like a water closet but with an outsize cistern immediately above and behind it. This cistern was filled every week by Tony Pascoe with fine, crumbly soil, which they dried in a little shed behind the laundry house. In fact, the flue from the copper in which the laundry water was boiled passed through the shed for the express purpose of drying this soil. Instead of a chain dangling from the cistern there was a crank lever. When you turned it, a measured quantity of powdery soil fell into the bucket, covering the fresh-laid contents, so to speak. When Pascoe filled the cistern with fresh soil-powder he took away the bucket and dug its contents into the vegetable garden. I emptied my mistress's night soil into this earth closet every morning. Her washing water I tipped out of a back-stairs window onto a little sloping bit of roof, where it drained away through the rainwater pipes into a large butt, or kieve, as we call it in Cornwall. Being soapy, it made excellent water for bordeaux mixtures for the potatoes and roses. Nothing was wasted.

After taking care of my mistress's night soil and washing water and — *eurgh!* — cleaning the receptacles, I took her orders for breakfast, which she ate in bed. That first morning, when I brought her washbasin back (the ewer being left in the kitchen to be filled with hot water later), she gripped my hands and felt the skin to see if it was still damp right above the wrists. I think she hoped to discover that I had not washed them properly. But I have never forgotten a story my mother once told me about a man at the town waterworks who did not wash his hands after going to the lavatory and who infected a large part of the town with dysentery — after hearing which I have always found it impossible to walk ten yards from the lavatory without washing my own hands. So Mrs T was disappointed of her grumble but pleased with my diligence.

In fact, that same sort of contradiction coloured every aspect of our relationship, making it very difficult for me ever to know where I stood with her or how she really felt about me. If she found me wanting in some little thing, she seemed to take particular delight in bawling me out and trying to make me feel small. But if she found I had done something well, without any special instruction, there was a sort of self-satisfied pleasure in her, as if she were saying, 'Well, what else would anyone expect from *my* granddaughter!' Of course, she never did utter those fateful words — not once in all the time I knew her — but that was what her attitude suggested.

I think she was fond of me in her own *very* peculiar way. If I hadn't felt that, I think I should have upped and left, not once but many times, during those first dreadful months. But she was a woman brought up to show as little emotion as possible — except that she had a good line in sneering and ill-tempered abuse. And outrage when she thought her social position was being attacked. So even if she had felt any slight warmth for me, she had no way of showing it.

Her breakfast was a leisurely affair. I, too, ate mine in reasonable ease though in only half the time she required. Then I attended to her dress for the day, turning the underwear that was warming before the fire and brushing out her bonnet with a light feather plume. Velvet was the worst, especially the black. I had to brush it with such care or it looked ruined. Also the velvet bonnets were usually trimmed with wire 'flowers' of black straw and raven's feathers, which she used to crush in her careless way. I was forever at them with the flower pliers or holding the feathers in the heat of the fire to help them straighten.

I always polished her shoes and boots the night before — that is, put the polish on and let it harden overnight. In the morning all I had to do was buff them. There was proprietary blacking, even in those days, but it was a shilling a bottle and so I was only allowed to use it on her patent leather boots. For all other footwear I had to make up my own polish, for which I took equal quantities of sweet-oil, vinegar, and treacle, plus an ounce of colouring — lamp black for blacking. (Later, when she would be out of mourning, I'd use burnt umber for brown leather, and yellow ochre for pale tan.) This polish was put on with a cotton pad and also left to harden overnight. It buffed up pretty well with a lamb's fleece the following morning.

What I loved about this work, right from those very first days, was that it was all mine. I had no overseer except my mistress. I knew I should never please her, not openly anyway, so merely to escape her wrath was the measure of my success. But her dressing room and bedroom were *my* little empire. Not even Mrs Bourdeaux tried to queen it over me there. And my sewing box was mine. And so were all my cloths and polishes. And all the pomatums and bandolines and hair restorers — all of which I learned in time to make from old receipts. And the brushes and combs, the silks and ribbons, the gloves, the crape — almost everything I touched. It was all mine and I was responsible to no one but my mistress for its use, care, and maintenance. I could almost have hugged her for giving me this little world of my own — a world where I never had the slightest doubt but that I belonged. I would have done so, too, if I had not also known that she had done it out of spite, to dance, as it were, on her husband's grave, who would ten thousand times rather have have taken us Moores back into the bosom of his family.

I had no direct evidence that my grandmother played an active part in what followed — though plenty were eager to slander her and say that she did. Certainly, to anyone who knows the ways of the world, it is hard to believe that the Poor Law Guardians would have acted as they did without first consulting her. And even if all she said was, 'Leave me out of it. You must do as you think fit,' then her words were, nonetheless, decisive. It is especially hurtful to think that while I was toiling away for her comfort — finding lost buttons, making old lace and crape look like new, taking her beautiful dresses and packing them in wrappers of clean calico until the period of mourning was out, and so on — she was at the very least conniving at the terrible events of that week in Porthleven. And saying not a word to me.

She let me discover it for myself, in the most harrowing way, when I made my first visit home in the middle of April, two weeks after coming to Fenton Lodge. Sunday, it was. Sunday the 13th April, 1890 — one date in my life that I shall never forget.

I had heard nothing from Marian in all that time — not even an acknowledgement of the five-shilling postal order I had sent at the end of my first week at Falmouth. But I thought that a *good* sign — meaning they were all too busy. I brought my second five-shilling contribution with me. I took Dan Nicholls's bus from Helston and, with hindsight, was aware of a sort of evasiveness toward me among those who knew us. But nobody said a word, not even Nicholls himself when he stopped at the Sunset Farm lane and mumbled, "You'll want to get off here, I s'pose, maid?"

And I set off blithely down the lane, full of exciting news about my new place and bursting with curiosity to hear how they had fared. My mind went back to the last time we had all been together, on the morning of my departure for Fenton Lodge. We gathered in a knot and gave each other many a hug and even more kisses. The threat of being broken up by the Poor Law, which had hung over us like a darkness ever since the day our mother died, had never seemed more remote.

My body can feel them now as I write of that odious memory: Teresa's bony little frame, skinny as a fledgling, clinging to me, shivering at the early morning chill and not really understanding it all ... Gerald's hazel eyes and the blue of Arthur's, looking up at me, understanding the fact of our leavetaking and believing my promises to return in two weeks' time, but not grasping how narrow an escape we had had, nor how slender were the threads on which all such promises dangle ... and Tom, playing the man, shaking my hand, squeezing my arm, nodding confidently in a spine-chilling imitation of our father's manner when *he* was turning on the charm ... and finally Marian, telling me not to worry even as she clung so desperately to me, wishing with all her heart that I could stay.

Just before I left them I said that I intended to conduct myself so perfectly at Fenton Lodge that our grandmother would see she had nothing to fear from our barbarism. Then, in time, she might express a wish to see them for herself ... and so, bit by bit, we might climb back into the family's regard and enter respectable society. Therefore, I could not help adding, they were to do nothing to blacken our good name but were to behave in the same exemplary fashion.

And so, uplifted by my own fine sentiments, I had set off up this same lane to begin my new life as a wage-earning maid. I turned to wave from the gate, and again from half way up the lane, and again from the top, where the hedges of Sunset Farm at last blotted out my view. On each occasion they were there, watching, waving back. Those scenes have haunted me ever since.

The moment I came within sight of the cottage I knew something was wrong — unless Marian had started taking in washing and was doing a special line in babies' clothes — for the hedges were dotted with nappies and little bonnets and swaddlings of every description.

When I was half way down the lane a woman came to the door, saw me, and darted back inside. Moments later her man came out and strode up the path to intercept me at the gate.

" 'Tin't nothing to do with us, maid," he called out as soon as I came within easy hailing distance.

I recognized him then as Joel Sellick. Mary, his wife, came back to the door and watched as, sick at heart, I slowed to a crawl and shouted back, "Where are my brothers and sisters?"

For reply he merely beckoned me forward.

I wanted to turn and run. I thought that if I went back to the top of the lane and started again it might turn out differently — giving God another chance, as it were. But, of course, like a mesmerized rabbit before a snake, I came on with feet of lead. The air seemed to have turned solid all about me.

" 'Tin't our fault," he repeated when my snail's progress had brought us close enough for conversation.

"Where are they?" I insisted.

"I said to Harry Angell, I said surely they'm all paid up for the year? And he said t'weren't so. He said he did give 'ee the use of the place rent-free for the year. But that's not the same as paid-up. He said it didn't hardly make sense to leave the place sit idle for a year — not after they come and took they off, see?"

"They? Who are *they?*" I asked, though I hardly needed to be told.

"Why, your brothers and sisters, o'course."

"No! Who ... oh, never mind. I know one person who'll tell me everything. You didn't hear where they've gone, I suppose — where they've been taken?"

He looked at his boots and shook his head. He knew very well, of course, but he wasn't going to say. That did not augur well.

" 'Tin't hardly no fault of ourn," Mary Sellick called after me as I turned toward Porthleven.

"No one in the village isn't blaming we," he added.

I just stared at them until they looked away. I wasn't trying to make them feel ashamed. I just didn't know what to say.

I walked straight past the foot of the steps that led up to the Angells' house. I knew that if I came face-to-face with them I'd only do something I'd be sorry for after. I thought of calling on Tom at the hôtel (not knowing that he, too, had been taken away) but decided to press on directly to the constable's house.

Phyllis Hoad must have been on the lookout for me. They had a useless little pocket-handkerchief garden in front of their cottage. Take two steps and it was already behind you. But she had the front door open before I'd even closed the gate. "Come-you in, my lover," she called out solicitously. "Hoad's gone up Antron about their bull but I thought 'ee might come home today."

"Home!" I echoed sarcastically. The truth of it was that Hoad couldn't face me, of course. He'd left this painful business to be handled by his wife. Village constables didn't make routine visits on Sundays — certainly not about bull registers.

"I know! I know!" she said in anguish. "There now. Sit 'ee down and 'ave a cup tea and I'll tell 'ee all about it."

She closed the door as I took my seat. I stared into the fire and almost intoned: "Is it bad, then?"

I remember thinking, *This is a comfortable chair and that's a nice glowing fire. How can I sit here, relishing these comforts while this dreadful business is unfolding?* But I did. I basked in the warmth of that fire, even as the chill settled around my soul.

"It could be worse, I daresay," she answered, though in a tone that implied, *But not by much!*

"And the Angells are behind it, I'm sure."

She picked up the ever-stewing teapot and poured two treacly black cups. That afternoon I was treated to heavycake, which she usually reserved for breaking news of bereavements.

"That Harry Angel," she said, "did come down here one morning, 'bout two days after you went over Falmouth, I believe, and he laid information concerning your sister Marian as a loose liver."

She eyed me warily, a little surprised, perhaps, that I had not started up and protested loudly. Instead I replied scornfully, "He neglected to mention, I'm sure, that he has several times attempted to seduce her for himself and was each time rebuffed in no uncertain style."

Behind her surprise I was puzzled to see a certain relief in her manner — until I realized she was glad not to have to explain these 'awkward' matters to me.

I believe our family was somewhat unusual in that respect. Our parents had never once spoken about sex to us. When Marian got her first monthly, my mother said, "Well, now you'll have to stop playing with the boys." And that was the only reference I ever heard to it. Most parents did at least tell their children that it was nasty ... dirty ... shameful, and so on. But we were never told such things. So we had no attitude to it at all, beyond the usual giggly approach of our own schoolfellows. But children are great mimics and, since the subject almost never arose (in our hearing, anyway) among grown-ups, it hardly surfaced among us, either.

Anyway, Phyllis Hoad was relieved she could talk to me without having to explain. "I thought as how there was something of that in it," she said. "He had that look in his eye, you know — sort of shifty and smirking, all to the one time."

"He pestered the life out of her to let him have his way," I went on. Even though it wasn't strictly true, Mr Harry Angell was now a legitimate target for whatever I could throw at him.

"I'm sure, my lover," she replied. "But you do know the way of the world. When a respectable, godfearing man who 'tends church every

Sunday and reads the lesson and takes round the collection plate ... when such a man says one thing and, on the other side, a ... a ..." She eyed me uncomfortably.

"A slum maid of eighteen," I said.

"Well ... I'd hardly say a slum maid, but you know what I do mean — the way of the world. When he says one thing and she says another, you know which one they'm all going to believe! Poor li'l Marian! Beside herself, she was. 'Send to Falmouth,' she told they. Send for you, she meant. You'd bear her out. But there's nothing do frighten our Poor Law Guardians like word of a young maid in danger of moral turpitude, as they do call it."

"So did they take her to the Union Workhouse in Helston?" I asked.

She shook her head unhappily and my heart, already low enough, sank yet further. "Not ...?" I could not say it.

She nodded. "She's up Redruth."

"But that's a *reformatory!*" I protested. "It's for criminal and wayward girls." My flesh crawled with horror at the thought of my poor darling sister being locked away among such horrid creatures. I wanted to run from the house and go by the swiftest possible means to Redruth to get her out.

I was too angry for tears. In fact, I think Phyllis Hoad was closer to crying than I was. She just kept shaking her head and sighing and murmuring, "I know! I know!"

"And the others?" I asked. "Have they all been sent into reformatories?" I dreaded the worst.

She shook her head more readily this time and even managed a little smile, glad to be able to set my mind at rest on at least that score. "Mind you, 'twas touch-and-go with your Tom," she went on. "They said potboy in a place that sells intoxicating liquors wasn't no work for a twelve-year-old lad, so he's been sent to a farm-training school up Saint Austell way, somewhere."

"Saint Austell!" I was horrified. It was about twenty miles the wrong side of Truro, which, in turn, was about ten miles north of Falmouth. "And why a farm-training school? He'll never be anything but a farm labourer, then."

Mrs Hoad bridled a bit at that and I kicked myself, remembering that's all her father ever was — and a fine man with it. "I mean he's never had the slightest interest in farming," I said lamely. "What about the three young ones?"

Teresa, it seemed, had been taken in by some Anglican Sisters, the Sisters of St Breaca, who was one of our Cornish saints about sixteen centuries backalong. The sisters had a nunnery in Penzance. They said the prospect of finding a family to adopt a little maid that age was good, though her tubercular hip would not help much.

She saved the worst news till last — or no, the worst news after that about Marian. She said that Gerald and Arthur had been taken to an orphanage in Plymouth — sixty miles away.

If someone had *wanted* to break up our family, they could not have done a better job. Marian branded as a loose liver and thrown into a reformatory in Redruth. Tom being turned into a farm labourer in St Austell. His two brothers in a Plymouth orphanage, where, no doubt, they'd be fed in due course as cannon fodder to the Royal Navy — the navy of flogging and weevil-infested biscuits. And poor little Teresa being given away like damaged goods to the first tradesman who wanted to rear an unpaid maidservant.

Mrs Hoad gave me all their directions, which she had already written down in case I called. I think she was surprised that I didn't burst into tears on hearing the news. Perhaps if the Sellicks had told me these tidings straight out, I would have done. But I had walked the best part of a mile with the forebodings of this catastrophe ringing in my head. And during that time my grief had hardened into anger. Even more than that, my anger, in turn, had run the gamut from frenzied rage — in which I would have killed Harry Angell or the Guardians or anyone else who'd had a hand in this monstrous deed, even my grandmother — to cold, calculating hatred.

Outwardly, of course, it made me seem far calmer than I was. But Mrs Hoad was not deceived. Later I heard she told Mary Sellick that the look on my face made her tremble for all who'd played a part in the removal of my brothers and sisters.

"What'll 'ee do now, maid?" she asked after a long silence.

I stared out of the window, feeling so numb that I wondered what those houses, those fishing-boat masts, those people were *doing* out there. "I can do nothing," I said flatly. "Not alone. But there is one person who can."

"Harry Angell?" she asked anxiously, thinking my mind was turning toward foolish acts of revenge.

I shook my head. "My grandmother. I must get back to Falmouth at once and enlist her aid."

I looked at the clock over the mantelpiece and saw I had only five minutes before the bus would return to Helston. I rose and thanked her for the tea and heavycake, and for the kindly way she had broken the news to me. As I went out by the door she gave me a battered little cardboard suitcase, which I recognized as Tom's. In it, she said, she and Hoad had gathered all the scraps and things that had got left behind when the family was taken away. I thanked her again but did not dare look inside, desperate though I was for some actual memento of them all. I knew I should be inconsolable if I did so.

As I sat on the bus back to Helston I gave free rein to my anger once more. Every torment I ever heard of I now visited on the Angells. I pitchforked them into pools of burning sulphur with all the gleeful devils in Hell to assist me. And when the physical torments palled in my imagination, I turned to more practical sorts of vengeance. I went to the Guardians (not even knowing who they were or where they met, of course) and denounced Harry Angell for the liar and lecher he was. And my words were so convincing that they sent the beadle to arrest the couple at once. And they didn't turn the Sellicks out. Instead, they got our family together again and let us stay in the Angells' house while they languished in gaol.

Everyone on the bus knew what had happened, of course. They all understood what I had discovered on that visit. I know as much because Dan Nicholls himself refused to take my fare — or, rather, didn't even ask for it. And I never knew him do that before. What they made of my outward calm I don't know, but I was hardly aware of them.

By the time I reached Helston I had exhausted my store of childish but satisfying fantasies and my mind was ready for plans that, though more sober and less exciting, were closer to the realm of the possible. I had forty minutes to spare before the Falmouth bus, so I went to the churchyard to let our mother know what had befallen us. Being all alone in that solemn place, I told her out loud.

Of course, I broke down then, with nobody to watch me, and if the grave had been two feet deep instead of six, I think I should have clawed my way through the earth and climbed into the box beside her. Never in my life had I wanted so desperately to feel the comfort of her embrace. She was all the warmth and love and comfort I had ever known. And I missed her.

Oh God, how I missed her!

I must pause now. I cannot continue.

If my grandmother knew what I had discovered in Porthleven, she gave little sign of it — just a kind of flouncing off-handedness that might have been guilt or might just have been inadvertence. She was working in the garden, out near the front wall, planting some new heathers in the rockery. Perhaps she was even waiting for me — though gardening was one of her passions (and, for what it did to her clothes and boots, one of my dreads).

"Why, Miss Moore, you're back earlier than I expected. All's well at home, I hope?"

I, entering by the tradesmen's gate, dropped a curtsy and walked on, not trusting myself to speak.

Despite her age she must have nipped down the garden, running on tiptoe, for she was waiting by the kitchen-yard gate when I entered. "All's not well," she said. "I can see it in your face." She eyed Tom's cardboard suitcase.

To distract her I asked if I might fetch her a scarf as I feared the afternoon might turn chilly.

She shrugged and said, "Well, if you don't *wish* to tell me ... of course ... I can't *make* you."

I did wish to tell her. Of course. But not when she was distracted by other things, and her head full of *Erica* this and *Genista* that. She was the sort of gardener who always uses the jawbreakers instead of the names we all know, like heather and broom. However, I saw I had no choice. If I delayed now, I'd only be giving her the chance to say, 'If only you'd told me earlier, child!'

So I laid the suitcase down beside the back door and, explaining that I didn't wish to distract her from her gardening, led her back to the front border where I'd first seen her. As we walked I told her about finding the Sellicks established in our old cottage and what Mrs Hoad had told me about the Guardians, how they'd split us up and sent us to the four corners of the Earth, or of Cornwall, anyway.

"You appear to take it very calmly," was all she said.

In fact, my composure seemed to unnerve her — which, in turn, encouraged me to continue in that way and not to break down, which I was perilously close to doing several times. People have often given me credit for much more maturity and strength of character than I actually possessed. They do not realize how much their own illusions about me have encouraged me to live up to them. I have so often been a prisoner of others' expectations. They would have been surprised if they could have lifted the top off my head and seen what uncertainty and weakness and turmoil was seething away inside.

And it was so that afternoon with Mrs T. She thought me unnaturally calm. I saw it disquieted her. And so I continued in that same manner. "It would be little use running round like a headless chicken, ma'am," I replied. "That wouldn't bring us together again."

"And d'you think anything else would?" she challenged me. "Once the authorities take a large decision of that nature they rarely go back on it, you know."

"I know," I agreed. "But I also know that I shall never rest until we are all united again, no matter how long it takes."

"Dear me!" she exclaimed. "You must not let it become an obsession, you know. That would never do. People who let their lives be ruled by obsessions are rarely happy."

I thought she was a fine one to talk — but she probably imagined that her wish to rise above 'trade' and be one of the grand ladies of Cornish society was more of an honourable ambition than an obsession. We all have such blind spots. For my own part I didn't mind what she called it — obsession, passion, ambition ... whatever. All I knew was I could never be at peace until it was done.

"If you'll excuse me now, ma'am," I said, "I must go and compose a letter to Marian. The first thing is to get her out of that hateful place."

"Be careful! The governor there will read every word you write," she called after me.

I was grateful for that warning. It would probably have occurred to me on my own but I might have wasted several drafts before then. Also it made me aware that I could let *them* — the governor and his staff — know a thing or two without making direct threats or promises, which they would only have laughed at probably.

Even so, I required many drafts before I felt I had achieved my purpose, which was mainly to ingratiate myself with the governor so that he would allow me to visit Marian. And I also desired to warn her between the lines to keep her slate clean. I kept the final draft, from which I copied that letter, just as I hoard everything else in my life. (Fear of loss runs deep in my veins!) So here it is, word for smarmy word, just as I wrote it:

My Dear Sister,

I went home to Porthleven this afternoon only to discover it is no longer that to any of us. Mrs Hoad told me all, including the vile slander Harry Angell made against you. Do not blame the Poor Law Guardians for what they did. When a sly, evil man like that lays such accusations, they have no choice but to put you in the care of your present governors, who, I am sure, have your "reform" and best interests at heart. If you are not consumed with anger and resentment, which will make you behave in a surly and foolish manner, be assured they will soon discover the truth about you — which is that you need no reforming at all. And then they will release you into some place where your many good qualities will have scope.

I expect you find yourself among many girls of truly depraved characters. But I know you will find the strength to resist any invitations they may extend to you to join in and become one of them. That, too, will show those now in authority over you what a grievous mistake they have made and they will be all the readier to make amends to you for your false imprisonment and to see you set back on that virtuous road which you and I know you never left.

And do not worry about Harry Angell. He will get his deserts before long. You are not by any means the only virtuous maid he has tried to ruin. I heard things in Porthleven this morning that would make your hair stand on end. People are muttering about him and I feel sure he will soon be unmasked as the whited sepulchre we have always known him to be. Do you recall the first time he attempted to seduce you, on the day of our mother's funeral? You said you thought Michael Carlin overheard him. Think back again now. Can you be sure? I know Carlin has no great fondness for our family but I don't suppose even he would stand by and see you falsely imprisoned for very much longer.

I enclose the five shillings I brought to Porthleven with me this morning, hoping to add it to the family's coffers. Did you get the five-shilling PO I sent last week? I wouldn't put it past that blackguard Angell to have kept it if it arrived after you'd been taken away, just as he has kept the £5 rent we paid him up until Lady Day next year. Perhaps your present guardians will not let you have the money at the moment. If not, I'm sure they'll keep it safe against your release, which, I repeat, will be soon. So stay as cheerful as you can and be assured, my dearest, you are never far from my thoughts.

Perhaps you don't know what has become of the others? I don't know if they took you away first, you see. Anyway, Gerald and Arthur are in the Sutton Orphanage, Ebrington Court, Plymouth. Tom was sent to the Tywardreath Farm School, near St Austell. And poor little Teresa was taken in by the nuns at St Breaca's in Penzance (Morrab Road, if you wish to write). They seem to think they can foster her to some family there. I shall be writing to each of them as soon as I finish this. I can imagine the confusion and misery they must presently feel, but we must none of us lose heart.

I'll send you more money when I can and I'll write again as soon as I may, telling you all about life as a lady's maid, which is hard but interesting and rewarding. Mrs Trevarton is a splendid lady and a fine mistress, severe but fair, and quite determined to train me to the best of her ability — and mine! I know she will not rest in righting this injustice when she understands the full extent of it. I am writing separately to your governor to learn when I may visit you, which I hope will be soon. Meanwhile, be of good cheer and have as little to do with your fellows as possible.

When you are released, as you surely will be as soon as they see their error in keeping you there, we can work together at reuniting all of us once more. Keep that thought before you in these dark hours before tomorrow's dawn!

Your loving sister,
Cristobel.

I showed it to Susan, mainly because I feared it was altogether too sanctimonious and transparent to be credible. I had to exaggerate the piety more than I liked because Marian was so impressionable and trusting. She'd have taken the letter at face value if I'd made it more subtle. But not even she could think I'd genuinely write in such terms as *this* priggish epistle. Also I never called myself Cristobel to her. That alone would show her I was putting it on. I doubted whether she'd realize it was for the benefit of the governor or wardresses or whoever censored their mail. But at least she'd guess I had *some* ulterior purpose. That would be just like me!

If nothing else, my remarks about Michael Carlin were as good as a mighty big wink to any as cared to see it. It wasn't true that he 'had no great regard for our family.' In fact, he was very sweet on Marian and would have married her if his parents had let him, which, of course, they wouldn't. What I was doing was telling her that if she answered yes to these promptings of mine, I could go and ask Michael if he'd agree to say he'd overheard Harry Angell make those accusations. He'd never need to perjure himself in court, though. I was pretty sure that if he said as much in front of PC Hoad, the constable would find a way of using the fact — naming no names — to 'persuade' Harry Angell to say he'd got the wrong end of the stick and that 'on mature reflection,' he'd misunderstood Marian's words. That, in turn, would make it easier for the guardians to reverse their decision and let her go — all without losing face, which I knew was important. Also, to let the governor read it now, over my shoulder, so to speak, would prepare him to accept it more readily when he heard of it officially.

The letter made Susan cry. She said she wished she had such a sister as me and she hoped Marian wouldn't let herself be dragged down by the company she'd find in that dreadful place. This amazed me. She thought I meant every word I'd written quite literally! Two years older than me and much more worldly wise in many ways, and yet she thought me sincere.

Pondering the difference between childishness and maturity made me realize that I had no real childhood, or not as others think of that word. When I refer to my *childhood*, I mean the years up to about seven. Ten at the outside. For the children of the poor there was no 'childhood' after ten. Indeed, it was only in 1885, when I was eleven, that the age of consent to carnal knowledge for a maid had been raised from ten to thirteen — and there were many whose thinking had not yet caught up with the law.

But I *was* a child in many ways, no matter how grown-up I may have felt at the time. The moods that consumed me in swift succession on that day in Porthleven returned to haunt me in very slow succession over the weeks that followed. In my anger at the Angells I devised evermore fiendish tortures for them — especially for him. And when those primitive fantasies no longer satisfied me, I imagined scenes from my future life in which we met, I being then a rich and influential lady while their fortunes had taken a tumble. Sometimes my revenge was subtle, as I gave them what few coins I happened to have in my purse.

Sometimes I was frankly brutal — I just opened my portals wide and let my hounds chase them down my long, long drive. Best of all was my subtle brutality, as when I graciously allowed them to move into our old cottage beneath Sunset Farm — provided they did not disturb the pigs I also kept in the place!

Even at the time I knew those fantasies of revenge were childish, but they were balm to my spirit and they helped sustain me through my long periods of misery. (And, talking of *periods,* those weeks in May 1890 were when I had my first visit from 'my friend,' as we called it. Susan told me it was an ill wind blows no one any good, meaning I was lucky to have a deeper woe on my mind. Her first visit had scared her out of her wits. She'd been fifteen at the time, which was very young. Most girls didn't get it until they were sixteen, like me, or even later.)

My sorrows were worst at night. Not so much when we blew out our candle and finished our little chats. I was still in control of my thoughts then and could limit myself to one or two sad memories — Teresa clinging to me for grim life that morning, almost as if she knew we'd soon be parted for ever, or Gerald, with his curly brown hair and hazel eyes, shy and reserved in company though he was the daredevil of the family, always ready for any lark or folly. I would lie there in the dark, carefully allowing such memories to surface in my mind, and then I'd treasure the inevitable tears until I fell asleep. Susan would sometimes hear me crying and would reach across and stroke my cheek or behind my ear until I was quiet.

But then there were dreams. One of the saints, I forget which, said we're not responsible for our dreams. I just wish we could shrug off the memory of them half so easily. Time and again I'd dream not just that we were all together again but that our mother was still alive (never my father, funnily enough — or not so funnily, perhaps). Usually these dreams plagued me just before waking and I cannot describe the bleakness I felt on opening my eyes and rising into awareness of where I was and what melancholy events had brought me there. I used to clench my eyes tight and try to wish myself back into that warm, sunny, happy dreamland just for a few minutes more. In one of those dreams my mother gave me a present of a beautiful tortoise made in highly polished gold. It had ruby eyes and there was a scintillating diamond set in the centre of each of its scales. Ever since then I cannot pass an antique-shop window without looking to see if they have it. I think I shall never stop looking.

It is amazing how people could live under the same roof and hardly ever see each other. Servants and masters, for instance, hardly ever met, and then mostly by accident. All the sweeping and dusting and polishing was supposed to be done out of sight, either before the family rose or after the gentlemen had gone out to work and the ladies had departed to their shopping or to charitable visiting. While the family breakfasted, we bolted down our own, much simpler meal and then dashed to make their beds and clean their rooms. We played Box-and-Cox with the house — one lot in while the other was out — and ne'er the twain shall meet. Most of the time we maidservants were in our own part of the house, cleaning things or mending them. Out of sight, out of mind.

I've been told of big country houses where there were many more divisions than the simple line between servants and masters — separate passages and stairs for male and female domestics, for instance, and some where even the upper and lower orders of domestics were kept separate, too. Those were houses where 'upstairs' servants rarely ran across 'below-stairs' ones.

Of course, the arrangements at Fenton Lodge weren't anything like so extreme but it was still possible to go days and even weeks without seeing any of the family or guests except those you served directly. Perhaps that wasn't so remarkable during the week, when young Master Mark was away at school (he was a weekly boarder at Truro Grammar). The only people in the house then were Mrs Trevarton and her cousin Stella — a Miss Stella Wilkinson — who was 'keeping her company through the darkest months of her grief.' Actually, the only dark thing about my mistress's grief was her clothing. The two of them had a high old time playing bezique and planning how to spend Mrs T's newly won access to the family's fortune.

At weekends, however — or 'Fri-to-Mons,' as they called them ('weekend' was considered to be a 'howwid Amewican vulgawism,' as I heard one of the foppish Stanton daughters say) — the house filled with visitors and Master Mark had to sleep on a camp bed in his mother's dressing room, which was a great inconvenience, not to say annoyance, to me. This was all during those early months of mourning, when the two eldest sons felt they had to come and support their mother at every opportunity — not because their mother needed it, nor even because they wished to, but because Society would expect it of them.

Archie was the eldest, being then about thirty-seven. A short, fat, bald man, pompous and prickly, he had already more than half taken over the management of the business before his father's death. His mother quarrelled with him endlessly. She wanted him to hand it over entirely to a manager and start living the life of a proper gentleman. His wife, Megan — a shrewish little Welsh witch, ten years his junior — took my mistress's side because she, too, smarted under the label of 'trade' and longed to be a proper lady. Unfortunately for their ambitions, Archie not only enjoyed the work, he was actually rather better at it than even his father had been. 'Old Mister Bill' had built Trevarton's up from next to nothing but he lacked the temperament to manage a big enterprise, which needs consolidation more than further enlargement. Fortunately for us servants, they left their children at home in Penryn. Four more spoiled and troublesome brats I never knew. Why the parents had to come and stay overnight at Fenton Lodge when Penryn is only two or three miles away I don't know, but I suspect those four children had a lot to do with it. Nannies and nurseries were grand buffers to keep a brood at bay but parents had to be very rich and utterly singleminded if they wanted to exclude their offspring entirely from their lives.

The middle son, Walter, could not have been more different. He was a partner in Trevarton & Jacko, solicitors, in Redruth, and I liked him from the moment I saw him, though he was a bit long-winded at times. But his heart was in the right place and you can forgive people like that for a lot of smaller drawbacks.

He was twenty-nine, a slim, dark, dapper man with a handsome face and lovely curly, glossy hair, which came down in short-clipped sideburns to the angle of his jaw. He was clean-shaven except for a pencil-line of a moustache — which was *the* thing. Walter, who was rising thirty, had recently married his partner's sister, Felicity Jacko. She was still only twenty but, being a tall, sinuous, dreamy woman like the females in Burne-Jones's and Rossetti's paintings, she seemed more mature. The pair of them were still hopelessly in love. I understood the *facts* of life but that isn't the same as understanding the feelings that go with them, nor what a grip they can get on people. I couldn't fathom why those two were always going for long walks over the headlands and coming back all muddy ... and touching each other at every opportunity, and springing apart when surprised in drawing rooms and corridors, and starting to yawn at eight in the evening. Innocent me — I even began to wonder if they weren't secret opium eaters!

Master Mark was even more handsome than his elder brother — and didn't he just know it! He had a dimple in his chin you could wedge a shilling into and it wouldn't fall out. And his lips looked as if they were chiselled in marble by one of those classical sculptors — fierce, even cruel, but very strong. His nose, too, had that same carved quality, with finely arched nostrils. His eyes were deep-set and, being pale blue, though his hair was dark, they seemed to be eternally blazing in the depths of their sockets. He was rising seventeen when I started at Fenton Lodge and everyone said he'd break many a heart before he was a grown man.

I didn't take to him at all, not as a person. But that didn't make me impervious to him as a *man*. I don't think a woman needs to actually like a man to fall under his spell. A hard man, even a cruel one, may make a better defender of his own home and children than a kindly but weaker one, and I think there's something in every woman which responds to that power, even against her more civilized judgement. Otherwise how d'you explain why so many women marry strong men who are beastly to them — and do it all over again if their first husband dies on them? So, I have to say that the first time I set eyes on young Master Mark, my heart did a little flutter, even though he was, strictly speaking, my uncle. The feelings he awakened in me just made me want to turn and run from the room in dire confusion.

It happened in his mother's dressing room, where he was wrestling with the camp bed — a stack of wooden Xs linked to a series of steel Xs, jointed like a lazy tongs.

"This blessed thing may be *intended* as the frame of a camp bed," he said to me, "but it doubles as an excellent finger-chopper-offer. Got any fingers to spare?" He smiled at me. "You're new here, aren't you?"

I bobbed a curtsy and said I was his mother's lady's maid.

"Ah yes!" he replied knowingly, but not as if he'd heard about *me*. He seemed to be referring more to his mother's new pretensions.

I had no idea whether the three sons knew about their errant sister, or her death, or her family. Perhaps the two older ones did but not the johnny-come-lately. Even so, did any of them know her married name was Moore? Did they know I was one of that clan? They showed no sign of it. Master Mark asked if my parents had neglected to give me a name, and when I told him, it seemed to ring no special bell. I was relieved. I didn't mind them knowing but I didn't want them to know that *I* knew that they knew. It would have been difficult all the time, with all of us knowing and nobody ever talking about it. Susan kept urging me to tell them — the sons, anyway — just to make them feel awkward and embarrassed. I wouldn't have minded that so much, but I realized that getting a good training as a lady's maid would set me up well in life, better than if I went into a shop or factory. So I was afraid Mrs T would sack me if I said anything to her sons. Susan offered to tell them herself but I still begged her not to. She said not to worry my head about Mrs T giving me the push. She'd dismiss every other servant in the place before sending me off. I thought she was just trying to encourage me by saying that. I didn't realize that she understood my grandmother a great deal better than I did.

Master Mark said it must be pretty hard, working for his mother. He said this with a lazy sort of grin, letting his tongue linger on his lip — obviously tempting me to be disloyal. With my limited understanding of life I felt he was going to be one of those men who loved getting women into his power. If they were young and pretty, the purpose was obvious. But such men could work just as hard on the old and plain, too. They saw *all* women as some kind of threat, so they had to forge these emotional chains, which they could tweak as a reminder whenever they felt challenged. Or wanted some favour off us.

These insights came mainly from books and conversations, but they put me on my guard. And in any case, I didn't fall for his invitation — because, of course, I could never forget he and I were kin, much as I might have liked to at times. In fact, I tried a little emotional blackmail of my own. I told him his mother was the soul of kindness. I explained that my own parents had passed over recently and she had taken me into Fenton Lodge and agreed to pay me more than I was worth, just so I could help with the upkeep of my orphaned brothers and sisters (not saying anything about the way the Guardians had broken us apart). It gave me a secret satisfaction to know I was talking to my own uncle about the death of his older sister and the fate of his nephews and nieces — and he hadn't the first idea of it.

He must have realized how out of character it was for his mother to behave in that way. But he was young, too, and, like me, accepted the vagaries of his elders quite readily. Like those of the weather, which was just as capricious. Besides, the important thing for him at that moment was that I had *not* fallen for his bait. So he now had a challenge on his hands, and Master Mark could no more ignore a challenge than a bird may ignore a juicy worm.

"But you must find her an *exacting* mistress," he said. "All the other maids have told me so."

In other words, *You'd be in good company if you agreed.* By this I realized he was trying to trap me, though I still had no idea why. That has always been a danger to me — to know that somebody wants something but not to understand why. So when I realized what Master Mark's game was, I, too, could not simply refuse his bait and leave it at that. I had to find out his purpose. Rather cheekily I asked him why on earth he imagined she might be a hard taskmistress — was she a hard mother to him?

He just sniffed and said it was impertinent to ask such a question.

I said, "Ah," and carried on with the camp bed. That involved pushing flat steel bars through loops in the canvas stretcher before fitting them over little studs that held the 'finger-chopper-offer' part at the correct size.

He just watched me. "You've done this before," he remarked.

When I told him I hadn't he said, "Well then, you obviously pick things up very quickly."

I was still smarting from his rebuke about my impertinence, so I thought I'd show him what I could do if I really tried. As I pressed the bars home over the studs I said, "*Some* may think so, but if I'm shown a bit of canvas with four loops thirty-four inches long and then four rods thirty-six inches long ... well, I don't need to go away and consult Euclid about what goes where." I straightened up again and added as an afterthought, "Sir."

He coloured up as pretty as a turkey-cock. I thought he'd explode, but then he burst out laughing and said, "By heavens, what a maid you are, Crissy!" He came round to my side of the camp bed and gave it an experimental push with his foot. It moved in one rock-solid piece. "Perfect!" he added. But all this was just a ruse. His real purpose was what followed.

He said, "Talking of knowing what belongs where — d'you know where hands belong?" And he slipped his around my waist and pulled me tight against him. "And lips," he added. "D'you know where they belong?" And quick as lightning he put his to mine and gave me a hearty kiss.

I only just managed to stop myself from running away. Perhaps at the back of my mind I had some inkling that these were his intentions all along. Perhaps I'd even worked out that his true purpose at this stage was simply that — to put me on the run so that he could enjoy all the thrills of the chase. Anyway, as I say, I managed to stop myself in time. Instead I just stood there as if carved in frozen marble, not breathing, staring with cold, unblinking eyes straight into his.

There was no passion in him, not of the tender emotions, at least. Just the joy of combat. Nor was there passion of that kind in me. Yet it was not unpleasant. Tom and I had pretend-kissed once or twice, just to see what it felt like. Only the last time he tried it he just giggled and tried to spit in my mouth, which left me with a distaste for the whole business. But this kiss with Master Mark was, I have to allow, not unpleasant. It was new, anyway. And he didn't feel a bit like someone to call 'Uncle.'

My complete passivity was something new to him, too. When it finally penetrated the thicket of his own self-satisfaction, he pulled a few inches away from me and stared at me, a bit puzzled, a bit hurt.

And still stony-faced — not angry, you understand, nor resentful, nor haughty, just totally blank — I said, "Will that be all, sir?"

He just scratched his chin and, turning from me, said in a thick, surly voice, "You may go."

So I did. I began to dread the school holidays, which would come in July. And yet, such is the caprice of human nature, part of me began to look forward to them, also.

On the Saturday before my next Sunday off I got a letter from Marian at last. Parts of it had been blanked out with indelible ink, which made it impossible to decipher by holding it up to the window or letting the sunlight reflect across it. The bits I could read added nothing to what I might have guessed anyway — that she was miserable and had no idea what accusations had put her into her present confinement, nor when she might expect it to end. In closing she begged me to come and visit her at the first opportunity. As if I'd have stayed away a minute longer than necessary!

There was one puzzle: I had written to her at the 'Redruth Girls' Reformatory' but her reply was from the 'Home for Wayward Girls.' I did not understand the significance of this until I was almost there.

The Sunday-excursion fare to Redruth and back was five pennies from Falmouth but only four from Penryn. I walked the three miles and saved the penny. Such were the margins on which we had to live. As for church, I went to the early service before breakfast but, not being confirmed, took no communion, which left me able to catch the first train at nine o'clock and be in Redruth by ten.

It was a great adventure for me because, although I had been on a train before, I only had our mother's word for it. For me, *this* was my first railway journey. It was a little branch-line train pulling just a few carriages, so you could actually feel each thrust of the pistons as a quite perceptible jolt under your feet — and under your situpon, too. At least, you could in the Third Class carriages, where the seats were of varnished wooden slats. There was only an old lady and a middle-aged labouring man in the compartment I chose. He had a clay pipe in his mouth but did not light it during the journey.

The first few miles from Penryn are the most dramatic, as the single-track line climbs a steep gradient, bursting out of narrow cuttings and soaring over steep, wooded valleys on equally narrow bridges. The man — a stonemason, I now learned — told me that to save money the railway company had built them of wood on stone piers. That was back around 1860. "Someday soon," he said, "one will collapse with a train on it. They they'll have to rebuild them all fitty-like."

After that, every time we went over a bridge (of which there are eight), I closed my eyes and held my breath. It never did happen, of course, neither then nor on any later journey.

The view that really took my breath away was of Truro Cathedral from the station platform, which is on a hill to the west and about level with the spires. It looks so toylike from there and you imagine you could just reach out and pick it up in one hand. I was so entranced it even put poor Marian's predicament out of my mind for a while. I found a machine they'd forgotten to empty for the sabbath and, when no one was looking, got a penny bar of chocolate for my belated breakfast.

The journey down the main line from Truro to Redruth, however, brought grim reality back with some force — it was a journey from a beautiful old market town, set amid green, rolling hills, into the heart of industrial darkness, where the hills still rolled but were bleak and without trees. The Cornish mining industry was in full swing, even on the sabbath, for the pumps had to be kept going and the stopes shored up while the miners were on their day of rest.

It was a gray, overcast sky, I recall, with only a fitful gleam of the sun every now and then. And the black smoke plumes from the tall mine chimneys rose and fell in a flat curve before the wind teased them to nothingness. The smell of soot and burning coal was everywhere.

I asked one of the porters where the girls' reformatory was and he responded (or so I thought), "Great sins or little sins?"

I started to tell him my sister had committed no sin at all, nor any crime, either, but had been sent there on the malicious report of a neighbour. However, he cut me short with the explanation that the reformatory had two departments. One, for girls who had committed actual crimes, was at a place called Great Sinns, a couple of miles north of the town. The other, which was a home for wayward girls not convicted of any crime, was at Little Sinns, half a mile closer to Redruth. So there was my little puzzle solved — Marian was a 'little sinner'! The 'Sinns' actually referred to a group of tin mines of that name and had nothing to do with the reformatory or the wayward girls' home — except, perhaps, through the sense of humour of whoever decided to build them there, long after the mines had closed.

The two institutions were at different distances along the same road, so he gave me directions sufficient for both and wished me God speed.

My way took me through the centre of the town (which required all of three minutes to cross) and then out through a rather run-down suburb to the Portreath road. There was still no real countryside, even beyond the last straggle of dwellings, for the land was scarred with mine halvans, artificial streams for buddling and vanning the crushed ore, and abandoned, derelict plant of every kind. A lot of the soil thereabout was poisoned with arsenic from the calciners, which burned off impurities before the ore was sent for proper smelting. Such a landscape would have seemed a fitting place for abandoned and derelict people, too.

There was no mistaking the two institutions the moment I came in sight of them. They stood, not quite half a mile apart, near the crest of a long bare ridge that flanked the road to the north. They were built of cold Cornish granite in a vaguely ecclesiastical style, which helped disguise the barred windows. They belonged to that High Victorian period when men believed that architecture could improve people's morals. Such a philosophy produced a bleak sort of grandeur. I tried to imagine myself — and, of course, Marian — being locked up in such a place ... wondering what this first glimpse of it would mean to me. One thing was certain — any thought that I might count as an individual, or have some individual value, would be crushed at once. Those stones were meant to bruise the soul. Argument and opposition, they proclaimed, were futile.

Each institution was surrounded by its own perimeter wall, also of cut and dressed granite, six foot high and with revolving spikes along the top. On the lower part of the slope, between that wall and the road, was a large vegetable plot, laid out with military precision and ringed by a fence of steel posts and wire mesh against the rabbits. The day being Sunday, none of the maids was working there, but one look at it revealed they spent many a weekday hour tending it and keeping it so trim and free of weeds. Cornwall is a paradise for weeds.

I was wondering if I should cross the fields to reach the first building, at Lesser Sinns, when a woman went by in an ass cart and told me to follow the Porthtowan road, which I had passed half a furlong back. It would take me to the front entrance. She asked me if I belonged there, which, when I thought about it on my way up the hill, was heartening, since it suggested that maids who did belong there were sometimes allowed out.

My spirits sank again, however, as I drew near the front entrance. The wall on this side was ten feet high, so I could see nothing but the slate roofs of the building itself. But there was the expected gothic arch, which framed a severe and viciously spiked wrought-iron gate and supported a large entablature on which was carved:

> God the All-Terrible! King, Who ordainest
> Great winds Thy clarion, the lightning Thy sword.

Even on a bright summer day it would have made me shiver.

I peered within, through the bars of the gate, but saw no one. I heard maids' voices, several dozen by their volume, singing, *Almighty, invisible, God only wise* — which I had sung at a much sprightlier pace in Falmouth earlier that same morning. I hummed along with them while I inspected the forecourt, which was dominated by a young horse-chestnut tree, about twenty years old — as old as the building, probably. It was all in new leaf, so bright green it seemed to burn. There was not a tyre mark on the gravel, which was raked smooth right up to the gate. On my side it was scored and rutted from the traffic. And, even though my own sister was wrongly held in that place, I could not help thinking that — for the sort of maid who *deserved* to be inside there — it was probably a very good thing. The stark difference between the damaged highway beneath my feet and the spotless gravel drive, which began precisely on the line of the gate, spoke louder and more to the point than the calculated sermonizing on the entablature above. I'm sure that many a parent with a daughter slipping beyond their control must have stood at that same spot and felt heartened at the sight of so much order and discipline.

There was a bell pull beside the gate. I looked at it but did not dare. Then I fell to thinking of our mother, which I had tried not to do too often, being afraid of self-pity and of missing some present advantage while my thoughts were distracted. I knew she was always there beside me, or hovering near, and I wondered what she would say about all this if she were there in the flesh.

Then an odd thought occurred to me, which had nothing to do with those present circumstances. I had now been four or five weeks at Fenton Lodge and never once, I realized, had I thought of my mother as a little girl there — moving about those rooms, sitting on my grandmother's knee to repeat her lessons ... standing before that looking glass and asking, 'Will I be pretty when I grow up?' ... pressing her nose to that pane and wondering if the rain would ever stop ... and generally doing all the things little girls do as they grow up. In thinking of it then, as I waited for the service to end, it was as if my mother had suddenly acquired an extra substance or a new coloration or something she hadn't possessed before.

And then, more than anything, I wanted her to *be* there, so that I could tell her about this new discovery — that she had a history before I was ever thought of, that she was *somebody* long before I existed. Such moments come to every son and daughter. It is how we learn to let go of our parents — and how we teach them to let go of us. And this very ordinary, commonplace discovery about our mother hit me with such force, and seemed to me so unique, that I was desperate for her to slip out of those invisible realms, show herself to me, and let me tell her all about it.

And so I learned an important truth about grief, as well. I couldn't have put it into words but the germ of it was sown at those forbidding gates. Grief is not about tears and self-pity. They are merely its occasional by-products. Grief is being cut off from all those opportunities to share. To share what? Everything! We live life in a kind of daze. It's a tale told to us not by a fool, as Shakespeare says, but by someone who speaks very fast — a thousand words a minute. We pick up mere smatterings. And it's only when we step back for a moment and share them with others — compare our muddled understandings with theirs, which are equally sketchy and imperfect — that we can begin to see the true pattern of it all.

Our mother had been the most wonderful person for that sort of sharing. She had turned her back on the conventional life she had been reared to lead. The veils of prejudice had been lifted from her sight. She saw things that others missed — things that I, too, in my turn, was beginning to glimpse as, in a way, I made the same journey, though in the reverse direction (even to that same childhood home of hers!). Of course, if she hadn't died, I'd never have started that journey, perhaps never have made these discoveries. But feelings trample on such nice logic. I *had* started the journey and I *was* making those discoveries — and she was no longer there to share them. *That* was the heart of grief for me. The tears, as I say, were incidental.

But they there were there on my cheeks — real tears — when the gatekeeper came from nowhere and asked me what I was doing. I was only vaguely aware of them but they softened his manner as I turned to face him. "You're not one of ours," he said in a gentler tone.

I showed him Marian's letter and explained my purpose there. He told me visits had to be arranged in writing in advance and that, in any case, a maid was not allowed any visitors during her first six weeks.

I asked if I could have a glass of water as I'd walked a long way.

He took me into his lodge, where a kettle was trilling on the hob. I warmed my hands at the stove while the tea brewed.

"What did your sister do to get sent here?" he asked.

I gave him a potted version of what had happened since our mother's death — saying nothing, of course, about the Trevartons and our connection there. All I said was that a charitable gentleman connected with our family had paid the rent for a twelvemonth and that the Angells had taken advantage of our affliction to pocket the money, get us out, and rent the cottage afresh.

"Harry Angell, eh?" he said, though whether because he knew the name or was merely committing it to memory I couldn't tell. He poured out the tea and gave me plenty of sugar, for which I was grateful. Then, apropos nothing, he said, "However ..."

He left the rest of the sentence hanging while he went out by the inner door and walked briskly across the courtyard. He returned a couple of minutes later to say that Marian's housemistress would see me when the service was over, which would be soon. The singing had stopped and the subdued hum and clatter of people moving around under discipline came drifting across the yard to us.

Marian with a housemistress! I thought. Just like rich little girls in stories. I wondered did she sleep in a 'dorm' where they held pillow-fights and midnight feasts?

I'd barely finished my tea when he said, "Here she comes. Miss Martin, herself."

At first I took her for one of the maids. Her short, spare figure was dressed all in black and she huddled her shawl tight around her against a chill breeze, which the courtyard somehow magnified into little wind-devils. I dropped a curtsy when she entered the lodge. I was all ready to say, "Good morning, ma'am," but the words deserted me at the sight of her beauty. She really was the most beautiful lady I had ever set eyes on. I had to fight an impulse to touch her cheek — to see if she was real.

"You are Cristobel Moore?" she asked. "Marian's sister?"

I saw she was accustomed to the effect her beauty had on impression-able young females of around my age. Her voice was less attractive — rather shrill and wobbly, in fact. I curtsied again and said I was. I also tried to explain that I had not known about their rules for visitors but she cut me short with: "And you are the authoress of this letter?"

It appeared as if by magic in her hand and she waved it before me. Her manner was amazingly impersonal. She showed neither hostility nor warmth toward me. I said I hoped it had not caused offence.

"On the contrary," she replied. Then, looking me up and down, she said, "But I supposed you were older than Marian. You certainly write like an older sister. Davies tells me you've come all the way from Falmouth this morning?"

"And not a bite to eat, ma'am," the porter put in, though I had not told him that.

"Is that true?" she asked me.

"Yes, Miss Martin." I didn't want to own up to using the chocolate machine on a Sunday.

"Well, you may take luncheon with us," she said. Cutting short my thanks she went on: "I'm disappointed to find you so young, Miss Moore. I had hopes of ... well, never mind. I must talk with you about your sister. Come!" She turned and walked back across the courtyard.

I looked at Mr Davies, as I now knew him to be called, and he tilted his head in the direction she'd taken. "Go on," he urged. "You're some star to her! Don't let it run to waste."

I trotted after Miss Martin, catching up with her at the main door, which was of oak, studded with iron rivets. Over it a clock gave the time as twenty-eight minutes to noon. An inscription beneath it ran: UT HORA SIC VITA.

"D'you know what it means?" she asked when she saw my eyes scanning the legend.

"*Vita* has something to do with *life,* I know," I replied. "And I'm guessing that *hora* means *hours.* Something about the hours of our lives being numbered?"

"Not bad." She nudged me indoors. "As the hours pass by, so pass our lives, perhaps? Life is but a passing hour? You weren't far wrong, you see. Now, sit there and make yourself comfortable."

Her study was immediately inside the entrance and its door closed behind us before I had more than the barest glimpse of the hall. I had an impression of a broad, uncarpeted staircase, bare granite walls, and over the half-landing a large gothic window, barred and filled with plain glass. I saw no people there, nor did it smell of girls — wayward or otherwise. It smelled of carbolic and cabbage.

"Now tell me what has happened, Miss Moore," she began. "Tell me everything you can remember and please try to leave nothing out."

Taking my heart in my hands I replied, "First, I should like to ask you, Miss Martin, why my sister is here at all? Has she done anything wrong? Has she been up before a magistrate?"

The housemistress waved her hands at me as if banking down the fires of my impatience. "We don't have all day," she said. "Simply accept for the moment that she is lawfully placed here under the provisions of the most recent Poor Law Act — of 1889, to be precise. Now please tell me everything that led up to her arrival here, as far as you are aware of it. Believe me, I have her best interests at heart. You do believe that, don't you?"

I told her I did — and then I told her *everything.* Our mother's story, our father's decline, their deaths, our resolve to keep the family together, my visit to Fenton Lodge, my grandfather ... I told her the lot — the way it had all started so hopefully and then had turned to dust and ashes.

As soon as I mentioned the Trevartons her expression changed — not markedly but enough for me to notice. Up until then there had been a sort of eagerness in her. But when I mentioned my grandmother's offer to me, her expression became set and rather grim. At the time I had no idea what a risk she was taking in seeing me at all. A prudent woman who valued her place would have sent me home without even seeing me. But women like Miss Martin are the salt of the earth.

Yet she was no fool. She said nothing that I could repeat to her detriment. She simply pointed out that old Mrs Trevarton had made no representations on Marian's behalf — leaving me to assume that my grandmother was rather content to leave things as they were. And from there it was but a short step to the surmise that the old woman had actually had a hand in the breaking up of our family. Just in case I didn't get the point, Miss Martin added, quite casually, "D'you think it might help if you asked your grandmother to intervene directly to bring you all back together again? The Trevartons have enormous influence in the county, you know. They could undo things as easily as do them in the first place."

I'd have had to be deaf and stupid not to understand her then.

Deflated, I said I thought there'd be little point in asking my grandmother to do anything on our behalf.

"I rather agree," she said with a wan little smile. Then, brisk again: "So we are left with the situation as it is. I am well aware that Marian does not belong here, and I believe without question that the situation arose in just the way you describe. But that still doesn't help us to deal with this business." She put her head on one side and said, "May I be quite frank about her?"

"Please," I replied, already half guessing what was coming next.

"I said that your letter led me to expect you to be her elder sister ... well, now that I've met you, I think you *are* — in all but actual years. The hours of your life are *not* like the hours of hers — *ut hora non sic vitae!* She is so thoughtless and impressionable! I fear that every day she passes under this roof, in the company of girls who are truly wayward and well advanced on life's downward path, the danger of her corruption can only grow. I was on the point of writing to you about it. I had hoped to find you fully twenty-one and able to take her into lodgings and keep her under your wing. But ..." There was another wan smile.

"I believe you flatter me, Miss Martin," I said. "But I must agree with you over Marian."

She nodded. "Good. Well, then, my next suggestion is this. I have an aunt — a married aunt — who lives to the north of London in a village called Hampstead. Have you heard of it?"

I dredged up the only thing I'd ever heard about Hampstead. "Where Keats lived?" I asked.

Keats had been our mother's favourite. He died even younger than she did — only twenty-six.

"Ah!" She gave her first genuine smile — a smile between equals. Social equals, that is, for we were most *un*equal in every other way. I was still a servant in a servant's Sunday drab, but now I had a toe over the threshold of her class. "Keats! 'Where youth grows pale and spectre-thin and dies ... where but to think is to be full of sorrow, and leaden-eyed despairs'!" She waved a hand at the walls around us. "And to think he never even set eyes on this place!"

I felt the hair prickle on my neck for I was remembering another snatch of Keats, which our mother had spoken only a week or so before she died: 'Where's the face one would meet in every place? Where's the voice, however soft, one would hear so very oft?' Had our mother known how we'd feel after she was gone? I was halfway through the quotation before I realized I was speaking it out loud.

"Yes," she said with a little catch in her voice. "Well!" And this time she had to force herself to become brisk once more. "My idea is to send Marian to my Aunt Alice in Hampstead, where she would be trained in domestic duties — possibly even as a lady's maid, like you."

What a dilemma! What a bitter-sweet proposal it was! Anything, even work in a fish cannery, would surely be better than Little Sinns. But ... London! Over three hundred miles — and twenty-five shillings — away by train! (And a single fare at that, for there were no Third Class return fares. The working classes moved. They did not visit.)

"I know," Miss Martin said sympathetically. "It hasn't exactly come out of the blue. My aunt did write to me about a month ago, asking if I had a suitable girl. Would you ... *object* if I sent her Marian?"

She laid an odd stress on the word. At the time I thought little of it. I was thinking mainly about what was best for Marian — and this offer was obviously it.

"Of course I shouldn't object, Miss Martin! I'd go down on my knees and thank you — and so will Marian, I hope."

"Good!" she exclaimed with obvious relief. "Well, no doubt you'd like to wash and brush up before luncheon. I'll put you and your sister on Matron's table. There's no talking during meals, I'm afraid, but you'll be able to smile at each other. And then afterwards you may promenade together on the road outside, provided you keep within sight of Davies's window."

I embarrassed her with my thanks.

T he only place where we were *not* in sight of the porter's lodge window was immediately outside the gate, right up against the wall — a most public kind of privacy. There, after that awful silence right through the meal, Marian and I broke down and, hugging to each other like cleavers in wool, cried our eyes out. But we embarrassed ourselves so much that it ended in a fit of giggles and then, feeling ever so much better, we walked hand in hand up and down the bleak stretch of road between Great and Little Sinns. I took my glove off so it would be skin against skin. There's nothing like the touch of one's own flesh and blood.

The warmth of her hand made me realize how lonely I had been since we were all together last. And if *I* had been lonely, who, in a way, had ended up in the best situation of all, I could just imagine how it must have been for Marian and how it still was for Tom, Gerald, Arthur, and little Teresa. I was filled with a rush of anger at everyone and no one for wrenching us apart.

"Have you written to any of the others?" I asked her.

"We aren't left to write till we've been in six weeks," she replied.

"You mean you're not *allowed* to write *until* then. Why are you 'talking common'?"

I don't think she was aware of it, actually. She had simply fallen in with local custom, as was always her way.

"Same thing," she said.

I didn't want to spoil the occasion with an argument, however mild. So I remarked that Miss Martin seemed a nice enough person. Marian replied that she was very hard and often caned the maids on their bare posteriors. I asked if she did so unjustly. Marian said no, but mercy wasn't her strong point.

"It must be very hard keeping discipline — knowing the sort of maid who'd be sent to a place like that," I pointed out. "I expect they're a bad lot all round."

I was surprised to see a sort of contemptuous pity in my sister's eyes. "You really believe that, do you?" she asked. "The world is divided into sheep and goats — or ewes and nannies, in our case?" She shook her head sadly and I felt rather small, especially after the way Miss Martin had built me up.

"What then?" I asked. "What are they really like?"

"Like people. The naughty ones are the ones everybody expects to be naughty. They don't like to disappoint, I suppose." She giggled.

I saw it would be a fruitless discussion. In any case, I wasn't in the least concerned for any other maid under that roof, only for Marian. "Miss Martin says you shouldn't be here at all," I told her.

She darted a surprised glance at me.

"Has she not spoken to you about it?" I asked.

She shook her head. "What did she say? She asked me a lot about our family, and our parents' deaths, and what had become of us all."

"Did you tell her about the Angells and how they cheated us?"

She shook her head again.

"Why ever not?"

"Because."

"That's no answer, Marian."

"Can't you see? If I blackened his name like that, it would look as if I was kicking back, out of spite, at those disgraceful things he said about me. It would only make people think he was telling the truth."

She had a point. I wondered if I had done right in telling Miss Martin about it. People will always believe the word of a Godfearing, property-owning churchman against that of an orphan adolescent maid of an inferior class — which is why we were so vulnerable, of course. "Have you told *anybody?*" I asked.

"Only June Goldsworthy," she replied. "She's my best friend here. I made her promise not to split."

"What did she say?"

"Nothing much, really," she replied — but so awkwardly that I knew it wasn't true.

"She must have said something."

"Well, if you really want to know, she said I'd as well be hanged for a sheep as a lamb."

It was a moment or two before the implication of these words struck home. Meanwhile Marian was adding, "She says her older sister does it and she's got her own apartment in Falmouth and it's lovely."

I was about to explode and say things like 'And you call this June Goldsworthy your best friend! No wonder Miss Martin wants to get you away from here as quickly as possible!' But memories of many previous clashes with my sister prevented me. Not that we were forever fighting. Quite the opposite. But on those occasions when we did, I never got my way by taking the high ground with her. Instead I said, "Miss Martin asked me if I thought you could train as a lady's maid, too. She knows a family in London who are looking for a good maid to train. I said I wasn't too sure about that."

She took the bait. "What?" she asked indignantly. "You think you're the only one with enough airs and graces to ..."

"It wasn't that," I assured her. "Honestly, Marian! As if I'd think like that! No — it was just the thought of your being so far away from the rest of us. And" — I hesitated — "you know ... London."

"What about London?" She was calmer but still prickly.

I sang a snatch of the old ballad: *"So to London Town she came. There she met another squire — and she lost her name again!* And that young lady ended up 'drownded,' if you recall."

"And you think that would happen to me!" she sneered.

I hugged her arm and said, "No! I was just being selfish. I didn't want you to move so far away. I still want to get Teresa back — and the boys. I want us all to be together again."

"But the Sellicks have got the cottage now," she objected.

Poor Marian! When a person lives so intensely inside each passing moment, she cannot take a longer view. "There are other cottages," I pointed out. "In fact, there's an empty one on the road up to Whitethorn. I can see it out of my bedroom window. You could get work somewhere in Falmouth, I'm sure. And so could Tom. And with my five shillings we could support the others between us and not be a burden on any parish. So I think there's a good chance they'd let us. If you read the newspapers, they're full of letters and speeches about the burden of the indigent and needy on the poor put-upon ratepayer — so they should be very glad that we're willing to relieve them of the four Moores they're currently burdened with. Five, including you!"

Marian was silent so long I had to prompt her: "What d'you say?"

She sighed. "There's not the slightest hope of us being all together again, Crissy. If you think that, you're living in a fool's paradise."

I knew then that it had been a mistake to mention London — which I only did to distract her from the shocking notions this June Goldsworthy creature had put in her mind. "So you're just going to let them split us up and you're not going to raise a finger in protest!" I said bitterly. "Much less *do* anything about it."

"Look what happened when I tried!" she responded angrily. "I lost my character and my liberty. It's all very well for you to talk, Crissy, but where were *you* when they came and took everyone away? You were supposed to find day work in Helston and pull your weight at home. Instead you took a nice living-in place with our grandmother, who only lets you come home ..."

"And five shillings a week, don't forget," I interrupted, beginning to feel angry myself, now.

"It's not the same as having you there, though. You weren't *there* when the men came and took us to scats and pieces. There was only me. Against five of them. You weren't there. We've no hope of getting back together. You're only making all this fuss because you feel guilty you weren't there."

Her brutal words had such a ring of truth that I was mortified. I *did* feel guilty for what they had done to my brothers and sisters. I always will. And perhaps I was trying to take it out on her. I felt so desolate, so ashamed, that I burst into tears once more.

Marian could not bear unhappiness in others — soft thing that she was. She put an arm about me and hugged me tight, saying things she hoped would comfort me. Every one of them was another nail in the coffin of my hopes.

"Try and look on the bright side, darling," she said. "The boys are learning trades and will be 'prenticed soon enough. Teresa will be taken into a good home with two parents who actually want her. And, if what you say about Miss Martin and these people in London is true, I may soon be as well off as you. We can all keep in touch by writing. We can keep each other's spirits up — you've no idea how wonderful it was to get your letters. Mind you, I don't know how you find the time! You're an angel ..." And so on.

The trouble is, it worked.

I'm two people, in fact: a realist and a battler. The realist in me responded to these honeyed words, agreeing that the picture they painted was probably the best that a powerless group of orphan children could possibly hope for, and that we were very lucky to be able to contemplate it even. We could have been put into orphanages and sent out to farms in the colonies, where the children were virtual slaves. We all knew youngsters who'd vanished like that, never to be heard of again. So Marian was right to say we were the fortunate ones — and we could, indeed, keep in touch by writing. Postage was only a penny, and we could all beg pen and paper. Teresa couldn't write more than her own name and a few simple words as yet, but if her new parents truly loved her, they'd surely let her draw pictures and they could add a few words of their own until she was able to write for herself. And we could pass each other's letters around until they fell apart. In short, it wasn't the end of the world.

Unfortunately, my spirit couldn't accept such soothing advice.

I did not realize that events would move so quickly. Perhaps it was just as well, for there had been enough tears already that day and if I had known it would be my last meeting with Marian before she went to Hampstead, there would have been floods more. I wrote to Miss Martin a few days after that visit, thanking her for her kindness and enclosing a note for my sister. She replied saying that Marian had left for London that very morning, taking my letter with her. No doubt, she added, I should be hearing from her when she had settled in. She gave me her directions, which were care-of a Mrs Morrell of Nether Hall, Windsor Terrace, Hampstead. She added that it was where Keats had loved to walk, recalling what we had said about the poet.

There was a curious postscript to her letter, saying she had been struck by Marian's sober and earnest behaviour after her return from our walk, which she ascribed to my excellent influence. She said she was always on the look-out for young females of good character, older than her charges at the Home for Wayward Girls, but not so old as to be unable to communicate freely. "It is not that my girls lack for good female examples," she added, "but, unfortunately, most of them are elderly and rather stern. They mean well but manage ill. Young women who can show, by their example, that life may be Fun without being Wicked or Criminal are rare. It is my belief, dear Miss Moore, that you will be such a young woman in three or four years' time and could be a great influence for good here; in what precise capacity, it would be pointless as yet to speculate, but please do keep some such vague possibility in mind meanwhile. And I entreat you not to lose touch entirely. Now that Marian has left here, you have no obvious reason for calling upon us, but please do so at any time you may find yourself in this neighbourhood. Mrs Trevarton's son is, I gather, a solicitor in Redruth, so it is not unthinkable that you may be sent here on an errand to him. And if you feel in need of advice that you think I might tender or some small service I might perform, please do not hesitate to ask."

All in all it was a most curious letter. I think she was aware that, having so recently lost a mother, my feelings might be especially vulnerable to the unspoken appeal between these lines. But why should she wish to make such an appeal in the first place? I did not even consider such a question then, of course. I was in too much of a turmoil (that is, equal parts of sadness, trepidation, and excitement) over Marian's swift departure. Later, in a calmer frame of mind, I thought she might have reached that awful moment in a spinster's life when the prospect of marriage has faded to almost nothing. Perhaps she had earlier been repelled at the thought of babies — helpless, bawling, vomiting little bundles of selfishness. Perhaps the notion that in me she had found a ready-made daughter, past the puking stage — mentally an adult but emotionally still a child — appealed to her.

Or perhaps she was just a conscientious housemistress and a kindly woman. One can be too clever by half when one tries to fathom the actions of others.

Anyway, with Marian gone — taking with her any realistic hope of swiftly reuniting the six of us — I felt I ought next to see what had happened to dear little Teresa. Perhaps I was wrong, though. At every stage in life girls are mentally and spiritually tougher than boys. They may cry more readily and bruise more easily but that means nothing. Boys soon learn to keep a stiff upper lip but that doesn't protect their souls from the scars. I should have gone to see Tom next. St Austell was no farther up the line from Truro than Penzance was on the down line. And I could have given Tom the fare to go and see Gerald and Arthur in Plymouth, which would have made him feel responsible toward them — and they toward him — and so it would have kept the five of us closer. But instead I wrote to him, telling him about Marian's bit of good fortune (as I expressed it) and said I was going to see Teresa on my next Saturday off, which would be on the tenth of May. (My days off had been changed from Sundays to Saturdays for Mrs T's convenience. But it was more convenient for me, too, since there were many more trains on Saturdays than on the sabbath.) I explained that that, in turn, would mean I could not see him until the twenty-fourth at the earliest, and even then it would depend on what situation I found with Teresa.

I also wrote to the two younger boys, of course. Arthur replied with a drawing of a dreadnought, which told me nothing beyond the fact that he could not be too unhappy. Gerald was only slightly more informative: They got jam on Sundays and he was learning to sew his own buttons on and darn his own socks. From Tom I heard only how exhausting the work was and how meagre the food. He was tired and hungry most of the time — after which his "Hoping this finds you as it leaves me at present" didn't seem very affectionate.

I was too young to read between the lines of these scrappy missives and see all that they did not say. I saw only the selfishness of boys — which is all I ever saw in our father, too.

Also, in fairness to myself, I have to add that my attempts to communicate with Teresa were far more worrying at that time. I had written three or four letters to her, care of the Sisters of St Breaca in Morrab Road, Penzance. I had even got the name of the superior there, a Sister Enuda, and had written to her, entreating her to pass on an enclosed note to my little sister. To none of these had I received any reply — nor even an acknowledgement of their receipt. You may imagine that I wasted no time that Saturday morning but caught the first train to Truro and the first down connection to Penzance.

I passed the postman going up Whitethorn Hill and he gave me a letter from Marian, postmarked Hampstead. I was so excited I wanted to stop and read it at once, but it would have made me miss the train. Then, by the time I reached the station I had grown so accustomed to putting it off that I thought I would keep it until I reached Truro, where I had an hour to wait between trains and intended walking down to see the cathedral, which is modern, of course, but looks centuries old. I could not have picked a more tranquil and gracious place to read so disturbing a letter.

Either Marian had an imagination to rival Hans Andersen or Miss Martin had no idea what her Aunt Alice was like. A rich widowed aunt must sound like a very safe and respectable creature. However, the fact that she chose to live in Hampstead, which even then had a raffish, artistic reputation, would hang a little question mark over her *absolute* respectability. I knew as much the moment I had read Marian's letter. But Miss Martin knew it not, it seemed.

In her very first paragraph my sister was cock-a-hoop with the clever 'stunt' she and June Goldsworthy had played on Miss Martin (as they imagined). There was a copy of the *Police Guide* in the porter's lodge, and the Goldsworthy creature had got to hear of it. (The *Guide* is a compendium of law as it affects the police and the general public, written in fairly plain English for the benefit of the sergeant on the desk. It is the bible for all officials who have legal dealings with the public.)

She and Marian had crept down there at dead of night and looked up the main provisions of Section One of the Poor Law Act, 1889 — which Miss Martin had mentioned to me and which I may then have spoken of to Marian. Anyway, it dealt with the power of the Poor Law Guardians over children.

The pair of them had copied out numerous paragraphs, the general conclusion of which was that the right of the Guardians to detain orphans ceased on their sixteenth birthday, unless that had been brought before the courts. Then, and only then, could they detain them until the age of eighteen.

Marian, though I had told her of Miss Martin's intention of sending her to Hampstead long before she and June Goldsworthy dreamed up this idiotic night raid on the porter's lodge, was convinced it was her 'cleverness' in leaving this scrap of paper lying around where Miss Martin or one of her assistants could find it that had forced the housemistress to realize they were breaking the law by detaining her there. Miss Martin's pure kindness in sending her to 'Aunt Alice' was thus reduced to the panic-stricken response of a frightened woman.

And as if that weren't folly enough for one letter, she went on to say that, even for children below the age of sixteen, the Guardians' powers were limited if there were parents, guardians, or near-kin willing and able to take care of them. She enclosed a fresh copy of the whole rigmarole — "in case you need some ammo in your fight for Teresa!"

So now it was *my* fight to get the family back together! Her idea of family was now a matter of brief reunions in some remote future when we were all grown up and had some control over our lives. Meanwhile Life itself beckoned and enticed her — especially as it appeared to be lived in Hampstead.

By London standards, I suppose 'Aunt Alice's' establishment was nothing out of the ordinary. But to me, as retailed in my sister's letter, it seemed shocking in the extreme. Mrs Morell (to give Aunt Alice her proper name) often wore no corsets, for instance, and did not greatly mind if her servants left them off, too. "Try it yourself one day," Marian wrote. "You've no idea what a torment they are until you leave them off. And the gentle touch of loose linen against your skin is sublime!"

Sublime! What a Nineties sort of word! I had to get up and leave that beautiful cathedral before I could read another word of this shocking letter — which was just as well, for there was worse to follow. Mrs Morell was a liberal freethinker and a great believer in female education. She insisted that all her domestics should enrol for one evening class a week at the Working Men's College in Great Ormond Street. She also insisted on their belonging to the Honor Club in Fitzroy Square, which was a club for better-class female servants. The subscription was fourpence a week for under-seventeens. Marian listed their activities in her letter: visiting doctor on Mondays, games on Wednesdays, gymnastics on Tuesdays, sing-songs on Saturdays, and poetry, embroidery, and mandolines on Thursdays. There was also a circulating library. She forgot to say anything about Fridays and Sundays, which was typical of her. All Mrs M's female domestics except the one on duty went there three or four nights a week. She paid their bus fare, which was a penny each way. I thought it was a scandal. Of course, there was a bit of jealousy on my part, especially when I heard that Marian had enrolled in a Useful Arts course at the Working Men's College. Her chosen subject was porcelain and pottery decoration, which I should have loved to do.

I read this letter several times on the train to Penzance, which enabled me to disentangle the strong rage of jealousy from my milder outrage at Mrs Morell's freethinking ways. I even managed to salvage a little superiority for myself out of my feelings when I realized there was, in fact, nothing to stop me from enrolling in a Useful Arts course down at the Royal Cornwall Polytechnic in Falmouth — which had the distinction of being the first polytechnic in the whole of England. (So there!) And I should be doing so under my own steam — not at the insistence of any employer! I felt a great deal better as I left the terminus at Penzance, having inquired of a porter the way to Morrab Road. I was not aware how much of that baleful letter had stuck in my brain — but I was soon to find out.

I had been to Penzance a couple of times with all our family but I knew little of it beyond Market Jew Street, which is where most of the shops are. The town divides naturally into two — a commercial half, built around a mighty harbour and facing east toward St Michael's Mount and the foreshore of Mount's Bay, and a residential half, full of hôtels and boarding houses and facing southward to the open waters of the bay and the English Channel. Morrab Road more or less bisected this residential area, running inland from the seafront to the hills around Chapel St Clare on the northern fringe of the town.

My quickest way probably led via Market Jew Street, the town's main thoroughfare, but I love the sea and resolved to stay as close to it as possible. I strolled along the wharf around the innermost part of the harbour for a furlong or so, past a series of warehouses and depôts until it ended at the lifeboat station. There I had to turn inland and thread my way through a warren of mean streets around the back of the gasworks. Despite a good sea breeze, the walls of the buildings were dank and patchy with green slime. The lanes wound this way and that, as if they were the last thing the builders of all these higgledy-piggledy dwellings had thought of. The oppressive, musty smell trapped among them made me realize that our family's poverty, which was as deep as anything around me here, had had certain advantages, nonetheless — sea air and sun to name but two. I was happy to find a ropewalk that led me down to the port once more, not far from the Trinity House dock.

The harbour was crammed with ships of every sort — colliers, cargo boats, the *Lyonesse,* the ferry to the Scilly Isles, just casting off, and hundreds of inshore fishing boats, either returning from one trip or getting ready for the next. The smells of tar, steam, fresh fish, and harbour mud all mingled on the briny air and filled my youthful head with romantic ideas of voyages and adventures — vague but all the more enticing for that.

I recall gazing at one big, rather rusty cargo vessel — probably just a little tramp steamer but huge-seeming to me — and spying a boy around my own age leaning against the stern rail, smoking a pipe and spitting a great quid of juice after each puff. Seagulls wheeled and mewed around him and when he caught my eye he gave a sort of diagonal nod of his head and winked jovially. He knew how I envied him his free, roving life (as I imagined it) and I suppose at that moment it must have seemed pretty good to him, too — what with the sun streaming down and the bay all mottled with pretty little white horses. I went aside from my direct path then, up on the walls of the old battery, to bask in that same sun and relish my one-day's freedom. Or just five minutes of it, anyway.

The fact was I did not relish this meeting with the nuns of St Breaca's. I could not understand why Sr Enuda had not even acknowledged my letters but it did not bode well. I knew I ought to be preparing certain words and phrases so that I wouldn't be taken by surprise and have to stammer and stumble through my thoughts when the time came. But I've never been very good at that sort of thing — what do I say first? ... what if they say this? ... or that? ... how can I get them to agree to so-and-so? — all that sort of thing. If I try to work things like that out in advance, my brain either freezes solid or I start imagining fantastic things — like ... I could ask Sr Enuda if she'd ever seen a school of whales in full flight across the evening sky. Just to flummox her. Stupid things like that, which only made me feel annoyed in the end. It was worst of all when, as now, I had absolutely nothing to go on.

The seafront was fringed by a modest little cobbled road known rather grandly as the Western Promenade. Morrab Road was quite new, too. In fact, the upper half, before the School of Art and Science, was still a lane through open fields and gardens. I had no difficulty in identifying the House of St Breaca, which was then the largest building in the new road — a granite house with a fussy gothic porch and large bay-window projections on either side. Three lay sisters were weeding the flower beds in front while a tall, elegant nun in a blue habit gathered a basket of flowers. Like any lady of the house, she wore kid gloves and wielded a pair of secateurs.

I approached her and dropped a curtsy. "Sister Enuda?" I asked in my politest manner.

"Yes?" Her tone was cautious, even wary.

"If you please, Sister," I went on, "I am Cristobel Moore."

"Yes?" Now she was curt, as if the name meant nothing to her.

"Teresa's elder sister. Teresa Moore — from Porthleven — a little dark-haired maid, aged five ..." I went on adding details, hoping for a moment when some sort of recognition would light her face.

But none came. Indeed, after a while she shook her head and cut across me, saying, "It doesn't mean anything to me, child, I fear."

"I was told she'd been taken into your care here. After our parents died. In March. I think she came here around the beginning of April."

She frowned in bewilderment. "Who told you all this?" she asked.

"The police," I replied — which certainly made her more attentive than before. "We were six in the family. Three of us found work and were supporting ourselves and the younger children, when a neighbour laid false charges against ..."

"The police?" she cut across me.

"PC Hoad, Sister. The village constable in Porthleven."

"But why would she have been brought here?"

"That's what he said. He didn't understand it, either, I'm afraid. D'you mean she wasn't?"

"I'm not saying that," she answered sharply — and for the first time I got the feeling she was being deliberately obtuse and evasive. Of course, my hackles went up at once and I had to take an equally deliberate hold of my temper.

"Where else might she have been taken, then?" I asked.

"I'm not saying she *wasn't* brought here," the sister continued. "It could have been while I was away. But if she was suitable for adoption, she'd have been in and out rather quickly."

I drew a deep breath and clenched my fists tight. Then, speaking in as careful and controlled a manner as I could, I said, "Well, someone must have written down something about it. There must be a record somewhere. I just want to know where she is."

She half-turned from me, reaching for another flower for her basket. "We're all very busy," she said. "You'll have to write. Yes — send in your inquiries in writing."

I sighed. "Not wishing to be disrespectful, Sister Enuda, but I've written several letters here this past month — all without a reply. The latest was directed to you personally. Besides, I'm here now. I've travelled two hours from Falmouth and it has cost me almost a florin. So, if it's not altogether too much trouble ..."

She turned and stared at me as if I'd crawled out from under a log. "Why! What an impertinent little creature it is! 'If it's not altogether too much trouble' — forsooth! How dare you!"

"You mean how dare I inquire after my baby sister's health and whereabouts?" I responded.

She saw then that I was not to be browbeaten with the sort of words and phrases that ladies of her class employed on servants, so she changed her tactics completely — and with a turn of speed that I had to admire. "You may give up all expectation of seeing your sister again or of tracing her whereabouts. Once a child is adopted, all links with its past life are severed — deliberately so, and for what I should hope are obvious reasons."

She tried to imply by her tone and glance that I was one of the most obvious reasons of all. But for that I believe I should have kept my temper. Instead, I said, "Then you *have* given her to another family?"

"I didn't say that."

"What did your words mean, then?"

She hesitated. Then, somewhat rattled — and annoyed with herself for letting me get her in that state — she snapped, "It no longer has anything to do with you. Legally you are no longer her kin. You have no *locus standi.*" (Or some such Latin phrase that was meant to impress.)

So it was to be a matter of law, eh!

I drew a deep breath to calm my racing heart and said, "Did you *ascertain* that both her parents were dead? And that her next of kin were failing in their guardianship?"

"Of course!" she snapped — then, realizing she had told a lie in which she might be caught out, she added, "The authorities did, anyway."

"But it wasn't the *authorities* that handed her over for adoption, Sister. It was *you!*"

"It's the same thing," she said. "Goodness — what a proper little barrack-room lawyer it is!"

"Did you find us — her next of kin — mentally defective? Or vicious in habit and mode of life — or in any way unfit to have control of her?"

These were direct quotations of the phrases Marian had copied from the *Police Guide,* of course. And though I tried to speak them as if I used them almost every day, phrases like 'unfit to have control' alerted her at once to their legal origin.

"It *is* a barrack-room lawyer," she said again, but not quite so loftily as before. It is usually a mistake to repeat an insult of that kind.

I pressed on: "Or had we been convicted of any offence against Teresa? Were we permanently bedridden? Or residing in a workhouse?"

"What *are* you talking about?" she asked angrily.

"You invoked the legal situation now that Teresa has gone for adoption. I am talking about the legal situation *before* that — the Poor Law Act of 1889 — which makes it quite clear that Guardians do *not* have absolute power to place orphan children … you know … here, there, and everywhere." I waved my hands vaguely toward the house. I was running out of steam and my heart was thumping away in a panic at my own boldness.

But also, I must admit, I was excited — even thrilled. If I *had* done the sensible thing and prepared for every possible discussion in advance, including one as hostile as this, I should never have had the courage to pursue it. But because she was so smug and superior, so sure she could use her own smattering of the law to bamboozle me, anger filled me with the power of ten — and then it was easy.

Also she was enjoying it, too. I've seen women fighting in the street — drawing blood, even — screaming and cursing … and all the happier for it. Sr Enuda was like that. The petals on the roses and Michaelmas daisies in her pannier trembled with her passion. "What's done is done," she said harshly. "If you think it can be undone, then you're nothing but a fool — no matter how clever you may think you're being. The Poor Law Act, indeed! What did you imagine you'd achieve by coming here today?"

The question made me think. What, indeed, had I hoped to do here? For a start, what had I hoped to find? I decided to answer that question first. "I had hoped to find a little charity in such a house as this, Sister Enuda. A little love …"

"Which is why you came armed to the teeth with the law, I suppose!" she sneered.

She had me there. But I have always found it best, when losing an argument, simply to ignore the other side's most damaging points and pursue my own. "A little understanding, even," I continued. "It was not very kind to tell me I am nothing to Teresa now, and that she is nothing to me. She is *everything* to me."

Sr Enuda was obviously of the same opinion as me, for she simply ignored this accusation. She turned on her heel and flounced indoors. It was such a juvenile action that, for a moment, I could almost picture the adolescent little maid she must once have been — goody-goody enough to have been made a school prefect but full of insecurity and quite unable to cope with any serious challenge to her authority. "If you want to bandy law with me," she called out over her shoulder, "put it in writing. This interview is at an end."

She was within an ace of falling to pieces. A terrible and savage glee filled me. I don't know if I actually bared my fangs and made talons of my fingers but that is what it felt like. I suddenly became aware of the three lay sisters — standing, kneeling, crouching at their work, watching me with jaws agape. I'm sure they'd never seen Sr Enuda go flouncing off in retreat like that.

But my feeling of triumph was short-lived indeed. I asked the lay sisters if they remembered a little maid with a limp, about five, with dark hair and deep-set blue-green eyes … and so on. At least one of them did. I could tell by her guilty eyes. But they were too frightened to speak. And in any case Sr Enuda threw wide a window at that moment and told them to get on with their work.

On my way down the path I bent and retied my shoelace near the guilty-eyed one. "Tell me!" I whispered urgently.

"She'm gone, my lover," she replied out of the side of her mouth.

"Where? What's the family's name?" I begged.

"Dunno," she answered reluctantly. But she did know, I felt sure.

"And *you,* girl," the superior added, "if you're not off these premises within ten seconds, I shall send for the police." After a long pause — too long to be effective — she added, "Then you'll learn all about the power of the law!"

At the front gate I turned and stared at her — a ghost of a woman behind the sheen on the window pane. Our eyes dwelled in each other's for a long time, in a childish contest to stare the other out — which, in the end, I let her win.

I walked back down Morrab Road too angry for tears, too bitter for mere sadness. Then my brain — the very same brain that had refused to prepare for that encounter — now began to replay it for me in all the ways it might have gone better. I should have started by saying what a lovely garden they had created out of what were mere fields only twenty years earlier. I might have given a hint that I was interested in becoming a nun myself. I should have let all her unpleasantness wash over me and have come back at her with love and cheerfulness.

And, of course, that developed into one of those stupid fantasies in which I now pursued Sr Enuda, night and day, year after year, with expressions of love and forgiveness, tending her on her deathbed and shaming her by my Christian example.

Then I *really* got angry with myself. Only the big, wide vista of the sea, and the screaming children playing in the sand, and a mongrel dog barking at a wavelet as if it were a living enemy ... the whole panorama of life going on around me, heedless of my hurt and rage — only this, I say, was able to calm me to the point where I could begin to take stock and assess how much damage I had done to my hopes of getting my darling sister back.

My first thought was then quite philosophical, really. I thought of how odd it was that life-as-we-expect-it-to-be is so different from life-as-it-really-is.

What sort of woman makes a reformatory superintendent? A grim half-man woman, surely — someone very like Sr Enuda. And what do we expect a nun to be like? A creature of sweetness and self-denial — a sort of Florence Nightingale to all the world. No prize for guessing which of the women who had entered my life recently came closest to fitting *that* bill!

I thought of Miss Martin's offer to help and knew that she was now my best — perhaps my only — hope of repairing some of the damage I had done.

I had no chance to see Miss Martin for another two weeks but I wrote her a note thanking her for what she had done for Marian, also for her very civil opinion of me, which I thought I had done nothing to deserve. I copied out just enough of my sister's letter to let her understand what a libertarian household her Aunt Alice maintained, in case she was unaware of it and had fond ideas of sending a truly wayward girl there for taming. I also summarized my meeting with Sr Enuda, covering my intemperate behaviour with the white lie that I had myself consulted a copy of the *Police Guide*, which I had discovered in my grandfather's library. I concluded by saying how much I would welcome her advice about undoing the damage and discovering my little sister's present whereabouts.

By then it had struck me that neither Tom nor Marian had made the slightest reference in their letters to our break-up as a family, much less to any active desire to see us all together again. Their unspoken attitude seemed to be that it was all up to me now. Marian was too busy exploring all the new possibilities that had now opened up before her; and Tom was too preoccupied with keeping *himself* together — never mind the rest of us.

So I was becoming reconciled to the idea that, for the moment, anyway, I would have to accept the *fait accompli* and simply do my best to keep in touch with the others. At least in that way we might reunite when we once again enjoyed freedom of movement. It was a bitter pill to swallow.

Teresa was the one who worried me most, because, being the youngest, she could so easily grow away from us and become a total stranger by the time she was of age. I tormented myself with visions in which she was adopted into some well-to-do family who would fill her head with snooty ideas so that she would look down her nose at her origins and have no desire to associate with a pair of sisters who were in service, much less with brothers who were labourers or, at best, mere artisans. Part of the torment, to be sure, lay in the fact that, if she *must* be adopted, I would not have wished her to be placed in a poorer home, even though she would not develop such airs and graces there.

Meanwhile, my training continued apace. To give my grandmother her due, she did nothing by halves and she taught me as thoroughly as anyone could. True, there was some self-interest in it, too. She desired a lady's maid of the highest quality. No duchess or royalty should have a better. So she set out to recast me in that mould and her attention to detail was relentless. Sometimes it was quite eerie.

I remember when she instructed me in the washing of blondes, which were fine lace trimmings, usually attached at collars and cuffs. I had to pick them off the garments and pull out every last trace of the cut stitches before washing them very lightly, using thin flakes of the finest toilet soap. Then I rinsed them in water with a little fig-blue, dried them, then redipped them in thin gum-water before drying them between layers of linen and ironing them.

The eerie thing about all this was that I recalled our mother showing me precisely the same procedure. She did all the fine finishing for several washerwomen in Porthleven and I used to help her. And she had shown me a trick in which she dissolved a little lump sugar in the final rinse water, instead of the thin gum. It made the blonde look as good as new and she told me not to pass on this little secret to any of the washerwomen. I told Mrs T of it, however, and she shot me the queerest look — as if I had read her mind — as if she had been on the point of telling me the very same thing.

And then, of course, we both realized what the link was. I could just see her telling our mother such tricks — perhaps in that very room — when she had been a maid the same age as me! Looking into that old woman's eyes, I could see she remembered it, too. The shock of it was doubly revealing, for it told me that since I had entered her household she had somehow managed to forget that I was that maid's daughter — not deep-down forget, perhaps, but at the everyday level.

I think, too, that it was the start of a slow change in her, one which eventually overcame her original thoughts and feelings about me — and even about my mother. While my grandfather had lived, he had been the one who regretted most keenly the deaths of all his other daughters. He was the one who hankered most to be reunited with the one maid who had managed to survive — but who had been lost to him by a death of a different sort. (Whether our mother would have reciprocated his desire I doubt. Perhaps she would have for our sakes, or when my father's decline into drunkenness was almost complete and she had come to the end of her tether. But to have done it for her own sake — never! She could be as stubborn in her opinions and implacable in her actions as anyone I ever knew; sometimes people have compared me to her but I know otherwise. I have had to fight a grim fight to retain my kind of stubbornness. Hers came naturally. And in all other ways she was more like Marian than me.) And, as so often happens inside marriages, when one partner desires something to the point of obsession, the other discovers a total indifference to it — like Jack Sprat and his wife. I'll bet that if Mrs Sprat passed on before her husband, he pretty soon developed a liking for fat — or if he had been first to go, there'd have been slivers of lean meat on her plate before long!

And so it was with Mrs T. While Old Mister Bill had lived, the unrequited longing to be reconciled with their daughter could be left exclusively to him; but the moment he departed, a little worm of that same emotion began gnawing away somewhere inside her — except that it was now too late. I was therefore the nearest substitute, and all the better in that I was not tainted by the original sin of disobedience.

How awkward life can be when it serves us tricks like that! We make bold decisions in a particular set of circumstances, being quite sure of our feelings ... then our circumstances change, our feelings change, but our decision is now unalterable. If my grandmother had been the strong, inflexible character she liked to suppose she was, she would have dismissed me the moment she felt the first twinges of that change coming on. But I think it rather fascinated her — not least the discovery that she could be swayed by new emotions at her advanced age. So I, the cuckoo, stayed in the nest beyond the point where she could bring herself to throw me out. And I continued to inhabit a mysterious sort of in-between land where I was both apprentice lady's maid and restored granddaughter — and yet, in some curious way, neither.

Mind you, this is pure speculation on my part, for we never got remotely close to discussing such things. At first that was because it would have been too painful, emotionally, for either of us. Later, I think it was because comment was no longer necessary in any case. We had reached an accommodation of our bizarre dual relationship that did not require any words.

Eerie moments like the one I have described (and there were, naturally, several others of a similar character) were by their nature fleeting. They did not call for either of us to readjust our basic attitude to each other. Indeed, I think we were not unusual in that. I'm sure there have been many occasions when ladies and their maids have developed an intimacy even deeper than the natural bonds between blood relations. The first sign that a more permanent change was occurring in my grandmother's attitude toward me came on the weekend after my visit to Penzance.

I had never kept secret from her my struggles to bring us Moores together. (I always called us 'we Moores' when speaking to her, to avoid the ambiguity of the word 'family' in that context.) I told her of my visits to Little Sinns and Penzance, though I said little of what actually took place there. And, of course, I never even hinted at my suspicion that she herself had played some part in it all. The part of me that suspected it and hated her for it had to play second fiddle to the rest of me, which needed the position, the training, and the money.

I also told her I hoped she would consider sending me, rather than one of the garden boys or any of the other maids, on errands to Redruth — so that, while Mr Walter was framing his reply, I could employ the time on a brief visit to Miss Martin. She replied that she would bear it in mind. "But *you,* Miss Moore, will also bear in mind that if you so much as hint to my son of your connection with our family, you'll be out on your ear with no character."

Again I wondered if the two older sons really did not know of our kinship, especially when all the servants and half the town did. It was such a family of fictions! However, I assured her I'd never do such a thing, not after she'd been so kind to me. (The odd thing is that I could bring myself to believe things like that at the time I spoke them!) But she remained unconvinced. She said she'd never met a woman yet who had the smallest sense of honour when those things closest to her heart were at stake — so I should never forget that her threat to kick me out backed up my promise to hold my tongue.

However, on that very next weekend, her threat was put to the test — and found to be quite empty! It came about in the following manner.

Having white-lied to Miss Martin about finding the *Police Guide* in my grandfather's library, I was astonished to discover that there was, indeed, a copy of the book there all the time. A moment's thought would have told me that it was not at all unlikely that a justice of the peace would get each new edition as it came out — especially a man like my grandfather, who would not want to be entirely at the mercy of the clerk of the court on matters of legal interpretation.

Mr Walter, who was paying the usual weekend visit, had sent me in there to get a copy of Ruskin's *Stones of Venice,* which his wife, Mrs Felicity, wished to consult on some point of architectural history. (He told me it was the book which, almost single-handed, had led to the visual destruction of Britain by all those ghastly Victorian buildings in brick-gothic. It opened my eyes for, in fact, I had rather liked brick-gothic until then.) While searching for the Ruskin book my eyes fell upon the *Police Guide* and I could not resist the temptation to find the passages Marian had copied. I was mainly interested to discover what she had left out of her précis.

It took rather longer than I expected because the index was so misleading. The relevant sections of the Act were listed under 'Work-houses,' not 'Children.' I was so excited to find it at last that I did not notice that Mrs Felicity, despairing of my return, had come to the library in person and was standing at the door, watching me, intrigued by my behaviour. When she saw the title of the book that so captured my interest, her curiosity would not be satisfied until I had explained all. And the more I explained, the more she wanted to know.

She was, as I said, a pre-Raphaelite sort of beauty, with a long, swanlike neck, the most luxuriant chestnut hair you ever saw, big, appealing eyes of a mysterious green, and an aristocratic, slightly roman nose. Her soft, dark-red lips looked like a calligraphic swash, they were so full of balanced curves and flourishes. She was the sort of woman whose very appearance is enough to overawe other women and make them accept opinions from her, take on commitments to her, and perform services for her — none of which would they even contemplate with most other women of their acquaintance.

She only needed to say, "And how did *you*, my dear Miss Moore, feel at that moment?" and I was off — telling her *exactly* how I felt then, and the next moment, and the next …

Even so, by some heroic effort, I managed to withhold all hint of our kinship with the Trevartons, though I think I must have told her every other detail of our parents' deaths and the breaking-apart of the six of us children.

At this stage I did not know how much her husband knew of our family's history. He would have been no more than twelve years old when our mother eloped with the groom, Barry Moore. Servants in the stables were usually known by their first names — unlike garden and indoor servants, who were always known by their surnames, even the maids. So the name Moore might not have registered with him, anyway. And, unless he picked up some gossip from the Trevarton employees — Bert Eddy, for instance, knew of me — he would have no other grounds for suspicion.

On the other hand, I could not believe that Mr Archie knew nothing of my origins and connections. But, as everyone said about him — in all things, not just in this instance — the more Mr Archie knew, the less he'd say. His silence was almost a guarantee that he knew. It was not easy for a maid my age, unversed in the ways of the world — and certainly in the ways of *their* world — to navigate a path through such treacherous shoals.

Anyway, I didn't know how much Mr Walter knew, so, rather than be caught out in a lie later, I told as much of the truth as I could, omitting only those facts that might connect me with the Trevartons and Fenton Lodge. Mrs Felicity was enthralled and, even though she had the Ruskin book in her hands by then — and had opened it at the section she wished to consult — she ignored it utterly and encouraged me with those mysterious eyes of hers to say more … more … more.

That was on the Saturday afternoon. She must have repeated some of it to her husband that night because, the following afternoon, when my mistress lay down and I had a couple of free hours, he watched me go out for a walk and then followed me.

In two hours I could make a very leisurely stroll down to the beach at Gyllingvase, which was a wild sort of place beyond the edge of the town. From there it was my habit to go up over the headland to Swanpool Point, down to the beach, and then along the lakeshore to Fenton Lodge — with lots of rests to stare at the sea and ponder on the ups and downs of life along the way. But I was not to be allowed such privacy on that day! I was going down the lane from Whitethorn Farm, when I heard his cry from behind me: "I say — Miss Moore! Do wait for me, there's a good girl!"

I knew at once what was coming and my heart fell into my boots. Mrs Felicity must have passed on everything I had said. And now he was going to get me to repeat it all. And — even worse, perhaps — to offer me his purely altruistic help in my struggle to discover what they'd done with Teresa. Of course, it was only 'worse' in one respect: If my mistress got to hear of it (and how, without letting him know the full truth, could I prevail upon him to say nothing to her?), she'd carry out her threat to dismiss me without a character. I could not think what to do, and I even contemplated denying the whole thing.

But that would have had the same dire consequence for me. He'd have gone indignantly to his mother, telling her of the 'cock-and-bull story' I'd made up to tease his wife … she'd hear the details and realize at once how close I'd come to blurting out everything ... and I'd be out on my ear, anyway!

Tell all or deny all — I was damned no matter what. There must, I thought, be a middle way through this minefield.

He wanted me to begin the tale at once, but I said it was a lovely summer day and I did not wish for anything but to breathe the sea air and feel the soft earth underfoot — at least until we reached the beach. Fortunately he was one of those men who know how to get more from a woman by letting her think she's having her own way. I say 'fortunately' in this case because it gave me time to collect my thoughts.

I saw the ideal place for our conversation when we were about a hundred yards from the beach — somewhere that would allow me to keep an eye on him while I spoke. The council had built a concrete wall to prevent further erosion of the land and some swimming enthusiasts had lately added a small flight of steps protected by a wooden rail. When we reached it I took one step down, then stopped and turned toward him, pretending to admire the view along the sands toward Pendennis Castle. He naturally stopped, too, and leaned against the return of the wooden rail at my side, staring out to sea. Then, I began my tale at last — or those bits of it that I had told his wife the day before.

Naturally, I watched his face like a cat by a mousehole. And I saw nothing in his demeanour to suggest that my tale was anything other than the tale of a stranger. There was no recognition of anything that touched him personally. I relaxed, thinking I now had the best of both worlds — I'd get the advice of a lawyer free and I'd not be breaking my bargain with my mistress.

"And so," he said when I had finished, "you were perusing the *Police Guide* in the hope of finding some hammer to crack this nut?"

I considered that this was a rather slangy, joky way of expressing my situation and just stared at him, somewhat coolly. He must have taken my blank look for incomprehension, because he then put it another way: "You want some legal means of getting your younger sister back from her new home?"

I nodded. "And of reuniting the rest of us, sir."

He looked at me as if I'd suggested climbing the Matterhorn. "But how would that be possible, Miss Moore? I mean, even suppose there were some legal instrument you could brandish that would force the agencies of the law to send your brothers and sisters back to you ... what then? There they are — imagine them — huddled in a group at

Falmouth station — all looking at you, saying, 'Well, now you've got us here — what next?' What d'you answer them?"

"We wouldn't huddle, sir. We'd dance. And no one would worry about what's next, believe me. We'd find something — just as we did before the Guardians broke us up. We've had a good schooling and we're not without resources."

His eyes dwelled in mine for a long moment but all he said was, "Hmm!" Then, more briskly — looking about us as if he'd half forgotten where we were — "This will take quite a bit longer than I thought. Where did you intend walking next? Pendennis Point and back, perhaps?" He gazed along the seafront.

The prospect was enticing but it would take too long, unless we stepped it out so briskly that conversation would be hard. So I told him I intended taking a more leisurely stroll just around Swanpool Head and back home again.

On my use of the word 'home' he jerked his head and looked at me curiously. Being a lawyer he was very quick to notice little variations of expected usage like that. He had, of course, already noted that my speech was more middle-class than it had any right to be. That was not so very unusual, mind. Lots of servants affected a gentility they were not born to, but they were themselves affected in other ways, too. My 'middle-classness,' if I can put it like that, was more natural.

"Very well, then," he said, taking my elbow gently and turning me in that direction. "Before we discuss what you might do, let me tell you a thing or two about the Law with a capital L — not the law of guardianship or the law concerning orphans but the mighty institution itself. Have you ever come across some stubborn article that refuses to budge — the lid of a jamjar, say, or a nut and bolt holding together something you wish to take apart?"

I smiled and nodded. "Almost daily, sir."

"And how d'you set about it? D'you go immediately to the toolshed and pick up the sledgehammer?"

I laughed.

"Well, that's the Law for you," he went on. "It's a sledgehammer. Always make it your last resort. I keep reading articles saying why don't we make the Law cheaper and easier to use? That's like saying why don't they make sledgehammers smaller and lighter, so that people could use them on little tintacks? The Law is *meant* to be big, slow, cumbersome, heavy, awkward, costly ... all the things people complain about at the drop of a hat. And why? To encourage them to try everything else first. D'you follow?"

I could see now that although his manner was still more frivolous than I would have liked, he was taking the problem itself quite seriously. "Even so, sir," I replied, "if I'm using a little hammer on a carpet tack, and the carpet tack proves to have a mind of its own, there'd be no harm in showing it I have a big sledgehammer in reserve, I'm thinking."

It was his turn to laugh. "I can see you're quite a terrier, Miss Moore. My wife was right."

I wondered what she had told him to prompt such an aside but did not ask.

"It also strengthens my original point. The more force of character you have, the less you need the force of Law. A strong woman may do things with her bare hands that a weak man could only do with a sledgehammer — to adapt our parable. Tell me more about yourself — if you don't mind. I'm not idly prying, I promise you."

"I'm sure I don't know what there is to tell, sir," I replied, beginning to feel uneasy.

"Well, to begin with, you are obviously better educated than your age and station would suggest. How has that come about?"

"Through the influence of our mother, I suppose, sir," I answered reluctantly. "Her family thought she married beneath her — though my father always had his own carrying business. Or did until the drink got the better of him."

"And what was *her* family? Might I have known them?"

"She was the one who educated us," I said.

He did not press his question, but he noticed my evasion. "Hmm!" he said again. Then, "Let us turn our attention to Miss Martin — whom I know, of course. Not socially, but we have enjoyed a number of professional encounters. I admire her greatly, I may say."

"She was very good to Marian," I offered.

"Yes, wasn't she!"

His intonation was so odd that I halted and stared at him.

"You know the phrase 'a sprat to catch a mackerel,' I suppose?" he asked with a light, sardonic smile. He was a very handsome man. If he had not been my uncle I should easily have become infatuated — as maids my age often are with men safely beyond their reach. I thought also of his younger brother — and then put him from my mind with some determination. Mr W continued: "Miss Martin is obviously after you. She said as much in her letter. You're the mackerel. Marian was the sprat."

"After *me?*" I echoed in amazement. "Surely I was not meant to take that seriously, sir?"

"I believe you were. And I believe you should. Why d'you think she wrote it otherwise?"

I did not want to repeat aloud my own thoughts about Miss Martin's spinsterhood and desire for a sort of step-daughter in me — even though I could think of no other explanation. I began to wish I had not told him so much about her letter. I only did it out of a sort of pride — to show him I needn't be in service all my life. I had other prospects.

"I don't know," I answered lamely. "Why?"

He screwed up his face in token of some effort. "I wonder how I may put this without fear of misunderstanding?" he mused aloud, but more to himself than to me.

We resumed our gentle stroll up the path to the top of the Swanpool cliffs. "It all goes back to a myth about the nature of women — or Woman with a capital W." Being a lawyer, he was fond of abstracts like that, I suppose. "A myth that has grown up over the past two hundred years or so. If you go back a few centuries more, you'll find quite different ideas about the nature of Woman. Chaucer and his contemporaries were quite certain that women were sly, mischievous, not to be trusted an inch, and if not actually *im*moral, certainly *a*moral. You understand the difference?"

I nodded.

He went on: "Man was then considered to be the higher, nobler creature whose task it was to guide Woman from darkness into light. But, somewhere around Shakespeare's time, you can see the start of a slow shift in attitudes — until today we're at the other extreme. Today we put Woman on the pedestal — the source of all goodness and purity, without whose radiance wretched Man would soon sink in the quagmire of his own innate corruption."

I wanted to laugh — thinking of how this man's own younger brother had wished to put me 'on a pedestal' — on my back was more like it! But, of course, Mr Walter wasn't talking about mere women like me. He meant real *ladies* like Mrs Felicity. Anyway, I couldn't see where all this was leading.

He brought me up sharp with his next question: "May I ask toward which viewpoint *you* incline, Miss Moore?"

I blurted out that I found both extremes pretty daft.

He laughed and said, "Quite so! That's why Shakespeare is so great. He had the good fortune to live between those extremes. We recognize the power of his honesty but we still cling to our own myths. Except that some of us are in professions which cannot afford to wear such blinkers. Miss Martin is such a person. She knows — more than most, I would say — that women are not natural pedestal material. She'd settle for simple, honest goodness of heart and leave all that blinding-angelic-purity business to the myth pedlars. I suspect that is what she has seen in you, Miss Moore — goodness of heart. In her world it's like finding a nugget of gold among barren rock. Anyway" — he rubbed his hands briskly and strode out a little faster — "I'm sorry to have laboured the point. All I really wanted to say is that I think you should look upon Miss Martin as your best ally in your dispute with the Guardians. She should be the first arrow in your quiver. You did quite right to send her that letter as soon as you returned from Penzance."

I thanked him then and wondered what we might talk about during the rest of our walk, for Fenton Lodge was still more than half a mile distant. Perhaps I could ask him *why* men wanted to put women on pedestals? But the words that came out of my mouth surprised me as much as they amused him. I said, "With all respect, sir, I should still like to know what the Law might say upon the subject — even if it must be the last arrow in my quiver."

"Aiee!" he exclaimed with a sort of strangulated laugh, pretending to tear out his hair. "If you aren't the terrier of all terriers!" Then he resettled his hat and put his arm around my shoulder to give me a reassuring hug. "Well, young lady, I'm not so familiar with the Poor Laws and matters of guardianship that I can just spout it off like that. But if you're going to crack this whip over me every time our paths cross, I can see I shall have to do a little homework."

"Oh, please, sir," I stammered. "I didn't mean to suggest I'd do anything so impertinent ..."

He cut me short with another hug and then let my shoulder go. "Have no fear of that," he said. "As a matter of fact ..." He drew breath to add something further — something light and airy, I suppose. But then, thinking better of it, he fell into a reverie, which lasted the best part of a minute. Then, drawing an even deeper breath, he said, in a rather halting manner quite unlike anything previous, "Let me now confess that I had another purpose in joining you on your walk today, Miss

Moore." He then went on to make several complimentary statements about me which were untrue as well as uncalled for. He continued: "I need hardly tell *you* that the death of a loved one is a grievous thing. We all have our different ways of coping with the shock of it. You, for instance, have found hard and demanding work to occupy your mind and exhaust your body — at least I hope you discover those benefits in it. My mother has no such advantage, I fear. *We* fear — my elder brother and I. And our wives, of course. True, she has her committees, her charities, and the reduced portion of her social life, which will return to its full measure when the conventions allow. But it is not enough. Her chosen way of dealing with her grief seems to be to hide all vestige of it."

This seemed to me a charitable way of saying that she didn't care a rap about her husband's death — which, *I* fear, was the truth. However … Mr Walter had to cope with his own grief, I suppose, and this was as comforting a lie as any.

"At first we thought it was genuine," he went on, "this callous, or at least indifferent, exterior she affects. But beneath it, we now believe, she is penning back her genuine grief and giving it no scope to express itself. We cannot see how any good can come of it. Indeed, we fear that one day, like the pent-up violence inside a volcano, it will erupt and do great harm, to herself, to others around her. It would be unfair to a young woman of your tender years not to warn you of this possibility. But we have a more selfish purpose, too. In short, we would be most grateful if you would keep an eye on our mother's … how may I put it without being too alarmist? Her state of mind? And let me or my brother know the minute you think our fears might be on the point of realization. I promise you, we would rather endure a dozen false alarms than ignore one genuine crisis. Or is that asking altogether too much of you? Please do not hesitate to say so."

I drew breath to assure him I'd do what I could but he added, "I should also tell you that we've talked this over with Miss Wilkinson, too. She agrees with us that the danger is at least potentially there. Of course, her visit will come to an end soon — in the next two months, anyway. But while she is here you may carry your misgivings to her in the first instance. *She* will send you on some errand to my elder brother or to me should she think it needful. And after she's gone … well, we shall cross that bridge when we come to it, eh? You will be more secure in your place by then and may safely take little initiatives of your own."

I gave him the reassurance I had been about to give him earlier.

Then at last he said that he ran across Miss Martin quite often at the courthouse in Redruth and he would, if I wished, discuss my purpose with her and see if they could come up with some way forward. From that moment on, I would have swept the ground before him and plundered every garden in Falmouth for petals to strew in his path.

But when we arrived home I was mortified to hear him discussing my revelations with his mother — which, of course, he had every right to do, since he knew nothing of our kinship with his family. But it must have seemed to her that I had skirted as close as humanly possible to revealing our secret without actually going that final inch. She was not to know how careful I had been. It must look as if I had broken my word in all but the most literal sense. So I expected the worst. At the very least my mistress should have summoned me and demanded an explanation for my apparent betrayal of her.

Yet nothing happened!

Not by the smallest glance or gesture or word did she refer to that damning conversation with her son. I did not know what to think then. One after another all the certainties in my life were being knocked out from under me.

Part Two

Falmouth Harbour

Eyeless in Gaza

The hardest thing at that time was to say nothing to my fellow servants. My dashed hopes, my all-too-realized fears, my small successes, my huge setbacks — of these I could say nothing to the Bourdeaux, to Mrs Gordon, to Trebilcock and Weeks, to Betty Coath, and Clarry Benjamin. The one exception was Susan Callaghan, my roommate.

They all knew that I was the mistress's granddaughter, of course. Those who did not remember my first visit certainly remembered my second one! But it was another of those things we never actually talked about. Life was full of things that everyone knew about, thought about, wondered about ... and never mentioned. But their possible resentment faded when they saw I was to be no favourite of hers and that she gave me as hard a time as any — indeed, harder in many ways because I was with her the most, more even than Mrs Bourdeaux, and got the first helping of tongue pie whenever it was being dished out. Mrs B herself once asked me if I didn't resent having to take the brunt of the mistress's spleen so often. Of course, she didn't put it like that — nor did she add, "You being her granddaughter and all" — but that's what she meant. I just said no, it was the way things were, and so on. But the question made me think, and I then began to realize that cross temper and fussing can be expressions of love, too, not merely of dissatisfaction.

Of course, I was also old enough to realize that such fancies might be no more than wishful thinking. A maid who's just lost her mother and family has a need for love that no one can understand who has not faced such loss. I was self-aware enough to see that. And yet from then on I felt that my grandmother's sharp, shrewish interest in me, her constant barrage of petty criticism, her unending tune of weary or exasperated sighs ... were all linked by a thread of love. Twisted love, of course, because she was beyond doubt a very twisted person emotionally, riddled with thwarted ambitions and dissatisfactions of every kind.

One example — which is actually rather comic — is that she couldn't even be ill properly. She was a powerful swimmer, an excellent horsewoman, and a keen dinghy sailor with the Greenbank Yachting Club — all of which activities would have been frowned on during the first three months of widowhood. So she tried to be ill, instead. Minor illnesses of numerous kinds were all the fashion among ladies then.

Most of them were an excuse for taking laudanum, which was a respectable form of opium addiction. But laudanum actually made her nauseous — which, being a genuine sickness, was not at all what she wanted. She would try to lie in bed, breathing shallowly and submitting to having her brow bathed with cool compresses — and all the while her constitution, which was as strong as an ox, was chafing against the enforced idleness until her every fibre was just shrieking with boredom. Illness joined a long list of thwarted ambitions for her! Eventually I plucked up my courage and dared to suggest to Doctor Mayer that he should prescribe a course of daily swims. He grinned, patted me on the back, and said, "Capital!" And life at Fenton Lodge was a great deal easier thereafter.

However, I was saying that when it became clear that I was a new buffer between the mistress's temper and the rest of the household, all resentment that my kinship might have aroused was instead dispelled and I was regarded, if anything, with sympathy. The harder she treated me, the nicer they became. It was quite amusing to see — especially after I began to suspect that a warped sort of love lay behind the old woman's rages. I felt I was being favoured by all sides! Perhaps I was the one who was becoming warped?

For all that, though, their general pleasantness toward me made it all the harder to say nothing of my one great ambition in life. Susan, as I say, was the exception. I told her almost everything partly because I'd go mad if I didn't share my frustrations with *someone,* and partly because I needed her spontaneous reactions in order to know how ordinary (or extra-ordinary) my behaviour was, for I had no yardstick of my own.

For instance, when I showed her Miss Martin's letter, she said, "I don't know how you do it, gel!" And she said the same again when I repeated my conversation with Mr Walter, except that this time she gripped me by the shoulders, as if she was holding me up like a dress she was thinking of buying — turning me toward the light and running a critical eye up and down me. "Yes," she said thoughtfully. "There *is* something about you. I don't know what. Can't put a finger on it. But you've got it, gel."

"What?" I asked.

"The same as what a cuckoo's got — whatever that is," she replied. "First Miss Martin — you're not with her more than half an hour and she's offering all the help she can give. Then Mister Walter, who wouldn't give *me* the time of day — offering the professional services of Trevarton and Jacko! And now Mrs T herself!"

"What's *she* done?" I asked scornfully, for I had just endured a particularly trying day with her. (That was before the daily swim brought the household temperature down.)

"It's what she's *not* done that's the interesting bit," Susan replied. "She don't know how careful you was with Mister Walter. She'll fly off the handle if you so much as lock one buttonhole stitch the wrong way. But what does she say about this? Not a dicky-bird! Face it, gel — you've got *something.*"

It could have turned my head — talk like that coming on top of all my inexperience of life. But the more I thought about it, the less I agreed. Miss Martin had *her* reasons for her admittedly unusual behaviour. It was nothing I had said or done. Mr Walter, too, was quite genuinely worried about his mother's refusal to show the grief he (but not I) felt sure must be bottled up inside her. He saw in me a diligent young servant who could be trusted with a simple commission to keep an eye on the old lady and let him know of any alarming development. In return for that he agreed to help me achieve something I desired. You don't need the mystic qualities of the cuckoo to enter into arrangements like that! Daily life is full of them.

The instance of my grandmother was a little harder to explain. I was so sure she'd fall on me like a hundred of bricks for speaking out to her son that her failure to respond in any way was almost worse. I felt my neck was stuck in a guillotine whose blade was just temporarily wedged. In the end I decided that she must have realized that my dismissal, coming on the heels of that conversation, would arouse her son's suspicions in a most awkward way. Also, it would leave me free to approach him and Mr Archie directly and blackmail them — emotionally, if in no other way — to help. By dismissing me she would free me from my pledge to do no such thing.

So there, too, I did not need any 'magic powers' to have done what I did. In any case, if I 'had something,' in the way Susan meant the phrase, why did it desert me at the two really important moments in my recent life — with Harry and Reenie Angell and with Sr Enuda?

However, by forcing me to think about it, she brought me to realize that the balance of powers between mistress and servant was not nearly so one-sided as it might look on paper. If my mistress really had made her private calculations of gain and loss along the lines I had supposed for her, then she and I were a lot closer to evens than I had previously imagined. And from then on I became a great deal easier and more confident in my daily dealings with her.

And that, too, was something that fed upon itself. For, if part of her hectoring manner was twisted love, the rest was plain, old-fashioned bullying. It was something I noticed in her that very first time we met — when I wanted to get the number of the fiver my grandfather had given me — how fiercely she went for me and yet how she backed down when I stood up to her. The same thing was happening between us now, only much more slowly and infinitely more subtly. Her outward ferocity remained for all to see (and hear), but its inner heart became more hollow with every passing week. By the end of that summer, she knew and I knew that the bluster was all bluff. The odd thing was that I never called her bluff. She would rant and rave and I would meekly accept it — and it was like a little daily pantomime between the two of us.

Underneath it all a quite different relationship was developing. It was something that neither of us wanted to face openly, though. I did not even wish to think about it. I was vaguely aware of it but I kept pushing it out of my mind whenever my thoughts veered in that direction. I guess it was the same with her. We clung to our pantomime because it had become familiar and comfortable ... because it calmed the understandable fears of the other servants ... because it let everyone know where they stood.

I had a spot of luck in getting to see my brothers — what you might call assisted luck. Mrs Felicity announced that she wanted to go to Plymouth to buy some new furnishings and she suggested that her mother-in-law and her Aunt Stella — that is, Miss Wilkinson — might like to come along, too. Aunt Stella was only in quarter-mourning by then, because the master had not been a blood relation and three months had passed. The three of them decided to stay overnight at a small temperance hôtel called the Drake, at the eastern end of the Hoe. It was quite unnecessary for them to take a maid along, but Mrs Felicity suggested that I should accompany them nonetheless. It would add to their comfort, she said, and hôtel servants were so unreliable — which wasn't true but it helped to justify the extravagance of including me in the party.

I say it was 'assisted luck' because, at the time she made her proposal, I was pretty certain Mr Walter had put her up to it. Mrs Felicity did not strike me as the sort of woman to consider a servant's needs or intentions spontaneously. But nor was she that other sort who, knowing how much I would welcome the chance, would sooner die than offer it. My mistress agreed because she knew how impossible her daughter-in-law became when thwarted in small things.

Our visit happened toward the end of June. In the meantime I hadn't been back to see Miss Martin, though I had, of course, written again. That was so I could save up to get two days off. I would need at least two if I was to go and see Tom in St Austell, which was half way to Plymouth, and then go on to see Gerald and Arthur at the Sutton Orphanage in Plymouth itself the following day. So, if I took just a couple of hours off at St Austell on our journey home, I could kill two birds with one stone — and without wasting precious days off.

It was a Friday, I remember, a warm, close day with veiled sunshine and little wind — the sort of day when everything you look at seems to be in wait, holding its breath for something to happen. As an upper servant I travelled Second, after settling my mistresses in the First (Ladies Only) and seeing they were equipped for all emergencies — that is, furnished with their hamper, their cordials, their novels, and their smelling salts.

They had a curious way of bickering, my grandmother and her daughter-in-law. Mrs Felicity was much too *ethereal* to descend to vulgar snapping. She liked to use barbed compliments, instead: "I *do* admire the way you plait your hair. I could never get away with it like *that.*" Or, "How *daring* of you to mix puce and violet ribbons, Aunt Stella — and in such jolly *profusion,* too!" Or, "I wish *I* were brave enough to read Mrs Gaskell *in public.*" The insult was always in the feather-light stress, never in the actual words. It drove my grandmother and her cousin wild because they were of a more straightforward generation and did not admire the new style. They were reduced to saying things like, "How *civil* of you to say so, my *dear!*" But they put the cattiest possible emphasis on the words, which showed they did not understand how to manage it at all. What they'd all be like by the time we reached Plymouth, which was more than an hour from Truro by rail, did not bear thinking about.

We were much jollier in the Second. I travelled with a farmer's wife, who was accompanying a consignment of eggs and butter up to her brother-in-law, who had a grocery in St Austell. Also a petty officer, rejoining his ship at Devonport. Also a dapper little man who told me he 'travelled in lady's underwear.' I laughed and pretended I'd never heard the joke before — but actually he really did. And beautiful samples he had in his suitcase, too. Our one remaining travelling companion, a dignified, rather reserved young lady who told us nothing about herself at all, would have bought several of his samples had they been for sale. As it was, she made a note of the shops in Plymouth his company usually supplied and the names of the items she liked especially. One, I remember, was a corset called 'Araby' — because it had little crescent moons cut out of it all around the top and bottom. It looked pretty enough in the suitcase but if a woman had any fat on her — and most of us did — it would have been dreadful. And it would have felt dreadful, too. I was just so amazed that a woman who seemed quite genteel could sit there calmly discussing things like that with all us strangers around, including a petty officer.

The farmer's wife got out at St Austell, of course. I had told her something of my tale and her parting words were for me to stop at her brother-in-law's shop for 'a bit chat and a bite,' when I went to visit Tom at the farm school — which, she also told me, was a fine institution and had given many a young fellow an excellent start in life. She was most likely only saying it to comfort me, but in that she succeeded and I felt buoyed up the whole journey.

The salesman pointed out Restormel Castle, which you can briefly glimpse near Bodmin Road. He said it was the most romantic castle in Cornwall but didn't explain why. Then he rested his suitcase on his lap and entertained us with several card tricks. He also told me and the other lady how people can cheat at cards — dealing aces to themselves and forcing rubbish on other players, and so forth. He showed us *five* different ways of dealing a good card into your own hand! The petty officer's fingers were twitching throughout this demonstration and at last he chipped in to show how to cheat with the three-card trick. He told us he'd seen simple *matelots* — as he called his fellow sailors — cheated of every last coin in their pockets by such shenanigans.

"And if you come across a game where a couple of ordinary bystanders are winning small fortunes," he added, "don't let them fool you. They're not ordinary bystanders at all. They're in cahoots with the dealer. Ignore the black looks he gives them as they walk off with their winnings. Some of them could act Sir Henry Irving off the stage!"

The reserved lady lost a lot of her reserve before we reached Plymouth — taking her turn to fool us with the three-card trick, and laughing and stamping her feet like a child when she managed it.

I'd never been 'up the line' before, so everything was novel and exciting to me. It was Cornwall all the way to the Tamar but the land west of Truro was quite unlike the Cornwall I knew and loved. My Cornwall was all rounded hills and granite — almost treeless except where woodlands had been preserved around the grander country houses. But up there, far from the tin mines' greedy furnaces, it was all wooded valleys and hilltop groves. In one place, there were tens — if not hundreds — of acres of rhododendrons, just reaching the end of their flowering.

The grandest sight of all, though, was man-made — Isambard Kingdom Brunel's railway bridge over the Tamar at Saltash. It's only a single-track bridge and the parapet on each side is so low that, when you're near the middle, you can look out of either compartment window and imagine you're floating in mid-air. And what a view! The Tamar, which divides Cornwall from Devon, is several hundred yards wide at that point, and deep enough for ocean-going vessels, too. If you look downriver, you can see what looks like half the Royal Navy at anchor. A good part of the fleet was still under canvas, so the distant view was hidden behind a whole forest of masts and spars and furled sails.

The petty officer pointed out the blue peter on one ship — his own, the *Ashanti* — and explained that it showed she'd up-anchor on the next tide. I'd lived in a seaport — Porthleven — practically all my life, but it was no more than a fishing-cove harbour. All I knew were fishing boats and small coasters. Vessels like these were either smudges on the Atlantic horizon or broken wrecks on the shores of Mount's Bay. Of course, Falmouth was one of the busiest seaports in the kingdom. It was the last place to which owners could send their ships to wait for sailing orders — and to gain a day or two on vessels sailing from Liverpool, say, or Southampton. So I'd seen a fair motley of cargo vessels since coming to Fenton Lodge. But even so, it was nothing like the sight of that grand fleet from the middle of that majestic bridge.

It was a foretaste, too, of surprises yet in store. The railway station is a mile or two from Brunel's bridge, but we seemed to be going through built-up areas almost all the way. I could not believe that so much country could be covered over in bricks and mortar. Mind you, it was a little misleading, because what we know as Plymouth is a fusion of three old cities: Devonport, Stonebridge, and the original Plymouth, which was the bit around the Hoe (where Drake played his famous game of bowls and all that). The railway line just happens to pass south and then east through all three. If it had gone east first and then south, it would have been in farmland all the way and even the three-in-one Plymouth would have seemed much smaller.

For all that, though, Plymouth was home to some ninety thousand souls — far and away the largest sprawl I had ever seen. Falmouth only had five thousand. When we finally drew into the station I own I felt dwarfed and rather lost. It must have shown in my eyes for, as we descended, the no-longer-so-genteel lady leaned close to me and said, "Just remember one thing, pet — you're as good as the next one and not so bad as most. That's my motto."

It's funny how an almost meaningless bit of mumbo-jumbo like that can put heart into you, nonetheless. I felt a new confidence as I went up to the Ladies Only, where the guard was just undoing the door with his special key. My three ladies emerged like shot from a barrel, as if they needed double the distance between them that their compartment had provided. Only the beautiful Mrs Felicity had a little smile twitching at the corner of her lips. I rode with her in one of the cabs to the hôtel, during which I was allowed to eat up their leavings in the hamper. She let me finish the wine, too. There had been six miniature bottles packed and only one was left, a light hock, very clear and golden. She saw me trying not to wrinkle my nose and told me it was "an acquired taste — you know — like strong cheese." After a pause she added in a murmur, "And men."

Then, more briskly, she asked what I had learned on the journey.

Perhaps it was the unaccustomed wine rushing to my head but I said, "I learned that I'm as good as the next and not so bad as most, ma'am."

"How modest!" she said.

When she saw that I took it as a compliment she added, "I mean the ambition, not you."

I just stared out of the window at the passing scene and finished a ham sandwich. I left the tomato because, like most people then, I considered them poisonous — not deadly, of course, but certainly not good for one.

The number of streets seemed endless. All those buildings. And all those unseen rooms in all those buildings — rooms that were home, or home territory, to one or other of those untold thousands of people. It was mid-afternoon and the pavements were thronged. The rapid succession of framed views made me dizzy. I tried picking one individual out of the crowd and imagined what his or her purpose might be. This one was going to have his tooth pulled. That one was on her way to pick up some shoes from the cobbler. Those two were going a detour to avoid a shop where their account was overdue. One party was obviously on its way to a wedding. So many different purposes driving so many different people — and all of them *in*different to me! I suppose mine was the almost universal reaction of a country-bred stranger to a large city but it seemed overwhelming and unique to me at the time.

My first realization — that it was an uncaring, even callous, place — soon gave way to something more encouraging: that I could be free here in a way that was quite impossible in a village like Porthleven, where everyone knew me. Even in a town like Falmouth, where I couldn't possibly know all five thousand, they'd jolly soon get to know *me* if I did anything out of the ordinary. Not that I *wanted* to behave like that, mind, but in a big city like Plymouth I'd have the freedom to do so whether I wanted it or not. And that made a difference to the whole atmosphere, the *feel* of the place. I wouldn't say such thoughts occurred to me all at once, then and there, but they were sort of hovering around me, half in my mind, as I began to relish my guessing game about all these people and all their diverse errands.

"Penny for your thoughts?" Mrs Felicity interrupted my reverie.

I almost told her but it seemed impertinent for me to say something like, 'I wonder if that woman's going to get a tooth pulled or fetch some shoes from the cobbler,' so instead I said something vague and halting, like, "I was wondering about all these different lives ... you know — if you think of a person's life as a line ... all these lines criss-crossing. What a tangle it all is!"

She said nothing but turned and stared at the busy world outside as if she were looking for something new in it. "Yes," she murmured at last. "And just think — if their *thoughts* were drawn as lines, what a leviathan of a tangle *that* would be! It would make that haphazard motley out there look like the most formal quadrille." She turned and smiled at me. "It's my favourite pastime, you know, Crissy — to sit at a café window and pick on some particular person out there" — she waved a patrician glove at the window without so much as glancing that way — "and invent an entire life for them. Tell me — have you ever modelled anything in clay?"

I was still so amazed that she had called me Crissy — and so casually, as if she had never called me anything else — that I had to replay her question in my mind before I could answer. She knew it, of course. She never did anything accidentally and she always knew precisely what effect she was having. I was about to tell her I'd just enrolled in evening art classes at the Royal Cornwall Polytechnic in Church Street — though I hadn't started yet — when she continued, "Professional sculptors, you know, make what they call an *armature* first — a skeleton of wooden struts and crumpled-up wire netting, roughly the shape of the finished model — which they then cover with the actual clay." Her hands mimed the process as she spoke. I could see it was something she enjoyed. Her fingers almost *loved* the air between them. "That's what I adore doing with total strangers from my café window — treating them as armatures on which I can create imaginary lives. D'you think you would enjoy that, Crissy?"

I would, of course, but not out loud and certainly not in her hearing. I said cautiously that perhaps I might.

She took it for a positive yes and went on, "We'll slip out and try it the moment we're settled at the Drake. I have a feeling that the other two ladies will wish to lie down for an hour or so. I'm afraid they found the journey *very* trying."

You may imagine how my mind raced while I helped my mistress and her cousin settle in their rooms at the Drake. Mrs Felicity saw to herself, with the assistance of one of those chambermaids whom she had called useless. Then she hovered around, waiting to snap me up the moment I had done. But that eagerness in her led me to the thought — indeed, to the conviction — that she had something much more interesting in mind than a trivial game of let's pretend at the window of some nearby café. I craved a few moments alone to pay a call of nature and used the occasion to cudgel my brains to think what her true purpose might be. For one awful moment I even imagined she had found out about my kinship with her in-laws and was going to confront me with it in some way. The thought had just flitted through my mind earlier, when she had called me Crissy. I dismissed it then as too far-fetched and I did so again now. But life, I was about to discover, does not know the meaning of the term 'far-fetched.'

She practically hauled me out into the street, where she bundled me into a waiting hansom. She handed the driver a piece of paper with some directions written upon it, then clambered in beside me. She was grinning like the cat that got the canary — just after the bird fell into the cream jug. She put an arm around me and gave me a quick, excited hug.

Before I relate what happened next I feel I ought — in her defence — to point out that the life of an upper-class lady of limited means was the most boring thing imaginable. Only a prisoner on a regime of silence could have had a more tedious time of it, I think. I remember one evening, after I'd been in service at Fenton Lodge for about three weeks, I flopped on my bed in a state of utter exhaustion and said to Susan, "If there's a life after this, *I* want to be a lady next time." But she told me that after I'd been at it a bit longer there wasn't a thing in *their* lives I'd envy them for. I didn't believe her then, of course, but I soon started coming round to her point of view. By the time of that visit to Plymouth I suppose I was about half way. I envied them their leisure but I pitied them for all the ridiculous constraints they put upon the use of it. For that reason, too, I suppose, I was never as angry with Mrs Felicity over what she did as I should have been.

Anyway, it soon became clear that whatever she'd written on that slip of paper, it wasn't the directions to a café — or not to the sort of place a lady might patronize. We soon found ourselves traversing a very mean quarter of the city. Fortunately I saw the street nameplate as we took the turning or I should have been taken completely off my guard — Ebrington Street, Sutton Ward, it read. My two little brothers were at the Sutton Orphanage in Ebrington Court, so I knew at last where she was really taking me. My mind began to whir.

This turn of events must mean that Mr Walter had told her the legal side of my story. Curiously enough, it had never occurred to me that he might. I supposed that, being a solicitor, he'd keep my business to himself, even though I was not a paying client.

The question that worried me was: Had she, being a woman, made the mental connection that her husband had not? In short, had she at last tumbled to the kinship between the Moores and the Trevartons?

Well, the answer to that would be a simple yes or no. The really important question would come next: If yes, what would she then *do* about it?

Clearly that depended on me — on my response to this 'delightful surprise.' Otherwise she would have acted already. So I was wrong about her cat-and-the-canary smile. That had been a smile of pure anticipation. I was the canary, still safely on the perch. The jug of cream was somewhere nearby, in Ebrington Court. And she — the feline — had yet to pounce.

By now I think I was every bit as excited as she was, but our manner of showing it could not have been more different. She could hardly contain herself. She sat beside me, shivering like a thoroughbred under starter's orders, whereas I became outwardly calm and grave — and yet I had the *double* excitement of knowing I was about to see my two dear little brothers once more and that Mrs Felicity was playing some kind of game with me, in which I must be ready to give as good as I got. My mind was racing, as I said, but my body was passive and my expression blank. It is not something I have learned or cultivated but it has always been so with me. It only happens when I feel threatened, mind. Other emotions — surprise, delight, grief, and so on — run their normal course with me as with everyone else. But threaten me and my outward demeanour grows calm at once. I have often been glad of the faculty but never, I think, more so than on that afternoon on our way to the Sutton Orphanage. It allowed me to consider other possibilities ... other ways in which she might have learned of our kinship.

Our mother eloped in April '72, at which time little Felicity Jacko could have been no more than two or three years old. So she could have heard nothing directly, even though such a shocking event would have been the talk of the county among people her parents' age and class for weeks if not months. Had she heard it indirectly, then? Sometime during the last few years?

Yes, that was horribly likely. Probably when she first fell in love with Mr Walter or he with her. Old gossip would have been resurrected before her parents would let her proceed with the courtship. Questions would have to be answered. Where was the bolted daughter now? Was there a legal marriage (for bastardy was a worse disgrace than poverty)? Even at the age of twenty she would have been spared such discussions but she had her own eyes and ears — and a mind like a surgeon's lancet. The name Moore might have stuck, being neither too common nor too uncommon to forget. And when Mr Walter passed on what he'd learned from his mother's new maid, well, two and two make five to any woman with a sharp mind like that.

Perhaps I was doing Mr Walter an injustice? He need not have told her a thing. The name Moore might itself have been enough for her. Put

it alongside my genteel speech and obvious refinement of education ...
that could certainly have been enough.

These and other speculations whizzed through my mind in far less
time than it takes to tell. We had probably trundled a mere dozen paces
by the time I had encompassed them all. It required even fewer for me
to decide to take the bull by the horns. "Do Arthur and Gerald know
we're coming today?" I asked calmly.

"Oh, you wretched child!" she exclaimed, though her eyes were
dancing merrily. She gave me a token slap on the wrist, too. "How did
you know we're going there? Or did you just guess? I might have known
you'd be too sharp for me."

I only hoped I was! "Ebrington Street," I said. "I saw the plate up on
the wall as we turned. And Sutton Ward."

She shrugged. "I should have erected my parasol or something — or
made you wear a blindfold. I did consider it, actually. Tell me, are you
angry? It *is* what you wanted to come to Plymouth *for*, isn't it?"

"Of course," I agreed. "And why should I be angry?"

"I don't know. Everybody seems to get angry with the things I do. This
must be the place."

She rapped the handle of her parasol on the roof just as the driver
was drawing to a halt anyway. "Be so good as to go and ring that bell,"
she told him.

With a great deal of wheezing and groaning, all designed to increase
his tip, he clambered down and gave the chain a pull. The horse hung
his head and the sudden silence exaggerated the creak of leather at
every little movement we made.

The bell was answered before its echoes had died. A little shutter at
head height opened and we could see a face behind the iron grille,
though whether male or female was not possible to say.

"Yes?" It was male.

The cabman gestured toward Mrs Felicity. She raised a weary hand
and beckoned him to come out. He, too, moved most reluctantly. He
was an old fellow with long, silky white hair spilling out beneath a
tricorn hat, which he'd put on askew in his haste. He wore an old-
fashioned beadle's frock coat and a leather apron such as blacksmiths
wear when shoeing horses. A very strange uniform, if that's what it was.
He had few teeth.

Mrs Felicity passed him her card and said, "I wish to have Arthur and
Gerald Moore brought out here to me. Kindly arrange it."

She was impressive, I must say. I would not have disobeyed her, nor even questioned the command. She had the same effect on the porter for, though he stepped back to argue, he took one look at her expression and went mumbling off to fetch someone braver, or with more authority, at least.

That person proved to be the matron, a large woman in her forties, more rectangular than rotund, and with the smallest, thinnest mouth you ever saw. The tones that issued from it were surprisingly bass. But even this formidable lady wilted a little in Mrs Felicity's presence. I'm sure she drew breath to say something outraged and demanding, but all that emerged was, "May I inquire as to your business here, Mrs Trevarton?" in a tone poised awkwardly between respect and belligerence. "I am Mrs Rogers, matron of this orphanage."

"And I am on the committee of the Camborne—Redruth Union, Mrs Rogers. As you know, we are paying the maintenance of the two Moore boys."

The woman's lips vanished but somehow words managed to come out of the remnant of that slit of a mouth: "It is customary to give notice of visits, Mrs Trevarton."

"Oh?" She sounded surprised. "We abandoned that system years ago. It encouraged the superintendents to keep the children in squalor and to spruce them up only for our arranged visits." Then she smiled. "But I feel sure you conduct no such system *here,* Mrs Rogers. One glance at you and I am filled with reassurance on that score at least."

The poor woman was trapped and she knew it — not that she yielded at once, mind. She said, "It is most irregular."

Mrs Felicity ignored her, saying, "I should so like to carry a favourable report back to my committee."

The matron repeated that it was most irregular and added that she would write to the Camborne—Redruth Guardians about it.

If the threat had any weight, Mrs Felicity did not show it. She just went on smiling as she said, "I understand you have a few vacancies, still. I need hardly remind you that we are one of the few boards in the West Country who are willing to fund places outside our own union."

Mrs Rogers went off with very ill grace but with no other choice than to accede to the request. I was torn two ways. Part of me exulted along with Mrs Felicity at her win over the matron. But most of me was fearful of the consequences it would have for my little brothers and their future treatment at the hands of that virago.

"Isn't this exciting!" Mrs Felicity said, rubbing her hands so vigorously that flakes of white kid polish fell to her lap.

It was, too — I couldn't deny it. Even more so for me than for her. The chance of seeing Arthur and Gerald again, which I had looked forward to so keenly and so hopelessly all these months — to have it suddenly thrust upon me like this was enough to outweigh all my misgivings, heavy though they were.

We sat and waited, straining our ears at every little sound from within. Ebrington Court was a dead end, so there was no passing traffic. The loudest sounds continued to be the wheezing of the cabman and the creaking of the leather bands that held the body of the hansom to its springs and chassis. At last I could bear the suspense no longer. I sprang down and went to pat the horse's head. Not that I was mad about horses. I just had to do something. But he was an old curmudgeon, quite out of love with humanity — like his master — and he shied away from my would-be-gentle strokes.

The old porter, thinking I was maid to this visiting angel of doom, came to commiserate with me.

"Do this sort o' caper happen often?" he asked under his breath while he held the nag's head for me to pat.

I realized that in a moment or two he was going to see me hugging and kissing my brothers and generally making an exhibition of myself over them, and — as the last thing I desired was to have another resentful official left behind us in this establishment — I told him, also under my breath, that I was the boys' sister and that I had no idea what game 'that one' was playing. "She said she was taking me to a café and instead she brought me here," I concluded. "I wish she'd have let me come tomorrow, in my own way, and honestly and openly — which is what *I* intended. Please tell Mrs Rogers so, too."

I don't know how much detail he took in but he did at least grasp that Mrs Felicity and I were not in cahoots in this business.

"Here they come, Crissy!" she called from her seat in the cab.

I skipped round the porter and ran headlong into Gerald, almost knocking him off his feet into an equally astounded Arthur.

"Whee!" I cried, lifting him up and whirling him round a full circle. When he was younger I'd been able to twirl him round and round until we both collapsed from giddiness, but now he was nine it was all I could do to twirl him once. I let him down and hugged them both to me and wished the moment would never end. I was determined not to shed tears in front of Mrs Felicity. But for that, I'd have howled my eyes out. Arthur cried but Gerald just sniffed and swallowed a lot in order to preserve his manhood. I was briefly surprised that the matron had not come back out with them, but then I supposed she could see nothing beyond further humiliation in an unequal contest with this haughty and well-connected lady from Redruth.

My brothers said none of the things you might have expected — no, 'How did you get here? ... Who's that lady?' and so forth. Not even, 'How long are you staying?' I confess that after all the heartache I'd felt at their loss, their indifference was hurtful. Arthur, drying his eyes, asked if I'd brought any niceys, meaning barley sugar or ginger fairings — which, of course, I would have done if only I'd known. Gerald stared past me, up the road, as if he'd often wondered what it was like up there. I closed my eyes and hugged them to me again, despairing of ever being able to tell them all that was in my heart to say. They felt very thin and bony — but then, they always had, I suppose. We were not given to over-eating, we Moores!

The air around us darkened and I opened my eyes again to find Mrs Felicity plucking the two boys from me. "*Now* we'll go and find that café," she said brightly.

The place she chose to take us to was on the western end of the Hoe, behind the big Orphan Asylum — which was where I had first thought my brothers had been taken. That end of the Hoe was rather disreputable. As well as the asylum there was a small prison, recently closed, some derelict barracks, a limestone quarry, and several rows of workmen's cottages, all higgledy-piggledy, with no proper roads between them. And on a stretch of open ground in the middle a Midsummer Fair was in progress, with roundabouts, a coconut shy, a helter-skelter, swing boats, and all the usual attractions — including a café, so she kept her word to me despite all.

The two boys, of course, had a marvellous time, thanks to this fairy godmother with her bottomless purse. But the longer the afternoon wore on, the more resentful I became — and with good reason, I think. The time I had available to spend with my brothers was limited. Every second was precious. The things I wished to tell them — *needed* to tell them — could not be said between a swing-boat ride and a hysterical romp in the Hall of Mirrors. They could not even be said over a plate of sticky buns and foaming mugs of ginger pop.

'I love you dearly. I think of you night and day. And don't worry, somehow, some way, I'm going to get us all together again the way we were ...'

How could I tell them such things when their eyes were on mounds of pastries with honey glaze and chocolate icing?

How could I tell them Marian's news or ask if Tom had written?

Or did they remember our parents in their prayers?

Or would they like to hear about Teresa?

Or were they keeping up with their lessons and why didn't they write more often?

Smiling Lady Bountiful was there between us at every point.

And yet I dared not fall out with her, dared not show the smallest hint of my resentment at what she was doing. Quite apart from what she might be capable of in her malice, I needed Mr Walter and his promise to work something out with Miss Martin. So I grinned and bore it all with the best outward show of delight I could conjure. I was getting quite adept at hiding my true feelings by then.

And, in fact, between her questions and mine, I did manage to learn most of what I wanted to hear — about their life at the orphanage, anyway. It was a strange irony of the times that most children who lost their parents, or who had to be taken from them for one reason or another, immediately went up in the world. They were kept cleaner, healthier, better fed, and better protected than most of them had ever been before. And better schooled, too. And, though that was hardly the case with my brothers, it was still true that they had more certainty, more stability, in their lives than they had ever known before. I'm ashamed to say I was somewhat less than delighted to make this discovery. In fact, it came as an unpleasant shock.

Another shock was to realize how much they had changed — to look at, I mean — in just a few short months. Not that they were pinched-looking or anything like that. They'd 'just growed,' like Topsy. Some of the change might simply have been my imperfect memory, but it showed me what strangers we would all surely become unless we could meet and see each other quite often. But how was Marian going to come down here from London to see these two? And then go on to visit Tom and me? And Teresa, once we knew where she was? And the same for Tom. Where was he going to get the money to go up to London?

I stared at those two poor boys, trying to burn every detail of their looks into my memory, until I embarrassed them completely.

The moment came at last for them to return to the orphanage. I think they were feeling a little sick with all the excitement, otherwise they would not have protested so feebly. As we rose to our feet, Mrs Felicity turned to me and said, "Well, Crissy, do we take them back or shall we keep them?"

Her tone was so light I felt sure she was joking. I just laughed, though I did not think it very amusing, and crouched to wipe the sticky off Arthur's face while he flinched and pulled a face like an old man.

"I mean it," she said as I straightened up again.

And I, still not entirely believing her, said something foolish about what would my mistress say?

She laughed harshly and said it wouldn't matter since I'd not be returning to Fenton Lodge, anyway. She'd rent a little cottage for us in Redruth, and I could get Marian to join us, and Tom — and then we could all set about looking for Teresa. "Isn't that what you want?" she asked sarcastically.

I don't know how close I came to madness at that most madcap moment of my life. It was not just what I wanted — it was *all* I wanted. Everything I'd dreamed of since our mother died and the Guardians struck. But there was something in her eyes, in her whole manner, that made me say a reluctant no. It warned me that she was not on my side. She was not fighting my battle but one of her own — something much darker and more obscure. My battle (and even at my tender age I realized this) could only be fought in the open, stage by tedious stage, building on the agreement of all parties.

The hardest thing of all was to dash the hope her words had kindled in the hearts of the two boys. They, of course, imagined that life with Lady Bountiful would be one long round of treats like this. "It'll be back to Porthleven," I warned them. "Bread and scrape. Meat once a week. Scaring the rooks for a penny a day — and that not yours to spend."

They lifted their disappointed eyes to Mrs Felicity but she, realizing I was in earnest, answered with a noncommittal shrug. We were a rather disconsolate party on our return to Ebrington Court. After tearful farewells on the pavement, Mrs F accompanied them within. I would have gone, too, but — being more mindful of my future visits, and reception, there — thought it more prudent to seek out the matron and assure her I had no part in that day's events. When she would not come to me I found the porter and impressed upon him yet again my innocence in what had happened and I begged him to let the matron know it, and how sorry I was.

When Mrs Felicity returned she found me sitting in the cab, staring blankly ahead, trying to look lost in thought. I wanted nothing more to do with her. But I might as well have spared the effort.

"You're a disappointment, Crissy, I must say," she began jovially. "It might have been quite an adventure to kidnap them back again."

"I'm sorry if I've given offence, ma'am, I'm sure," I said, not even trying to make it sound sincere.

"Oh, come on!" She dug me with her elbow. "You needn't pretend with me."

My bewilderment was genuine but she took it for play-acting. "Does my mother-in-law *know* you're her granddaughter?" she asked.

My mouth went dry between one heartbeat and the next, though the interval felt like a year. "I never mentioned any such thing to Mister Walter," I said at last, carefully ignoring her question.

"Him!" she exclaimed contemptuously. "He hasn't any idea of it. He wouldn't tolerate the situation for one moment, if he had. You'd be out on your ear, so you'd better not let him know a thing about this."

I couldn't believe he'd simply get me dismissed. I thought it more likely that he'd insist on bringing us openly into the Trevarton fold. But I *had* to know — and so I durst not do the slightest thing to antagonize her, for she was plainly in rather a feverish, volatile mood that day.

Meanwhile she was murmuring, "The best place to hide a watch, they say, is at the clockmaker's. Was it your granny's idea — or yours? You still haven't answered my question — *does* she know?"

I nodded. "She knew from the very beginning." Then, staring directly into her beautiful eyes (and wondering yet again if that were the light of madness shining out of them), I added, "She'd dismiss me at once if she ever found out I'd told *you.*"

"My God!" she shrieked, half standing up in the cab, and shaking her fists at the skies.

Her parasol rattled out on the cobbles and a hopeful urchin handed it back up. She was so consumed with her own private rage that it was left to me to give the lad a penny.

"Drive on," she shouted at the cabman, as if he had been wrong to stop at all. Then, turning to me, gripping my arm, she said, "How can you accept such a situation, Crissy? Doesn't it sicken you?"

I shook my head but said nothing.

"Why ever not?" She took a grip on her anger and even forced a little smile. "Tell me. I'd like to try to understand your point of view."

I explained that the only thing that mattered to me was to get us *all* together again ... that my mistress's offer to train me as lady's maid *and* allow me five shillings a week was far and away the best offer I could expect (I wanted to say *genuine* offer but still thought it wisest not to antagonize her) ... and that beggars couldn't be choosers.

She just laughed at this. "But I've offered you an instantaneous solution — your own cottage in Redruth ... Ah, I see! You thought it was just a whim on my part? Perhaps you think I have no funds of my own? Well, let me assure you I have! I may not be as rich as the Trevartons, but I'm richer than one of them — the one who married me! I'll give you a *pound* a week — and the cottage, rent free. By deed of covenant, if you wish, so it can't be revoked. Now what d'you say?"

I just closed my eyes and shook my head.

"Still no!" she exclaimed. "I wish I understood you."

I laughed grimly. "You're not alone. I wish the same about you. Why would you do such a thing when it would tear the Trevartons apart?"

"*Because* it would tear the Trevartons apart, you goose! Or at least it would tear the veils from my husband's eyes. He thinks his mother is some kind of saint — can you believe that?"

"She's not a bad old stick," I replied lamely.

"Not a bad old stick," she sneered. "Don't you realize *she's* the one who broke you up, you Moores?"

"You don't know that," I protested.

"I'm the only one who *does* know it. What have Arthur and Gerald to do with the Camborne—Redruth Union, eh? Nothing! You belong to Helston and the Lizard. So why is Camborne—Redruth funding those two lads? And Tom at Tywardreath?" She answered herself even while asking the question — by patting her own breastbone sharply and repeatedly. Then she continued: "And who put *me* up to it? Who is paying a precisely compensatory amount as a charitable donation into our funds? Who spun me a cock-and-bull story about a debt the Trevartons owed to the children of some former servant? How convenient that the name covers both the firm and the family! I took her to mean the firm, naturally. How d'you think I know so much? More than *you* told me! D'you think my husband revealed it all? Shame on you! He has more honour than you credit him with."

My blushes gave me away.

But that change in me, from guarded truculence to an embarrassment more in keeping with my age, had a profound effect on her. The bantering tone evaporated. The sneering ceased. She put an arm around me and hugged me to her side. "My poor, dear Crissy," she said gently. "You don't know who to believe now, nor whom to trust — nor where to turn next, I'm sure."

The emotional assaults of that day had all been too much for me, and this was the final straw. The tears I had not even admitted were imminent, now fell in abundance. I just buried my face in her shoulder and felt her other arm go about me — and then somewhere far above me I heard her voice saying, "Even now you don't know the half of it. But never mind. Never mind. Enough's enough for one day."

L uckily for me, my mistress and her cousin were still resting — in fact, snoring — when we returned. I suspected that Mrs Felicity, who had brought the wine bottles with her from Redruth, had laced them with something more powerful than what was on the labels. Just before dinner both ladies woke up in a testy humour — which did not improve when they learned they had snoozed through a whole afternoon of shopping opportunities. They snapped at me. They snapped at Mrs Felicity. They snapped at each other through several rounds of bezique before retiring once again to their beds.

I was all for retiring, too, but Milly, the hôtel maid whose room I had to share, suggested we slip out for 'an evening on the town.' It sounded very bold when she first mentioned it but all it consisted of was walking up and down Union Road, clinging tight together and ignoring all the catcalls and advances of the 'matelots' — and surreptitiously glancing at the fancy ladies of the town, who were plying their trade quite openly, even though it was an hour before sunset. Their antics seemed to fascinate Milly but she could only come down here to witness them when, as now, she had a companion to chaperon her. Our feelings were a mixture of distaste and awe. I would have felt more kindly toward them if they had not been so cheerful, so swaggering, and so well dressed — like stately galleons with sails of silk. They were known politely as 'Unfortunates' but anything less unfortunate-looking would have been hard to find in Union Road that evening.

But, for all their outward elegance, their business was coarse — a horrid let-down of all my vague and beautiful imaginings about private acts between men and women. I had my own make-believe lover, of course. Sometimes he was French, sometimes more exotically remote. Arabian or something. And if he did rather resemble Master Mark, I never called him that and tried not to think of him too closely. But what we did in each other's arms was all very misty and wishy-washy — nothing like what takes place in the farmyard. However, the encounters Milly and I glimpsed in the little alleys and courts that led off Union Road that evening were grossly agricultural. I observed them only because it was an education and a warning and I could not understand Milly's fascination with them, for, by her own admission, she had witnessed them many times before.

"Could *you* ever do such a thing?" she asked with hushed voice — and, I thought, with a certain sly interest, too.

"I suppose if it were that or starvation ..." I replied vaguely. "What were they before they started on this life, I wonder?"

Milly, who had a liking for the dramatic, said most of them had been maidservants at one time — sinfully used and then cruelly abandoned by the young masters of the house. She'd seen it happen. The 'good, kindly' households were the worst because they'd lull a maid into a false sense of security. She'd fondly imagine she was liked and wanted for herself, not just because she had good muscles and a willing disposition. But as soon as she got belly-up and dared to point the finger of accusation against the precious young master, there were suddenly seven doors, each with seven locks, between her and anybody who mattered in that same 'good, kindly' household.

On our way back up to the Drake I asked her how she knew all these things. I think she had been waiting all evening, nudging me ever so gently toward that question, because it let her tell me the one thing she'd been dying to get off her chest ever since she'd discovered that Cousin Stella was a Wilkinson and that my mistress was her paternal cousin — and thus a Wilkinson, too. Milly told me she'd once worked as a maid in the house of Roger Moynihan, the well-known Falmouth artist, whose first wife, Esther, had committed suicide about twenty years ago. This Esther had been a Wilkinson before her marriage, and she'd also been one of *them* — the gay ladies we'd just been spying on in Union Road. Esther told the whole story to old Ma Harding, her housekeeper, who nursed her after an earlier suicide attempt. She had made several before she succeeded. And Ma Harding had told Milly.

At this point I said that Wilkinson was not an uncommon name, so why should this have anything to do with *my* Wilkinsons?

She asked if the name of Nancekuke House, near Redruth, meant anything to me and I had to admit it was where 'my' Stella Wilkinson lived when she wasn't visiting us.

Milly smiled with grim satisfaction and continued. Apparently Esther's parents had managed an inn in Redruth, back in the early Sixties, and both of them had been suffocated by fumes, down in their cellar, when Esther was about eighteen. Her father, who would have been an uncle to Stella, was also one of the Wilkinsons of Nancekuke House. Despite their wealth, they refused to help poor orphaned Esther. They'd cut her father out of the family for going off and doing something dirt-common like managing a public house and that was that. She was no kin of theirs! Thank heavens Milly and I were walking arm-in-arm up Lockyer Terrace at that moment, so she couldn't see my expression. I could steel my arm not to jolt or stiffen but I wouldn't have guaranteed my face not to give me away.

Anyway, unlike us Moores, young Esther had been brought up as a genteel lady. She soon found that legal copying work and addressing envelopes didn't pay well enough to keep her in gloves, never mind meat and shoe-leather. So, when starvation brought her low enough, she had to start trading on the only asset she had left. And even though she'd later entered into a respectable marriage to a respected artist, she could never overcome the shame of it.

I was obviously made of more reticent material than poor Mrs Moynihan, née Wilkinson, but it was only by the skin of my teeth that I avoided blurting out my own story at that juncture. I did briefly wonder if Milly had heard of it by some other means and was only telling me all this in order to bring it out. But I didn't see how she could.

Milly was meanwhile taking ghoulish delight in the thought that guilt and shame left stains on a person's soul that not all the seas and oceans in the world could wash out. It was an awesome thought for me, too, that a woman who had been forced into the gay life, though rescued and made respectable again by such a good man as Roger Moynihan, could nonetheless be so burdened down by her guilt that she'd end up doing herself in. I wished Marian, in particular, could hear the tale and I resolved to tell it her in my next letter. But I could think of nothing to say to Milly that would match the depth of my thoughts.

After a long silence she said, "I pity men, really, don't you? Or I pity any man who gets married. Women are like cats. Put a bowl of milk before us and stroke our fur the right way and we'll purr — no matter who it is. Faithfulness isn't in us. Men'll never understand that. They're more like dogs. Once they've fixed their devotion on a particular person, that's it. They may stray and wander and get up to all sorts of mischief but they'll always come back. Everyone talks of doglike devotion, don't they. But you never hear of *catlike* devotion!"

I laughed and remarked that you often hear of a cat-and-dog *life* — otherwise known as holy wedlock.

She said, very firmly, that she was *never* going to marry. She was the first woman I had ever heard utter such a sentiment — so defiantly, I mean. Of course, I'd heard old spinsters say it in quite a different tone, but that wasn't the same. Milly was the one who put into my mind the idea that I'd one day have an actual choice in the matter of wedlock.

At that time, though, it was just the tiniest seed. I was far more interested in this revelation about the Wilkinsons, with whom, I suppose, I could claim some remote sort of kinship. It was odd to think that on the day I visited Marian at Little Sinns, our promenade took us to within a mile of Nancekuke, the Wilkinsons' ancestral home, where all these dramas, so reminiscent of our own, had unfolded.

I wondered what relations were they of ours. Then, with something of a shock, I realized that if Esther's father, the despised innkeeper, had been Stella's uncle, then Esther would have been a cousin to *both* of them — to Cousin Stella and my grandmother, too — to say nothing of being a third-cousin to me!

But I was less interested in my remote connection with her than in the first-cousin bond between the unfortunate (and Unfortunate) Esther and my two ultra-respectable ladies. Suddenly the ferocity of my grandmother's response to our mother's elopement was explained. It must have made her fear there was some bad seed in the Wilkinson stock, which kept bursting out in each generation — and in the female line, too — enticing one or other of them down into the Low Life. If, indeed, she had come to believe such a thing, then Harry Angell's slander against Marian would have seemed only too probable to her. It now seemed as good as certain that she was, indeed, the prime mover in the events that had put my elder sister into the care of Miss Martin.

I did not welcome this new understanding of my grandmother's motives. The things Mrs Felicity had told me that afternoon had helped me make up my mind about her — once and for all, or so I had hoped. She was a bully and a tyrant — and my enemy, too. Also, Milly's comment that women are like cats had struck home with me, for did it not exactly describe my situation at Fenton Lodge? They had set a bowl of warm milk before me and had stroked my fur in the right way, yet it kindled no devotion within me. I was already telling myself I must be more independent — in my attitude, of course, not in the sense of leaving the Trevartons and earning my living elsewhere. I was still, above all, a realist. I just thought I needn't purr so much.

But now, the more I understood that my grandmother was, in a way, *compelled* to behave as she had done toward us, the harder it was to condemn her for it and to make her the villain of the piece, the source of all my family's woes. I had the feeling that one day I might understand her so well I shouldn't be able to blame her for anything at all. And then I got annoyed with myself for this weakness — and with Milly for starting it.

The ladies, having missed a whole afternoon's shopping, decided to stay on in Plymouth until Monday. I was given leave on the Sunday to go to St Austell to see Tom. Mrs Felicity wrote me a note for the superintendent. She also secretly gave me the money for the fare, saying her husband would wish it. I didn't believe it and my doubts must have shown. Later she said it was a reward for my discretion over our jaunt with Gerald and Arthur. But, since she had made no secret of it herself, that couldn't have been true, either.

Deep down I knew she was waging some kind of feud against her mother-in-law and she was just keeping me sweet as a potential ally. Of course, I wanted no part of it. I had battles enough of my own. But I did need the money for the fare, so I accepted it and, to that degree, compromised myself with her. But then I was compromising myself in the same way with my mistress — tending her every wish, taking my wages (and what are they but bribes to do something we would not otherwise choose to do?), though knowing she was the main instrument of our family's disintegration. Oh, well …

Fortunately there was my work to stop me brooding about these embarrassments. And my few hours of leisure were filled with my one great obsession. The train was a stopping train so I had more than an hour to think things over before we reached Par, a mile or two short of St Austell but the nearest station for Tywardreath. And it was then that I first began to admit the truth that had been obvious to everyone else from the outset — that my dream of getting us all back together was no more than a dream, at least in the foreseeable future. It was Mrs Felicity's offer of help that opened my eyes. A little cottage of our own, free of rent, a pound a week income, and all her considerable influence to undo the evil work my grandmother and the Angells and the Guardians had done between them — what more could I ask for!

It was the combination of desperately wanting to say yes, while knowing with equal despair that it would never work out, which made me face the truth. It would never be *allowed* to work out. Mrs Felicity was a bitterly frustrated woman. Young and inexperienced as I was, even I could sense that. My situation provided her with the chance to rebel, disguised as an act of charity. She had chosen cleverly, too, for it was not such an obvious act of charity that all the world would applaud her. That was the last thing she wanted. Universal applause would have been just a different kind of prison to her. She wanted *passion* in her life — passionate debate, passionate support, and passionate antagonism. With herself at the calm eye of the storm. And we Moores were ready-made for such a *cause célèbre*.

I didn't think it out in so many words, because when you're thinking silently to yourself you don't actually need all the words to see the full picture quite clearly. But if somebody had sat facing me, asking all the questions, pressing me to follow every point to its conclusion, I think I could have expressed it all, just like that. Funnily enough, though, instead of warning me off Mrs Felicity's offer for good, it made me wonder whether I shouldn't take her up on it after all. I mean, knowing what her real motives were was like being on my guard. Knowledge is power. I could exploit her obsession just as easily as she could exploit mine. These ideas were beginning to form as I trudged up the hill to the Farm School — a good, stiff climb of almost two hundred feet in only half a mile.

It was an ordinary farmhouse, facing southwest over the waters of St Austell Bay. The day was warm and hazy and there was a succulent sweetness on the sea air — a compound of woodbine and elderflower, both of which were then in full bloom. God forgive me, but I slipped into thinking how perfect life would be if I had no responsibilities toward my siblings!

When I reached the front gate I could see the barrack-like buildings that had been added at one end of the original farmyard to make accommodation for the boys. Its sheer walls were of dressed granite. The windows were tiny. And the roof was of machine-cut slate devoid of all character.

There was no one in sight. The farmhouse door was open, as were several windows. Even without the boys' block I would have known this was no ordinary farm, for I never saw a Cornish farm with a flower garden before. And I never saw a flower garden so completely free of weeds, either. It was fully a quarter-acre but the beds were crammed with snapdragons, michaelmas daisies, columbines, love-in-a-mist, honesty, poppies, goldenrod — just about every common flower you could think of. But they were all marshalled like soldiers on parade. Somehow, for all its brightness and colour, it was even bleaker than the grim dormitory that loomed in the background.

From the yard behind the house came the sudden squeal of a pig. For a second it sounded so human that my heart leaped into my throat. I had a picture — straight out of *Uncle Tom's Cabin* — of the whole school assembled round there to witness the punishment of one of their fellows. When I realized it was only a pig I had to laugh — and to admit that I was letting my ideas about the place be dictated by the grim architecture and the even grimmer regimentation of the flowers. It would be better to wait and see. But see whom? I had stood there at the gate for several minutes now and still no one had appeared at the door or the windows.

Then I heard a strange sort of muttering-rumbling sound coming from somewhere behind me, back down the lane I had recently followed. And then the apparent desertion of the place was explained. They had all been to chapel!

They were at first no more than a brown crocodile — well named — occasionally glimpsed among the winding hedges. As this brown beast turned the final bend it resolved into some thirty youths with ages ranging from twelve to sixteen. All were wearing the uniform brown tweed cap and jacket with gray flannel knickerbockers, gray socks, and brown boots. And they all had uniform haircuts and uniform faces.

I searched among them with mounting panic for Tom and saw only thirty pairs of strange eyes — curious, admiring, and — some of them — frankly lustful. It made me blush and lower my eyes at the very point where I should have discovered him next. Thus it was his cry of "Crissy!"

that led me to him — that and the superintendent's cane, which descended on his head from behind with a force that his cap did little to cushion. He yelped and I could see him struggling not to cry.

The superintendent was meanwhile striding across toward me, saying, "What are you doing here, you impertinent baggage? Go away! There's no place for you here."

I curtsied and handed him Mrs Felicity's note, which he took reluctantly, turning it over several times and examining the seal minutely to see if it had been tampered with. "Is this your character?" he asked. "I told you there's no place here."

"If you please, sir," I replied, "it's a note for you from Mrs Trevarton — of the committee of the Camborne — Redruth Union."

He was not pleased. "On the sabbath?" he asked severely.

"She believed it to be your visiting day, sir," I said timidly. He looked away, awkwardly — like a man trying to deny the undeniable. I added, "Perhaps she is wrong and I have wasted my money?" I held out my hand for the return of her letter.

"No," he said crossly. "It *is* visiting day." His tone implied that it was a great inconvenience to him if people were going to actually *use* the facility. "Whom do you wish to visit?"

"My brother, sir — Tom Moore." I pointed to him.

"I know Master Tom Moore," he said sarcastically. "Moore's the pity, I may say!"

He actually expected me to laugh with him at this feeble pun. I did manage an encouraging smile, which, in turn, took a slight edge off his unpleasantness. "Very well," he went on curtly and beckoned Tom to join us. "What's in your bag, Miss Moore?"

I opened it and showed him — a couple of pasties I'd bought at the station buffet in Plymouth — the only place open on a Sunday — and two bottles of pop. All he said was, "Hmm!"

Tom had meanwhile joined us and stood shuffling from foot to foot, just beyond easy reach of the superintendent's hand. He was grinning broadly but his eyes were begging me not to disgrace him — not to throw my arms about him, hug him, kiss him ... all the things I was longing to do.

"Do you know this person, Moore?" the superintendent asked — as if the smiles that were splitting our faces were not answer enough.

"Yes, Mister Vingoe, sir, please sir, she's my sister, sir," he said breathlessly. His voice was sweet in my ear but it pained me to hear my brother reduced to speaking in so servile a manner, and to a man of no very great importance.

"Very well," Vingoe said. "She's brought you croust. You may sit and eat it in the long meadow. At least one of you must be in sight of the matron's window at all times — is that clear?"

"Yessir Mister Vingoe sir," Tom answered in one long rush.

He still had not opened Mrs Felicity's letter — but then I realized he wanted this permission to be *his,* and to be seen to be his, not something he was forced to grant after reading what she had said.

I curtsied again, being too angry at the implication of his last words to speak. What low creatures he must deal with if he could set such conditions for a meeting between brother and sister! And how dare he lump us with them! I was slightly annoyed with Tom, too, for not showing the slightest resentment. But it did not last three seconds of our being alone together.

The bolder among his companions made catcalls after us, clearly thinking it worth the sting of Vingoe's cane on their heads and shoulders. The crocodile wound its way down the side lane — their equivalent of the tradesmen's entrance — to the yard at the back. Meanwhile Tom and I walked in the opposite direction, farther uphill to the gate into the long meadow. As soon as they were out of sight I risked slipping an arm around his shoulder and giving him a hug.

His need for some physical affection after more than three months of separation was as great as mine but in his case it was tempered by the fear of being seen by his fellows and all the teasing he'd later have to endure. But there was a place just inside the gate where a hawthorn, infested with traveller's joy, gave us all the shelter we could desire. And then we hugged each other and cried softly and dabbed each other's tears and squeezed each other's hands until we could be calm again. Then we continued into the meadow and found a place free of ants, thistles, nettles, and all the other irritations of a country picnic.

"No need to ask if you're happy here," I remarked.

"Why, 'e in't too bad, I s'pose," he replied in as broad a Cornish as I'd ever heard.

It shocked me more than even the sight of him smarting under Vingoe's cane. "Why are you talking in that common fashion all of a sudden?" I asked. "Not to impress *me,* I hope!"

He sniffed and hung his head awkwardly to one side.

"Do they tease you if you talk properly?"

"I do talk proper," he said defiantly. "Proper Cornish. Nothin' wrong wi' that. Wurrz that pasty to, then?"

We munched in silence awhile, both being ravenous. They were good pasties, almost as good as home made. I realized I was going to have to curb my tongue. I didn't want us to fall out over lesser matters when there was so much of importance to be settled.

When our hunger was blunted I told him briefly about seeing Gerald and Arthur the day before — saying that they'd settled in well and were getting enough to eat. "Talking of which," I concluded, "at least *you* don't look too starved."

" 'S all right," he conceded grudgingly.

"Well — if you couldn't eat adequately at a farm school, where could you?" I remarked.

We were talking to each other like strangers. We both sensed it yet there was little we could do to avoid it. We were a family no more, seemingly. We did not have that daily contact, those shared experiences to keep us intimate with each other. A family is like an unending civil war, with no clear aims and perpetually shifting allegiances. We had none of that left. Only 'Did you see ...? Did you hear ...? Tell me!' It wasn't the same sort of thing at all. I had a struggle not to weep all over again, not in happiness this time.

The ginger beer was all shaken up by the journey and the marbles were hard to push off their seals. Tom spat into the neck of his bottle, which helped. He was able to let the gas out a bit at a time. I could not be so unladylike and lost a good mouthful before I got the neck between my lips — and a *very* ladylike sight I must have been then, I must say!

Our laughter was some compensation for the little wedge of strangeness we both now felt between us. I went on then to tell him all about the mess I'd made of my visit to St Breaca's. He replied with the interesting piece of news that his best 'cooze' at Tywardreath was one 'Orace Brokenshaw, who had also come from St Breaca's. I told him Marian's news, too — all of which I'd put in my letters, of course, but telling and listening is different from writing and reading. Finally I mentioned Mrs Felicity's offer, though I immediately hedged it around with all my misgivings and the thoughts I had had on the train from Plymouth that morning.

"What d'you think, Tom?" I asked. "Am I being foolish to look a gift horse in the mouth? She'd only be trying to use us for her own ends but shouldn't we turn the tables on her and use her for our ends? What d'you say?"

He shrugged awkwardly. "Marian do seem 'appy 'nuff. Her'd get all nurley if you was to bring she back from Lunnon now."

I clenched my fists and bit the end off my tongue at this shower of uncouth speech. "We could manage without her," I said. "Just you and me. Think of it — no rent to pay. And twenty shillings a week under deed of covenant."

"I 'ad one o' they but 'e died," he said sarcastically — a catch phrase meaning, 'You're talking over my head.'

"It means Mrs Felicity couldn't turn it on and off like a tap," I explained (hoping it was true). "It means she binds herself to pay. Honestly, Tom! Anyone would think you were *happy* here! Don't you *want* us to be a family again? Don't you even want to *try?*"

He just hung his head to one side and leaned away from me, as if I were a howling gale. I saw then that in only three months they had broken his spirit — not by much — they'd left enough to make him a useful son of toil but not enough to go joining a trade union or anything threatening like that. Bend with the wind until the storm had passed — that was his motto now.

I realized then that there was nothing I could do — no point in even trying to rally him. The damage was already done. Perhaps it hadn't taken much to do it. I don't think I'd ever seen him put to any really severe sort of test. He'd defended me once when some rough boys started teasing me on the way home from school. He'd fought like a ferret and sent them home sore — and taken his own punishment at their hands, too. But that was different. It was something immediate — fists up and sort it out now. He could still do things like that, I felt sure. His spirit was broken but not cowed. However, the capacity for a long, dogged, relentless struggle was just not there — and I could not honestly say it ever had been.

I gave up trying then. A more open failure would only infuriate me and leave him feeling dejected. So I turned the conversation to other things. I didn't even revert to the subject of Teresa — where I really needed to hear someone else's thoughts and to have him urge me onward in my battle with the nuns. Instead I asked if he was being bullied by the older boys.

"'Ardly now," he said grimly and showed me several not-quite-healed scabs on his knuckles.

"'Ardly now — seein' as 'ow you do talk some proper, eh?" I laughed and tousled his hair.

He had the grace to laugh, too.

And the rest of our time together passed in the same mood of happy triviality. He promised to write to Marian, to me, and his two younger brothers — and I'm sure he meant it at the time he said it. I hid my disappointment as best I could, which was well enough to keep it from him, anyway. My most desolate moment came when we paused behind the shelter of the traveller's joy for one final embrace. His body felt so strong and wiry — it annoyed me all the more that his strength did not run through and through him.

We parted at the front gate, since he was not permitted in the garden except when actually working there. I went up to the front door, pretending to inquire whether Vingoe had any reply for Mrs Felicity. My real purpose was to thank him in the most refined and ladylike manner so he would be left in no doubt as to what sort of people we Moores really were.

Alone with me — that is, with no gang of boys before whom he had to strut his manhood — he was a different person altogether. Also (since no human motives are ever unmixed) he was anxious to discover at first hand what report I was going to carry back to the woman he assumed was my mistress. "Pray come inside, Miss Moore," he said, dry-soaping his hands with nervous eagerness. "Tell me how you find your brother? He is well, I trust?"

I glanced over his shoulder at the clock. "My train back to Plymouth is at six, sir," I replied.

He looked at the clock, too, and saw there was no time for a cosy hearthside chat in the farm parlour. "Allow me to escort you down to the station, then," he said.

I told him he was most civil but I had no desire to discommode him in that way.

He insisted, however, and so we stepped it out together. He pointed out a smudge of smoke and a plume of steam, several miles away among the hills to our west, and said it was my train, standing in St Austell station — which meant we had plenty of time before it came down the hill to Par. I didn't entirely believe him about the smoke and steam but I already knew we were in good time. The next train after this one wasn't until nine and wouldn't get me back to the Drake before midnight. I'd never hear the end of that.

As soon as we were on our way he repeated his question about Tom's health. I assured him my brother was stronger and healthier-looking than when our mother had died.

"*Both* your parents died, I understood," he said.

I agreed but said nothing as to why I'd spoken only of her death.

"The regimen at Tywardreath is strict," he went on. "I grant you that. Strict but fair."

My spirits fell as it struck me he was going to spend the entire walk down the hill in trying to dictate the 'report' he imagined I'd carry back to Mrs Felicity. I racked my brains for some way to prevent him.

Perhaps it was because I'd already blazed that trail in my mind, not once but twice, that same day. Anyway, it occurred to me that here was a man who wanted something badly of me — the assurance of a good report to a member of an important committee in his life. And here was I who needed something, too — namely, all the help I could get from whatever quarter might offer it, in discovering Teresa's whereabouts. Whether Mr Vingoe could be of the slightest assistance to me there, I doubted. But, since Tom's best 'cooze' had come to Tywardreath from St Breaca's, there was at least some connection between the two establishments. So I'd gain nothing by holding my tongue. Also I could put an end to his dreary monologue of bashful self-praise.

So I told him of our break-up — being careful not to criticize the Guardians or anyone he might consider his allies — and of what had happened to Marian ... of my friendship (I dared to call it that) with Miss Martin ... of my visit to the youngsters in Plymouth. In short, I gave him a truthful if slightly rosy picture of myself until I came to talk of my youngest sister. Then I told him what a stupid fool I'd been and how, quite inadvertently, I'd angered Sr Enuda — and so had jeopardized my chance of ever finding out where Teresa had been sent. I did not need to state the request in so many words. He put on his most soothing manner and told me he knew the good sister quite well and — while promising nothing — would see what he could do.

I thanked him then and told him how happy I was that Tom was in such firm but caring hands. I would not have said as much after our initial encounter, of course, but — given that Tom had to be *somewhere* and could not or would not come to live in Mrs Felicity's promised cottage — I actually meant it now. His offer of help saved that day from despair. It would otherwise have been a very dismal ride back to Plymouth that evening.

W hen our party returned from Plymouth I told Susan at once of Mrs Felicity's strange antics. Susan and I enjoyed a little *conversazione,* as we called it, every night between prayers and sleep, where we went over the great and stirring events of our little day and set the whole world to rights. I added that I was sure our mistress was aware of her daughter-in-law's antagonism — well, she'd have to be a simpleton *not* to be — and I also thought she had a shrewd idea that Mrs Felicity had tried to recruit me to her side of that sweetly smiling, deadly battle between them.

Susan must have mulled it over all day because at our next night's *conversazione,* she told me it showed how much Mrs T had changed.

"If such a thing had've happened any time before the master's death," she said, "you'd've got given ten minutes to pack your bags and vamoose. She wouldn't even have brung you back here from Plymouth. She was much more ruthless in them days."

"I wonder what has changed her?" I mused aloud.

We talked and talked that night and at last decided that it was because the 'freedom' my grandfather's death had allowed her was proving to be a bit of an illusion. She had actually *needed* all those constraints — the financial ones, mostly — which she had thought so irksome when he was doing the imposing.

Of course, by *our* standards there never had been a time when the Trevartons needed to worry about money at all. They had always been rich beyond our imaginings. But the rich think differently. There was a man in Devoran who committed suicide around that time because he lost a hundred thousand pounds in a share swindle. I thought it perfectly understandable until it came out that he still had another four hundred thousand left! But my mistress continued to find it understandable, even after that. They do think differently.

Anyway, to get back to the way Mrs T had changed when Old Mister Bill's constraining influence was no more. We decided that she was only now beginning to realize how much she had needed those constraints — the way a woman needs a corset to feel properly dressed. (I tried Marian's suggestion of going without and found it physically more comfortable, but mentally it was agony.) So she was having to constrain herself voluntarily in ways that he would once have imposed upon her!

" 'Cos he was always there, see," Susan said, "like a wall, all around her. She knew she could do as she pleased — so long as she never went outside the wall, of course. He'd always be there to defend her so long as she played the game and stayed inside. But now the wall's gone. Or *she's* the wall. She's got to be her own sentry, walking her own battlements, like the rest of us. Without him, she needs allies. So she can't just chop your head off like what she would have done in the good old days. If the enemy's trying to bribe you, she's got to go one better to keep you loyal, see?" She giggled. "You're sitting pretty, my lover!"

I was too much of a born pessimist to let such nonsense go to my head, but I had to admit there was at least a grain of truth behind Susan's dramatic exaggeration. My mistress continued to be severe with me, but severe in a careful way — never pushing me to the brink of rebellion, always choosing points on which I truly did need instruction and correction.

Also, she was very careful never to leave me an opportunity of being alone with Mrs Felicity. So, on the Sunday she allowed me to go over to Redruth to see Miss Martin — toward the end of that July — she made sure that both Mr Walter and his wife were at Fenton Lodge.

Miss Martin had changed, too. She wasn't exactly severe at our previous meeting but there had been a sort of remoteness about her, a proper solemnity that went with the grave responsibilities of her office. I could not imagine one of her girls making some giggling confession and her responding with so much as a smile. There's a word — *gravitas* — just made for her. But today she was all smiles as she met me at the gate, and she actually took my arm in a most companionable way as she led me across the courtyard. It surprised several of the girls, too — I could see.

She took me all over the school — showed me everything and explained its purpose. I was amazed at the neatness of the place, the shine, the polish ... everywhere. The girls' beds were stripped to their bare mattresses with the sheets and blankets folded into a tight box-shape of about fifteen inches cubed: blanket, sheet, blanket, sheet, with the underblanket tucked tight and wrinkle-free all round it. They didn't need looking glasses. The shine on the dark-stained pine floor was good enough to let you comb your hair and straighten your tie by. All their clothes, too, were neatly folded over bits of cardboard and plywood to make them sit square and tidy — and all in the same order so that the mistresses could see at a glance if anything was missing.

I thought it was just for Sunday, to give the maids employment when ordinary work would be forbidden. But Miss Martin said it was like that every day of the year. The same degree of order prevailed in the schoolrooms, the laundry, the kitchens … all over. During our tour the maids were promenading in pairs in the back courtyard. A few who had visitors were out on the highway, walking up and down under the watchful eye of Davies at the window of his lodge.

Miss Martin and I stood at the tall window on the main half-landing and stared out at the pairs in the back courtyard. It was a warm day, even for July, and they were in summer frocks and blouses — all uniform, of course, and most of them rather ill-fitting. Some strolled arm-in-arm, heads leaning inward like well-matched carriage horses. Others were a yard or so apart and clearly not talking to each other. But they were all in pairs.

"Chatter, chatter, chatter!" Miss Martin sighed.

"What *do* they find to talk about so ardently?" I ventured. All I really wanted to hear was what progress she, perhaps assisted by Mr Walter, had made in tracing Teresa — if any. But I felt I was in her hands now. She had clearly discovered something of interest, otherwise she'd hardly be all smiles.

"Mischief," she replied. "See those two?" She pointed out a pair of maids at the farthest corner of the yard. "Just turning toward us. One fair, one dark. Carrie and Dorothy — 'Dot and Carry' they call themselves, of course. There you see two of the best pickpockets in Cornwall! The constable who collared them told me he followed them through Wendron Ram-Buck Fair last year and didn't see them take a thing. If he had, they'd be at Great Sinns now, not here. But when he stopped them at the end of their stroll they had two watches, a purse, and five handkerchiefs between them. At this moment they're probably discussing where they went wrong (from their perverted point of view, of course) and how to avoid being caught with the loot on them next time. I often wish I could become invisible and go out there among them — and listen to what they're actually saying."

I asked her what happened when she went out among them, *not* being invisible.

She laughed and said, "What d'you think! I hear snatches of improving verse, quotations from the Bible, declarations of penitence — all as straight as a pig's tail! And the moment I'm out of earshot, they go back to hatching some future villainy. At this moment Carrie is probably suggesting they recruit two or three other girls during their enforced stay here — to form a chain along which to pass their ill-gotten gains the moment they ill-get them. The police can't watch everybody and if they pounced on either of the actual pickpockets, they'd find no evidence to bring into court."

"But if you know that ..." I began.

She cut across me, shaking her head and smiling ruefully. "I don't know it. But that's what *I'd* be thinking if I were in their boots." Then, seeing the shock on my face, she added, "To look after little criminals properly, my dear, you've got to think like a big criminal yourself. There's no place for sentiment or naïvety here. Come on — let's go and take a dish of tea. I'm being a very bad hostess today. I know what you're longing to hear — but I thought this might interest you, too?"

I assured her it had been most interesting — which was true. But it was also true that I was bursting with curiosity about Teresa. And so, to steer the conversation in the right direction, I told her of my visit to Tom at Tywardreath — and of the flower beds whose military precision would not have been out of place at Little Sinns. "It was horrible," I concluded. "But also necessary, I suppose."

She darted a glance at me. "You understand that now, do you? Girls have come back here and told me they go on boxing their sheets and blankets for weeks after leaving — though all the time they were with us they longed for the day when they'd be able to stop. Chaos is in all of us and we each must find our own way of coping with it. The girls who come here have really been less successful than most — and that's the only large difference between us. I hope I'm not shocking you again?"

I shook my head and told her she was putting into words a few thoughts that had been hovering around me for some time, without quite settling. I also decided I would later ask her advice on having to play pig-in-the-middle with the two Trevarton ladies.

She was a Mif, I was pleased to notice, for I had decided lately that the milk-in-*last* ladies were not nearly so congenial. The maid who made our tea and toasted our bath buns (the *valette-du-jour,* as Miss Martin called her) carried our tray out to a part of the front courtyard that had been so landscaped with privet and escallonia as to form a sort of private terrace. There I sat beneath a sunshade, in the balmy summer air, eating the lightly spiced bun and sipping a fragrant tea, and trying to avoid the thought that my life had become interesting, challenging, and varied — in a word, *rich* — since our mother's death.

"Well now!" Miss Martin said briskly. *"Revenons à ces moutons* — to our sheep! Or to one little lamb in particular."

I realized I was holding my breath. "You mean Teresa," I said, letting it out in a rush.

"Yes — Teresa. You must prepare for rather a shock, I'm afraid."

I did not dare look at her. "Bad news," I said glumly. I knew it, of course, otherwise she would have told me at once. Now her earlier smiles meant nothing.

"Good and bad. The bad part is that she has gone rather a long way away. The good part is that she has been adopted by one of the best families in the county — eminently respectable. In fact, they live quite close to Redruth. Or used to live, rather. The best part of all is that *he* is a surgeon and is confident he can make your sister's hip quite well again. Isn't that nice?"

It was, of course, and I said so, but I was also worried by her talk of 'rather a long way away.' I asked her where precisely they had gone.

"To India," she replied. "General Sir Redvers Wilkinson has just been appointed Surgeon-General to the Indian Army. Apparently, according to my informants, he and Lady Wilkinson had been toying with the idea of adopting a child for ..." She noticed my expression at that point and her voice trailed off.

"General ... *who?*" I asked, thinking I must surely have misheard.

"Ah!" she exclaimed, full of gravitas again. "So the name *does* mean something to you. I wondered." The smile returned to her lips as she added, "Would you care to enlighten me, my dear?"

Enlighten *her!* My own head was spinning with the possibilities opened up by this revelation. And yet some part of my brain must already have leaped ahead of my conscious thoughts because I next asked — in fact, you could say I *heard* myself asking — the one question that mattered: "Were you able to find out whether my mistress, Mrs Agatha Trevarton, played any part in the affair?"

She shook her head. "Not I. But I believe Walter Trevarton did — your uncle. Tell me — is he aware of your kinship? In your letter you asked me not to mention it — and I didn't of course. And at our first meeting I felt quite sure he was unaware of it. But the next time we met — the day before yesterday, in fact — I was much less certain. There was a marked change in his demeanour. In fact, I have to tell you that he's ... well, 'withdrawn from the inquiry' sounds ridiculously dramatic. But he said he'd rather not have anything more to do with it."

"For any reason?"

"Yes — though he mentioned it only indirectly. He said when he told you he'd do his best to discover Teresa's present whereabouts, he had no idea his own family had been instrumental in her adoption. Now that must surely mean his mother — in view of what *you* told me when we first met. Or is there something I don't know?"

I explained the Wilkinson connection then and we established that the General was, indeed, one of the Wilkinsons of Nancekuke House, not two miles from where we were then sitting. I wanted to ask if Teresa had actually been there when I came to visit Marian, back in April. But courage failed me. I knew what the answer would be, anyway.

We agreed, unhappily, that the Wilkinson connection made Mr Walter's words ambiguous. 'Family' could mean either his mother or — through her — the Wilkinsons, his maternal forebears. Of course, I had never heard of this General Sir Redvers Wilkinson, so I could not say how close his kinship was to my mistress.

"But let us suppose it is of the closest," said Miss Martin, who had a splendidly logical mind in matters like this. "Suppose he is actually your grandmother's brother — which would make him Mister Walter's uncle. Why should that *embarrass* him in quite the way it did? I can't see it. I mean, such an adoption would imply nothing underhand."

I then voiced the thoughts that were clearly on her mind but which she would rather not speak aloud. "Would a general and his lady adopt the crippled daughter of two dead paupers — in the normal course of events? Is it at all likely?"

She thought it over and shook her head. "Hardly! Unless ..." Again she hesitated.

I completed the thought for her: "Unless they knew of some kinship."

"Quite."

"But how would they come to know of it — in this case?"

She sighed reluctantly. "It's hard to avoid the conclusion that your grandmother told them. It is certain that she influenced the Helston Guardians to place your sister at St Breaca's in Penzance. They'd never have agreed to it unless she — or someone of her social standing — had guaranteed the necessary funds." Watching me carefully, she went on adding other relevant facts: "The Guardians' records of adoption are open to inspection, of course. The convent's are not — as you yourself discovered! And if *I* know these things, you may be sure that Mister Walter knows them, too. It cannot have been long before he discovered that all trails lead back to Fenton Lodge. I wonder what he's planning to do about it?"

It was the perfect moment to tell her what had passed between Mrs Felicity and me in Plymouth a month earlier.

She closed her eyes, shook her head, and gave a brief, unamused laugh. "If ever you feel in need of honest, *straightforward* villainy, Miss Moore," she said, "do come and join me here!"

I was within an ace of crying out "Done!" If she had held her silence a little longer, I'm sure I should have struck the bargain at once.

But she was her brisk, businesslike self again as she said, "And what has happened since? Has Mrs Felicity repeated her offer to you? It is entirely self-serving on her part, of course, and you were quite right to turn it down. I think you showed great strength of character. It must have been very difficult."

I explained how my grandmother had made intercourse impossible between her daughter-in-law and me. Then, embarrassed by her praise, I went on to tell her what thoughts I'd had on the way to see Tom.

"You see," I said, "now I know Mrs Felicity isn't really trying to do me a kindness but only wants to use me for her own ends, it does sort of free me from being obliged to her, doesn't it. She's almost inviting me to use her for *my* own purposes, don't you think?"

She chuckled again, genuinely this time. "D'you recall what I said earlier about the necessity — in such a place as this — of meeting criminal thoughts with criminal thoughts of one's own? As long as they remain just thoughts, of course."·

I was crestfallen. I must have been secretly hoping for her permission to *use* Mrs Felicity, even though any chance of getting Teresa back with us had now gone. (It had gone on a Peninsular & Oriental vessel via Suez, to be precise.)

"D'you think Mrs Felicity will try again?" Miss Martin asked. "She's rather young to take on someone as formidable and experienced as your grandmother. One has to admire such recklessness — though one stands well back from the arena, if one can, of course. She might very well try again."

"You mean a more experienced woman would not?" I ventured.

"Certainly not. Have you ever been fishing?"

"Only in rock pools."

"It's the same thing. You throw in a good piece of bait — and this offer of a rent-free cottage and a pound a week was *very* good bait —

and you wait to see if the fish bites. If it doesn't, the experienced angler moves on. One doesn't throw good bait after bad."

"What d'you think I should do if she does repeat her offer?" I asked.

"Exactly what you've done so far, my dear — follow your instinct. It hasn't let you down yet. Actually, the person to be worrying about — or not worrying, perhaps, but *thinking* about — is the lady's husband. Your Uncle Walter. It would be wise to assume that by now he *knows* he's your uncle, too. What d'you think he'll do about it?"

I told her what Mrs Felicity had said he'd do if he ever found out — insist on ending my employment at Fenton Lodge and instead give me some kind of education more suitable to a Trevarton.

My neutral tone as I explained all this puzzled her. She asked why I didn't do something to *make* it happen — just in case she was wrong and Mr Walter had only tumbled to half of the truth. The Wilkinson half, that is.

"I gave my word I'd never tell either of her sons," I explained. "Nor even drop the vaguest hint."

She made me recount the precise circumstances of that promise and then pointed out it was no such thing. "She said you'd pack your bags and leave if ever you told him. Your subsequent promise was not absolute. It was based on that condition. So *of course* you'll pack your bags and leave when Mr Walter discovers the truth! He'll insist on it. It's a closed circle. Your grandmother's condition fulfils itself — leaving your promise sterile and untouched. Ethically, you are quite free to tell him. If you still decide not to, it must be for other reasons."

She knew, of course. I don't think there was a single nook or cranny of the human soul she had not explored during her years at Little Sinns. She certainly understood the soul of the adolescent maid, with all its selfish hunger for an object of devotion and sacrifice. Those words of hers brought me to the brink of a discovery I might not otherwise have made for weeks, if not months.

"She *is* my grandmother," I said. "She may not treat me as her grandchild — much. She may even forget I am that to her. But even so it matters. It matters to me. I am of *her* family. She is eaten up with miseries. I would not want to leave Fenton Lodge until she has become a happier person in herself."

She closed her eyes and shook her head slowly. I was surprised to hear a sort of catch in her voice as she said, "Oh, Crissy!" — calling me thus for the first time — "Family, eh! *Family!*"

W hat with the trains and the walk from the station, I didn't get back to Fenton Lodge until gone nine that evening. The news of Teresa's adoption and the strange circumstances surrounding it left me more bewildered than ever. It goes without saying that I didn't know what to think. In fact, I hardly knew what to *feel,* even.

I had spoken of my little sister often enough to my grandmother. Well, not *often,* perhaps, but certainly more than once. And she had never so much as breathed a word about the General and Lady W although she was the one who persuaded them into it and arranged everything through St Breaca's. Did she imagine I was *never* going to find out?

With hindsight I remembered an odd look or two from Cousin Stella Wilkinson, when I came back from Penzance that time, but it was nothing I could blame myself for not taking up.

I chewed the inside of my lip raw on the train home that evening, wondering what my grandmother's motives were. If hers really had been the guiding hand behind the dispersal of the six of us, what did it show? Was there a pattern?

Well, there certainly was with the boys. She'd pushed them off into places from which they'd never rise above the level of labourer or artisan, unless by extraordinary effort on their part. But her treatment of us girls was quite different.

She'd sent the eldest to a reformatory — and that was the end of it as far as she was concerned. I didn't count Marian's later removal to a good home in London, for my grandmother had nothing to do with that. But nor had she shown any pique or chagrin when I told her of it. Indeed, she had smiled ever so slightly, which puzzled me at the time but now I saw why. Marian scrubbing workhouse floors would very gladly join up with me in my plans to get the family back together. But Marian living the life of Riley in free-and-easy Hampstead, with her evening classes and her nights out at the Honor Club, would be a much more reluctant ally — as, indeed, she had proved.

Me she had placed in a sort of halfway house — offering to make me one of the most privileged of domestic servants, with the chance of an excellent match when the time came. For it was well known that ladies' maids, who knew all the rules of etiquette and well-bred behaviour, were greatly sought after by aspiring shopkeepers and merchants with more guineas than graces. She had done me a slight favour, you could say — if, like her, you believed that our mother's rebellion had cast us permanently out of the family.

But Teresa, at five, had presumably been 'rescuable' still from the taint of that same rebellion and the social disgrace that went with it. Or was she simply too young to present a challenge to the only family that mattered to Mrs T?

I had to smile at that thought. The general and his lady may not have known it when they agreed to the adoption but they would certainly be aware of it by now: Teresa bore out everything anyone ever said about the nature of the youngest child in a large family. It either lets itself be cowed, like piggy-widden, or it fights its corner like a little terrier and never lets the big dogs deny it a place at life's table. Teresa was a champion in the second group. In fact, put her among half a dozen little terriers and she'd make them look like piggy-widdens. I just hoped she had been cunning enough to wait until they were well on the way to India before she opened the valves and gave full vent to her personality.

But, that minor satisfaction apart, the rest of my thoughts were a gloomy reflection on my grandmother's cunning. She had sorted us out quite ruthlessly — like apples that had lain in a barrel next to one rotter (our father, of course). I could see her doing it. No tears, no smiles — just a good housekeeping chore, grimly done.

Those were my conclusions as I alighted from the train at Tregallas Halt. I was so angry that if Fenton Lodge had been anywhere within half a mile, I should have gone storming in and handed in my notice at once. But, as I strolled through the lanes that wound over the hills and dales between there and Swanpool, the whole thing began to seem too neat, too pat. The grandmother I had come to know — and to pity if not exactly to love — was nowhere near so simple. Also there was a nagging little thought at the back of my mind, a thought I did not wish to face just yet. I did so before that walk was done, however. Some calm and secret part of me must have realized that if I was about to do something so heedless as to hand in my notice, then I had jolly well better face it.

And *it* was the much less palatable alternative that *I* was the cause of all that had happened. Perhaps the old woman hadn't given two hoots about us until I came bursting into her happy home and threatened to pull it down around her ears. She really had forgotten our mother so successfully that, by the time she died, her passing was just another entry in the Poor Law Register. Then in walks little Crissy and she isn't with Old Mister Bill an hour before he fetches out pen and paper and starts writing a codicil to his will! (I hadn't forgotten that — though there was nothing I could do about it.) The resulting argument kills the old gentleman. And then the cause of it all turns up again the very next day and — however unintentionally — creates a scene that none who witnessed it will ever forget. And who could blame the old lady if her next thought is: *Dear God! There are five more like her at home!*

It isn't the Middle Ages. She can't give a feast and make us all drink from poisoned chalices or drown us in butts of malmsey. Besides, people of her class have far more effective institutions nowadays for dealing with problems like us — as she very swiftly demonstrated! This possibility did not shed a kindlier light on my grandmother, but, by making me the unwitting cause of our misfortunes — as the one who roused her out of her former indifference — it became hard for me to sustain my rage.

And I thank heaven for it, too, because — as it turned out — I should have made a fine fool of myself if I had simply gone storming in without learning what dramas had unfolded during my few hours' absence from Fenton Lodge.

Mrs Bourdeaux told me my mistress had retired already and was not to be disturbed. She looked as if she would say more but, after several hesitations, decided against it — no doubt knowing that Susan would tell me whatever it was anyway. I listened for a minute or so at the old lady's boudoir door and realized she was sitting writing at her desk. She had a reluctant fountain pen that had to be 'encouraged' every now and then to feed a little more ink to its nib — hence the repeated sounds of her fist lightly hammering her blotter and the little gasps of annoyance that accompanied it. I could not imagine what she might be writing but I was fairly sure it wasn't another codicil in my favour!

I should have left off my eavesdropping as soon as I realized what she was at but, unfortunately, Master Mark spotted me there and, realizing I was in a situation where I could not cry out, came swiftly and silently up behind me and took a disgraceful liberty. The misfortune was his, not mine. If we'd been in a situation where I could have spoken to him, I'd have done so, and he'd have retired with no hurt to anything but his pride. However, he left me with no choice but to put into practice what Susan had told me about 'how to stop a geezer's mouth from watering and make his eyes water, instead.' Unfortunately (again for Master

Mark), she hadn't told me about doing it gently. I thought he was just play-acting — lying on the floor, writhing and groaning like that.

Anyway, I got back to the servants' hall without further interference — where Susan immediately seized my arm and, grinning from ear to ear, said, "You look exhausted, my lover. Time you was tucked up in bed!" Her sparkling eyes promised a whole budget of scandal.

On our way up the back stair we peeped into the corridor and caught a glimpse of the poor young master crawling into his bedroom. I explained what had happened and *then* Susan told me about the extreme sensitivity of a man's 'family jewels.' Of course I wanted to rush back and apologize and do what I decently could to soothe his pain, but Susan pointed out how impossible it would be in the circumstances. And anyway she wanted to tell me what had happened between the old lady and her son and daughter-in-law while I'd been gone.

Mr Walter and Mrs Felicity had arrived just before luncheon, having first attended church in Penryn with Mr Archie, who had then joined them in a family delegation to Fenton Lodge. Mrs Megan, Archie's wife, had decided not to take part — wisely, as it turned out.

Sunday lunch was almost always a cold buffet because the Trevartons did not believe in putting servants to unnecessary toil on the sabbath. So there were no servants in the dining room and no one overheard their discussions until they became quite heated. Even then they kept shouting things like, "Keep your voice down for heaven's sake — d'you want the whole parish to know!" — which they managed to comply with briefly but long enough to leave some gaps in comprehension.

However, putting together what I had learned from Miss Martin with what Susan now told me, I surmised that Mr Walter had learned not only of his mother's efforts to get this unknown Teresa Moore adopted by her uncle, General Sir Redvers Wilkinson (yes, he was her uncle even though he was almost ten years her junior), but also of the child's kinship with the Trevartons. And of course, the moment he knew Teresa was his niece he knew the same of me and Marian — and that the three boys were his nephews. I suppose a good lawyer would know half a dozen ways of mixing a smile and a threat to get any information he wanted, either directly or through his cronies in the police. Anyway, he must have discovered what extraordinary efforts his mother had made to divide us up for good. But the thing that really shocked him — just as Mrs Felicity said it would — was to realize that his mother was employing her own granddaughter and training her up as a lady's maid.

Mr Archie took his mother's side. As I suspected, he'd known it all from very early on — thanks to the rides I had from Bert Eddy and the gossip at Trevarton's. He was probably unaware what had befallen each particular niece or nephew, and almost certainly didn't care, either. The family business was his entire life and he didn't want any business with the family to interfere! He saw nothing particularly wrong with my employment in his mother's household and he thought his younger brother was making too much fuss altogether. The argument between the pair of them had been at times as heated as that between Mr Walter and his mother.

Mrs Felicity had taken no part in these tribulations. Or if she had, she'd kept her voice down and none of the servants had heard her. But I was certain her rôle was not as passive as her silence suggested. She would have done nothing directly and openly against her mother-in-law but she'd take the first private opportunity to ensure her own wishes were not thwarted. I knew she'd stop at nothing to humiliate Mrs T and I was afraid she saw me as the perfect instrument.

"I don't understand you, gel," Susan said when we had talked our way round and round this maze of passions and plots. "There's the Old Lady what's done her best to destroy your family — she's even got your little sister carried off to the other side of the world — and there's Madame Felicity who wants to spend her own money bringing you all back together again — and now she's got Mister Walter on her side and all — and you say you don't know *what* to do nor where to turn!"

"They're all devils," I replied. "Better the devil you know than the devil you don't. At least I know the Old Lady's brand of devilry."

Susan just sniffed at that. "Just don't you *never* talk to me in future about your bright dreams of bringing your family all together again one fine day. You could walk out of this house tonight — take that cottage what she's offered — get the boys back, and Marian, if she'd come. And don't tell me a lawyer like Mister Walter couldn't arrange it, him being your uncle and all."

On the face of it, she was right. Was I just being a coward? Even worse — a selfish coward?

If only my grandmother had been the wicked ogress of pantomime and fairy story! Then it would have been so easy to take sides and strive to undo what she had done. But the truth was that we were all of us better off — materially, anyway. And we all faced a brighter future than we would have if we'd just been left on our own. Even Tom, whose prospects as a twelve-year-old pot boy in a pub, paying all his earnings into the family kitty, had not been too great.

I explained all this to Susan and eventually, and rather grudgingly, she agreed I did have a point.

At which, of course, my mood swung round to the other side and all that mattered then was *family*. We belonged together — for richer for poorer, for better for worse … and all that. Those marriage vows are about family, too, not just the couple at the altar. *Families should be together no matter what!* That was like a great glowing text in the sky for me. Its heat shrivelled up all those smaller calculations of comfort and self-interest.

I fell asleep that night as confused and miserable as I'd been at any time since our mother's death.

Things happened at Fenton Lodge that no one ever mentioned. You were left to work it out for yourself that so-and-so must have said such-and-such to whatsername, which is why she's acting a bit cool toward you-know-who. Something of that sort happened to me the very next morning after my unfortunate encounter with Master Mark. I met him on his way down to breakfast, while I was going to tidy his mother's boudoir. I was so mortified I didn't know where to look. I wanted to tell him how sorry I was and so on but the subject was so embarrassing I couldn't even think where to start. But I needn't have worried. *He* apologized to *me!*

He reached out a hand to touch my arm and stop me going on by, and he said, "I can't begin to tell you how sorry I am, Crissy."

Not 'Miss Moore' but 'Crissy.' That alerted me. This encounter was no mere continuation of past encounters. He was signalling a difference.

"I didn't know," he added. "I had no idea."

Was he fishing? Susan told me he'd been excluded from yesterday's family confab. In fact, because sailing was allowed on the sabbath, as distinct from racing, he'd taken a dinghy and gone pottering around in Carrick Roads with a chum of his, Tony Fox. So he couldn't have heard anything directly. Therefore someone must have told him something after he came back — indeed, *after* he took that liberty with me. But who? And how much?

That's the way you had to think all the time in the Trevarton household.

"Nor did I!" I replied emphatically, hoping he'd take my meaning. When I saw he didn't I added, "Or I'd have slapped your face, instead of what I *did* do."

"Oh, that!" He blushed — and rubbed his cheek as if I *had* slapped it. (He could hardly rub the other place!) "I deserved it — but that's not what I was talking about. I meant I had no idea that I'm your uncle." He swallowed heavily as if he'd got a huge confession off his chest. Then he gave a little, nervous smile, begging me to say something.

I said, "Your mother forbade me to tell you — or your brothers."

"And yet all the servants knew!" He raised his hands helplessly, as if to say, 'What folly!'

I smiled at him, trying to put him at his ease, and said, "I never *thought* of you as my uncle, even though I knew you were."

His embarrassment faded rather quickly. "I certainly never behaved like one, either. You really should have said."

"Would you have believed me? Anyway, that's not the point — which is I should never have accepted your mother's offer — or at least not her conditions. It should all have been in the open. The whole family should've known. And agreed. Of course, it's easy to say that now."

"Gosh!" he exclaimed. "I don't know where to begin. There's so much I want to know — about you, your brothers and sisters — you know. And *my* sister, too. I've only heard hints — I mean, I only learned the truth last night, after ... you know."

"After I should have slapped your cheek!"

"Put it like that, yes. I kept waking up in the night, thinking, *Something big has happened ... something stirring ...* And then I'd remember — I've got all these nephews and nieces I've never even heard of! It's like a discovery scene in a melodrama. Or it's like finding there's a whole new wing built onto a house you've lived in all your life. No, I don't know what it's like. It's like nothing that ever happened to me before. What are you going to do next?"

That question shook me. While he'd been gushing on about this wonderful new discovery, I had realized that it must have been Mrs Bourdeaux who told him. She had a soft spot for him, having no children of her own, and often used to carry him a glass of warm milk and honey last thing at night. Perhaps she twigged what had happened between him and me? Anyway, she was the only one who'd visit his room at that hour, and she was the only servant who'd dare tell him the truth about us.

And whose side was *she* on? I wondered.

Then there was his question: What *was* I going to do next? The idea that it was up to me to act had not even crossed my mind. I was so far out of my depth in that household I thought it safest to drift with their currents until I felt a bit of solid ground beneath me once again.

But he was right. I really ought to take the initiative or I'd be swamped by all those family cross-currents. His family, not mine ... and yet it was mine, too! That was the whole point. My head began to spin. I wanted to talk it over with someone. With Mark, probably. As usual, I felt I wouldn't know what to think until I'd listened to myself testing several possibilities out loud — and with someone else there to provide a bit of discipline.

"Could we discuss it after luncheon?" I suggested. "While your mother takes a nap? I'm supposed to be putting fresh camphor in the furs but I could do that tonight instead. Oh, no! I can't. Monday is my polytechnic evening."

"The good old 'polly,' eh! What d'you do down there?"

"Useful Arts. It's just a general drawing course at the moment."

"Ah! I suppose an uncle may walk with his niece unchaperoned?"

I dug him with my elbow. He leaped away from me as if in mortal terror that I was about to assault him again.

"At least I seem to have done no permanent damage," I remarked.

He drew breath to make some risqué or flippant reply, but then he seemed to realize we'd left that sort of world behind — the world where young masters try their luck with servant maids, who rebuff them or not as the case may be. All he said was, "Until this evening, then."

All that day I waited for my grandmother to say something. But she behaved as if nothing untoward had happened. She must have known that her dispute with Mr Walter was all over the house — and that Susan would certainly have told me about it — and with some embroidery. But it was a day like any other as far as she was concerned, outwardly, anyway.

She asked me if I'd had a pleasant time with Miss Martin, so I thought if that was all we were going to discuss, I'd give her something to think about. I'd have loved to tell her that Miss Martin would welcome me with open arms among the staff at Little Sinns, though in what precise capacity she had not said. However, there were plenty of maids my age who were teaching in dame schools all over the country, and with no more education than I'd received, so she wouldn't have questioned it.

However, I thought that would be a little blatant, so instead I just went on and on, bubbling with enthusiasm for the institution, the girls, their deportment, the wonderful work of reform and rehabilitation, and so forth — and above all I sang the praises of the wonderful Miss Martin. It was easy for me, too, because I believed every word.

Eventually the old woman told me I'd said quite enough, but by then, I think, she'd grasped what I was really saying — that dismissal held no terrors for me at all. She knew that, despite her enormous influence with the Helston Guardians, the Camborne — Redruth Union was part of her daughter-in-law's fiefdom. It was therefore a doubly safe haven for me, should I choose to go to Little Sinns.

I think it was the first time in my life that I managed to put ideas of such importance into another person's mind while seeming to speak of something quite different. I saw that my grandmother was actually wise to say nothing to me on the subject we both knew was uppermost in our minds. To speak of it openly would change the feelings between us for ever — and neither of us (I also realized) was quite ready for that yet. However, in this more subtle way we could explore the possibilities of the situation ... do a little probing around the margins ... and all without running that risk.

Came seven o'clock that evening and I set out for my drawing class at 'the good old polly.' It was true that an uncle could walk his niece unchaperoned, but in a whispered consultation at teatime that day Mark and I had decided that *this* uncle and niece had better leave the house separately. He was waiting for me at the bottom of Swanpool Hill, where we could either take the main highway and go into town along Wood Lane or follow a little farm track that meanders among some fields and, if you follow it across several highways, eventually comes out by the observatory at the end of Woodhouse Terrace. I had tried going that way once but been forced to turn back because the bit where it dipped under the railway line was exactly like the terrifying scene that rose in my mind when our mother first read us the tale of the Billy Goats Gruff. They, you'll recall, used to attack travellers through their territory. (I know they lived on a bridge and this was a tunnel, but children's minds don't bother with minor details like that.)

"Well, this *is* nice," he said, offering me his arm.

I told him I didn't think that was a very good idea and he said, "Perhaps not." Then, falling in beside me, he went on, "All the same, it is nice. You're more like a sister, I feel, than a niece. A fellow needs sisters. You know what happened to mine, I suppose? They all died before I was born — except Monica, but I was only two when ..."

"And Selina," I pointed out. "My mother."

"Yes — of course! Sorry — that's the whole point, isn't it. But she died — I mean, eloped — but we were always told she'd died — three years before I was even born. I still can't believe that all the while I was growing up — you know — running over these fields ... paddling down there in the sea — all that time I had a real live sister not twenty miles away. What was she like? D'you mind talking about her? Don't if you'd rather not."

I felt the hair prickling on the back of my neck. He was the first Trevarton who showed that he felt some genuine kinship with our mother. Archie had been nineteen and Walter twelve in the year she eloped, so they must actually have known her quite well. But neither of them had shown the slightest interest in her life after that — how she had lived and what she'd been like with us, her children. It was guilt, of course. They had known of her existence but had done nothing to help her. Mark was free of that.

I took his arm then.

He pulled a face and said, "Oh, so now it *is* wise all of a sudden?"

"No, it's just that you're the first member of your family to want to know what our mother was really like."

"Didn't my father?" he asked at once — and then answered himself. "No. I suppose he wouldn't have wanted to press such questions on you, not straight after she died. He must have thought there'd be plenty of time for that — poor man. He never got over her elopement — or so ... er, so I was told."

"By Mrs Bourdeaux!" I shook his arm impatiently. "She told you last night — when she told you everything else. Why not say so! You're a terrible family for letting slip as little as possible. Did she also tell you there was an almighty *spleen* at Fenton Lodge yesterday — between your brother Walter and your mother — all about employing me as a domestic servant?"

"You'd rather not tell me about your mother, then?" he countered.

"No, no, of course I want to. I'll tell you now." And, for the next ten minutes or so, as we wandered up the long, gentle slope among the hay meadows and market gardens, I did my best to convey an impression of the sister who had vanished from Fenton Lodge three years before he was even born. I described her gentleness, her strength, her almost permanent bewilderment among people who never accepted her as one of them and others who rejected her as no longer one of them. I told him about a time when she burst into tears one afternoon in the middle of Helston — on the doorstep of the Angel, it was. She greeted a girl she'd been to school with and the woman just looked straight through her and walked on. I was about five and I ran after the woman and kicked her — which brought tears to *her* eyes, too. But our mother took me home and whipped me for it — not very hard, because she knew I did it for love of her, but hard enough to teach me that there's ways and ways of showing it.

In no time, it seemed, Mark and I arrived at the summit of our walk, with a view right across the harbour and Carrick Roads. St-Just-in-Roseland, miles away on the farther shore, shimmered vaguely in the evening haze. It was a quarter past seven — about an hour before sunset. Scarcely a breeze stirred the air, which was drowsy with so many mingled scents. There was tar and salt and seaweed from the bay, hibiscus and succulents and all sorts of exotic shrubs from the wealthy gardens in Wood Lane, and the unforgettable, unforgotten smell of haymaking from the pastures all around. Gulls mewed raucously from nearby chimneys while high above us a whole choir of skylarks was trilling away.

"They always remind me of auctioneers," Mark said. Then he raised his voice impossibly high — higher even than a little girl's squeal — and piped, as fast as he could: "Come-on-now-gentlemen-what-am-I-bid-for-this-fine-bit-of-turf?"

It sounds silly now but it was ever so funny at the time. I was so weak with laughter I had to rest on a stone bollard at the top of the zigzag path that led down to the churchyard.

Drawing class lasted two hours, with a five-minute break when two of the ladies sold lemon cordial, which they brought with them. Mark said he'd go for a long walk around Pendennis Point and call back for me at half-past nine.

The polytechnic was an imposing building in the classical style. It had an entrance like a theatre, so that the building itself was a little way back from the street. Upstairs one whole side was given over to a long gallery, where they held exhibitions not just of pupils' work but of items of general Cornish interest — mining and archaeology and the history of the seaport and things like that. In between times it was *our* classroom — the general-drawing class.

We couldn't draw from the life because we were a mixed class, but naked Graeco-Roman goddesses and athletes in pure white plaster were considered decent enough. Also, as Mr Moynihan, our master, said, "They didn't need paying and they kept more or less still."

That was the first evening I'd seen him since Milly told me all about him and his first wife — the unfortunate Esther Wilkinson who was some sort of kinswoman on my grandmother's side. He'd been at the Royal Academy for the summer exhibition and we'd been supervised by a man called Charlie Murphy, who painted signs and shopfronts all over town. He'd taught us how to draw York roses, Lancaster roses, castles, anchors, elephants, and all the traditional decorations you get on gypsy caravans. It had been quite interesting but we were glad to get back to some real drawing. Everyone said we were so lucky to have a real academician to teach us. Mr Moynihan said he did it because it kept his feet on the ground — though we all knew he did it really to find free models for his Cornish genre paintings.

He was a very hard taskmaster. Two hours was all most people could take of his teaching because he drove us like slaves and hardly ever praised our work. That evening he ignored me for the whole of the first hour, though he sat at everyone else's donkey and drove them, one by one, into despair. We were drawing *Discobolus,* the naked Greek discus thrower, caught in mid-spin just before he releases the discus. It's the most difficult subject of all, I think, because it's a perfect knife-edge balance of sculptural stillness and athletic motion, so, if you fail to capture either, you fail altogether. And there were a dozen and a half of us there that evening, busily proving it.

Roger Moynihan set the scene and then left us, saying, "Just incriminate yourselves quietly. I'll be back in fifteen minutes." He had a smoke on the fire escape and then returned, seated himself at some hapless student's donkey, looked at the drawing, slumped, and intoned, with a sort of weary edge, *"When* are you going to start drawing?"

And then he took the pencil out of the student's hand, just to show he wasn't using a magical one of his own, and he'd do a little sketch up in the corner which was sheer magic. Just a few flowing lines, a little bit of hatching, and there was *Discobolus* pulsating with life and making the student's own feeble effort look so tawdry.

He worked his way around the class, not going in order, so you never knew where he'd pounce next, while I sat there, making my drawing worse and worse with every new line. As we came up to the five-minute pause I just wanted to throw my pencil across the room and tear up the paper and go and join the needlework class because it was something I knew I really could do.

And then he pounced.

He stared impassively at my drawing for ages, long enough for my racing heart to come back to near-normal. By then I was looking at my effort with some hope, thinking actually it wasn't too bad. The proportions were right and the light and shade suggested the anatomy pretty well. And I don't think Moynihan himself could have improved my perspective of the discus.

I thought he agreed with me, too, for he looked up with a little smile and said "Mmm!" in a tone bordering on faint approval. But then he said, "Drawing, Miss Moore, is an act of worship. You come in here each Monday evening to pay homage to a miracle. To life! To the world! To the tumbling, tossing, restlessness of things ..."

Well, 'life' and 'the world' were words I could take or leave. They were the sort of big, windy ideas *anyone* could reach for. But when he said 'the tumbling, tossing, restlessness of things' it sent a shiver down my spine. It was like a gimlet that drilled through the crust of my commonplace ideas about Art and Beauty and so on and penetrated right through to what it was *really* all about. Not just life but *my* life.

My life was one long tumbling and tossing restlessness, so were my thoughts, and my feelings. And my ever-changing hopes for our family. Even the meaning of 'family' itself was beginning to tumble and toss, especially on that evening, when Mark had spoken of feeling like a brother to me and his words had struck an echo in my heart.

And there was Roger Moynihan, not measuring anything, and not really drawing this plaster cast in front of us, but capturing perfectly that elusive balance between repose and energy. When he drew a muscle it wasn't just a squiggly line with a bit of hatching in the right place, it was a knot of tension in a living arm. His pencil really was a magic wand that put us all in touch with the mysteries of life — or whatever it is that lurks beneath the surface of mere appearances and provokes that unending restlessness.

Mr Perrow, a chandler's apprentice who happened to be on the donkey next to mine, looked at my drawing as we broke for lemon cordials, and said, "You're pretty good, you know."

I was flattered, of course, even though I knew he was only trying to butter me up to go sparking with him in King Charles the Martyr's churchyard after classes, which he'd done with several of the girls. But flattery was the last emotion I wanted to feel just then. Roger Moynihan had just helped me to see something important — or rather, to glimpse it. Already I could feel my mind losing its grasp of part of it. If I didn't hold on firmly, I'd lose it all. So I just said, "How can you look at *his* drawing and then at mine and say a thing like that?"

He sneered that I was teacher's pet and turned his back on me.

Mr Moynihan didn't return to my donkey that evening but at the end of class he asked me if I'd like to sit for him on my next free afternoon. I felt a terrible urge to blurt out that he wouldn't want me near his studio if he knew of my kinship, distant though it was, with his first wife — to say nothing of the parallels between her father's social disgrace and my mother's. Moynihan was a notoriously loquacious painter who chatted away all the time he worked. So I was afraid I could not spend several hours in his presence without letting slip something that would tip him off. So, like a fool, I told him that I'd *love* to but unfortunately my only free time was on the sabbath. He just laughed and said, "Good egg! If I worship any kind of creator, which I doubt, then it is entirely through the tip of my brush!"

So that was that. When Mark collected me after the class, I passed on this news to him most apologetically, as if I had already promised him that afternoon — which, in my own mind, I had.

"You'll need a chaperon, anyway," he said easily. "What's the painting? One of his scenes of Cornish life?"

I said it was called The Cocklepicker and I'd have to stand on the beach wearing a tattered skirt that came down to just below my knees, showing off my calves and ankles. At my age it was still something I could *just* decently do, though in my mind I already felt much too old for such a display. However, art had its own rules and it was a great honour to be immortalized by a real academician, so I wasn't going to make any bones about it.

Mention of my naked calves and ankles put poor Mark into a fine old quandary. A few days earlier, before he knew I was his niece, it would have brought on a flurry of suggestive words and guffaws, I'm sure. Now he hardly knew what to say, though he realized he could not let it pass entirely without comment, either. In the end he said something that took me by surprise.

"What a fool I've been!" he said — not jestingly, either. Nor bitterly. Just rather sadly. "Shall we go back via Custom House Quay? There's an oyster stall there. D'you fancy half a dozen Helford oysters and a glass of porter?"

It sounded wonderfully grown-up. He didn't need to ask me twice.

"Or a bowl of cockles," he added as we changed direction. "Get you in the right frame of mind for old Moynihan?"

I dug him with my elbow.

"You are an extremely aggressive young female, you know," he said. "Kicking your mother's old school chums ... nearly ruining my marriage prospects ... lashing out with your elbows at every other word I say! D'you think you're really cut out to be a demure little lady's maid?"

I'm sure I blushed to the roots of my hair. I was glad of the night, for it was now a good hour after sunset. "Why did you say you'd been such a fool?" I asked.

"Oh, that." He became serious again. "Because of the way I behaved to you before — seizing you and kissing you ... taking liberties — it isn't at all what I really wanted, you know."

"You gave a good imitation, then — that's all I can say. What *did* you want, if not that?"

"This," he said, slipping his arm through mine. "Just to be friends. It's jolly hard just to be friends with a girl. Or for you to be friends with a boy, I suppose. The world expects otherwise."

"*Sus*pects," I corrected him.

"Exactly. That's what's so perfect about us, being uncle and niece *and* boy and girl at the same time. We can't get all soppy with each other. It's not allowed. So we *can* be just friends, good friends, the very best of friends, without either of us ever needing to suspect the other of ulterior motives. Don't you agree? Do say yes, *dear* Crissy!"

I was not nearly so sanguine. He might have been a few weeks older than me but I knew better how easily people deceive themselves. And others — but especially themselves.

I said yes, however, as he asked it of me.

After the oysters and ale we took the long way home by way of the Falmouth Hôtel and the seafront between there and Gyllyngvase beach. The night and the splash of the tiny waves made conversation easy. I asked him what had passed through his mind on his stroll round Pendennis Castle, while I had been drawing my plaster-cast athlete.

"Did you ever wonder," he asked, "if you were adopted — if the person everyone says is your mother actually isn't?"

"Is that what you were thinking about?" I countered uneasily.

"I often think it," he replied. "Probably because there's such a gap between me and Walter."

"There wouldn't be if Sarah and Monica had lived," I pointed out.

"Sarah was born only three years after Walter, and Monica only four years later. I came along a full seven years after her — by which time my mother was forty — forty and a day, to be precise. That's why I wonder sometimes if she really is my mother."

These thoughts disturbed me. I did not wish to lose a nice safe uncle, who was also devilishly handsome and conveniently of an age with me, on the very day that he found me. I was surprised that he raised the topic, too, especially after his earlier delight at discovering our kinship at last. What could he hope for by denying it now?

"Whose son are you, then?" I asked.

He gave a self-deprecating laugh. "Probably my mother's — I mean, the woman I've always called my mother. But just supposing ..."

"Supposing what?"

"My sister Catherine," he said hesitantly. He was realizing that it was one thing to hatch such thoughts and quite another to speak them aloud. I must have been the first person he had ever shared them with.

"She died at the age of thirteen or fourteen," I pointed out. "She fell from her horse."

He made no reply.

We had reached the seafront by then. The moon, almost full, was rising over a smooth, rolling sea. We stared at it awhile and then I took his arm to turn him for home. "Didn't she?" I prompted.

He sighed. "That story seems to have gained currency. In fact, though, she had turned eighteen when it happened — whatever *it* was. It could have been a fall from a horse."

"You mean there's some doubt?"

"Lots. She was a consumptive — or so they said. She went to Switzerland with my mother for the entire winter. I was born there in the January of that year — eighteen seventy-four. She 'fell off her horse' nineteen days later. I've often wondered."

"That's *all* you've got to go on?" I asked scornfully.

"Catherine wouldn't have been the first young lady to suffer a sudden and hitherto quite undiagnosed illness at around that age — one that required her to spend at least six months abroad in hope of a cure. And remember — it was seven *years* since Mamma had had Monica. It's enough to make anyone wonder."

One of us had to say it: "So we might be cousins, then — you and I — not uncle and niece."

"Mmm." He squeezed my arm and, gazing skyward, said, "Makes a difference, what!"

I pulled my arm away. "It means we may no longer walk about unchaperoned — until we know what is fact and what is fancy."

He chuckled dismissively.

"It jolly well does," I assured him.

"But we already know what is fact," he said evenly. "The truth may be quite different but the *fact* is that the world insists I am Agatha Trevarton's son, and the world must accept the consequences — namely, that you and I may walk unchaperoned as long as we are decorous about it. In other words, we should find some rather private place when we kiss."

"Kiss?" I echoed in surprise.

"Like this!" He drew me in among several tall clumps of pampas grass growing in front of Gyllyngdune House, slipped his arms about me, and lowered his lips to mine.

It was quite unlike our previous kiss. In fact, it was such a sweet sensation, and so much more thrilling than my wishy-washy imaginings, that I could not resist him as I ought to have done. But in my heart-of-hearts ...

No! I will not make lame excuses for myself. There was a boldness in my spirit and a strength of desire in my body that combined to make his advances irresistible. I surrendered my lips to his with a swiftness and a passion that took him aback. It took me aback as well. For a moment or two — and quite a long moment it was — I would have done anything he wanted. If he had fished up my petticoats, like the men I had seen with the Unfortunates in Union Road that night, I should have kissed him all the more passionately and done nothing to hinder his purpose — for, indeed, it would not have been his purpose alone.

But that long, giddy moment passed (fortunately without his realizing it had ever been there to seize) and that calculating imp who must have saved many a maid from ruin resumed command of me once more. I broke off the exciting contact of our lips and flung my arms about him, hugging his dear head tight against mine.

"Whoo!" he gasped in my ear.

The tickle of his breath almost undid my resolve again.

He must have sensed it for he stopped panting soon enough and the next thing I felt was the hot, moist tip of his tongue exploring the whorls of my ear. I would never have imagined that such pleasure was possible. It sent stabs and darts of ecstasy through and through me, from the soles of my feet to the crown of my scalp, setting all my flesh a-tingle. I buckled at the knees and, if he had not been holding me so tight, I should have collapsed to the ground.

"Oh, Crissy!" he murmured. "You're so ... you're just the most ... I don't know. I don't know."

I put the tip of my tongue in his ear then, and was rewarded with another gasp of pleasure.

And yet there was a difference. When he had done it to me it was like a loving act, something I wanted to go on and on. But when I did it to him it was more like an invitation. And I didn't want it to go on and on. For one thing I didn't like the taste! I was pondering some tactful way of telling him to wash more thoroughly in future when he turned my face aside and went to work on my other ear, closing his lips around the whole lower half of it, suckling on the lobe, and running his tongue up and down the back of it.

This time I almost swooned at the pleasure of it — not just darts and thrills but a vast, warm glow that filled every part of me, every little sinew. Before I could stop myself I loosened the two top buttons of my bodice, saying I was so hot I could hardly breathe.

My ear was suddenly cooled as he returned his lips to mine — which made it easier for him to slip his hand inside my bodice and run his nails lightly along my collarbone and up over the slope of my shoulder. No man had ever touched me there before and I would never have believed that so simple a caress could give rise to such profound pleasure. Once or twice a loose finger strayed an inch or so lower, but took no further liberty than that.

How long we remained, kissing and caressing in that fashion, I had no idea, but the moon was well up when, with my bodice rebuttoned, we stepped back upon the clifftop drive and resumed our walk.

"Well," he said cheerily, "I think we're a jolly responsible couple — well able to spoon without a chaperon and without o'erstepping the bounds of propriety."

"Yes," I agreed. "I could kiss and kiss like that for ever — and be perfectly satisfied by it and never want ... you know — more."

"Mmm," he responded vaguely.

I knew it was not at all what he had meant but at least he now knew what *I* meant.

I lay awake that night, savouring the memory of our embraces, wondering if he really was no more than my cousin — and (to my shame) not caring much if he wasn't. Either way, I was determined not to risk 'breaking my ankle' with him, as the saying has it. So the way ahead was simple. If he truly was my cousin, our courtship might well ripen into marriage. If he was my uncle, it wouldn't — and I should have gained a valuable faculty for self-control, like learning to swim with water wings.

Then, as the memory began to fade, I felt a little pang of regret that, in gaining a beau, I had lost a companion. That pleasing prospect of uninhibited talks — honest, frank, and free of emotion — began to recede. In its place loomed that amorous hunger to be alone, to touch, to kiss, to dip a toe into the waters of that Rubicon which all lovers must one day cross.

But I need not have worried. August, with its long, late twilights, is not the month for clandestine lovers who merely long to embrace. And in any case it happened that Mark had been sincere in his earlier assurance that he hung upon my words as much as upon the lips that spoke them. We spent far more time in conversation — setting the whole world to rights — than in actual spooning, though I allow we had our share of that as well.

I could not keep these changes in my life from Susan's notice, of course. She knew nothing of our canoodling but even so she thought it dangerous for a young uncle to be so much in the company of his equally young niece. I assured her that our intercourse was of the noblest and most intellectual kind. She, being a year older, greeted this with supercilious amusement.

About the time that I began to keep company with Mark, she took up with a young photographer's assistant called Jim Collett, who had finished his apprenticeship a year earlier. She said it was much better to be a maidservant in the country than 'up Lunnon,' because there you usually had to ask permission to entertain followers, which wasn't always granted. And even if it was, they had to come into the servants' hall where the housekeeper could have her eye on them. But in Cornwall, country ways still prevailed and maidens and their swains could go out walking in the lanes and fields in the old, time-honoured way.

So she would patiently listen to my assurances of Mark's and my purity and then she'd regale me with lurid accounts of how she'd fought an epic battle with Jim's wandering hands. But when one epic battle succeeded another — and all were described with the monotonous sameness of those magazine stories — I began to suspect that it was mere wishful thinking on her part. I'd seen Master Collett a couple of times and exchanged a few pleasantries with him, and he did not strike me as the wandering-hands kind of young man at all. Rather the opposite. He once showed me a book of Rossetti's poems, which he'd brought with him for his walk with Susan. I felt sure the only groping he ever did was through the pages of love's dictionary, seeking words to express the power and majesty of his emotions.

He was not a handsome young man — at least, not in the obvious way that Mark was. But he had a good countenance, earnest and intense, and he radiated a kind of inner strength. But then, as if to contradict that, he sometimes wore a slightly bewildered air, bordering on the forlorn — as if he knew he had misssed something in life but could not rightly say what. Occasionally our eyes would meet and I'd get the feeling he was about to ask *me* what it might be. He never did, though.

However, wishing to know him better (so that I could the better judge Susan's lurid accounts of their trysts, of course), I suggested that the four of us should go out together one afternoon. In fact, I suggested the afternoon on which I'd agreed to become The Cocklepicker for Roger Moynihan. Susan demurred until, rather impertinently, I suggested that we should pose on the sands together. Then the prospect of immortality on canvas persuaded her. I was impertinent because I spoke without first asking Moynihan.

He was quite put out when I told him, but his grumpiness evaporated as soon as he saw how pretty Susan was. Then he couldn't wait to get us both into our costumes and down to the beach — barefoot and in short, ragged skirts and petticoats. It was a funny thing. We both felt shamefully naked as we dashed across the highway at Greenbank and then down over the rocks, all under the snooty and startled gaze of the Yacht Club members. But the moment we were on the beach, standing in shallow pools of water — in short, in the proper setting for such dresses — we felt completely natural and unflustered. Also rather annoyed and impatient with Mark and Jim, who couldn't take their eyes off our naked calves and ankles — as if they looked any different from their own limbs!

But after a while, they got bored with just standing there, so Mark went to the club jetty and took a rowing boat, in which the two of them went sculling around in the slack water between Greenbank and Flushing, the village on the far bank, about a quarter of a mile away. To set a limit to Moynihan's monopoly of us, they called out that they'd decided to treat us to a strawberry-cream tea in Flushing at four.

"That's your employer's youngest son, isn't it?" Moynihan asked when we were alone — give or take a shifting population of curious children and occasional nannies. He was only sketching us that afternoon, so he was even more talkative than when he was painting.

"Mark Trevarton," I said.

"I wonder if he knows that he and I are distantly related by marriage?"

"The other young man is Jim Collett," I added. "He's working as an assistant to ..."

"I know," he interrupted. "Stanton's Photographic *Artists!*" He spoke the word with contempt. "One of our modern oxymorons — like '*Humane* Butchers' or '*Invisible* Menders'!"

I thought I had successfully got him off the subject of kinship but he was a dog with a bone. After a brief silence he went on, "My first wife, God rest her, was a Wilkinson — and so, I believe was your mistress, that young lad's mother?"

I was expecting it, of course, but Susan wasn't. He noticed how she twitched and looked at me. Then he was like a dog with a whole skeleton. "Didn't you know that?" he asked her.

"No," she replied awkwardly. "I mean, I was thinking what a small world! You know, sir — the way one does?"

He stared her out and said, "Does one?"

I hated him for that sort of skill, because at the beginning, when all she did was twitch, he really had nothing to go on. But by pretending to know absolutely everything about it, and staring at her with those all-seeing-artist's eyes, he got her to the point where she'd blurt it all out just to make him stop.

"We try not to pry into our employer's private life," I told him.

He just chuckled. "Bravely said! But you're not on trial here, you know. You've already got the position. And you're holding it very well!"

I smiled then as if he had just said something more enlightening than witty. "You're quite right," I replied. "I'm not on trial, am I!"

A mood of utter recklessness overcame me. What was I afraid of? Why shouldn't he know of my kinship with the Trevartons? The only people who didn't know of it by now were strangers who'd be entirely indifferent to the fact, anyway.

He was eyeing me curiously, for my reply seemed to promise some revelation. "What follows, then?" he asked.

"It follows that if you are related by marriage to ..."

"Crissy!" Susan cut across me urgently. "Think!"

"Think what? It's no secret any more — if it ever was. The workers at Trevarton's always knew. So did all the other servants at Fenton Lodge. The only people she wanted it kept from were her sons — and even one of them knew all along. And so do the other two, now."

She just raised her eyes to the clouds, as if to say that nice arguments like that were beside the point.

But I, for my part, no longer saw *any* point in all that secrecy. All it did was induce a sense of shame, which was quite unjustified. So I turned back to Moynihan, who was now on tenterhooks, jaw open, and said, "It's nothing to get all excited about. I read once that absolutely everybody in England can trace at least one line back to William the Conqueror, so we shouldn't be surprised to come across accidental kinships in other directions, too. And the fact is, Mister Moynihan, if you're related by marriage to Mark and his mother, then you're related to *me*, too." I turned to Susan and added, "There!"

"On your head be it," she said gravely.

We both stared at Moynihan then, who had knocked his easel askew in catching the pencil that had fallen from his grasp. When he had all straight again he set the pencil down and walked across to join us. "How can that be?" he asked. "Explain."

I obliged him. That is, I gave him a bare outline of the situation.

"How utterly fascinating!" he murmured. "Come on — you must change out of these clothes at once and tell me all about it." He was already back at his easel, folding it up and tucking away his pencil. "D'you mean to say that your grandmother, Mrs Trevarton — *the* Mrs Trevarton who sits on all those charities, which strive so earnestly to educate poor families and keep them together — that she sees nothing extraordinary in employing her own orphaned granddaughter as a menial in her own household?"

I bridled. "I wouldn't call myself a menial. Nor would the wealthy shopkeepers who court me for my mistress's custom, either!"

He laughed. "That's even richer, don't you think!" He led us back across the rocks.

Susan tried to attract the boys' attention but they were busy chatting with the ferryman at Greenbank jetty.

Moynihan's wife, a muscular, roly-poly woman called Francesca, was gathering blackcurrants from a bush in the front garden. "Oh dear!" she exclaimed at seeing us return so soon. "Isn't it working?"

"Swimmingly, my dear!" He put her in her place with a kiss on the forehead. "They're just going to change and then I shall deliver them into the arms of their swains upon yonder bright strand!"

I could have wept. To see this man whom I had almost revered as a god — who, as an artist, was, indeed, very like a god in his powers — to see him behaving in this so-ordinary fashion — saying that his wife was, in effect, just a little domestic doll, not worthy of sharing this exciting discovery about the Trevartons — and not even saying it *to* her, which would at least have been honest, but to *us,* which made it doubly demeaning to her … well, it made my blood boil, I'm afraid.

So, although I was acutely embarrassed once again to be standing there in that short dress, with people stopping in the street to stare at us, I stood my ground on the path beside her and said, "The fact is, Mrs Moynihan, your husband has discovered that I am Mrs Trevarton's granddaughter and he cannot wait to quiz me on it."

He looked daggers at me but I no longer cared for his approval — or disapproval, either. She stared at me in surprise, as was to be expected. And yet I felt she was putting it on. I think she already knew and had kept it from him. In other words, she had done to him the very thing I had just found so contemptuous! I felt rather foolish then and began to regret my impetuous action. In fact, I regretted having opened my mouth at all.

She must have known my tale before I told it, because her first question was the sort you ask after mulling the situation over for quite some time: "Tell me, Miss Moore," she said, "why d'you suppose your grandmother proposed such an arrangement in the first place?"

"Oh, *I* was going to ask her that!" Moynihan cut in petulantly, just like a thwarted child. If he'd stamped his foot, the picture would have been complete. The situation was suddenly so comical I had a job not to laugh out loud.

His wife turned to Susan then. "You probably know her better, Miss Callaghan. Why do you think she did it?"

Susan was getting over her annoyance and beginning to see the funny side of it, too. "Cheap labour, I reckon," she replied, rather flippantly.

Mrs Moynihan only smiled and shook her head at that. "Not interesting," she said firmly.

"Come on!" Moynihan exclaimed. "This isn't right at all. You two girls go up and change back into your own frocks and then we'll *all* go over to Flushing for that strawberry tea."

We set off again five minutes later, back in decent skirts that swept the pavements on behalf of the municipal council. We crossed the road and sauntered down the jetty, where we had ten minutes to wait for the ferry. The boys had to row like demons to get the dinghy back to its berth and then run back to join us.

"Does young Master Mark know he's your uncle?" Moynihan asked as they rowed away.

"Of course," I replied. "Otherwise I'd still be bound by my promise to his mother to say nothing about it."

"And yet he ..." He waved his hand awkwardly. "And you ...?"

"Our friendship is purely platonic," I said.

"No such thing!"

"Roger, dear!" his wife interjected with a laugh more argumentative than humorous. "I do think Miss Moore is entitled to know best."

"No such thing," he repeated even more firmly. "Take it from me — platonic stuff and nonsense! It doesn't exist."

"No go, eh?" Mark asked breathlessly as he and Jim joined us, just in time to board the ferry.

"On the contrary," Moynihan replied. "Miss Moore told me ..."

I interrupted rudely, thinking it had better come from me. "Mister Moynihan wondered if you knew that his first wife was a Wilkinson — of the Nancekuke Wilkinsons — which would make you and him kinsmen by marriage."

"Oh really, sir?" Mark did a splendid imitation of a young man showing deep interest in the affairs of his elders. "Who was she — your first wife, I mean? I've never heard anyone mention the connection at home." His voice trailed off as our expressions made it clear he had committed an unintentional *faux pas*. "Oh, I say," he added. "I'm awfully sorry."

Moynihan was the least troubled of all. "Not at all!" he exclaimed. "I'm glad. It shows it's no longer common gossip. I'm grateful to you, Mark. The truth is, she took her own life."

Mark closed his eyes and looked as if he wished to sink beneath the waters all around us.

"It's over ten years ago now," Moynihan went on. "So it's hardly a burning issue. Anyway — that's the connection between us. Her father — rather like Miss Moore's mother — your sister — ran off with ..."

"Oh, you know about that, do you?" Mark asked glumly.

"I do now. That's what made it impossible to continue sketching. I want to hear all."

Mark turned on me. "You *told* him?" he demanded coldly.

"It's no secret any more," I replied.

"Hah! Lots of things aren't secret but we still don't go about blabbing them to all and sundry."

I flared up at that. "Don't you shout at me!"

"We hardly count as 'all and sundry,' young fellow," Moynihan put in, also annoyed at his tone. "My first wife, Esther Wilkinson, was your mother's cousin."

"That must be Stella," Mark said. "Stella Wilkinson. She's staying with us now."

"Stella's *another* cousin. My first wife would have been your first cousin once removed. And to that extent we are kin — rather slender, I admit, but something more than 'all and sundry,' eh?"

Mark rounded on me again. I was the one he wanted to get. *"You* couldn't have known all that," he accused me. "And yet you blurted your whole story out to him."

"As a matter of fact, I did know all that," I replied.

Moynihan stared at me sharply. His quick mind was thinking: *If he's lived at Fenton Lodge all his life and never heard the tale, whereas you only came there a few months ago, and yet claim to have heard it — what's been going on?*

We reached the Flushing jetty at that moment. Mark sprang up on the quayside to grab the painter. As soon as we were all ashore, though, he gave a stiff little bow and said, if we didn't mind, he'd take a little walk to Trefusis Point and back. He'd join us later.

I took a step forward, meaning to go with him and give him a piece of my mind. But Susan was even quicker. She shot me a glance that said, *Better leave this to me,* and trotted off to catch up with him.

Jim Collett stared after her, then looked at me, then at the Moynihans.

Roger Moynihan had an enigmatic smile on his face. "Such drama!" he said. "Oh to be young again! Well, we're too early for tea, so I'll tell you what — you two could wait for them here while Francesca and I go and look at the memorials in the church, eh? See you in half an hour?"

J im Collett leaned against the railings beside the ferry steps, gazing upriver. I studied him, trying to think of an original way of saying, 'Penny for your thoughts?' Every so often he half closed his eyes and I knew he was composing the view for a photograph. I said, "Mister Moynihan doesn't have much opinion of photography."

He just smiled at me — pleased, perhaps, that I had read his mind — and then he gave a little toss of his head.

It's odd how impressive a small gesture like that can be. It said, 'Live and let live.' Or it said, 'Come to that, I don't think much of Mister Moynihan as a photographer.' Or, 'It's much too nice an afternoon to waste in fruitless discussion.' Somehow it gave this young man a status equal to the great artist, who had so far dominated our afternoon.

Also — I'm not very proud to admit it but it's the truth — the thought that he was much too good a young man for Susan was never far from my mind. I tried to suppress it but it would not go away. All she wanted was someone to have romantic experiments with. She'd encourage Collett to the point of danger and then she'd cry halt. To be fair, he was probably just as keen on those experiments as she was. He'd hardly be normal otherwise. But the week after she said stop they'd discover they had nothing else in common. I durst not pursue these thoughts because Susan was my best friend.

"Mister Moynihan is not thinking much about the art of photography this afternoon," he said. "Nor about his own art, either."

"What, then?" I asked.

He shrugged and turned to face me. "Some game of his own."

He had one thing in common with Roger Moynihan — they both made you feel they could see beneath the surface of things and get to the inner reality. He went on: "Ten minutes ago he couldn't wait to ask you more about your unusual situation. But then he saw how much it annoyed Mark, so he tilted the board in that direction instead. If he were truly interested in your story, it wouldn't matter about Mark running off like that. We could be strolling around Flushing now — you, me, him, and his wife — and he could be asking every question under the sun. But now he'll wait until Mark is back in the fold. He wants to watch his expression, too. Not that I blame him, mind." He gave a little, self-deprecating laugh, which as good as said he'd do the same.

"How much has Susan told you?" I asked. "About my situation?"

"She told me about the family squabble a couple of weeks ago."

I was taken two ways by this. I was glad he knew — I wanted him to know — and yet I felt annoyed at Susan for telling him.

Then he spoiled the simplicity of my anger by saying, "Mark told me rather more — just now. Have you been to Flushing before, by the way? Shall we stroll around a little? It's quite pretty."

"Mark!" I exclaimed, falling in step at his side and picking up the thread again. "I can't make him out at all."

"In what way? I haven't met him before this afternoon."

"He's the only one among the Trevartons who's shown the slightest interest in our family — the Moores. Even his brother Walter, who thinks his mother a disgrace for making me a lady's maid ..."

"Yes, what do *you* feel about that?"

"Oh, well ... in the beginning I thought it very generous. But now ... I don't know."

"What changed your mind?"

Reluctantly I told him it seemed to have happened after I started evening classes at the polly. Then I realized that was much too simple. "It hasn't a single cause," I added. "Perhaps it started when Walter's wife, Felicity, tried to interfere." I explained all about that and went on: "It slowly dawned on me that when people see a new situation like this, their first thought is how they can use it to further their own wishes. Even Miss Martin, who is one of the finest, noblest people I know, can't help stirring my dissatisfactions in the hope of getting me to leave the Trevartons and go and work with her."

Then I had to explain about Miss Martin, too. So Susan couldn't have told him very much, after all.

"Why don't you do that?" he asked. "It's possible she only said that about waiting a couple of years because she knew you wouldn't come now, anyway. She was getting her bid in early, so to speak. Also, the help she gave Marian was a good way of not losing touch with you, wasn't it! Have you considered that?"

I shook my head. "Anyway, I enjoy my work at Fenton Lodge. And I'm good at it."

"The same would be true at Little Sinns. I think you'd be able to turn your hand to most things, Miss Moore."

"Also I like Mark — especially now he's stopped being silly. You know what I mean? The fact that he's my uncle makes it impossible for anything romantic to ... you understand — between us. And we both realize it. So we can truly be just friends. It's good for one's spirit, you know. Very liberating."

"Don't protest *too* much," he warned with a sly smile. "Next you'll be telling me you don't mind Susan going off with him now."

For some strange reason my heart began to pound. It was true — I *didn't* mind what Susan had done. But only because it left me alone with Mr Collett. And then I realized that Susan hadn't left me alone with him. Roger Moynihan had done that. Before the silence became oppressive I blurted out the first thing that came to me: "As to that, Mister Collett, I should have thought *you'd* be the one to object to her present behaviour."

"I would have," he replied, "if she'd left me alone at the quayside."

It was a nice thing to say, and it was nicely said, too. I began to feel calm again — still excited but no longer flustered. "Moynihan maintains it's impossible," I said, reverting to our earlier exchange. "Platonic friendship, I mean. What d'you think?"

His laugh had an overtone of comic despair but I could not tell whether it meant *Where do I begin?* or *How could you be so naïve?*

"Well?" I insisted.

"It's your life," he replied awkwardly. "If I say anything — anything at all — I'll risk being lumped along with Miss Martin and Felicity Trevarton and all the other people who just want to *use* your situation for their own ends."

"I don't see that at all," I protested.

"Good," he replied. "I'm sorry. I interrupted you just now. You were saying about Mark. On the one hand he's the only Trevarton to show any interest in you Moores, but, on the other ...?"

"And in our mother," I added. "She was his elder sister, of course. He's asked me loads of questions about her. None of the others has. But he's made me realize I didn't know her very well. For instance, I don't know *why* she ran off with my father. I know she loved him and he was very handsome and so on — but I don't think that's a good enough reason, do you?"

"You have no idea at all?"

"It's not the sort of question you ask your parents, is it — why did you choose this good-for-nothing drunkard?"

"Was he always a good-for-nothing drunkard? Stop me if I'm asking too many questions, by the way."

I touched his arm. "Don't be silly, Mister Collett. No, he was quite a different character before he took to drink ..."

And so I began telling him about my father — how we once had a house of our own — down St John's in Helston — the successful little haulage business he had started to build, which had also contributed to his downfall, because when the *Sprue* was wrecked on Loe Bar, he had the means to carry home enough wine to drown a dozen Dukes of Clarence in. I told him of the failure of the business and our removal to Porthleven. And our mother's taking-in of washing and how she was so good that it threatened to put others in the village out of business, until she came to an agreement with them to do all their fine finishing and delicate work for them — which, you could say, was the start of the training I was now continuing at Fenton Lodge.

And in between I told him of my brothers and sisters — little tales of our growing up, and what they were like, and where they were now. In the end I suppose he knew as much about us as Miss Martin or Mrs Felicity or anyone, although I'd spent much longer talking with them. He was not only easy to talk to but very quick on the uptake.

We wandered right out of Flushing while I was prattling on — not up the Mylor road, which would have taken us past the church where the Moynihans were, but up the river bank to the part they call Little Falmouth, where the oyster beds are and the lane ends. We stood for a moment admiring the ribs of a small sailing ship being built at Ponsharden, across the river. I tried to make out the Trevarton depôt in Penryn but it was almost a mile away and the heat haze was too dense. We could see a rusty, iron-hulled boat at the quay — a smear of red — but that was all.

Then, as we turned and made our way back to the harbour, our talk drifted on to poetry and books we liked. He said he thought I might like *Tess of the d'Urbervilles* for its picture of the rise and fall of important families. I said I thought its closing words blasphemous — where, after describing Tess's hanging, Hardy added something about the President of the Immortals having finished His sport with her. It was, in fact, our mother's opinion, because I had not then read the book. She also said Hardy hadn't the guts to say 'God.'

He said, "But just think about it, Miss Moore. Think back over your life and the tale you've just told me. Take from it as much evidence as you can of a benevolent God and put it in one pan of the scales. Then take the evidence for Hardy's view — that the gods, if they exist at all, use us for their sport. Put it in the other pan and tell me which of those two pans now weighs heaviest?"

"That is a very bleak view of life, Mister Collett," I told him, though I could not answer his actual point.

He laughed. "Only if you wish never to grow up."

We were approaching the square above the harbour by then. I could see the Moynihans waiting for us at the jetty — also Susan coming back with Mark in tow. In fact he was literally in tow for she had hooked the handle of her parasol round his arm — as a sort of joke, I suppose — and was leading him toward us as a farmer might lead a bull to market. Personally, I did not find it very amusing and only just managed to stop myself from taking Jim Collett by the arm, which would have been a childish demonstration of pique, demeaning to us both. Also, as he had just made me rather acutely aware, I *did* wish to grow up.

"As a matter of fact," he said, "I'm going up to London next week. There's an exhibition of new cameras and negative materials. May I carry a message from you for Marian?"

I thanked him then, rather offhandedly, I'm afraid. My coolness had nothing to do with him. It was caused by the grass and dead leaves Mark had been too careless to brush off the back of Susan's dress. The knees of his trousers, too, showed traces of dust and earth that required some sort of explanation. But Collett, though he appeared to notice nothing of this treacherous evidence, took it in good part. I think he was intrigued by Susan's and Mark's behaviour now that they had joined us. They were being joyful and carefree in rather too blatant a manner. When they were not searching each other's eyes for encouragement they were looking at us as if to say, 'It's all his (or her) fault, really. *I* don't want to behave like this.'

Moynihan was delighted because he thought his manipulations had brought matters to the point where some kind of explosion was now inevitable. He didn't know that Jim Collett had seen through him from the start and had no intention of providing sport for earthbound mortals, too. As the great artist led us away for our postponed strawberry tea, Collett touched my arm and murmured to me, "Don't play his game, eh?"

Susan heard the fag-end of this warning and exclaimed in a deliberately common voice, "Ooh! Playing games, eh? What games, I wonder?"

Mark put his finger on her lips and said, "Shush now! No one's playing games. Not any more. Isn't that right, Collett, old bean?"

Everyone looked at Collett — except me. I went on looking at Susan, who, not noticing me, reached out with her lips and kissed Mark's finger as he withdrew it. *Then* she noticed my eyes upon her and froze for a moment in panic-stricken guilt — before trying to recover the situation by pulling a clownish face, rolling her eyes as if to say, 'Whatever next!'

"The whole of life's a game," Collett said vaguely. "Or a sport, which is much the same thing."

He smiled at me when he said 'sport,' so everyone knew the word had a particular significance between us. I felt I had to explain, in case others jumped to unfortunate conclusions, so I told them how we had been discussing the ending of Hardy's novel, with its talk of human life as mere sport for the immortals.

That made Moynihan look at Collett with a new respect. It dawned on him that he was not dealing with some shallow-minded apprentice to a trade he, in particular, despised.

And, curiously enough, that made *me* look at Jim in a new light, too, although the evidence for it had been there all along. I suppose that sudden gleam of respect in Moynihan's eye gave it a focus, for I saw that Jim Collett had the makings of rather an impressive man — a man who could think for himself, who was not taken in by fame (Roger Moynihan) nor by superior social position (Mark Trevarton), but who would always stand up for himself — and, indeed, *be* himself.

Mark apologized rather curtly for his earlier behaviour, saying he was sure the Moynihans would understand his desire for certain episodes in his family's history to be kept private. He had no idea why the artist and his wife were so disconcerted by this remark but it was clear to me that *they* thought he knew all about Ethel Wilkinson and her life as an Unfortunate before her marriage to Moynihan. They must also have thought he was warning Roger that any teasing or embarrassment he, Roger, might try to dish out would be returned in kind.

They were not to know that Mark was quite incapable of devious behaviour like that. Indeed, it was the best thing about him. But, just to make certain of it — to give no point of leverage for any mischief-making the man might yet contemplate — I took Mark's arm and hugged it warmly and said, "I'm sorry. I shouldn't have behaved as if my feelings were the only ones that mattered. Everybody's feelings are important — isn't that true, Mister Moynihan?"

And so our strawberry tea was one long peaceful truce, with nobody trying to score points and nothing said that would not have been said among six chance acquaintances who had no skeletons to hide. We returned to Greenbank and parted on the most amicable terms, agreeing to return one evening soon and resume our pose for The Cocklepickers.

However, I had not forgotten the grass on Susan's dress, much less that fleeting kiss she had given Mark's finger when he hushed her up. I understood her well enough by now to know that her attitude to trouble was to keep her head down and say nothing if she thought it might just give up and go away — the way I used to be. On the other hand, if she knew that wasn't the way of things, she'd meet it head on — bull at a gate. I was intrigued to see which course she'd take with me.

On our way back through the town, just outside Jim Collett's lodgings, he suggested that, as Susan and I had the evening off, too, we might all go for a swim at Swanpool Beach. Mark added the proposal that we should take some chops and sausages down and cook them over a driftwood fire. While Collett went indoors to collect his towel and costume, the three of us planned how to raid the larder for our picnic and get out of the house unnoticed. Mark bravely volunteered to take all the blame for it afterwards, for our theft would surely be noticed.

Our plan succeeded and he went off with the booty, making directly for the beach. Susan and I changed quickly into our bathing costumes — or, rather, into two of hers, for I had not yet saved enough to buy one of my own — and got dressed again over them. Then we sauntered out for an apparent evening stroll in the opposite direction. But of course we doubled back as soon as we were out of sight over the headland. It was then that she asked me what Jim and I had talked about while she had been soothing Mark.

I started to reply but she wasn't very interested. Her question was a pretext for a conversation *she* had in mind. She was simply waiting for me to finish. So then I told her we talked about novels and poetry and things, and she said, rather heavily, "I can well believe that!"

And then she waited on tenterhooks for me to ask the obvious reciprocal question — what had she and Mark talked about ... how had she calmed him down, and so on. Which I did.

But instead of answering me she began to quiz me about my real feelings for him. Did I wish he *wasn't* my uncle? Did I think *he* wished he wasn't? If he and I were the only two castaways on an island, would we soon forget the prohibitions of civilization? And so on.

I'd have been mentally deficient not to see what was behind all this. She wanted to suggest a swap.

Panic!

All my logical faculties said, *What a good idea! Agree and have done with it.* But, unfortunately, these affairs have little to do with logic. Every other faculty within me resisted this siren song of Susan's. I was attracted to Jim Collett — how could I deny it? But I did not want to say a last farewell to Mark (whom I could no longer consider my uncle, anyway) until I was a great deal more sure of Jim. If that meant war with Susan — even a sweet, subtle, female war — so be it!

"Did he kiss you today?" I asked suddenly.

"No!" she said at once — but her face gave her away.

"What was all that grass on your skirt?" I persisted.

"What grass? Anyway, I asked you a question, and you haven't answered me yet."

We were both aware we'd have to join the two young men very soon, and pass an amicable evening with them no matter what our true feelings might be, so we could not risk the up-and-down ding-dong toward which this conversation was inevitably progressing. So I merely said, "Let's drop it for the moment, eh? As far as this evening goes, you're with Jim Collett, I'm with Mark. All right?"

She grinned ruefully. "All right."

"Only one thing ..."

"What?"

"When we take up this conversation again, don't pretend you have no idea what grass I'm talking about."

She tossed her head and looked away. But I knew it was only to hide a smug little smile.

The men were waiting on Swanpool beach — the small, eastern portion that was not visible from Fenton Lodge. Jim Collett held up both hands and declared, "'O nymphs more bright than moonshine night!'"

"'Like kidlings blithe and merry!'" I responded, completing his quotation, for I knew the song well.

Mark and Susan stared at each other in bewilderment.

Not a good beginning.

My apprehensions lifted, however, the moment we went in for our dip — though Susan spoiled it by showing off, quite unnecessarily.

I'll tell you a strange thing about Porthleven. Although it's a fishing port and almost everyone who lives there has some connection with the sea, it's almost a matter of honour *not* to learn to swim! The fishermen all claimed that the ability to swim had never saved anyone from drowning. It simply prolonged the agony of it. Our mother, being the woman she was, said she'd never heard such nonsense. And in summer, on those few days when we had the leisure for it, she took us over to the rocks on Breage side, where there were pools of every depth from knee-deep to dive-in, and made sure we mastered the dog-paddle and breast stroke.

To my chagrin I discovered that Susan's mother — or someone — had helped her to master the trudgen, which is much faster than both. Soon she was farther out to sea than I would ever have dared to go. If she had stayed by me, the men would have hovered about us, too. Her bit of swank, however, faced them with a choice.

"After you, old chap." Mark gestured toward Susan's bobbing head, a hundred yards beyond us.

Collett pulled a face. "I'm not that good a swimmer," he confessed.

Mark set off at once, in an ungainly flurry of limbs and thrashing water. The moment his back was turned, Collett grinned at me and swam a few skilful strokes that gave the lie to his earlier modesty.

"You may have to go and rescue them both," I warned him.

"I wanted a further word with you, Miss Moore," he replied.

"Oh?" I said nervously. "I can't imagine what about."

He grinned. "The Royal Cornwall Polytechnic."

It was so far from my thoughts that, for a moment, the words had no meaning. "The polly?" I managed to say at last.

The sun, setting behind the hills that beetle over Swanpool, played with a curious effect on the wavelets all around us, especially when I turned and faced the darkling sea to the east. Its rays seemed to fill them with a sort of liquid fire, a lambent, ruby lustre that briefly infused each transient crest and left me feeling I was suspended somewhere out of time and space. I could think of nothing further to say to him. I was so fascinated by the unreality of everything — the suspension of everyday nature and all its laws and constraints.

"I was impressed by Moynihan today," Collett went on, apparently unmoved by the cold fires in which we were plunged. "When I saw his last exhibition I thought he was an extinct volcano. But now I think he may be moving again. D'you suppose he could teach me a thing or two about composition? Would it help if I joined your classes on Monday evenings — beginning tomorrow?"

"*His* classes," I said.

"If you prefer. I can't see your expression. You're just a silhouette from here."

I swam a few strokes until we were level.

"God, but you're beautiful!" he said.

My heart turned over. I wanted to be so suave and poised, to say something light and witty ... but all that came out of my mouth was, "You shouldn't say such things, Mister Collett."

"Why not?" he asked pleasantly. "It's the simple truth. You are one of the most beautiful girls I've ever seen."

"But you're Susan's young man," I objected. I knew I was being very simpleminded and green, and I hated myself for it, but I felt these things had to be said now or we could drift into all sorts of complications.

He stared out to sea for a moment or two, where Susan and Mark were having a splash-fight, with lots of laughing and coughing. "D'you think so?" he asked.

"She's behaving disgracefully today," I complained. "I wish I'd never brought her along."

"Ah! Then indirectly you wish *I* had never come along, too!"

"No!" I protested. Then, "Yes! Oh ... *I* don't know. But she *is* behaving disgracefully."

"Unwisely," he said, then, seeing my surprise at such a pettifogging correction, added, by way of explanation, "The bits of grass on her dress? The marl on Mister Trevarton's knees?" He smiled. "I think I am no longer Miss Susan Callaghan's young man — if, indeed, I ever fell into that category."

"Category!" I laughed at his use of the word. "Hardly that!" I said. "I'm sure she only has one follower at any time."

We had drifted into the lee of some half-submerged rocks, where I found I could stand in water up to my shoulders. He, however, lay back, stretching at his ease in the calmer water, and said, more to the sky than to me, "I'm not greatly concerned with how many followers *she* may have at any given time."

"She has always spoken of you with admiration and affection," I said.

He just chuckled at that.

I told him it was all too easy to ruin a maid's reputation by sniggering at anything people said to her credit.

It stung him into standing upright — on the same rock as me. Unfortunately it was rather a small rock so we were rather too close for comfort. However, he stared me in the eye and said, "D'you think chapter and verse would be kinder? Very well, Miss Moore. Let me tell you frankly that I think Miss Callaghan, today, got from Mister Trevarton — in ten minutes — what she failed to get from me in ten weeks."

His eyes flashed angrily — but was it anger at Susan for rejecting him, or at me for being such a conventional ninny? I quailed before it yet I could not stop myself from pointing out that no gentleman would ever say such a thing about a lady.

"A gentleman?" he said icily. "Well, now, if you want a *gentleman* ..." And he waved a scornful hand in Mark's direction.

Suddenly he laughed and all the tension between us evaporated. *"Do* you want a gentleman, Miss Moore?" he asked playfully.

I responded in the same light vein. "I want *everything,* Mister Collett."

"I'll see what I can arrange," he said. Then, taking me by the hand — delicately, as if to do no more than stay me against the pluck of the water — he added, "We can walk ashore along this shelf, you'll find. Let's go and light a fire."

We lit a fire, all right — a fire of outrage that burned for weeks. And not on Swanpool beach, either, but up at Fenton Lodge. To hear my grandmother and Mrs Bourdeaux carry on, you'd imagine that the four of us had stripped to the buff and danced a witches' sabbath round the little pile of burning driftwood on which we grilled our chops and sausages that night. Our real crime, of course, was to have been observed by one particular lady with a lively imagination and a loose tongue. The tale she carried around Falmouth, from one At Home to another, soon reached my grandmother, and then there was no pacifying her.

The men escaped lightly. Jim Collett was forbidden to call at the house and Mark was sent off with friends of Mr Archie's on a walking tour of the Lake District. The attitude was that boys will be boys but girls must never be anything less than ladies. The severest punishment was reserved for Susan and me. We were 'gated' — a posh term for 'imprisoned in the house' — for the rest of the month. No letters, no callers, no free time, no communication, and no talking except on business. I was surprised we were left sharing the same bedroom, but we had to leave our door open — which forced us to move our beds tight together and converse in whispers.

There was no reasoning with my grandmother, though I tried. I pointed out that it was the duty of servants to obey. "If Master Mark required me to iron a shirt for him and I refused, you'd scold me for it, ma'am," I said. "Yet when he requires Callaghan and me to accompany him to the beach and cook a dinner for him and his chum, you send *him* on a walking holiday and vent all your anger on us!"

This was no treachery against Mark. It was what we had all agreed on when the cold sea water had brought us to our senses and we realized that hot water of a domestic kind would soon be pouring down upon us.

The old woman shrivelled me with a look that said, 'You don't expect me to dignify such drivel with an answer, I hope?'

The severity of our punishment made me bold — on the lines of 'in for a penny, in for a pound.' In fact, I had half a mind to give in my notice and trust that Miss Martin would take me in. What stopped me was the thought that she was in some way beholden to Mrs Felicity for her place. And, though I knew *that* young lady would do almost anything to spite her mother-in-law, I doubted she would do it openly. Also, she was about as reliable as a rubber nail. So I hung there in a nervous limbo, unwilling to hand in my notice yet careless of provoking my dismissal. I said, speaking not to her but to one of her dresses, which I was picking over for lint, "I just wish there was a list somewhere of those commands we are to obey and those we are to ignore."

"Your very impertinence condemns you, Miss Moore," she replied. "I shall not bandy words with you but I can see it is my duty to instruct you — in this as in so many other matters. There is a ruffian at the core of every man, over which the code of a *gentle*man forms the merest veneer. Scratch it and it comes away. And none can scratch it better than a pretty servant maid in her teens — unless it be *two* pretty servant maids in their teens. I speak bluntly because I am astonished you do not already understand as much. What you two maids did at Swanpool on Sunday night was the very height of folly. Who knows where it might not have ended but for the lucky chance that you were observed!"

"We were not aware of being observed, ma'am, so that can't have ..."

"As I said — I shall not bandy words with you, miss. Kindly be so good as to hold your tongue."

I think I have never felt such blazing hatred for any other human as I felt toward my grandmother at that moment — not for my father in his worst drunken bout ... not for the Angells in their triumphant theft of a whole year's rent. I was within a whisker of handing in my notice on the spot — and devil take the consequences. But then I thought I could hurt her more, and worry her more, by asking if Mark were truly my uncle or, as he and I were both now convinced, merely my cousin. I enjoyed a brief daydream in which I added that the question was of more than academic interest to us — which would really have put the cat among the pigeons! But I lingered so long in enjoying the thought of this bombshell that the moment for action passed.

She, knowing nothing of what was going through my mind, assumed that I was submitting to her command. That annoyed me particularly but I took comfort from the thought: *If only she knew!* — which, I then realized, is the daily solace of servants everywhere. For the first time in my life I became a true servant — not outwardly, which I had long been, but in my very soul. It frightened me. I saw that I must escape, somehow, before the grayness invaded every part of me and I became like Mrs Bourdeaux, watching 'my betters' anxiously, my head full of mutinous thoughts I would never dare express.

"That will be all, Miss Moore," she said, primly triumphant.

But I no longer cared. I was already drifting from the room, my mind gripped by the horror of this revelation. It was no longer important to score points off the old woman, nor even to state my own opinion, whether she accepted it or no. I simply had to get out of this life. I mean this way of life. I had to stop masquerading as a servant before I actually turned into one.

But where? And how?

Go to Little Sinns? Become a teacher-wardress-assistant? Too vague a prospect. I would not be allowed to see Miss Martin for at least another month and I wanted an answer *now*. If I were a boy I could run away to sea. But where can a girl run away to? Union Road, Plymouth — or Vernon Place, Falmouth, where the nightly scene was the same?

I was not thinking of genuine possibilities for escape. I was merely touching the brick walls that held me where I was. In fact, as I realized when I had touched them all, there was only one exit door for a girl in my situation: a walk up the aisle to the altar.

I thought of Mark, and then I thought of Jim Collett, and then of Mark again. But what did I know of either?

Mark was a handsome rogue, full of self-confidence, easy to talk to, a wondrous lover (at least as far as kissing and canoodling went) — but he had put Susan on her back in the grass inside ten minutes and done God knows what with her. I should never know peace of mind with him.

Jim Collett was good-looking, quiet, profound, and nobody's fool. He also thought I was beautiful, which Mark had never said. Any *sensible* girl would have chosen him against Mark. But that was to ignore the physical side of love, whose power and wonder I was only just beginning to experience. What if I should choose Jim (or any other man) for his strong and noble qualities and then find myself ... not repelled but simply unmoved by his physical qualities and acts?

I stood there on the landing, my forehead pressed to the window pane, staring out at the garden with unseeing eyes. Where could I turn? Who could I confide in?

My mother!

I suddenly felt her presence beside me, as powerfully as on that morning when she turned my steps toward this, her childhood home. I knew then that at some crisis in *her* life, she, too, had stood at just this spot, with her forehead pressed against the identical glass, at her wits' end over what to do next. Something of her presence still lingered here.

There was a little gasp from my grandmother's door — the door I had closed behind me only seconds earlier. I turned to find the old woman staring at me, with such a strange expression on her face. My scalp tingled. For a moment we were naked to each other — more than naked — we were one flesh, caught in horrified contemplation of itself. We were united by the living presence of that dead woman who forged a link between us which we could never break.

That bond lay far beyond the reach of love or hatred — or any of those emotions that governed our daily intercourse. The violent feelings she had aroused in me a few minutes earlier were suddenly as chaff in the wind. They vanished. But nothing of any warmth replaced them — just the certainty that, come what may, we were yoked together in ways that only another death could break. Did she understand that, too?

If she did, she could not face it. Whatever she had come out to the landing to do, she now thought better of it and returned immediately to her room — leaving me to my own communion. Again I laid my forehead to the cold glass and let my unfocused eyes roam about the scene beyond. But my mother had gone. In her place was a cool, reasonable presence — my own mind, struggling to compensate me yet again for her loss. Long ago she had fled from this house in search of happiness ... had lived in tolerable bliss for five years and suffered another thirteen in misery. So if she truly had been there, inside me, a few moments earlier, it was to warn, not encourage.

I could not forget what Susan had done. She knew there was something special between Mark and me, yet she had as good as stolen him from under my nose that afternoon in Flushing. However, it made *my* decisions easier for, if she acted without thought for me, why should I consider her?

So it seemed to me that if I took a liking to both men equally — or, rather, took an equal liking to them for their very different qualities — and, furthermore, if I was in no particular hurry to make up my mind, then I should be free to go out with either, or both, or neither, entirely at my whim. And at every opportunity that offered. And even if she could bring seven gypsies with their crystal balls to prove I'd settle with Jim in the end, I still wasn't interested in the swap she had engineered and handed to me with her take-it-or-leave-it air.

Only the fact that we were fellow sufferers that month allowed us to maintain our former friendship. Even so, it was only half the friendship it once had been for it was now without trust. She described to me in vague but feverish detail what she and Mark had done at Trefusis Point that afternoon. It was on the tip of my tongue to trump her with Jim Collett's ungallànt comment that she had got Mark to do inside ten minutes what she had failed to persuade *him* to do in ten weeks, but I resisted nobly. In any case, I did not believe her.

I think what happened was that she spied him half-reclining in the grass, tiptoed up behind him so that he would have no time to rise, and flung herself down beside him. Possibly they kissed — briefly. But that any actual impropriety took place I beg leave to doubt. True, in Mark's estimation I might be more of a lady than Susan — and she more of a 'bit of fluff' than me. And a gentlemen is trained to protect a lady from her own amorous desires, whereas a bit of fluff is fair game, anywhere and any time. But even so he would not fall with such indecent haste. At least, I did not think it likely.

Therefore he was most unlikely to have made any commitment to her, such as young rogues make to win the favours of light-heeled scatterbrains like Susan.

Therefore, I concluded, I should do nothing, and say nothing, to disturb the unnatural peace between us — until I had cause. I simply let her think I had accepted the new situation, just as she had engineered it.

Susan, for her part, had no plan at all, I'm sure. But then she did not need one. She was such a *natural* fighter, as swift and as instinctive as a cat. The moment I let her think I did not mind what she and Mark had done, she began to dwell on it in endless whispered rhapsodies after we retired to bed each night. I *knew* she was lying and yet her fictional 'Mark' — by sheer force of repetition and circumstantial detail — took on a life of his own and began to replace the Mark I still knew and loved. I feared that when the real man returned I should accuse him of scarlet sins that flourished nowhere outside Susan's wishful thinking.

And I dared not repay her in kind for my line had been that Jim Collett and I had experienced nothing more than an intoxicating meeting of minds. It was nearly, but not quite, the truth. For on the Monday after our picnic-swim on Swanpool beach — before word of mouth turned it into that witches' sabbath and the heavens fell in about us — Jim joined Roger Moynihan's drawing class at the polly. More to the point, he walked me home afterward. Still more to the point, he took my arm most of the way.

It seems such a little thing when set down like that: He took my arm. Yet it was as thrilling to me as a passionate kiss with Mark would have been. No — it's wrong to make comparisons like that. It diminishes them both. 'Passionate, hot-blooded, amusing ...' these are words that go with Mark. 'Strong, tough, stimulating ...' these are Jim Collett's hallmarks. Mark and I are easy equals. Jim is nobler and finer than me in every way. When he says *I* fascinate *him,* I simply cannot believe it. He is one of those people who impress simply by being. He does not need to do anything remarkable nor say anything profound, he just needs to be there and everything is changed. At least, that's the effect he has on me. The moment he comes into a room I want to move to his side — like when he came into drawing class that first time and sat down next to Jacqueline Trebilcock even though the donkey next to mine was empty, I almost died of jealousy and frustration.

So there it is. I've let the cat out of the bag. My ramblings about these two lovely men have accidentally brought me to face the truth. I *do* love Jim, not Mark. I love him hopelessly, unbelievingly, fearfully. My greatest fear is that he will somehow find me out — discover how unworthy I am of even his slightest affection. And that is why I cannot give up Mark — because even if he did find me unworthy in this or that respect, I know jolly well I could turn on him and cry, 'Snap!'

Also, to be sure, I will *not* be dictated to by Susan.

At the beginning of September I was permitted to resume my art classes, but only on the strictest terms. Mr Moynihan was to sign a note to the effect that I had attended the class from such-and-such a time to such-and-such a time, both the hour and the minute to be recorded in his own hand. I then had twenty-three minutes in which to return to Fenton Lodge or risk a further week's gating. This, of course, was to prevent me from seeing Jim Collett, unless he were willing to jog-trot and pant at my side all the way home.

What childish folly! Did my grandmother really think Moynihan was the sort of man who'd play that game? I cannot believe it. The whole thing was done for public show. Moynihan himself thought it vastly amusing. He wrote out a sample with the times left blank and told me that since no one at Fenton Lodge had any paper in his autograph hand, any near-copy would do, and I was a good enough draughtsman by now to forge his penmanship perfectly.

Then Jim Collett arrived and my heart began beating in a dozen different places in my chest.

"Ah, Mister Collett!" Moynihan welcomed him back effusively. "Have you spotted any good compositions while you were away?"

This referred to a good-humoured little argument they'd had when Jim first joined the class — on the Monday after our fateful swim at Swanpool beach, which was before I got gated and before he went to London for that photographic exhibition — and to deliver my promised letter to Marian. Jim had said he wanted to develop his sense of composition and improve his photography. Moynihan had pointed out that you couldn't actually compose pictures with a camera, all you could do was select views that happened, quite accidentally, to be composed already. Jim merely dipped his head and smiled, as if to say, 'Just you wait and see!'

Now, with Moynihan trying to tease him again, he produced his answer. He winked a hallo at me as he took a stout manilla envelope from his pocket. He opened it with a magician's flourish and drew forth a half-plate photograph, which he handed to Moynihan. Craning my neck over the man's shoulder, I saw it was a photograph of Flushing taken from the artist's own front gate — or almost. But something about it was not quite right. Moynihan looked at it in bewilderment for a moment, and so did I. Then we realized what was wrong. For the Greenbank Hôtel had apparently vanished, and in its stead was a large oak tree. And not any old oak tree, either, but a photographic copy of one that Moynihan himself had painted in the days when he was more pre-Raphaelite than Impressionist. It was therefore realistic enough to pass as an actual photograph at first glance. I knew it well for it hung in the entrance hall of the Passmore-Edwards Library, down on Falmouth Moor. Of course, it helped that the whole composite picture was printed in what they call 'soft' focus, which, if you didn't know, you might think was just badly focused. Anyway, it spread a sort of gauzy, romantic haze over the scene, which helped the tree blend in perfectly.

It took Moynihan almost half a minute to work out what Jim had done — and then to understand the point of it. Then he turned to me and, with an amused lift of his eyebrow, said, "Birds of a feather, eh!"

Since we had only just been speaking of my forging his handwriting in the notes to my grandmother, it was not hard to grasp his meaning. But his lumping the two of us together like that thrilled me, and I suppose it must have showed. Anyway, Jim and I settled side-by-side to draw that evening's plaster cast — the head of Laocoön and one of his hands grasping the serpent's throat — and I was almost willing to agree that the pain of our month apart was worth the intense joy of merely being together again. Not speaking. Not even looking at each other much. Just *being* there. The whole of that side of me nearest him tingled, the way your hands tingle when you reach them toward a chestnut-roaster's fire at a street corner on a cold winter's eve.

Moynihan knew very well what was going on between us, of course. Hadn't he been there from the very beginning! When he sat down and looked at my effort he said, "You should allow yourself to be distracted more often, Miss Moore." He tapped his brow. "The greatest enemy of good drawing sits up here in the brain, you know. The brain gets *ideas.*" He pronounced the word with disgust. "And it thinks that drawing consists of getting ideas and putting lines around them. So the secret of good drawing is find some obsession that will kidnap our brains for a spell — thus freeing the hand and the eye to get on with it unhindered. That's why I talk too much — or hadn't you noticed?"

Amid laughter Moynihan showed me where my sketch fell woefully short of perfection. Then we broke for refreshments. Jim and I retired to a corner, where he produced Marian's reply to my letter. Alas, it, too, fell woefully short of the perfection I craved from her.

I wanted Marian to tell me — as I had told her — of the pain of our separation ... how she thought of me every day — and Tom, Gerald, Arthur, and Teresa. And how she had written to them ... heard from them ... treasured their replies. I wanted her to copy bits of their letters and to let me know what she, in turn, had replied to them. I know that a letter is a cold proxy for the rough and tumble of family life but it was all we had. I wanted to feel that whir and buzz of *us* again, the dearest half dozen in the world. Instead Marian's letter gave me a few obligatory sentences about missing the rest of us and thinking of the happy times we had known — followed by pages of the even happier times she was presently experiencing. She had made ever so many friends at the Honor Club. I really ought to try to get away to London for a few days. They were all longing to meet me, this paragon of duty and competence she'd told them all about, and we'd all get on so toppingly together. She'd been to the music hall in Camden Town where she'd been picked up by two Jack-ashores and only just rescued in time by Sophie Forrest (I'd love her!!) before she could suffer a Fate Worse Than Death (!!!?). She'd decorated her first plate at the Working Men's College, using on-glaze colours, but it had cracked in the kiln. She had been sent home for using unseemly language, so all she'd say now was, 'Botheration!'!! And so on and so forth — page after page of empty-headed *fun,* liberally dosed with exclamation marks.

It quite spoiled the rest of that evening, at least until it was time to leave. A better humour returned when I forged the first of Moynihan's notes to my grandmother. It took three goes, and a lot of lip-licking, before I made something passable. Moynihan himself watched with his usual aloof amusement. He said, "'Are you in a hurry, darling?' murmured the lover to his lass. 'Or shall we take the *short* cut through the woods?'"

Jim chuckled but I ignored the jibe. I allowed us forty-five minutes instead of my grandmother's niggardly twenty-three. "I am in no hurry," I said.

The moment we were outside, Jim took my arm. I could hardly breathe. I wanted him to take all of me, to lift me in his arms and carry me. Or at least hug me half to death. But the street was full of eyes. And, twenty yards later, the churchyard of King Charles the Martyr was full of young Mr Perrow, the chandler's apprentice, spooning with Jacqueline Trebilcock ... and so we had no choice but to saunter on as if our hearts were not galloping and our limbs not trembling and our stomachs were still where the anatomy books said they'd be.

"Well, er, what did you think of Marian?" I asked hesitantly. "I mean, was your photographic exhibition all you had hoped for?"

He laughed, a little immoderately. I realized he had been holding his lungs rather full — like me. "Very successful. I learned a lot. Otherwise I'd not have been able to dodge Moynihan's oak tree into that photo. Some of the things one can do nowadays are amazing. I reversed the negative of the tree and used it as a mask, or shield, when printing the view of Flushing. Then I printed the tree into the masked area — having blacked out the rest of all that neg. There's no end to the tricks an ingenious person might do."

"You are amazing," I told him. We were mounting the narrow, windey footpath that leads up through the churchyard into New Street, which is actually a little cul-de-sac of a town square.

"Am I?" he responded, slightly surprised.

"Yes. I've often asked Mark things about sailing — technical things, you know. What *luffing* is and stuff like that. And ..."

"All I know about luffing is you have to duck your head when you do it. Or you regret it."

"Yes, well, he didn't even tell me that much. His attitude is that, as I'm just an empty-headed female, there's no point in confusing me with science. Most men are like that. But not you."

"Ah, well, I can return the compliment and say that most women are not like *you,* Miss Moore."

"Crissy," I suggested.

There were little squishy noises from his throat as he swallowed heavily. His breathing was shivery, too.

"And what about Marian?" I asked again.

"Ah, well, I could see her letter was a disappointment to you," he replied diplomatically.

"Which you fully expected it to be," I said.

"I'm afraid so ... Crissy." He gave a little laugh at the ease with which my name came out.

"D'you think I'm just flogging a dead horse, Jim — wanting to get our family all back together again?"

"No." The response was immediate. "It's *you.* You couldn't do otherwise, could you. You wouldn't be Crissy if you gave up."

We sauntered across the little square to the footpath in front of the posher houses, where up-and-coming petty tradesmen ape the manners of the really posh houses in Florence Terrace and Wood Lane.

"Did you discuss it with Marian — or she with you?" I asked.

He nodded. "I wanted to, of course, from the very beginning. But I waited until she brought it up, unprompted — just in case she'd think you put me up to it."

I gave his arm a tender squeeze, by way of saying my thanks. Few other men would even think of the possibility. "And?" I said.

"She feels very guilty, of course — because she's having such a wonderful time up there. You're not entirely dissimilar, you know, you and she. You both have the same enormous zest for life and the same unquenchable spirit ..."

"But she's all bubbly and fun while I'm grim and implacable. I know!"

He put his arm right around me and hugged me against him, shoulder-to-shoulder. "That's not even worth refuting," he said scornfully.

We were in the darkest part of the square, half way between two guttering gas-lamps. I swung round in front of him, keeping in contact all the way, and then pulled him to me, leaning back at the same time against the area railings of one of the houses.

Without thinking or willing it I turned my face upward to his and he looked down at me and our lips were so close that mine tingled at the warmth of his nearness and thirsted for their touch ...

And then they touched and I closed my eyes and the whole world and everything in it shrank to that one point of silken contact between us — which he broke almost immediately to murmur, "Oh Crissy, Crissy, Crissy! How I love *you!*"

I knew I should reply — tell him I loved him, too — but something elemental and formless within me had forgotten how to make words. All it let me do was whimper and reach my mute, enhungered lips across that gap, craving to adore him more, and more, and more.

We squandered most of the extra time I had allowed in 'Moynihan's' note — as Jim reluctantly pointed out at last.

"I don't care if we stay out till midnight," I said. "I don't care if I never go back there."

"Well, I do," he told me. "Because if you get kept in again, I shan't see you next week, nor on Sunday. Will you get this Sunday off?"

I said I wasn't sure. The truth was, I really felt I ought to go and see Miss Martin again, to get a better feel of how things stood between us and how dependent she was on Mrs Felicity's goodwill. But if he gave me the alternative of spending my free time with him ... well, it would be no choice at all.

"Do try," he urged. "I'd like to take you over to Redruth to meet my Aunt Eph and Uncle Jim. They brought me up after my parents died."

I promised I'd do my best. Susan had never even mentioned this uncle and aunt. Probably he'd never even told her about them — much less suggested that he should introduce her to them. I felt honoured.

I asked how long ago his parents had died. He said he had never known either. His mother died in bearing him and his father had been carried away by a congestion of the kidneys shortly after that. "Aunt Eph and Uncle Jim were my only real parents," he added. "Or the only ones I've known. But they always insisted on the 'Aunt' and 'Uncle' because, they said, it kept the memory of my parents alive."

While he spoke, someone lighted a lamp in the downstairs room of the house behind me. Its sudden glow flushed his face and sparkled in his eyes. He seemed so marvellous to me that, once again, I was filled with a dread that he would one day soon discover all my inadequacies and cast me aside. The adoration in his gaze was little insurance against that awful day.

He withdrew a little, turned my face toward this new illumination, and touched my cheek as if he could hardly believe I was really there. Then, reluctantly, he took my arm and pushed me into resuming our homeward walk.

Since New Street was a cul-de-sac for all traffic, other than occasional pedestrians like us, many of its inhabitants did not bother to draw their curtains. So window after window revealed to us little vignettes of domestic snuggery. Such tranquil lives they seemed to hint at. So well ordered and secure. I thought of the way money came into and went out of my hands and it made me marvel that people could ever manage to save enough to gather so many *things* around them — books, ornaments, pictures, domes of wax fruit, palms and aspidistras, tapestries ... never mind the useful things like tables and chairs, beds and wardrobes. As for a piano ...! Modest as it all was, it seemed impossibly far beyond my reach. And yet, just as I knew Jim was *my* man, so, too, I knew that one day none of this would be beyond us.

"Actually ..." Jim broke our silence at last. "You may think that Marian's letter paints a rather giddy picture, but underneath it all she misses you dreadfully."

It was one emotion too many. I felt tears prickling behind my eyelids. But the last thing I wanted at that moment was to cry, so I took a firm grip on myself and asked him how he could possibly know such a thing.

"Because she never stopped talking about you," he replied. "And I, of course, did nothing to hinder her."

"Oh dear!" I was pleased, naturally, but also full of foreboding. "What did she say? Too much, I'm sure."

"Too much to remember. Shall I tell you what has stuck out most in my mind? You probably won't even remember it, yourself. It happened when you were just a tiddler."

"What?"

"When Tom was born. You were still living in St Johns, Helston, then, I think?"

"Yes. What about it?"

"D'you remember what you did when you were brought into your mother's room to see baby Tom for the first time?"

"Of course not!" I laughed. "I wasn't even four years old. I'll bet Marian doesn't remember, either. This is something she made up."

"It doesn't have that ring of invention. I believe it, anyway. I believe it of *you.*"

"What?" I pinched his arm in my impatience.

"She says you leaned over and kissed your new little brother — rather dutifully — and then you went over to your mother's dressing table and picked up her hand mirror — and you looked at yourself in it — and you said, 'Cris-to-bel' — just like that!"

It seems odd, but I had never heard this tale before. And yet, as Jim said, it did not have the ring of invention. I wondered why Marian had never told it to me, not even to tease me. Perhaps since our parting she, like me, had been going over and over her memories of our family life, good and bad, and this had come back to her suddenly.

It gave me a sharp pang in my chest. I wanted to fly up to London, then and there, and creep into bed with Marian and lie at her side, as we had done so often, talking the night away — only this time about all our memories, those precious moments that would vanish forever unless we breathed life into them continually. I suddenly saw it would be no use our waiting until we were all grown up and could make our own independent way to a family rendezvous. Our shared memories of all those little living moments would by then be like pressed flowers in an old maid's herbarium.

Jim, God love him, had told me this tale in a light-hearted vein. No doubt he'd been hoping to say how like me it was — how, even at that tender age, I wasn't going to let any outside event crush me or take away my individuality … something flattering like that, anyway. But he was quick to sense my mood and so said nothing.

There was a steep climb up the steps past the Oddfellows, then a further flight of steps up to the lower end of Wood Lane. We were hastening too fast for talk. When we had regained our breath, a little way up Wood Lane, I said, "So you have no brothers or sisters?"

He knew what I meant. It was as if he had been inside my head, listening to all my thoughts, during the previous five minutes. "*I* want to help, Crissy," he said simply. "Marian won't be much use to you — not because she doesn't want to help — but it's not her nature. Let me be her deputy, eh? Because I really *do* want to see you as happy as she is."

Mark returned from his lakeland walks the following Sunday afternoon, but I missed him because, being back in my grandmother's good books, I was given the afternoon off to go to Redruth. She, of course, assumed I would visit Little Sinns, and I said nothing to disabuse her. She already knew I would not see Mrs Felicity because she had gone to London for a week or so.

Jim met me at Penmere Halt but the train, an Excursion Special, was crowded and we could do no more than sit side by side, touching and holding hands. He looked very dapper, with his narrow check trousers cut to the latest fashion, fawn kid gloves, a bamboo cane, a shiny new Celluloid collar, and a tie that could double as a spare bootlace if one should chance to snap. I was proud to be seen with him and glad I had put on the better of the two dresses my grandmother had passed on to me by way of marking that my punishment was over. They were not her dresses. Mrs Bourdeaux thought they must once have been my Aunt Catherine's. I did not inquire too closely but they were certainly in the fashion of the Seventies, when she would have been about my age. I just altered the shoulders to a more modern and feminine line and took out a large piece at the back of the skirt so as to fit the smaller bustle we favour nowadays. But I did not adapt it to the very latest in modern fashion. That's a mistake lady's maids find it all too easy to make because, naturally, we have to *know* our fashions inside out if we are to do our work properly. It leads to a lot of sneering behind the backs of those silly girls who slip over the boundary between knowing a thing and doing it. Anyway, Jim approved of the result and that was all I cared about. Aunt Eph and Uncle Jim, I gathered, were sticklers for dressing well on Sundays.

They lived half a mile or so west of the station, in a small semi-detached house on the corner with Rose Row. I realized I had passed it, all unawares, on previous visits to Little Sinns! It gave me a shivery feeling to think that I had stepped so innocently past the very house where the man I now loved most in all the world had grown up. All his sorrows, all his joys ... his fears, his rages — all had come and gone there, leaving nothing that I had detected as I passed on by.

As someone came shuffling up the passage to answer Jim's knock at the door, he stepped to one side, pushed me to the middle of the top step, and flattened himself out of sight against the house, between the doorway and the bay window.

"Go on!" he said.

The door swung open on creaking hinges to reveal a stooped, gray-haired woman, thin and worn. She had a flowered (and floured!) pinafore over her dark Sunday best.

"The room is let," she said.

I was annoyed with Jim for his tomfoolery, mainly because I didn't know whether it *was* tomfoolery or whether he was testing my quickness of wit in some way. I wasn't exactly angry but my feelings were pretty sharp, for all that. I thought, *If he wants to play silly games, he can't object to anything I say.*

"Are you Mrs Collett?" I asked. "Mrs *Jim* Collett?"

"Ye-es?" she admitted warily.

I smiled and, raising my voice and tilting my head toward Jim's hiding place, said, "Well, if *young* Jim wishes to give *me* that same name, he'd better stop playing silly games like this!"

She caught on at once. She pulled open the bow of her pinny and drew it off her in a single sweep of her hand. Then she stepped out onto the footpath and stared at Jim with a look in which exasperation and merriment fought with each other. Merriment won and she flung her arms around him for a brief maternal hug, saying, "Oh, Jim — when will you ever grow up!"

He winked at me over her shoulder as if to say, 'I'm only like this with them,' but I was amazed to see him like this with anyone — this wise, mature, serious young man I'd come to know and love. I suppose children are always children to their parents. And other people's expectations are bound to colour the way we behave.

I was glad to have discovered this unexpected side to him, though. It was the one element — or the most important one, anyway — that had been lacking between us so far: the ability to let himself go and be a little childish now and then.

"Ooh, but you're getting light as a feather, Aunt Eph!" he said, wrapping his arms around her small, compact frame and hugging her off the ground.

"Stop that this minute!" she cried out sharply, her face turning red with delight. "Oh, you are a scamp — you did give me a turn!" When he put her down at last she pulled her dress straight and said, "Come-us on indoors now — and you do the thing properly — introduce this maid to your uncle and me. What must she think of us?" She took my arm and led me indoors at last, murmuring, "What must you think of us, Miss Moore?"

So! Not only was our introduction a formality, but Jim must already have told them something of me. And unless he had popped over here one evening during the week, the conversation could only have taken place between that Sunday in Flushing and the evening class at the polly six days ago — in other words, *before* he had even kissed me or told me of his love.

I said, "I think you and your husband must be two saints, Mrs Collett."

"Paint?" A voice came from the foot of the stairs.

My eyes, growing accustomed to the gloom, made out a tall, lean old man in a black Sunday suit that he must once have filled rather better than he did now.

Aunt Eph turned to Jim and said in exasperation, "Well?"

Jim, staring at the old man, said, "I've brought Miss Moore to show off to you, Uncle — and to you, Aunt, dear."

Then, at last, he introduced us properly. As they ushered us into the parlour, Uncle Jim asked, "Who said that about paint, then?"

Aunt Eph raised her voice. "Young Jim met Miss Moore at painting classes. Where they do learn how to *paint*. You know — pictures and that, not walls and windows. He told us — remember?" To us she added at normal volume: "Gone a bit deaf, poor soul."

"Deaf?" he shouted at her. "I aren't deaf, woman. Shut the door and bring us a dish o'tay and some fuggan."

From the little Jim had said about his adoptive parents I gathered that the old man had been something of a petty tyrant in his own home. If so, deafness and advancing age had conspired to cut him down. I was quite shocked, when we were settled in the parlour, to see him in full daylight, for I knew neither of them was yet sixty. He, at least, looked twenty years older than that. And the shock was made no smaller by the strong family likeness between him and Jim. Was this, I could not help wondering, my husband-to-be, forty years on?

The parlour was cold, even on that rather warm autumn afternoon. It was like those historic rooms they rebuild in museums, where you peep in and feel nothing of ancient life, only a modern lifelessness. I wondered when anybody last sat in the chair I now occupied. I don't mean the bric-a-brac all around us was antique. Quite the opposite — it was hideously modern, most of it. Plaster antlers, jugs with funny faces, Celluloid fans that were given away with Lipton's tea last year, the lid of a biscuit tin with an oleochrome of *Sunset over Naples Bay* on it, a shoe-horn painted to look like silver-filigree inlay — it was all cheapjack tinware from every travelling fair that ever set up its stalls on Tolskithy Moor. None of Jim's photographs were on display, I noticed. But that was only fitting. Jim had grown so far apart from his adoptive parents that his prints would have done nothing but emphasize the gulf that now yawned between them.

I had an awful premonition that one day my own little Teresa might visit my married home and stare at my ornaments with similar feelings of distress.

We exchanged platitudes until Aunt Eph returned with tea and cake. Then Uncle Jim said, "Your father, Miss Moore, was 'e one of the Moores of Praze-an-Beeble?"

I said he was.

"His sister do have the post office over to Nancekuke," he went on.

It was the first I had heard of any of his family — which is odd for Cornwall, because the first thing any two Cornish people do when they meet, anywhere in the world, is to compile each other's genealogies. I knew my father had relations, of course, but the implication had been that, once he fell into drunken ways and started going to prison for it, they had severed all links with him. And with 'that-there flighty, high-quarter 'oman' who had driven him to drink. And with all her brood.

My surprised expression must have suggested to Aunt Eph that I had not understood her husband. "She'd be your aunt," she explained. "Aunt Ellen she'd be to you."

"Our father never spoke of his people," I said apologetically. "I *thought* there was a sister but I was never sure."

It was all the prompting they needed. Over the next ten minutes they told me all they knew. I learned, for instance, that my aunt Ellen had married another ne'er-do-well, a man called Billy Ivory, who had 'gone to Americay as a Cousin Jack' — that is, as a Cornish miner whose skills were prized over there once the easily mined lodes were exhausted — "and 'e never showed 'is face in Cornwall again," Aunt Eph concluded.

Whenever Uncle Jim stated the bare bones of a fact, Aunt Eph added the living flesh with phrases like, "She never married, poor soul ... He had a wall eye they could never seem to cure somehow ... And that boy never laughed again!" My paternal relations, it seemed, inhabited a world in which desirable things *never* happened. Nonetheless, I also learned that my father's father had died before I was born — that his wife Mary, my other grandmother, whose maiden name had been Jeffries, still lived (as far as they knew) and was housekeeper to a vicar up near Jamaica Inn — that her sister Jane, a great-aunt to me, was married to a farmer near Goldsithney — and that my father had had a brother called Anthony, who was in the Royal Navy. They did not know whether he was still alive or not.

There was my inheritance, then — the paternal half with its tendency to split apart and never come together again, and the maternal half seeming doomed to gather itself into itself, as the Wilkinsons had gathered Teresa and my grandmother had gathered me. There was no need to ask which side I took after, with my yearning to gather all of us together again.

And, by coincidence, that same question — which family did I take after — was the one uppermost in the minds of Aunt Eph and Uncle Jim. I did not realize it until after we parted that afternoon, when Jim and I were strolling back to the station and he said, "They've really taken to *you,* Crissy." After a second or two he felt he had to add, "As I knew they would, of course, once you and they actually met."

"You mean your description of me had filled them with doubt?"

He laughed awkwardly. "Not that. Just the fact that you're a Moore — Barry Moore's daughter. Can't blame them, I suppose, even though Uncle Jim's own father — my grandfather — was hanged up Bodmin as a common criminal."

"What for?" I asked in surprise.

"Burglary and coining, I was always told. God knows what else — probably his worst crime was to get on the wrong side of most of his neighbours. They'd have been on his jury."

"Well, I liked them, too," I told him.

"Really?" It was his turn to sound surprised. "They're pretty dull sort of people, I think."

"But good. They're good people. You shouldn't disparage them by picking on their weakest point. Why did you take fright and hide after we'd knocked at the door?"

He laughed but glanced warily at me. "That wasn't fright, my darling — or not in the way you mean it. I had a sudden feeling it was all going to go badly, right from the beginning, if I just stood there beside you and said, 'Hallo, Aunt Eph. Remember Miss Moore? When I told you how much she means to me and how I hope to marry her one day, you said no good could possibly come of it? Well, here she is. Shake hands.' I could see that wasn't going to work."

I had to laugh, not only at the comic picture he painted but also at the happy thought about our marrying one day. And although it was the sabbath and we were in Redruth's main street, and dressed in our most respectable clothes, I also had to throw my arms around him and kiss him for dear life.

"All the same," I said as we resumed our walk, "you took a risk. I might have made the most awful idiot of myself."

"No you wouldn't," he replied calmly. "I think that, in some ways, I know you better than you know yourself. And that's one of them. There is *no* situation in which you would make an idiot of yourself."

This was balm to my spirit, of course, but I wanted him to get back to what he'd said about marrying one day. I didn't want him to propose just yet. It was much too soon for that. But I wanted us to acknowlege the possibility, because there was so much we could then talk about — what we thought marriage was *for,* what sort of home we wanted, what was the best size for a family, and so on. And if he was going to branch out from Stanton's and set up in a studio of his own, could I help — or did he think a wife's place was at home and she should have nothing to do with 'his' business?

But it was probably too soon to talk about things like that, too. Not because I hadn't made up my mind and wanted him to help me. Quite the opposite, in fact. When it came to marriage, these were the questions that exercised me most, the questions on which I had the strongest possible opinions — so strong, in fact, that nothing he could say would alter them. That's why it was too soon. I might blurt them out and put him off altogether!

As summer rolled over to autumn and autumn gave way to winter, life at Fenton Lodge settled into a routine — not a fixed routine but the usual one of gradual change. Sudden shocks had no part in it. The earthquake promised by Mr Walter and Mrs Felicity over my employment as a 'menial' did not happen. Nor did the much smaller but still painful upheavals feared by Mrs Bourdeaux. It seems that we love big dramas as long as they visit other people's lives. We will settle for much smaller theatre in our own. We'll huff and we'll puff but we'll leave the house standing.

I'm sure my grandmother knew I was seeing Jim, but she must have realized there was no way of stopping it short of gating me permanently. Also, perhaps, Mrs Bourdeaux might have put in a good word on his behalf. Or, since old Stanton, his employer, was a relative of the Foxes, and Mrs Elizabeth Fox was a particular friend of my grandmother's, she might have received a favourable report through those channels instead. Or as well. Anyway, there was no more quizzing me as to whether we were couranting together. But nor was her earlier prohibition withdrawn. The permission to break it was — like so much else in that strange household — never put into actual words.

Mrs Felicity was the biggest surprise to me. She had seemed so vehement — and so venomous toward my grandmother that time in Plymouth — that I truly feared she was beyond the influence of reason. I mean, it would not have surprised me if she *had* huffed and puffed and blown the house down, even at the risk that bits of it might fall upon her. But, after her brief visit to London (which, it was now whispered, had been to see a man in Harley Street), she and Mr Walter went off to Italy for the whole of September — that is, as soon as they entered half-mourning. And even after they returned, early in October, their visits still seemed to coincide with my absences.

It even occurred to me that she was perhaps waiting for *me* to take the next step. She must have known that the Great Family Argument was overheard by every servant in the house and that they would surely have passed it on to me with all the usual embroidery that servants know how to add. Was she expecting me to respond in some way? If so, she must have taken my inactivity as a vote on my grandmother's side of their argument.

How little she understood us! My grandmother and I had few obvious features in common but we were alike in one important way — we were much more prone to burn on a long, slow fuse than to flare up at once, even when the provocation was great. I did not for one moment believe that the old woman's continuing silence after Mrs Felicity's outburst meant that it was over and done with as far as she was concerned. Silent watchfulness was in our blood.

But which blood was that? The only inheritance she and I had in common was from the Wilkinson line. She was a Trevarton by marriage and a Moore not at all. I decided I must learn more about 'us Wilkinsons.' Unfortunately these thoughts occurred to me only after Cousin Stella had gone back to her grace-and-favour cottage at Nancekuke. She gave me a tip of one guinea, which I invested in the Credit Union. The picture in my mind as I paid it over was of that domestic world Jim and I had peeped into through the windows in New Street that evening. It was the first money I did not mentally dedicate to the reunion of our family. Except that, in my inmost heart, Jim was *family*, too, by now — he was its next phase, in fact, since a family is a living, breathing thing.

But not everything in my life revolved around Jim. That autumn, Roger Moynihan began to court me strongly. I don't mean romantically, of course. I mean he tried to persuade me I was missing my vocation by becoming a lady's maid. I had a great talent for drawing, he said. It was a crime to ignore it. He was going against his own principles in saying this. He believed that the only thing to do with artists was to discourage them. "Let 'em starve," he'd say. "It narrows the field. Start encouraging them and you won't see the honey for the wasps." Yet he did all he could to encourage me to give up my secure future at Fenton Lodge and take up Fine Art instead — as opposed to Useful Arts. I asked him what I'd live on and he spoke vaguely about various scholarships and bursaries and exhibitions and endowments that were 'available.' I replied that if people had to give four different names to the same thing, it was to cover a severe deficiency in each individual one of them. He laughed and said he saw he'd never pull the wool over my eyes. So I said I'd stay where I was, thanks very much.

Unfortunately, human nature doesn't always pay heed to human reason. I could make up my mind easily enough but my spirit took more convincing. Jim and I continued to attend the Monday evening drawing classes — in the *Useful* Arts course — but every time I sat at my donkey there was a new rush of excitement within me that had nothing to do with Jim's nearness. I felt something stirring to life that had not been there before. The power of suggestion! Moynihan had tipped a few drops of poison in my ear and this was their effect. Drawing was no longer a struggle to get the marks on the paper looking vaguely like the object out there. I could do that without even trying by now — to the envy of my classmates but to my own despair.

Jim, who was a pretty good piano player, said that something of the sort happened to him while he was learning that instrument. He reached a stage where he could play almost anything from sight. Others used to congratulate him but *he* could hear that, for all its competence, his playing was wooden and mechanical. It had everything except that mysterious element called verve or life or sparkle ... that *something* which makes you sit up and say, 'Yes! Now I've got it!' His playing certainly had that verve by the time I got to know him and I asked him how he'd managed it.

"Practice," he replied — rather uncomfortably, because it tended to support what Roger Moynihan was urging me to do.

As to *that* argument, Jim refused to take sides. Mark almost commanded me to put it out of my mind. He said there were already too many bad artists in every branch of the arts. I went to bed that night seething with anger at his arrogance — and determined to go to Moynihan the very next day and tell him I was on. But I woke up next morning grateful to him for having brought me to the brink of that decision, which had looked so attractive from a distance but much less so now that I was close to it. Also, Mark made me aware of the seductive power of a strong-minded man. How easy it would be to yield to Mark's bossy certainties — heap all my problems on his shoulders and stop worrying, worrying, worrying ...!

By contrast, Jim's constant refrain of 'Well, what do *you* think about it yourself, Crissy?' was much less satisfactory to me — or to that part of me which wanted someone strong to take over my increasingly clouded and fragmentary life and shake it back into some sort of order. In fact, however — in his own subtle way — Jim was just as positive as Mark. Still using his own experience as a pianist, he said he'd now reached the stage where he was fairly pleased with himself. "However," he added, "it's only the mediocre artist — in any field — who can claim that. The truly great artists are *never* satisfied. They always strive for more and more and more perfection. Then beneath them comes a much larger group who will never be truly great but who will also never settle for being happily mediocre, either — like me and my piano playing. That's the dangerous group for you, Crissy. I don't know whether or not you'd ever be among the truly great. No one can tell that. But, knowing you as little as I do, I'd stake my life that you'd be in that second group of permanent malcontents. D'you *want* to be a permanent malcontent?"

So he flattered me into not risking myself.

Also, I suppose, deeper forces were at work within me — dark suspicions about what art does to the soul. There were people in the class who could remember Moynihan's first wife, Esther, who had killed herself about ten years earlier. Before that she had a long history of nervous afflictions, which, of course, they blamed on her guilt at her previous life of shame — though there were dozens of other women similarly afflicted who did not have the excuse that they were reformed Unfortunates. Anyway, the thing that struck me, listening to their gossip, was that through all the ups and downs — the shouting matches, the dashes to hospital, the stomach pumps, the languorous convalescences — Roger Moynihan had continued to paint with unhindered vigour. She had finally hanged herself — not taken poison, as many said. And the very day he cut his wife's body down from a tree in their garden — while she lay there, waiting for the coroner's men to come and collect her — he finished a painting that had to be dry in time for the summer exhibition. In a century from now, the people who see that painting and take pleasure in it aren't going to think the worse of it — nor of him — for such callousness. But that's small consolation to those who have to live with the artist and the demon that drives him — or her — to do such callous things.

I didn't want to become like that. I wanted to be Jim's wife, the mother of his and my children, the maker and keeper of our home. If any demon was to rule me, other than that, it was my desire not to lose touch with my family.

And there, too, Jim was the greatest assistance. One evening, early in October, he handed me a piece of paper on which he'd written General Sir Redvers Wilkinson's address in Mysore. Also, since Jim was nothing if not thorough, there was his full title and list of honours, and — the master touch — some paragraphs copied from *Manners and Rules of Good Society* by A Member of the Aristocracy (19th Edition) telling me how to address a baronet correctly.

Except that it didn't. It said that I should address a general as 'Dear General Blank' if I was a member of the upper classes but just as 'Dear

General' if I was not. It also said I should address a baronet as 'Dear Sir John Blank' if upper class, otherwise just 'Dear Sir John.' It did not say how *anyone* should address a general who was *also* a baronet. Nor did it say whether a niece who happened to have fallen out of the upper classes into the lower ranks but who remained a niece still counted as upper class for the purposes of letter-writing. I think if people are going to make rules, they should make them thorough or they should forget them. Rules that let you 'get by' in ninety percent of cases and leave you floundering for the rest are a nightmare.

In the end I decided to begin my letter to him: 'Dear Great-great-uncle Redvers and Aunt Araminta ...' I'd discovered her name meanwhile but I didn't think *she* would take kindly to a string of great-greats in front of it. The main text of the letter went through a good dozen drafts before it satisfied me — and Jim. He made me blunt my more savage barbs and kept bringing me back to my main purpose, indeed, my *only* purpose, which was to let them understand that if they tried to exclude me from all intercourse with Teresa, they'd be storing up trouble. It had to suggest that they'd find in me a good friend — or an implacable foe. Our final draft — the one I actually sent — read:

I'm sure it will surprise you to hear from Teresa's elder sister — just as it surprised me to discover at last what has become of her. We should have been spared a great deal of distress had we learned directly of your adoption of her. However, now that we know of it, may I say how pleased we are. Teresa will henceforth enjoy prospects that would have lain impossibly beyond her reach but for your generous action. How could we be anything but delighted?

Our one great fear is that, being so far away from us in person, she will also grow away from us in spirit. We were a loving and close-knit family when we lived together. We still are, despite our separation. I spend almost every penny I earn on postage and train fares, keeping in touch with my elder sister, Marian, who is in London, and my three younger brothers — Tom, at Tywardreath, and Gerald and Arthur in Plymouth. I enclose likenesses of us, which I have sketched from memory (except the one of myself, of course), trusting that you will give them to Teresa with all our love. We want her to know that our silence all these months has been through ignorance of her whereabouts, not neglect of her memory, which is as dear to us as it ever was.

I would rather have enclosed a letter for her but have held back for fear that you might think it impertinent of me. That would distress me more than I can say. If I desire anything more than to be a friend to you — one who warmly appreciates your kindness to at least one small sprig of the Wilkinson line — it is that I desire to be no more separated from Teresa than geography dictates. In short, I respectfully ask your leave for us to correspond with her and to send her what little gifts we can afford at Christmas and on her birthdays.

My greatest struggle was to find the right note for a closing paragraph. Conventional words — perhaps a reference to India's fatiguing climate or a word or two about Cousin Stella — rang hollow. And anything on the lines of a 'by-the-way, my drawing master is Mister Roger Moynihan, who is not unknown to you, I believe?' looked like the clumsiest sort of veiled threat that I could tip skeletons out of cupboards if I wished. In the end I decided to leave it just as it was, despite its abruptness, and simply add, 'Your respectful great-great-niece, Cristobel Moore.'

I still had doubts about the wisdom of writing in such a vein right up to the moment we posted it. Jim and I actually held it between us as we slipped it into the pillar box. We pushed it in with a sort of ritual gesture and then looked at each other.

"Now we know," he said, "how that daughter of the house of Levi felt when she launched the infant Moses upon the Nile."

Marian and I agreed we'd not give each other anything that Christmas. We had little enough money to spare and decided we should use it for the comfort of the boys, who needed it more than we did. For our Tom I got a good, strong fishing line and keep net. For Gerald there was a book of soldiers and their uniforms down the ages, all in oleo-colours. If you cut carefully around the uniforms you could put them on the soldiers, who otherwise stood to attention looking rather sheepish in their underwear! And to Arthur I sent a box of simple magic tricks, including a game in which he could fish with a magnet on a string for paper salmon whose eyes were iron studs. I told him if he got good at it, his brother Tom would one day show him how to do the real thing. I wanted them to go on thinking of each other like that.

I also told them of my letter to General Wilkinson, saying that I expected a reply daily but had heard nothing yet.

I considered long and hard about whether to get anything for Jim. Presents were given only between members of a family, with few exceptions. Susan and I, for instance, would exchange handkerchiefs or a little flask of rosewater, because we shared a room and because, though I had decided for Jim, Mark was still making passes at me from time to time — and she knew it. Our friendship was, therefore, fragile.

But Jim! What to do about Jim?

We behaved like a betrothed couple, completely at ease in each other's company. I no longer felt inadequate in comparison with him — not because I had discovered feet of clay on him but because he made me feel so special. I think the courtship that leads up to betrothal is the most difficult of all. It's like swimming when you know you can't yet swim. Before a man can confidently ask a woman to marry him he must have sampled the sort of intimacy that an engagement entails. It's rash to ask for a whole plate of curry before you've tried a little spoonful or two. And it's the same for her. How can she accept him unless she's gained a little experience of that same intimacy? But how to get it?

Wouldn't it be marvellous if once in a while it was all right to say, 'Let's have a temporary betrothal, just this afternoon — to see if we like it — and then, if we do, we can try it for a day or two next month … and so on, until we're confident enough to make it permanent'?

Actually, come to think of it, it wouldn't be marvellous at all. It would be purgatory! Walking on eggs would be bliss in comparison.

I don't know what the answer is. Just muddle forward and hope for the best, I suppose, which is what Jim and I were doing, anyway.

None of which helped solve my dilemma.

We were deeply in love — of that I had no doubt, neither of my own feelings nor of his. One day — soon, perhaps — we should become formally engaged. But until that happened, it would be presumptuous of me to buy him a present for Christmas — as if I were hinting at him to hurry up and make his proposal. I know he'd never entertain such a suspicion seriously but even if it merely flickered through his mind and was firmly dismissed a second later, I'd still feel mortified.

In the end I got hold of one of his handkerchiefs — by 'accidentally' pricking my hand on some wire — took it home to wash, and 'forgot' to bring it back for a couple of weeks. During that time I embroidered a rather swell monogram on the initials JC. I could give it back to him as a present if he gave me one or I could just pretend it was my way of apologizing for keeping it so long. I was pleased that he kept asking for it, though. I like a man who takes care of his clothes and knows what he's got. Mark, by contrast, had four blazers and I'm sure he thought they were all the same one. And he'd wear his socks until they'd walk out of the house by themselves if Susan or I didn't put out clean ones for him. *And* take away the old.

We had a lovely servants' party in the hall on Boxing Day, which was a Thursday. The best thing about it was that Jim was formally admitted as my follower at last. I asked my grandmother if I might bring him as my guest, and she said yes as if she'd been expecting it for some time. So at last he was formally introduced to my grandmother. Before that he'd merely raised his hat and bowed to her a few times in the High Street.

He played the sprightlier tunes on the piano. My grandmother, the only other competent pianist among us, was still in half-mourning and felt she could not go beyond the slower, sentimental pieces. It suited me very well, though, because I danced those with Jim and was free to choose from the entire male field for the lively ones. Tony Pascoe, the under gardener, who was only twenty-three, was a wonderful dancer. And so was Philip Weekes, my grandfather's old valet, who came back to us for Christmas and was asked by Mrs T so stay on as under butler to old Bourdeaux.

Mark danced quite a bit with Susan, though he seemed rather ill-at-ease. Her mood changed very noticeably, too, as the evening wore on, but I was slower than usual to notice it because of the most wonderful things that happened to me. There was a cold buffet supper of all the Christmas leftovers, including my favourite 'gerty-meat,' which is a Cornish kind of haggis. I gorged myself on that. Then there was a sort of pause, since nobody felt like dancing again straight away. Mrs T played carols and everyone sat or stood around her, singing their hearts out. Then Jim whispered in my ear that it was rather hot indoors and wouldn't I like to slip out into the backyard for a breather? Well, I didn't say no!

I thought I knew his purpose but I couldn't have been more wrong. We *did* kiss and cuddle, of course — a lot — but that wasn't what he had in mind. After a while he fished in his pocket and said, in an oddly nervous, faltering way, quite unlike his usual confident self, "It's a Christmas present ... well, in a way. I mean it's for a lot more than just Christmas, you know."

Then, as I fumbled with the wrapping and opened it, he added, "It's for life, I hope."

It was a little cardboard box, full of fluffy cotton wool on which rested … well, I knew it was a diamond by its sparkle, even before I saw the ring. Nothing sparkles like a diamond.

"It was my mother's," he told me.

I was paralyzed. The long-awaited moment had come at last, and yet it took me utterly by surprise. None of the words I had prepared in the daydreams I had woven around it was any longer available. My mind seemed to have fallen through the surface of the night to a place where it could only watch what was going on. I couldn't take part any longer. I watched myself take up the ring and hold it into the light coming out by the scullery window. There was a full moon that night but it was hidden for the moment behind a skein of cloud.

I heard him say, "You know which finger I want you to wear it on, Crissy. You know what I'm asking."

I did, of course, but I could not seem to shake off that strange numbness which had stolen over me. I did not even know my true feelings, they were such a blend of fear, bewilderment, and ecstasy. This was a moment I had dreamed about and planned and savoured for so many days and so many nights, yet its coming caught me so unawares that I knew not what to say.

"Darling Crissy," he murmured, slipping an arm about me and drawing me tight to him. "Don't cry! This is supposed to be happy."

I didn't know I was crying. I wasn't sobbing but there were tears on my cheeks. I sniffed, rather glutinously, and he tugged at the hanky in his breast pocket.

"No!" I exclaimed, galvanized at last. And I dived into my bodice pocket and pulled out the little present I had embroidered for him.

"Finally!" he cried out, and began at once to dab my eyes and cheeks. Only then did he notice my handiwork. He stopped and peered at it closely. "But it's exquisite!" he said, kissing me on the icy tip of my nose. "Is this my answer?"

"No!" I pinched him playfully and said, *"This* is."

And I slipped the ring round the third finger of my left hand — the one named Davy Gravy in the nursery rhyme. It fitted as if made for me.

The moon had been waiting on that moment for she suddenly burst forth in all her splendour, turning us and our world to silver and painting a scene I shall never forget — nor ever wish to, either.

Jim stood there, his face just inches away, smiling serenely, staring into my eyes, full of wonder and unable to believe that this moment had finally come — and that I had said yes, just like that. All the world knew that modest girls always asked for 'a day or two to think it over.' It was considered wanton — indeed, almost lewd — to accept at once.

Jim's mind must have been travelling along those lines. When we had kissed again, to seal our bargain, he said, "If you'd rather think it over... you know ...?"

I grinned at him and said, "Getting cold feet already, eh?"

"No!" he exclaimed vehemently. But then he broke into a grin, too, and said, "Our first quarrel!"

It wasn't, actually. We'd already had several. But I knew what he meant. Our other tiffs had all been about impersonal things that didn't really matter. Art and stuff like that. I hugged myself tight against him and said, "I've had five months to think it over. If you'd asked me to marry you that afternoon in Flushing, I'd have said yes."

He swallowed heavily and I felt his adam's apple bob up and down against my ear.

"Did you think of it then, too?" I asked.

"Before then," he whispered. "From the very moment I saw you, I knew you were the one — the only one. It's probably ungallànt to say this, but I only walked out those few weeks with Susan because it brought me near you and kept alive my hope of getting nearer still. I felt such a traitor but I couldn't help it." He gave a slightly embarrassed laugh. "Yet in a funny way, the moment we started couranting properly, you and I, that desperate need to ask you to marry me — before someone else noticed that you are far and away the most marvellous girl in all the world and got in first — it just evaporated."

"Until tonight."

"No. Until last week. Aunt Eph told me she and Uncle Jim had courted almost twelve years before he proposed. She said all the love had gone out of it by then. So then I went straight upstairs to my mother's old jewel box, took out the only jewel it contained, and ... well, now it belongs to the only jewel in my life!"

I cried again at that, a little, anyway, and we kissed and murmured sweet nothings until Susan, speaking from the still-room window above us said, in a comic Cornish accent, "We'm all nurley with they there ol' slow dirges th' ol' 'oman's playing, my lovers. We do want zummat spronsey now."

She was 'spronsey' enough herself that evening yet I detected an edge of desperation to it. I knew her well enough by then not to take her high spirits at face value.

It was just the same later, when we were in our beds and chattering away about my engagement — on the surface she was all bubbly and gay, underneath she was on edge. I could sense it even in the dark.

Eventually I asked her outright what was troubling her. At first she tried to deny she was feeling at all out of the usual, then she said it must be the full moon, and only after a great deal of wheedling from me did she unbend at last. In a hesitant tone she asked, "Your mum and your dad ... can I ask you something about them?"

"Yes?" I responded with a sort of half-questioning wariness.

"I mean, did it go wrong between them from the start? Or was it all right for a bit? And for how long? I mean, you had a nice house and your own general you said, up until you was about six, wasn't it?"

"As far as I could tell it was all right. I mean, what does a six-year-old know about things like that?"

"And if he hadn't ... you know ..."

"Gone on the booze."

"Yeah. If he hadn't done that, d'you think they'd still be ... I mean, would he have a good business? You might be on the up and up, still, don't you think?"

"Why d'you want to know all this, Sue? Why tonight in particular?" I had a horrible feeling I knew the answer.

"D'you think marriage between people of different classes ... no — I mean, was it the booze as did for him? It wasn't because they came from different classes, surely? That wouldn't of mattered if he hadn't taken to the bottle."

"But *why* did he take to the bottle, eh? That's the real question. I've often wondered. Was it because of the strain of living with a spouse who knew more, who could do more, and who was much more at ease with people in general than he was?"

Susan swallowed heavily. "D'you think that was it? But I wouldn't never feel like that."

"As I said — what does a child of six know? I had a perfect father for six years and a devil for the next ten. Imagine dying and not one of your children sheds a tear at it — not even the five-year-old!"

"Don't!" There was a shiver on her voice.

"Is all this to do with Mark?" I asked.

"You needn't say it in quite *that* tone," she grumbled. "He could do a lot worse than me."

"And you could do a lot better than him," I said. "Has he actually proposed marriage? There must be something in the air tonight!"

"It's the moon, like I said. Anyway, I suppose you think you're the only one entitled to be engaged," she said in a huff.

"Of course I don't, pet! If you sounded as happy about it as I am about me and Jim, I'd swallow all my doubts and ..."

"It's not as if I *wanted* it to happen." She cut across me.

"What did you want then?"

"Fun, of course."

"What sort of fun?"

"Oh, Crissy! *All* sorts. He's got money. He's good-looking. He's got perfect manners. He's nice to talk to ... I mean, we can talk, you know, him and me. We can really talk."

"So why not marry him? Did you say no?"

"I said I needed time to think about it."

"Time for his mother to get to hear of it. How serious *is* he?"

"He said we'd have to run off to Gretna Green because of his age. He's got money of his own."

"And how long would that last?"

"Oh!" she said in exasperation. "I suppose you think you're the only one entitled to marry *at all* around here?"

"But I thought you *didn't* want to marry him! Make your mind up!" After a pause I added, "Besides, you're talking as if Jim and I are tying the knot tomorrow. I expect it'll be years yet."

"I know, I know!" she snapped.

"Well then," I said, my feathers still ruffled. "I don't know what we're quarrelling about. You tell me Mark has proposed and you seem miserable about ... actually, why *did* he propose tonight? Did you tell him about Jim and me? Were you spying on us long enough to realize that's what we were doing?"

I spoke these last words in a sort of jesting banter, hoping to cajole her into a happier mood. But I might as well have saved my breath. In the same morose tone she said, "I told him something all right, but it wasn't that."

It wasn't telepathy. Her intonation said it well enough. For a moment I was too flummoxed to answer her. Then I said, "So you had that fun after all!"

"He did," she replied. "I thought if we were standing up, I couldn't get ... you know." She burst into tears. "Oh, Crissy, what am I going to do?"

I climbed into bed with her and held her for comfort. I thought it over for a while but there was really only one right answer. "I think you should go and tell Mrs Trevarton everything — you and Mark together."

"I couldn't!" She was appalled at the thought. "And not with Mark there, either."

"I know it won't be easy but it's for the best. If you run away together, how far will you get? And even if you reached Gretna Green, you've got to live there a month before ..."

"A month!" Her horror at this news revealed she had been seriously considering Mark's ridiculous offer.

"I don't know the exact length of time. Maybe it's two months. But I do know you can't just turn up one day and get married the next. Anyway, what future would there be in that?"

"A whole month," she repeated feebly. "Or two! Oh, Jesus!"

"And if you just let matters drift until it starts to show? How long has it been?"

"Dunno." She sniffed back the flood of tears that had drained into her nose passages.

"You must know," I said, bewildered. "Unless ... you mean it happened more than once."

"Not more than once a night!" she replied sarcastically. Then, with a giggle, "Not often, anyway."

"So you have no idea when it actually ... you know ..."

"Blimey, I've got no idea *how* it happened, never mind when. He's always been the perfect gentleman. He's never done it inside me — always got out in time. I thought what with that *and* standing up always, we'd be safe." She let out a great sigh.

"So you could be two or three months gone already?"

She buried her face in my bosom and tried not to answer.

"More?" I asked relentlessly.

"Don't you despise me now?" she asked. "I've been scared to death of saying anything. I thought you'd never speak to me again."

Naturally I was hurt that she could think me that sort of person, but it was good for me to see myself through another's eyes. It made me realize that I was something of a whited sepulchre. "Of course I'll speak to you," I said. "And help in any way I can. I'll do anything to help. Would you like *me* to tell Mrs T?"

"No!" she almost screamed.

"She'll have to know," I pointed out. "It's bound to come out sooner or later — as the midwife said. She won't go easy on you but she'll be fair. You've said yourself often enough that she's a fair sort of woman."

"Yeah, well, fairness is one thing, but when it comes to sheltering the sons and heirs in a family, fairness goes out the window."

I drew breath to argue but she went on: "Don't try and talk me out of it. I've seen it happen. The place I was at before here … or the place before that … I forget. Anyway, one of the maids — only sixteen she was — younger than me. She got belly-up by the youngest son — and mind you, they was the nicest, kindest masters and mistresses you could ever hope to meet. Until then! We all said it. We was like one big happy family there. But the minute poor little Mary said she was carrying *their* grandchild — *bang!* Up went the shutters like you've never seen them go up before. Young John or whatever his name was — yes, I believe it was John. Anyway, he'd been a bit of a naughty boy, no doubt of it. Tut, tut, and tut again! But as for Mary, she was the Whore of Babylon all of a sudden. 'Course they'd all suspected it from the start. That's what comes of taking in such creatures and giving them a lovely home and five pound a year! She'd been the seductress — just like Eve in the Garden of Eden. Dear, innocent little Johnny hadn't a chance! So don't tell me about fairness, Crissy. I've seen it working."

"What happened to her?"

"What d'you think! They got her certificated as a mental and moral defective — that's what. The babby got took off her by a religious couple up Newquay way and she's scrubbing floors and doing the laundry in the loony bin at Trescobeas. And no five pound a year for her, neither!"

I was exasperated, not only at the awfulness of it all but at the hopelessness that Susan radiated like a furnace. "But Mrs T would never do that to you," I objected.

"Mothers'll do anything — anything — to protect their sons."

"We wouldn't let her," I said.

"Yeah," she sneered. "Well, you tell me how to propose to stop her — and then I might just listen."

Part Three

Penzance
after the
Great
Blizzard
1891

Crossing the Rubicon

I took Jim to meet Miss Martin and told her of our engagement. I thought she would be disappointed for, as a married woman, I would be unable to join her at Little Sinns. A married woman could not be employed in a salaried position anywhere. But, if she was disappointed, she hid it well.

Privately she told me she found Jim 'impressive.' She said she could not see him remaining an assistant at Stanton's for long. *That* possibility, I realized, had not even crossed my mind — I mean, I had never for one moment thought he would remain an assistant there. The same was also true of me. Always at the back of my mind was the feeling that my present life was all temporary. I would not be a lady's maid for ever. I would not be separated from my family for ever. And — happiest of all — I would not be a spinster for ever, either.

But what time limits governed these temporary situations? *When* would I become Mrs Jim Collett? At our present rate of earning it would take years and years for us to save enough to start a home, a family, *and* our own photographic business. I began to see why Miss Martin was not too disappointed, after all. She had every reason to hope I might yet join her at Little Sinns and stay at least for a few years. Jim and I talked it over on our walk back into Redruth. Should I hand in my notice at once, I wondered?

It was a cold, blustery January day with low clouds scudding over the sky, threatening rain but never delivering it. The advantages of moving from Fenton Lodge to Little Sinns were undeniable. It would be a big step up for me, both socially and financially. My salary, on the local government scale, would be forty pounds a year with free board and lodging. I should also have a day off every week rather than every fortnight — and that meant the full twenty-four hours. So I could keep up my Useful Arts course *and* see Jim each week. I could finish at, say, five o'clock on the Monday, take a bus to Falmouth, arriving in good time for the evening class, lodge the night at Jim's boarding house, where they were very used to commercial travellers taking rooms for just the one night, and be with him for breakfast and luncheon the following day — and still be back by five on the Tuesday.

The disadvantage was that we'd be out of easy reach of each other for the remaining six days of the week. True, he could come over on

Sundays and spend the afternoon with me at Little Sinns, but I'd still be on duty while he was there. This drawback was more mental than actual for, though we lived in the same town, we saw little of each other — alone, that is — during the week. If I was sent on a message into town, I'd always drop in at Stanton's in case Jim had five minutes to spare. But usually it was just a nod and a wink and he'd vanish into the studio or darkroom. Again, he sometimes cried in at Fenton Lodge of an evening, where he was permitted to sit and read to me while I got on with my sewing, but Mrs Bourdeaux didn't really approve. She liked Jim well enough but she thought it set a poor example. Anyway, the atmosphere was never easy and, as I said, we had no chance of being left alone.

Our discussion of these points was briefly interrupted when we called at his aunt and uncle's. We mainly wanted to show off the engagement ring and let Aunt Eph shed a tear or two. Poor Uncle Jim was rather asthmatic, though, and we didn't stay.

The other disadvantage of my moving to Little Sinns, as I pointed out when we resumed our walk back into Redruth, was the thought of breaking the news to my mistress.

"Your mistress!" Jim exclaimed scornfully. "She's your grandmother. She should be delighted to see you going up in the world. Why d'you show such tenderness for her feelings? She never bothered a scrap about yours."

He was right, of course, but it wasn't the entire truth. Just as shot silk can be both blue and red, depending on how you look at it, so was my relationship with the old woman shot through and through with contrary emotions. To call her my mistress did not deny she was also my grandmother, but there was no way of explaining these things to Jim. He liked the world to be black-and-white — like his photography.

There was a similar ambiguity, I must admit, in my feelings about Mark. I could have explained my feelings about my grandmother if I had only been able to find the right words, but I could never have explained how I now felt about Mark.

I knew how I *ought* to feel, of course. I loved Jim. I was his wife-to-be. He was the earth, the sky, and the stars to me. He was a finer man than Mark in every way, and of his devotion to me there was no shadow of a doubt. Mark, on the other hand, was well on the road toward becoming that scourge of modern society — the rich and idle young man. Susan loved him. A cynic might say she had no choice but I think it was genuine on her part — and she swore it was genuine on his side, too.

Neither of them had the first idea what to do about her condition but a sort of fatalism had settled over them. Nothing showed as yet, and the birth was six months away (actually, it was only five but they preferred to think of it as six), which, at their age, seemed like half a lifetime.

All in all, then, it was a situation no sensible outsider would want to get mixed up in. And yet some frighteningly primitive part of me was furious at Mark for giving me up and turning to Susan instead. Perhaps it was the *way* it happened that provoked me so — to go running after him that afternoon in Flushing and come back looking so smug, with grass all over her dress and everyone thinking it only took her ten minutes to seduce Mark away from me. The insult to my pride!

Anyway, sometimes, when I met him about the house, I was desperately tempted to play the coquette and lead him on and make him suffer, too — all out of a childish desire for revenge. I wasn't proud of these desires but I couldn't drive them away.

These thoughts and feelings — about Jim, and my grandmother, and Mark and Susan — swirled around my head a hundred times a day, of course. So, on that afternoon in Redruth I didn't have to think them through, plodding step after plodding step. They were so familiar that they flashed by in less than five seconds. But a five-second pause in a conversation is long enough to break its thread and make one look as if one has nothing to reply.

"Well then!" Jim was surprised that I seemed to have conceded without our usual ding-dong. "You'll hand in your notice soon?"

Fortunately I was spared the immediate necessity of answering him because we rounded a corner and almost literally bumped into Mrs Felicity. She stared at me the way you do when you come across someone you know very well but cannot immediately place. Then her eyes lit up and she exclaimed, "You!"

I introduced Jim and she said, "Ah yes!" as if she'd heard a great deal about him — which she probably had. They had spent Christmas with her parents, so, what with that and their Italian holiday and so forth, she and I had not met since the day of the great family argument over me, which was now over six months cold. "Are you hoping for a meal?" she asked. "There's nowhere in Redruth open on a Sunday."

It wasn't true, of course. There were three hôtels for a start. But she probably meant they were beyond our means. Anyway, her real purpose was to add, "Come home and take pot luck with us? There are so many things we need to talk about."

I demurred, saying that we had to make sure of our bus but she waved my words aside, promising to send us home in her carriage. "Mrs Bourdeaux has told me about a codicil your grandfather wrote on the night he died," she added casually. "He intended to leave you a thousand pounds. Did you know that, I wonder?"

Of course Jim was all ears at this. Felicity, who was about to turn twenty-one — and thus just six months older than Jim — was deploying all her feminine charm in his direction and he was responding to it. I said, rather more scornfully than was polite, "That old servants' gossip!"

"Apparently not," she replied evenly. "I said the same, of course, but she showed me a draft that your grandfather wrote before he made the actual codicil, which he then got her and Bourdeaux to witness. She says your grandmother tore the thing up the very next day and burned it — but she knows nothing about the existence of this preliminary draft." Ominously she added: "Yet!"

"What?" Jim was scandalized. "What's all this?"

"It's trouble, darling," I told him. "It's poison. It's money for lawyers and barristers ..." Secretly, though, I was intrigued to hear all this, for it was the first direct evidence that Mrs Bourdeaux had, after all, known of my grandmother's action in destroying the document.

"It's trouble all right," Felicity said. "For old Mrs Trevarton. It'll mean prison for her, I shouldn't doubt." Give her credit for it — she was quite frank with us.

Too frank, in fact, for Jim now began to sense that she was somewhat unhinged, at least on that one topic of her mother-in-law. He started making the apologetic noises I wished he had made from the start.

But I knew his bull-terrier spirit well enough by now. He might have his doubts about Felicity but he'd not let go of the revelation she'd just made. So, partly to stop him from plaguing the life out of me to tell him all, and partly to let him see what a dangerous ally Felicity would be in any move against my grandmother (whom he, too, disliked heartily), I accepted Felicity's kind invitation. We took a hackney from the station.

Their house, 'The Acacias,' was at West Raven, on the western fringe of the town. It stood on a hillside, facing out over the Tolskithy Valley. The acacias for which it was named were in fact Robinias, or False Acacias, which have lovely feathery leaves in summer. In winter, however, they have dark, bare branches, liberally furnished with thorns — a forbidding sight against the darkling January sky. The wind keened through them, making me long to get indoors and stretch my hands toward the nice, warm fire whose glow I could see in one of the rooms.

The interior was a living monument to modern — and quite clearly Felicity's — taste. If Jim had been wondering how strong her personality was, the answer was here all about us, stamped on every square inch. It was like walking into a jungle — not an actual jungle but one that had been rearranged and stylized by an embroiderer, with lush foliage and twining tendrils teased out into heraldic patterns. Green was the overall effect, of course, but not the stolid pastoral green of our Cornish wood and field. Instead there was cool eau-de-nil and dark terre-verte and hot chrome green — the *decadent* colours that were all the fashion. Many people spelled the word 'decay-dent,' for the pronunciation was the same and the sneer was all too easy to make.

Her furniture was the strangest I'd ever come across — in reality, that is, for I'd seen numerous photographs and line blocks in magazines. It was all rather tall and thin. The wood — mostly fumed oak and limed elm — was made to look as if it had been squeezed out of a tube rather than carved by chisel and smoothed by rasp and sandpaper. The frame around the mirror over the mantelpiece looked more like a piece of silver-coloured driftwood than the product of human hands.

Mr Walter must have noted our arrival when the hackney pulled up for he was standing, his back to the fire, with a ready-prepared smile. "Cristobel!" he exclaimed. "What a fortunate encounter! I was on the point of sending you a note to be sure to call on us when next you visited Miss Martin. And this must be Mister Collett, about whom we've heard *so* much."

Formal introductions over — and my engagement ring duly admired — he turned back to me and asked, "Did my wife mention the extraordinary conversation we had with Mrs Bourdeaux recently?"

Recently? I could recall no recent visit of theirs to Fenton Lodge. Did it mean that Mrs B herself had come over here to meet them? That would explain how they had heard 'so much' about Jim, too.

"You risk getting your head snapped off, darling," Felicity warned. "Cristobel thinks the whole thing is a lawyer's conspiracy."

"Aha!" He beamed encouragingly at me. "Didn't I always tell you — she has more good sense in her little finger than all the Trevartons in Cornwall." To Jim he added, "Don't let her slip away, my boy."

Jim laughed awkwardly and said he didn't intend to.

Our host plunged a hot poker into a pewter jug of madeira that was standing in the hearth. It hissed and sizzled, filling the room with the most soporific aroma. The mulled wine soon mellowed the day and put us in a much more relaxed mood. We sat down and stretched the soles of our boots toward the flames. I watched the steam rising from mine and felt more contented with the world than I had for some time. (I had recently been deliriously happy, to be sure, but contentment is something different.) Felicity went out to tell the cook we'd be four to dinner.

Mr Walter meanwhile said, "Let's leave the codicil business until later …"

"No," I said. "Let's leave it altogether."

His eyebrows shot up. "It's a thousand pounds," he reminded me.

Jim turned to me and repeated the words with an edge of reproach: "A thousand pounds, love!" He meant we could get married as soon as we wished if we had that much in our pockets.

But I knew better. I won't say I'd been thinking about it for the past six months but my mind had occasionally circled around the problem. Also I was a more avid reader of the Law Reports than he was. The sports pages were more to his liking. So, rather wearily, I decided to kill the subject off once and for all. I turned to Mr Walter and said that if he'd put a mere five hundred pounds in my hand that week, I'd play whatever part he desired of me in any law suit he wished to bring and he could keep every penny of the winnings.

He just laughed, of course.

So I reduced my demand to two hundred and fifty and told him that not only was I serious, I was also making this a test of *his* seriousness — a three-hundred-percent return on an outlay of two hundred and fifty.

He gave an exasperated sigh and said it wasn't that easy.

"Well, *I* never thought it would be," I told him — with a glance at Jim to make sure he was following. "I'm much more interested in hearing from General Wilkinson about Teresa — and the legality of all that."

In other words, I was telling him that if he wanted to put right what he perceived as his mother's wrongs, the torn-up codicil was a non-runner as far as I was concerned. I'd read *Bleak House* and knew all about Chancery and the law's delays. But if he wanted to do something about Teresa's adoption, I'd be at his side all the way. I didn't necessarily expect him to bring her back to England but at least he might find some way to force the Wilkinsons to allow us to keep in touch with her. I'd settle for that. The point registered with him, I could see.

But for Jim the prospect of that thousand-pound bequest was still too alluring. "It looks, sir, as if you think Crissy would have less than a three-to-one chance of winning in any legal challenge to that codicil?" he remarked.

Mr Walter tilted his head awkwardly. "As I said, it's nothing so straightforward as that."

"It would never come to court," I put in. "I think the only strategy that might work would be to *threaten* a lawsuit and trust to my grandmother's fear of public shame to make her pay over the thousand pounds. Or a large sum, anyway."

It was not Felicity's strategy, of course. She so hated my grandmother that *only* a public humiliation could have satisfied her. Nor, I think, would it have been Mr Walter's strategy, either. He wanted to end the scandal of my employment as a 'menial' (in his eyes) at Fenton Lodge. Earlier last year he would probably have wanted her to apprentice me in some genteel shopkeeping trade and, upon my qualifying, to set me up with a little business of my own. Now my engagement to Jim provided an even speedier answer.

But I could not have lived with myself if I helped Felicity to spite the old woman. And, less nobly, I admit I was too proud to accept the enforced charity that Mr Walter would have extracted. I was determined we should make our own life in our own way, Jim and I.

Something of my determination must at last have communicated itself to Mr Walter. He stared at me. He glanced at Jim. And he saw he had lost his chance.

"Tell me what you know of Teresa's adoption," I said. "May I ask if you played any part in it?"

Felicity returned at that moment and said, "No!"

I continued to look at Mr Walter, who shifted uncomfortably and said, "I advised against it — at least, against the *way* of doing it."

I was on the edge of my seat by now. The drowsy, mellowing effect of the mulled wine had quite lifted from me. "The *way* of doing it?" I echoed his emphasis. "You mean arranging matters so that the authorities would conclude that the next of kin — Marian, Tom, and I — were incapable of looking after the three young ones?"

He nodded.

Now I felt as cold as ice. "So when I told you my pitiful tale ... when was it? Back in May last year, sometime — you know the time I mean — you already knew very well who I was? You already knew every detail I thought I was revealing to you?"

"I warned you!" Felicity hissed at him.

I persisted, however. "Then what," I asked, "was that celebrated family argument about at the end of July?"

"Oh!" Felicity exclaimed sarcastically. "D'you mean there's actually something you *don't* know?"

I turned to Jim and said, "D'you see, darling? D'you see now?"

He smiled back at me and nodded slowly by way of an answer. I don't think I ever loved him as much as I did at that moment. Spontaneously, without any signal between us, we rose in perfect unison to leave.

"See?" A bewildered Felicity echoed my words. "See what?" To her husband she said, "D'you know what she's talking about?"

"I'm saying ..." I began, but Jim cut across me. Speaking with chill dignity he said, "She's talking about being used, Mrs Trevarton. You, your husband, Crissy's grandmother — even, God rest him, her grandfather — have done nothing from the beginning but use the Moores and *their* family crisis for your own individual ends."

I wanted to throw my arms around him and hug him half to death.

"It's wrong!" Mr Walter intoned like a man in pain.

We all turned to him. "May I ask in what particular?" I said.

"*We* are wrong. I was wrong — most of all — I was wrong. And you, Mister Collett, are absolutely right. May we start again, Crissy? Can we treat this as a clearing of the air? We are a family, after all. Families can survive such disputes."

"Family?" I sneered. "No one is going to tell *me* what that word means. I know only too well what *my* family is." I turned to Jim. "We can still catch the last bus if we run."

"I really can help you over Teresa," Mr Walter said quietly. "And I want to help you, too."

A pair of traction engines could not have torn me more effectively in two. I stared at Jim in an agony of indecision — hoping he'd forget all those times when I'd insisted this was *my* problem and I didn't want to get him involved in any part of my family's misery. (It was a typical keep-my-cake-and-eat-it wish on my part, of course!) But that evening was the first time I actually longed for him to make a decision on my behalf about *my* family.

"Stay for supper?" Felicity saw me teetering and looking toward Jim for a decision. "Cook will be *so* disappointed if you don't."

Jim nodded gravely. Then, with a light, slightly mocking smile on his lips, he added, "I'm sure you'll understand, however, if we sup with a long spoon!"

elicity's advice was better than Uncle Walter's, I think. But it was still tainted by self-interest — hers, of course. He told me that, legally, the Wilkinsons were on fairly shaky ground over their adoption but, the world being what it is, people like them would always defeat people like me — unless I was prepared to give up everything else in my life and become a sort of monomaniac tigress fighting to get back one of her cubs. In the end the Law would have to yield her up to me, but it would be a long and costly struggle. I'd have to find some sympathetic barrister who'd take on my case for nothing. In short, Walter showed me daylight through an open door but, as I gratefully approached it, he kept adding these steel bars until, by the time I arrived, the day was quartered into dozens of little squares, all too small to let me pass.

Felicity, by contrast, advised me to accept the situation as it was and to play instead on the Wilkinsons' guilt and their good nature. They had been somewhat unwilling accomplices in Teresa's adoption — or, rather, in my grandmother's manner of carrying it out. If I could slip a little wedge between them and keep tapping at it gently ...

I showed her then a copy of our letter — Jim's and mine — to the General. She said it was an excellent start. I had to keep reminding myself that her honeyed advice was tainted by her overwhelming desire to isolate and score off my grandmother. It could, however, provoke her into revealing a telling truth at times, so I couldn't simply set all her advice to one side. I just had to be careful, that was all.

I asked her what, in her opinion, the Wilkinsons' response would be. She thought it over and said I might not get a direct reply to this particular letter. There was just enough of an edge to it to put the wind up them. In which case, they'd almost certainly write to old Mrs T in the first instance, asking who was this young person and what sort of trouble might she be able to cause? I should therefore expect to hear from her first — and not in the friendliest terms, either!

All our conversation took place over a sort of buffet dinner in which we served ourselves — to avoid having servants around to overhear us. The informality produced a surprisingly friendly atmosphere, considering our earlier quarrel. Felicity remarked on it at one point and said that some arguments could clear the air, and it was good to know that we

could all speak frankly and not hold back and give as good as we got —
and still remain on amiable terms when it was over. It struck me as
curious — the way she could come out with things that were so obviously
true they were platitudes ... and yet she'd leave you with a feeling of
distrust. She spoke obvious truths for obscure purposes.

However, the atmosphere became relaxed enough for me to murmur
to Jim — while we were helping ourselves to the bread-and-butter
pudding and the other two were out of earshot — "Should we mention
Susan's 'little difficulty'?"

He did not answer at once but when we were seated again he looked
across at me and nodded.

"Uncle Walter," I said, calling him that for the first time. "Aunt
Felicity." I looked at each as I spoke.

"Oh?" He raised an amused eyebrow and waited for more. She said
nothing, nor did her expression.

"This is a *very* family matter, so I hope you won't mind the intimacy of
my address. It concerns another uncle of mine — your brother Mark."

"Oh God!" Felicity let out her pent-up breath. "What now?"

Her response surprised me. I asked what he had ever done to
provoke it.

"Never mind!" Walter cut in impatiently. "What about him?"

"Well, in the first place, he'll *murder* me if he ever learns that I am the
source of this information. So if you choose to become involved, as I'm
sure you will, I'd be obliged if you could somehow leave him with the
impression it came via his mother or Mrs Bourdeaux. Please?"

"Very well, my dear," he said. They both nodded a promise.

"Remember my mother?" I began. "The way she ran off with ..."

"Tell them straight," Jim cut in.

So I did. "Mark wants to run away with Susan, marry her, and set up
home somewhere."

Walter almost choked on his mouthful. Felicity rose in her seat but
Jim got there first and thumped him on the back. With watering eyes
and a strangulated voice he managed to look at me and say, "What?
Where? Susan the upstairs maid?"

"She's expecting his child," I went on. "Next June or July, she thinks."

"She *thinks?*" asked a scandalized Felicity. "She *thinks* it's his child?
She *thinks* it's next June or July? I'll tell you what *I* think!"

I could feel a long, fruitless argument coming up so I turned to her
and said, "There can be absolutely no doubt of it, Aunt. June-July is as

certain as these things ever can be. And it's unquestionably Mark's. I'd not support her in so serious a lie. Mark has no doubt of it, either."

Walter lowered his head into his hands, too shocked to think straight, much less to speak. Even without my abandoned opening remarks, I feel certain he'd have thought of my mother and her elopement — though she was not carrying at the time. He must have thought that some cosmic evil spirit presided over his family's affairs of the heart. Or was he remembering the strange circumstances surrounding Mark's own birth? I longed to ask him.

Felicity lost none of her poise. "Did you *know* it was going on?" she asked me. "I mean were you aware they were running that risk? Where did they go? Did they do it in the house itself? What was Mrs Bourdeaux doing all this while? Has she been told?" Her fingers were going pittapat on the tablecloth, counting back nine months from July. "It happened last October-November!" she exclaimed, scandalized all over again. Then, in complete contrast, in a voice so quiet and calm as to seem sinister, she murmured: "If November, she's not yet three months gone, though."

Walter, alerted by her sudden change in tone, looked up and said, "No!" very firmly.

Her tongue flickered out like a snake's — in and out, not side to side — and she replied, still in that eerily calm voice, "It'd be for the best."

"No," he repeated even more firmly, matching his calm to hers. "Absolutely not. Put it out of your mind, now and forever."

She glanced at us — not to include us in the argument but to see whether we understood. We did, of course, but perhaps our expressions concealed the fact. "Very well," she said. *"Pas devant les enfants."*

My blood boiled at this, of course. I longed to tell her — in French — that we were not children and that we understood perfectly well. A month earlier I would have done so, too, but wearing that darling ring on my finger had made me grow up rather fast. I merely said, "They both want the baby," and left her to decide whether my apparent response to her unspoken suggestion was deliberate or accidental.

"They are under age," Walter protested. "Not for marriage, I mean, but for parental consent. They can't marry without that."

"Not even in France?" I asked — hoping his knowledge of French law was as slender as mine. From the way he bit his lip, I guessed it was. My main purpose, of course, was to conceal Mark's and Susan's intention to run away to Scotland and marry under their less restrictive law. I felt justified in revealing their predicament but not their actual plans. A smile from Jim told me he understood and approved.

"How much money has he?" Felicity asked her husband.

"Enough," he replied grimly. "A couple of thousand. More, with the interest that's since accrued." He banged the table with his fist. "Oh *why* did Uncle Emlyn not put it in trust until he was twenty-five? We all warned him but he had this absurd philosophy that a young man could learn to spend money wisely only if he began by frittering it away foolishly. I ask you!"

"Can Mark be made a ward of court? Or can she?"

"I don't know. Probably. Obviously it's something to consider."

"And urgently!"

He screwed up his eyes as if in pain. "The main thing is to prevent them from doing anything foolish and irrevocable. I don't like these dramatic solutions. Ward of court! It would all be so public. The best solution is for the girl to be sent away to the country somewhere — up in England — and to be set up in a small business — a village shop or something ... find a husband of her own sort who's willing to take her on. It would be expensive, of course." His expression brightened and he actually laughed a little. "We could make sure it cost every penny the boy possesses. Then Uncle Emlyn's philosophy would come true in one fell swoop! The money would be gone. The boy would have learned his lesson." He rubbed his hands like a man preparing for action and looked at me. *"That's* the thing to do, eh ... Niece?"

I shrugged noncommittally. "They are in love, Uncle," I warned him.

On our way back to Falmouth, Jim and I took full advantage of the luxury — and privacy — of the Trevartons' carriage. After ten minutes or so of passionate kisses, however, I could sense a certain restlessness in him. His heart and soul might be in our love-making but his mind was elsewhere. I, in my infantile jealousy, supposed he was thinking of Felicity, who had certainly not hidden her talents under a bushel that evening. Those fears were, of course, a revival of my earlier insecurity — my pessimism that Jim would, in some obscure way, 'find me out' and realize how inadequate I really was. And, because of that, I was afraid to offer the traditional penny for his thoughts.

And so one of the most momentous days in our lives — in terms of its revelations, decisions, and turning points — ended with a bewildering sense of estrangement between us, a gap that not all the kissing and cuddling in the world could bridge.

Full marks to Felicity for her understanding of human nature. She'd have made a far better lawyer than her husband, I think — though he was astute enough. Her prediction that my grandmother would hear from the Wilkinsons before I did proved correct. The letter arrived before that month was out — on Wednesday, 28th January, to be precise. I have good reason to remember the date, as will soon become clear.

It was ten to eight in the morning of a crisp winter's day. There was a light powdering of snow over the roads and fields, which is something we don't see every year down in the far west. I stood at the window at the head of the stairs — over the entrance portico — waiting for the sunrise, which would happen in about five minutes. My grandmother could not bear to be wakened before sunrise in winter.

We could not see the eastern horizon from Fenton Lodge. Swanpool headland was in the way. But there was not a cloud in the sky that morning — indeed, the vault of the heavens was already blood-red, an omen of storms to come — so I knew I should see the change of colour as the rising sun gilded the walls of Pendennis Castle, which was just slightly north of east from that window. I should also see it redden the rocks and bare-branched trees on Pennance Point, away to my right.

I remember thinking how curious it was that Susan's baby had been conceived (like many of Falmouth's firstborn) in one or other of those places — either in the thickets of rhododendrons between the castle and the battery on Pendennis, or among the leaf-mouldy undergrowth and ferny hollows of Pennance. She said she couldn't be sure but by rights it ought to be Pennance. Not being Cornish, she pronounced it *penance,* whereas we say *p'nance*. 'Penance,' she said was just about right for her!

I was letting my mind run along these inconsequential lines so as to avoid another omen of storms to come — not the shepherd's-warning red in the skies above but the letter from India that lay among the rest of that morning's post on the tray I was about to take in to my grandmother's bedside.

It required a supreme effort of will not to open that letter and brave the old woman's wrath. After all, a little devil within was whispering to me, the Wilkinsons had no right to reply to *my* letter in this way —

trusting that Mrs T would deal with me and stop me being such a nuisance to them. It was *not* their private affair. They had broken the law, or at the very least had stretched it to its limits. And should *I* then act as their helpless messenger — being forced to carry unopened a correspondence designed to thwart me, to cheat me of my legal rights once again?

I lifted it, slipped the edge of my thumbnail under the corner of the flap ... and hesitated.

The sky changed from blood-red to bronze. Saved by the dawn! It was time to carry in her early morning tea. I decided on a slightly more honourable course than the simple one of intercepting the letter. I slipped the envelope into my pinafore pocket, opened my grandmother's door, and started to carry out my plan before I could have second thoughts. It was so reckless — so unlike me! Yet I was suddenly filled with a most wonderful feeling of calm.

"Good morning, Mrs Trevarton!" I called out with the sort of joviality she hated at that hour. "It's a crisp winter day and a white world outside." I planted the tray at her bedside and set about pouring her cup of tea.

"What? Eh?" She groaned as she fought her way back to consciousness. Her cheeks were sunken and gray — a sign she had been having bad dreams. The product of a bad conscience, I often thought. "Don't be so cheerful, gel. You know how I detest it at this hour. What's that?"

"Your tea," I said, placing the cup at her side.

"No — *that!*"

She made a snatch for the letter but I stepped nimbly back. "It's from your Uncle Redvers," I said.

She, of course, was not used to thinking of him as 'Uncle' so her face creased in bewilderment.

"I'm going to read it to you," I added matter-of-factly as I drew wide the curtains.

She blinked at the sudden brightness but her eyes soon grew accustomed to it. During that time she realized at last who I was talking about — and what I had just said. Her expression darkened and she reached out an imperious hand. "You'll do no such thing," she snapped. "Give it to me at once!"

I took it out of my pocket.

She relaxed, grimly satisfied that her will had prevailed.

I stuck my nail under the gummed-down flap.

"At once!" she roared.

I slit the envelope open. "Postmarked Mysore, twelfth of December last," I remarked. "Mine to him got there pretty quickly, then."

"Yours to him?" she echoed, but the peremptory tone was now absent from her voice.

I think that was the moment when she realized this was no juvenile game of mistaken high spirits on my part — something she could quell with a few sharp words. There was a sudden watchfulness in her gray, basilisk eyes.

"Dated the same," I said, beginning to read the contents. "'Dear Agatha ...'"

"Give it to me, gel." Now her tone was low and menacing. "If you persist in this defiance, I shall make you very sorry for it."

I ignored her. "'I enclose a copy of a most vexatious letter from Christobel' — misspelled, I see — 'Moore. I thought you said you could manage her? It really is too bad. Minty was quite prostrate on reading it and ...'"

"Cristobel!" My grandmother spoke my name with quiet menace. I could not remember her ever calling me anything but 'Miss Moore.' It almost threw me off my stride. "This is your last chance. If you persist in this trespass upon my private correspondence, I shall have you whipped. I mean it."

I leaned against the brass rail at the foot of her bed and stared straight into her eyes. I honestly no longer cared whether she meant it or not. I was free of her at last — emotionally and in spirit. I was quietly drunk on my freedom. "Don't you understand?" I asked.

To my amazement she lowered her eyes and said nothing.

In something of a daze — being unready for her submission — I returned to the letter: "'Minty was quite prostrate on reading it and took to her bed for several days. When Miss C went to St Breaca's and made all that fuss' — that must be me ... Miss C — ' and made all that fuss, I told you we should call it off. Sister Enuda got the measure of her at once. She wanted to call it off, too, you remember? But no — you insisted you could control her. And now this!' New paragraph. 'What are we to do? Frankly, I'm inclined to put Teresa in charge of the first family back to England, with a label round her neck directed to you. She does nothing but mope for her brothers and sisters anyway, though lately she's been settling down better, I must allow. We were just beginning to entertain some hope of becoming true parents to her when this letter arrives out of the blue and we are all at sixes and sevens again.' New paragraph. 'By the time you receive this we shall probably have settled somewhat, and for the second time. But you really must do something' — underlined — 'about Christobel. As you'll see, she hints in her letter to us that she might be willing to accept the status quo as long as she and her brothers and sisters may correspond with Teresa. Reasonable enough on the face of it. But is it just a ruse to keep in touch and poison the girl against us at some later time, once we have made her truly our daughter? What we know of your Christobel's behaviour so far does not inspire confidence.' Aaargh!"

I gave a strangulated cry of frustration and tossed the remainder of the letter at my grandmother — unread, though there were several pages more of this maudlin twaddle. "How could you?" I asked her. "The man's nothing but an old maid. In fact, that's an insult to old maids. How could you entrust your granddaughter into his care? You make me *sick* — all of you!"

The bed shook.

I realized she was trembling with rage.

She moved so swiftly that I became aware of events in the wrong order. There was a crash of china behind me that seemed to have nothing to do with her. Then I saw a huge, dark octopus-shaped wetness materialize on the wallpaper behind her. Then a cup whizzed past my ear. Then I saw her arm move.

"Out!" she shrieked, finding her voice at last. "Get out of this room! Out of my sight! Out of my house!"

I was already gone.

Mrs Bourdeaux hurried past me out on the landing. "What ever is the matter this morning?" she asked, half-fearful, half-excited.

"Last autumn I wrote to General Sir Redvers Wilkinson in India," I explained. "You know who I mean?"

She nodded tersely.

"I've just read Mrs Trevarton his reply."

I realized she assumed it was the General's reply to me, for she would certainly have been furious to know I had opened and read a letter addressed to our mistress. Before I could explain, however, we became aware that the old woman was no longer shouting her curses after me. In fact there was a strange silence from her bedroom. Perhaps she'd found something of interest in the portion of the letter I hadn't yet read.

"I'm going to pack my things, Mrs Bourdeaux," I said wearily.

"Don't!" she called back over her shoulder as she hastened to my grandmother's bedroom. "Don't do anything irrevocable yet."

But I was quite determined to leave that day. I'd have luncheon with Jim and we'd send a telegram to Miss Martin. The sense of relief was enormous. I smiled, for I knew exactly what Jim was going to say. The last words he had spoken to me on the subject of leaving Fenton Lodge and going to work at Little Sinns was that I'd no doubt find my own way of breaking the news *gently* to my grandmother!

I packed the trunk first, with all the things I should not immediately need. I could send for it in a day or two. My overnight requirements and the things I should wear during the first week went into a gladstone bag, light enough for me to carry into town. I was halfway through filling it when Susan slipped into the room and said, "What ever happened this morning? Did she throw a cup of tea at you? There's tea all over the wall behind her."

"Like an octopus."

"Yeah!" She laughed and then became serious again. "Doctor Mayer's here. It looks pretty bad." Her eyes took in the scene and her jaw dropped. "You're not ... not leaving?"

I nodded. "What looks pretty bad? My grandmother?"

"A plethora of blood, they say." She tapped her temple.

"A stroke?"

She shrugged. "What's going to become of us? She can't talk. She can't move none of her left side. She can just scribble on a pad a little. She can't read anything you hold up to her but she can hear — a bit. At least, they think she can. I don't know what's to become of us."

I put an arm about her shoulder and gave her a little hug of encouragement. "Buck up," I urged. "You know what *could* become of you — if you were sensible. You'd have a nice little business of your own. And a house. And your baby."

"But I love him and he loves me," she replied. "We want to get married. We're *going to* get married."

"And *your* friends will laugh at you for getting ideas above your station. And *his* friends will cut him because they can't invite him anywhere without his wife — and they won't invite you. We've been through all this, Sue."

"Why are you leaving?"

"Mark can afford it, you know. And he jolly well ought to pay — the way he's used you."

"Where are you going?"

I told her then, about my letter to the Wilkinsons and their reply and what I'd done with it. And the more I explained the more her jaw dropped and the harder she stared at me. Almost every statement of mine she greeted with "You didn't!" or "She never!" or some such empty contradiction. Finally I told her of Miss Martin's offer and said I'd be taking it up and working as a teacher at Little Sinns for the next few years.

"And you mean you could have gone there at any time over the last few months?" she asked. "Why didn't you?"

"How could I? Just suppose I'd been over in Redruth today — with that letter coming from India and me knowing nothing about it!"

"And that's why you stayed?" she asked incredulously.

She still didn't understand how I felt about my family.

I went and had luncheon with Jim and we composed a telegram ready to send to Little Sinns, saying I'd arrive on Friday. I delayed only because Mrs Bourdeaux made such a special point of asking me not to go just yet. And, as things turned out, she had a far better idea of what was going on than I did.

I returned to Fenton Lodge that evening and asked her several times if I might see my grandmother but she said the old woman was adamant — I was not to go near her.

When I awoke the following morning I saw my trunk, all packed and standing by the door, and I realized I had no duties there if my grandmother still refused to see me. I rose nonetheless and went down to see if I could help the housekeeper.

I met her standing by the window where I had stood a mere twenty-four hours earlier, tempting myself to open that letter. The moment she saw me she gave a wan little smile and, gliding toward my grandmother's bedroom, beckoned me to follow. She must have been waiting for me.

As I entered the room I knew my grandmother had died during the night. Death has such an unmistakable presence. And the stillness of a dead person is not the stillness of a table or a rock, nor even of a waxwork figure. It is a stillness like nothing else on earth.

I went to her bedside and, not knowing what else to do, touched her on the brow. It was cold and waxy. She had been dead for some hours.

I knelt and prayed for a few minutes — trying hard not to think all the selfish, or self-centred, thoughts that would naturally crowd one's mind at such a moment.

When I had finished, Mrs Bourdeaux nudged my arm and I saw she was offering me a sheet of paper. "I think you ought to read this before I burn it," she said.

It was penned in the housekeeper's hand and it read: 'Codicil to my Last Will and Testament. I, Agatha Trevarton, née Wilkinson, widow of William Trevarton of Fenton Lodge, being of sound mind and being convinced of my own imminent decease, do hereby revoke that portion of my Last Will and Testament in which I have bequeathed the sum of one thousand pounds (£1,000) to my maid Miss Cristobel Moore. The said thousand pounds is instead to be distributed equally among my surviving children.'

There followed a scrawl that might charitably be called my grandmother's signature. Beneath, to witness, were the undoubted signatures of Mr and Mrs Bourdeaux.

A lamp still burned at the bedside. The housekeeper picked it up and carried it over to the fireplace, where the fire had burned itself out overnight. "Come on," she urged me.

"I don't understand," I said, not moving from the bedside. "A bequest to me? The one from my grandfather?"

"No. It's simple enough. She destroyed the codicil your grandfather wrote — as you know. But then she got an attack of conscience and rewrote her will to leave you the money after all — so that, although you were denied the benefit of the bequest as long as she might live, your curses should not follow her into eternity. But last night she took against you so strongly, she no longer cared. So she wrote that." She pointed to the sheet in my hand. "And now, if you please, we'll burn it, too." She laughed grimly. "Surely you see the justice of it, don't you?"

Very soon after I came to Fenton Lodge I realized that my life as a young, unmarried servant girl was a great deal more free than the lives of my mistress and her friends — and of their young, unmarried daughters. Convention bound them hand and foot. The magazines called them 'ladies of leisure' but their days were as regulated as those of any convicts at hard labour, and even their genuine hours of ease were fraught with perils — watched over by servants indoors and by a thousand unseen eyes outside. No wonder they were ailing most of the time.

My modest inheritance of a thousand pounds revealed that money, too, was something of a mixed blessing. People talk about the power of money, meaning the power of the rich to get things done, to have their own way, to prevail over the poor. All I can say is that trying to grasp that power and hold it is like trying to trap quicksilver.

If you haven't got money, you can't argue about what to do with it — which makes life very simple. You manage without it as best you can and you buy your pleasures by the pennyworth. You plan your life a week ahead and you leave the real future to the gods — or to Hardy's President of the Immortals. But an inheritance changes all that. It doesn't so much give you *a* future, it gives you a dozen possible futures and suddenly *you* have to choose. It took me some time to realize this — consciously, anyway, though I suppose that underneath my immediate happiness the thought was nagging away, as thoughts always seem to do with me. It's a good thing that wills take such an unconscionable time to go through probate.

My very first reaction was, naturally, that Jim and I should marry as soon as possible. People would shake their heads when the news got out, and they'd watch my shape over the coming months as eagerly as we were starting to watch poor Susan's! And, when I disappointed them on that score, they'd no doubt predict all kinds of disaster, attendant on our unseemly haste to get to the altar. But they couldn't peer into our hearts and minds and see how closely bound we already were in spirit. Jim and I were so absolutely right for each other and so happy in each other's company — happy in a firm, calm way — that we could sometimes walk an hour together hardly saying a word. How dull, some might say. But we returned from such promenades refreshed, invigorated, and with our love eternally renewed.

But for some reason, which Jim was unwilling to share with me, he rejected my offer. No — even that is not true. He didn't exactly reject it, not outright, not in so many words. But he didn't accept it, either. He just gave a confident little smile and said he was already pursuing one or two other lines of inquiry (which he would also not share with me) and could we leave it at that for the moment?

If only he had said, 'Rest assured, my darling, we shall be married as soon as possible — into our own home and with our own little business for support.' That's all I wanted to know. I didn't care a hoot whether it came about thanks to my money or through some clever scheme of his. But by excluding me from his plans he made it seem that my money was his last resort, the last thing he wanted to touch. And, by the same token, it implied that he thought me altogether *too* eager to help him — who was dearer to me than life itself — which, if it had been true, implied that I had no faith in *his* ability to raise the capital. What a tangled web!

None of this was said, of course, but such thoughts went round and round in my head and they must have occurred to him, too.

Perhaps it was just as well, I consoled myself bleakly. I was sick in love with him to the point where I risked losing my own self entirely. Or, not entirely but to a dangerous extent. A touch of emotional independence might be no bad thing. The trouble is you can *think* such thoughts easily enough but it doesn't help you to *feel* them. And the sadness of this tiny estrangement between us continued to make me melancholy whenever we were not actually together.

To bring us closer I decided to take lodgings in the same boarding house as Jim. He had lately moved to a new landlady up in Woodhouse Terrace, overlooking the whole of Falmouth Harbour. But then — typical of me, blowing all ways at once — I decided that might be dangerous — not just in the obvious way but because there were other decisions I ought to take, about my family and what to do now that I could afford to bring us all together. And if Jim was going to arrange his affairs without consulting me, then I should decide mine alone, too, before risking such closeness. For the meanwhile, then, I stayed on at Fenton Lodge as a sort of phantom companion — that is, a companion to nobody. To the ghost of my mother — and of hers. I was not waited on, nor did I wait on anyone else.

Even so, the Bourdeaux began to treat me as the mistress of the household — because, I suppose, they felt rudderless without *someone* to occupy such a position. They tried going to Mark for their daily orders but he was so shaken by his mother's death that he just said they were to do whatever they thought she would have told them. So then they began turning to me. But not in a straightforward way. Mrs Bourdeaux never said, "What are your orders, ma'am?" or anything so obvious. Instead she'd find some occasion to meet me 'accidentally' somewhere about the house, and then she'd say, almost off-handedly, "I thought we might turn out the box room this morning," or, "It might be a good idea to get the sofa reupholstered, d'you think? Now we're likely to have few callers for a while." It was a curious way of carrying on, almost as if I were an alternative housekeeper — not the *real* one but one waiting in the wings, as it were, one who had to be included and kept up to date on the domestic arrangements. Of course, I never queried her decisions or made alternative suggestions. Nor did I so much as hint that I was giving my approval. My attitude was that I appreciated her courtesy in keeping me informed. No more than that. It sounds odd when I try to describe it now, yet it seemed easy and natural at the time.

But in my heart-of-hearts I knew that staying on at Fenton Lodge was really just a way of postponing any decision. I was grateful for one fact, though — that an inheritance of a thousand pounds wasn't large enough to interest any of Falmouth's upper-crust mothers with an impecunious younger son who needed the support of a well-dowried wife. With a mere thou' coming my way I remained not-quite-a-lady. Had I inherited twenty thou', you may be sure that my Trevarton lineage and the fact that my mother had married respectably and had not been 'a ruin'd maid' at the time of her elopement would be remembered on every hand. And then I should have been found chaperons for every hour of the clock and there would have been a miraculous draught of invitations with every post. The big wide world that now opened before me would have been reduced at once to the drawing rooms of Wood Lane, Florence Terrace, and Alma Crescent. And doctors of the mind, the body, and the soul would have been engaged to argue me out of my betrothal to that common little photographer's assistant.

It was the unexpected arrival of Cousin Stella at Fenton Lodge that finally stirred up some action. She claimed she had returned because, while Mark remained at the house, it could not run without a mistress — which I interpreted as meaning he would find a mistress of his own if she were not there to stop him. Secretly I suspected that her meagre life as perpetual dependant at Nancekuke made even this semi-exile beyond the Falmouth suburbs seem attractive.

In fact, between us we considered every reason but the obvious one — which was that Walter and Felicity had spoken to her about Susan's interesting condition and she realized that *something* had to be done before it became too obvious to pass off as a mere putting-on of weight.

Her original intention was to come on the eighth of March, a Sunday, but the weather turned bitterly cold and, by the following morning the famous Great Blizzard had started. It snowed a day and a night without stopping, and the accompanying gales smashed up ships in every 'safe' anchorage around the coast. The harbour gates at Penzance were wrenched off their mighty hinges as if they were a child's toy. And no traffic moved, not even on the railways.

I'm ashamed to say we had rather a jolly time of it at Fenton Lodge. We had a well-stocked pantry and plenty of firing, and, to raise poor Mark's spirits out of their melancholy, we played games and charades, and read stories aloud all that day. At teatime, when the blizzard abated to a mere storm, Jim fashioned a pair of snowshoes out of tennis racquets and struggled over to join us. He and Mark spent the evening in the cellar, making a toboggan out of old floorboards and gas-piping. He delayed so long that he ended up kipping with us for the night, sleeping in Mark's room.

Later, when Susan and I were in our beds, she giggled and said it was all wrong — she and Mark should swap beds for the night. She must have thought I was shocked, for I made no reply. The truth was, so many responses occurred to me that I was left tongue-tied. I had so often wanted to ask her what it was like to *lie with* a man, as the Bible puts it, but now that she'd offered me the best chance I was ever likely to get, the words deserted me. Also the suggestion that I might *lie with* Jim (of course, I'd often thought about it in my own mind — but I mean the suggestion coming from outside like that) ... it made my heart flutter so wildly that, even if I'd had the words on the tip of my tongue, I'd have been too frightened to utter them.

Anyway, as I was saying, the Great Blizzard made it impossible for Cousin Stella to come that Sunday — indeed, all that week. And we took advantage of the snows to exhaust ourselves outdoors — on the toboggan ... in building a snowman ... in snowball fights ... and a grand igloo-making contest. By the Friday, though — Cornwall being Cornwall — the snows had all but gone, leaving sodden little remnants under hedges and round corners, where it had drifted deepest. And Cousin Stella moved in on the following Sunday, the day before the anniversary of our mother's funeral. She announced she would be staying until Archie, Walter, and Mark decided what to do with the house, which they had inherited equally under their father's will.

Probate would not be granted for some time on my grandmother's will, so I still did not have any money of my own. In fact — on paper — I was about twelve stomach-churning pounds in debt. The family agreed that it would have been quite inappropriate for me to remain as a 'menial' in Mark's household, so Walter's solution, as executor of his mother's will, was to advance me a pound a week. Actually, he said I could have whatever I needed. The pound a week was my decision. I dearly wanted to go and see Marian, of course, but not if it was going to run me even more heavily into debt. In any case, Miss Martin was going to pay her Hampstead aunt a visit at the end of April and she had asked me to accompany her then.

I did use my new-found leisure to pay a couple of visits to my brothers, both Gerald and Arthur in Plymouth and Tom at Tywardreath. I found them all much happier than they had been the previous summer — which I had, in any case, already gathered from their occasional grudging replies to my letters to them. I thought Gerald and Arthur were a bit on the thin side, but they were energetic and lively and, from what I saw of their schoolwork, doing very well at the three Rs, too. Part of me, I'm ashamed to admit, was crestfallen at this. Had they been miserable and ill-used, it would have spurred me to do something about it. The temptation to leave well alone was getting stronger with every month that passed. I did not mention my windfall to the two younger ones — which, I suppose, was another aspect of 'leaving well alone.' I saw no reason to unsettle them until I actually had the money and, indeed, knew whether or not Jim would be needing it for his — I mean *our* — business.

I did tell Tom, however. He, too, was now happily settled in at the farm school. He admitted he'd been bullied quite badly at the beginning but once he'd knocked old Cobbo's teeth out — old Cobbo being the ringleader of the bullies — he'd been left alone. I said I hoped he had not become a bully himself. He smirked and said some of the 'young 'uns' deserved the odd toe-tap. He then explained that a toe-tap was where a gang of you hold a boy down while one of you grips his bare foot in one hand and smashes the other fist down on his toes as hard as you can. The 'young 'uns' he mentioned were either his own age or a few months younger at most. I had sometimes despaired of understanding boys when we had all been together as a family. On that afternoon I think I gave up altogether.

He was delighted at the news of my inheritance and came out at once with plans for a pig farm. Magnanimously he added that I could go partners with him — as long as I didn't interfere. We could start small, he said, and he knew just the place — on the banks of the Cober, at the foot of the hill called Castle Wary, due east of Helston. For an outlay of a mere fifty pounds we could build sties for five gilts, who would produce a hundred weaners a year between them, which we could fatten on for bacon at fivepence a pound or pork at sevenpence or more. We could make a clear profit of forty pounds a year, which, if we ploughed it back, and continued to plough it back for the next ten years, would make us the biggest pig-farmers and pork-butchers in Cornwall.

"Farm-to-table," he said, his eyes all aglow.

He had it all worked out to the last little curly tail. I had a terrible sinking feeling that it was going to cost me fifty pounds (at least) to retain his affection and teach him what Burns said about the best-laid schemes of mice and men. Just as a test I asked him if he wanted to start at once or would he wait until I'd got a house where the whole family could be together once again. His face fell and I saw that the rest of us had no place in his dreams at all — except me as what he called a 'sleeping partner' — i.e., a cheap and friendly banker.

I returned to Swanpool that evening to find a letter from Marian describing some beautiful 'and really very sensible' clothes that were presently in a sale at Shoolbred's in Tottenham Court Road and could I possibly advance her the five pounds, which she would promise faithfully to pay back before Christmas?

But I digress still further.

It was, as I said, Cousin Stella who broke this logjam of plans and expectations — my own and everybody's else — by her sudden arrival for an indefinite stay at Fenton Lodge. From the very beginning she treated me as a sort of unofficial — and even unacknowledged — companion, which inevitably meant that she, for her part, became my unofficial — and certainly unacknowledged — chaperon. I did not greatly object to this curtailment of my liberty, which was modest in any case. I have already remarked that unbounded freedom (like modest wealth) is not the blessing one might imagine it to be.

She asked for me to be seated with her at dinner on the evening of her arrival. It was the first time I was served by any of the staff in that house and I must say I felt uncomfortable to be taking my meat and vegetables from dishes held by Bourdeaux and young Weeks. They had both ribbed me so often in the servants' hall — and I, them. But they now assumed the dignified mien of an assize-court judge. I tried winking at Weeks but he pursed his lips severely and looked annoyed at me. What curious creatures we are!

Cousin Stella (as I was now asked to call her) watched me carefully during that first meal, no doubt assessing my ladylike qualities. I don't think she had any actual plans for me at that stage but the possibility that she might have to develop some sooner or later must already have crossed her mind. A young maid alone in the world and with a thousand pounds suddenly dropped into her lap was a potentially loose canon that would have to be secured, one way or another — preferably by marriage. I must have passed her scrutiny without too many poor marks for she made no comment.

She liked what she called 'a glass' of port after her meal, by which she usually meant a good half-decanter. (So, too, by the way did old Bourdeaux, who was delighted to have her back in the house, for her raids on the decanter gave him what Weeks called 'covering fire.' The bottles fairly flew out of the cellar.) She did not drink it at the table, as men like to do, but she'd sit by the drawing-room fire taking sip after sip and staring into the flames with eyes that grew ever more misty as glass followed glass. And occasionally she would sigh.

I, with my horror of alcohol ever since the wine from the *Sprue* turned sour in our bath, paced her sip for sip in elderflower cordial and sketched little fragments of still-life here and there about the room.

After her thirtieth sip, and her third heavy sigh, she turned her eyes upon me and said, "Susan, eh! What's to be done about that gel?"

"Ah!" I was taken by surprise and did not know whether to fall in with her at once, or to feign ignorance, or to do what most women would have done, I suppose, which was to ask delicate, probing questions to discover first how much *she* knew.

"The present situation cannot continue for very much longer," she said. "Her condition is already apparent — at least to one who has been away from this house for some months. Perhaps you would notice it less, being here all the time."

If either of the elder Trevarton sons had canvassed my opinion, I'm sure I should have answered them quite straightforwardly. But Cousin Stella was a Wilkinson and I could not forget it. An Agatha Wilkinson had broken my family up. A Redvers Wilkinson had kidnapped my youngest sister. And now here was a Stella Wilkinson asking me how she could best interfere in the life of one of my dearest friends: "What's to be done about that gel?" It was the wrong question at the wrong time and I was the wrong one to answer it.

I said, "What *is* it about you Wilkinsons, eh? Why must you forever interfere in other people's lives? You leave nothing but misery in your wake — and it doesn't even make you happy!"

She set her glass down abruptly and her eyes filled with tears.

I was mortified, of course, and full of shame at my outburst. I sort of fell across the carpet, landing on my knees in front of her, saying, "Oh *do* forgive me, Cousin Stella. That was quite unwarranted. You are the one Wilkinson who has never interfered in anyone's life as far as I know. I had no right to vent my anger on you. Say you forgive me — please?"

I touched her cheek and bit my lip and prepared to smile if she'd give me the chance.

She actually laughed! She also cried, or, rather, she blinked away her tears and dabbed them into the crocheted mittens she always wore of an evening, but she laughed as well.

"I shan't forgive myself so easily," I said, rising to my feet again. "But I'm glad you haven't taken it amiss. You're the last person in the world I'd want to offend."

"The reason I'm laughing," she said as she dabbed her eyes one final time, "is that — of course — the one topic I truly wish to discuss with you, my dear, is your own family and the lamentable consequences of ... well, you put it with devastating candour, but who can deny it? — the consequences of Wilkinson interference. But I thought it might take days, if not weeks, of getting to know you before I'd dare raise the matter! I should have known better. Your grandmother did warn me."

Her last remark puzzled me and for one idiotic moment I wondered if she'd been attending séances and playing with ouija boards.

She saw my embarrassed hesitation and added in a gently reproachful voice, *"Before* she died, actually. Did you think we never discussed you, Agatha and I?"

I apologized once again, resumed my seat opposite her, and sipped my cordial. It reminded her of her port, which she picked up again with new relish and drained in one. I rose, crossed the room, and returned with the decanter, which I left on the table at her side.

"Perhaps just a little tot to help me sleep," she said as if it would be her first of the evening. She filled the glass to within a hairsbreadth of the brim, leaned over and sipped it down to a safe level, and then sat back heavily in her chair. "Agatha was terrified out of her wits by you," she said.

I let the words echo several times in my mind and still believed I must have misheard her.

"She was," she asserted when she saw that I could only stare.

"Of me?"

"Of you."

"But why?"

She shrugged. Her expression hinted she was already wishing she hadn't mentioned it. "Because you did — terrify her, I mean."

"But I had no intention of it. I'll swear such a thought never once occurred to me."

"I can believe that!" she exclaimed with a sort of heartfelt hollowness that only deepened my bewilderment.

"I don't wish to frighten anybody — except myself at times, perhaps. When I think I deserve it."

"And when *do* you think you deserve it?"

I'd made the remark without really thinking, the way one does. "Oh," I replied vaguely, "when I say nasty, untrue things like I said to you just now. Sudden, vicious temper like that — it frightens me."

"Ah!" Her voice softened and a faraway look came into her eyes. "You don't remember Muffet, do you?" she said. "Little Miss Muffet."

"The nursery rhyme?"

"No, the cat. Agatha's cat. She said you reminded her of Muffet."

I remembered a stone out in the garden, engraved with the words *Little Miss Muffet.* It had never occurred to me it might be a pet's grave. "Why?" I asked.

"She was a strange cat — little Muffet. Well, all cats are strange but she stood out even so. She was one of the most beautiful creatures you ever saw, for a start ..."

"Well, *there* we part company already!" I exclaimed.

She waved this away as mere false modesty, not worth a comment. "She was black from head to foot except for white paws and a white shirt front. Very neat and delicate." She patted her bosom. "She'd often come in here of an evening — if we were sitting like this — she'd come in here and absolutely *beg* to be taken up." Suiting action to words, she bent and raised an imaginary cat up to her lap. "You'd stroke her ..."

Cousin Stella stroked the invisible cat so realistically that the skin prickled on the back of my neck as I struggled to assure myself there was no actual cat there.

"And she'd purr ... and purr ... and purr. And then all of a sudden — in mid-purr even — bang! She'd flip her head right round and sink her teeth and claws into you!"

"Oh! Thank you very much for the comparison!" I said sarcastically.

She laughed. "Don't misunderstand me, dear — anyway, it's not my comparison but Agatha's. Muffet didn't do it to hurt. I mean, she didn't draw blood. Well — not usually. She would if you went on and on and provoked her to — but normally she didn't. She'd just get her teeth in so far and then stop."

"I still don't see ..."

"It wasn't the savagery. It was the suddenness of the transformation. It reminded one that just a fraction of an inch under that sleek, very domesticated fur — and beneath the meek and civilized 'please will you take me on your lap?' — was a magnificent untamed creature of single-minded purpose. That's what reminded her of Muffet when she first met you — have you forgotten? When she had to lock you in the attics to cool off?"

"There was not the slightest necessity ..." I began. Then I gave up, for we were getting nowhere. "It doesn't matter now. Jim Collett has patted me on the head a thousand times since then and I've never sunk my teeth into him once — so there!"

"Ah," she said, slightly embarrassed.

"Surely someone has told you of our engagement?" I asked.

She nodded and smiled.

"Another topic you were going to work around to one fine week?" I suggested.

"Too many." She smiled into her glass and then downed it as she had its predecessor. "Topics, I mean," she said — in case I supposed she meant glasses of port! "Tomorrow, if this improvement in the weather continues, we shall go for a nice long drive. To Helford perhaps."

I said, "To Helston churchyard, I think."

I made up a small wreath of my grandfather's hothouse carnations and wrote two little tickets of remembrance, one with his name and one with ours, me and my brothers and sisters. My good angel urged me to add my father's name to the dedication — he was, after all, interred in the same plot — and my grandmother's name beside my grandfather's, but I could not do it. A year was too soon. The scars had not yet healed.

Cousin Stella noticed the omission. She asked if she might add her own name to that of my grandfather, but when she handed me back the ticket I saw she had added my grandmother's, too. I said nothing. As for the omission of my father's name, as soon as we were off in the gig, she said, "He was a good man at heart, you know — your father. I thought that whole business could have been handled so much better."

I asked her to tell me about it for it was something our mother had spoken of sparingly.

"Your grandparents were too close to see it," she said. "It was quite obvious to everyone else that your father was a cut or two above your ordinary coachman-groom. Did you ever know his people?"

"No," I admitted. "Not until recently. Jim's aunt and uncle told me something about them. His sister is the postmistress at Nancekuke, funnily enough."

She was amazed. "What — Ellen Ivory? I've known her for centuries but I didn't know that!"

"She was born Ellen Moore. She married Billy Ivory ..."

"Yes, I know all that. But I never knew she was a Moore — much less Barry's sister. What else?"

"He had a brother, Anthony, in the Royal Navy, who may or may not be alive, still. They think his mother *is* still alive, Mary Moore. She was a Jeffries. She's housekeeper to some vicar up Bolventor way. That's all. Ellen Ivory is the only one they knew of hereabout."

"Well, well, well! We knew nothing of that. Your father was a mystery. But — had it been properly managed — it could all have turned out so differently. Agatha was to blame for that, I'm sorry to say. But Bill was at fault, too. He should have been firmer with her instead of letting himself be dragged along in her wake. The follies we commit for love! It was all folly — and all because of love. Barry did the honourable thing when Selina was all set to run away with him. He went directly to Bill and confessed the whole thing. He asked for her hand in marriage in a straightforward, honourable fashion." She shook her head sadly. "That was the moment when it could have been saved."

Then she turned to me suddenly and asked, "What would you have done, Crissy? Try to put yourself in your grandparents' place now. The coachman comes to you out of the blue and asks for your daughter's hand — what's your answer?"

I was not ready for such a question. My mind had slipped into the sort of semi-trance in which a child listens to a fairy tale. Had I been five years old, my thumb would have been in my mouth and my eyes wide open. "I'd have ... well, I suppose I'd have said yes," I stammered.

There were only two possible answers — yes or no. My grandparents had said no, so yes had to be right.

Cousin Stella dismissed this with a single sarcastic grunt. "What old Bill should have said was neither yes nor yet no. He should have said, 'Here's fifty pounds, my lad. Go off and start your own business. Stay away from my daughter for three years. And if, at the end of that time, you've got five hundred put by and the business is thriving, I'll double it. And if you still wish to marry her and she still wants you, I'll throw her in for nothing!' That's what he should have said. Poor Barry would never have gone to the bad, then. The pain of three years' separation would have tempered his mettle. Success like that would have given him the self-confidence he later sought at the bottom of a bottle. And acceptance — social acceptance — would have welded him into the Trevarton family. It would all have been so different."

By now I was having to breathe deeply and keep swallowing and sniffing to stop myself from bursting into tears. I had a sudden picture of my father — our father — standing before that dear sweet man, our grandfather, waiting in agony for his reply. The scene was before my mind's eye, as real as the day. It was our father as I could *just* remember him — handsome, tall, confident ... impressive. I felt desperate to burst into their long-lost world and take them by the arms and shake them and shout, 'Stop! Think! This is the moment on which *everything* depends — all our lives. Do it right!'

I believe I must have been on the verge of fainting. There was a sort of distant, muted roaring in my ears — deep inside them — and everything around me suddenly assumed the crystal-sharp clarity you often get in dreams. I could not see the hedges — the totality of things — but I could see each tiny green bud on every twig, and every silver dewdrop on each blade of grass. It lasted only a second or two (I think) and when I emerged from it a great pall of sadness settled over me, over us, over the whole of Cornwall. It was a rather impersonal sadness — not mine but something universal, like air and sky. It was more than the sadness of realizing that I had no possible means of going back to a time before I was born (which sounds absurd when you put it into actual words) and breaking into that scene and setting our family's history off on an entirely different path. It was also the sadness of realizing that I myself actually *was* in a scene like that — now — this afternoon — tonight — tomorrow ... In fact, I was living in one all the time. I was held for ever in a situation that some as-yet-unborn child of *mine* might feel just as desperate to break into, fifteen or twenty years hence, and shout warnings in *my* ear ...

It was the first time in my life that I became aware that decisions are for life. Poverty had led me to feel they were good for a week at most.

Cousin Stella, slightly embarrassed that her re-enactment of a battle she must have fought, in her own mind if not with my grandparents, had produced such an emotional effect upon me, began to gently mock the idea. "But perhaps all is for the best," she said airily. "The Trevartons, as you know, were unlucky with girls. You and Marian would both be in great demand for dynastic alliances — no love matches for either of you! And even young Teresa ..." Her voice trailed off with deliberate delicacy. "Talking of whom ..." she said. "Or shall we not? Which shall it be — a certain love match with Mister Collett ... or Teresa?"

I had to laugh. Sometimes, if you're going to manipulate a person's feelings, the best way to do it is openly and blatantly. "They're two sides of the same coin," I replied. "What I want to do is to marry Jim and use part of my inheritance to bring Teresa back to live with us — and Gerald and Arthur, too."

"And Tom and Marian?"

"I'd give them fair shares — say, a hundred and fifty each. Something like that — which would leave a bit over, which would pay for a proper grave for our parents."

"So you'd be giving Mister Collett a reach-me-down family! What does he think of the idea?"

"We haven't ... I mean, I haven't actually put it to him, yet. Not in so many words."

She stared at me in surprise.

"The inheritance has really brought nothing but division between us," I explained.

"Ah! When was it ever different?"

We had traversed the whole of Goblin Bank by now and I was having to haul hard on the brake as we went down into the valley before the equally stiff climb up to Penjerick. Between gasps of effort I explained that Jim didn't appear to want any of my money to help him set up in our own photographic business. That is, he wanted money, of course, but he wanted to raise it on his own.

"Ah! How like your father — he was just the same. And he managed it, too. A wise woman never tries to help a man who's sure he doesn't need it!"

I borrowed a trick of hers, then, which was to ask an awkward question when she was least expecting it. "Tell me why my grandmother took me on as her maid," I said. "Especially if, as you claimed last night, she was somewhat frightened by me."

Perhaps it was a common trick among all the Wilkinsons. Anyway, it didn't take her in the least bit aback. She handed me the reins for a turn and said, "Aggie wanted you where she could keep an eye on you. I didn't know about Bill's codicil until Mrs Bourdeaux told me of it the day I came back. But it explains a lot. It proves that Bill recognized you Moores as *family*. Aggie would have interpreted that as a danger, a threat to *her* brood of Trevartons — or the ones that survived — Archie, Walter, and Mark. So she arranged for the six of you to be scattered abroad, here, there, and everywhere. But in you she saw a particular danger — the way you came straight here after your mother's funeral, demanding your rights ..."

"But I didn't!"

"Well, that's how she saw it. Understand that." She touched my arm gently, as if warning me not to explode. "When it comes to *family*, dear, there's no such thing as truth. There's only the way people see things. She saw you as a threat — you in particular. She knew she'd never have a day's peace if you were over the hills and far away, plotting and scheming to get your brothers and sisters back again — which you *would* have done!" She laughed grimly. "Not that she got much peace *after* you came to Fenton Lodge, either!"

We reached the top of the hill, by the first group of cottages in the hamlet of Penjerick, and I stopped to let the horse get his wind back.

"Also," Cousin Stella said cautiously, "in her own odd, unsatisfactory way, I believe she loved you. Feelings in a family are never simple."

Her voice gathered intensity as she spoke. I was about to protest at this obvious ... well, I shan't call it a lie — let's just say misunderstanding — but her intensity compelled my silence.

"She was born with very little love in her make-up, poor Aggie. And most of that was quenched by the loss of her daughters. She had five of them. You know about all that, I'm sure?"

I nodded. "They all died except my mother," I murmured. I was itching to ask her if Catherine had been Mark's real mother.

"Quite. Aggie hated you at sight. She *knew* you were a threat to the Trevartons. Yet — because of her sad history, I suppose — she could not simply let you go. And then, over the months when you were her maid, something in you fanned and rekindled that last little spark of love in her bosom — and then she really was in despair! We talk euphemistically of death bringing peace — I honestly think it was the only peace she could ever have known after that."

The tears that had never been too far from me since we set out that morning now began to fall. I wept quite silently, in silent shame. There was so much I had not understood before — even about my father, but most particularly about my grandmother and that awkward bitterness which now stood revealed as love, or the nearest thing to it of which she was still capable.

"There!" Cousin Stella said, not soothingly but almost in triumph, as if she had hoped for this outcome. She made to take back the reins but I braced myself, sniffed the salt from my nostrils, and cried "Hoo-ap!" to the horse.

We left Penjerick behind us at a smart trot. The day suddenly brightened. Inexplicably a load had been lifted from me. "What was my mother like before she eloped?" I asked suddenly, but not to startle her this time.

"Rather like your sister Marian," she replied. "Judging from what you've told me."

I could not remember telling her much about Marian at all, but perhaps she was just letting me know in a gentle way that disgruntled servants talk, and so do frustrated housekeepers and tiddly butlers and merry mistresses, and so word gets around anyway.

"Selina was gay and rather feckless. She had a smile for all the world, and a heart to match. That's why no one believed she could be so serious about Barry Moore, you see. Bill was quite sure that if he just said no, she'd mope for a day or two and then be her old bright self. He thought it was one of her happy whimsies — no more than that. And so everyone was quite shattered when she took it seriously and eloped with the fellow. It broke their hearts. Ah well!"

We saved a couple of miles by cutting a corner, passing through Trewoon farm. The farmer wasn't pleased and told us not to do it again, but he didn't turn us back.

Once we gained the main Falmouth — Constantine road we took up a smarter pace.

Cousin Stella said, "Why *did* you come to Fenton Lodge that day? I know Bill went over and put carnations on Selina's grave. Aggie told me of it. But you weren't to know that. What brought you?"

"Our mother told me to go there."

She looked at me sharply. I know people think I'm not quite right in the head, on this one particular point at least, but I *know* my mother spoke to me that morning after her burial. I was *there* and the scoffers weren't. I explained all this to her.

"Are you getting your own back for last night?" she asked wryly. "When *you* thought *I* had been communicating over the Great Divide with Aggie?"

I just tried to laugh it all off. But she wouldn't let it go. "And now we're going to visit her grave again — a year to the very day! What will she advise you to do about Teresa, I wonder?" she mused.

"I think she'll advise me to listen very carefully to *your* opinion on the matter, Cousin Stella," I said.

"Oh, but you are a *Wilkinson!*" she exclaimed with mock petulance, as if 'wilkinson' were a common noun, like 'pest.'

I laughed and asked what on earth she meant by that.

"I mean you have an absolute obsession with family — anything to do with family matters."

"What about you then?"

"It doesn't show in all of us, dear. Nor does it come out in every generation. Marian doesn't have it. Nor did your mother."

"She loved us."

"Oh, but it goes far beyond mere love! It's what I said — obsession. It's bigger than love and hate put together. It's everything ... it's *family!* You know what that word does to you! You have it. Aggie had it. Even dear Redvers in his watered-down way has it."

I thought that 'watered-down' was the best description anyone could imagine for the man who had revealed himself in the letter I read out to my grandmother. I laughed out loud — and then, of course, had to explain why. In fact, I always carried the letter in question around with me, in my pocket book, because it was too dangerous to leave about the house, even in a locked drawer. I passed it to her and she read — and digested it — in silence until we arrived at Constantine.

I've never been able to make up my mind about that village. In some way, which I can't quite put my finger on, it is not like any other Cornish village I know. Perhaps it's because not one of the roads leading into it also leads straight out again. It's something you don't expect to find in a small village of fewer than a hundred houses. It's as if the settlement had once been a fortress, from which every last trace of the original outer walls has long since been effaced. But that sense of a tight little community, embattled and ramparted, has somehow persisted down the years. When we stopped to water the horse we considered knocking at one of the cottages for a 'dish o' tay,' but something about the huddled houses and cheek-by-jowl gardens made us put it off until we reached Gweek, a few miles farther on.

The first thing Cousin Stella said to me once we were on our way again was: "You've had this letter for six weeks, my dear, and you still need *advice?*"

"Why?" I asked, wondering what I had missed. What could be so obvious that she saw it at once?

"Simply post them that ticket with directions to Fenton Lodge! Let them tie it round her neck and send her back with the next family bound for home!"

"Oh," I said bleakly, for I had, of course, considered that.

She was surprised I did not leap at the idea. Perhaps she was right in thinking me a true *Wilkinson* in her sense of the word. Perhaps Sir Redvers and I were more truly Wilkinsons than she was. Reading between his petulant lines, which were, in my opinion, more aimed at scoring off my grandmother than at expressing his true feelings, I could sense that more of him wanted to keep Teresa than to let her go. And if I were right in that, then my Wilkinson instinct told me that nothing would stiffen his resolve better than a provocative act like sending out such a ticket — especially from an 'impertinent and vexatious creature' like me!

Cousin Stella was not at all put out to have so much cold water poured over her brilliant idea. She merely asked me what else I had considered doing.

The honest answer — despite my earlier brave words about marrying Jim and bringing Teresa back home (method unspecified!) to live with us — was that I was tending toward the idea of leaving her with the Wilkinsons out in India — as long as they allowed us to correspond. But Cousin Stella's remarks about my 'obsession' made me too ashamed to confess as much. Instead, I said, hesitantly, "The one remaining weak link in the chain is the convent in Penzance — especially Sister Enuda. I had no idea my visit put her in such a fright. I thought I simply made her angry -- and, since anger is one of the seven deadly sins, I assumed she went off like that rather than lapse from grace."

Cousin Stella's laugh stung me.

"It's jolly well what she *ought* to have done, isn't it?" I challenged her. "As a good Bride of Christ, I mean. It makes life impossible for others when even nuns set out to deceive. Anyway, if she *is* feeling rather uneasy about the way she let my grandmother hustle and bustle her into getting Teresa adopted, I thought I might go back and have another word with her?" I made it sound like a question so as to provoke some opinion from her.

"And then?" was all I got.

"Well, I thought that if I started by being terribly apologetic, and saying I had no *idea* of the true circumstances of the adoption, nor of the way my grandmother had *steamrollered* everyone, and what *must* she have thought of me and would she *ever* forgive me and blah-blah! If I did all that fawning and grovelling and then asked her if she could suggest a way out of the mess ... well, I mean she must have given it *some* thought meanwhile, wouldn't you say? I could at least get an idea of the way her mind is working?"

When she said nothing I prompted her: "Well?"

"Crissy," she said. "Sometimes you frighten even me!"

Then I thought I might as well be hanged for the sheep as well, so I asked her straight out if Mark were truly my grandmother's son.

Her only response was to close her eyes and shake her head. As a gesture it was so ambiguous that either answer — yes or no — could have followed. In fact, all she said was, "That old canard — is it still going the rounds, eh!"

"You mean it's not true after all? He really is my uncle. He's not just my cousin?"

It took a little time for the words to filter through. Then she looked at me, as sharply as before. "Is it important for you to know?"

I could feel the muscles at my temple flexing and my teeth aching with the pressure of my jaw. "Not for me," I said, for I knew what she was thinking. "But it may be for him."

Her eyes fixed themselves in mine. "I see," she said. "Then I'd better tell you, hadn't I. Poor Catherine *did* go to Switzerland to have a baby. And it was a boy. And his name was Mark. But he is buried with her in the same coffin in a little Lutheran churchyard just outside Berne. Aggie had given birth to a baby boy of her own, two weeks earlier. He had not been named when baby Mark died so she gave him his name. Ah me! It is not difficult to see how the rumours began — nor, I suppose, why they have never died down."

As we entered by the churchyard gate my eyes began an anxious search for our parents' grave. I thought memory was playing tricks, for where I expected to see lank grass and weeds, with perhaps just a glimpse of the simple wooden marker and four corner posts the parish had supplied, there stood a handsome slab of pink marble framed in a gothic arch of granite. It is not a large graveyard and I knew I could not possibly be mistaking one part for another. My immediate thought was that *this* was how they treated a pauper grave — they gave it to the next family that came along waving enough money for a proper burial.

I turned to Cousin Stella, a bitter comment on my tongue, only to find her smiling at me the way parents smile when they lead an unsuspecting child into a room where they have a treat prepared.

"You knew!" I accused, caught between annoyance and delight.

She smiled and nodded.

"But you let me bring these!" I shook the now unwanted spade and shears I was carrying. "And when I said about using some of the legacy for ..." I gestured toward the grave and gave up. "Who did it?" I asked.

"Who do you suppose?" she asked in return.

Cousin Stella herself? Archie? Not Walter — he was capable of it but he would have said something, too.

"I told you," Cousin Stella added. "She was a very tangled, enigmatic character, your grandmother."

I rested the tools against the hedge just inside the gate, and went back to the gig for the wreaths. When I returned, Cousin Stella said, "I'll just wait up here," and made for the church door. But I took her by the hand and said, "Please?" My feelings were in turmoil. I should have wanted to be alone with that simple mound and the wooden marker, but ... *this!*

She took my arm. "Why, child, you're all a-tremble," she said. "Aren't you pleased?" She waved her free arm toward the grave.

We were close enough now for me to see it was a no-expense-spared monument. The pink marble, which looked like butcher's brawn in jelly, was no simple slab. It had been carved and polished into an elongated scroll, supported on each flank by columns of black marble, flecked with iridescent blue. And the granite of the surrounding arch was of the fine-grained type that allows for the most intricate carving.

The monumental masons had made the most of it, for the arch had twining granite roses climbing up and through it. They were so detailed you could see every thorn.

The inscription was carved in the sort of capital letters you see in illuminated manuscripts and the grooves were filled with gold leaf. The dates of my mother's birth were there: 5th July 1854 — 12th March 1890. For my father it just said, 'in his forty-third year.' I could have supplied the exact dates. Somehow that made me feel more excluded than anything else in the monument now before me.

Cousin Stella's question was still on the air. The work must have cost three hundred pounds if it was a penny. I wanted to say that one-tenth of its price wouldn't have come amiss on the *eleventh* of March last year, but she was so pleased with what my grandmother had done, and so eager for me to show delight in it too, that I said, "Pleased and overwhelmed. You know what I was *expecting* to find here."

There would be no advice for me from our mother today. I could feel that her spirit had fled from this Trevarton grave as it had fled from her Trevarton home nineteen years earlier. My grandmother had reached across the Valley of the Shadow of Death and claimed her daughter back. This tomb was neither an act of charity to us, the children, nor a belated apology to our parents. It was a proclamation to the world — to people yet unborn who, in years to come, would pass this way — that 'Selina Moore, née Trevarton' had been a person of substance. Here she proclaimed in stone, after her death, all that she had denied in life, before it. It was the final triumph of that hypocrisy whose steady drip had etched all love from her soul and led to such a bitter death.

But I had the last laugh. In trying to steal our parents from us, the old woman had unwittingly moved them closer than they had been for many a long year — in my heart at least, which was the only lodging thereabouts where they still might linger on. I turned to Cousin Stella and asked if I might borrow her fountain pen.

She hesitated. It was a new, patent Waterman that never flooded the page and she was ridiculously proud of it, and possessive beyond reason. But she saw my trembling chin, which I could not control, and she silently handed it over. I added my father's name to both tickets and gave it back to her. Then we laid the wreaths on the graves and said a silent prayer. I think she was surprised I did not weep. But what should I have wept *for*? True, all that could die of our mother and father lay buried there beneath our feet. But all that could be wept over had been banished by marble and granite and gold leaf. Just before we turned to go I said, "I *shall* get Teresa back — and Gerald and Arthur, too. All of us together again. I swear it."

"Yes," Cousin Stella said soothingly as we walked back up the slope, "it would comfort them, too, to see it, I'm sure."

I said nothing to disillusion her. I had not been talking to her, anyway.

I asked Cousin Stella to come with me to St Breaca's in Penzance but she said she didn't wish to cramp my style. I could quite see that it would make things awkward for her one day with Sir Redvers, so I did not press the invitation. She advised me that courtesy demanded I should write a note to Sr Enuda, ahead of my calling — which was true. On the other hand, it would also give the woman a chance to reply that on no account would she receive me, which, since I intended going, no matter what she might say, would make me seem very rude. And if I mentioned an actual day, she could take the additional precaution of arranging a distant visit of her own to coincide with it. I therefore set courtesy aside and went unannounced.

I did, however, write a brief note which I carried with me, to be handed in when I arrived at the convent. It followed the lines I had described to Cousin Stella — saying how ashamed I now felt about the way I'd behaved last time ... would she ever forgive me, et cetera ... and might we now discuss an amicable settlement of the problems my grandmother's hasty actions had left behind?

Again I went by train — Second Class this time, even though I was paying for myself. In Truro there had been a slight drizzle but at Penzance I found the day dry and breezy. So I decided to walk the mile or so to Morrab Road, taking the more interesting route through the docks, as before. The ticket collector asked me my intentions and then advised me to go via Market Jew Street, instead. Not only would it be quicker, he said, but there was some excitement down the harbour because a man-of-war, the *Ashanti,* had split a mast off the Wolf Rock yesterday and she'd come in to make a temporary repair. The captain had given the crew shore leave until midnight.

He was discreetly warning me to avoid the harbour, of course, for Jack-Ashore is inclined to be boisterous with nubile young females. However, no nubile young female who'd lived in Falmouth for a year needed telling about the ways of Jack-Ashore — nor how to circumvent them without too much bother. The harbour area held no terrors for me. Besides, I remembered the name — HMS *Ashanti*. It was the vessel the petty officer had pointed out as our train passed over Brunel's bridge across the Tamar, on my first visit to Plymouth. So, on the offchance I might bump into him — and wondering if he'd remember me — I set off along the wharf toward the Trinity House quay.

The hour was barely noon. There was a mackerel sky above, which let through dramatic shafts of sunlight that played over the harbour and the sea in tumbling golden columns. A fresh salt breeze wafted in off the bay, the dying remnant of the squally storm that had dismasted the *Ashanti*. But the scene around me on the landward side reminded me of Union Street in Plymouth on the night Milly took me down there to chaperon her while she indulged her fascination for the creatures of the night. What a red-letter day she would have had there in Penzance that morning, where it was all going on in the full light of the sun!

Notwithstanding the ticket-collector's fears, the jolly tars left me alone, give or take a ribald comment or two. And, indeed, I *could* give or take a ribald comment or two — 'How are you off for dripping?' ... 'Does your mother know you're out?' ... 'Every Judy needs her Mister Punch!' ... 'Thank God we've got an army!' ... and so on. But a sailor can see as well as any other man the difference between a hem that sweeps the cobbles and one that shows a pretty ankle and a frothing of lace petticoats. So I — and a couple of lassies from the Salvation Army — passed through those mean, sad streets without harm. I thought that's what Milly should have done — borrowed a Salvationer's uniform, or even just an armful of their newspaper, *War Cry*. She could have passed freely among them then without fear. I came at last to the ropewalk that leads down once more to the harbour — and all without the most distant glimpse of my petty officer.

Actually, I think the difference between Unfortunates and other women is much more than the mere height of a hem above the ground. I found it hard to think of them as women at all. I don't mean I despised them particularly, or saw them as denizens of a nether world — though aspects of their behaviour would have excused one for thinking so — rather that they seemed like a third sex or a new branch of the human race. Or mechanical creatures on a stage. Then, my mind going ahead to St Breaca's, I realized that my feeling about nuns was identical! Nuns were the other side of the same coin, perhaps, but it *was* the same coin.

The Unfortunates despoiled the sacred spirit of love by offering its counterfeit so promiscuously. But the nuns detracted from it by going too far the other way and then calling their abstinence holy. I was so deep in these thoughts that I walked past the end of Morrab Road and had to turn back!

No lay sisters worked in the garden that day. My previous visit had been in mid-May, the month when every bed and border shouts, 'Weed me! Feed me! Heed me!' But now, at the end of March, the plants were indulging in that deceptive, green-budded calm before their riots of spring. As I entered by the carriage gate an upstairs window flew up and, for a moment, I thought the sisters were throwing a bed down — not exactly upon me but intending to block my path. It was, however, just a large feather mattress, which they were shaking out to air. Its lower end came to a halt just above my reach. The sight of a luxurious feather mattress jarred with my notions of cloistered austerity.

"Yes?" a shadowy figure called down at me from the dark interior of the room, or cell, or whatever it was. "What do *you* want?" She made it sound as if I were the tenth importunate caller that day.

Any social unease I might have felt at just turning up out of the blue, was instantly absolved by her rudeness. Rather than shout back I waved the note I had prepared.

"D'you expect me to read that from here?" she cried. "What is it?" She came toward the window but tripped over something and almost fell through the opening. If the mattress had not been there, she would have tumbled headlong out.

I gave a little gasp of impotent horror and held my hands up as if to catch her — a futile gesture but it's the sort of thing one does.

"Don't fuss!" she muttered crossly as she struggled back to her feet. She seemed to speak more to the mattress than to me. It crossed my mind then that she might have found a spare bottle of communion wine but I put the thought from me. It's not the sort of thing one wishes to believe of a nun.

"It's for Sister Enuda," I said hesitantly.

"She's gone," she replied brusquely and vanished from sight.

A moment later, however, she returned and knelt in the opening, bringing her chin to rest upon the feather mattress. I saw she was a woman in her fifties, not unlike Cousin Stella to look at but quite different in voice and accent. Her tone was deep and she had a strong West Country burr, though of an educated character.

She stared down at me with great, mournful eyes. "Moore?" she asked. "Are you the Moore girl?"

"I'm Cristobel Moore, yes, Sister … er? I'm afraid you have the advantage of me."

"Sister Berrion. How d'you do."

"How d'you do. You say Sister Enuda has gone?"

"Over the hills and far away — or at least as far as Saint Columb. We have another house there, you know."

"No, I didn't know that. Er … has she just gone for the day?" I thought she might have got to hear of my visit, by some magical means available only to nuns, and decided not to meet me.

"No — for good," said Sr Berrion. "For better or for worse but certainly for good."

"And who is the new superior, if I may ask?"

She dipped her head gravely. I thought she was giving me permission to ask but then it dawned on me that she was acknowledging the rôle herself. "Will you tell me how you knew my name, Reverend Mother?" I rejoined. "I say, may I come in? This is rather awkward — and I see that the front door is, in fact, slightly ajar."

"Good gracious!" she said. "Is it? I'll meet you downstairs. Wait in the hall."

It was as cold inside as out and yet there was an atmosphere of warmth in the house — austerity minus that special chill one usually associates with the word. Simplicity is what I mean, perhaps? I had never been inside a nunnery before but our mother had. She did a special annual laundering of sacerdotal vestments and altar cloths for some Catholic nuns in Camborne and she had often described their house to us. I think she envied them their life without men — and without children, too, though she would have kept all hint of it from us. I looked for the eternal flame and the holy water and that statue of the Virgin but saw none of these things. There was a painting of St Breaca, a cross in one hand, a sword in the other, slaughtering a whole pack of Cornish unbelievers.

Sr Berrion came down the stairs with the sort of dignified caution that always gives tipsy people away. "Our patroness," she said when she saw my interest. "Everyone else has gone to Land's End for the day — a treat for the youngsters, you know." She came to rest beside me — a small woman who barely reached my shoulder — and stared up at the painting. "She was Irish," she explained. "All our Cornish saints were at that time, of course. The Christian message had only just reached them over there and it got them so excited they felt they had to go out and convert the whole world — even us Cornish, though we had already been Christianized for centuries by then. And *that"* — she pointed at the carnage so lovingly depicted in the picture — "seems to have been their favourite method of conversion."

She wandered on into the refectory, the first room off to the right of the hall. "I wasn't expecting anyone to call today," she said. "I'm turning all the mattresses as a penance and the effort seems to have made me a little light-headed."

Perhaps I was being unfairly suspicious, then? But I thought not. I knew only too well how cunning and plausible an addict to the bottle can be. I told her I was very good at making beds, especially feather beds, and offered to help. At first she demurred but it was a token. She soon caved in and accepted. My visit was obviously cutting into her unhindered drinking time, so the sooner I was sent away, the better.

Between us we made short work of the beds. There were only six nuns in the house and she had already turned two of their mattresses. For good measure we turned the children's mattresses, too. There were twenty of them, sleeping head-to-tail in ten beds with hair mattresses. As we finished I said jokingly that I thought nuns would sleep on such paliasses as well.

Her rather surprising reply was, "I never wanted to be a nun, anyway." She gripped my wrist and gazed deep into my eyes, saying, "Don't let anyone ever force you to do something that you know in your bones is not right for you! You're a kind, helpful girl, Miss Moore, or you wouldn't be up here with me. And you have an impulse to self-sacrifice, too. So you'll be especially vulnerable to the danger I'm talking about. No, don't try to argue. Enuda warned me about you."

She loosened her grip and slipped her arm through mine to lead me back to the stair. I asked exactly what Sr Enuda had said.

"Your grandmother, too," she went on. "She wrote to warn us about you before she died."

She must have felt my arm twitch for she chuckled and said, "You didn't know that, did you! Oh yes, she said you'd stop at nothing to get Tessa back."

"Teresa."

"Yes, her. So I can't say I haven't been expecting you — but not, I must say, today. You'll take a cup of tea with me?"

I said that would be pleasant. There was something very appealing, almost childlike about her. The alcohol had obviously loosened her tongue but I guessed she was, in any case, garrulous by nature. I don't think she told me anything during the hour or so we were together that she would not have said within a week of acquaintance in the normal way of things. I'm sure all the other sisters knew she had no real vocation. That would account for the happy atmosphere I felt the moment I entered. Feelings like that linger even when the people who create them are away for the day.

When she said they had *all* gone to Land's End, she did not mean the lay sisters, of course. Like domestics in other houses, they hardly counted. She rang a bell and asked one of them to bring us some tea and cake. The lay sister curtsied like any tweeny. Sr Berrion led me into the room to the left of the entrance, which proved to be her study. Discourteously she went before me — to sweep up a flask of whisky, I realized. She pretended to tut-tut over a carelessly discarded book but I saw the sparkle of the glass and the amber sheen of the fluid as she slipped it to the back of the bookshelf and rammed it home with the allegedly offending volume — a fat *Dictionary of the Bible*.

"You have pictures of saints but none of the Virgin Mary, I see," I remarked, making conversation.

"Why should we?"

I explained what our mother had told us about the nuns in Camborne.

"Oh — Catholics," she said dismissively. "Anyway, Berrion means 'virgin' in Cornish, you know. The village of Buryan, out Land's End way, is named after her. It's in the Domesday Book."

I did not see the connection — or the relevance — of this but fortunately the lay sister came in at that moment with plates of caraway and madeira cake, saying that the tea was just drawing and she'd return with it 'dreckly.'

I was torn now between asking what the *present* reverend mother's attitude might be to her order's treatment of Teresa and what else my grandmother might have said in that letter.

"You mentioned a letter?" Sr Berrion said.

I almost replied, 'No, *you* did,' when I recalled the note I had prepared for my encounter with Sr Enuda. I passed it over, not least to gain some time for myself to think. I decided that the indirect approach — asking about my grandmother's letter — might nonetheless provoke Sr Berrion into revealing something of her attitude to the Teresa affair.

The teapot and cups arrived during this interlude and I took the liberty of pouring. Milk in first.

Sr Berrion folded my letter and tossed it casually onto her desk. "Are you sincere?" she asked, relishing her first sip of tea. I felt her brain was no longer the least bit fuddled.

I finished my mouthful of caraway cake, which really was excellent. "In my apology?" I replied. "Yes, Reverend Mother, of course I am. I really see no point in raking over the past and talking about blame — especially as the principal ... what can one call her? Agent? Actor? My grandmother, anyway — especially as she is no longer with us." I meant, of course, that we could blame her without actually saying so. "The main thing is to find some amicable and honourable way of reversing the damage."

I went on to explain about my grandmother's bequest. Her surprise revealed to me that the old woman's letter to Sr Enuda had not been complimentary about me. However, as Sr Berrion was quick to point out, the fact that I was *now* able to support Teresa did not mean that St Breaca's had acted wrongly *then,* when I had more faith than cash.

I smiled and shook my head sadly, trying to suggest that she still had not grasped the point — but that it was my fault for not making it clearly enough. "There's no question in my mind but that St Breaca's acted correctly throughout," I assured her. "However, as you yourself have just pointed out, Reverend Mother, that was *then* and this is *now.* It's a question of what to do for the best — *now."*

She eyed me warily and asked what I might have in mind.

"Well ..." I spoke haltingly as if I were thinking it up as I went along. "It occurs to me that if you — as a new superior here — were to write to General Sir Redvers Wilkinson to say that you had been going through last year's diary — or commonplace book — or however you keep your records of these things — and that the haste in which Teresa's adoption was carried out and the manner in which certain corners were cut ... all this has left you feeling uneasy to say the least. You realize, of course, that he had been posted to India, but even so ... even so ... You would, of course, have consulted Mrs Agatha Trevarton as the prime mover — that was the name I couldn't think of just now: prime mover! You would have consulted her as the prime mover in the business had it not been for her sad death. Hence your letter to him as the person *next most responsible.* Something along those lines, perhaps? I'm sure you could phrase it a great deal more tactfully."

Her smile was sphinxlike. "Anything else, Miss Moore?" she asked. "Any more pearls to cast?"

"Well" — I continued with every show of reluctance — "you might also say — which is true, I'm sure — that the most disturbing aspect of the case is the fact that Mrs Trevarton did not reveal to anyone here that she was Teresa's grandmother. Surely your order would look askance at any grandmother who placed her own grandchild for adoption with you — even if she did pay all the expenses? Perhaps you'd be *doubly* uneasy if she agreed to do that?"

I meant, of course, that Sr Enuda jolly well ought to have been made uneasy by it — not that I blamed the poor woman, for I knew how formidable my grandmother could be when she wished.

Sr Berrion, who was stone cold sober by now, was fascinated at these suggestions. She did not for one moment believe I was thinking them up as I went along but that did not detract from their effectiveness. "What would such a letter achieve?" she asked bluntly, to see how far ahead I had considered the business.

"From the General's latest letter to my grandmother," I said, "which I had the painful duty of reading aloud to her on her deathbed, it was clear that the Wilkinsons were not as ecstatically happy with their adopted daughter as they had hoped to be. Also that he, too, was having second thoughts about the way the whole business was rushed through. At one point he said he had a good mind to tie a ticket round Teresa's neck, with directions on it to my grandmother's house in Falmouth, and send her home with the next family for England. So I think a little nudge from here — along the lines I suggested — and a little olive branch from me — perhaps with the hint that my grandmother left me the bequest expressly in order that I might bring our family together again ... well, Reverend Mother, it would make it so much easier and pleasanter all round than going to law, don't you think? All our secrets being made public! None of us would emerge very well from it. What d'you think?"

Her smile was grim. "If it weren't for my vows, young madam, I'd tell you precisely what I think! However — part of me is still worldly enough to see the sense in what you say."

"You'll do it, then?"

She raised both hands high and wide, facing toward me. At first I thought it was a holy benediction but then I realized it was a very secular gesture of helplessness.

One of the minor reasons that Cousin Stella had 'promoted' me — or, rather, allowed me to drift up by imperceptible degrees — to the exalted rank of unofficial and unpaid companion was to give me sufficient authority to deal with Susan and her 'little problem.' It was growing larger every day, and in every sense of the word. All the servants knew of it by now, and there were rumblings of discontent among them. Especially the women. Mrs Bourdeaux said it would do her own reputation no good with a future employer if word got out that a maid had become *enceinte* under her stewardship — especially if the wretched girl had not been dismissed without a character as soon as the fact became known.

The fact itself would not be held against her, for everyone knew the way of the world. Real ladies feel no sexual passions at all. Their share is redistributed in extra measure among females like Susan, inhabitants of the lower ranks of society. Such creatures, driven by their augmented demon, could swiftly overpower any poor man's resistance. The natural nobility and moral strength of properly brought-up young gentlemen was no match to them. "Poor Mark!" the world would say, forgiving him at once. "Still, he's learned his lesson and he'll be a better man for it now — especially since the canker has been cut out of the household and sent on its way."

So God help the household that did not cut out that canker as soon as it manifested itself!

Betty Coath, our other upstairs maid — and even little Clarry Benjamin down in the scullery — both took their cue from Mrs Bourdeaux and began grumbling that Susan's condition was a threat to their future livelihood. Something had to be done, and soon. Mark and Susan still talked of running off to Scotland but I was fairly sure that his good sense would assert itself in time. It would remain mere talk, a romantic dream that revealed his innate good-heartedness. Susan still dreamed of an elopement, but that just showed her dismal understanding of human nature, despite her apparent worldly wisdom. Indeed, she was losing touch with reality altogether, for she was now savouring the idea of becoming a 'lidy.' She seemed to have forgotten how scornful she once had been toward Society and all its petty rules and restrictions — not to mention its snobbery and cruelty.

Cousin Stella, bless her, was a cut above the common herd. It was unthinkable to her that Susan should simply be turned out into the cold. In her view, Mark was just as responsible for Susan's condition as the maid herself was. Mark had money of his own, not to mention his expectations from his parents' wills, so it was only right he should be hurt in pocket, too, by making proper provision for Susan and the baby. I was delegated (to put it kindly) to knock some sense into both of them. For that reason, Cousin Stella did not insist that I move into one of the main bedrooms of the house. Others assumed she left me in the same room as Susan so as to prevent any nocturnal rambling by Mark — who might reason that no one would miss a few more slices off an already cut cake, as they say.

I knew very well what *ought* to be done. I had not changed my mind from the very beginning. Susan should go away and have her baby and Mark should settle a large enough sum upon her to let her bring the child up — by owning a small shop, for instance. If the baby made her less marriageable, the income would make her more so. Together they'd balance out. If only Susan could get rid of the illusion that she loved him — and the delusion that he loved her!

I decided to ask Jim what he thought I should do, even though the subject of the future was not exactly a happy one between us at that time. I had to be careful about it, though, in case he suspected I was really talking about us and only using Susan and Mark as stalking horses. Funnily enough, it was he who raised the matter first, not me. It happened one Wednesday early in April, when he got the afternoon off and we went to one of the art galleries.

Falmouth was fortunate in having three noted families of art connoisseurs who generously allowed their collections to be seen by the public at certain times — the Foxes of Grove Hill, the Foxes of Tregedna, and the family of the late rector, William Coope, at Gyllyngdune House. Rembrandt, Raphael, Leonardo, Titian, Vandyke, Correggio, Claude, Poussin ... almost all the great masters were represented between them. And there were lesser masters like Andrea del Sarto, Annibale Caracci, Bassano, Wouwermans, and Backhuysen — superbly gifted artists who nonetheless made you realize why men like Rembrandt and Titian were so revered. Even the poorest of them was so far above me in talent that I could look at their works without a twinge of envy or despair. Any comparison would have been just too laughable. In fact, Roger Moynihan's effortless mastery of pen and brush was far more disheartening to me because, although he could never hold a candle to the old masters, he was still far superior to me and my feeble efforts.

Jim liked Claude and Poussin best because, underneath the surface serenity of their landscapes, he said, there was always something dark and menacing going on. Also, more practically, he liked to analyze their compositions as an aid to his own work as a photographer. I liked the portraits best, especially the Rembrandt self-portrait at Gyllyngdune and Titian's *Ignatius Loyola,* which was at Grove Hill. I liked to gaze at them until everything else in the room turned into a blur and they were liberated at last to float in an unreal space. It seemed to make them more real.

These paintings also showed me how each of us is at the mercy of those who live on after we are gone. It didn't apply in Rembrandt's case, of course, because his was a self-portrait, but our thoughts about Loyola are now more or less dictated to us by what Titian and his fellow masters chose to tell us. I don't know anything about the real Loyola except that he's a Catholic saint. But the Loyola I *do* know something about was zealous, a master of logic, inclined to be arrogant, and very sure of himself and his importance in God's plan for the world. But I only know these things because they're all there, captured to perfection in Titian's brush strokes!

I tried to explain this to Jim, because I thought his approach to paintings was much too practical, too photographic. 'What's in it for me?' he asked of each one.

"Jim? Just supposing ... I mean, if I died today ..." I said as we left Grove Hill and strolled up Wood Lane.

"Hush!" he cried in horror.

"I was just wondering what you'd tell people about me, years from now, when you're old and grey?"

He slipped an arm about my waist. "Dear Crissy," he said. "Such a thing to worry about!"

"It's not worry. It's just ... I don't know — curiosity, I suppose. What are people going to remember about my grandmother, for instance? What are Gerald and Arthur — and Teresa — ever going to *know* about her, now? Only what I tell them, and you, and Mark, and so on. But what can I say about her? Lots of things I couldn't even find words to express. Sometimes I could love her, sometimes I'd hate her — but was that really her or mostly me? Sometimes I'd look at her and say to myself, 'You're a stranger. I don't know you at all.' How do I sum that up? I'll just say something vague like ... I don't know — 'She was a complicated woman, sometimes generous, sometimes mean beyond belief.' And then when Teresa grows up and has children and they ask what was their great-grandma like, what'll she tell them? 'I don't know. I never met her. Your Aunty Crissy did but she could never make her mind up about her.' And then — a hundred years from now — even that will be forgotten. She'll be reduced to a name on a bit of paper that our great-grandson stumbles across one day in an old family deed box. Just a name on a spill for a servant to light a fire with — isn't that *dreadful!* Don't you think it's dreadful?"

"No." He laughed. "I think it's hopeful. You should tell all this to Susan, not me."

"Why?"

"Because of the fuss everyone's making about one little bastard baby. A hundred years from now, who will care? It's what we *do* with our lives that counts. William the Conqueror was a bastard child but I'll bet it was a rash man who mentioned it to his face!"

My hopes, which had leaped up when he spoke Susan's name, seemed dashed again. "Don't you think she ought to go away and have it quietly — and then let Mark set her up in a little shop or something?"

"Do you?" He seemed surprised.

"Everybody does," I said. "Cousin Stella ... Mrs Bourdeaux ... all the other servants ..." My voice trailed off. He looked at me with such disappointment that I felt just about *so* high. "What's the alternative, then?" I asked.

We had reached the corner with Melvill Road. "Shall we go on to Gyllyngdune?" he asked.

I said I'd seen enough paintings for one day.

"Just to the seafront then." He took my arm and we set off at a jaunty pace down the hill.

"What's the alternative?" I repeated.

After a pause he said, "D'you remember telling me a couple of weeks ago about your drive over to Helston with Cousin Stella? The picture you had of your father and grandfather at that fateful interview? How you wanted to go back in time and tell them they were on the brink of choosing between happiness and disaster for everyone? Well, I think we're at precisely such a point now with Mark and Susan." He paused and then said, "No argument?"

I butted his shoulder with my head. "Go on."

"They can do all the sensible things that Mrs Bourdeaux and the scullery maids want them to. But if they do, Susan will pine for her lost love forever and Mark will turn into the sort of idle-rich young man who gets servant girls into trouble and does the decent thing by setting them up in little tobacco kiosks all over England."

"Or?" his silence forced me to ask.

He laughed slightly nervously. "Yes. That's the awkward bit — because it involves you and me, my love. D'you think Mark and Susan could actually be happy together?"

"But it's out of the question."

"Never mind that. Do they *like* each other? Do they get on? I'm pretty sure Mark is genuinely fond of Susan, but what about her?"

"Oh, she *loves* him, of course," I sneered.

"And it's all fake?"

I could not say it was, so I said nothing.

Jim continued: "Suppose that instead of setting her up in a *little* business he were to set *himself* up in something rather larger — something in which she could help him? As wife and partner — would that work, d'you think?"

The skin at the back of my neck began to tingle. 'It involves you and me,' he had said. "Go on," I told him. "This business ... would it have anything to do with photography?"

When he laughed I added, "As if I needed to ask!"

"Tony Snell thinks it's an idea worth pursuing. He's known Mark since schooldays."

"Of Snell and Angove — the lawyers?" I'd often passed their office in Arwennack Street.

He nodded. "They've been advising me."

We were on the bridge over the railway and paused to watch a train pass beneath us. Wreaths of steam and sulphur-reeking smoke swirled around us as the train clanked on toward the terminus, half a mile away.

"The first trippers of the year." Jim's eyes followed the train. They had the same predatory glint that creeps into farmers' eyes when they look at a flock of sheep.

"You were saying — Snell and Angove?" I prompted as we set off once more toward Gyllyngdune.

"Yes," he said, taking my arm again. "Between us I think we've exhausted all the regular, conventional ways of raising capital — without success. Actually it's the easiest thing in the world, raising money. All you have to do is to promise the man who lends you the stuff that you'll work every hour of the day and night and give him all your title deeds and shares — and ninety-nine percent of the profits. You'd be amazed at the number of wealthy men who are willing to part with a couple of thousand on such terms!"

"And you think Mark would be any different — once all the usual professional advisors had finished with him?"

"Could be. Not would be. But that's why it's important to know how well he and Susan would get on, really. Because I wouldn't be offering him a business partnership ... I mean, that's the least of it. The main thing I'd be offering — or which *we* would be offering if you agree — is a way out of his present dilemma. From his point of view he can either kiss Susan goodbye, and kiss goodbye to a couple of thou', and set her up in a business for which she is probably quite unsuited — and, in any case, it would pass to some other man if she got married again ... or he can put his money into his own business, keep Susan, keep the baby, and become a useful member of the working classes."

We crossed the road and he helped me over a stile, where a footpath leads across the field and down to the Cliff Road along the seafront. I looked swiftly about for bulls, as I always do when entering any field, but there was only a little grey donkey, who came trotting swiftly toward us and stopped a cautious ten paces away. I tried to make friends but it kept backing away as I advanced.

"What do you think?" Jim asked.

"What will Mark actually *do?*" I replied. "And where is this business to be?"

He shrugged, implying that such details hardly mattered as yet. "It can't be within fifteen miles of Falmouth — that's my gentleman's agreement with Stanton's. But that still leaves a lot of Cornwall — and a lot of trippers."

I gave up trying to befriend the donkey and took his arm again. We were almost across the field by now. "What is this fascination with *trippers?*" I asked.

He looked suspiciously at the donkey and then, pretending it might be an eavesdropper, he put his lips near my ear and murmured, "We're going to make a small fortune out of trippers — you and I — *and*, if you agree, Mark and Susan as well."

I laughed because his voice tickled. Then I kissed him and said, "Oh yes? How?"

He rubbed noses with me and said, "How?" — like a Red Indian. "Be serious!" I said.

We climbed another stile and were on the seafront at last, or, rather, on a low, twenty-foot cliff above the mixture of rock and sand called Gyllyngdune beach.

"Like this," he said. "Imagine you're a tripper and we're down on the sands and this is a bright summer's day." He ran backward on tiptoes until he was about ten paces off. Then he held an imaginary camera to his eye and said, "Smile, please! Snap!"

He turned an imaginary key on the side of his imaginary camera and then pointed to the empty road beside me. "There's another tripper. Snap! And another. Snap! Let's walk slowly right along the beach, snapping every tripper as we go." He held out a hand to me.

"What good will that do?"

"Let's just do it — you'll see."

Laughing, I joined him, saying, "I do understand words, you know. There's no need for a charade."

"There is — because this is something absolutely new. Something no one's ever done before in the entire history of the world. At least, I don't think so. I hope not. Maybe in America. They've had these new cameras there a couple of years already."

"New cameras?"

"Yes." He stopped and showed his to me, holding it so reverently that I almost convinced myself it was there. "There's the lens, see? The focus is fixed between about eight feet and infinity — on a bright day, anyway. That's the viewfinder — a bit crude but it's adequate as long as you don't bend the wire. And that's the trigger. You cock it like this ... click! You point it like this. And you snap like this ... snap!"

"What about the plate — the negative?" I didn't know much about cameras but I did know they all had to have plates.

But, it seemed, I was wrong. He smiled and shook his head and said, "Not this beauty! It's got a roll of Celluloid instead of glass. The unexposed negative is painted onto one side of a long strip of Celluloid, which they roll up once it's dry. You unroll a bit of it in front of the lens, like this ..." He turned the imaginary key on the side of the camera again. "Snap! And roll on another bit to expose. Each exposure is only the size of a postage stamp but you have to be careful to wind on enough so that they don't overlap. It's easy once you get the hang of it. *You* could do it, without any training at all. Try!"

And he thrust the 'camera' into my hands.

I laughed and pushed it away.

"Careful!" he cried in alarm, pretending to catch it before it hit the ground. This time he put it into my hands and made me take it. "Now wind on the negative."

Sheepishly I complied.

"That's enough. They're very small, each neg. Now cock the trigger — just pull on that bit of cord. That's right. When you hear the click, it's ready. Now choose your view — take Pendennis Castle there. 'The splendour falls on castle walls!'"

"Snap!" I said proudly and handed him back the 'camera.'

"Wind on," he said. "Always wind on after you snap. Didn't I say it's easy? *Even Mark* could do it!"

He laughed and clapped his hands. This time *I* caught the camera, handing it back to him with a look of silent reproach.

"Quite right," he said severely. "We haven't finished our work for this afternoon. There's room for a hundred exposures on this one roll of *film*. That's what they call the Celluloid — film. So ... snap-snap-snap-snap-snap! Now the whole roll of film is exposed. I've taken portraits of a hundred trippers, all right?"

"Or Mark has," I said.

He nodded. "Or you have. Or Susan — *after* the great event. So here's my changing box — did you ever see one of these?" He squatted and pretended to open the lid of something about the size of half a teachest. "See this little box inside? There's a couple of spare rolls of film in that but I mustn't open it until I've shut this lid again. So I pop the camera in and do just that. It's completely impervious to light. And now I roll up my sleeves and stick my arms inside the box by way of these long sleeves of black material with elastic at the ends. Still no light can get in. I pick up the camera, open the back of it, pull out the holder with my exposed film, pop it into this other little box, close the lid, open the box with the unexposed film rolls, take out one — which is already in its own holder — slip it into the camera, close the camera, close the box ... check again that everything is closed tight ... withdraw my arms, open the box — and *voilà!* The camera is ready to use again."

He handed it to me.

"Now let's see what happens to the exposed film in this tin. Here's a young lad on a bicycle, waiting to take it from me — or from you, or Mark, or whoever is taking the *snapshots,* as they are called. He rushes it back to the studio. Pedal-pedal-pedal." He panted like a dog. "Develop-develop-develop! Print-print-print! Dry-dry-dry!" He glanced anxiously at his watch. "Just in time! Here are a hundred prints all ready to take down to the railway station — where the departing trippers can see them and marvel *and,* let us hope, buy them at a shilling a time."

"A shilling!" I couldn't believe it. Photographers didn't even look at you until the word *guineas* was mentioned.

"A shilling," he repeated firmly. "At the height of summer there are at least a thousand trippers a day who visit any respectable Cornish resort. If we snap only half of them and only half of those we snap buy our prints, it's still more than twelve quid a day! And the materials would cost less than one pound." He became completely serious then. "Of course, there are lots of details still to be worked out. And it would only be for a couple of months each summer. For the rest of the year, we'd operate like an ordinary photographic studio — portraits, weddings, christenings, and so on. Also I want to do views of picturesque Cornwall and print them by collotype on ordinary paper. Once they're framed and behind glass you can't tell them from real photographs — and you can get five thousand prints off one collotype nowadays. They could sell for a guinea each."

My laughter puzzled him. "I thought it wouldn't be long before the talk got round to guineas," I said.

He took my arm and we started walking toward Swanpool Head. "So what d'you think?" he asked anxiously.

"I think we should use my thousand pounds for capital and forget Mark and Susan."

"The two of us couldn't do it alone," he replied.

"Hire an assistant, then. Or two — or however many it needs."

He shook his head. "Assistants can't be relied on. I know. I'm one myself. Look how I'm letting Stanton's down!"

"But you've finished your apprenticeship — *and* worked out the promised year."

"That's not how they see it."

"Anyway, with what they're paying you they can hardly be surprised if you want to go off and better yourself."

"Ah ha! And with what we'd be paying *our* assistants we could hardly be surprised if they go off and better *them*selves! We'd even be teaching them how to do it. These new Eastman-Kodak cameras aren't expensive, you know. They could set themselves up in competition to us in no time.

Everyone who works in this new business I'm proposing *must* have a personal stake in it. It's just too easy to copy."

I made one last effort: "Then offer our assistants a small share of the business to start with — plus we could give them a little bit more for each year they stay."

He halted and turned me to face him. "Why not Mark and Susan? It's such a natural alliance. You and he are related. We're all good friends. You like Susan, don't you?"

I had to admit it.

"He's got more money than is good for him. If he doesn't put it to good use — *and* roll his own sleeves up and get stuck into something practical and worthwhile — it'll corrupt him and ruin him. It happens every day. As I said, it'll save his soul, save Susan's good name, and save a little baby Trevarton — who will be your cousin, incidentally."

What could I say in the face of so much zeal and good-heartedness? I should have felt such a dog-in-the-manger for continuing to put my objections. And besides, what objections could I now make? Only that I had an awful foreboding at the prospect of such a partnership.

So, with half of me seething in silent protest, I smiled and spoke the only truth I could at that particular moment. I said he was a far worthier human being than I could ever hope to be.

"You approve, then?" he asked.

"We can give it a try," I agreed.

"So will you sound out the ground with Mark — or shall I?"

The following day was the first truly warm day of the year — breezy, but warm. I was already having second thoughts about the way I had volunteered to 'sound out the ground' with Mark and I realized that, the longer I held back, the more reluctant I'd become. So, brushing all my misgivings aside, I suggested to Mark that he should take Susan and me across the Fal to St Mawes, where we could have a bite of lunch at the inn, take a little stroll out to the ruined castle there, and come back home in time for tea. I meant us to go by the regular ferry-boat, of course. The dinghy was his idea.

It was a mistake but in the end, I think, it saved the day. It got Susan out of the way while I seduced Mark — with the prospect of untold wealth, I hasten to say, not … you know.

We left the gig at the Yacht Club and set off across the harbour in high hopes. People had made such a *thing* of Susan's condition that she took every chance to deny its very existence, much less its influence on her. She had terrible morning sickness sometimes, but she'd grit her teeth and say it was nothing and insist on carrying on as if she were on top of the world. All the way down through the town I'd tried to make her agree she'd be far more comfortable in a nice big steamboat ferry, but she wouldn't hear of it. It was no more than a couple of miles, she answered blithely, and the sea looked quite calm. She'd be perfectly all right and we were to stop fussing.

We'd hardly gone half a mile, though, before her cheerful chatter died down and she turned a distinct shade of green about the gills. In the middle of Carrick Roads, with less than a mile to go, she parted company with her breakfast. How I managed not to follow suit I don't know, but she was half dead by the time we arrived and I was ready to go straight back — on the steamer, of course — and home to bed. Lunch at the inn was no longer on our agenda.

A chastened and apologetic Mark supported the pair of us along the little path that led over the headland to the castle, which is like a baby brother to the much grander fortification on Pendennis Head, opposite. It looked invitingly solid, despite its dilapidation, and the warm-coloured stone, grey with an orange cast, was less forbidding than the words 'granite castle' might suggest.

"Feel like exploring, sausage?" Mark asked Susan when we arrived at the base of its wall.

The spot was in full sun, and sheltered from the wind. She sank gratefully upon a large, fallen stone, leaned against the wall, closed her eyes, and raised her face to the sun, murmuring, "Just let me sit here and breathe."

"You go," I told Mark, taking the rug from him and spreading it out on the grass. "I'll stay here with Sue."

"No!" she protested. "I'm not *ill*. I'll recover all the sooner if I can just lie here and have a little snooze, all on my ownio." She smiled wanly at me and stretched out flat upon the rug. "Go on — honest! Don't do anything *I'd* do!"

"She's amazing," I said to Mark as we squeezed between the rotting planks someone had once put there to stop trespassers like us.

He didn't reply.

"Don't you think?" I pressed him.

"Ouch!" He pretended to stub his toe but I knew it was to avoid answering me.

When we reached the parapet we crossed to the far side, where, with the breeze on our faces and the sun at our backs, we could gaze out across the mouth of the Fal to Pendennis Castle and the harbour — two mighty features that obscure the rest of the town from that particular vantage. I was disappointed. Only the very topmost fringe of Falmouth was visible. I could see Woodhouse Terrace above a thicket of masts and rigging. I'd swear I could even make out Jim's lodgings. Also Beacon Hill, of course, high above the Yacht Club. And Greenbank and Flushing, away to our right.

"How long ago that seems!" I murmured, pointing across the bay. "That afternoon last summer in Flushing."

He leaned on the battlement, rather close to me — uncomfortably so — and said, "Mmm."

"Was that when you and Susan ... you know?" I asked.

"Good God!" he exclaimed.

I had meant was that when he and she had first kissed, but his shock showed he thought I was asking if that was when they first ... you know! Then *I* was shocked that he could think such a thing of me. "I meant *kissed,*" I said — which only made it worse, because now we both knew what he had assumed.

Then he laughed. "Well, why *not* talk about it!"

"Certainly not," I replied.

"All right, then," he said affably. "Don't."

He whistled a formless tune through his teeth and drummed his fingertips on the stone. "I know why you've brought us here today," he said at length.

"I brought you?" I asked in surprise.

"You suggested it. I know you want to talk me into parting with Susan and paying for her confinement and setting her up in a little shop or something. So you needn't deny it. Cousin Stella's put you up to it, hasn't she."

"Poor Cousin Stella!" I said.

It was not the response he expected. My tone promised something subversive, something Cousin Stella would certainly not welcome. (And it was true — she most certainly wouldn't! But that was a battle for another day.) Mark turned and stared at me with sudden interest. "Do tell."

"It's a wild idea," I said nervously. "Jim would probably *kill* me if he knew I had even breathed a word of it to you." (This was the line Jim and I had agreed upon, to save any embarrassment between them if Mark unexpectedly said no.)

"What?" Now he turned to face me, all else forgotten. He grinned and rubbed his hands.

"His plans. Ever since he told me, I can't stop thinking about it. To me it looks like the answer to *everything* — to your problem, to Susan's, and to his. But, of course, you and he may not see it that way. Nor might Susan." I looked him directly in the eye. "Forgive my asking but you *do* like her, don't you, Mark?"

"I love her," he said belligerently.

"I know that. But do you also *like* her? D'you get on together? Is she a *chum* as well as a ... you know?"

"Ah." He scratched his head. "Yes, I suppose so." He smiled. "Yes. We do."

Suddenly I felt a pang of the old jealousy. Would I ever be rid of it? If only he *had* turned out to be my cousin! Even now, knowing him to be my uncle, there are things about young men like him that make young girls like me forget those bounds of restraint. He was so handsome and so ... just so easy and nice and everything. All of which was quite independent of my feelings for Jim. I mean, I loved him as madly as ever. I had an ocean of love for him. These feelings were just a bit of froth blowing about on its surface.

I drew a deep breath and returned my gaze to the safer distances beyond his face. "Love," I said. "Yes, well, that's the most important thing, I suppose."

And then I went on to tell him about the new business Jim had described to me yesterday, pausing every so often to assure him I'd be scalped if Jim ever found out, and swearing him to secrecy, and so on. I was surprised at how quickly he picked it up. I don't think I'm *that* brilliant at explaining things. He even pointed out something that had not occurred to me. He said, "There should be two people down on the beach. The second one should go along behind the photographer handing out leaflets telling the victims — sorry, I mean the subjects — to get to the station in good time. So they can look at the photographs and decide whether they want to buy them. You know how, when the whole family's having a good time down on the beach, you leave the packing-up and the going-home to the very last minute."

For the first time since Jim had proposed what I was sure would be a disastrous partnership, I began to feel there was just the smallest chance that he might be right after all. I would never have expected my rather empty-headed, hail-fellow-well-met uncle to make such an astute point — and certainly not so quickly.

He was quick to see the general point, too. "I suppose I'm the sleeping partner who puts up the capital?" he said.

"The partner, anyway," I agreed. "But I don't think you'd get much sleep — not if things work out the way I thought they might. You put up the capital. Jim puts in his ..."

"Isn't your thousand enough?" he asked. "How much will it need, for heaven's sake?"

"Of course mine's enough," I replied. "It's what Jim's counting on. But that won't help *you*, will it — you and Susan. This is *my* proposition now. If you agree, I'll find some way of putting it to Jim. You provide the money. He provides the skill. And all four of us will slave day and night to make a success of it. You see? Mister and Mrs Trevarton and Mister and Mrs Collett — four *working* partners. Welcome to the working classes, Mark! You and Susan get each other. The baby gets a good name. And we all get rich beyond our wildest dreams. What d'you say?"

He licked his lips and grinned at me. "Actually, I've just thought of something else."

"What?"

"The leaflet we hand out — that should also say they can have extra snaps to send to their friends at a shilling each. Just pay in advance and leave their name and address."

Susan said no. She said it the moment Mark put the first bones of the plan to her. She said it again when I tried to flesh them out. She said it several times on the journey back, which she and I made on the steamer, leaving a disconsolate Mark to take the dinghy back by himself. She was quite adamant that she wanted to be a 'lidy.' I'd like to think it was good sense that made me refrain from pressing her but actually it was a blend of disappointment and exhaustion.

"Wants to be a lady?" Cousin Stella echoed when I told her what had happened. "I think it's only fair to let her know what she's letting herself in for, don't you, my dear?"

The twinkle in her eye was all I needed to set me off in the right direction. How wonderful it must be to be a wise old lady like that, to be above the hurly-burly, and to see ways out of life's morass which those who are in it up to their necks cannot hope to glimpse! "I'll start. You take over," I suggested.

"Admirable, dear," she replied.

My chance came a couple of days later, when Susan thought we had forgotten the Collett — Trevarton partnership. She climbed into bed that night and stretched luxuriously. "It tickles!" She giggled. "I dunno — it's like a little tadpole or ... something a bit bigger. A tiny goldfish, mebbe. Yeah — a tiny goldfish swimmin' inside of me. Ooh!" She giggled again.

"Sue?" I ventured. "When you are mistress of this grand household you're planning ..."

"Oh yeah!" She turned eagerly toward me to play her other favourite game. One was with the baby-to-be, the other with the life of privilege that lay ahead of her as Mrs Mark Trevarton. "What now? Isn't it funny to think I'll be a lidy, what was never born to it, and you, who was — in a way — will be a tradesman's wife!"

"Hilarious! Listen — suppose an upstairs maid in your grand household got herself into your present condition ... would you be very understanding or very strict?"

She replied without even thinking: "Oh, very understanding, naturally. After what I've been through myself."

"Really?" I responded in a surprised tone.

"Shouldn't I be?" she asked, also surprised.

"Well, of course you *should* be — from a charitable, Christian point of view. But it would be terribly brave of you. It'd be just the sort of thing all the ladies in your new circle would be waiting to pounce on — all your new so-called *friends.*"

There was a long pause and then she said, "Pounce on? What sort of thing d'you mean?"

"Signs of moral laxness. You know the sort of hypocritical things they ... well, we've spoken about it often enough in the past. That's why I think you're being absolutely heroic about it, honestly. I don't think I'd have the courage or the stamina to go into the lions' den — or the lionesses' den, I should say, because it's those lawdidaw ladies who'll be ready with their claws all honed and polished, waiting for just one tiny slip on your part."

After another painful pause she said, "You're right, gel — as ever! You just watch me. I'll be so strictly moral and pure from now on that Mrs Ormiston-Chaunt herself would look up to me."

I reached across the divide between our beds and patted the outline of her shoulder. "That's my girl!" As an afterthought I added, "I hope it will be sufficient."

"Well, what more could I do?" she asked in a slightly panicky voice.

"It's not really a question of *more*," I said. "Nor even of *less*. It's that most awkward target of all — the one labelled *Just Right!* I remember things our mother, God rest her, used to tell us — when she ran out of bedtime stories — about life in this very house in the Good Old Days. Her memories are so much more vivid, so much sharper to me, now that I can picture the actual rooms where they took place. Things that used to make us laugh ... well, I mean, they're still funny to *me*, of course, because I think that whole *world* is comical, but ..."

"I wish I knew what you was talking about," she interrupted.

" '... *were* talking about' or *are*, not *was*," I said. "That's just the sort of thing I'm referring to. If you don't give the lionesses a big, juicy moral lapse to feed on, they'll pick on little things like that instead. I remember Marian asked our mother once if she didn't regret having given up the old life, and she said never for the smallest part of a single second. She told us how she once presented an older married lady to a younger one instead of the other way around. She said all the air in the room suddenly turned to ice crystals and the way my grandmother spoke to her afterwards! It made her feel like the most stupid, incompetent, miserable little worm in creation. She cried for hours and hours. Just for a silly little thing like that!"

Susan said nothing.

"Of course," I added to comfort her, "no one will do that to *you*. Or not to your face, anyway. And once you pick it up, you'll be as bad as all the rest, I'm sure." I chuckled. "Our mother said that's what happened to her — she became as bad as all the rest. She and Corinna Dick spent a whole morning once, laughing at a pompous visitor at the Falmouth Hôtel who had his visiting cards *glazed!* 'Can you imagine it?' she said to us children. 'I actually used to think it *important* whether visiting cards were glazed or unglazed, or thick or thin, or one-and-seven-eighths inches (good chap!) instead of two-and-one-eighth inches (horrors — what a cad!), and whether PPC cards could decently be sent by post ... and so on.' Once she stood outside a house agonizing for a *quarter of an hour* whether to send in her mother's card or her father's — because she was calling to solicit a contribution to a charity. She couldn't decide if that counted as a business call or a social call. If business, she should send in her father's card ... or wait a mo' — do I mean her mother's? I can't remember. But *you* probably know, Sue."

"Me?" she asked in surprise. "Why should I know a thing like that?"

"Because you're the one who can't wait to join these ridiculous ladies with their ten million rules — only two thousand of which are written down in the etiquette books. The rest you're just supposed to know, somehow. By magic, probably."

"She should have sent in her father's card, I'm sure," she said then. "Seeing as how it was business. It was business, wasn't it? Raising money — that's business."

"I've just remembered," I told her. "It *was* a business call — but, for that very reason, she should have sent in her *mother's* card! The *only* time a married lady can send in her own card is for a business call. An unmarried one, of course, sends in her mother's in lieu. Ah me! I don't envy you, Sue, but I admire your bravery, that I will say."

There was the longest pause of all before she responded. "All right, Miss Clever-boots! I know what you're trying to do. I suppose that Cousin Stella put you up to it, but you're wasting your breaths, both of you. I'm going to marry Mark and I'll do whatever it takes to become a real lidy. I'm *not* going to spend my days amid the stink of photographic chemicals with a husband who can't even put Esquire after his name. So put that in your pipe and smoke it! I'll take my chance with the lionesses, ta very much."

The clock down in the hall struck midnight.

"Good heavens!" I exclaimed. "We'd better get our beauty sleep — or I shan't be fit for a life of useful toil and you'll be no match for that pack of lionesses, either!"

I don't believe she slept at all well that night. The following morning she was almost in tears when, after breakfast, she hesitantly asked Cousin Stella if she'd give her lessons in etiquette.

Cousin Stella, to whom I had already outlined our previous night's conversation, agreed at once, of course. "I think we'll start with familiar terms of address to members of the aristocracy."

It was a brilliant choice. The number of aristocrats that even a woman as exalted as Mrs Fox might encounter in a year would be in the low twenties, and the number with whom she'd be on familiar terms would be even smaller than that. But Susan was not to know such things, of course. The suggestion opened up before her an enticing vista in which she hobnobbed daily with dukes — or with baronets at the very least. Little did she know what a nightmare of an obstacle course lay ahead of her!

I brought them cups of tea and little sweetmeats throughout the morning, so I was able to keep fairly well abreast of the 'lesson.'

"Dull Men Eat Very Brown Bread," Cousin Stella began. "That will help you remember the order of precedence in the English peerage, my dear: Duke, Marquis, Earl, Viscount, Baron, and Baronet. Of course you never actually *call* a baron 'Baron' unless it's a foreign title. An *English* baron is addressed simply as 'Lord' So-and-so. The confusing thing is that viscounts, earls, and marquises are *also* called 'Lord' So-and-so. Baronets, on the other hand, are 'Sir' …"

It was a good start, to judge by the gloom already shadowing Susan's eagerness to learn.

On a later visit to the room I heard Cousin Stella say: "The wife of a peer is always 'Lady' So-and-so. If her Christian name happens to be Mary, for example, you must never, never, *never* call her 'Lady *Mary* So-and-so,' for that would imply that she is the daughter of a duke, a marquis, or an earl …"

Susan just stared at Cousin Stella's lips. Her own silently mouthed the words a fraction of a second later. Her tea grew cold in the cup.

Later still: "The Earls of Devon are an exception. The earldom has no subsidiary titles for the eldest son to take on as his courtesy title. So he simply takes the family name — Courtenay. He's known as Lord Henry Courtenay, Lord John Courtenay, or whatever his Christian name might be. His *wife* will also be Lady Henry Courtenay or Lady John Courtenay but his *sisters* will be, for instance, Lady Caroline Courtenay, Lady Margaret Courtenay, and so on. And if a sister should marry a commoner, she keeps her courtesy title. She'd become Lady Caroline Smith, for example — wife of plain Mister Smith. It's quite simple, really …"

I think I never saw poor Susan with so long a countenance.

Coming up to luncheon, I overheard Cousin Stella saying, "Well, Susan dear! That's the easy part over and done with. This afternoon, I think we'll get our teeth into something a little more challenging, eh. Leaving Cards and Paying Calls. I think you'd better bring pencil and paper for that."

Dear Susan was a determined young lady, I'll grant her that. For two increasingly terrifying days she stuck it out, battling gamely to remember that Duchesne is pronounced 'Dukarn' and Hertford, 'Harfurd' ... that a lady *never* called her husband plain 'Smith' or 'Mister S' but always 'Mister Smith' ... that a wife's sister has precedence over a husband's sister if the wife cannot act as hostess herself and a deputy is needed ... that an assize judge has precedence over a high sheriff — indeed, that a high sheriff has *no precedence whatever* outside his own county ... and that ...

But enough!

Such, at least, was the poor girl's conclusion by the Friday evening of the following week. She sank into bed, complaining for the ninety-tenth time that her head was spinning with "'oom to acknowledge when driving in an open carriage, and 'ow to address an Indian prince, and did the younger sons of knights go in before doctors of divinity, and I don't know what-all, I'm sure."

"You'll soon get the hang of it," I said encouragingly. "One magic moment will come when it all falls into place, and all your suffering will be over. You'll see."

"How much of it do you know, Crissy?" she asked.

"None of it, thank you very much! Nor do I want to. As far as I'm concerned, my mother had the right attitude — it's a sad, empty sort of existence that needs filling with twaddle like that! If ever I must write a letter to a bishop — which I can't see myself doing, but you never know — but if it should happen, then I'll pop down the library and look it up in one of the books. Then I'll forget it again directly. Life's too short, I say. Give me good, honest people who aren't sneering at each other all the time. 'Ooh! Did you see that? She used the wrong knife and fork! Tsk-tsk-tsk!' Still — to each his own. It takes all sorts to make a world, and it'd be a dull old place if we all thought the same."

"Actually ..." Susan said hesitantly.

"What? I hope it's not more of your wretched *etiquette*. I've had quite enough of ..."

"No — honest! In fact, I think I've had enough of it, too. You know what you was saying — about Mark and me going into partnership with you and Jim?"

"Yes?" I made a guarded question of the word.

"Well — where would it be? I mean ... Falmouth? Newquay? Penzance? St Ives?"

ometimes a whole month goes by and you look back and wonder what happened. Not a single memorable event stands out. And then, for no particular reason, everything changes and there are months like that April, with two weddings to arrange (both, admittedly, very modest and quiet), premises to rent, and lodgings, a legal partnership to be agreed, and my long-awaited visit to Marian to be fitted in. That we managed it all was a miracle.

In fact, it wasn't my London visit that had to be fitted in, for that had been arranged before everything else — so everything else had to be fitted around it. Jim's gentlemanly understanding with Stanton's — that he would not set up on his own within fifteen miles of Falmouth — ruled out Truro, Redruth, Camborne, and, though only just, Helston. Since the business we proposed to set up depended so heavily on tourists and trippers, that left only Penzance, St Ives, and Newquay.

Jim (perhaps feeling a little guilty at the brusque way he had turned down my money) now asked me to look at all three places, with our new enterprise in mind, of course. My father had taken me to St Ives once, before he tipped the business down his throat, but I had forgotten it. Looking at it now with newly opened commercial eyes, I thought the summer trade there would be brisk enough but the winters would be dead. Newquay offered the best possibilities, summer and winter, but it already boasted a well-established photographer, plus a go-ahead newcomer who could very quickly steal our thunder.

Penzance also had its well-established studio, Gillott's of Alverton Street, but Gillott himself was the last man to compete in our chosen field — not that that would stop him from complaining that we were competing in his, mind you. He wore Celluloid cuffs and a high-wing collar and bowed his customers backward into his salon, which smelled of mothballs. You could be photographed against backgrounds like the Matterhorn, a country cottage, a Greek temple, or in a twiggy bower under a romantic moon — everything that Jim had learned to detest during his apprenticeship at Stanton's. Penzance had no other full-time photographer, and certainly not one in our chosen field.

Jim, Mark, and Susan accepted my assessment of the three towns. So Penzance it was. I was flattered, of course, but also slightly unnerved. I had imagined I was simply making a preliminary survey and that the final inspection — and decision — would be Jim's and Mark's. Susan expressed regret, saying she thought St Ives was 'a better address.' On her baby's birth certificate, she meant. But Penzance it was.

In this fit of falling over to be nice to each other, Jim and Mark came to what I thought was the most dreadful decision — namely that we should rent a very large house, big enough for us to divide between us *and* provide our studio, darkroom, waiting room, etc. I tried to argue against it, thinking that Susan would naturally agree with me. After all, what sane woman wants to share a house with even the best of her friends and that friend's husband! But the idea of living in a *big* house appealed to her more than the idea of sharing it repelled her. So I was outvoted. I said no more but decided to bide my time. Come what may, I would not tolerate such a situation for more than a few months — during which time I should contrive, by hook or by crook, to show the others how wrong they were.

However, I did not want them to be able to say afterward, 'Of course, Crissy's to blame for our failure. She *never* liked the arrangement. She was against it from the start and she made jolly sure it didn't work.' I thought I could box a bit cleverer than that.

It was the same when they came up with an even more preposterous suggestion — namely that the four of us should get married on the same day, too. What woman wishes to share that most special day in her life with another — no matter how dear a friend? Unless, of course, she's about to part company with a healthy, full-term baby! I could quite see why Susan favoured the suggestion — which meant that, once again, I was completely outvoted.

However, I realized that this ridiculous plan would be fairly easy to thwart. Susan would rather be married alone, with the baby still inside her, than in tandem with the baby at her breast. A judicious extension of my visit to London, one or two little hitches with the lease of our big house, even a diplomatic chill on the kidneys ... anything would do.

So there was no more enthusiastic supporter of those two insane decisions — to share a house and a wedding day — than Crissy Moore!

Choosing a suitable house was slightly more difficult. At first sight the obvious location was out on the western edge of town in the Morrab Road area. It was near the pleasure gardens, the beach, and the two big hôtels — the Mount's Bay and the Queen's. But the obvious place is not always the best, and it certain wasn't in this case. There is a beach of fine golden sand, a couple of miles long, on the eastern side of Penzance, between the railway terminus and St Michael's Mount. It had its own railway station at Long Rock, so people going there might not come into the town at all. If we were intending to 'catch' day-trippers with the lure that they could take their own holiday photos back with them, it would be hard to manage such a service with delivery boys on bicycles and our studios at one extreme edge of our 'fishing ground.' A location between the two main beaches was therefore our obvious choice.

Susan, who had a perfect right to agree or disagree on what was to be as much her home as mine, disagreed. The houses around Morrab Road and Cornwall Terrace were far more select and genteel, in her view, than those along Chyandour Cliff, on the eastern edge of town, which was my preferred area. Perhaps it really had been a cliff once. Now it was just a road, twenty feet above the railway lines. Susan said she didn't want her baby lying out in the garden with a constant rain of railway smuts falling on him. (It was going to be a boy, of course.) She would have settled for somewhere a little farther out, near the Eastern Green, at the start of the long golden beach. There were one or two select and genteel houses there, she said. But I felt it was just too far out of town to attract local business, on which we'd depend in winter.

It was deadlock. The men — wise for once — said they'd rather we settled it between us. So I took out a pack of cards and suggested we cut for it, she and I. I was glad I'd paid such close attention to the little tricks the travelling salesman had shown us on the train to Plymouth that time — also that I hadn't previously revealed them to Susan. So, Chyandour it was. Susan took several days to get over her huff but I did right.

Actually, the reason I chose Chyandour was that lots of houses were then building in that area, so, when the time came for our two families to split into separate homes — as I was determined we should — we'd still be close enough together to make the business side of it easy.

Susan wanted to pick the house at once, of course — before I went to London with Miss Martin. But, as a seeming sop to her dented pride, I said it was only fair that she should have the main choice — and take her time about it. Since I had chosen among the towns, she should choose among the houses. She was mollified by this and accepted the commission. I knew I was safe enough because Jim would never make any binding agreement to a house I had not seen and approved.

On both visits to Penzance I was sorely tempted to call at St Breaca's and see Sr Berrion, not simply to discover whether she'd written to the Wilkinsons in India, though, of course, that would have come up in our conversation. She also interested me as a woman, despite her addiction to spirituous liquors, which usually finishes a person for me. I resisted the urge, however, because I felt she was not the sort of woman to welcome such 'interference,' as she would see it, especially after she had given her word about writing to India. It was too early yet to expect any letter back from the General, so I thought it best to wait. If I still had a little goodwill among the nuns in Morrab Road, I'd squander it when the reply came. Susan, who was now an expert on such matters, said I should leave a card with the words, 'To inquire after progress?' written above my name. But, as I would not have a card until after my marriage, her advice was of curiosity value only.

I could see difficulties ahead about living under the same roof as Susan, even for the briefest few months. She was so contemptuous of 'trade,' as she called it, and wished to give the impression that Mark was merely 'slumming it' in photography — as if it were just an eccentric hobby of his. Her dreams of going in to dinner on the arm of a duke — or a baronet at the very least — died hard. The curious thing was that if anyone should suffer from such delusions of grandeur, it ought to have been me. Our mother really had 'come down' from the fringes of that glittering world. But she had been so contemptuous of it — and so convincingly contemptuous, too — that I could not raise the smallest interest in the quaint customs of polite Society.

Often I would remind myself of the little orphan waif who had knocked with such terrified bravado at the front door of Fenton Lodge, a mere thirteen months ago, and who had thought Susan Callaghan the last word in worldly wisdom. *If that little creature could see me now!* I thought. For truly, my fortunes had improved out of all recognition. But amazement of that kind is impossible to sustain — especially when you reach a pinnacle that seemed unattainable when you were down there in the foothills. It becomes even harder to sustain when you scale that seemingly impossible height, only to realize that it, in turn, is the merest foothill to the *real* pinnacle of your life, which *still* beckons you onward and upward, as unattainable as ever.

And what if my fortunes had gone the other way? If I were now one of those ladies of the night, like that Esther Wilkinson, my cousin twice-removed, who had walked the streets of Penzance before she married Roger Moynihan — what then? I should probably look back on that virtuous orphan-waif of a year ago with equal amazement at going from *that* to *this*. And it, too, would probably be just as hard to sustain.

On the other hand, perhaps the naïve young Crissy who turned up at Fenton Lodge that fateful afternoon was not quite as naïve as she wanted the world to suppose. Perhaps she would not be in the least surprised to see what changes a year had brought. She did, after all, insist on knocking at the *front* door!

It was strange that my thoughts should have been running along those lines — about all the ways in which life can treat an orphaned girl left to fend for herself. Just before I set off for Redruth, where I was to spend the night before our London visit with Miss Martin at Little Sinns, Jim gave me an envelope with Stanton's monogram on the corner — the sort of envelope in which they deliver portraits to customers. "Thought this might interest you," he said.

It was a portrait of a woman in her early twenties, taken back in the Sixties to judge by the dress. There was something familiar about her. She was fair-haired, probably blonde, since pale ginger came out darker on film than a blonde of the same shade as measured by the human eye. She looked relaxed, remarkably so for a sitter of those times, when exposures were anything up to a minute and heads were clamped in discreetly hidden iron frames. There was a world-weariness in her eyes and a watchfulness, too, as if she had seen much and now trusted little.

"Is it fancy dress or really from the Sixties?" I asked.

"Why?" he countered.

"I feel I've seen her before. The eyes are like my grandmother's. But it can't be her. She'd have been in her thirties by then."

"The eyes are like yours, too. Cover up her hair and it could be you."

I did as he suggested and then laughed. "It *is* me! You fraud! You took one of my photos and dodged it into some old negative you found at Stanton's — the way you did with Moynihan's oak tree that time." He could easily have got an image of me because he had taken a number of photos of all three of us, posing as trippers, to display as come-all-yous for our all-in-one-day service when we got started. "I'm glad we live now and not then, though," I said. "What awful clothes!"

"It's Esther Wilkinson," he told me. "I was going through the old negatives, because we sell the glass plates to the nurseryman at the top of Killigrew Road. He scrubs off the gelatin and uses them for cloches. Anyway, I came across that. The catalogue says 'Miss Esther Wilkinson. Engagement portrait. Send account to R. Moynihan, Esquire ...' and the same address as today."

The penny dropped. *"That's* where I've seen her before, of course! His portrait of her on the back landing! You remember? Where I strayed by-mistake-on-purpose, and he got quite annoyed with me."

"Old Moynihan must have seen the likeness at once — the minute he saw you sitting in class at the polly." He tickled me under the chin. "And you fondly thought it was your skill at drawing that interested him!"

"It was!" I insisted. All the same, our likeness was such that my sudden appearance in his class must have given him quite a shock. Also it explained why Francesca, his present wife, had given me such an odd look every now and then. She was so Italian in appearance I had merely supposed she was of that Latin temperament which sees passionate intrigues behind every glance and smile.

I stared at the photograph, into those world-weary eyes — and I had judged them world-weary before I knew her identity, so it was not a case of finding what I expected to find. I was searching for other traits, other clues to character. This young woman, orphaned like me, had died by her own hand before I was born. She had been rescued by one of the most genial and interesting men in Cornwall and yet she had been compelled by some even more powerful influence toward that dreadful act. There was no hint of it in that eve-of-engagement portrait, of course. Yet behind those eyes the fuse on that fearful time-bomb must have been sputtering slowly down toward its moment of detonation. In the circumstances, the similarity between us was unnerving — give or take my unruly blonde locks and her sleekly disciplined tresses. I already knew I had my grandmother's eyes, but to discover that I had practically *all* of her cousin Esther's features would have been slightly unnerving even if she had lived happily and died a natural death. The thought that there was *something* hidden in my flesh that shaped it along preordained lines, giving me no choice other than to resemble her ... well, it was like carrying my own personal cloud around on an otherwise sunny day.

Family! It seemed I'd never be free of it. It was an octopus — or a multipus — that grew a new tentacle every month. I shivered and handed the photograph back to Jim.

"Keep it," he said. "Show Marian — see if she gets the likeness."

I knew I'd keep it anyway. Even if he had accepted it back, I'd have asked for it again sometime. Having Esther's photograph in my own keeping gave me the illusion of controlling that elusive kinship between us, which now extended far beyond mere genealogy.

I went over to Little Sinns on the last Saturday in April. It was a year, all but two days, since my first visit there, when Marian was one of the 'little sinners' and girls like June Goldsworthy were trying to talk her into becoming a bigger one. Miss Martin was even more excited at the prospect of 'our London adventure,' as she called it, than I was. My life had been rather full of excitements lately, whereas hers had run along the same predictable grooves. It had not lacked dramas, I'm sure, but they were all of a muchness. Snuffing out rebelliousness in the human spirit has much in common with laundering dirty linen day after day — and no one could claim that is an interesting sort of occupation.

I still did not understand her friendship for me — I mean why she had picked on me so particularly. Her daily life was almost entirely taken up with girls my age and older, so why me? I was glad of her interest, naturally, but that's not the same as understanding it.

She had moved a spare bed from one of the dormitories into her own room. It was, she said, the one Marian had occupied during the few weeks she had been there. For a woman who lived a life of discipline bordering on harshness she had an oddly sentimental streak. When I opened my suitcase to get out my nightgown and toothbrush her eyes fell on the photograph Jim had given me. She was curious, as I could see, but too well bred to inquire about it. I passed it to her and said, "Guess who?"

She carried it to the oil lamp at her bedside, peered at it for a moment, then frowned at me. "Is it some kind of trick photograph — you know, like the fox with hawk's wings and a fish's tail?"

"Why?" I asked, because I wanted her to say more precisely what she thought of the woman in the picture.

"If it is, I'd guess it's your head superimposed on an old photograph — or it's you in fancy dress."

"It's my cousin twice removed — my grandmother's cousin. She died before I was born. Isn't it extraordinary?"

She looked at it again and then at me. "Very."

"She was a niece of General Sir Redvers Wilkinson — the one who's adopted Teresa out in India, although he's the younger. She married Roger Moynihan, the artist, over in Falmouth."

Miss Martin became uncomfortable at this news. She obviously knew of poor Esther's history. She looked again at the photograph, as if to see whether she had missed some clue.

"A history like hers leaves no mark upon the features," I said as she handed it back to me. "Though there is a sort of cold or cynical cast to her eyes, don't you think?"

"Yes," she said without looking at it again. "You know her story, then, I gather?"

I nodded and laid the picture back on top of my suitcase. "I'll hide it under one of my dresses," I said. "I don't want Marian to see it as soon as I start unpacking."

As soon as the words were out I realized they provoked a question as to whether I'd left it on top deliberately for her, Miss Martin, to see. The simple fact was that I hadn't realized we'd be sharing a room. But simple facts are feeble when more interesting variations are around. She looked at me curiously and I guessed her mind was already working along those lines. I hadn't really wanted to continue talking about Esther Wilkinson but now I had to say something to round the conversation off.

"I saw a portrait of her once," I said. "By Moynihan himself, of course. But I saw no likeness to myself then. It was his personal vision of her, naturally. The camera sees things differently. Jim says it *sees* nothing, which is why it can show us everything. An artist sees something and then has to suppress everything else in order to make us see it, too."

"He's a most interesting young man, your Mister Collett — but then *you* wouldn't be interested in him if he weren't, would you! What did Mister Moynihan's painting tell you?"

"It was full of love and tenderness. I remember thinking I'd give anything to be loved like that."

"And now you are!"

"Yes." I took up one of her hands and hugged it briefly to my cheek. "D'you know it's a year ago come Monday that I first visited Little Sinns? Can you remember that day? I don't think I'll ever forget it. May I wash in this bowl?"

"Of course! I'm sorry." And she fussed around, filling it with cold water from the ewer and topping it off with a little hot from the kettle one of the girls had brought up earlier. "I certainly do remember that day. You looked so frightened."

"I was! I feared that, if they were able to lock up Marian for nothing, they could do the same to me." I stripped to my chemise and washed my face and arms vigorously. Usually I flannelled myself all over, every evening except bath nights, but I was too shy with her there.

She wasn't, though. She stripped off everything and washed all over, smiling quite unselfconsciously at me. Then I felt ashamed of my false modesty and did the same. She had a beautiful body, like a Canova, pale as alabaster. She was the first completely naked grown-up I'd ever seen. It made me wonder if Jim and I would undress in front of each other — perhaps even undress each other! Or would he be too shy? Would it be up to me to decide that sort of thing?

Meanwhile, Miss Martin talked on about her impressions of me that day — words it would be far more embarrassing to record than my meditation on the subject of our honeymoon. "Penny for 'em?" she prompted when she realized I had merely been saying yes or no for some while.

"I was thinking I am sometimes not very kind to Jim," I replied. I was dry enough by then to slip into my nightgown. "We were talking about our honeymoon last night and I said I didn't think we could afford to take one in the middle of summer, which is our bread-and-butter time. I said we should postpone it until around Christmas. We need the money, because it'll take time to build up a year-round photographic business."

"But surely your partner has plenty?" She laughed. "And *you're* not exactly poor now."

I tipped some of her toothpowder onto my hand and dipped my toothbrush in it. The foaming tickled my palm. "That's what Jim said. But I don't think that's the right attitude."

She was just finishing her teeth by then. "Don't you *want* a honeymoon? Not even a couple of days off?"

I could only make noises round the foam but she thought I was avoiding an answer. "You're such a puritan, Crissy!" she said.

The word shook me, not because of its unfairness but because, in one instant, it swept aside all my bewilderment — chiefly about myself — and showed me a truth that, for a moment, paralyzed me. Or, rather, it paralyzed my muscles but left my mind racing. "Puritan ..." I murmured.

"Yes." She was watching me intently.

"Yes," I echoed. "It's what I've become, not what I really am. Because of having to. Because it's the only way I can achieve ... because people expect ... oh dear!"

"Take your time," she said. "Sit down and I'll brush out your hair."

"No. You sit down and I'll brush yours. I'm the lady's maid. You'll see how good I am."

She realized I had to be *doing* something so she accepted the offer. "Good at everything," she said as she sat before her dressing table — showing that she already half knew what I was struggling to say. Will I ever understand human nature as thoroughly as she does?

Anyway, it helped me begin. "It's what everyone expects," I said. "They say, 'Oh, Crissy, you're so mature for your years' ... No. They don't even say for my years. Just 'so mature ... so level-headed ... so competent' ... Jim says it. Cousin Stella says it ..."

"I say it," she put in quietly.

"But it's like patting a puppy-dog on the head for doing something well. He does it again — to get another pat. And again and again and again." I unpinned her buns and let the coils of her hair unroll, which they did rather reluctantly. She had fine, silky hair. "I *long* to have a honeymoon, yet I say 'No!' so that people will say, 'What a sensible, frugal, no-nonsense gel she is!' I've turned into a performing puppy-dog. Miss Goody Two-Shoes, twice nightly *and* matinées!"

She laughed. "But you're not the only one, Crissy."

I thought she was going to say she was the same, and I was suddenly afraid of it — too much intimacy and pouring-out of hearts too soon, I thought. "You remember that letter I wrote to Marian the week after she came here?" I asked.

She nodded. *"That* could have been signed 'Miss Goody Two-Shoes,' all right!"

"But it worked. It made you realize that Marian wasn't what they said. It led to ... well, our friendship. To this." I gathered her long hair into one hank and brushed it out.

"But surely you didn't think I was *deceived!"* Her eyes danced merrily in the looking glass. "I started to say just now that you're not the only one. I've known dozens of girls like you. Hundreds. Girls who have never had a childhood. They're earning money from the age of five. Or looking after the house and even younger siblings. They're mature and responsible and worldly wise at *ten* — never mind ... what are you now? Seventeen, is it?"

I nodded.

"You're an old lady, my dear! But very few of the girls I'm talking about could have written that letter you wrote to Marian — even if they had the education and vocabulary. That required something more than untimely maturity. And that's why I became so interested in you. And why I had hoped you'd come and work here with me." She handed me a bow to tie her hair in a tail. "Don't take this amiss, but you have so much in common with the girls in this house — the same lack of a real childhood — the same maturity beyond your years. But you have that something extra, which is quite indefinable."

I laughed grimly. "I don't think it is. I think it *is*, quite simply, the childhood I never had. It's clamouring for some attention now that I no longer have to count every penny."

She rose and, thanking me, went to her bed. On the way she paused and stared down at Esther Moynihan's portrait. "She had to grow up rather quickly, too." Then she changed her mind and came back. "I'll brush out your hair now," she said.

When I was seated she went on, "About this honeymoon. Could it also be that you're a little afraid of it — of being alone with a man in those circumstances? And lying in bed with him? You know what I'm talking about?"

I blushed. "Well, I hope I'm mature enough for *that!*"

"Ah." She seemed disappointed. "Well, anyway, did you happen to notice a book in my shelves down there? Called *What Every Young Wife Should Know.* Would you like to borrow it?"

I told her there was a copy at Fenton Lodge.

"I see. You've read it from cover to cover, I expect?" There was a missionary zeal in her eye.

I felt weary all of a sudden, but I realized we had to get this out of the way, here and now, or it would turn into a kind of Chinese torture lasting all week. "I haven't found that book particularly useful, I'm afraid," I said.

She asked why and I told her it was the sort of book that wanted to be terribly well liked by absolutely everybody. It wanted to be frank and open and honest and yet it didn't wish to hurt religious people's feelings. So it was mealy-mouthed, furtive, and vague, and it *still* offended religious people by discussing such matters at all.

I thought she would leap to its defence but all she did was ask if I could think of a particular example.

Only one came to mind. "There's a bit where he says — I'm sure it's written by a man — he says something like what a good thing it is for husbands and wives to sleep in separate rooms. Freedom-loving people like the English might at first find such an arrangement mean-spirited, he admits, but the nobler parts of our consciousness ought to inform us that it is the only way of resisting temptation when it grips us too strongly. And yet, he adds — in a typical, wishy-washy attempt to be all things to all readers — the connecting door between those separate bedrooms ought *never* to be shut. I ask you — what a simp! It's like saying thieves should be thrown into gaol — to satisfy the puritan moralists — but the door should never be locked — to please the libertarians. Oh dear me!"

"Why are you so sure it's written by a man?" she asked, gathering my hair and tying a bow around it like hers.

"I don't know. The atmosphere? It's full of fear — fear of women. Didn't you feel that when you read it?"

Instead of answering me she asked, "And how would *you* rewrite that particular passage, Crissy?"

Well, of course, I had asked for that! Flustered, I just said something vague like, "If you ask me, I think his whole theory is wrong. He seems to think that people have a higher nature, which is to be encouraged at every turn, and a lower nature, which is to be crushed at all costs. To me that's wrong."

"Self-sacrifice for others is not somehow higher than, say, stealing from others?"

I didn't mean that, of course — and she knew it — so I didn't bother to answer. Instead I climbed into bed, stretched luxuriously, and said, "Oh, Marian! If your bed in Hampstead is only half as comfortable as this, you're in clover!"

Miss Martin climbed into her bed and turned down the wick to a small glow. "I know it sounds silly but I'm afraid of the absolute dark," she confessed. "D'you mind?"

"Of course not. We only ever had nightlights when we were very ill. To me it's the height of luxury."

"You didn't answer my question," she said.

I sighed. "I'm not talking about stealing and murder and things like that. They harm other people. But what husbands and wives get up to doesn't harm anybody. If a husband and wife *don't* have separate bedrooms and make full use of their 'conjugal rights' — as the divorce reports call them — who is harmed? And why all this talk of 'higher' nature and 'lower' nature? Is Sister Berrion *higher* than me because she keeps her virginity for ever — while I'm just keeping mine until Jim and I are married? I resent that."

There was a long silence. I peeped at Miss Martin and found her staring at the ceiling. The tiny flame of the lamp beyond her laid a fine line of silver down her profile, as in a painting by La Tour. Her expression was unreadable by it.

"Now I've offended you," I said. "I'm sorry."

"No, dear, not in the slightest," she replied. "I ought to have known better — that's all."

"Better than what?"

She just chuckled.

I took an enormous risk then, speaking as soon as the notion crossed my mind and before I could have second thoughts. "Were you ever engaged to anyone, Miss Martin?" I asked.

She jerked her head and stared at me sharply. Now her ear was limned with silver and there was just a glint of light on the outer edge of her right eye. "What makes you ask that?" she said.

"I don't know. You were talking the way Marian used to talk when she had a great secret to tell but she wanted me to ask questions and pick away at it."

Miss Martin stretched her arms above her face, fingers twined, and yawned. Or mixed a yawn and a chuckle. "Well, you're quite right in one respect, Crissy. It *is* a secret. But I don't want you to pick away at it. If I tell you, will you keep it absolutely to yourself?"

"Of course I will. Cross my heart and ..."

"There's no need for that. Your word is enough. It's nothing shameful but I just don't see why anybody else should need to know, that's all. I was not only engaged once, I was actually married. In fact" — she drew a deep breath and took the plunge — "legally I still am, I suppose. I haven't seen him for ten years. I don't even know if he's still alive."

By now the whole bedroom was whirling round my head. The revelation was so unexpected, so unlike anything I might have guessed about Miss Martin, even in my most extravagant fancy, that I still couldn't relate it to her. "How ...? What ...? I mean, who ... golly!" was all the sense I could speak.

"I was completely unprepared for marriage," she said evenly. "I mean, *completely* — you know?"

I made a sort of noncommittal but sympathetic sound. To express surprise would have been like making myself out to be superior in some way — although, mind you, I've never understood those cases of absolute ignorance one reads about from time to time. Like that army captain who was cashiered for telling a girl it was an exercise to improve her singing voice. I'm sure she had at least *some* idea what he was doing to her.

"That's why I was concerned for you," Miss Martin went on. "I'd hate it to happen to anybody else — especially to someone I'm really ... well, really very fond of."

I laughed, partly out of embarrassment. "That sounds as if your next words would be 'despite your ...' something or other."

"Yes, well, despite your lack of need for my well-intentioned advice. It's most aggravating when one has wound one's courage up to distil one's life experience — only to find it is not needed after all."

"Oh, I'd never say that, Miss Martin. I'd happily accept all the advice anyone can give me — and most especially from someone *I've* grown rather fond of."

"Despite ...?" she suggested.

"Despite her alarming tendency to think rather more highly of me than I deserve!"

It was her turn to laugh — also partly out of embarrassment. Then, after a short silence, she said, "I suppose giving advice is like saying what I'd do differently if I could start all over again. I'm thirty-two now. I married Paul Martin — he was no relation, by the way, and Martin is my maiden name, too, but it has been a convenient confusion since we parted. Anyway, I married him when I was eighteen after being engaged to him for two years and knowing him for three before that — on and off, you know. His people lived a few doors away from us — this was up in Plymouth. In the Seventies. It wasn't a very passionate courtship. He was getting on for thirty when we married, but I suppose he'd had his eye on me for some time and thought I'd suit him very nicely. I was thirteen when he took me to the fair. He was twenty-four then. We went sailing quite a lot. And bicycling parties. The usual things, you know. I was sixteen when he took me to my first civic ball. I was flattered by his attention, of course. What young girl wouldn't have been. He was somebody quite senior in the borough council — on the civil-service side — tipped as a future head of administration."

"May I ask where he is now?" I interrupted.

"Standing in a jungle somewhere," she replied. "A plan in one hand and a whip in the other, no doubt. Anyway, he was twenty-nine and I was eighteen and we married in some style and went to Normandy for our honeymoon. I suppose my mother thought he was old enough to enlighten me on the rituals of the marriage bed — and I'm sure he was delighted she'd done nothing in that line herself."

She swallowed heavily and there was a sort of shiver in her breath.

"You needn't tell me if you'd rather not, Miss Martin," I said. "I'll understand, honestly."

"No, no — I want to. Listen, d'you think you could bring yourself to call me Harriet?"

Once again surprise reduced me to silence. Despite the warmth of our friendship there was a great difference in our ages. But I think I was even more astonished to discover she was called Harriet. I hadn't thought of her as having any particular first name, but Harriet was one of my favourites.

"You're shocked," she said.

"No ... Harriet. Dumbfounded. If ever I'm blessed with a little girl, I've already decided to call her either Harriet or Charlotte — my two most cherished names. Now it'll definitely be Harriet."

She moved nearer to me between her sheets, close enough to touch my brow. "You're not just being diplomatic?"

"Cross my heart and ... oh, sorry! No, I'm not."

"You're such a *natural* diplomat," she said. "It's just that there's nobody left in my life these days who calls me by my Christian name — and I'd like it to be you. Anyway, where was I? Oh yes — my *wonderful* honeymoon in Normandy!"

There was another awkward pause. I said, "You thought he must have been glad your mother had not enlightened you?"

"Ye-es." She sighed. "It's so bizarre — what Paul did. Have you ever seen an illustrated edition of *Treasure Island?* Or any book with pictures of treasure chests in? You know those old-fashioned treasure chests with the half-barrel tops and the heavy brass fittings? Paul had one of those — full of jewelled girdles and diadems and bangles and strings of pearls ..." She saw me staring at her wide-eyed and added, "All theatrical tawdry, of course. Worth a fiver at the outside. And on our wedding night in Normandy — or the night after, because we slept apart on the ferry boat — he took off all my clothes and sat me in a chair and very slowly decked me out in these sham jewels. It took about an hour. And then he sat and gazed at me from all sorts of angles, murmuring things like 'Beautiful ... glorious ... magnificent ...' — which quite flattered me at the time. And then he retired to his own room, leaving me to take it all off and pack it away. He did that two or three times a week for about a year. And I, in my ignorance, thought it was what all married couples did. So when we'd been married a year and there was no baby on the way, my mother — crimson with embarrassment — asked me if Paul was performing his marital duties properly. And, of course, I said yes — several times a week, in fact. So then she arranged for me to see her doctor, without Paul knowing, of course — in case the *fault* were mine! Her doctor was away so I saw a young locum, who got the full story out of me."

A dreamy quality invaded her voice as she went on. "He was a young man. I was a young woman. So I suppose what happened was inevitable. So then there *was* a baby on the way. Paul was livid about it — but, of course, couldn't say a word, which only made him angrier still. He threw me downstairs one day — and that was the end of the baby ... the end of *all* babies for me ... Though I still take no chances."

"Oh, Harriet!" I cried out in anguish, reaching into her bed, feeling for her hand, to take it in mine. She wouldn't let me, though — and the significance of that little afterthought passed me by at the time.

"I'm all right," she said stiffly. "I'm all right. There was a question of criminal proceedings and also of a civil action, but it was all resolved by his agreeing to go abroad and stay there for the rest of his life. My parents haven't entirely disowned me but we have nothing to do with each other now. Paul sent money for a while but when I started working here, nine years ago — I was just an assistant then — I asked him to stop. I can't deny the allowance was useful but I felt sick every time it came and slept badly for several nights, so in the end it wasn't worth it."

She reached out for my hand then and gave it an encouraging squeeze — also a little push away from her. "So now you know, Crissy. The full, ghastly truth."

I stared at the ceiling. "If you hadn't told me yourself," I said, "I could never have believed it. You always seem so serene. He was mad, wasn't he — your husband. He must have been."

"He was certainly ... how can one put it kindly? Damaged? How or when I don't know. It's the one great mystery of my life — what happened to Paul to make him like that?"

"If only you'd known," I said.

She nodded slowly. "It wouldn't have helped the situation then, but I'd like to know now."

"No, I mean if only you'd known the proper thing to expect of a husband, he wouldn't have been able to cheat you like that."

She appeared not to hear me. "I think he was afraid," she said. "Of women, I mean, not just of me. I know what you mean when you say that book was written by a man. It *is* filled with fear. And Paul's fear of women is the nearest I can get to an explanation. Outwardly he was a fine gentleman and a well-liked civil servant. Inwardly he had an opinion of himself as something low and mean and vile — consumed with lust. Since he feared to discover that I might be the same, he put me on a pedestal and adorned me and worshiped me from afar."

Then she answered my earlier comment: "I don't think that my knowing what a proper husband should do would have been of the slightest help to a man like that. In every *other* respect, you see, he was a perfect husband to me — kindly, attentive, considerate, amusing, intellectually stimulating. He always supported me in public, even when I was wrong, and then he'd point out my error privately afterwards in the kindest way. He broadened my horizons and gave me enormous confidence to be myself — which I had previously lacked. Oh, I owe him a great deal. I can't deny it. I don't wish to deny it. *But...!"* She laughed. "The cost was not worth it."

"And there was no sign of it — this 'damage,' as you call it — *before* your wedding?" I was thinking of my own situation, of course.

"What could possibly be a sign of something so grotesque?" she asked. "D'you remember that painting by Burne-Jones about six years ago — *King Cophetua and the Beggar Maid?* The moment I saw it — the king looking up admiringly at the remote and beautiful beggar girl whom he's adorned in silks and finery — I thought, *Oh dear — Burne-Jones, too, eh?* But that's probably a dreadful calumny on the man. In fact, I think Paul's malady was just an extreme form of something that's mildly present in many men — maybe all men. They seem to have this need to put us on pedestals, adorn us in beautiful things, look up to us, make *us* a sort of standard of nobility." She laughed drily. "And as long as it's mild, I suppose we're only too happy to go along with it."

"We certainly enjoy adorning ourselves in beautiful things," I said. "Talking of which, Marian asked me to lend her five pounds to buy a costume she saw in a sale. I didn't reply. Perhaps I ought to have done — before some latter-day Paul Martin comes along and volunteers his purse instead!"

And so we fell to talking of Marian and Hampstead and all the things we hoped to cram into our five days in London ... until the pauses joined up and words turned to snores.

Harriet and I travelled up to London in Second Class Ladies Only compartments. There was only one through-train on a Sunday and that was an overnight sleeper leaving Penzance at five in the afternoon. We caught the nine-o'clock from Redruth, which went as far as Plymouth, arriving shortly before midday. There we had just over two hours to wait before the London train — which gave us time to go down to the Sutton Orphanage and take the two boys out for a quick luncheon, all of which I had arranged in advance.

My pleasure at seeing them again, and both looking so well, too, did not survive the entire meal. Their table manners shocked me, as did their gluttonous appetite. The latter I could excuse, for I don't suppose there's an institution in all the world where boys of that age rise from the table swearing they couldn't touch another morsel. But their inability to close their mouths when eating, and the way they clutched their knives and forks like savages at a kill, and Gerald's new habit of wiping his nose on his sleeve, shocked me deeply. Harriet was offended, too, I'm sure, though she passed no remark at the time.

"It seems I shall be able to make a civilized home for them none too soon," I said when we had made our goodbyes and the two of us were on our way back to the station.

"I didn't say anything while they were there …" she began.

"But you were as shocked as I was, of course."

"No, no! I have to correct far worse faults than that every day — and from girls, too — girls twice their age. It's institutional life does that for them. I'll bet it's a year since those boys opened a door with anything other than the toe of a boot! What I meant was I said nothing about their coming to live with you. Do they know about it yet? I wasn't sure."

I shook my head. "It would only fret them. They have no real sense of time. I'll wait until a week before it happens — and even *that* will seem an eternity to them. Besides, I want Teresa back first."

"Ah," she said, as if that were significant.

"Because she's had the biggest wrench of all of us, you see? I don't want her returning to a home where Gerald and Arthur have already spread themselves — going into *their* playroom and pushing aside *their* things to make room for hers. I want her completely established and belonging and … *there* before either boy comes back."

On the train, where we had the compartment to ourselves for the first hour — as far as Newton Abbot — I said, "I sometimes wonder if I should have those two boys back at all."

"Goodness!" she exclaimed. "Here's a change of tune!"

"I mean have them full-time. You see, I *could* afford to send them to Truro as weekly boarders. They seem to like institutional life. Tom loves it, too. He's not looking forward at all to leaving Tywardreath — which he'll have to do this autumn. Besides, there's Jim to consider. He's marrying me, not the whole Moore family."

"What about Tom, then?" she asked. "Where will he go when he leaves Tywardreath?"

"There are several nurserymen and market gardeners around Gulval, which is only a mile from where we'll be living at Chyandour Cliff."

She chuckled and said, "So all you need do is entice Marian away from Hampstead to some work in Penzance and you'll have your family complete again!" Seeing my face she added, "Isn't that what you've wanted all along?"

I nodded glumly. "It's what I wanted in the beginning. But what *is* my family now? Time changes the very ground beneath me. Jim's my family — or very soon will be. So is Mark. Even the General is my family — though rather remotely. But still …" I sighed.

"And not forgetting the young girl whose photograph is tucked away in your bag," Harriet said. "She, too, is kin to you. Her life has certainly influenced yours far more than has any other Wilkinson — including the General *and* your Cousin Stella." My surprise made her add, "Certainly! Has Cousin Stella never spoken about her, and that dreadful time for your family?"

"Only in very vague terms. Why? Do *you* know about it? Well, I suppose everyone in Redruth must."

"I perhaps know a little more than most because I have the privilege of knowing Mrs Vosper Scawen — Jane Scawen. Wife of the Helston lawyer. You've heard of her surely?"

"The dynamite woman? The one who built the hanging gardens at Trevivian, over on the Helford?"

"That's the one. She was a very close friend of Esther Wilkinson — or Moynihan, as she became. Her suicide followed several failed attempts and Jane Scawen nursed her back to health each time."

"How did they know each other? I heard Mrs Scawen was a foreigner. From Yorkshire or somewhere."

Harriet laughed. *"That* sort of foreigner! Yes, but her mother was from down here — from Falmouth, in fact. If you think *your* family history is complicated, you should go into hers one day! Anyway, her father brought her down here after her mother died, precisely in order to escape all those complications and scandals. He thought her mother was from Wales, you see — because she'd covered her tracks very well! But, as I say, she was from Cornwall. So the poor man brought her right into the lion's den. But that's all died down now. The thing I was going to tell you about Jane Scawen was that at the very moment of her arrival — when she'd just stepped off the train at Penzance — an innocent of eighteen — she struck up a conversation with Esther Wilkinson, who was plying for custom just beyond the station entrance. Can you imagine it? Little Jane hadn't the first idea about that side of life, of course. Her father was beside himself with fury — though it didn't stop him from becoming one of Esther's regular customers. In fact" — she looked all around the compartment though we were still obviously alone — "he died 'in her arms,' as they say, though they carried him downstairs to the barber's shop and made it look as if he'd expired there. The lengths people will go to!"

I took a deep breath, having forgotten to breathe for almost half a minute by then. "The barber's shop in the little lane above the gasworks?" I inquired.

She thought it an odd question and told me she had no idea. "Why?" she asked.

"It's uncanny, but I passed it only the other day. On my way from the station to Morrab Road. It's in that sort of area — between the town and the port. It makes me shiver to think of all the dramas that have gone on in all the houses one passes every day — and you never know about them until you hear some little detail like this. Just think — Mrs Vosper Scawen's father died in the arms of my cousin twice-removed in a room I walked past just last week — and I'd never have known the first thing about it unless we'd had this conversation here, today, in a train a hundred miles away from Penzance!"

She chuckled. "It's not just dramas in houses, my dear — it's in families, too. There's not a family in the land that doesn't have at least one such skeleton rattling away in its cupboards."

I recalled then how this present conversation had started. "You didn't explain how Esther Wilkinson had more influence on my life than ..."

"Oh yes! Well, her shame left a deep scar on the whole Wilkinson clan. You see, what's *supposed* to happen to a girl who becomes an Unfortunate is ... well, misfortune! Overnight she should lose half her teeth, become addicted to laudanum and gin, dress in filthy rags, look ten years older, and die horribly within six months. She is not supposed to start accruing more capital than all the younger brothers in her family put together. Nor to start looking the picture of bonny good health. Nor to out-dress all her sisters and cousins. Nor to reveal to all the world that an independent-minded woman with a strong will and a cool head for business can manage very nicely thank-you without the supposed protection of a father, a brother, *or* a husband. Above all, she is not supposed to look down on the rest of the world with the cool, cynical gaze you rightly see in her photograph!"

I was sitting on the edge of my seat by now, of course. Every muscle in my body was tense. Harriet became aware that, despite the camouflage of sarcasm, she had revealed more of her innermost passion than she had intended. It was on the tip of my tongue to ask her how, believing these things as ardently as she did, she could spend her life breaking the independent minds and strong wills of the young women in her care. But then I saw a kind of panic in her eyes, a mute plea to change the subject, so instead I said, "It's pretty amazing, in the circumstances, that Mrs Scawen continued her friendship with Esther after her father's death — I mean, when you consider the manner of his dying!"

"Ah!" She gratefully accepted this line of escape. "You'd have to know Jane Scawen herself to understand that. She's the nearest thing to a saint I've ever met. *Tout comprendre, c'est tout pardonner.* But — as I was about to say — Esther's failure to follow the path ordained for Unfortunates by Society, was an even greater scandal to the Wilkinsons than her way of life itself. Like you Moores, she was the offspring of a love-match the rest of the family had bitterly opposed. So when you Moores, like Esther before you, were orphaned and rumours of Marian's moral delinquency reached your grandmother's ears ..."

"But that was all trumped up!" I protested.

"I know, dear." She patted my hand soothingly. "That was obvious to me within ten minutes of her arrival at Little Sinns. Feckless, yes. Easily swayed to good or bad. But morally delinquent, no. However, your grandmother must have thought history was about to repeat itself. That's why she moved so swiftly to spread you as far apart as possible and made sure that ..."

"With Felicity Trevarton's help," I pointed out. "That's one thing I've never understood. Felicity loathed my grandmother with a depth of feeling it would be hard to exaggerate. Why, then, did she fall in so readily with her schemes?"

"Have you seen her lately?" Harriet asked.

"No, not for some time. I've been avoiding her."

"Why?"

I shivered. "There's something about her. She pretends she'll move heaven and earth to help you but you know in your bones, somehow, that she won't do anything that doesn't serve her own secret purposes, too. Even if it would cost her nothing, she wouldn't lift a finger beyond that. I still don't know why she was so helpful to my grandmother."

"And how d'you think she feels toward you? D'you think she's been avoiding you just as much as you've been avoiding her?"

I laughed drily at the possibility. "My grandmother's bequest to me must have taken her aback."

"Does she know the whole history of guilt that lay behind it?"

"Yes. Mrs Bourdeaux told her everything. She knows my grandmother died full of hate for me. But people will always ignore uncomfortable facts, anyway — won't they. If she's determined to believe my grandmother and I were as thick as thieves at the end — conspiring against her — she'll simply ignore things like that. I just have to think of all the ways she could make life unpleasant for me ... and try to be ready for any one of them."

These thoughts distracted me several times every day, so it was easy for me to speak of them while my mind secretly followed quite a different line — one prompted by the question that had been on the tip of my tongue a few minutes earlier: How could Harriet, holding one set of beliefs so passionately, act in such a contrary manner at Little Sinns? Perhaps she didn't! Perhaps she had little private talks with certain selected girls — girls with 'independent minds and strong wills' — and taught them how to conform in all outward aspects while they continued to rebel in secret!

I had only ever seen Harriet at work from the viewpoint of a visiting friend. I decided I must ask Marian how she had seemed from the other side of the table. At Newton Abbot, as I say, we were joined by a party of three ladies on their way to a choir festival in London and our books suddenly became more interesting than any conversation we might hold in such company.

The sun dropped below the horizon two hours before we reached London. I had no idea England was so vast. From Redruth to Paddington Station was a journey of ten hours with just the usual halts at stations. Because of our long break between trains at Plymouth, we would be taking over twelve hours — and even then, London was still fifty miles or so short of the east coast! I'd seen England in atlases, of course. In fact, I could draw the outline of the British Isles from memory and had often done so for the infants when I was helping in dame school in Porthleven. But nothing could prepare one for that endless sequence of hills and valleys, woods and streams, towns and villages which stretches beside the line for hour after hour, the whole way to London. Had we left Cornwall around sunrise at six, we could *just* have squeezed the journey in before sunset. But here we were, somewhere in the Cotswolds, two hours short of the city and the sun had already gone. The porters came along the platform at Didcot and lit all the lamps in the carriages. The friendly smell of the lamp-oil flame was added to the aroma of that strangely fish-tainted steam you get on railways. I think it's something in the lubricating oil they use.

I pressed my nose to the window, pulled my bonnet down to shield my eyes from the lamp, and gazed out at the darkling landscape as it trundled by. Something almost magical happens to the world during those brief moments of late twilight — something I should love to be able to paint one day. The colours sink into a uniform darkness and the objects in the landscape lose their character and definition. But before they melt away entirely, they breathe and move! You can understand where all those legends come from, about creatures that are inanimate by day, mimicking stones and dead wood and other natural formations, but which stir themselves to life as darkness falls. There comes a moment when the whole landscape seems to stir itself in that way, when trees, hills, rivers, and even houses, are all liberated to wander the earth until dawn. Then the night becomes an unknown country, punctuated by pinpoints of light whose brilliance is a mockery, because they reveal nothing. Indeed, like will-o'-the-wisps, they deceive, seeming near when far, or far when near.

Then the moon rose. It had been full the previous night so it was still bright enough to make sure the landscape settled down and behaved properly once again. By the time we reached the outlying villages west of the capital — places like Southall, Ealing, and Acton — it was well up in the sky and turning everything to silver and black. Gaslit rooms in passing cottages revealed tantalizing little snippets of life, but I no longer felt myself excluded from it all — as I had that evening last September when Jim and I peeped in through the windows of New Street on my way home. Soon I, too, would have a house of my own (*all* my own, not the half one the others were planning), and then *I* would be able to say things like, "Butter the cat's paws before you come up, dear," and do all those other little warm, domestic things that whisper, "I belong here!"

"You *are* in a pensive mood, Crissy," Harriet said as we reached Kensal Green Cemetery, which is the start of London proper. She nudged me as she handed me my overcoat. "I expect it's chilly outside."

The choral ladies had already fussed themselves into their coats — and galoshes, though it was not even threatening rain. Now they sat at a loss for what to do next. From the railway map in the timetable I knew there was a station called Royal Oak about a mile before Paddington — and we hadn't passed it yet — so I just said in a pretty offhand manner, as if I made this journey every day, "Oh, there's plenty of time yet, you know," and I did not start putting on my things until Royal Oak flashed by. I imagined that the three ladies looked at me with admiration as a metropolitan habituée, but I don't suppose they did, really.

Underneath it all (I can admit it now) I was madly jealous of Marian because London was her home and she was going to be so casual about its wonders while I would have to school myself not to gawp and gasp at every turn, and to hide my surprise — and even my delight — at everything novel I saw. I had been reading up on London, especially Hampstead and Fitzroy Square and the West End, ever since Harriet invited me to join her. I practically knew whole pages of *London Old and New* by heart. And *Grant's London Sketches,* with illustrations by 'Phiz.' Oh, she wasn't going to make *me* feel like a Cornish bumpkin!

There is something exciting about arriving at the terminus of a railway line. Even little Penzance has it, but it is nothing when compared with the thrill of arriving into Paddington. Our train had passed through the whole of southern England, sweeping up travellers as it came. And now they all come pouring out of their carriages, all wanting a porter at once, and a cab, and not to lose even one of the eight children they have brought with them.

"Count the bags again," cries one anxious father. "I'm sure it should be twelve."

"Sit there until Mamma comes back and don't you *dare* move!" An anxious woman shakes a finger in a frightened little boy's face.

"Where has that wretched fellow got to now?" snaps a peppery old man with a waxed moustache.

"Guard! I need half a dozen men to get my equipage off the wagon," calls a gentleman who has brought his carriage to Town with him. He is already looking out anxiously for the horses, which should have been there on our arrival and clearly aren't.

A stout porter with a walrus moustache goes by with a trolley full of bloodstained game — rabbits and hares, mostly, with here and there a farm goose or a brace of ducks. He ignores all calls upon him, as he is entitled to do, for these are express goods.

A middle-aged lady holds up a placard on which she has written, *Barnaby's Uncle?* She holds it above her head and peers into every passing face, anxious for any response other than the curiosity or merriment that meets her on every side. What is the story there? I wonder. Amused, Harriet murmurs to me that 'Barnaby's Uncle' sounds like one of those party games where several people end up with sprained ankles.

Just beyond the throng, waiting in the gloom for a train to pull in on the next platform, stand three convicts in heavy iron shackles, their shaven heads bowed under the cold eye of a burly warder.

And over us all hang vast clouds of smoke, swirling among the open tracery of the cast-iron arches and drifting upward into the great vaults of glass that span the platforms. Where it spills out at the open end it turns the bright silver of the moon to a dull, sulphureous yellow and blots out the stars completely. They do not twinkle so much as sputter and vanish.

"Crissy! Dear, dahling Crissy!"

Jerked from my reverie I turned to see my lovely sister advancing upon me, arms raised high, smiling from ear to ear, and ignoring the rest of the world as if it were there on sufferance, where she walked by right. "Welcome to the great wen!" she cried as she flung her arms about me and hugged me half to death.

I almost burst into tears. I was determined to be so grown-up and casual, but the feel of her dear self in my arms again and the music of her voice swept all those brave intentions aside. However, I managed to blink and sniff the worst of it away and say, in a voice far steadier than my nerves at that moment, "You remember Miss Martin, of course."

As she broke from our embrace she said, "You've grown!" looking significantly at my bosom.

Harriet, who couldn't see Marian's eyes, took it as a general comment, so I passed no remark and hid my embarrassment.

Marian turned and bobbed as pretty a curtsy as anyone could wish. To her surprise, Harriet put an arm around her shoulders and gave her a little hug. "You've grown, too," she said, patting Marian on the forehead to make clear which department she was referring to.

I said, "Marian's ever so grateful for all you did for her, Harriet. Aren't you, Marian?"

My sister's smile faded and she assumed a languid hostility I remembered from our early teens. "I'm perfectly capable of expressing my gratitude in my own way and of my own volition — thank you, miss!" she said sharply.

"Oh, send for buckets of water!" Harriet said gaily as she threw her arms about our shoulders and bore us across the platform, out of the general press of the throng. She did not seem to be aware of the chained prisoners standing there. Perhaps she thought that was where the cabs drew in. By the time she did realize it, we were almost in danger of bumping into them.

All they could see was the silhouettes of three women against the lighted platform beyond. But by that same light we found ourselves staring into three faces brutalized by their regime and enhungered by the deprivation it enforced on them. Human minds trapped inside the bodies of dumb animals could not have stared out more piteously than they. Their faces will haunt me for ever, I think.

"Now then! Stand back, ladies, if you please!" Their single warder found his voice at last.

Harriet's arms fell to her sides and we retreated separately in some haste. "I'm so sorry, my dears," she said. "I only saw them out of the corner of my eye and I assumed they were cabmen. How dreadful! Where *is* the cab rank?"

"I have Mrs Morell's carriage waiting beyond the barrier," Marian told her.

We found a porter and showed him our bags. He followed us out to the concourse. I asked the collector if I could have my ticket back once he'd punched it, to keep as a souvenir, but he just smiled and shook his head. I asked him what would happen to it and he said all tickets had to be 'reconciled.' At which point I gave up.

"How can tickets be *reconciled?*" I asked the other two as we moved on. "With whom have they quarrelled?"

"It's probably a great deal easier than reconciling *sisters!*" Harriet said heavily.

Marian and I looked at each other and laughed. "Nothing can do that, Miss Martin," my sister said gaily.

A barefoot beggar came up to Harriet and, cupping his hands, asked for 'any loose coppers' she might have. She was just about to open her purse when Marian, with the dexterity of a conjuror, produced a small printed card with the heading *The Mendicity Society* upon it — and some other printing. "Go to the address on this card," she said. "The officials there will ..."

"I know the officials there!" he sneered. As he turned away he tore the card in two and dropped it.

"You!" Marian thundered. "Come back here this instant!"

He turned and stared at her uncertainly, sizing her up.

"If you don't do as I say," she went on, "I shall find some *loose coppers* for you all right!"

As he shuffled back she said, "Pick up those bits and put them in that litter basket there."

He obeyed in silence, head bowed, looking at no one. But as we paid off our porter and climbed into the carriage, Harriet nudged my arm and pointed him out again. He had returned to the litter basket and was fishing out the bits of card, which he then dropped on the pavement once again, grinning all the while to himself. "There's hope for that man yet," she murmured.

Marian, who had also seen this act of petty defiance, said, "The reason he wasn't interested in the Mendicity Society is that the officials there make inquiries into people's circumstances before they hand out subscribers' money. He almost certainly would not pass their scrutiny. Some of them make a small fortune, you know. Why — he's probably richer even than Crissy!"

I turned and gave her a playful punch, which she smothered in another tight hug.

"Pax?" I suggested.

"Pax," she whispered, giving me a quick kiss on the ear.

Harriet winked at me, which I had never seen her do before.

Mrs Morell reminded me somewhat of Cousin Stella, though she was a good ten years younger. But she had the same benign smile and well-padded figure, and the same short, blonde hair. She sat and chatted with us while Harriet and I — ravenous despite our lunch with the boys and those long hours of doing nothing but talk and read — polished off a delicious steak-and-kidney pudding between us. Nothing I know beats suet crust in kidney gravy.

I'm sure she had a thousand things to discuss with her niece but while I was there she confined her conversation to general topics — what was happening in London, a few tentative plans for the next day or two, and so forth. When we had finished she took me up to my room — a guest room next to the one Harriet was in — and said she was permitting Marian to share the bed with me while I was there. She cut short my thanks, saying, "You have a great deal to tell her, I understand."

Marian, who was waiting out in the corridor, overheard her and began badgering me at once. "Tell me! Tell me all — I want to hear everything. Is it good news? Is it about Teresa? Have you seen Tom and the other boys?"

"I'm getting married," I said.

It brought her flow to a halt. She frowned. "But I already know that. You wrote and told me just after Christmas."

"No, I mean a date is set — the twenty-ninth of May."

"*This* May?" Her jaw dropped. "You mean ... a *month* from now?"

I nodded. "D'you think Mrs Morell would let you away to be my bridesmaid? Down in Penzance?"

She gave a scream of delight, flung her arms around my neck, and attempted to spin the pair of us in giddy circles. I stood my ground, trying to remain serious — but also wishing I could give way to unrestrained behaviour as easily as she always could. I began to realize how much I had missed Marian — all rivalry apart. I needed her wildness in my life, too — her madcap audacity. I needed both to admire her for it and protect her from it, though the fact that she had survived a year without me, apparently unscathed, showed how little she needed what protection I could give.

"D'you know it's exactly a year to this very day — well, in an hour's time it will be — since we last saw each other?" I asked.

"Oh, at Little Sinns!" she replied, waving a dismissive hand. "You're marrying *Jim,* of course? You haven't taken up with another? No, you wouldn't! I like Jim. He looks spiffing. The girls here all fell head over heels for him when he came to see me that time. D'you think he'd send us his photo if you asked him?"

"That's why I didn't send you a fiver for that costume, you see," I white-lied. "It'll be a very simple affair, this wedding. We're going to marry at the register office in ordinary clothes and so if you're going to be bridesmaid ..."

"Not in church?"

"Jim's a freethinker."

"But you — you're not, are you? Why should his faith — or lack of it — prevail over yours?"

"It will be cheaper in a register office," I explained.

She burst into laughter. "In that case, I suppose one could say your faith *does* prevail, too." She crossed the room to the washstand. "She's even given me a guest towel," she said in amazement. "Will you wash first or shall I?"

"I'm covered in smuts from the train," I said.

"Shake! I'm covered in smuts from London! You go first. We have to wrap everything in calico, you know, before we put it away in a chest of drawers. The smuts penetrate, even in a closed drawer."

I stripped to the buff and began my usual all-over wash. As I lathered and flanelled away I told her about Mark and Susan, and how we'd disabused Susan of her ideas about becoming a lady, and I was just starting on our plans for the photographic business in Penzance when I noticed her standing directly behind me, head cocked on one side, peering intently at my legs.

"What is it?" I asked in alarm, looking down to see if My Friend had come early this month and caught me unawares — which had happened once before.

"Oh ... nothing," she replied airily, beaming a smile at me and looking everywhere *but* at my legs.

I continued telling her about our plans while I towelled myself dry — and then I caught her at it again — staring at me with ill-concealed curiosity. She was stripped to her skin by now, too.

"What *is* it?" I asked crossly, stepping out to where I could see myself in the long, oval mirror on the wardrobe door. "Nothing!" I decided irritably. "As usual."

"Exactly!" she laughed but I did not give her the satisfaction of explaining her humour. Instead, I told her how, once we were all settled in at Chyandour, I'd take Gerald and Arthur back to live with us, once Teresa was safely back in the fold, that is. I did not mention the nonsense about sharing a house because I did not intend it to last more than a month or two.

I paused to let her prompt me with the obvious question — as to how Jim would feel about that — but instead she said, "When a girl's had a shake with a man, her knees won't go back together, you know. She can put her ankles together but not her knees. It's a well-known fact." While she spouted this twaddle she surreptitiously (but oh-so-obviously) placed her own ankles in contact with each other and straightened her long, slender limbs to show me an inch of daylight — or gaslight — between her knees.

"Marian!" I said wearily. "Your knees *never* touched. You were always bandy, remember?"

She was miffed. "Not as bandy as this," she said, turning her toes inward as much as she could — to make it worse yet.

"I suppose you're trying to tell me you've done It — yes?"

She tossed her head and grinned at me in the washstand mirror. "Shan't tell you, now."

"Good!" I heaved a sigh of relief. "Can we go back to talking about *important* things?"

"Like *your* wedding and *your* home and *your* Jim ..."

"And *your* brothers and sister, Marian. And *your* future, too." My mouth was so dry I had to dip my toothbrush in water before it would pick up any powder. Then it was so wet it foamed like new-brewed ale and ran down my chin.

"Mad dog! Mad dog!" She pointed at me and laughed. Then she kissed me on the cheek and whispered, "Sorry, Crissy. You just invite it sometimes. Take life a bit easier, eh?"

"*Have* you done It?" I asked, thinking I ought to humour her a little.

"Me? Nope!" She grinned ruefully and shook her head. "How about you, then?"

I grinned happily and shook my head. "It can wait. Have you got a particular friend?"

She shrugged. "Lots."

I rinsed my mouth and put the brush to dry. "That means no *particular* one," I said as I climbed into bed. There I stretched ecstatically, straining every muscle until I shivered in all four limbs and it felt as if I had lemonade in my veins.

"I keep thinking something better will turn up," she admitted as she climbed in beside me. "Gawd 'elp us!" she added in assumed cockney. "There *must* be something better than what I've met with so far. Or d'you think I'm too choosy?"

"I couldn't say. D'you think Mrs Morell will let you come and be my bridesmaid?" I asked.

"Dunno. She's a bit strange. Mind you, so's the whole of Hampstead. It's not like any other part of London. Everyone says so."

"In what way?"

"Well, it's all rich people round here but they're not like other rich people. It's all artistic ideas and philosophy and æsthetic things with them. Because of some landowner here about fifty years ago who wanted to cover it all with houses and streets, like the rest of London. But the people living here already, I mean they were all rich and had friends in parliament and so on. So they stopped him."

"How?"

"I don't know. Something to do with entrails. And a will. He had to break some entrails and they stopped him."

"Entail?" I suggested. "He had to break an entail to a will?"

"Could be." She giggled. "I knew entrails didn't sound right. You ask Mrs Morell. She's got it all down pat."

We put out the lamp and then she reached out and drew back the curtain beside the bed. "Mrs Morell was born in a farmhouse up Fitzjohns Avenue, there. It's gone now, but the late Mister Morell was born in *this* house. Isn't that nice! And I'll tell you another thing — see that great big building beyond the trees? That's the home for orphaned soldiers' daughters. That's where Miss Martin started, before she went to Little Sinns. Did you know she was married once?"

"No!" I laughed as one laughs at gossip that amuses but does not finally convince.

"It's true. He was a colonial governor or magistrate or something and he died of yellow fever."

"Well, she's never said anything like that to me," I said truthfully.

"And you're very 'in' with her now, eh? Calling her Harriet and all! She always did like you, mind. Couldn't stop talking about you before I left Little Sinns. I'd have murdered the pair of you if I hadn't been sent here — just for a bit of peace."

"Oh, Marian!" I flung an arm round her neck and buried my face in her hair where it spilled out over the pillow — and suddenly found myself crying for no reason whatever. Really sobbing.

"Here, here, little kitten," she said, running her fingernails up and down my spine. She hadn't called me that for years. Mind you, I hadn't cried like this for years, either — not with her, anyway. "What's the matter, eh? Tell it all to Big Marian."

"They've built the most awful grave over Mother and Father," I said.

"Is that why you're crying?"

"No. Oh ... I don't know. It's just that there's so much to tell you, and I want you to know it all, and see it all, and feel it all. And I can't. There's just too much. I want you to *be* there. Our lives are slipping apart."

"Oh, I don't know," she replied jovially, determined not to be sucked into my more solemn mood. "We seemed to take up pretty much where we left off, I thought!"

When I swallowed it sounded as if half a dozen ligaments in my neck were breaking. Marian gave a start and pulled away from me. "What was *that?*" she exclaimed.

I laughed and rolled away from her, onto my back. "I don't know." I stared at the ceiling. The street lamps in Fitzjohns Avenue made a sort of blunt-lace pattern across the plaster.

"Our lives would have slipped apart, anyway," Marian said. "Brothers and sisters can't go on living under the same roof all their lives. It's just not natural."

"Yes, but Tom's only ... I mean he's not yet fourteen. Gerald's ten. Arthur will be nine next month. And Teresa's only just turned six. *Our* lives might slip apart in the natural way of things, yours and mine, but we owe them something better, surely?"

After a pause she said, "What's Jim think about your plans to bring the young ones to live with you? Does that include Tom, by the way?"

I explained about trying to get him work with the nurserymen and market gardeners around Gulval. "He fancies his independence now," I said. "He could lodge somewhere else and just come to us for Sunday lunchtime and holidays. That would be a natural slipping-apart, wouldn't it? Don't you think we owe them that?"

"We?" she echoed. "I don't see what I can do up here."

I said nothing to that.

"I'm very happy here," she added.

"I see that," I told her.

"Listen," she went on urgently. "I'll come down to Cornwall and I'll be your bridesmaid — if Mrs Morell will agree. But I'll be coming straight back."

"Of course," I said.

"I know you! You'll get me down there and go to work on me and try and make me stay. Well, I won't."

"I'm glad you're so frank, Marian. It's important to have no mis-understandings, right from the start."

There was an edge of hysteria in her voice now. "I *know* you," she repeated. "When you go all sweet-and-reasonable like this it's because you think you've won already. But you're wrong. I won't stop in Cornwall more than a day after your wedding. I won't."

"Fine," I said.

During the night I got up to use the chamber pot. She followed me. As she got back into bed she said, "I won't!"

And when I woke up the following morning I opened my eyes and found myself staring straight into hers — wide awake already and just waiting for me to come back from the land of dreams. "I honestly won't!" she said.

I was a great disappointment to Mrs Morell, I fear — for the first day, at least. She had planned so many exciting things for us to do and see. But Jim had given me certain commissions, too, and it was more than my life was worth to come back empty-handed to Cornwall. So she reluctantly agreed it would be best for me to get the dullest chores out of the way first so that we could call the rest of the time our own. Therefore, armed with a well-lined purse and a sixpenny map of London, I set off shortly after ten to turn my list of photographic requirements into ticked-off purchases.

The 'Hampstead Yellow' went every fifteen minutes from the High Street to Oxford Circus, so it didn't matter if you missed one. The most you'd ever have to wait was fifteen minutes. How different from Cornwall, where there were hours between services and some places only had two a day, anyway. It was a bright morning, typical for late April, with flocks of fleecy clouds drifting across the sky from the west, none of them promising rain. I went upstairs on the bus, to be out in the open and not miss any of the sights. Unfortunately I was distracted in this by the two women in front of me, a younger one of about twenty and her Mamma, as I gathered.

The whole way down to Tottenham Court Road (fare threepence), they were arguing about *Middlemarch* by the late George Eliot. My ears pricked up at once because it was only a month or so since I had read the story. I was trying to read everything I could on marriage — not *What Every Young Wife Should Know* and such rubbish, but marriages with real people like the Casaubons and the Lydgates in *Middlemarch*.

The daughter thought the story dull because it had neither villains nor heroes — nor heroines nor *femmes fatales,* either. It was all about a comfortable, tolerant, middle-aged *bourgeoisie.* I was thrilled to hear a word like *bourgeoisie* actually being spoken as part of an ordinary conversation, not produced and paraded as one or two people down at the Falmouth polly tended to do. I realized I was listening in to my first (and probably only) Hampstead literary conversation.

At least, that is what it appeared to be at the beginning. Soon, however, I realized that something much more devious was going on between these two women and after that, I'm afraid, the passing scene — my first daylight glimpse of London — passed almost without notice on my part. The mother told her daughter she was being petty-minded to demand overblown rubbish about villains and heroes in a story so full of the problems of real life. She mentioned the unhappiness of the Lydgates' marriage as an example — and how Rosamund's delusions contributed to it.

"One can only blame the poor woman's upbringing," she said. *"There's* a real-life villain for you if you like — bad upbringing! Rosamund was taught from her earliest years that marriage should bring security, comfort, and liberation from all life's financial worries — especially to a girl of such beauty and social position. She comes to believe it is her divine right, almost. And therefore, when her marriage to Lydgate clearly delivers nothing *but* financial worries, she shuts her eyes to the evidence all about her and goes on insisting that what *ought* to be so, *is* so. Result — disastrous collapse of marriage!"

From the way the daughter's neck turned bright pink at this homily I guessed the mother's rebuke of Rosamund's extravagant delusions had found a more personal mark in her. If so, I admired the mother's courage in this indirect criticism of her daughter's upbringing — for she herself was, I presume, at least partly responsible for it. Or perhaps this was her stepdaughter and she was getting in a dig at her true mother?

Anyway, the daughter responded that Rosamund was worth ten of Lydgate any day. His distinction was purely intellectual — she granted him that — but in all matters of taste, feeling, and discrimination he never rose above the vulgar country surgeon that he was.

I felt I now had an excellent portrait of the daughter's husband — or husband-to-be? Perhaps some 'eligible gentleman' chosen for her by Mamma and Pappa?

Mamma repeated her assertion that Rosamund was a walking encyclopedia of delusions — the notion that she was worth ten of Lydgate being just one more proof of it.

At this the daughter radiated the sort of contained explosive pressure you feel near a railway engine when it's all fired up and ready to go at a good steep incline. When her Mamma praised Dorothea for being above the vulgarity of the two Lydgates, she would have none of it. Dorothea was just as deluded in marrying Casaubon for his 'fine mind' as Rosamund had been in choosing Lydgate for his 'fine social prospects.' And look where it got her! Another disastrous marriage! "Dorothea should have married Will Ladislaw from the start," she concluded. "But then, of course, there would be happiness ever after — and poor Miss Eliot would have absolutely no story to tell!"

I had not realized until then that 'George Eliot' was a woman. I read the tale thinking 'he' was a bit of a mysogynist, in fact. But knowing 'he' was really a she made it all right because all women have a fair streak of natural misogyny in their make-up, anyway.

While I was rearranging my thoughts about *Miss* 'George' Eliot, the daughter turned and smiled acidly at Mamma — meaning, of course, 'If only you and Pappa would allow me to marry *my* Will Ladislaw' — whatever his name might be — 'there would be happiness ever after — and you would have absolutely no rebukes like these to deliver'! From her profile, masked though the upper half of it was in a fine net veil, I could see she, too, was a beauty — so Mamma's jibes at Rosamund, the undoubted beauty of *Middlemarch,* had an extra cutting edge to them.

I longed to interrupt and tell Mamma that her daughter was quite right. I myself was going to marry my equivalent of Will Ladislaw — because there was no parent or guardian in my life to say yea or nay to it. And it was going to be happiness ever after. And it wouldn't be a dull story at all — well, maybe to our neighbours but not to Jim and me. And I thought there would be a lot more happy marriages in the world if people were left free to court in peace, without being surrounded by chaperons and suspicion all the time, and to marry for love. Unfortunately the bus reached St Giles's Circus at that point, where it turned into Oxford Street. My first port of call was to a house in nearby Greek Street where they sold imported German lenses. So my quarrelling ladies never got the benefit of my immense worldly experience!

But their conversation lingered with me long after they had gone. I thought the daughter had had the best of the argument in the end. As we were trotting down Tottenham Court Road she had conceded that Rosamund had been partly at fault in accepting Lydgate. "Both of them were wrong," she said. "They saw marriage only as a social and professional institution. They ignored the obvious fact that marriage is also between individuals — who have individual needs and ambitions."

Life is full of casual eavesdroppings, most of them shallow or meaningless. But that final statement of the daughter's really struck a chord in me. In a way, it was the same point *I* had been itching to make. But because she put it in different words, she set me thinking about my own forthcoming marriage with Jim — and how much of that was a matter of social and professional convenience. Had I truly begun to appreciate him as an individual with his own needs and ambitions? Had he considered mine, too — especially my hope of getting the family together again? What if our personal ambitions were absolutely at odds? If my ambition to reunite our family were to make him unhappy, one of us would have to give way. Did I love him enough for that surrender to be mine? Was my soul great enough to make my sacrifice absolute — in the sense that I would never reproach him with it nor resent the fact that his needs had prevailed over mine? All of a sudden, my blithe hopes of living 'happy ever after' were beginning to look rather thin.

I quickly dispatched my list of purchases and gave directions for their delivery to Nether Hall, Hampstead. I then had a quick helping of whelks, jellied eels, and bottled brown ale at a stall in Leicester Square — 'The Cheapest Bite in the Kingdom' it said over the awning — and went on to Trafalgar Square, where I intended to catch the 'Chocolate Chelsea' to Bethnal Green (fare fourpence), to see the National Portrait Collection, which Harriet had told me she did not wish to visit.

When I began art classes at the polly I had tried doing little sketches of people and had proved hopeless at it. Lately, however, I seemed to have found the knack. It came to me suddenly that what you had to do was to forget the pencil in your hand — or crayon or whatever it was —

and forget even the paper you were drawing on. You had to try to see it as a misty sort of film, behind which was a hazy view of the person you were drawing. I mean, the features had to be already *there,* however dimly seen, before you began. Then all you needed to do was turn their fleeting presence into something more permanent. Sometimes, after sketching a person's face, I'd look at my hand and think, *Good heavens! I've been holding a pencil all this time!*

Anyway, that's why I was going to the portrait collection — because, as is always the case with things one is good at, I was beginning to take an increasing interest in the art of portraiture.

But my heart wasn't in it that afternoon somehow. The daughter's final words on the bus that morning were still churning away in my mind's ear. I wanted to get on the next train to Cornwall and tell Jim everything I'd heard and all the thoughts it had put into my head. I took a disconsolate turn or two round Landseer's pussy-cat lions and Nelson's pillar and then caught the 'Carlton Yellow' to Kentish Town, changing onto the 'Hampstead Yellow' at Camden Town. That was ninepence squandered in bus-fares in only four hours — so the Scotsman's joke about London being a ruinously expensive place ('I had nae been there an hour when bang went saxpence!') was no joke at all!

Shops, offices, houses, churches, chapels, breweries, cattle pounds, music halls, and little green squares — all passed by, cheek-by-jowl, on that long uphill drive to the heights of Hampstead. The map says Euston, and Mornington Crescent, and Haverstock Hill, and Rosslyn Park, and the very resonance of the names seems to lend each area a distinct and instantly identifiable character. But it's an illusion. The bricks and mortar — and the cobbles and paving stones — form one continuous band of dwelling and occupation that swallows up the whole. London is a great blur of bricks and mortar trapped in a net of half-appropriate names.

I arrived back at Nether Hall only to discover that Mrs Morell and Harriet had just gone out to take her dogs for a walk on the heath. Marian told me I'd easily catch them as the sheepdog was rather old and they always followed the same walk. I'd probably find them before they even reached the Consumption Hospital, but if not, I'd see them crossing the West Heath to the Suburban Hôtel at the Vale of Health, where they'd stop for tea on the terrace overlooking the ponds.

She was right. I caught up with them in Frognal Rise, just beyond the hospital. They took the speed of my return as an unspoken compliment and welcomed me to join them. I wanted to tell them of the conversation I'd overheard and all the thoughts it had sent tumbling through my head but Mrs Morell had thoughts of her own tumbling through her head, which she was even more determined to express.

She told me what I'd already learned the previous night from Marian — that she'd lived in Hampstead all her life, having been born at Mount Farm, half a furlong up the hill from Nether Hall, which had been her late husband's family home. Last night, on Marian's lips, it had seemed no more than an interesting fact. Now, seeing the nostalgic gleam in Mrs Morell's eyes and hearing the wistful tone of her voice, I felt a pang of jealousy. How wonderful it would be, I realized, to live in one place all your life. And to grow up in full view of your future husband and his home — which would one day be yours. It was already too late for me to do that — born in Helston, reared in Porthleven, courted in Falmouth, married in Penzance. I was already a convicted globetrotter!

Mrs Morell told us the story Marian had tried and failed to tell me last night — how Sir Thomas someone, the lord of the manor, had wanted to make a fortune by building all over Hampstead Heath — which he couldn't do without breaking the entail on his estate. That would have needed an act of parliament. But Hampstead village had already been colonized by several dozen rich families who enjoyed the green spaces and didn't want London's filthy tide of the Great Unwashed lapping at their magnificent gates. And it was true. I'd seen more grand mansions in the half-mile I'd just walked than you could see in any ten miles in Cornwall. These rich people had enough friends in parliament to block Sir Thomas's plans, so to spite them he'd dug sand and gravel and clay and loam all over the Heath, which he could do without legal restraint, apparently.

"The place looked as if ten battles of Waterloo had been fought over it," Mrs Morell told us, waving her hand over what were now rolling green pastures once again. "He died only just in time to save the place. His son, Spencer, was much more accommodating. He gave the Heath to the public in perpetuity and was, in return, allowed to build on all the land around us at Nether Hall. He turned our little farm track into Fitzjohns Avenue, which is named after a farm they owned in Essex. It ought to have been called Mount Farm Avenue, by rights. And the moral of that — as Alice said — is: 'Give a lot to get a lot.'

We had a splendid, breezy walk over the regenerated Heath to the Vale of Health. The Suburban Hôtel looked like a five-storey dockside warehouse with a few turrets from a castle stuck onto it in odd places and then limewashed all over. From its topmost turret you could see not just the Crystal Palace but far beyond it to the South Downs, half way to the sea. I went up there on my own, to enjoy the most distant view I was ever likely to see in my life. There was a man up there with a telescope — a big one on a tripod. He told me that on a clear day like this the homes of more than ten *million* people were in view!

He let me look. I became fascinated with what a telescope does to a landscape — the way it flattens the perspective and simplifies all the colours. Never mind ten million people — it was like ten million paintings by Corot out there! Everywhere you looked. I wondered if Jim had ever thought of coupling a camera to a powerful telescope. He might get some very artistic landscape photos that way and people would wonder how he did it.

The man refocused the telescope on a group of young men playing cards on a blanket in the grass beyond the pond. I could see every card in one man's hand and it was so close I almost shouted out, 'No, no! Play low!' when I saw he was about to play the queen on his partner's already-winning knave.

"Think what fun God must have!" the man said to me as I left him to his vigil. It was a dreadful blasphemy but I couldn't help agreeing.

I told the others about it when I joined them on the terrace for tea; it was one floor up, on the roof of the dining saloon. Mrs Morell said it was a typical Hampstead comment.

The terrace overlooked one of the larger ponds on the Heath. Already this early in the year there were eight or nine rowing boats out — four sculls and the rest with parties of up to six. One had two gaudy young women and their swains, shrieking with laughter and horsing about. "Ghastly East Enders," Mrs Morell said scornfully. "It makes one wish Sir Thomas had owned the land down at Southend Green as well. They'd never have built that wretched railway station, then. You should just see the frightful people it brings up here in summer!" She shuddered fastidiously.

She brightened quickly, however, when Harriet asked me what I had done in London that morning. I told them all about the conversation I had overheard on the bus and the thoughts it had stirred in me. "The thing is, you see," I said, "if I make a big sacrifice for Jim's sake — like giving up my hope of getting the family together again — is he then *obliged* to make a comparable sacrifice for me when the occasion comes? And wouldn't that tarnish my sacrifice? I mean, it's a bit like saying, 'I'll only give you a present if you'll give me one back.' I mean, that's the *unspoken* thought in our minds when we give each other birthday presents and things, isn't it, but it'd spoil it if we said it out loud. So what I'm asking is — is marriage like that, too? Are there unspoken rules about 'I'll sacrifice for you this time if you'll do the same for me next time'? Because if there are, it would spoil it if I said it out loud. But if there aren't, then we ought to make it a spoken rule that would be *un*spoken from then on — but you'd have to speak it in the first place, wouldn't you?"

Mrs Morell waited for more and then said, "Finished?"

I bit my lip guiltily and nodded.

"Do you think Mister Collett would welcome this sacrifice from you?" she asked.

"No. He says he'd love to see me happy and to have Teresa and my brothers living with us — which isn't quite the same thing as saying it would also make *him* happy. I'm sure he would be happy, mind. I'm only picking this as an example because it's something I want more than anything else in all the world — well, that and Jim, of course. I mean, it would be the biggest sacrifice *I* could possibly make for his sake."

"Hmm!" She stared out across the pond, where the Ghastly East Enders had now lost both their oars and were paddling frantically with their hands toward where one was floating. A gentleman sculler, dressed like a forty-year-old schoolboy, carefully rowed around it and carefully did nothing to help them, either. "If Mister Collett were even more eager to make his sacrifice for your sake than you are to make your sacrifice for his, would you deny him that pleasure?"

I shook my head ruefully. "It isn't the sacrifice itself that worries me, Mrs Morell. It's afterward. Either of us could do it in a great surge of love and glory. But after — as month followed on month and the years rolled by — could I stop the bitterness from eating into my heart? Or could he?"

"Well?" she pressed me. "*Could* he? How well d'you know him? You must have some opinion, surely?"

I thought of Jim. A picture of his dear, darling self filled my mind. I knew what a good man he was — and what a good wife I was going to be to him. And what a rich, interesting life we were going to make together. And I knew that, even if he did not relish the prospect of playing father to my reach-me-down family, he would not, in the fullness of his days, regret it. "I think he could," I answered. "But that isn't the same as *knowing* he could. If only marriage weren't so irrevocable! I think engaged people should be allowed to set up home together without everybody tut-tutting and getting the vapours."

Mrs Morell laughed and turned to her niece. "Another very *Hampstead* sentiment! Either it's in the very air we breathe, Harriet, or you sent me the wrong sister."

Harriet turned to me and said, "You're asking for a guarantee about people, dear. But there's no such thing — as I found out to my cost. And so did your mother before you."

Mrs Morell sat bolt upright. "You have told her about Paul?"

Harriet nodded. "I judged it right."

"You took a chance!"

"That's right — I judged Crissy and then I took a chance! Isn't *that* the very point you were about to make to her with regard to Jim Collett?"

Her aunt relaxed and smiled once again. "Yes," she sighed and turned to me. "One makes one's judgements and then one takes a chance. I was lucky. I had thirty happy years as a result of the chance I took. Harriet didn't — and nor, I gather, did your poor mother. But we cannot help it. We have to take that chance. We are driven by this compulsion to hold little babies in our arms — and buy them school uniforms — and grieve at the risks they, in their turn, take with their lives!" She looked up over her shoulder at the telescope, whose end projected among the castellations on the tower. "What fun God must have with us, indeed!"

I t seems monstrously ungrateful to say it but I could hardly wait to get back to Cornwall. The seven days I spent in London were the most enjoyable of my life. Mrs Morell was a marvellous hostess to me and could not have been kinder. And Harriet and I became firmer friends than ever. Since Marian had never felt like my elder sister — because she had hardly ever behaved like one, either — I can say with some truth that Harriet became the elder sister I never had.

We did all the obvious things, of course — the crown jewels, the National Gallery, the Kensington museums, and so on. I discovered a new painter-hero in the print room at the Victoria & Albert, called Samuel Palmer — the only etcher *ever* to have captured the mystery and secrecy of moonlight. And he managed it in water colours, too, where you have to use the whiteness of the paper and the thinness of the paint to suggest light and air!

I wished I had not read so much about London in advance, as a sort of country cousin's defence against my metropolitan sister. Mrs Morell considered that letting Marian and me sleep together was concession enough — especially if she was to be given three days off to be my bridesmaid the following month. So Marian had to carry out her normal duties while Harriet and I, and sometimes Mrs Morell, too, went around London together. It meant that almost everything we saw was already half familiar to me. I felt like Rip van Winkle, because *London Old and New* is full of engravings of the town as it was in bygone days. So Piccadilly, in my mind's eye, was a wide, empty street peopled by bucks in ruffs and knee breeches and ladies in towering wigs, all trotting around in phætons. Well, it all *looked* the same. Devonshire House was still there, and the Burlington Arcade, and the Royal Academy. But the dark clothing of modern men and the dreary dresses of today's women — mostly brown and gray-blue and wishy-washy mauve — and the impossible crush of the traffic (not to mention the awful stench of horse dung and urine!) ... all these turned its expected beauty into a nightmare. Harriet and I walked the full length of the street and we overtook a whole fleet of omnibuses, even at our leisurely stroll. It was worse than Church Street in Falmouth last January, but that was when they had to dig up the gas main. In London the streets are packed like that all the time. I don't know why they put up with it.

The event I enjoyed best — apart from discovering Sam Palmer — was my first dinner party, or the first one where I went in on the arm of a gentleman instead of fighting off the arm of a hired footman. (Actually that happened to Susan, not me.) He was a Mr Dalziell, pronounced *dee-ell*, a barrister at Lincoln's Inn and greatly in demand at dinner parties at that time because the notorious Baccarat Scandal, in which the Prince of Wales was to appear as a witness, was about to come to trial and he was able to tell us all the inside gossip around the Law Courts. People could talk of nothing else, even in Hampstead, which was supposed to be so cultured and disdainful of London's High Society and its trivial obsessions. Somebody had accused somebody else of cheating at cards at a house called Tranby Croft — or perhaps it was a Mr Tranby-Croft who owned it? Anyway, careers were ruined and writs flew. No one would have heard a word about it if the Prince of

Wales hadn't been there. He had bet a few shillings on some hands and now the Great British Public was up in arms about it. I had no patience with the whole affair. The Great British Public itself spends more on gambling each year than it lets the government spend on education!

I managed to get in a civilized word or two to Mr Dalziell about Sam Palmer's etchings, explaining how his technique of wiping the surface of the plate very clean before printing it made the black lines sparkle and gave the scene that silvery brilliance you get with moonlight. It wasn't my own discovery. A man in the print room at the V&A had pointed it out to me, but I didn't think it worth going into such minor details. He had also showed me how other artists leave a thin film of ink on the plate to give an overall tone to the print. Dalziell was most interested in this and said he had a number of etchings in his chambers at the Albany and would be delighted to hear my obviously expert opinion of them. I was flattered, of course, and arranged to call by the following afternoon, thinking it must be all right because you can hardly get a man more respectable than a barrister. But Mrs Morell made me send my regrets instead. Apparently an invitation from any bachelor (even from a barrister!) to a lady to 'see his etchings' is a code for an assignation among à la mode people in London! I wonder what might have happened if I had said nothing to her about his invitation and had gone in all innocence to his 'set' of chambers in the Albany. Now, alas, I'll never know.

I hinted as much to Harriet on our return journey to Penzance, which we made on the first Monday in May — a month before my wedding. There was no through train to the far west on Sundays apart from the sleeping-car express, which left at midnight on Saturday. A berth would cost five shillings and, since sleepers were First Class only, our supplement to convert from Second Class would be a pound. So, though I *ached* to sleep on a train while it puffed and whistled through the breadth, if not the length, of England, I knew I should regret the extravagance when it was over. We did, however, pay the supplement so that we could travel on the Penzance Corridor Express on the Monday. It had a restaurant car for First Class passengers only. We left Paddington at the very civilized hour of ten-forty in the morning and arrived at Redruth at the equally congenial time of six-thirty that evening. And I think that to dine on mock turtle soup, followed by oyster patties, followed by haunch of mutton, followed by charlotte à la parisienne, followed by dessert — all for two shillings and eightpence a head, and all while being whisked at magical speed through the rolling hills and plains of Somerset, is something everyone should experience at least once in their lifetime. *And* we saved two shillings and fourpence each over the cost of a night berth on the sleeper!

It was while we were tucking into the oyster patties that I admitted to wondering what turn events might have taken if I had gone to Dalziell's set in all my innocence.

Harriet hesitated a moment, seeming slightly flustered. Then she recollected herself and laughed. "Don't imagine you're the first young woman who, on the eve of her marriage, begins to wonder about a quick *affaire* with a forgettable young man before it's too late!"

"Did you ... before your wedding?" I prompted, all agog and half expecting another astonishing confession.

"Of course not," she replied. "If I had, I'd have known at once there was something distinctly odd about Paul's idea of marital relations. And I'd have been spared a great deal of misery, too." She smiled. "My aunt was very taken with your idea of permitting trial marriages. In fact, she was very taken with you altogether."

"Well, I liked her, too," I responded, slightly embarrassed, though I don't really know why.

"When she told you to keep in touch with her — after you're married — she meant it, you know. She doesn't say that sort of thing to every Tom, Dick, and Harry who stays."

"Dalziell was a very handsome young man — well, thirtyish-young, anyway," I said, partly to change the subject and partly because her earlier response had intrigued me.

"Charming," she agreed off-handedly. "To me, thirty *is* young."

"And attentive."

"Very." Some linesmen doing Sunday repairs became of absorbing interest to her.

I persisted. "Also, despite being a barrister, he was rather frivolous, so there would have been no risk of any long-lasting attachment."

She turned to me with amused weariness. "All right, you can stop your ferreting. I suppose Marian told you?"

"No," I replied.

She saw my surprise was genuine. "Good for her," she said. Then, frowning, "Bother! I've given myself away now, haven't I! Actually — this is the truth, now — my first thought, when my aunt stopped you from making that visit, was that it was even more dangerous to send

Marian with your note of regret. So I intercepted her in the Euston Road and took the note myself while she went to the Honor Club. It was only when I was approaching the Albany that I thought, *Why not?* On my own behalf, I mean."

"Golly!"

So here was the confession after all — and not about some remote *affaire* in the past, before her disastrous marriage — but about the day before yesterday. "In other words, you didn't go that long, long walk to Archway and back!"

She shook her head and smiled like a cat with cream. Then, defensively, "Why shouldn't I take what opportunities I may?"

"Why not, indeed, Harriet! I wouldn't criticize you for it — not even secretly to myself, honestly."

I tried to imagine her and Dalziell *in flagrante,* as they say, and could not — not *my* Harriet but another one whom I was just beginning to know. One day, perhaps, they would coalesce. For the moment all they could do was coexist, slightly overlapping, in my mind.

After a pause I went on, "Only one thing puzzles me ..."

"Yes?"

"What d'you do about ... I mean, how d'you avoid ... *consequences,* you know? Not you *personally,* of course, because I remember what you said. But *me.* How would I?"

"Ah!" She relaxed. "I've been wondering whether or not you'd ask me that. I've been itching to tell you because I think it's something every woman should know. But not until *she* itches to find out! And as for me, I still take precautions, no matter what the doctors told me that time."

"But how?"

She glanced rapidly all about us and then said, "I'll show you when we're back at Little Sinns."

What she showed me was a plain pill box, filled (or, actually, not *quite* filled) with what I thought was vanilla fudge. No writing on the lid. She said it was a simple mixture of quinine bisulphate and cocoa-butter. She got them from a chemist called Rendell in the East End of London and she wrote down the address for me. "You just pop one into your vagina *before* congress," she said casually.

When she saw my shock she grinned and added, "I'm always very careful to be quite specific nowadays. I once told a girl to pop them 'up her front passage.' It didn't stop the babies but it made the most dreadful mess in the hallway!"

Mulberry was the name of the house Susan had chosen for our consideration while I was up in London. I stayed at Little Sinns that Monday night and joined the other three on the Penzance train at Redruth the following morning — which I had arranged by telegram. Even though we had the compartment to ourselves, it felt very strange to be kissing Jim in front of the other two. And so early in the day, as well. It was not the first time we had embraced in their company, mind, but after eleven days' separation we were both eager and yet strangely shy — almost as if we had forgotten how we fitted together and where arms and lips went and so on. Also it was a foretaste of the way things would be in our shared household — a prospect I was beginning to loathe, though I managed to hide it from them.

"Is that what you mean by lenses, old chap?" Mark shouted when he thought our embrace had gone on long enough. "No wonder you wanted to get your hands on 'em!"

Apparently Jim had bored them to death all the way from Falmouth about how he was looking forward to getting his hands on the new German lenses — not a word about wanting to see me again, of course!

I handed the precious things over to Jim, who at once went into raptures, putting on his special cotton gloves and holding them up to the light and focusing the passing scene upside-down on the palm of his hand and marvelling at the smooth action of the lamellæ in the stop rings. "You can go down to eff-one-twenty-eight!" he said in tones of awe. "I could do close-up pictures with quite a depth of field — like a pinhole camera."

"For what type of customer?" Mark asked.

Jim shrugged. "I hadn't thought that far."

At the Penzance terminus our quickest way to Chyandour was up the steps, past the booking hall, and out to the street. But I pretended I wanted to see the harbour and slipped out by the luggage entrance instead. I tried to imagine the scene as it had been half a century ago, when Jane Scawen, then Miss Jane Harvey, had come to Penzance with her elderly father — the story Harriet had told me a week or so back. I forgot to say that I had shown Esther Wilkinson's portrait to Marian but got cold feet when it came to telling her the full story — because I knew she'd tease me with it in some way. She just agreed that the likeness was extraordinary and that was that. Anyway, my kinship with that poor self-murdered woman had taken a powerful hold on my imagination.

I leaned against the stone beside the entrance, just about where I imagined Esther must have been standing on that day, and closed my eyes on the year 1891. The sun was shining square on the wall, so I pretended I was enjoying its warmth. And there they all were in my mind's eye — the gentlemen in those absurd stove-pipe hats and waistcoats that looked as if they were made from horse-blankets ... fishermen in smocks (well, no change there) ... and the ladies in those impossibly vast crinolines, looking less like belles than bells — bells with their clappers wrenched out and stuck upside down on top, to form their peg-doll bodices and heads. But I was wearing a crinoline, too — shorter than the others and showing a well-turned pair of calves and ankles encased in expensive leather boots. My bosom, décolleté, was but thinly veiled down to my cleavage and sinful perfume rose around my nostrils ...

My heart began to pound, not in the imaginary past but here and now. I opened my eyes guiltily and saw Mark, standing not two feet away from me and staring at me with such a curious amusement. "What's all this?" he asked.

"What's all what?" I replied crossly, heaving myself away from the wall and starting our walk around the station to join the others.

"Susan sent me to see if you were all right."

"Why not Jim?"

"She said not to worry him."

"Can't a person just enjoy a bit of sun?"

"A bit of fun?" he asked eagerly. "Say the word!"

I laughed. *"Do* grow up!" I was about to warn him that if he continued such tomfoolery, Jim would soon have second thoughts about sharing a house. But then that gave me an idea, so I held my tongue.

"What about a last fling before our marriage? Or first fling in your case ..."

"Marriagezzz," I interrupted.

"Your last chance for a first fling, eh?"

I began to walk faster. "You've got a nerve — talking to me like this." We rounded the corner and I was dismayed to see how far along Chyandour the other two had progressed. "Anyway, you're my uncle, so it's doubly disgraceful."

He chuckled. "I'm not, you know."

"You are." I was about to tell him what Cousin Stella had said but something about his air of confidence unsettled me. "What makes you think otherwise?"

"A little bird."

I halted and turned to look him straight in the eye. "You mean someone has told you you are not my grandmother's ... not Agatha Trevarton's son? Someone who *knows?*"

He nodded. "Someone who knows." The supercilious smile seemed fastened on his lips. I have to admit that they were extremely kissable.

"Someone who was there?" I insisted.

He shook his head but the smile remained. "She wasn't there."

"Felicity!" I exclaimed and started walking — indeed, almost running — at once. I don't know why I felt so threatened, but all I wanted was to be with Jim and feel safe again.

Mark caught my sleeve and pulled me back to a sedate walking pace. "Don't run," he said. "It looks so guilty, don't you know. And that would never do."

"Ah!" I sneered. "Your nasty little one-track mind can grasp at least that much, can it?"

"Of course! Also, I've changed my mind about a last premarital fling. I can see you're much too noble. But perhaps you'll feel different after your honeymoon. You'll have done your duty by Jim, then."

"Well!" I was furious with him now and just wanted to hurt him all I could. "A *duty*, is it? That's what Susan does for you! No wonder you married a housemaid — or intend to!"

He gasped as if I had kicked him in the stomach. His bewildered eyes searched mine as if to ask how we had suddenly fallen into such a fury. There was the briefest moment during which, if he had apologized, we could have kissed and made up. Or made up, anyway. But it passed. And then he just wanted to hurt me in return. "Actually, I wouldn't dream of taking your virginity," he said coldly. "Jim deserves every drop of it. You'll make him pay dear enough for it, I know."

I stopped and faced him once again, this time clenching my fists ready to blood his nose if need be. "What d'you mean by that?" I demanded.

"Nothing." He lowered his eyes and shrugged awkwardly.

"I might have known it," I said wearily as I walked away.

"D'you think he *wants* your wretched little brood under his roof?" he shouted after me. "Flighty Marian and Pig-keeper Tom and three little waifs beside — d'you think he actually *wants* them?"

When I failed to respond, he ran and caught me up.

"Has Jim actually said as much to you?" I asked calmly — surprised at how calm I managed to sound, considering the utter turmoil his words had stirred within.

"I've said too much already," he mumbled.

I turned and gave him a brilliant smile. "How nice, *Uncle* dear — after such storms as these — to end on a note of serene agreement."

He puffed and gasped at my side for an otherwise silent while. I suppose sailing does not provide as much exercise as ordinary housework — at all events he was quite shockingly out of condition.

"Oh God, Crissy!" he said at last. "I'm sorry. It wasn't true. I just wanted to lash out. Say you forgive me — *really* forgive me — not this silent acid-sweetness?"

"None of it was true?" I asked, watching him closely once again. "Felicity said nothing on the subject?"

He desperately wanted to reassure me now, to get back in my good books, but he knew his eyes would let him down. "No. That bit was true — but not the rest. Jim has said nothing. Nor even hinted it."

"And Felicity?"

"She said Archie told her I was Catherine's son. She and my mother … I mean, our grandmother, Agatha, were both expecting at around the same time — and both out in Switzerland to minimize the scandal in Catherine's case. Grandmama had her baby, a boy, a week or so earlier. He was baptized Mark just before he died. They used his birth certificate to legitimize me — and his baptismal certifcate, too."

It had a ghastly ring of truth. A baby born to a forty-year-old woman was far more likely to succumb than one to an eighteen-year-old. And perhaps Catherine really had died in a fall — not from a horse, to be sure, but down a flight of stairs, say. A 'fall from a horse' would be a good riposte to any who might suspect she'd been with child. In fact, if anybody but Felicity had come out with this tale, I'd have been forced to concede its greater probability. But now I'd back Satan himself in a truth-telling competition with that particular woman.

I said nothing to Mark, though. He was and always would be my uncle and I no longer cared *what* he believed about it. "Pax?" I suggested as we turned the corner into Lanoweth Road. We had almost caught up the other two by now. They were no more than twenty paces ahead.

"Pax!" he agreed.

Jim greeted us with a casual, "Slowcoaches!"

Susan brushed some imaginary lint off Mark's lapel — the sort of gesture a woman makes to show a man she loves him even if she isn't saying so.

The rage that had flared between Mark and me only moments earlier was well and truly gone — but not, by me at least, forgotten. I could not get it out of my mind that Jim might have said something about my 'brood of pathetic waifs,' or whatever the phrase had been. Only the much more disturbing news about Felicity drove it from the forefront of my mind.

Our possible future home — Mulberry, as I said — was in Lescudjack Crescent, a stately semicircle off Lanoweth Road. All the streets in that part of Penzance lie on the steep slopes of Lescudjack Hill, once the site of a mighty castle. Mulberry itself was one of ten almost identical houses put up in five semidetached pairs by a speculative builder called Wallis, about two years earlier. Only three had so far been let. The variations were in the fretwork on the bargeboards and the capitals on the columns supporting the porch roof. Devoran, the half-house to Mulberry, had acanthus. Mulberry itself had vine leaves.

"It should be mulberry leaves," I said.

Susan pretended to be shocked. "You a Cornish gel, born and bred — and you don't know your own lingo! Oh dearie me! Mulberry's nothing to do with leaves or trees — quite the opposite — it means 'bare hill top' — which I s'pose was before Mister Wallis came along. Lescudjack means 'monastery in an elder grove.' And Chyandour means 'near the water.'"

I laughed and accused her of making it up, but she said Wallis himself had told her. "He knows all them ... I mean, *those* Old Cornish words."

"What's Devoran mean?" I asked. "Apart from being a village between Penryn and Truro?"

"Two hills," she replied, with an odd sort of smile, slightly arch.

"Has anybody taken it?" There were no curtains at the windows and a dew-decked cobweb straddled the front door.

"We could have that instead if we want," she told us anxiously. "It's the same except it's a mirror-image."

"Mulberry looks fine," Jim said. "What does Penzance mean, I wonder? 'Pen' means hill, I know that much. But what's 'zance' when it's sober? Did he tell you?"

"Willis says it could either mean 'holy' or 'bay.' A lot of Cornish words have two meanings. I s'pose people were very poor in those days."

She turned the key in the lock and pushed the mound of her baby indoors ahead of her while the rest of us tried to work out the logic of her last remark. The idea that people might be so poor that they didn't even have enough *words* to go around was a novel one to me.

Despite my quarrel with Mark and the disturbing things he had said, my mood was buoyant. In the first place, I knew he'd quite understand if I now asked him to marry as soon as possible and not wait for Jim and me. And in the second place, Devoran next door was empty. I felt sure Mr Willis would be open to a private arrangement with me to keep it that way for a month or two more.

So I was free to enthuse over Mulberry all I liked. And, indeed, had it been Jim's and mine alone, I should have enthused quite genuinely. Though untenanted for two years, it felt tinder dry — which is as rare in Cornwall as false teeth for hens. Morning sunlight was streaming in through the windows at the back of the house. In the afternoon it would be the turn of those in front. The whole place was so light and airy that it lifted the spirit just to walk in, empty and echoing as it was.

"We could take it furnished at forty pounds a year," Susan said. She had already told us that the unfurnished rent would be twenty-eight. "It sounds a big jump from twenty-eight to forty, I know, but I don't think we could rent the same amount of furniture separately from anyone else for only twelve quid."

Only twelve quid!

But she was right. Furniture of the quality demanded by the sort of families who would live in these fine houses would be eight pounds a year per family at least.

"This would be adequate for a studio," Jim said of what would normally be the drawing room. "Unless there's a big enough room in the basement?" He looked at Susan.

"The basement's all kitchen and scullery — and pantry and coal cellar," she told us. "Because of the slope of the hill, the basement is only basement from the front. Round the back it's the ground floor, looking out over the garden. We're not allowed to hang out washing — or so Wallis says. But Mrs Collis, our next door up, had hers out the day he showed me over, so if no one complains, we could hang ours out, too, I expect." She patted her stomach and added, "There's going to be quite a bit of it, one way and another — at least from *our* half of the household!" She smiled archly at me again. "And soon enough from yours, I shouldn't wonder."

"Talking of *half* the household," Jim said. "How are we going to divide it? By floors, I suppose?" His eyes canvassed my opinion.

I mystified him by shrugging and saying I had no strong feelings on the matter. I wanted *them* to do the choosing, so that they couldn't blame me later for suggesting a division that I knew would fail.

"Let's see the extent of our little empire first," Mark suggested.

Nothing more was said about dividing the property until we had looked into every room — and every tiny cupboard and closet and built-in press in the place. And the more we saw of it, the firmer grew their opinion that here was a house in which we could all live in harmony *and* run a good business, too. I agreed — oh, how I agreed! And in my imagination I mirror-reversed the layout of each floor and thought, *This will be Teresa's and here's where Gerald and Arthur will sleep — and this could be Tom's and that one Marian's if they got work near by ...*

When we had completed our tour and were back downstairs again, Mark — flexing his muscles as our accountant, stock-keeper, and general business manager — said crisply: "To sum up, then, we have a studio, an office, a waiting room, and — with a little extra plumbing — a darkroom on the ground floor. Let's call this the ground floor, eh? To avoid confusion. The basement is all kitchens and things like that. Up on the first floor we've got four bedrooms and a bathroom — and a *water* closet! The pipes to that will give us plumbing and drainage for the ground-floor darkroom, by the way. No dressing rooms but one can do wonders with folding screens and curtains and a bit of give and take on all sides."

"Dressing rooms are a bourgeois fad," I pointed out — wisdom I had acquired in Hampstead. It certainly stopped the conversation for a moment or two.

Jim frowned at me and shook his head slightly, but I saw nothing amiss in my remark. Why should husbands and wives need to creep behind screens or vanish into separate rooms to put on or take off their clothes — especially when, *after* taking them off, they often share the greatest possible intimacies in the marital bed?

"On the second floor," Mark went on, "we have what is clearly intended as a nursery, a nanny's room, a housekeeper's sitting room and bedroom, another water closet, and a small sitting-up bath. And then four garret bedrooms for maids and a box room. And a space for the water tanks."

Susan was the first to speak. "I s'pose all four of us would rather live on the first floor?" she said. "So do we draw lots or what?"

"Hold your horses!" Jim put in. "Perhaps you and Mark should talk it over separately, and me and Crissy, before we decide. But I'd like to suggest that we just draw lots for which *side* of the first floor we occupy. You two one side, us two the other. I suppose you noticed that the pair of bedrooms north of the corridor have connecting doors, and so do the pair on the south, too? In other words — there'd be a bedroom and private sitting room each."

"And what about the one bathroom and the one *wc*?" Susan asked.

He didn't answer her directly. "We'd look upon it as if we were boarders in a lodging house. I've lived in boarding houses for years. There's seven of us where I am at the moment, sharing one bathroom — men and ladies. And one *wc*. We seem to manage without rancour. And if seven relative strangers can manage it, surely we four friends ought to be able to? We could try it, anyway, and if it didn't work, *then* we could draw lots to see who moves up to the second floor. Shall we discuss it or take a vote now?"

"Neither," I suggested. "Let's mull over the idea to ourselves and talk about it on the train back to Falmouth. We're supposed to be starting a *business* here. We should be talking about that, surely? If needs be, we could all sleep happily in tents on the lawn, I'm sure ..."

"That's another thing he's forbidden in the lease," Susan said. But when she saw my expression she added, "Sorry!"

Jim, thinking he understood my petulance, said, "The second floor will be for Gerald and Arthur, of course. And Teresa if we have the good fortune to get her back. And Tom and Marian if they come to visit. I mean *when* they come to visit."

I managed to smile gratefully at him even though my heart was crying out, *Too late! Too late!* "To business," I said. "What we've got to do today is measure up the ground-floor rooms — see if they'll take all the equipment — find out how easy it'll be to make a darkroom at the back ... things like that."

Jim looked at Mark and said, "She'm right 'nuff, boy!" and Mark replied, "She i'n't wrong."

While they called out the measurements I did sketch-plans of the rooms and Susan wrote down the figures. When she handed the first completed plan back to me she looked quickly all about us and whispered, "By the way — Devoran means *two breasts!*"

We decided to take the house furnished, at forty pounds a year — which made me feel weak at the knees when I thought of so much money going out all at once. Little did I know then what other expenses the month would bring! I had a word in Willis's ear and, for a fiver deposit on our eventual rent — and not a word to anyone, please — got him to hold Devoran, next door, in readiness for a move that could not come soon enough for me.

Jim had to work out his notice at Stanton's until almost the end of May, so, to begin with, it was only the three of us, Mark, Susan, and me, who went to Penzance each day. I took good care never to be alone with Mark, after his behaviour on that first day — though now he seemed to want to pretend it had never happened. Jim came with us on Sundays and on his day off, which varied week to week. We soon discovered that 'furnished' means 'equipped with about a quarter of the things you'll actually need.' Everything else, from bed linen to saucepans, had to be begged, borrowed, or otherwise acquired.

A lot of it we were able to transfer from Fenton Lodge. Cousin Stella had contracted the disease called independence during her time at Swanpool. The idea of going back to being a grace-and-favour dependant at Nancekuke House had no appeal for her. That, and a mutual liking which had sprung up between her and the Bourdeaux (not unconnected with port wine), induced her to set up her own establishment down on the Helford River at Port Navas. She said it was just far enough from Redruth for only the best of her old friends to keep up their acquaintance. The three Trevarton brothers then decided to let the Lodge furnished — but with hired furniture, not their good family heirlooms, which they divided among them. So Mark and Susan acquired more than enough in the way of bed linen and domestic utensils, the surplus of which we, in turn, were able to borrow. In fact, it was one aspect of our communism of which I could wholeheartedly approve and it even softened my resistance to the idea in general. Not enough to make me change my mind but enough to make the situation bearable for the time being. First and foremost we had to keep every spare penny for the business, whose day-to-day cash requirements were still mere guesswork on our part. But, if the advance-capital requirement was anything to go by, they would be hefty indeed.

For studio work, Jim got the very best Timmerman bellows camera on an Eddystone tripod. Also a pair of carbon-arc spotlamps by Swan — the latest thing. They would allow us to make indoor portraits that looked as if they were taken in bright sunlight, even in the depth of winter. Gillott's, down in Alverton Street, had nothing like it. Most expensive of all was a whole-plate enlarger from Prefect of Poplar, which was something else Gillott's didn't have. The really up-to-date photographer no longer needed to clamp the paper and plate together in a printing frame and hold it up to the sunlight — which, of course, meant that the print could only ever be the same size as the negative. The new dry-gelatin bromide papers from Eastman's were so sensitive that you could use relatively dimmer man-made lighting — as in an enlarger. So really vain people could now have their faces enlarged to the size of a house if they wanted.

But the main part of our business was, of course, the 'snap shots,' as people called them, of trippers and parties on the two beaches. The plan was for me to go down to the station each morning to meet the tripper-trains and excursion specials. There I'd hand out leaflets explaining our service and advising those who wanted to use it to look out for 'our master photographers in their special black-and-white hats,' who would be patrolling the beaches until three o'clock each afternoon. All the pictures they took would be ready to collect at the station after four o'clock. Anyone wanting to leave earlier could make arrangements to call at Mulberry and collect theirs.

'Our master photographers' would, in fact, be Jim. Mark wanted to do the developing and printing so that he could stay near Susan and their new baby, who was obviously going to be spoiled out of his very life. In the mornings Jim would be wearing an old-fashioned stovepipe hat painted with black-and-white stripes. In the afternoons, a bowler, similarly adorned. Christopher Wallis, our builder's fourteen-year-old son, who was an aspiring amateur photographer himself, had volunteered to be our bicycle boy at weekends and when the school holidays came round. On weekdays a lad called Tim Willett would be the 'despatch rider.' Jim would also cover the couple of miles between the two beaches by bicycle.

He had modified the 'Kodak' in two important ways. First, he had put a carrier on the front, to take an extra lens for people who wanted a closer view of themselves than the 'Kodak' usually provided. It could not focus clearly under about ten feet, and not at all under six, so the usual 'snap' showed the subject in the middle distance, often with the face too small to be easily recognizable. Our leaflet explained this refinement and we had even gone to the expense of making a 'zinco' illustration to show the difference. I did the original drawings for it, using Sir Henry Irving as my model, because everyone would know his face at once. Jim's other modification was a stout, telescopic strut on which he could steady the camera. People think that with an amazingly quick exposure, like one-tenth of a second, even a man with the palsy could take a clear picture. But the truth is quite the opposite. Even a man with (as he thinks) a rock-steady hand can move enough in a tenth of a second to cause a slight blurring.

Jim's original idea of using a light-proof box for changing the films in the 'Kodak' proved impracticable. The box was too cumbersome to ferry from beach to beach. So we bought four 'Kodaks' instead. Two would be in use at any one time — swapped, turn and turn about, between the beach and the darkroom. The third would be a reserve in case Jim got more requests than he could handle. Then Christopher would deputize for him on one of the beaches while I stepped in to help Mark go mad in the darkroom. The fourth was just a spare in case one of the other three failed.

What with one thing and another, then, our expenditure on equipment alone came to £482 17s. 4d. Carpentry and painting and furnishings on the ground floor — to make the office, waiting room, studio, and darkroom, came to a further sixty-odd, not counting the replumbing, which cost another fifteen. So, on the ground floor alone, we got rid of almost six hundred pounds in less than a month! That sum would have kept my mother and us six children for ten years, until even little Teresa was ready to go out into the world.

It was a good thing we exhausted ourselves in work and daily travel, otherwise I should never have managed to sleep. But Jim and Mark were incredible. The more we spent, the happier they seemed to be, Jim especially. When he walked around the finished studio and ran his hands lovingly over the polished brass and mahogany of the new Timmermans, he seemed three inches taller than the humble assistant who showed people into Stanton's creaking old studios.

After two weeks, though, the inconvenience of daily travelling began to tell on poor Susan and, since the bedrooms were furnished by then, she and Mark decided to start living there at once. The wedding was quiet, as was natural in the circumstances. He did not even tell his brothers, nor Cousin Stella. Jim and I shared the modest festivities of their wedding breakfast but, as I explained it to Susan, it broke my heart that we could not go to the altar — or, at least, to the registrar's desk, together. For, to fall in with Cousin Stella's arrangements, I had *promised* her I'd stay on at Fenton Lodge until the last Friday in May. On that day, Marian would be coming down to Penzance, ready for my wedding on the following Monday. So, from the middle of the month onward, I travelled alone each day from Falmouth to Penzance — which proved to be much more fruitful because, instead of chatting and daydreaming aloud to each other, I was free to get on with writing lists and planning the day's work.

Thus I kept my mind busy, when it might otherwise have dwelled gloomily on Mark's hurtful words that I would make Jim pay dearly for my hand by foisting my family upon him. As for Felicity, I did not know what to think. Nor did I want to reopen the topic with Mark. But it fretted me to wonder how had he and she come to discuss such a subject at all. Did he ask he out of the blue, just for something to say? Or had he a darker purpose? Or had she started it? Was the darker purpose hers? The whole gamut of possibilities was wide open — from the complete innocence of both parties on the one hand to sinister motives in both on the other — and *different* sinister motives at that!

It would not have done to brood on such matters, but nor was it wise to forget them entirely. Happy as I was in managing the day-to-day business of setting up our new home, it was not the sort of month I would like to live through again.

For the last three days — Tuesday to Thursday — I was entirely alone at Fenton Lodge. The Bourdeaux were surprised I stayed on but I think Cousin Stella understood that I needed to commune with my family's ghosts. Not spectres in white sheets, of course, but lingering memories and feelings, leftover fragments of vanished lives. At first it felt a bit spooky, wandering round those uncarpeted rooms and passages with a guttering candle in my hand, my footfall echoing in rooms that had so recently been crammed to overflowing with bric-a-brac of every kind.

Here I remembered my first glimpse of my grandmother — which almost wasn't a glimpse because the sweep of my eye had taken her in as just one more ornament, lost among so many!

And there was where Mark had kissed me that time, and I, guilty with my unshared knowledge, let him, just to see what it was like. And all the troubles that had flowed from that one moral lapse!

And here my grandmother died, cursing me — and carrying that curse with her into eternity. I squared my shoulders now, daring her to return, this 'witching hour, and finish the business one way or another. "Come on!" I murmured at her memory. "It's just you and me. No one will ever know."

Outside, under a waning moon, a vixen yapped sharply, bringing echoes from across the pool below. And now, too, I heard the distant thunder of the waves — which had probably thundered just as loudly in my ears, though entirely unnoticed by me, for the past year and more. As nature is swift to reclaim an untended garden, so, too, her sounds reach into the echoing shells of such houses as this.

And is madness waiting, too, out there — ever ready to trickle inward upon the untended mind?

I must allow, I would have none of these thoughts if Susan were here with me, or even if I knew little Clarry Benjamin was sound asleep up there in her garret.

Madness? Perhaps not.

Eccentricity, then — its English cousin. Am I going to be an eccentric old lady?

I feel I have been prepared for nothing in this life, except, it seems, to be ready for anything and everything. Here I am, alone for the first time in … God knows how long … it could be for the first time ever. I don't mean alone-on-a-walk, or alone-in-the-bath, or that sort of alone. I mean this sort of alone — as it stole over Robinson Crusoe on his first night ashore. Here I am, *this* sort of alone, and what is the thought that pops into my mind? That I am prepared for nothing! I feel I have no inner resources — no faith, no morality, no goal.

No faith? I can believe in nothing outside love and family.

No morality? For my love's sake and my family's sake I would cheat the world and sell my soul.

No goal? When I have my brothers and sisters around me again — as I most surely will … what then? That is no goal for a lifetime's dedication. Not a true ambition at all. It is merely a wish to put the clock back fifteen months and thumb my nose at those who broke us up, both the dead and their living helpers.

What when that wish is granted? It is the destiny of all families to grow up and dissolve their union. I am closer in affection to Marian and Tom now than ever I was when we lived in three cramped rooms and fought one another for every private inch.

I have been prepared for nothing — not even for the inevitable divorce of siblings!

I sat on the stairhead, peering down into the corridor where our mother must have passed to and fro every day of her life for eighteen years. Did nothing of her rare magic linger there, caged in those old stones? She hated her early life but not the home in which she lived it. She loved these walls, this womb of refuge. Oh, ungrateful stones that have kept naught of it here for me!

"Mother?" I whispered, daring her, imploring her to come from wherever she was and tell me what to do now. At least she could tell me whether or not I should give up my hope of reuniting us all and, forsaking all others, cleave only unto Jim.

Oh Jim! Oh my darling Jim — how I love you! I'd do that for you. I would, I would!

Is it love — this yearning for him, this great, aching hollowness I feel inside me at the very thought of his dear person? Or is it just what *she* felt, too — nineteen years ago, when the ladder reached up to the sill of that window there, and she almost fell into Barry Moore's arms in her haste to be joined with him?

Oh, Mother, come quick and tell me! If anyone should know, it would be you!

At lunchtime on that last Thursday in May, Jim took his hat and coat off its peg at Stanton's for the final time. The bad feeling over his leaving had turned to acceptance by now. The fact that he was setting up his business in far-off Penzance no doubt helped. Old Mr Stanton actually gave him a box of dry-gelatin plates as a going-away present. "And I trust that none of *our* patrons will end up on one of these!" he said as a sort of joke and warning combined.

Jim and I met for lunch, which we took at the Falmouth Hôtel, the poshest in town. It cost us five shillings — which had once been my earnings for an entire week — but what was that to a couple who had managed to get through the best part of a thou' in the past month! We had a half bottle of medoc with the meal, too, not enough to go to one's head but sufficient to mellow the day. I had good reason for hating wine and, indeed, had not let the stuff past my lips until I stayed at Mrs Morell's with Harriet. Even then I had not greatly cared for it, though I did come to realize it was foolish to loathe it as fiercely as I had done. Now, for the first time, I found myself actually relishing its strangely mellow sharpness and the gentle afterglow it awakened in my throat.

When I told Jim, his eyes went wide in mock alarm and he warned me I was on the slippery slope that drags a person down from humanism into hedonism. "However," he said, advancing a counter-argument, "wine and honeymoon do rather belong together." His tone was flat, as if the observation had only a passing relevance to us.

"Honeymoon?" I echoed. I could feel my pulse suddenly hammering in my temples.

He smiled. "Not for us, of course. But we might take a working break, perhaps — a *hard-working* break where we can forget the petty details of the business and concentrate on the grand strategy? I thought that a day or two away from the hurly-burly — and away from our esteemed partners, delightful though their company is — might not come amiss. Somewhere you and I could snuggle down on a far-flung island, out of the sun and out of the wind, and ... you know."

"And *what?*" I struggled to keep a straight face.

He sighed. "Well, there's so much to sort out still. How we match negatives in the darkroom to faces and names on the beach, for instance. And what about people who want additional prints to be posted on after them? There's so much that's still undecided. We need a couple of days alone together — just you and me and a bottle of wine — and a loaf of bread, perhaps — to discuss all these matters at length. And at breadth. And in depth, come to that."

I kicked him under the table. "And so?"

He began to admire one of his fingernails. "And so I've booked us a room at the Castle for next Monday night, and tickets to the Scillies on the *Lyonesse* next Tuesday, and a room at the best inn at Hugh Town until the following Saturday ... all very provisional, of course. I suppose we may cancel without *too* great a forfeiture."

"Have I ever told you how much I love you?" I asked.

"Love?" He became alarmed. "Lord, but there won't be any time for *that,* I'm afraid. As I said, there's so much we need to settle about the business. I know you wouldn't *dream* of taking four days off just for the sake of love, so I've arranged a very business-like agenda for each day."

I thought that if teasing was to be the game, two could play. So I went all frosty and asked him if he thought it right to arrange such things without a word to me.

He admired a different nail. "Actually," he drawled, "it rather came about by accident. I was down at the steamship company on quite a different business ..."

"Oh yes!"

"Yes, indeed. The *Lyonesse* sails out each Tuesday and back on the Saturday. It occurred to me that, if they'd let me on board in the hour before they sail, I could take pictures of passengers standing in heroic poses at the bows or with their hands on the wheel — that sort of thing — and the prints would be ready and waiting upon their return to Penzance. Not a pot of gold, I agree, but a useful trickle of extra revenue. And so, to dispose the master favourably toward me, I started out by buying a couple of tickets for next Tuesday's sailing. I had *absolutely no idea* we might actually make use of them. It was a simple business expense — a bribe, if you like. But there they are." He drew them from his breast pocket and laid them on the table. "It'd be an awful shame to waste them, don't you think?" He lifted his glass. "To wine and honeymoons!"

I lifted mine. "To elegant liars!"

After lunch we strolled back to Fenton Lodge along the Cliff Road, where, a mere two months earlier, Jim had told me of his plans. Remembering that day, I could not believe we had achieved so much in the intervening weeks.

Jim slipped his arm around me and said, "You *are* a funny sausage, you know! I suspect that underneath this cool, calm exterior there seethes enough passion to launch three grand operas — yet your first thought, always, is to rush to deny it. You *know* you want us to take a honeymoon. You did from the start."

I just stared ahead and kept a straight face.

"I felt it the very first time I mentioned the subject," he went on. "Yet you said no as if you absolutely meant it. Why?"

"Oh!" I leaned my head hard against his shoulder. "You know! Honeymoon! Everyone looking at us — at me. The hôtel maids sniggering behind my back. Crossing the Rubicon ... leaping the great divide ... all that. And me with no work in my hands."

"So you thought that if you got up at seven and cooked our breakfast and then straightened my tie as I leave for work at eight, and gave me a quick peck on the cheek, and then went out to the wash house with a bag of laundry — then people would look at you and say admiringly, 'Now *there's* a woman with the right ideas!' Is that it?"

It was a horrid parody but it wasn't actually wrong. "Anything's better than all that sniggering," I replied.

"Curiouser and curiouser," he murmured.

"What now?"

"I cannot imagine anybody *daring* to snigger at you — not even behind your back. And for you to say 'No honeymoon!' because of such fears is as good as running away, isn't it? And I can't imagine you running away from anything, either."

I sighed, because he was right, of course. "It's just ... *honeymoon!* You know! Having nothing *else* to do."

"Than what?"

He wasn't being deliberately obtuse. His tone made it clear he just wanted me to say it. So I took a deep breath and obliged. "You know — after all these months when 'being good' meant keeping our clothes on and our hands away from ... certain places — suddenly 'being good' means the very opposite. It's too much all at once."

"We can soon take care of that," he said calmly. He lifted his hand from my waist and crooked it round my head — which was still against his shoulder — to look at his watch. "In about five minutes, at a guess."

When he put his hand back it was rather lower than before.

"D'you think ...?" I said.

"We'd be alone at Fenton Lodge, wouldn't we?"

I nodded.

"And we are getting married next Monday?"

I nodded again.

He held my arms as if he feared I might hit him after his next question: "And perhaps you still have some of what I thought was vanilla fudge — until I tasted it?"

I stopped in my tracks and stared at him. "You *ate* it? But when ... how ...?"

He laughed. "The very first day we were at Mulberry. Mark and I were measuring up, you were drawing, and Susan was writing down the figures — remember? And you asked me to bring you your handkerchief from your bag ..."

The implications of his discovery — and of his question, 'Do you *still* have any left?' — were just beginning to dawn on me. Did he think I *always* carried those things around? And that I might have used even one of them — never mind all — in the last four weeks? I just wanted the ground to open up and hide me.

"You knew what they were?" I managed to ask.

"Not until I tasted it. I know the taste of quinine and I couldn't imagine why anyone would want to put it into vanilla fudge. And it just so happens that one of Ma Harvey's favourite niceys is fudge." Ma Harvey was his present landlady. "She makes it every week. So when she gave me some, I told her the last lot I'd had tasted of quinine — and then she started laughing. I thought she was going to die, honestly! But she calmed down after a while and explained it all. So that's how I came to know. Have you still got it with you?" He patted my handbag.

That was better. Perhaps that's what he'd asked before, and I — in my guilty panic — had misheard. "Did you tell her *how* you came by it?" I asked anxiously. "Did you say it was in my bag?"

He shook his head. "Of course not. *Have* you got it with you? This is for the third time of asking."

I had to laugh then. I said, "Perhaps — like calling the banns — it *is* the sort of question that must be asked three times! They're in my dressing-table drawer at Fenton Lodge."

"And do you know of any just cause or impediment why we should not use them?"

"No," I replied.

All my fears — how idiotic they were!

My heart was racing and yet I felt serene. We sort of drifted the rest of the way in a golden, summery haze. Whenever I had thought about it before, I had felt so sure I was going to be awkward and embarrassed, and that it would hurt, and that I'd faint or break down in tears … and that the whole thing was going to be sordid and awful, and we wouldn't be able to look each other in the eye for days after. And yet it was exactly as Susan had once described it in our whispered, late-night *conversaziones* — better than an extra lie in bed of a morning, better than chocolate (better even than real vanilla fudge!), better than dancing. Wonderful beyond words.

Who would have thought that such pleasure — such *capacity* for pleasure — lurks all unsuspected inside us there! Because it isn't like food, where you've got only so much appetite and it dwindles away as you satisfy it. I should think that if we hadn't had to go over to Penzance the following day, we should hardly have had the energy left to walk up the aisle, or at least up the steps of the town hall, the following Monday!

Part Four

Penzance Promenade

The Promised Land

I think a wedding should either be a big, slap-up 'do,' costing a hundred pounds or more, or it should be small and intimate. Ours was small and intimate — as quiet and modest a wedding as we could have wished for. Indeed, there was just Marian, as my bridesmaid, and Mark and Susan as witnesses. The only other person I really wanted there was Harriet, but she said she never attended weddings and was sure I'd understand. Of course I wanted Teresa and my brothers there, too, but I'm talking about those people I could realistically have invited.

It would have been nice to have Cousin Stella, who had been such a good friend to me, but Jim said he'd have to ask his aunt and uncle then. And Mark didn't want any other Trevartons there because he hadn't yet told them that Susan now shared their illustrious name. So there we were, just five of us at the registry.

I know such occasions are supposed to be reverential and almost sacred — the Most Magical Moment in a girl's life and so on — but the Fates, or Providence, or whatever you like to call it, had obviously decided otherwise in my case. Our mother used to tell us a fairy tale about two knights who fought each other to the death because, when they met face-to-face on a forest path, underneath a shield that was hung up in the branches of a tree, one of them declared it was made of gold while the other maintained it was silver — with all the usual manly insults to back up their claims. After their combat, as they lie bleeding to death, the breeze gets up and the shield starts to twist in the sunlight — revealing to the pair of dying hotheads that it is, indeed, silver on one side and gold on the other.

In future, when I think of our mother's fairy tale, I shall at once be reminded of our wedding ceremony in Barnicoat's office in Penzance town hall. He, with his back to the window, saw two young people solemnly plighting their troth — and how we managed to retain our solemnity I'll never know. For what we — facing that same window — saw over his shoulder was a dog and a bitch in the back courtyard, carrying on in the way dogs and bitches are wont to do. The contrast between Barnicoat's face as he spoke of the solemnity and indissolubility of the marriage bond and the dog's face, with its glazed eyes and its tongue hanging out in a stupid, drooling grin, was comic beyond words.

So in future, when I put my hand on my heart and say I shall never forget our wedding ceremony, I shall mean one thing by it while my hearers will probably understand something quite different — which is fitting, in its way.

We gave way to our mirth in the street afterwards, and continued in the growler on the way to our wedding 'breakfast' at the Queen's Hôtel on the Esplanade. Though not quite as posh as the Falmouth Hôtel, it was every bit as expensive — 12s. 6d. for the five of us — but, as Mark said, you can only die once, too.

Marian rather hogged the limelight at table, with her stories of life in London and all the well-known people who lived in Hampstead — giving the impression that she rubbed shoulders with them every day. Susan kept glancing at me, surprised I was taking it all so calmly, for Marian seemed to be making a special play for Jim's attention, almost flirting with him, in fact.

Of course, I would have responded pretty sharply if I had not twigged very early on what game she was playing. She was still afraid I was going to badger her to come and live in Penzance. So she was flirting like that with Jim in order to force me to think twice.

Jim, who is as susceptible to female flattery of that kind as any other man of spirit, responded as one might expect.

I let their miniature 'affaire' continue until Susan's pointed glances at me became annoying, and then I said, "Marian, I haven't breathed a word to Jim — yet — about the possibility of your moving in with us and helping with the business. But I'll do so now if you like. You seem to get on like a house on fire!"

Marian blushed and Jim had the grace to go red at the tips of his ears. There was no more flirtation.

"Yes, what about all that?" Mark asked me. "We haven't heard a peep out of you all month, not about that, anyway."

"About what?" I asked.

"Getting the whole Moore clan together again."

The nerve of the man! You'd think he'd never said a word about Jim only putting up with my ambitions and not really sharing them.

Then Marian said a peculiar thing. She said, "Could we go and look at this place where the nuns took Teresa? Is it near? I'd like to see it before I go back to London."

I said it was, in fact, just around the corner, but I was puzzled as to why she asked.

Jim said, "Let's do that. I've not seen it, either."

It didn't please me at all — not the sort of thing I wished to do on the Most Magical Day of my life! On the other hand, I did not wish to quell this unaccustomed show of interest in Teresa by Marian — even though I suspected she knew full well that that was how I'd feel.

So we settled up, paid our calls of nature, and went out to the promenade, where we strolled a hundred paces or so to the junction with Morrab Road. "There it is." I pointed out the convent and hoped that, seeing what a dull, ordinary-looking building it was, Marian would be satisfied.

But she walked a few paces up the road and then glanced back at me. "Shall I catch up with you?" she asked. "Which way are you going?"

Of course the two men would not hear of her walking even that short distance unprotected by their chivalry, so they followed her and Susan and I followed them. I asked Susan if she wouldn't rather just sit in the sunshine, offering to wait with her if she liked. But she was determined not to let the baby 'interfere,' as she put it. Despite her desire to be a 'proper lady' and to ape their ways in every possible direction, she had also read somewhere that pampering a lady through her *enceinture* and treating her like an invalid only weakened her constitution and turned all her useful muscles to flab. And if she feared anything more than not living like a lady, it was not living at all. So fresh sea air and healthy exercise triumphed over drawn blinds and smelling salts.

By the time she had pointed this out to me — not for the first time by any means, I may add — we were approaching the carriage gate of St Breaca's. Two lay sisters, raking the gravel, watched us with a strangely indifferent curiosity.

"So there it is," I said to Marian. "Now let's go back and walk along the sands."

But she leaned over the gate and said to one of the women, "Would Sister Berrion be at home by any chance?"

I was amazed she had even remembered the name. She had seemed more interested in her curling papers when I told her of that incident.

The lay sisters exchanged glances and giggled. The last time I had seen two females giggle like that they had been seven years old and swapping smutty jokes. One of them pulled herself together and drew breath to answer when she was interrupted by the shriek of an unoiled sash window being raised up on the first floor of the house.

It was Sr Enuda!

"Miss Moore?" she called out, as if she did not trust her sight over that distance.

I went forward to the garden gate, which was near enough for me to talk loudly rather than actually shout. "I'm Mrs Collett now, Sister Enuda," I replied. "This is my elder sister, Miss Marian Moore. We didn't mean to disturb you — I'm sorry. She just wanted to … you know … see Saint Breaca's." When she made no reply I added, "I hope you don't mind?"

She held up a finger in a somewhat ambiguous gesture and vanished from sight.

"Is that the nun who's supposed to be scared to death of you?" Marian asked.

"I told you," I answered. "Sister Berrion was drunk. Or mad. Or even both. She said whatever came into her head."

I skipped back to the lay sisters and asked what had happened to Sr Berrion.

To my horror one of them drew a finger across her own throat while the other said, "She didn't never ought to have been a nun."

"Dead?" I asked fearfully.

They laughed again. "No — kicked out."

"She'm now teaching up the girls' school."

Sr Enuda reappeared at the main door to the house. I never imagined I should be relieved to see her, but I was. The thought of having to speak with the near-lunatic Sr Berrion had deterred me from visiting this place ever since, though I had not realized how much until now.

Sr Enuda came rather solemnly down the path to greet us. "You two can find some gravel to scratch at the back of the house," she told the lay nuns as she approached.

They curtsied and left us reluctantly.

I made the introductions. She nodded solemnly at each instead of shaking hands — part of what it means to shun the world, I suppose. "I've no news for you," she told me the moment I had finished.

"I wasn't expecting any," I assured her — which wasn't strictly true, though it would be mid-July before one could fairly accuse the General and his wife of being dilatory in replying.

"Good," she said.

"May I ask if *you* have written to the General, Sister Enuda?" Marian put in. "Sister Berrion promised to do so but we understand that she has left?"

Sr Enuda glared at her. So did I, though there was a lot more admiration in my eyes than in the Reverend Mother's. "What should *I* write to the General?" she asked coldly.

Marian smiled at me as if to ask if we could believe our ears. Turning back to the Sister, she said, "That our late grandmother, God rest her soul, in her haste to do the right thing, had inadvertently done the wrong thing, instead. That was the gist of what Sister Berrion promised to write."

It was plainly the first Sr Enuda had heard of it. It crossed my mind — and I'm sure it crossed Marian's, too — that Sr Berrion's departure had probably been rancorous and painful. It might not have stretched to a lengthy and detailed conversation about Teresa and my visit and the undoubted illegality of what they had done. In fact, it would have been thoroughly understandable if Sr Berrion had said nothing at all, but had simply left Sr Enuda to dig her own grave.

For her part, the Sister was quick to recognize the olive branch Marian was holding out. "I must say," she replied, "you have a refreshingly different attitude from your sister." This with a cold sweep of her eye toward me.

"Perhaps we might discuss it further indoors?" Marian suggested.

The woman looked at the five of us with mild alarm.

Marian, to make her point clear, turned to us and said, "You people go for that stroll on the sands. I'll catch you up." To Sr Enuda again she added, "I don't expect we'll need to detain each other for long."

The woman's only response was a guarded nod.

"Are you *sure* about this?" I murmured to Marian.

She winked and let herself in by the gate.

"What about old Marian, eh?" Jim said as soon as we were at a safe distance to talk.

"I hope she knows what she's doing," I responded.

"She had that poor old penguin eating out the palm of her hand," Susan put in admiringly.

Oddly enough, I had never seen the likeness between nuns and penguins before. I can't think why, but I hadn't. And I was in such a highly wrought state that day I was set to have hysterics, right there in Morrab Road. Only that Jim hit me rather too hard on the back, as if I were having a coughing fit instead of a laughing one, stopped me.

We kept to the prom because Susan said walking in the sand was *too much* exercise.

"What can Marian tell Sister Enuda that I can't?" I asked anxiously.

"All the things that the woman would simply shut her ears to if you were to say them?" Mark suggested.

"God, it's over a year ago," I grumbled. "Why should she bear a grudge that long? Anyway, she started it. She attacked me. You can see how belligerent she is. She doesn't give anyone a chance."

"That's why Marian took *her* chance before the woman could withhold it," Jim put in.

I rounded on him. "Oh, that's right! Stick up for her!"

"I shall." The smile never left his face. "I've got the greatest admiration for your Marian. I always have had." That was his idea of a joke, because, of course, he'd only met her that once. Anyway, he went on, "D'you think there's a chance she'd come and live at Mulberry? She's so jolly." He turned to Mark. "How about you, old fellow? You wouldn't object to sharing the place with one more niece, would you? Hardly notice it among so many!"

"I should jolly well say not!" Mark agreed. "Especially one as pretty as Marian."

If I hadn't spied Susan grinning her head off, I might have exploded then and there. Instead, I reined in my temper and pointed a warning finger at Jim. "Have a care, young man!" I said. "Your jokes may return to haunt you!"

He glanced at Mark, all innocence, and asked, "Am I joking? Did it sound to you as if I'm joking?"

I walked ahead of them in silence for a hundred yards or so. What glances they may have exchanged I neither knew nor cared. Then I felt Jim's hand grip my elbow to slow me down. "Come on, Crissy," he said soothingly. "This isn't like you at all."

"I had no wish to go to that nunnery — today of all days. What did Marian want to suggest it for? And why did you and Mark have to go with her? She walks all over London alone. She's perfectly capable of negotiating one furlong in Morrab Road."

"She obviously has a plan. Teresa's her sister, too. And you can't say *she's* off to a bad start. No — sorry! I meant you can't say she's off to a *bad* start."

"You were right the first time," I said glumly. "The thing is we had all day Saturday and all day yesterday when she could have popped up to see the nuns. Why didn't she? She didn't say a word about it. Why wait until now?"

He pulled me to a halt then and turned me to face him. Mark and Susan ambled tactfully on by. "You and Marian are unalike in so many ways," Jim said, "that it's easy to overlook the few ways in which you are almost twin souls."

"Such as?" I challenged him. But my anger had gone.

Eyeing me warily he said, "You are both arch-manipulators, even though your methods are quite different. She's obviously petrified that you're somehow going to manipulate her into leaving London — where she's equally obviously having the time of her life — and coming to live down here. So, of course, she behaves like this! She flirts with me and she wades into *your* arrangements wearing ten-league boots."

"And you flirt back," I said.

"Of course I do! It's pleasant. It's harmless. And it makes a point with which I agree wholeheartedly: She belongs in London."

"You don't want her down here at all."

"That's not true. I don't want a miserable Marian — a miserable, *manipulated* Marian — down here. And she would be." He tickled me gently under the chin. "I don't want *any* miserable females from your family in my life ... eh?"

I felt a familiar prickling behind my eyelids as I leaned my head against his chest and hugged him to me — or me to him. "I don't want *any* of this," I said. "Let's go on to Newlyn and pay a fisherman to take us to the Scillies now, this afternoon. I don't care what it costs."

"We could go to the Castle now," he suggested — the hôtel where he'd booked us for the night.

I giggled. "Everyone would know."

"D'you still worry about that?"

I was tempted, but then there was Marian to think of. She was catching the ten-to-five to Plymouth, where she'd transfer to a sleeping-car train, in which, though it arrived in London just after four in the morning, she could slumber on until eight. I was paying, of course — or, rather our late grandmother was.

Jim didn't press the point because he'd gained his end by then and I was cheerful again.

Marian rejoined us shortly after that and we hired a cab for Susan while the rest of us walked beside her, chatting all the way to Newlyn, by which time we'd worked up a good appetite for tea.

"Well?" I asked Marian once Susan was settled in the cab — which was actually an open dog cart out for hire.

"Well what?" she responded.

"You know very well. Did you get anything useful out of Sister Enuda? Any promises? Even a small admission or two?"

"She admits they acted in haste. She agrees that Teresa will probably be *happier* with you than with a couple of oldsters who could be her grandparents — though she doesn't see that a child's happiness is of any great importance when she would be far better off materially left where she is. D'you know he's worth nearly half a million — old General Sir Redvers? And he said he's going to leave most of it in trust to Teresa. D'you think *we* aren't being just a teeny bit hasty, Crissy, dear? None of the Wilkinsons seems to live very long. And it's not everyone who has a little sister worth half a million!"

I had deliberately avoided looking at her during this appalling speech — hoping to freeze her out by my silence. But when at last I turned to protest, she flung her arms about me and laughed and said, "Oh, Crissy!" several times in a tone of jocular despair.

Then she thrust me at Jim and said, "*Do* something about her before you bring her back from the Scillies ... won't you?"

How do you spoil a maid's honeymoon? There are some people who think it amusing to send a telegram in advance to the honeymoon hôtel, saying that the lady is an invalid and will require a sedan chair. Or if the couple have booked into an hôtel overlooking a lake or the sea, they will write in the name of the husband to say that his wife's parents were both drowned and the sight of large expanses of water now fill her with thoughts of utmost melancholy — for which reason they would prefer a room at the back of the building from which not even the most oblique glimpse of the water is possible. But I can now tell these pranksters an even better way: As the honeymooners' transport is in the act of departing — be it from railway platform or harbour quay — you come running up toward it waving a piece of paper in a state of excitement, shouting words that the happy couple cannot possibly make out, what with all the hissing of steam and clanking of engines and screeching of gulls and such like.

In my case it was Sr Enuda, or it could have been one of her nuns — a *penguin,* anyway, as Susan called them — who came waddling up the quay as fast as a penguin *can* waddle, waving a piece of paper and scanning the crowded decks of the *Lyonesse* as well as anyone wearing two huge starched blinkers can scan anything.

She was obviously looking for me. I yelled. I waved. I attracted a deplorable amount of attention from our rather snooty fellow passengers, who did not come to Cornwall to be exposed to that sort of behaviour, but not so much as a glance from the good nun. In any case, Mark got to her first.

Marian had gone back to London the previous night. Susan was at Mulberry, resting. So Mark was the only one on the quay with any idea of the connection between the lost-looking nun and the energetic young hoyden on the ferry boat. He said something to her. She clutched the paper to her breast and her wimple shook. He spoke to her again. The hand holding the letter half unpeeled itself from her bosom. The wimple did not move. He spoke yet again, and this time the wimple nodded and the hand released the letter to him.

He read it swiftly and then held a brief conference with the nun. He read it again and then spoke with her further, and rather longer, too. I think I was holding my breath all this while, until my protesting lungs forced me to breathe once more. Then for one long, dreadful moment Mark appeared at a loss. He looked up at our ship, which was now a couple of furlongs out to sea, then at the paper, then at the nun, then at the sky, then at us again. Finally he held the paper above his head — in fact, he held both hands over his head in the attitude of a triumphant pugilist and executed a little victory dance on the spot.

"It looks like good news — whatever it may be," Jim said, slipping an arm around me.

I smiled back at him and said, "Yes, it must be." But I could not help remembering that long, hesitant moment before his show of joy. If it was such *obviously* good news, why pause at all?

"There'll be a telegram waiting for us at Hugh Town," Jim added.

Well, I *did* buck up at that. In three or four hours, I'd know the best and the worst of it. I could easily curb my impatience for that length of time — or so I thought.

Actually, it would have been better if there had been no submarine cable to the Scillies — if I had known for sure that there was no possible way between today and our return, next Saturday, for me to discover what had been written on that piece of paper. I could then have put it from my mind and thrown myself heart and soul into the enjoyment of our honeymoon — three and a half magical days away from the hurly-burly cares of the world (planning the strategic side of our business, as Jim had promised — ho-hum!).

But three *hours!* To ask a person to forget that she's going to learn something possibly quite momentous about a stolen little sister in a mere three hours' time is asking for more than flesh and blood can render. I tried. We both tried. Jim, who had once had a walking holiday, going right around the coastline from Penzance through Land's End to St Ives, pointed out all the features and places he could remember. He said that in the coming winter, when our business slackened off, we could leave Mark and Susan to hold the fort while we took the odd couple of days off and went bicycling all over the peninsula, which was as different from the Cornwall we knew as you could imagine.

For a while he succeeded in distracting me with these dreams but then he stood me in the bows and took pictures of me on his 'Kodak' from so many aspects that I knew he was just looking for the best 'shots' and angles for our future trade. So then I thought, *If he can't leave our cares behind, why should I!* And so I fell to wondering about that bit of paper which Sr Enuda had thought important enough to bring (or send) to the quayside.

Perhaps Sr Berrion had written to the General after all? Or maybe Felicity had muddied the waters? Or had my second letter to the General — the one I wrote as soon as I knew of my grandmother's legacy — prompted him to write to Sr Enuda, asking her to stand shoulder-to-shoulder with him in an alliance against me?

I meant against *all* us Moores, of course — Marian, me … all of us — including Teresa. Teresa most of all. I must not again fall into the error of thinking this was my private struggle against the Indian Wilkinsons.

Perhaps Sr Enuda was being so (relatively) pleasant to us, merely to put us off our guard? They must know that the longer Teresa lived in the General's household and the more they pampered 'their' only child, the less willing she would be to come home to us — and the more easily they could induce her to plead with me to leave her where she was. In those circumstances it wouldn't matter which of us had the law on our side. If Teresa pleaded to be left to stay in India and I had the entire House of Lords behind me, nothing would make me bring her back.

From that point on, my thoughts went rapidly downhill. I decided morosely that my chance of ever seeing my dear little sister again, before she grew up and grew away from us entirely, had probably already gone. I had frittered away this past year in my own selfish

development. I should have put the recovery of Teresa above all else —
above the comforts of life at Fenton Lodge, above friendship with
Harriet, above art, even above Jim. I should have been a cabin-maid on
a ship to India, and then bluffed my way into being an auxiliary nurse at
some hospital in Mysore … something, *anything* that would have got me
within speaking distance of my dear, darling Teresa …

Fantasies of all the heroically uncomfortable things I might have
done jarred so harshly with memories of the interesting and richly
rewarding life I had actually led. And now it was too late. Surely that
was the most dreaded pair of words in the language: too late!

"That's a glum face to be taking with us to Hugh Town," Jim said.

"Hugh Town," I echoed.

"Is there anything wrong with Hugh Town?"

I forced a smile then. "Oh, I was just dreaming. Impossible dreams."

"How impossible?" he asked.

"The Taj Mahal by moonlight?" I offered.

He hesitated. Then he saw what I was really saying. "Ah!" he replied.

"Why didn't Mark jump up and down with joy at once?" I asked.
"What was all that … that confabulation between him and the nun?"

"We really have to wait, darling." He gave me a hug. "It's not long
now and he'll surely send a telegram."

Shortly after that we cleared Land's End and it was like nosing into a
different ocean — which, in a sense, we were. I mean, we were leaving
the Channel and going out into the Atlantic — except that deep salt
water is deep salt water wherever you are and you don't expect a couple
of names on a map to bring about so dramatic a change.

It was a bright summer day with lots of blue heaven shimmering
through skeins of thin, high cloud, and lots of little white horses playing
over the sea all around us. There was no sign of rough weather on any
horizon, nor had we experienced any for the past several days. But
there clearly had been a storm somewhere out there, for, as soon as we
came out of the lee of Land's End, the ferry began to roll and yaw across
what looked like hills and valleys of shimmering green water. It was no
illusion, either, as a glance at the Longships light, a mile or so off Land's
End, confirmed, for the seas were breaking upon the reef in explosive
white sheets that rose almost as high as the lighthouse itself.

"Keep your eye on the horizon," Jim advised me. "When you feel the
deck beginning to rise, bend a little at the knees. And then, when it
starts to fall again, straighten yourself out."

How bending at the knees, which produces a rise and fall of three inches, can compensate for the motion of a deck that is falling and rising what feels like three *miles,* I could not imagine. And yet it worked! It's just that first bit of acceleration, up or down, which causes the trouble — when the deck seems to fall away from under you or, on the contrary, seems all set to fire you up among the clouds. Soon I was bending and straightening like an old sailor, hardly noticing I was doing it. I even got the knack of giving way on each knee at different times, to counter the rolling motion, too.

The trouble is, the sea is so fascinating when it displays even a tiny bit of its power like that. It distracts you from your troubles so that seasickness can then creep up on you unawares.

I'd grown up near the sea for most of my life — and actually within a stone's throw of the high-water line since the age of seven. I'd seen huge storm breakers hurl themselves up the sixty-foot cliff at Tyrock — and then be carried half a mile inland on the wings of the storm. But I'd never been out on the ocean itself before. I'd never seen swell as great as this with no land near, on which it might break. The white horses didn't count as breaking waves, for they were just little frothy things, whipped up by the stiff sea breeze. The green hills and valleys that lifted the *Lyonesse* to the heavens before plunging her deep into the abyss again were a quarter of a mile apart and as tall as a church. Some seemed as tall as a church *and* its spire.

There was a general drift toward midships, where, people said, the pitching and tossing would be least noticeable. We joined it at first but I soon felt we had been better off at the bows, where, though the motion was greater, you could see exactly what was coming and when it would hit you. So we returned there, feeling rather superior, and marvelled at the power of the sea and the audacity of our little steamer as she skittered sideways up and down those great, shivering flanks of green. We both felt dreadfully nauseous, of course, but our pride just about managed to keep us and our breakfasts together and we disembarked at Hugh Town suffering the oddest blend of ravenous hunger and appetite-stifling queasiness.

When you see them on the map, the Scillies look like a hundred islands scattered over the Atlantic roughly in the shape of a comma. But when you're among them you can see that only about twenty of them have any grass. The rest are just rocky outcrops, and the outlines of the comma-shape can't be seen at all. Hugh Town, the so-called capital, wasn't even as big as Porthleven, but the inn was comfortable and the people there friendly. Best of all — there was a telegram waiting for us with Mr Johns, the proprietor.

As soon as we were alone in our room I tore it open with trembling fingers. To show what a state I was in, my immediate thought was that it must be a hoax because, although it was signed 'Mark,' the handwriting wasn't his! All it said was, 'Good news awaits your return next Saturday. Try to keep busy meanwhile.'

I stamped my foot in vexation. "He could have said *what* good news," I said. "About Teresa? About our business? About Susan? He could have said."

"I didn't realize we were expecting quite so *much* good news," Jim commented. He took the paper from me and counted the words, including the name and address. "Eighteen," he said. "He just got in under the shilling!"

That annoyed me still more, even though it was exactly the sort of thing I'd have been likely to do. "He could have left off about keeping busy," I pointed out. "Then he'd have room to add 'about Teresa' or whatever. Can we send him a telegram back? It would teach him to be so thoughtless. Or we could send it reply paid."

Jim just laughed as he took the telegram from me and folded it away into his pocket. "It's good news. Let's just leave it at that until Saturday, eh? Are you hungry?" He looked at his watch and then tested the springiness of the bed with his splayed fingers. It was the way a furniture salesman might demonstrate a bed in a shop. Everything Jim did was managed with a professional smoothness and aplomb.

The boy came up with our suitcases. Jim tipped him sixpence, which pleased the lad no end.

"We'll get good service while we're here," Jim said, lifting my arms around his neck and putting his hands on my posteriors. "But nothing's too good for my darling wife. Shall we eat or go for a walk?"

I wriggled tight against him and kissed his neck beneath his ear.

"A walk, I think," he said, giving me a quick kiss back and then letting me go. "Work up a good appetite, eh?"

I picked up his hands and put them back where they had been. "And what was all that in aid of?" I asked.

"That, I hope, was working up an even better appetite," he said. "Do you object?"

"Let's make it a long, long walk," I said. "For the best appetite of all."

Jim had brought one of our 'Kodaks' along and Mr Barratt, the pharmacist at Hugh Town, who was also a keen amateur photographer, let him develop and print the shots we had snapped — Crissy on Bryher, Jim on Annet, Big Waves on St Martin's ... and so on. He had no enlarger so they were tiny prints, which we had to admire through a magnifying glass. The 'big waves' could have hidden behind an ordinary drinking straw. Barratt sneered at the 'Kodak' as a toy camera but I explained to him how we proposed to use them in our business this summer. I suggested that if he got an enlarger, he could do something similar here, only more leisurely, since people had to stay three or four days at least.

Jim was angry with me for letting the cat out of the bag but my opinion was that the more photographers there are, offering our sort of 'snap-shots-today' service, the better it will be for all of us — as long as they don't do it in Penzance! I mean, the fact that you can get donkey rides on the sands at St Ives doesn't harm the donkey rides at Marazion, does it! On the contrary, it helps. The first thing children say when they arrive at any old beach these days is, "Can we go on the donkeys now?" They expect the rides to be there. But, knowing what awful stick-in-the-muds most English people are, I'll bet that the original people who offered donkey rides on a beach somewhere back in history had a very thin first season.

"Which is better?" I asked Jim. "A world in which I've got to meet trippers off every train and *explain* our service and try to *persuade* them to give it a try — or one in which they say, 'Oh look! There's the black-and-white-hat man — smile everybody!' "

He saw the point in the end and even suggested that Barratt should wear a black-and-white hat, too — which rather shocked the man.

He was rather shocked with me, too, I'm afraid, when I asked him if he stocked Rendell's Quinine Pessaries — just in case the dozen I had left in the box weren't enough. I could tell that he was the sort of man who believes that such matters should be left to Providence. But we couldn't afford that luxury. Our business was, for the moment, the most important single part of our marriage and we wanted it well established before we risked starting a family, especially with Teresa and my brothers in the offing.

He said there was definite proof that 'those wretched things' didn't work. The archbishop of Canterbury had persuaded Rendell to make one-in-ten of them deliberately ineffective! They're so mealy-mouthed, some of these pious people. They wouldn't even condemn Satan outright — just assure you he didn't go to a very good school.

My little argument with Jim set me thinking, though. It struck me that we hadn't really considered our business from the customer's point of view at all — or only in a very general way. However, I waited until the Saturday morning before I spoke, when our minds were inevitably turning outward again to the life and the business that beckoned us back there in Penzance. We enjoyed our usual dawn kiss and cuddle and then I asked Jim, "How are we going to make the typical day-tripper think, *Oh yes! I simply must take some of these 'snap-shot' things back with me today?*"

"What's wrong with your little leaflets?" he asked in return.

"I don't think they're quite enough. Remember — these people have never seen anything like us before. What d'you suppose the man-in-the-street — or his wife — thinks of when they see the word 'photograph'? Or 'photographer'?"

He propped himself on one elbow and stared at me, more baffled than curious. "Portraits?"

"Expensive portraits — things that cost half a week's wages for some — mounted in card with bevelled cutouts and decorative gold borders … that's what any word with 'photo' in it means to them. Words like 'photograph' or 'photographer' have got little pound signs hanging all over them for people like that. *We* know different, but they don't. So that's the first hurdle we've got to leap."

"How?"

"You're going to think I'm mad, but I believe we should avoid any of those words. Photograph, photographer … photographic — we should ban them!"

He laughed. "Good morning, madam — may I take your … er — guess what?"

I said, "… your picture. May I take your picture for a shilling!"

I may have pointed this out before, but I often don't know what I'm thinking until I actually hear myself saying it. As soon as I heard these words in my own mouth I sat up and clapped my hands. "Got it!" I cried. "That's what we tell them — *Your Picture for a Shilling!* That's our slogan. We'll just have to paint over our advertising boards and do them again. We'll call ourselves 'The Shilling Picture Studio'! Won't it sound as if we've been in business for years, eh! Everyone knows *The Shilling Lives* — you can buy them at every station bookstall. And there's Shilling Hats ... Shilling Dinners ..."

"Shilling Funerals," he put in.

I hadn't heard of them. "Where?" I asked.

"Ours for a start. I think it's implicit in this suggestion of yours."

I pouted. "You're not taking this seriously."

"It would help if you put some clothes on."

Which is what I did — an hour or so later.

At ten-thirty that morning we re-embarked on the *Lyonesse* in a mood of wistful regret. It was a perfect day for leaving the Scillies — gray, overcast, drizzly, and with a dead-calm sea. Being unable to go on deck we splashed out the extra two shillings for a place in the saloon, where Jim read two back-numbers of the *Photographic Trade Weekly,* which he'd brought with him and hadn't so much as glanced at yet, and I used up almost a whole propelling-pencil lead on various new drafts of our come-all-ye leaflet and the advertising boards we intended to prop up at various places, like at the railway station and the entrance to each of the two main beaches.

The drizzle had passed over by the time we got back to Penzance. There, although I was desperate to learn what had been in that letter Sr Enuda or her minion had been waving the previous Tuesday morning, I got the cab to turn in at the station, where I took Jim up the platform and asked him to imagine he was a tripper arriving to spend the day on the beach. We walked back down toward the entrance and I pointed to where I thought our advertising signboards should stand. Then I showed him two little sketches I'd done on the boat. They were for boards that, when painted up, would measure about two feet by three.

One, which I had done using the solemn sort of lettering you associate with expensive studios, read 'Collett and Trevarton — High-Class Photographic Artists. Our peripatetic photographers will, upon request, take impromptu portraits of you and your loved ones in alfresco poses and situations ...' and so on.

The other had the much gayer lettering you get on music-hall song sheets for numbers like *Hi! Tiddley hi!* or *Catch 'em all alive-oh!* and it said, 'The Shilling Picture Studios — Your Picture for a Shilling! Look out for our wandering Snap-Shooters in their jolly black-and-white hats! Constant patrols on all main beaches!'

"Well?" I asked.

"I think we'd better bring Mark down here and repeat this demonstration for his benefit," he replied.

We returned to the cab, which had to take the long way round, up Lescudjack Road, because the horse would never manage the hill up from Chyandour. It made me realize that the fire engine would also take longer to reach us if the house caught fire — which was slightly more risky with our arc lamps and electricity. I'm sure such a thought would not have occurred to me — or not so instantly — before my marriage. It just shows how new responsibilities can change a person.

There was so much to juggle, and so little time left to juggle it in! When Mark came out of Mulberry holding what was obviously the nun's bit of paper, I almost said to him, "Can't it wait?" In fact, I started saying it and had to turn it into a joke. While I read the brief note I heard Jim ask after Susan and learned she was still two-in-one.

The good news — if indeed it was — was that Lady Wilkinson, the General's wife, was returning to England in July and would be staying for part of the time with her in-laws at Nancekuke House. I turned the paper over to see if there was more, but the reverse side was blank.

"Is she bringing Teresa with her?" I asked Mark.

He shrugged. "That was the first thing I asked the nun — Sister Culanus. She didn't know."

I frowned. "Culanus — that's a man saint, surely?"

Keeping a solemn face he said, "Nuns aren't supposed to have any sex. Talking of which …"

"Talking of Teresa," I insisted hurriedly, "was it just this sexless Sister Culanus who didn't know? I mean, I presume the Reverend Mother has received some kind of communication from the General? Or from someone at Nancekuke?"

He smiled tolerantly at me and said, "Funnily enough, *I* thought of that, too. So I went and asked Sister Enuda. But apparently not. The fact that Lady W is coming next month is all they know — not even the dates. That's why I didn't put anything more in the telegram — otherwise we'd have been conducting this conversation at a penny a word!"

"Te-ea!" Susan called in two notes from the window. She had obviously been watching Mark and me talking, and had guessed our conversation correctly, for the first thing she said to me, after the expected hugs and 'All right, are we?' and winks, was: "We think it's a hopeful sign, don't we, Mark."

"Yes, Susan," he replied.

"Dear old Minty Wilkinson!" Susan went on sarcastically, pronouncing the name rather as my grandmother used to, which I thought was sailing a bit close to the wind, since she was only just over three months' dead, and Mark was there beside her. But he seemed not to notice. As we sauntered into the waiting room she went on: "Obviously she needs to have a chin-wag with Sister Enuda, about you-know-what, but they daren't put a word of it on paper. So, no names, no pack drill, as the sergeant said. That's hopeful, surely?"

I stared out of the window, drumming on the sill, turning this information over in my mind as I sought for other, less rosy explanations. I couldn't think of any but I was sure they existed.

"No?" Susan prompted me again.

"I cannot feel that your sister-in-law, Felicity Trevarton, is entirely out of this picture," I said. "Her hand is in it somewhere. What's the first train to Redruth tomorrow?"

I thought Jim was rather preoccupied that evening but I assumed it was because the holiday was over and we were once again facing the challenges of real life. He behaved almost as if he wished we hadn't taken the break at all — which peeved me a little, I must say. Anyway, when I got into our bed and lay on my back and put my hands behind my head and slightly bent one thigh and let it fall gently against him ... he just carried on reading!

"Well!" I said after a silent while. "There's a first time for everything, I suppose."

"Eh?" He made it seem as if he were coming back from miles away.

"No, no — you carry on," I told him.

"It's quite an important article," he replied.

"How could I doubt that!"

He was reading from the issue of the PTW that had come while we were away. He folded it with that air of martyrdom you often see husbands adopt toward their wives in public. 'Look at me, everybody,' it proclaims. 'See how long-suffering I've learned to become!'

Whenever I'd observed it in the past I had promised myself no husband of mine should ever behave in such a fashion — and now here was Jim doing it in the very week of our wedding!

How could I stop it, here and now? How could I make sure he never, ever did it again?

The most important thing to do is ignore the hint. Don't rise to it.

I just smiled dreamily at the ceiling. "D'you remember that wonderful lunch we had at the Falmouth Hôtel?" I asked. "Thursday before last?"

"Mmmh?" His tone hovered uncertainly — reluctantly, even — between his earlier resentment and a nervous, what's-she-got-up-her-sleeve? curiosity. (Actually I was wearing a sleeveless summer nightdress, but that's beside the point.) He lowered his journal a significant half-inch and glanced sidelong at me.

"I meant to remark about it at the time and then forgot. I seem to remember we had *other things* on our mind? That afternoon, at least. Anyway, d'you remember that couple at the next table? You said the husband looked as if he'd crawl back under the carpet as soon as they got home again?"

"Oh ... yes?" Curiosity was getting the upper hand now. The journal fell to the counterpane.

"D'you remember how she ticked him off all the time — but oh-so-lovingly? 'Tuck your tie away, my dear. You know how hard it is for me to clean.' And, 'Use the toothpick, please, my angel. When you suck your teeth like that it gives me *such* a headache!' Remember?"

Jim chuckled. "My favourite bit of that conversation was when *he* said, 'Come to the point, please, my dearest, sweetest darling. When you beat about the bush like this, it gives *me* such a headache, too!' D'you remember him saying that?"

I dug him with my elbow — but at least his martyred look had gone. "The point is," I told him, "the thing I meant to say at the time, is I wonder how they got from all the wonder and glory of their wedding day to *that* state of sarcastic ... what can I call it? Not warfare. Not even subdued warfare."

"Stale...mate?" he suggested, with a light pause between the two syllables. "Holy deadlock? How do *you* think it came about?"

"I think *he* started it."

"Naturally."

"I used to wonder why some women put up with husbands who are the opposite of that poor chump. The absolute tyrants. D'you know, there's a fisherman in Porthleven called Cap'n Blight — though everyone calls him Cap'n Bligh, because of the mutiny on the *Bounty*, remember? Anyway, he counts all the buttons in his wife's needlework box ... he makes her stack all the towels, all folded in the identical way, in the airing cupboard — and all the sheets — so he can stand in the doorway and count them — which he does the minute he returns from sea — along with everything else in the house! D'you know, he once asked her how she managed to get through five eggs in only four days! And ..."

"Very well, darling! I see the man clearly — he's practically in this room by now."

"Well, the thing I was going to say is that Mrs Blight absolutely adores this martinet of a husband. She won't hear a word against him. I was talking about it with Susan once and we decided that women will tolerate men like that — even imagine they love them — because strong, hard men will do a good job of defending the domestic nest."

"Even if they make life inside that nest a living hell?"

"Yes, even so."

"Are you trying to tell me that I should take a leaf out of ..."

"No!" I said, horrified. "That's just one type of wife and one type of husband. There's also the other extreme — where the man is never anything but sweet and gentle and kind and understanding and blah-blah-blah. He tells himself that *his* domain is the great wide world, so the house is hers and all that's in it. He never counts anything, never questions her, defers to her in all matters domestic. The other extreme, as I said."

"Do such paragons of understanding exist?" he asked.

"Of course not!" I laughed. "But that doesn't stop the dear, kind, misguided fellows from trying their best. They just do it outwardly and bottle up their frustration on the inside, you see? And what happens when the bottle's full? They let it all pour out in the form of the martyred look that man had at the Falmouth Hôtel last week. And their acid-sweet way of talking to each other."

"And *I* was wearing that martyred look when you came to bed just now, I suppose?"

"Yes. For the very first time." I snuggled up and kissed him just below the ear. "I hope it'll also be the last. The alternative is to spit it out."

"And risk a blazing row?"

I swallowed heavily. "Is it that bad?"

He thought it over and then gave a single, dry laugh with little humour in it. "It felt like it ten minutes ago. But now ..." He reached out and took my hand in his. "Oh, Crissy, you have a way of ... You have a way."

I kissed him again. "Diddums! Have I cheated you out of an enjoyable little simmer?"

Now it was he who swallowed heavily. "The thing is — do you really have to go to Redruth tomorrow? Can't it wait? With everything we have on our plates here — can't Teresa wait just a day or two? Not even a day?"

What a difference four little words can make: 'Not even a day?' Until Jim spoke them he was making a simple request to me — an unreasonable one in my eyes but a reasonable one in his. Something worth discussing calmly, anyway. But those four extra words turned his question into the sort of non-question that lawyers ask in court. And, of course, it filled me with panic at once.

Here it comes at last, I thought. *What Mark taunted me with that day we first saw Mulberry.* My only thought was to come out fighting.

"Oh, very well," I replied, in that light tone of voice which isn't light at all. "Of course I can wait a day. I'll go on Monday. There's a bigger choice of trains then, too."

It angered him exactly as his weary martyrdom had annoyed me. "If that's what you thought I meant," he said with a martyr's sigh, "very well — go on Monday."

If he'd been the wife and I the husband, he'd have added something like, 'But don't expect to find your supper on the table when you come back — that's all!'

Then he committed the one really unpardonable sin in my book: He turned his back on me and made all sorts of noises feigning sleep. Or semiconsciousness, at least. Little swallowing noises and sniffs and the sort of chomping dogs do by the hearth.

Perhaps I persisted because the situation was so novel — and novel situations always have a certain excitement, no matter what. So there I was, staring at a pyjama-cliff, the rude back of the man I loved — and of course I still loved him to distraction — and desperately desired him, too — and yet I was seething and spitting with fury. I could have killed him, as well.

Instead, I punched him between the shoulderblades with the soft edge of my clenched fist. He told me later that I'd actually struck him very hard but I think it was mainly the surprise, because pugilism is not really in my nature. I still think it was quite gentle. Anyway, he spun round in the bed, which pulled the clothes half off me, and gripped both my arms at the wrists so as to pin me to the mattress.

Should I be ashamed of the deep, visceral thrill that seized me then? I, still possessed by my towering fury, lay there, pinioned and helpless, staring up into the flashing eyes of an animal I had just provoked beyond all reason. And I was *thrilled* to see it! So was he.

We astonished each other so much that he relaxed his grip a little. I ought to have felt pleased at that. I should have relaxed and let him build on that no doubt unintentional act of calm. Yet all I felt was renewed fury, tinged now with a desperate disappointment. There was an uncaged animal loose within me, too. *She* wanted this belligerence between us to go on. She exulted in its very excess.

She it was who slipped from that loosened grip and made a grab for his hair. She it was who let go when she had pulled it hard enough and whipped up those red mists of rage behind his eyes once more.

He gave vent to a roar, grabbed my offending arms, and pinned them back beside my head. Then, to stop me squirming away from him, he placed a ton of knee across my thighs.

I let out a squeal of terror and tried to bite his wrist. My teeth were the only weapons I had left by now — save one, and I did not want to start thinking of *that* as a weapon.

My cry made him aware of the outside world again. "Shut up, you blithering idiot!" he hissed, moving his hands, and mine, out of reach of my teeth. This brought his chest within butting distance, as I began at once to demonstrate. He fell on me then, all ten tons of him, and then suddenly he said, "Oh my God, Crissy, what's happening?" and he was kissing me and biting me and I had my arms around him and then my legs and I was kissing him and biting him back and we were laughing and snarling and biting and rutting and then hours and hours later, when he really was just going off to sleep, I sat up and said in horror: "The pessaries! We forgot the pessaries."

As I started to rise he said very quietly, but very firmly, too: "No!" And he pulled me down to him and caressed me tenderly and kissed my tears until I fell asleep.

My last thought, just before dropping off, was not about the astonishing thing that had just happened between us, nor about the astonishing things that might be going to happen inside my body between then and next March ... I mean, that's what I ought to have been thinking about, I know, but my actual thought was that we had no pessaries left, anyway — and, what is more, I had remembered the fact perfectly well earlier that same evening.

J im had to take me forcibly down to the station after lunch the following day — to catch the two-twenty, which would arrive at Redruth shortly after three. To my surprise, he bought two tickets. When he saw my raised eyebrows he said, "My real mistake was to imagine that Teresa is nothing more than *your* sister."

As we walked up the train in search of an empty compartment I said we ought to try to arrange a little quarrel *every* night.

"*Little* quarrel?" he echoed.

Unfortunately the train was rather crowded so we couldn't continue the conversation. In fact, he read the rest of his magazine while I glanced through the back numbers. A gentleman sitting diagonally opposite was quite put out to see me reading something that wasn't about knitting, pokerwork, or finding a hundred-and-one ingenious uses for old candle-ends. The look he gave me when I finally met his eye was almost one of hatred. Why do we frighten them so much when what we want is so little? All the same, it made me feel proud of Jim, who never for one moment questioned my ability to play any part the business might demand and who never thought me wonderful for being able to stand on my hind legs and talk. It was easy enough to feel a great warm upwelling of love for him when there was nothing much to do — as on the Scillies — but to feel it there and then, with a hundred other preoccupations waiting to claim my mind, well, that made it ten times more genuine. I think until that moment — despite all the times my innards had seemed to melt away at the very thought of Jim — I had not fully grasped why it is so important and so wonderful to be in love, why we think it more precious than life itself, and why it is the one obsession that has haunted our kind ever since we rose above the tribe of apes. Suddenly I felt that if *we* were together, Jim and I, nothing would ever defeat us.

Poor man! I don't suppose for a moment that he understood why I gripped his arm so fiercely as we walked up the platform at Redruth, nor why I could not answer his "What's brought on all this, then?" for the ache I had in my throat and the prickling behind my eyelids.

"We are going to get her back," I said when I could speak again.

"Of course," he agreed.

"No matter what."

"We'll murder if we have to." He meant it as a joke but I didn't argue.

After a decent interval he asked, "Have you thought what you're going to say to Mrs Trevarton this afternoon?"

"She might not even be there," I replied. "In which case we can walk on to Little Sinns and take tea with Harriet. Or call on your aunt and uncle, perhaps?"

"Talking of Miss Martin," he said, "d'you think she gives those quinine things to any of her girls when they leave?"

It was odd that the question had never occurred to me but the more I thought about it, the more likely it seemed that she did. "Very probably," I answered. "It'd be only sensible."

"She does take risks!"

I thought of Mr Dalziell, the barrister at the Albany, and agreed.

"She'd be sacked if one of them peached on her," he went on. "What'd she do then?"

Another possibility I hadn't considered. "She'd go to her aunt's in Hampstead and be her companion," I said. "Until she married, anyway. I bet someone would snap her up within the year."

He laughed but said nothing.

"What?" I asked.

"This illusion all you women suffer from — that it's the men who do the snapping-up!"

Felicity was, as it happened, at home that afternoon. She was — or pretended to be — quite pleased to see us. She was playing croquet by herself on the lawn at the back. Walter, she told us, had gone to call on a client who was dying — "for the fifth time in as many weeks!" she added between her teeth. I could not tell whether it was Walter or the client whom she disbelieved.

She took a pair of mallets from the box and asked us to join her. She warned us to keep our voices down because, although we could not be seen from the front, and were unlikely to be observed from the sides and back, if we were heard doing anything so sinful as playing croquet on the sabbath, the business would suffer for it.

Jim remarked that it was a pity no games were mentioned in the Bible. Children were not allowed to play with toy animals on a Sunday — unless they belonged to a Noah's Ark game, which was popular for that very reason.

We then indulged a pleasant fantasy in which a long-lost book of the Bible was discovered under St Augustine's tomb at Canterbury —

which spoke of the Israelites' intense passion for croquet, shove-
ha'penny, poker, football, cricket, fly-fishing …

"… and baccarat!" Jim said, bringing the list right up to date, for,
while we had been lost to the world on the Scillies, it — the world — had
been lost to all else but the scandal in which the Prince of Wales was
involved. It was the first time an heir to the throne had gone into the
witness box in several hundred years.

I hadn't bothered to read anything about it but Felicity, now it was
mentioned, could speak of nothing else. She was shocked at my ignorance
and went to some pains to cure it, for I had hardly listened when the
Hampstead people were all a-flutter over it. The case, I now learned,
was all about an incident at a private house-party somewhere up in
England, where some army officers had spied on a colonel in the Scots
Guards and then accused him of cheating. They cooked up a scheme
whereby, if he gave a solemn undertaking never to play cards again,
they'd hush it all up. If he wouldn't do that, they'd go to Doncaster races
and denounce him. Why they couldn't denounce him from the comfort
of their own firesides, I don't know, but that's what Felicity said. The
colonel not only refused, he sued his accusers for libel — which is what
all the fuss was about.

The case was still going on but Felicity said it was a time-bomb that
was going to blow up in the faces of the royal family and bring them to
their knees.

"Sceptre and crown will tumble down," she said gaily. "That old
harridan will be gone. England will be a republic before the turn of the
century. Can't you feel it in the air?"

All I could feel in the air was that the anger and venom she had once
directed against my poor grandmother had now found a much grander
target. Or harridan.

I kept trying to think of ways to let her know Mark had blurted out
everything she'd told him — or lied to him — about his being my cousin
rather than my uncle. But it was impossible with Jim there, not only for
the obvious reason but because he'd naturally assume I was dropping
hints about Mark's marriage to Susan, which was still secret. Very
frustrating. I concentrated on the croquet.

I had never actually played the game before — only tapped the balls
around a bit when clearing up after my grandmother and her friends.
But I soon picked up the rudiments and, by a series of flukes, found
myself in a position to roquet Felicity — that is, put my ball hard against

hers and pin mine down with my foot while I gave it a sharp crack with the mallet. The impetus, through my trapped ball, sent hers off into the shrubbery. When I did it for the third time, she lost interest in the game and suggested it was well past teatime. We dropped our mallets where we stood, leaving them for the servants to tidy up. Felicity probably thought nothing of it but to me it was one of life's little luxuries.

"I don't suppose you've had word from the Wilkinsons?" I asked casually as we made our way up to the terrace at the back of the house.

"Which Wilkinsons?" she asked, equally casually — which probably meant she had, and that she knew precisely what I was talking about.

"Any of them, really. I thought I might have come back home to find a little note waiting for me from Cousin Stella, just to let us know how she's settling in at Port Navas. Perhaps it's a little early, though."

"Yes," she said drily. "Honeymoons are like that, aren't they — seem to last for ever! Oh, *why* did you bring Mister Collett with you today? I'm dying to hear how it all went!" She smiled coyly at Jim to show she was really joking — and then icily at me, to show she really wasn't.

When she went to wash hands, Jim said, "I can find an excuse to go, if you like. She might tell you more if I weren't here. I could go to my aunt and uncle's — and you follow?"

"D'you want to?" I asked — foolishly, for his face made it clear he did not really want to leave. However, I desperately wanted a word with Felicity alone, so I said that was perhaps quite a good idea.

He made his excuses to Felicity when she returned, and her protestations of disappointment were insincere enough to send him on his way. She let me show him out so that I could mollify him with a kiss. "Remember," he murmured just before I closed the door, "you may not welcome her help, but you're going to need it whether you want it or not, when it comes to getting Gerald and Arthur out of the Sutton."

But for that sobering warning, who knows what might have happened when Felicity and I were alone at last?

"Tell me!" she said breathlessly when I returned. "Now that you're one of *us* — isn't marriage absolutely sublime! Tell me all, I want to hear all. Did Jim do his marital duty well and truly by you?"

I took her hand between mine and looked her in the eye, forcing myself to smile. "We were the scandal of the Scillies," I assured her. "Morning, afternoon, evening, and night!"

"Oh, stop!" she gasped, rolling her eyes heavenward. "You wicked girl! But look what a bonny colour it's given you!"

I continued in exactly the same tone, so that the words were out before she even started to grasp their meaning, "Why did you tell Mark he was my cousin instead of my uncle? You know it isn't true."

She took a long, bewildered moment to come down from out of the clouds. Then, soberly, she said, "But it *is* true."

I shook my head.

"Archie told me so. Ask him if you like."

For the first time my confidence began to be shaken. Passing the word on to Mark would only be malicious if it were a lie — and if she knew it to be a lie. Perhaps I had misjudged her all this time?

"What does Archie know of it?" I asked. "He wasn't there. Cousin Stella was — at least, judging from the way she spoke about it."

Felicity's gaiety returned at this. She gave a long, tinkling laugh. "But she wouldn't tell you the truth anyway, dear! What a gullible goose you are at times — and so astute at others! I suppose it's because you *want* to believe Mark's your uncle!" She grinned and her eyes twinkled with scandalous suspicions. "Why? Did he try anything exciting? He was delighted when I told him — like a dog with two tails ... if that's not too graphic a simile! I hoped he'd go so far as to propose marriage to you. Too late now! But don't cut him out entirely, will you. I'm sure Jim Collett is a splendid husband, but you never know."

Only Jim's parting words prevented an explosion at that point. "I'll bear it in mind," I said. And then, taking an enormous chance, I added, "The reason I asked whether you'd heard from *any* of the Wilkinsons was that Lady Wilkinson, the General's wife, is intending to visit Nancekuke next month."

"When?" she asked, her eyes like saucers. "I mean exactly when?"

"I don't know. That's why I asked if you'd heard anything."

If she had, she was wasted this side of the footlights.

"Not a whisper," she assured me. "Will she bring Teresa with her?"

"I don't know that, either." I went on to explain how I came to know even the little that I did. But at one point I forgot myself and said, "Mark asked Sister Enuda ..." and she was onto it like a pouncing cat.

"But how could he? He's up in Newquay — with one of his chums."

That must have been what he told his brothers. I could not think of an explanation quickly enough.

"He isn't, is he," she said. "He's with you in Penzance! I knew it! Walter and Archie think he's still a little boy. I'll bet he's married that Callaghan girl, too."

I sighed. "If I confirm all these wild guesses, Felicity, he'll never speak to me again. And actually" — I brightened — "that would solve everything at a stroke, wouldn't it!"

"I'll call on you one day at home this week. Is he living in Penzance, too? If you tell me where, I can accidentally stroll past and accidentally see him."

After that, there was no point in holding back the truth. I could not forbid her the house, and the moment she called in she'd see for herself the way things were. So I explained.

"All four of you *together?*" she asked in scandalized delight. "Under one roof?"

"Like lodgers in a boarding house."

"I have never been a lodger in a boarding house. Oh, Crissy! Now I simply must come calling. Next Wednesday, yes? That's settled, then. What a knife-edge of emotional excitements you tread! And next month, too, when Lady Wilkinson comes home, perhaps with little Teresa in tow!"

Then I saw I had missed the key to Felicity's character. In all the time I had known her, it had never occurred to me that she was utterly absorbed by the *romance* of each and every situation. There was no grand, all-consuming passion there at all. She had not hated my grandmother. She was not involved in any vendetta against me. She merely gave the appearance of it at certain times because the temptation to stir up other people's passions — *genuine* passions, unlike hers — was too great to resist.

I saw then that the whole world existed for Felicity for no other purpose than to provide her with an unending string of emotional wonders. There was no cruelty in it, nor even any malice, for she never really believed that the participants in those dramas were real people with real feelings. We were like actors in a theatre. If we pricked ourselves, *she* did not bleed.

Suddenly I realized it was impossible to dislike her for it — any more than one could dislike a baby for sicking up its milk.

"So you've heard nothing of such a visit — looming or actual?" I asked. "D'you think you'd be likely to? Or do they keep themselves very much to themselves over there at Nancekuke House?"

"I shall make it my business to find out *everything* now," she promised.

"Please don't," I responded in some alarm. "Please do nothing you wouldn't ordinarily do. If word of it reached them — that you were inquiring after Lady W, for instance — they'd know at once you were going to tell me."

"But how will you find out without help from *some* quarter? They do keep themselves very much to themselves, as it happens."

I thought that Sr Enuda might cooperate, if I could build on the little foundation of goodwill Marian had bequeathed me. That was my best bet. However, I mumbled something about Cousin Stella, instead, which appeared to satisfy Felicity.

I felt in my bones, though, that she was going to ignore my pleas and conduct inquiries of her own. She was desperate to be a spectator to my drama — to any drama, actually, but especially mine, since she had been at the ringside from the start.

As I left her that afternoon she said, "If you need somewhere nice and *safe,* my dear, somewhere to hide, you can always come here. I hope that goes without saying."

This suggestion shook me. She was quite right, of course, but it was something I hadn't wanted to think about too deeply — not even when I said I'd do absolutely anything to get Teresa back from the Wilkinsons.

Jim must have been looking out for me. As I hastened down Green Lane toward the corner with Rose Row, he came out to meet me.

"You'll never guess!" he said with every sign of delight.

"What?"

"I'll let Aunt Eph tell you."

Nothing in the house had changed, of course. The same gloom darkened the hall and passage. The same dusty silence settled over the parlour and all its bric-a-brac. But Aunt Eph and Uncle Jim were genuinely happy to see me — and she was just bubbling over with the good news her nephew had promised me. He, of course, had told them all about Lady W's forthcoming visit to Nancekuke and all the uncertainties surrounding it.

It turned out that Eph was a friend since childhood of a certain Hannah Pawley, whose very much older sister, Maria, had married Henry Wilkinson. She was that Maria whom the snobbish family had considered too low-class for them to acknowledge. He was the Henry who, cut off without a penny in the traditional manner, had become landlord of The Stag public house, in whose cellars he and Maria had been overcome by fumes. Their deaths had left eighteen-year-old Esther Wilkinson to make her own way in the world — with what tragic results I knew only too well.

What an inbred lot we are down here in Cornwall! And even where we aren't inbred, we've all inherited each other's lives and stories. I'm sure I could cross any threshold west of Truro, quite at haphazard, and, inside ten minutes of 'tay and a bit chat,' I'd have established *some* thread, no matter how fine, linking me and that household. Here was a case in point: My great-great-uncle's wife had a younger sister who was and is a lifelong friend of the lady of this house, who is my husband's aunt and foster mother!

Aunt Eph asked how I felt about the Wilkinsons and their behaviour over Teresa.

"I intend getting her back no matter what, Aunt Eph," I replied. "She'll come and live with us in Penzance — and Gerald and Arthur, too. The trouble is, I only know that Lady Wilkinson is coming back from India for a visit. When — I don't know. Nor for how long. Nor even whether she'll bring Teresa with her — which is the most important thing of all, of course."

" 'Course 'tis, my lover," she replied. "Tell 'ee what — that Hannah Pawley I mentioned just now, she's married to Bert Rapson who do work up at Nancekuke home farm. He's foreman there. And his sister Mary, she's been upstairs maid to the Wilkinsons there most of her life — and there's no love lost between her and them, I can tell 'ee! So I can very likely drop 'ee a postcard, this time tomorrow, with everything you do want to know."

She cut short my thanks and said family was family, when all's said and done.

I t was a disaster, that Monday — the first day in the life of The Shilling Picture Studio. In fact, it was so awful we decided to call it a trial run and make the Tuesday as our *real* inaugural day. It wasn't our fault. The rain simply bucketed down all morning and, though it cleared up after lunch, it was too late to bring forth the trippers. Poor Jim had to stay out there, cycling in heavy oilskins or standing under his umbrella, watching the raindrops burst in sloppy silver stars on the sodden beaches. He popped into the hôtels and got a little trade that way, otherwise we should have had only three takers all day.

However, it was not entirely wasted — nothing ever is. When I took our customers' prints down to the station in time for the six-forty up train that evening, one of the departing trippers, who had listened to my explanation that morning but had not asked Jim to take his photograph, saw two other parties looking at their prints – with shrieks of delighted laughter, I may add – asked to have a look for himself, and then told me, "I'd have gone for a set of my own if I'd known they came out like *that!*"

There was another man there who gave us a useful bit of advice, too. In fact, come this time next year and I'm sure we'll be able to say that he saved our bacon.

He was a salesman in a number of lines of what he called 'fancy hardware' – a cockney. Susan would have wept to hear him, I'm sure. He'd watched me explaining our service to trippers that morning and, by chance, he was leaving on that same evening train. When I'd collected our miserable three shillings he came up to me and said, "I've been watching you, love. You're not bad at your job but I could tell you things about selling that'd put your trade up ten times – even on a day like this. Fancy a drink? I can as easy catch the eight-ten as this one."

I said if it was business, would he mind if my husband joined us – I could send one of the porters up the road to fetch him.

He just laughed and said, "Listen – I'm married, too. It's not a crime, you know."

I don't know what he meant by that but the words somehow made it easier for me to accept. And not send for Jim. Anyway, I later discovered he wasn't married at all, he just claimed to be whenever it suited him.

We went into the private bar of the Railway Arms – the private bar because it was one of those strict establishments where they kicked you out if you tried to talk business in the public or saloon bars. I insisted on buying the drinks though. He took a pint of Rosewarne's Export.

His name was Cass Potter, he said. I asked him what Cass was short for and he laughed and said Cass was always short for a monkey. He'd had a cast-iron tip on Common, which had won the Derby a couple of weeks ago at eleven-to-ten, but he could have got a bet on at four to one – ah me! I realized that Mr Potter wasn't going to tell me anything he didn't want to. But I'm sure that what he did tell me was worth a lot more than a monkey – however much that may be.

"I've been selling all my life," he said. "A bit of this, a bit of that. At the moment, like I say, it's fancy hardware. You're selling photeys ..."

"Pictures," I corrected him.

He frowned.

"Photographic portraits for a *shilling?*" I went on. "Who'd believe that! You remember that hoaxer — what was his name? Theodore Hook? Stood in Oxford Street all afternoon offering genuine pound notes for half-a-crown — sold no more than five. People wouldn't believe us, either, if we said anything about photographs for a shilling. So we don't sell photographs. We sell shilling pictures, instead."

He chuckled happily. "Who thought all that out, eh?"

I scratched lightly behind my ear and said, "Modesty forbids."

"Cheers!" He took a well-rehearsed swig of his ale and gasped with satisfaction. "Well thought! You'll understand what I'm going to tell you, then. The secret of all selling — you know what it is?"

I took a sip of my own drink, a half-pint of ordinary mild-and-bitter, and shook my head.

"The secret of all selling is: Don't sell it — give it away!" He opened his suitcase and drew out one of his lines — a carving knife that looked as if it had been made for a Scottish baronial hall, except that the 'stagshorn' handle was of moulded Celluloid. Aunt Eph would have loved it. No, that's cruel.

Anyway, he said, "This is my best line. There's a fork to match." He plonked that on the bar counter, too. "First time I call, I *give* that to the shopkeeper — the set. 'I don't want to sell you any of these,' says I, 'until you've satisfied yourself about their quality. And I don't want you selling nothink of mine, without you believe in it yourself. So what I'm gonna do is this — I'm gonna *give* you that set! It's yours to keep — free, gratis, and for nothink — whether you order any more from me or not. But when I come back here in two weeks' time, I'm confident I'll have a satisfied customer in you — and that you're going to have many more satisfied customers, thanks to the order what you're gonna place with me! Could I say fairer than that?' And that's how I leave it. I've never been disappointed of a good order when I go back — never!"

I didn't quite believe *that* but I could see his general point was good.

"*Give* them something for free," he said, "even if it's only a bit of paper — that bit of paper you was dishing out this morning. You got it on you now?"

I fished one out of my bag and handed it to him. He read it slowly, with a critical frown. "Not bad," he conceded at last. "You again?"

I just patted my hair this time.

"But here's where you could improve it, see." He pointed to the line where it said that the pictures were a shilling each. "Now if you was to say instead something like, 'The usual price for these pictures is fifteen pence but if you present this leaflet to our snap-shot man when you ask him to take your photey — sorry, picture! — he'll mark you down for a special concessionary price of one shilling only.' See what I mean? Immediately this bit of paper is worth threepence! And yet you've given it away. In fact ...' He pulled out a stub of indelible pencil, licked it, and drew a little star up in one corner of my leaflet, across which he wrote: 'Worth 3d!' He surveyed it with pride. "There! nobody ain't gonna throw that away now, are they!"

The idea intrigued me but I could see one snag. "We can't manage two different prices — one for people *with* this leaflet and one ..."

He waved me to silence, a look of pity in his eyes. "'Course you don't!" he said scornfully. "You charge everybody a bob. That bit of paper is just the come-all-yous, as the Irishman says."

"People might complain," I objected. "If they took the trouble to save their leaflet carefully and then they see someone without one getting the same concession."

"You just wink at them and say, 'Me mum always said I was too soft for my own good. I need someone like you, sir — or madam — it'll probably be a madam, too, come to think of it! — to harden my heart.' Get a bit of patter, you can't go wrong. You never done no selling before, eh?"

I shook my head.

"Well, you'll soon pick it up." He laughed richly. "A few more three-shilling days like this one and you'll *soon* pick it up!"

After another gulp or two, however, he became thoughtful again. "'Course," he said, "there is a completely different way you could go about it."

"What's that?" I was glad I was only sipping my half-pint. Mr Potter seemed to have a lot of mileage in his fertile mind.

"I don't know your business at all," he said diffidently — and with genuine diffidence, too. "I've seen these 'Kodak' box things, though. 'S'matter of fact I was thinking of adding them as a line. I don't know what the film costs you, being in the trade, nor the printing paper — bromide, is that right?"

I nodded.

"But I would have thought your biggest expense ain't the paper and film, it's putting that camera chappie down there on the beach."

"My husband," I said.

"That don't mean he works for nothing, does it! In fact, I'm right — that *is* your biggest expense. Who else is working? You must have someone else in the darkroom, developing and printing, right?"

Again I nodded. "My husband's partner. Then there's his wife and me drying the prints and putting them in envelopes and writing the customers' names ..."

"Gawd's truth! So you've had four of you working all day — or, rather, *not* working all day but ready, willing, and able to work, right? And all for what? Ninepence each! You'd do better up the zoo helping blind monkeys to peel bananas!"

"You've got monkeys on the brain tonight, Mister Potter," I said.

He laughed and went on, "No, but you see my point, love. You *could* all have been working fit to bust."

"How?"

"Doing what you're all equipped to do — or what you're sitting there and twiddling your thumbs, *waiting* to do. Why not just get on and do it — flat out? Your hubby could just snap *everybody!* Don't wait to be asked. Just walk along the beaches — snap! snap! snap! — right, left, and centre. Have an assistant walking along behind handing out the leaflets. Nice job for you. Keep an eye on Number One — see his eyes and hands don't stray!"

I chuckled at that. "And I'd have to take all their names, too?"

"No! Forget all that. Just take the shots. After every hundred — or fifty, or whatever you think — bung the camera back to your partner in the darkroom and start on the next hundred."

I laughed at the idiocy of this scheme — yet knowing very well that Potter was no idiot at all. I laughed at the contradiction. "What are we supposed to do with all these prints?" I asked.

"Exhibit them. Build a little kiosk down in front of the station — just across the road here. Octagonal, see. One window and seven panels, each about three foot by two. Make your prints three inches by two and you'll get a hundred and forty-four on each panel — enough, I should guess, to show a whole week's snaps. Some people stay two or three days, you know. Some a whole week. But they all come and go by train. Or almost all. So that's where you catch 'em. 'If you can see your picture here, it's yours for a bob!' Put that up over the kiosk and your fortune's made. People will see 'em coming and they'll see 'em going, too. The moment they arrive at the station they'll think, 'Oh, I must get one of them!' You won't need no leaflet. Remember that geezer what said 'e'd 'ave got hisself tooken if only he'd seen what they looked like? And you don't need to sell 'em all. Nor even 'alf of 'em. If you only move one in three ... what's that? Forty-eight bob a day — which is a bit more than three bob, eh! And what's your season? A hundred days? That's two hundred and forty quid, my darlin'! And there's two hundred and fifty-six days left to count it in." He sniffed and glanced furtively all around us. "You 'aven't got room for one more, 'ave you? I always fancied being rich, myself."

He bought the next round, honours even, so I arrived home feeling rather mellow, though we now had only two-and-ninepence to keep the wolf from the door. It just about paid for supper for the four of us. Jim was a bit cool toward me because, of course, Penzance being Penzance, some kind friend had dropped by and told him I was seen drinking at the Railway Arms with a travelling salesman who was more often seen in the company of ladies of easy virtue. Fortunately, I was able to show him the leaflet on which Cass Potter had drawn the star and the legend, 'Worth 3d!' and I laboured all the points the man had made before he licked his little indelible pencil.

Jim bucked up at that and said it was an excellent idea. Funnily enough, I was the one who got a bit 'shirty' then — as Susan would put it — because why should I have to explain myself for dropping into the Railway Arms for a quiet drink with anyone I like? Especially on business. There are hundreds of people Jim could take in there for a drink and no one would come running to me to split on him. All right, there aren't all that many women he could see on business — except one sort, and then, I suppose, some kind woman friend would come and tell me. But, putting that aside, is it my fault that so few women are in straightforward, regular business? I thought he was very unreasonable to take the attitude he took in the first place.

So I said nothing about Cass Potter's much more exciting suggestion — partly because I wanted to think about it a bit further and work a few more figures out on paper so as to be ready for every objection, and partly because I could feel that he and Mark were so dedicated to their own ideas for the moment that we'd have to lose quite a bit of money before they'd be ready to consider anything so simple and so revolutionary as taking everybody's picture and throwing away two in every three.

When I woke up the following morning I realized it was the first night since my family broke up that I hadn't gone to sleep dreaming up one scheme or another to get us all together again.

T uesday was little better than Monday. Nine shillings was all we made, and this time there were three people who said they'd have ordered their pictures if only they'd known how nice they turned out. I suppose everybody who starts a new business goes through a phase like that. You *know* you've got a brilliant idea that nobody has ever thought of before. So you draw up plans, rent the premises, buy equipment ... all that sort of thing — quite convinced you're going to make your fortune. Then the big day dawns and you feel the mayor himself should come down and cut a ribbon or unveil something to mark this most important day in the life of your town ... but you open for business, anyway. And then *nothing* happens. And when the sun sets on the day, you're rather glad that no one seems to know you're alive because you just want to find an accommodating rabbit hole, like Alice's, and fall into it and find a bottle of something that will make you ten feet tall without effort.

I don't know which was worse — standing at the window that Tuesday evening, looking out over the gray slate roofs of Penzance, glistening with rain that had no right to be so heavy in June, *hating* that whole indifferent world out there ... or getting up at six the following morning so as to have breakfast out of the way and everything done in time to go down to meet the nine-thirteen from Truro and thrust a leaflet into the hands of the one astonished tripper who'd be on it if you were lucky. And he'd probably be blind — the one tourist who hadn't been able to look at the sky before he set out.

But Wednesday dawned — at ten past four! — and that was when my day began. Specifically, it began with the crowing of the cockerel belonging to the Roseveares, our next-door neighbours but one. It woke me, as always, but I did not go back to sleep at once, though I usually managed it. That morning I just lay there, knowing that something was wrong. After a while I realized what it was. I hadn't drawn the curtain fully last night. There was a good six-inch gap — and it was a pale, unblemished azure from the sill right up to the ovis! Not a cloud to be seen. I was so excited I almost woke Jim to show him the miracle, but he looked so *gorgeous,* lying there fast asleep that I hadn't the heart.

I say he looked gorgeous. He had a dark stubble on him as thick as arrishes after a corn harvest. His hair was all tousled and matted over his forehead. The way he was lying pursed his lips up as if he was imitating a budgerigar. And saliva was weeping gently from one corner. But I still thought he was the most wonderfully gorgeous heap of manhood a girl could imagine. If he'd been drugged asleep, I'd have cradled him in my arms and showered him with kisses. Instead, I just lay beside him, carefully not moving but imagining I was doing all that.

After about ten minutes, though, with the blue in the sky growing stronger and stronger, I realized there was no possibility of getting back to sleep. Ten minutes of gloating over the fact that this unkempt treasure of a sleeping man was all mine was a permissible self-indulgence. Fifteen minutes would have bordered on the sinful. Twenty minutes would have been outright moral turpitude. I slipped from between our sheets just in time to save my soul.

My share of the housework was done by five. Then I made a cup of tea and a slice of toast and marmalade and went out into the back garden, scanning the sky anxiously for any sign of a change. If the malevolent gods who had guided our destiny over the past two days had any say in it, there'd be high cirrus by five-thirty, white cumulus by six, darkening by seven, and all floodgates open by eight. But the high vault of the heavens remained one great dome of blue from horizon to horizon. The air was so still that the plumes from the engines firing up in the shunting yard below rose in eerie vertical lines like flossy puppet strings. The sea was stippled with a mass of confused wavelets but there was no underlying swell to give it any real movement. Farther off, toward the Mount, it was so calm that the dark, conical mass of the abbey brooded over its own mirror-image in the bay, which had now turned to a wide sea of gold in the rising sun.

A ridiculous wave of optimism spread over me. Today was definitely going to be different. Today would efface the disasters of Monday and Tuesday. I knew I ought to stay at home and write a new draft of our leaflet, incorporating all the points Cass Potter had made — before, that is, he got the absolute brainwave about snap-shooting all and sundry and never mind if two-thirds of them don't buy. I was still saving that for a time when we could all be slightly more optimistic about the business. But I was far too exhilarated to settle down to anything so good and useful. I wanted to skip through the town, ringing the crier's bell and shouting, "Today's the day, everyone! Rise and shine!"

Well, at least I could go for a walk. Down to the station, I thought, along the wharf, up round the gasworks, down to the Trinity House

dock, past the Battery, along the prom, up Morrab Road, along Alverton
Street to the Green Market, back down Market Jew — and home
James! I'd probably tire myself out by then and want to go back to bed. I
have lots of energy in the mornings but little stamina. Come the evening
and *all* I have left is stamina. One day the two will coincide!

I left a note for the others on the kitchen table and went out by the
back door, which, unlike the front door, had no bell on a spring to
announce our customers. As I passed the empty Devoran next door I
murmured, "Won't be long now!" That's how optimistic I was!

I was surprised at how many others were up and about at a quarter-
to-six of a morning. The milkman from the Wherrytown Dairy was
doing his round. The boy from Pascoe's Bakery was delivering fresh
loaves to the boarding houses along Chyandour. There was even a
crossing sweeper out, gathering up the horsedroppings before the
householders all about us could steal it for their gardens. And Victor
Jacks, one of our postmen, was out making his first delivery of the day.

"Got a letter from your sister up Lunnon for 'ee, missus," he called
out cheerily as I went down North Road. He handed it to me after
looking at the postmark. "Posted onto the train at Paddington at four-
thirty yesterday afternoon, and now there 'tis, in your hand, afore six
this morning — and all for a penny! My old grandad 'ud never have
believed it, and 'e worked in the Royal Mail all 'is life. In they days, the
mails stopped at Marazion and they only brung them on to Penzance
once a week. You want they others, do 'ee?"

'They others' were all bills and business post, so I just took Marian's
letter and asked him to deliver the rest as usual. I wondered what could
be so important that she went down to Paddington to post it onto the
train itself, but I waited until I could sit on the little stone bench by the
harbour — where I had once tried to picture the scene as Esther
Wilkinson had seen it. Now, the only imaginary picture that interested
me was one of our kiosk standing there, plastered all over with Shilling
Pictures and just raking in the money.

Marian's letter read:

Darling Crissy,
It must be in the air. Or you've got what Mary Beckerleg used to
call a 'gardening angel'! Just pin back your ears and listen —
because it all starts a year or two ago. One of the girls Miss Martin
helped once, a few years ago, got a job up here in Hampstead,

through Mrs Morrell, of course, working at Pearce's, a haberdashery in the High Street. Her name was Diana Roche. The son of the proprietor, Colin Pearce, fell for her, and they got married last year. She's the one Miss Martin went to call on the day before you went back to Penzance. She was about to have a baby, remember? The Pearces were very snooty about the marriage at first because, although Diana is the daughter of those Roches who own the big haberdashery in Boscawen Street, Truro, she had been a bit of a naughty girl, which is why she was sent to Little Sinns. And the haberdashery connection is why she was taken on at Pearce's. But anyway, all that was over and done with soon after the wedding, and by the time she swelled up with what they hoped was a son and heir, she could do no wrong.

Unfortunately, just a few weeks ago, Diana died giving birth, though the baby lived — name of Anthony. Miss Martin asked her aunt to represent her at the funeral but she had a bad cold and sent me, instead. It's funny how little things lead to big ones. All that happened was that the baby cried. And it all followed from that.

Mrs Pearce, Colin Pearce's mother, bent over the cradle — I should say this was at the funeral tea, after the interment — anyway, she bent over the cradle and was overcome with grief at seeing the poor little motherless mite. So, as I was standing the other side, I picked him up instead — and it was love at first sight between the two of us! To prove it he punched me in the nose and laughed. Of course, he wasn't even a week old, so it wasn't a real punch, nor real laughter, either. But he did stop crying and he gave that lovely sort of shivery sigh very young babies give after they've cried a lot, and, well, *I* fell in love with *him,* anyway.

And that was that, I thought. Except that when I got home that night I found I had milk! I couldn't believe it, and I'm sure you won't, but it's true. And I still had milk the following morning, so Mrs Morrell said it was an omen (she believes in things like that) and she wrote a note to Mrs Pearce, and it happened they were going all round the houses looking for a wet-nurse who was clean, sober, and reliable. There's lots with one or two of those qualifications but not many with all three. So Mrs Morrell lent me to the Pearces while they went on hunting for a proper wet nurse at more leisure.

I should of told you all this at your wedding but, as you'll learn, things were at a very delicate stage with me then and I was scared that if I breathed so much as a whisper, it would all come to nothing and I'd be a laughing stock. That's where we're different, you and me. You tell the whole world, years in advance, what you're going to make happen, and that's how you force yourself into doing it, no matter what. I could never do that because I don't have your strength and I know I'd fail. So anyway that's why I kept mum, even when you made that remark about the size of my bosom! What would you of said if I'd told you I was nursing a baby 'up Lunnon'! And the wiles I had to employ to get round the back door at Bowen's in Market Jew Street to borrow a breast-pump to relieve the pressure! Still, that's another story.

Where was I? Oh, yes — I tell you, it's a funny thing to have a baby at your breast that never grew in your own tummy! I feel like the virgin queen, and the Pearces treat me like a queen, too — not a servant at all but a real member of the family. To start with I only went round there every four hours to feed him, including nights. They're only a couple of hundred yards away and I can take a short cut up Shepherd's Passage. I didn't do any other nursing — bathing him and changing him and that — because they're quite rich tradesmen, with scats of servants. They've got several branches in North London. Then they gave me a room to sleep in so I didn't have to walk at dead of night, because everyone in London still remembers Jack the Ripper, even though his murders were all miles away from here.

And then — now this is a bit scandalous, so take a deep breath — poor Colin Pearce, who's still in deep mourning, of course, started to fall in love with me! And me? Well, I've fallen for him, too! Of course, we can't do anything about it. He hasn't even talked to his sister, Maureen, and they're as close as two lips. I think she suspects. And I even think she approves — especially of the fact that we're doing nothing to cause the slightest whiff of scandal. And believe me, I love Colin so much, I'm not going to do anything to upset that applecart. The only time we even touch is when I hand him back little Anthony. But, on the other hand, when I feed the dear thing at dead of night, when all the house is fast asleep, Colin comes in and watches me. He sees my exposed bosoms and gazes on me very fondly, and I feel no shame in it at all. I think of the innocence of Adam and Eve before the time of the serpent. It's something quite lovely and I hope you're not laughing to read it.

In fact, I had tears in my eyes, I thought it was so beautiful — but she probably wouldn't have (or 'wouldn't *of,*' as she puts it) believed it if I told her. Anyway, her letter continued:

But the upshot is, I mean the reason I'm going to take this letter down to the mail train at Paddington so you'll get it tomorrow morning, is that the Roches have made Colin an offer. They were there at the funeral, of course — out of their minds with grief because Diana was their only child — and if it hadn't been for Anthony I think they'd have lost the will to live. But he is now the world's darling, being their only heir. So what they've proposed to Colin is that he should come down to Truro — bringing Anthony with him, to be sure — and become the manager of their store. Old Daniel Roche's health isn't too good and he was thinking of retiring anyway. His daughter's death was almost the death of him, too. They were going to sell up but now the idea is that Colin will inherit in trust on the father's death and absolutely on the mother's.

Well, you can see where this is leading and why I say you must have a 'gardening' angel. Let me tell you about Colin before I tell you what is planned. This is strictly between us so don't breathe a word to anyone apart from Jim. You know what Cornwall is like and how easily word might get to the Roches, by routes you'd never believe possible. Colin is not the most handsome man in the world, except to me. I don't mean he's ugly but when you paint his portrait I'll have a word in your ear first about one or two little improvements you could make! He's twenty-eight years old, an inch or two taller than me — so, five-foot-nine, say, with his shoes on — he carries a little importance in front of him but he's not what you'd call fat. He's not fat about the face, at all. He has brown hair, receding rather badly, but he has sent for a cure for it from a doctor in New Orleans in America 'about whom all the advertisements speak very highly,' as he says in his dry, witty way. He doesn't set great store by it and I don't care one way or the other. Bald or fuzzy-wuzzy, he's the only man for me.

His eyes are the nicest thing about him, big, brown, and gentle. When he looks at me I feel a soft warmth all around me. His nose, I have to admit, is his worst feature. It is too long, too thin, and it veers off toward the left at the end. However, he has a fine, crisp tenor voice and he says if his nose were broader he would lose that timbre.

His mouth is, well, a mouth — not chiselled, not rugged, not Cupid-bowed, not thin, not thick — just a mouth. If it's perfect in anything, it's in being perfectly nondescript. His chin, at least, is firm and manly — and clean-shaven beyond the mutton-chop side-whiskers, which fluff out at the angle of his jaw. He dresses well, in good-quality suits — which he has to for his business but would in any case, I think — and is fastidiously clean in his person.

So that is Colin Pearce. Now to his plans. He told me of the Roches' suggestion two nights ago. "You must already know, Miss Moore," he said, "that I hold you in the very highest regard. The fact that I say no more for the moment is only in part because of convention. I loved my dear Diana and my grief is such that I feel I shall never surmount it — though observation of others who have trod this desperate path before me, assures me I shall, in the fullness of time. Indeed, a few weeks ago, in the days immediately after Diana's death, I was so deep in my despair that I would fain have ended it all. Had you not come along, I think I should have done. You have turned despair back into grief. And while that grief is on me, you will understand I can say no more. And nor, I think, would you trust me if I did.

"But when that grief has run its course — which may happen within the year that convention has set aside for it to do so — I hope I may name those sentiments of tenderness which now I dare not, sentiments you, and you alone have awakened in my sorrowing heart ..." And so on. When I say he spoke to me thus, I mean some of his sentiments were spoken, some were written down — enshrined, I would say — in a note he left with me that night. I've run them together here but I expect you can tell one from the other. Anyway, spoken or written, the sentiments are his.

And the long and the short of it is that I am engaged as Anthony's nurse and will shortly, in the first week in July, be accompanying my new 'master' to his new abode in Truro! And the unspoken promise between us is that, when the period set aside for mourning is over, he will cease to be my master and become instead my lord and master. Whether I, in the meantime, become his mistress or not ...

But no! I'm sure I have already shocked you quite enough, darling Crissy. The unspoken promise between us? I hear you ask. Between me, the original giddy miss, and a man still beside himself with grief — an unspoken promise? Have I taken leave of my senses? Yes, very probably. All I know is that, of the many foolish and scatterbrained things I've done in my life (and your list of them would be far longer than mine), nothing ever felt more sensible and promising than this. My life seems full of points where I have to decide — this way or that? And I'm given only moments to make my mind up. In those circumstances all I can do is trust my instinct. And my instincts about Colin make me say Yes with all my heart.

But take heart yourself, little one! All is not lost. I truly am only his son's nurse as yet and have no intention of becoming his mistress, at least until that unspoken promise is down on paper. (I do not say I have no <u>desire</u> in that direction, but that is where desire and intention part company — and intention shall prevail!) So you will have all the opportunities you could wish for to scrutinize my darling man and approve or disapprove as you will. And if you disapprove, I shall listen most carefully. I may not <u>heed</u> you, but I shall listen.

And now I want to hear all about your honeymoon, and I do mean <u>all</u>! Spare me no blushes, please. And what news of Teresa and the Wilkinsons? While trying to sleep on the train going back (and let me tell you, though you may think me ungrateful, sleeping on a railway train is an overrated pleasure, even First Class), I had the wildest dream in which our dear little sister was in the next carriage with the General and his Lady, and it was locked off from ours, and we had to risk life and limb, you and I, to rescue her! It was vivid enough for me to wake in a sweat. I hope, in reality, they will return her to us in a more tranquil and orderly fashion.

Say nothing of this to Tom yet. I'll let him know my directions, and go to visit him, when we move to Truro. Perhaps our house is large and will need a good gardener!

There were the usual endearments at the end but my eyes simply skipped over those and leaped back to where she spoke of 'our dear little sister.' The whole tone in which she wrote about us, her siblings, was so unusual — for her — that I would have forgiven her a dozen acts of genuine folly. (And I did not think her acceptance of Colin Pearce's offer in the least bit foolish. Poor people like us have to take risks that comfortable, bourgeois onlookers would naturally consider rash.) But 'our dear little sister' — and then thinking like that about Tom! Dear, sweet Marian!

The second post, at eight-thirty, brought a card from Aunt Eph, but Victor Jacks, the postman, spared me the effort of reading it. "That Lady Wilkinson's bringing your li'l sister home to Nancekuke in three weeks," he said cheerily as he mounted our front steps. I was polishing the brass plate that announced the high-class end of our business, where the only shilling in sight was the one that turns a pound into a guinea. He lowered his voice to add confidentially, "And that Mrs Collis next door — her sister's just 'ad 'er fourth. A boy. They belong to 'ave girls so she'm 'appy 'nuff."

I read the card nonetheless. It said, 'Her ladyship is visiting near Illogan for a month from 24th inst. Bringing the young lady with her. Hope this is of interest. Call again soon. We don't get many visitors.'

The village of Illogan was actually nearer Nancekuke House than Nancekuke village itself. I looked at Jacks in weary despair — of ever keeping a secret in Cornwall, I mean. "How d'you get from *this,* to Nancekuke House, Lady Wilkinson, and my sister?" I asked. "Not one of them is actually mentioned."

He chuckled. "I was born and reared over to Illogan," he replied. "So that's how the name caught my eye, see? Then ' 'er ladyship' — well, they aren't ten-a-penny, not there. Round Carclew and Perranarworthal, yes, but not round Illogan ..."

"All right! I grant you that. But Teresa, my little sister — how d'you know about her? I only ask because I'm curious."

"Ah, well, that's a bit o' luck, see. My missus do 'ave that li'l sub-post-office in Trewithen Road. We got Royal Mail red in our blood, my family. So I do 'ave a handy arrangement, see, where I belong to deliver north Penzance mornings and west Penzance afternoons." He winked. "Including Morrab Road."

I could not imagine St Breaca's receiving any important mail in the form of an open postcard, so I assumed some of the letters Victor Jacks delivered suffered from being stood too near the spout of the kettle. I said nothing, however. The most important thing is to know how the world actually works, because only then do you stand some small chance of persuading it to work in your favour.

I smiled my broadest smile and said I was very grateful to him for bringing me this excellent news.

"Why, 'tis only my job, missus," he replied.

"Ah no!" I protested. "I've known many a postman who 'only does his job' — and a right surly bunch they are, too. But people like you, with pillar-box red for blood, *can do so much more!*"

He knew what I was saying, well enough, but to point him in the right direction, I added, "I expect her ladyship will be coming over to Penzance to meet with the nuns. They must be getting very worried about the way they broke the law last year — the way they adopted my little sister, you know."

"'Ow's that?" he asked, open-mouthed.

"Oh, it would take far too long to explain. We're fighting them, my old man and me. Teresa's proper place is here with us." The clock struck the quarter-to. "Good heavens!" I exclaimed. "I must fly. I'll tell you the whole grisly story one day — if I win Teresa back." After a pace or two I turned and added, "I've got Post Office red in my blood, too, you know. My late father's sister is Ellen Ivory."

He laughed and winked. "Say no more, maid!" he called after me.

I hoped I had poured Teresa's name into his ear often enough for it to catch his eye, as well. Short of actually offering to pay for the gas that boiled the kettles, I don't know what else I could have said.

That morning the nine-thirteen was packed with trippers. I managed to hand out leaflets to about thirty of them but there must have been a hundred more who didn't even notice me, who had their minds on one thing only — a mile of sun-drenched sand. However, half a dozen of them came back into the station, having seen someone's else leaflet, and asked for their own copy. So we were getting somewhere. This time, too, I'd brought with me a dozen duplicate prints Mark had made from the negatives we had so far exposed, explaining that these were 'some of our satisfied customers.' (In fact, they were *all* of our satisfied customers!) So people could at last see what we were offering. Such an elementary thing to do — and yet none of us had thought to do it! The worst people to explain anything are the ones who know all about it. And the worst of all must be those who actually invented it.

I was hardly home twenty minutes when little Timmy Lester, whom we had engaged to cycle between the beach and Mulberry, turned up with the first dozen negatives to be developed and printed. It showed how dependent we were on the weather. In the first hour of this sunny day we had already done as much business as on the previous two rainy days put together. The only one who wasn't entirely happy with this was me, though I didn't show it. I feared that success would fossilize our system in its present form, and I was sure we could do much better if we followed Cass Potter's suggestion — namely to take promiscuous snap-shots rather than wait for actual orders.

The ten-fourteen from Redruth, the train Felicity had promised to take, arrived at just gone eleven, which was ten minutes after the night-sleeper from London. I met both trains with leaflets, so it was the busiest time of the morning for me. I saw Felicity standing back, greatly amused to see me in this, for her, novel rôle. I handed out four dozen more leaflets between the two trains — almost half of them to the rather snooty people on the night-sleeper, who came for the week, or even fortnight, rather than for the day. Watching their amused response, I realized our leaflet was rather too close in tone to others of the kind that promise a combined cure for baldness and cancer, or a patent chimney-flue that never needs sweeping. Their interest, despite this, made me think we should do a more refined and genteel leaflet for them. Perhaps Susan would care to write it, I thought unkindly.

"You're a marvel, Crissy," Felicity said when I was able to talk to her at last. Fortunately, hers was the last incoming train of the morning so I was free until after lunch, when I had promised to go and help Jim down on the beaches.

It sounds churlish, I know, but her praise only made me wonder what she wanted of me. "This day is the real marvel," I replied. "You should have seen me standing here yesterday — I felt like a bailiff at a wedding breakfast."

Outside, I made for the cab rank. She claimed to be shocked at my extravagance and said that on a fine day like this she would not dream of doing anything other than walk — by which she apparently meant sauntering so slowly that the snails began to whizz by. She linked her arm in mine to ensure I did the same.

"I know a true lady never perspires," she said when we emerged onto Chyandour Cliff. "But I should certainly *glow* if we went any faster than this. Why, it's like being at Cap d'Antibes!" And she waved a lordly hand toward the sunstruck beach and picturesque bay beyond — presumably ignoring the railway shunting yards and warehouses in our immediate foreground.

"Cap d'Antibes is where Walter and I went for *our* honeymoon," she explained. "You know where it is, I suppose? On the Côte d'Azur — heavenly! Completely unspoiled. We actually stayed at a little *auberge* at Juan-les-Pins." She pronounced each French word with a sort of vinegary precision.

"I quite enjoyed *Sainte-Marie,*" I replied, making St Mary's sound like somewhere in France.

She frowned for a moment and then laughed, thrusting me away and dragging me back. "You're right," she said. "I was trying to swank. Actually, it doesn't matter *where* one spends one's honeymoon, does it. I often tell Walter we ought to go back there because I'm sure I wouldn't recognize the place again. We hardly stepped out of doors the whole time. We were a scandal!" She gazed expectantly at me.

I said, "I already told you about our honeymoon, Felicity. We were a scandal, too. Honours even, eh?"

She pouted. "Yes, I know, but such generalities!"

It was so blatant I could only laugh. "It's all I'm going to say. Have you heard anything about Lady W's visit yet?"

"Alas!" she said vaguely. She was annoyed that she had insisted on walking now, since I was clearly not going to give her chapter and verse on our honeymoon capers. "This *ménage-à-quatre,*" she went on. "Do you actually *like* it?"

I was on the point of telling her about Devoran next door when I thought better of it. Why should she know anything more than was strictly necessary for *my* purposes?

"It's working out far better than I dared to hope," I replied — which was, in fact, true. It wasn't so congenial that I'd abandon the idea of moving next door, but all my worst fears had so far proved baseless. Of course, the four of us were still living in a kind of mutual honeymoon with one another, too.

Felicity was charmed by our house, mainly because we had done nothing to it yet apart from move in the absolute essentials — bed, washstand, aspidistra, and so on. Everything was still possible. She bristled with ideas and promised to send us a wonderful new German book she had come across, called *Das*-far-bigger-something-*Buch,* which was all loose colour sheets in a box and absolutely *crammed* with suggestions one could hand to 'one's colorist' before one set him loose on 'one's decorations.'

"But I was forgetting, Crissy," she concluded. "You're so nimble with your brush and palette, you could probably do it all yourself."

Timmy Lester brought more than four dozen more exposed negatives up for printing while Felicity was there, so she gained a satisfactory, if distorted, view of the business we were doing and the earnings we must be enjoying.

Since she had no Wilkinson news for me, and I had no honeymoon confidences for her, she didn't wish to hang on in Penzance until the four-fifty up-train. So we walked down the hill, more briskly than we had come up it, to catch the two-o'clock, instead.

"What news of Tom — and the two young fellows?" she asked as we set off. "We haven't said a word about them."

We hadn't said a word about Marian and Teresa, either, but I didn't point that out. "I'd like Tom to live near by," I replied. "I'm looking out for some suitable position. He enjoys the work and he wants to be in the open air. So I thought one of the market gardens round Gulval might do. He could spend Sundays with us if he liked."

"Bringing all his dirty laundry with him, no doubt!"

I laughed. "What are sisters for? It's a small price to pay for being a family again."

"Yes ..." she responded vaguely. "You say he'd spend Sundays with 'us' — meaning?"

"Gerald, Arthur, and Teresa, of course."

"Ah yes. Of course." Her tone became even more vague and her eyes began an uncomfortable survey of the skyline.

"I don't want the boys back home before Teresa, though. You know how they establish *territories,* so I want the place to be *hers* before it becomes theirs, too. I don't imagine there'll be any difficulty in extracting them from the Sutton when the time comes?"

"Well ..." she replied dubiously. "*Paying* orphans aren't all that numerous. It does help swell their coffers."

I laughed at this absurdity. "You mean I might have to *buy* my own brothers out — as if they had army commissions?"

We both laughed — but I knew jolly well what she was really saying. She was warning me it wasn't going to be plain sailing, not if she could help it. The boys were in the Sutton thanks to *her* manipulations. Her reputation was behind that arrangement.

Then it occurred to me that if warnings were being dished out, I had one for her. I bided my time until she was about to board the train; then, in an apparent afterthought, I said, "By the way, Felicity — do the trustees of the Sutton know that Gerald and Arthur are related to you and Uncle Walter?"

"Related?" she echoed in surprised distaste.

"Well!" I gave a slightly baffled laugh. "You *are* my aunt, you know — and theirs, too."

I truly think it had never occurred to her. I mean, she knew the *facts*, of course, but she had never seen their implications. Our mother had been dead to the whole family, to her brothers and, even more, to their wives. For almost twenty years her very existence had been expunged from the Trevarton mind. Felicity had simply acquired that same attitude along with her wedding ring.

"*Do* the Sutton trustees know?" I repeated.

"Oh ... that," she replied uncomfortably. "I'm really not at all sure, you know."

But I was.

Our successful morning under that sizzling sun had spoiled Jim for the afternoon's lull. When I joined him, soon after lunch, on the Penzance beach at Wherrytown, he was talking about the earlier flood of work being just a flash in the pan. The dismal trade of the previous couple of days was more like what we should expect, he said.

"All these people!" he waved a hand over our vista of the beach. "Why *don't* they want a picture of themselves — especially when it's only a bob?" He gripped the 'Kodak' angrily and shook it at them. "I'm offering you immortality for a bob, you idiots!" he said in a strangulated shout. Then, to me, he added, "If only one could snap a shot and immediately pull a finished print out of the side of this box! Something I could push under their noses and say, 'Look! *Now* d'you see!' Then I'm sure they'd *all* buy prints. Most of them, anyway. It's the hour or so's wait between the click and the 'ooh-look!' that's killing us."

Well, I reckoned I was never going to get a better chance than that! I touched him on the arm. He turned and found me staring at him in admiration. "You're a genius," I said. "You've hit upon the answer, of course. That's *it!*"

"What's it?" He looked down at the camera. "There's no way of modifying this to churn out washed-and-fixed prints!"

"No, no — I'm talking about the *other* thing you said. That's the bit of pure genius."

"What other thing?"

"About taking the prints first and *then* offering them for sale! D'you mean to say that it's so obvious to you, you don't even see how brilliant it is?"

"Well ..." he answered vaguely as he turned again to stare at the beach. It wasn't the sands at Blackpool but it was a crowd of several hundred. I could see the idea was beginning to take with him.

I think there's some part in all of us that can grasp ideas before they get turned into words. Bang! Just like that — all at once and not plodding from this step to the next. I think that part of Jim had already grasped the idea and now it was seeping up into his everyday thoughts, bit by digestible bit.

So I said nothing.

"You mean ...?" he murmured, biting his lip, running his eye along the half-mile of sands, from the Battery toward Newlyn Rocks.

"Let's try," I suggested, as if he had already put it into words — or as if words were no longer necessary by now.

"Here?" he asked. "But the business has gone dead here. I was just about to go back to Marazion Beach."

"But that's perfect, darling! If business is dead here — in the way we've been doing it up to now — and we try this brilliant *new* way of yours and find it's not dead after all, then we'll know just how brilliant it is. Come to think of it, bringing the dead back to life is one of the standard miracles, you know."

He frowned. "Hang on — let's just get this straight. You're suggesting that we ..."

"No! I'm not suggesting anything. I'm just putting your suggestion into a lot of plodding old words so that simple minds like mine can understand it. What we do is we go up to the Battery steps, down onto the sands — or rocks it is there — and you walk along the beach snap-shotting people ... snap-*shooting* people? Taking snaps of everyone in sight, anyway. How many left on that film?"

He consulted his notebook. "There are about fifty on this camera — half gone."

"Take the lot! Then switch to the other camera. How many snaps have you left on that?"

"About sixty when young Lester brings it back. But see here, Crissy, we can't just ..."

"And I'll follow behind, giving out leaflets to anyone who catches my eye. And I'll explain what you're doing to those who ask. I'll tell them there's absolutely no obligation to buy but their prints will be down at the station for every train from the four-fifty onwards."

His eyes were already sparkling at the prospect. "I don't think it's really *my* idea," he said diffidently.

"It's *our* idea, then — if you prefer," I answered in a dismissive tone, as if it hardly mattered. "But I shall always think of it as yours."

"Bit of a cheek, though," he went on. "Just going up and snapping people out of the blue, eh?"

I laughed. "That's the sort of thing Mark would say. *One* partner with gentlemanly feelings is quite enough, I'm sure."

"Ah!" He pulled a face. "Talking of Mark — he'll think we've gone raving mad down here."

"And he'll stop thinking it when we come back from the station with more money than we hoped to make in a week. I'm *sure* this is the way to do it, Jim!" I jumped up and down on the spot in my excitement.

For the next half-hour we walked the full length of the beach, snapping more than a hundred shots of trippers — parties and soloists. Some people grumbled, but fewer than I had feared. One barrack-room lawyer tried to tell me we'd taken his property. His appearance was his property, he claimed. I told him appearances can deceive, and then got well away before he realized the remark was meaningless. On the other hand, several people came after us and asked Jim to come back for a posed picture. One family started a fashion for taking off their boots and rolling up their trouser legs or plucking up their skirts and standing in the shallow water for a laughing family group.

Some sort of telepathy must have been abroad because, about half-way along the beach, we found parties actually ready for us, tall ones at the back, kiddies in front. Ladies were combing their hair and prinking their collars and cuffs and turning anxious faces to their hubbies, asking if they looked all right.

We snapped so many that we got ahead of poor Timmy Lester. Jim had to go up to the Queen's and 'borrow' their broom closet as an emergency darkroom to change the film. When Timmy came at last he brought a message from Mark that we were to stop at once as he couldn't possibly cope. So all we did was stop sending the boy back with more. We snapped another couple of dozen and then Jim went racing off on his bicycle to go and help with the developing and printing.

On my way back home I picked up a couple of idle fishermen, who couldn't sail for lack of wind, and, with their help, brought a couple of hired trestle tables down to the station yard. I made it all right with the station-master first, of course — a Mr Frederick Lyons. He was a bit shirty to begin with but when I dropped the name Trevarton (big customers of the Great Western Railway!) he listened to reason. And my reasoning was that if our little experiment today was a success, we should erect a permanent (or all-summer) kiosk in the station approach — for which we should expect to pay the proper rent.

Mark and Jim must have toiled like galley-slaves to get all the shots developed and printed — and dried — in time. But at twenty-past four, half an hour before the first departing train, they came down to the station with close-on twelve dozen snapshots. We dealt them out like three packs of playing cards on the trestle tables, which I had covered with green baize cloth. Thank heaven there was still no breeze or we should have been in trouble! Actually, they weren't as random as playing cards, they only looked like it. The two men had had the sense to keep the snaps in order, so that when we laid them out, still in order, people would find that the position of their snaps on the tables corresponded pretty closely to where they'd been sitting on the beach.

Penzance had never seen anything like it. Twelve dozen pictures all spread out like that! Just about every tripper who'd been on the beach that afternoon — it was like a bit of captured history. I thought we ought to make another set of prints and lock them away somewhere, or give them to the library to look after, so that a hundred years from now people could open the box and look at them again — just the way we were looking at them in the station yard. Nothing else could bring that day back so vividly. They'd peer into those faces and say, 'Who were you? Where did you come from? What stories could you tell?' And only then did I realize that all of them would be dead by then, along with Jim and Mark and Susan ... and me. All dead!

"Are you cold?" Jim asked in surprise.

I came back to the here-and-now with a bump. "No, I was just thinking about ... you know — photographs and ... immortality."

"Oh, that again!" Jim laughed.

Mark said there'd be more money in photographs and *immorality*. He and Jim both laughed at that.

And then the hordes descended and there was no time for either tears or laughter. Looking back on it at the end of that day we agreed that our entire business practically got reinvented over those trestle tables that evening. Some people saw their snaps, took them up, and left a shilling in the place of each. Mark started collecting them as soon as they were laid down but I said leave them a while because it showed people what to do without the need for us to explain it again and again. That gave us time to deal with the others.

Some wanted extra prints, to send to their families and friends — which, of course, they couldn't have on the spot. So, on the spur of the moment, Mark got them to write their names and addresses on the back of the single print we had done, and to pay in advance. The bit about paying in advance was a splendid idea, I thought. On the same spur of the same moment I said it was a shilling for the first print but only sixpence for any subsequent one.

The other two glowered at me for that, but a lot of people heard it and then they started ordering extras, too. And people obviously talked about it going into the station because others, who'd already paid for their prints and gone, came back with orders for more. So the glowering at me stopped.

When the four-fifty had gone, we covered the snaps over and left the trestles beside the cabmen's shelter while we went to the Railway Arms for a celebratory drink and a hot pasty. Then Mark went home to tell Susan the good news and start on the extra prints, which would have to be done that night so as to leave the decks clear for another brilliant day on the morrow.

Jim and I stayed on to serve the later trippers, who would be leaving by the six-forty. By the time they had departed we calculated we had sold a hundred and eight snaps and taken orders — and cash! — for about fifty extra prints. Our takings for the day came to seven pounds, sixteen shillings. Deduct three shillings for the hire of the tables and tips for the fishermen, and not quite a pound for all other expenses — film, chemicals, Timmy Lester's shilling, and so on — and we made over six pounds ten clear profit! To make that same profit in one day from an investment in Consols, say, at three and a half percent, you'd have to invest something like *seventy thousand quid,* so it was amazing, really, that our feet were still touching the ground.

What kept us sober, though, was the realization that we could not continue for many days with the sort of inspired muddle and improvisation that had somehow seen us through the day. We had a serious and far-reaching *re*-organization to plan and carry out before too many more fine days had dawned.

Not that we could have *too many* fine days, anyway.

T hat first month after our marriage was even more hectic than the one before it. *Everything* happened at once. Jim's brilliant idea (inspired by a little telepathy from Cass Potter via me) about snapping the shots first and selling them later was so successful that, within a week, our trestle tables went back to the repository and we had a grand wooden kiosk right by the station approach. We abandoned Marazion beach for this season because it would have meant hiring another photographer, another errand boy, and building another, smaller kiosk at Long Rock station — as well as getting a studio assistant for Mark, who could just about handle the prints from Penzance beach on his own. We thought we should learn to walk before we ran — or, in our case, to run before we sprinted flat out. We never topped seven pounds again but we regularly cleared five. I don't suppose there were many small businesses in the town that were making thirty-five pounds clear profit each week.

One evening, between the first and second departures, I amused myself by colouring in some of the unclaimed prints left over from yesterday. I used ordinary water-colours but dissolved in a collodion spirit instead of water. One of the trippers saw it and asked if I could do the same on hers. I was a bit reluctant to start all that because if you make a mess, it's not like proper water-colour where you can sponge it out, let it dry, and start again. With collodion it's right first time or nothing. So I said, with a sort of sympathetic smile (as if I was just an ill-paid servant of the Shilling Picture Co who was really on the customer's side), "I'm afraid they charge double for colouring in the picture. But you can do it yourself, you know. All you need is ..."

"Done!" She cut me off with a flourish as she plonked *four* shillings down on the counter. "I want both snaps coloured in!"

I knew then I should have said half-a-crown — which is what we decided to charge for it when we started offering the colouring service to one and all. And it worked in very well, because I had nothing to do in the slack periods between the three evening up-trains, so I'd lay all the snaps for colouring out on the kiosk counter, and I'd mix up a bit of cerulean blue, and I'd go dab-dab-dab-dab ... across the lot of them — and that was all the skies coloured in. Then darker cobalt blue and ultramarine for those that showed a bit of sea. Sometimes I'd get an

artistic flush and I'd put in streaks of viridian green, too. Then pale
ochre for the sand (which is an improvement on Nature because the
Penzance sand is more of a warm grey than anything) and dab-dab-dab
again with thin gamboge for the hands and faces. Also the limbs of the
kiddies. And then I'd do the 'specials,' as I called them — the bits that
needed solid colour because they showed up black on the print — the
scarlet stripes of the blazers and cricket balls, for example, and any
strong colours on ladies' parasols. Roger Moynihan would have had a
fit, I'm sure, but I'll bet my humble little camel-hair brush earned as
much in an hour as his grander squirrels and oxes and hogs ever did.

One day I was lost in my work when a gravelly cockney voice said,
"You've licked all the colour off of your lips, lady," and I looked up to
see Cass Potter standing there. "So you've been and gone and done it,
eh!" he added.

"We've been and gone and done it," I replied. "And I think we owe
you not just a drink but a slap-up, blow-out meal. Come on home with
me. We could even give you a bed for the night."

He pulled out his watch and said he had no time. He had to catch the
eight-ten, the last up train of the day.

It was then half-past seven — an hour before sunset. There were only
a few stragglers to come for their snaps so I closed up my counter but
left the display panels unshuttered and took him across to the same
private bar we'd used before — from where I could keep a sideways eye
on things.

He pretended to be sad to hear we were doing so well. He said he'd
taken a real fancy to me and had hoped, if we were really down on our
luck, that I'd chuck Jim and go off with him. I'd never been flirted with
in that way before, but I caught on pretty quickly and so played along
with him. Of course, he'd have been scared out of his wits if I'd taken
him seriously and offered to go off with him anyway. All the same I
thought it sad that a bright, amusing man like him couldn't have a
simple, honest friendship with a female. He had to keep up that stream
of mild innuendo and sly banter all the time.

I say I played along with him but I also tried to probe for weaknesses
in his façade — some place where he might show a more honest version
of himself than this eternally cheeky chap. And I found it at last when I
began to speak of my family — my brothers and sisters — and how we'd
been broken up and my determination to get us all back together. Then
he got so interested that he said he wouldn't bother with the train, and if

there was still a slap-up meal going, he'd take it, thanks. But he wouldn't stay the night. He had his own regular arrangements if ever he got stuck. I didn't inquire too closely for I could imagine what they'd be.

He watched while I served the last stragglers, and whistled when I put the day's takings in my purse. I asked him not to mention that it had been his idea in the first place and described how I had persuaded Jim to try it. Cass very gallantly said it *was* Jim's idea, anyway, because the notion of a camera that would not only snap a shot but would then deliver a finished print off the negative was ten times better still. Jim should work on that one, he said.

I introduced him as the man who'd *started* us on the right road by suggesting some changes to our leaflet. He was very good company throughout the meal, which was just pork casserole and beans followed by a summer trifle, and he regaled us with many near-the-bone stories of the travelling salesman's life. There's a hôtel in Truro with a notice on the dining-room door saying 'Guests caught bringing spirituous liquors into this room will be kicked out — thank you!' And there's a landlady in Falmouth who has little handwritten cards in each bedroom asking patrons not to replace the chamber pot under the bed after use, 'as the steam rusts the springs.' He and Susan got on particularly well and shared reminiscences of Limehouse and the Mile End Road till they saw us yawning. He concluded the meal with a naughty-but-nice song called 'So Her *Sister* Says,' as sung by Miss Jenny Valmore.

With some reluctance, Mark and Jim went off to the darkroom to do that day's batch of extra prints, ready for me to post the following morning. One day, a week or so earlier, we had let it go, because Mark said he could easily catch up the following morning. In fact, it had taken almost three days to catch up properly, so it was now part of our religion never to let the moon go down on unfinished business.

Susan retired to bed at once. Her time was very close by now and I lost count of the number of times I woke up in the dead of night. She only needed to turn over in her sleep, the creaking of the springs was enough to waken me. Anyway, off she went. And then Cass became that rare, serious self I'd begun to glimpse down at the Railway Arms.

"I've been thinking what you said — about getting your brothers and sisters together again," he said. "How are you going to do it?"

I explained all the complications, then — how Felicity, who was a problem in herself, was involved in keeping the boys at the Sutton — and the part the nuns of St Breaca's had played in Teresa's kidnapping

— and how Aunt Eph was helping ... pretty well everything, in fact. He listened in silence and then said, "It still doesn't tell me how you're going to get them back, love. Why don't you trust this Felicity mott? What's she ever done to make you nervous?"

I didn't really want to explain, and even if I had, it would have taken too long. So I just shrugged awkwardly and said, "Nothing really. It's just a feeling I have about her."

"Good!" he said approvingly. "I trust your feelings. You think she'd pretend to help and then trip you up at the last minute?"

"Yes — not necessarily out of malice. She could even do it out of curiosity. She'd be full of apologies afterwords. But too late, of course."

"You want a diversion. Make her watch your left hand" — he flourished his own left hand before my face — "and all the time you're working with the right!" He opened his right hand to reveal a tin of snuff. "And *then,*" he went on, "just when she's sure it's your right hand she's got to stop — hey presto!" He opened his left and and there was the snuff tin! Then he opened his right hand again and it was empty!

I gave a baffled laugh and asked how he'd done that.

"It doesn't matter," he replied. "The only thing you need remember is that I *did* do it — and you've got to do the same with your darling Felicity. Keep her happy chasing yesterday's echoes while you stay one jump ahead."

It filled me with a rosy glow — just the thought that I might be able to do something like that to Felicity. Of course, I hadn't the first idea of any details, but you can skip all that part when you're enjoying a daydream.

He cut into my reverie. "D'you think Lady whatsername will bring your Teresa to Penzance with 'er — assuming she comes to the nunnery at all, I mean?"

Again I could only shrug and confess my ignorance. "I don't know her from Eve — and that's the whole problem. The way the General writes about her she's a wilting flower, totally dependent on him — but then perhaps she's learned that he likes to think of her that way, and so obliges him. She might turn into a right old dragon the moment he's gone. I've seen that happen."

He chuckled richly. "No flies on you, gel," he said.

"Lots of women develop amazing powers when their husbands aren't around to save them the bother," I pointed out.

There was a touch of the old Cass Potter as he made his eyebrows go rapidly up and down, saying, "You mean, I'm still in with a chance?"

Then he watched in mounting alarm as I crossed the room to where he sat in Jim's armchair. And he pushed me away in panic when I made to park myself in his lap. I laughed and drew up a nearby chair. "From now on," I told him, "I'll call your bluff every time you joke like that."

He drew out a handkerchief and dramatically mopped his brow. "Next time I see *you* coming," he mumbled, "I'll take refuge in the nearest hornet's nest."

"I was saying that Lady W may be a tougher old turkey than I imagine. Sometimes I think I'll go down on my knees and beg her. Sometimes I think threats might be best. Or just plain reasonableness? There's nothing to go on, see? Anyway, I have to get to Teresa first and talk to her — without her ladyship or her nanny ..."

"Anna."

I looked at him in surprise — not amazement, for nothing about him would really amaze me. "You *know* them?" I asked.

"No! Anna — that's what they call them in India, nannies." Then he frowned. "No — anna is their money, isn't it — annas and rupees. But I know it's a word *like* anna."

It came to me then. "Ayah!" I exclaimed. "What on earth are we talking about this for? How does it help?"

"Ayah!" he echoed. "That's right. It always helps to have the right words, ducks. You mean if Teresa don't want to come back, you won't take her?"

"She's six now, getting on for six and a half. She's old enough to know what she wants."

"What she wants, maybe," he said. "But not what she *needs*. Only you and Marian can say that for her. And — take it from me — what she needs is 'er brothers and sisters around her. I don't care if you all fight like Kilkenny cats — or like most brothers and sisters I ever knew — she needs yer! And you need 'er. Take it from one as knows."

"You?" I prompted him.

He glanced nervously toward the door and licked his lips. "Don't let this go no further," he said quietly, "but your story ... I mean ... well, it could be mine, too, give or take a few details. Only I never 'ad your get-up-and-go. Not in them days. And now I never hop on a bus or train, never walk down an unfamiliar street, never plonk me backside on a bar stool, without I'm looking round for Albert and Hetty and" — his voice began to crack — "Millie and ..." He could not go on. "Oh gawd!" He sniffed heavily and wiped his eyes with a curious upward sweep, using the flat of his hand — as if using his knuckles would be too openly juvenile. "Don't mind me, love." He stirred uneasily.

"But I do, Cass," I said, using his Christian name for the first time. He looked up at me sharply.

"D'you object?" I asked.

He smiled and shook his head. "Funny," he said. "There's no one else who does. They've all gawn. What was I going to tell you ...?"

"Crissy."

He grinned more broadly. "What was I going to tell my own little Crissy — my favourite gel in the west? Oh yes! You said about being reasonable just now. What would you call reasonable?"

"Well, this I'll-get-her-back-whatever-the-price attitude may do wonders for my fighting spirit but it might be the very last thing Teresa wants — or needs, even — to follow your distinction. It could be that living in India with her great-great uncle and aunt is the best thing that could befall her. And if, when she's twelve and they want to send her to school back in England — well, she could only go back to India in the long summer hols. For all the other ones she could come here. That's what I call being reasonable."

Cass shook his head. "That's not what I call being a family at all."

"She could inherit a considerable fortune from the General one day," I added.

He darted a sharp glance at me. "You never said *that!*" he exclaimed. But then he slumped again and said, "Money! I never knew it bring any family together yet."

On the second of July I had another card from Aunt Eph to say that her ladyship had arrived and 'the giglet' was with her. Victor Jacks insisted on delivering it personally into my hand. As he did so, he winked and said he thought the following Tuesday, the seventh, was going to be an interesting one in the life of St Breaca's. And I was torn in two. Half of me rose with joy to think that, one way or another, the long heartache of my separation from my brothers and sisters would shortly start drawing to a close. The other half sank into near-despair, for these developments could not have come at a worse time. July and August were the two great holiday months of the year. Half our annual business would probably be conducted in the month of July alone, with another forty percent coming in August.

And Mark and Susan's babies were due any day now. Yes — *babies!* Doctor Eccles had put his auscultation tube to her tummy and heard two distinct heartbeats. The poor girl certainly looked big enough for twins — even triplets, which the doctor said could not be ruled out.

Mark and Jim were working all the hours God sent, beyond midnight sometimes, to clear the extra prints people ordered. Nor was I idle, what with addressing the envelopes, making sure the right prints went into them, and writing up our ledger — not to mention the colouring, not all of which I could manage between trains down in the kiosk. On top of that there was the normal business of housekeeping, keeping cook happy and two generals busy. Only Florrie, our first general, lived in, fortunately, but that meant the other two were paid higher rates. And also the marketing, which I tried to get done between nine and ten, after which I had to be down on the beach with Jim.

We saw more of each other than most husbands and wives, being together a good twenty hours of each day, which I am not sure the institution of marriage was designed to withstand. Things were on a knife edge with us many a time and only the fact that we were still newly-weds — and the pleasing chink of shillings and sixpences each evening — saved us from several distressing scenes. But I knew that if I was to say I'd take just a morning off to go and see Lady W, there'd be an explosion. Or worse — he might say, 'Very well, dear — if *you* believe our business can get along without you, right at the very peak of our short season, then go! Mark and I will stumble along as best we can.' There's a lot to be said for husbands who simply lay down the law and give the wife no choice!

The Monday before Lady W was due to visit St Breaca's — with or without Teresa — I was sitting disconsolately in the kiosk, with the collodion spirit drying on my brush, as I pondered my hundredth unworkable plan to be in two places at once. Then I spied Cass Potter sneaking into the Railway Arms.

"Mister Potter!" I called out. "Cass!"

He stopped as if I'd thumped him on the head and then slunk guiltily across the road to me. "I wasn't avoiding yer," he said as he drew near. "But you looked as if you didn't want company."

"I don't," I sighed. "But you're different."

"That's what I like to hear. Fancy a quick one? Drink, I mean."

I looked at the time, said, "Why not," and washed out my brush.

Over my usual half of mild-and-bitter I poured out my woes. When I'd finished he asked me what I did in particular when I went down on the beaches with Jim.

"Smile mostly," I replied. "Explain there's absolutely no obligation to buy the snaps he's shooting but they're there if they want them. Give out our leaflets. Pacify those who seem to think Jim is stealing their souls and carrying them away in his infernal box. In short ..."

"In short," he interrupted me, "nothing *I* couldn't do."

I just gaped at him, filled with a sudden, wild hope. "You?"

"It's selling, isn't it? I could do it with me eyes shut. I could sell down at the kiosk, too. What I couldn't do is colour in them pictures like what you do."

"I could still do that," I said, not able to believe my luck. "And looking after the house and all that side of it. Oh, Cass! Would you? Could you? Name your price — I'll give you *anything!*"

"'Anything?' asked Sir Jasper with a roll of his moustachioes," he said heavily, rolling his eyes and panting like a dog.

I pushed his indiarubber nose like a button. "One day you'll get such a shock. Some innocent young girl is going to take you seriously."

"Or so I 'ope!" he said in a stage whisper, putting the back of his hand obliquely to his lips.

"But seriously-seriously ..." I said.

"Seriously? I mean it. July's a rotten month in fancy hardware. Coloured buckets and spades is just about yer lot. I always take a holiday 'round now. Usually up Southend — meet me old chinas — tell 'em how I'm winning the war. Penzance'll make a nice change for once. Besides ..." He hesitated.

"Besides what?" I asked.

He grinned. "Never mind. It'll keep. Tell you when it's over — when you're sitting there with little Treeza on your lap. *That's* what I want to see, gel — so don't you disappoint me."

And so it was arranged. He wouldn't hear of taking money for it — not even commission. In fact he became a little cool when I mentioned it again. He said that helping to bring my family together again would heal his conscience over all the things he failed to do when his own was broken up. I still didn't press him for details about that. I thought it was what he'd been going to tell me when he said, "Besides ..." Anyway, I didn't have to look *this* gift horse in the mouth — he opened it so wide, and laughed so delightedly when I accepted, that I could count every single tooth.

Jim took a bit of persuading, especially when I brought Cass home without consulting him first. I admit it was going a bit far but time was so short. Anyway, his main argument was that we are a family business and don't want any outsiders barging in.

Family!

The word pursues me every day of my life. It haunts my dreams and colours my days. I am never free of that dear leech — the family!

Of course, I saw red and said I hardly needed reminding about the obligations of family *business* — giving the word a stress that was not lost on him. I dearly longed to tell him that the system we were using — of taking promiscuous snap-shots on the chance of selling them after — was entirely Cass's invention, but I resisted the temptation, thank heavens. It would have hurt him a lot because he had meanwhile come round to accepting that he was its original genius. Instead I reminded him that he had said that if *I* thought the business could afford to do without me, I was free to go and do whatever had to be done about Teresa. And I said I thought I'd done everything possible to see that my 'desertion' did no harm.

Only then did I remember he hadn't said any such thing. That was in one of the imaginary arguments I'd had with him. However, he was so tired he'd forgotten whether he'd said it or not. So that was that.

Actually, that wasn't quite that. It turned into quite a blistering row — all conducted in semi-whispers under the bedclothes so as not to upset Susan or embarrass poor Cass. And then we made it up in our usual way, which was an even greater ecstasy to us than on any previous occasion. The trouble was, we still enjoyed our normal conjugal pleasures on other nights — nights when there was no furious rage between us — but they were watered milk to the scalded cream of 'making up' after one of those rows. I began to suspect that we were coming to depend on them for what you might call the 'spice' in our lives.

Despite that rather heavy night, though, I was up at four next morning, doing all my chores for the day, leaving lists for Mrs Begley and Martha Morgan, our living-out cook and general, and wondering would it be tempting fate to air the bed I'd bought for Teresa. I was mad to start so early, of course, because Lady W would hardly catch any train before the ten-fourteen — assuming she came by train at all. That would bring her to Penzance at just gone eleven. If she came in her own carriage, she'd hardly set off before ten, either — so eleven o'clock was about the earliest she'd get here by road, too.

But reason can't fight feelings, so by half-past eight I was standing outside the School of Art and Science, which was as far away as one can lurk in Morrab Road and still have a clear view of the nunnery. Also the Penzance Free Library is next door, so I wouldn't stand out so much there as I would if I waited at the other end of the road, down near the prom. By eleven o'clock I'd lost count of the number of kind people who told me first that the library didn't open until half-past nine, then that it was open, in case I hadn't noticed.

Someone in the school must have thought I was a lady of the town who'd strayed a bit from my usual haunts between the gasworks and the harbour. Or maybe it was a person in one of the houses opposite. Anyway, *someone* got word to the police, who sent an embarrassed young constable out to move me on.

One pearl from the wit and wisdom of Cass Potter is that the best lies stick as near the truth as possible, so that if your victim looks into this or that detail, his findings are likely to confirm your honesty. I told the young fellow my real name and address and said I was waiting for my great-aunt, Lady Wilkinson of Nancekuke House, to collect me in her carriage, as we were going together to call on St Breaca's. She must have cast a tyre or something and had to find a blacksmith to shrink it back on again. I hoped it was nothing worse than that.

I also hoped — after he'd gone away, satisfied for the moment — that she wouldn't be too long now. Because the oddities of my half-truths would soon begin to dawn on the young fellow.

I did learn one good lesson, though — which was that if ever times got so bad with me that I was tempted to go out and join the ladies of the town, I'd have this memory of the most uncomfortable and boring three hours of my life to warn me against it. And that was on a pleasantly warm summer's morning with a light zephyr to temper the fire of the sun. How they stand out there in the pouring rain or with a frost deep enough to crack the very pavement under their daintily shod feet I can never understand.

Anyway, I endured three hours of purgatory there. The night-soil cart visited the convent. So did the postman, and several unidentifiable male callers who were probably tramps looking for a soft touch, and the butcher, and a horse and cart with a package from the railway, and the postman again … but no cab and no private carriage.

When Lady W did finally arrive I almost missed her because at twenty-past eleven a group of young ladies came out of the school and set up sketching easels on the pavement near me. And then I saw what a perfect fool I'd been. In my annoyance with Jim, in my eagerness to do my chores and leave Mulberry, and in my obsession to be 'on watch' at least two and a half hours before my quarry could possibly arrive, I had overlooked the most obvious excuse for any young female who needed to haunt a particular stretch of pavement to do so without bringing the law down upon her! I was even contemplating asking one of the girls if she could rustle up a spare easel and drawing board for me when a grand open phæton went bowling by with a *very* grand lady sitting in it — shaded by a parasol held by a little Indian page at her side. The poor young fellow must have held it aloft all the way from Redruth. Of Teresa there was no sign.

I followed them at a discreet distance, almost sure that they were who I thought they were — and very sure when the carriage drew up outside St Breaca's and the page sprang out and helped his mistress down. The front door had swallowed her by the time I drew level. Not knowing how much time I had, I plunged in at once without finesse. The driver had gone around the back of the nunnery, presumably to pay a call of nature. The boy, less inhibited, was widdling against the wheel. He finished just before I arrived and grinned at me rather sheepishly as he tucked his privates back up into his doublet.

"That's Lady Wilkinson's carriage, isn't it?" I asked him.

"Yes, Memsahib," he replied in a pleasant, slightly clipped singsong.

"Good," I said. "I'm supposed to be meeting her and Sister Enuda here. I'm Teresa's sister. How is she?"

"Very well, Memsahib. Very chicky!" He grinned and made a mime of strangling an invisible little person of his own height.

Then I realized he had said 'cheeky.' However, that was all the conversation we had because the coachman came out at that moment and, as soon as he set eyes on me, came running back to the carriage.

It's funny how much a little thing like that can give away. Why else would a great clod of a driver pick up his boots and *run* to stop a couple of people passing the time of day — unless his mistress had said something like, 'Keep your eyes peeled for a young female, rising eighteen, tallish, slender, with long, fair hair and, whatever you do, don't let her talk to my page!' What else would explain that look of panic in his eyes as he drew close?

I smiled broadly and, putting on the dialect, said, "Did 'ee knaw this-yur li'l bwoy, 'e do come from India?"

He relaxed a little, taking me now for a mere passer-by who, by chance, happened to fit the dreaded description.

"Gusson!" he responded with heavy sarcasm. "Well I never!"

"That's not up England somewhere, is it?" I asked. "India?"

"Not last time I heard," he replied flatly. He was beginning to suspect I was teasing.

"And how's my little sister, Teresa?" I asked, back in my normal voice once again.

His jaw dropped. He pointed at me but no words came.

"Never mind," I said. "I'll ask Lady W herself." And I turned in at the front gate.

I was two paces up the path before he found his voice. "You aren't left do that!" he cried in an odd mixture of anger and fear.

"Just watch," I told him.

Sister Enuda must have spied me from her study window for she met me at the door, which she opened no more than twelve inches and then barred with an acre of dark-blue serge. "If you don't go away," she said, "I shall call the police."

One of the problems of being a woman whose every order is obeyed under discipline and without question is that you stop preparing yourself for the alternative — that someone will simply push open the door and walk past you, for instance, as I now did. "I've already spoken to them," I said, pleased to hear how calm I sounded. Of course, I had fought a thousand such battles with her and Lady W during the past few weeks, until my stomach had lost the power to go on sinking. "I mentioned both your name and Lady Wilkinson's — my great-great-aunt. Where is she? In your study, I suppose."

"I am here."

The hall darkened as light ceased to flood in by way of the open study door. Its jambs now framed a woman so large, so static, and so old-fashioned in dress and appearance that I might have taken her for an enormous enlargement of the sort of negatives I found Jim throwing out of Stanton's cellars one spring-cleaning day.

"You are Christobel Moore, I take it," she went on icily.

"That was my maiden name, Lady Wilkinson," I said, keeping my tone pleasantly level but cool. "Or do I call you Great-aunt?"

She was furious at getting off on the wrong name and stared daggers at Sr Enuda as if she were to blame. To people of her class such absurd details have an importance that ordinary, sane people can hardly credit. This caused her to pause rather a long time before she replied, so that her "You most certainly may *not!*" sounded too much of an afterthought to be convincing.

And Sr Enuda spoiled it further by speaking at the same time: "She is Mrs Collett now, Lady Wilkinson."

As the Reverend Mother was unused to disobedience, so Lady W was unaccustomed to being spoken to while she herself was speaking. "What?" she asked tetchily. "Who is ... what?"

I waited until an uncharacteristically stumbling Sr Enuda began to explain and then *I* spoke over her: "Or Great-great-aunt, then?" I suggested. "You *are* my great-great-aunt, you know."

"Be quiet!" she snapped at me — though, unfortunately, she was looking at Sr Enuda at the time.

The nun gave up and turned on me instead. "What did you say about the police?"

Such petty amusement as I had begun to feel evaporated at once. "Haven't you called them?" I asked. "I thought you said you had."

"I said I *would.*"

"Police?" Lady W snatched a tiny handkerchief from her sleeve and dabbed her mouth with it.

"Please do so, then," I said. "It will save saying everything twice."

"Will somebody please ..." Lady W started to say, only to be cut short by Sr Enuda, who looked nervously up and down the hall, saying, "We simply cannot discuss this matter out here," and most reluctantly ushered me toward her study.

"Did you really imagine you could keep me out of it?" I asked her in a confidential murmur as we approached the awesome figure of Lady W, for whom the word 'Memsahib' had surely been especially minted.

"What is this?" she asked, refusing to budge. "Will you kindly explain what is going on?"

The question was directed at me but I invoiced it onward to Sr Enuda, who said, "This young lady has plagued the life out of us ever since ..."

"Yes, yes! She has done the same to us. What I wish you to explain is why you do not eject her and call the police?"

"Believe me, Lady Wilkinson, there are good reasons why we cannot do that."

I was surprised and delighted to hear it — or rather to hear it confirmed by the 'enemy.' For, although I knew it to be true according to the strict letter of the law, I also knew to my cost how easily the law can be *flexed*, shall we say, by those who can hook a little finger through the right buttonhole and murmur a word or two in the right ear.

"I should like to hear them," the old woman bellowed.

"I don't suppose you would." Sr Enuda was rallying well. "And certainly not out here — so will you *please* step aside!"

Lady W was astonished into complying. By the time she realized she had made an important concession — not to Sr Enuda but to me — I was inside the study and the nun was closing the door.

And locking it!

I did not realize how alert I was to danger — alert in all my senses — until I caught myself automatically checking on the locks and catches of the windows. Why should I run? And where to? I don't know, but I was ready for it, if necessary.

"Now will you explain?" Lady W thundered.

I did not sit down until both had seated themselves — a civility that annoyed her.

"It is precisely what I was about to tell you before this interruption." Sr Enuda glanced at me — a glance strangely devoid of malice or ill-feeling. "And it is really nothing different from the views I have expressed to you by letter, Lady Wilkinson — indeed, they were more than views, they were counsel's opinion. A very eminent counsel. And it cost us a great deal of money to obtain — as I also pointed out in my letter."

"Yes!" Lady W waved an angry hand, as if to swat the words before they could settle on her veil. "Well, you wasted forty guineas there. We, too, have counsel's opinion — as good as. The Deputy Assistant Advocate-General of India, no less. And his opinion is quite different, let me assure you."

I was sitting to one side of Sr Enuda's desk, almost at her right hand. Between us was a pad of notepaper and, of course, she had pen and ink. She must have thought I was scribbling her a note for, after an initial glance, she paid me no more attention. But what I wrote was a 'pay-bearer' cheque for forty guineas, drawn on Bolitho's, our bankers in Market Jew Street. She was so embroiled in her I-said-you-said exchange with Lady W that, when I asked, "Have you a twopenny revenue stamp, please, Reverend Mother?" she merely pointed at the top drawer, between us.

Only when I licked it, stuck it on, and signed my name over it did it begin to dawn on her that I was up to something more than mere note scribbling. By then I was done. I laid it face down on the sheet of blotting paper before her and then invited her with a wave to turn it over and see.

Another pearl from Cass. Somehow — the way these things happen after a few small drinks — we got to discussing roundheads and cavaliers, and the Civil War. And Cass said, "The thing about any civil war is that it keeps putting the ultimate question in the mind of every general — 'Is this the right moment for me to change sides?'" Then came that rich gargle-laugh of his.

But he's right. I never saw that same question writ more plain on any woman's face than I saw it on Sr Enuda's when she read my cheque.

But the look she gave me was the one she'd have given if I'd made it out for a million guineas instead of forty. She thought I couldn't possibly have so much!

"They'll honour it," I promised her. "Didn't you know my grandmother had left me part of her fortune?"

Lady W, aware by now that her contribution to the I-said-you-said round was falling on deaf ears, said, "Honour? What's this talk of honour — from the brat of a coachman, eh? Do you dare to lecture us on honour, Mrs ... Mrs ...?" She clicked her fingers in vexation.

It was too much for me, of course. Cass had warned me not to lose my temper, but that woman had gone too far. I drew a deep breath to steady my voice, for I was quivering with rage, and said, "I believe the daughter of an honest coachman might have *something* to teach the aunt of a common prostitute, Lady Wilkinson — if only that pots should not go about calling kettles black!"

I thought she would die of an apoplexy on the spot — and so, I'm sure, did Sr Enuda. But now I had the bit between my teeth I felt good enough for a gallop. I turned to the nun and said, "When you placed Teresa in Lady Wilkinson's care, were you aware that her niece was a common prostitute — and walked the streets in this very town, in fact?"

"Stop!"

Lady W realized that an attack of the vapours was going to lose her what initiative she might still have. "How *dare* you mention that incident?" she asked me.

"How dare *you* slight my late father's memory?" I asked. Then, turning again to Sr Enuda: "Please control her if you can! Stop this stupid name-calling."

"Is it true?" Sr Enuda asked with bated breath. The horror of this extra twist of the knife was just dawning on her — not only an illegal kidnapping to explain away but *this* too!

"I never knew the creature." The wattles beneath Lady W's chin rattled drily. "She took poison years ago, long before I married the General. It's of no bearing."

"I'm afraid it is, Lady Wilkinson," Sr Enuda said. "It is a material fact that should have been disclosed at the time of the adoption. It would not have ruled you out, I hasten to say. But it would have taken the decision out of my hands and placed it in those of the bishop — who, I feel quite confident, would have found in your favour. Nonetheless ..."

"In the three days we had at our disposal?" Lady W asked incredulously. "My *foot!* In any case, Mrs Trevarton — my niece Agatha — *she* knew all about it."

"But the decision was not hers."

"Ha! You say that now! You were happy enough to endorse it at the time. You know very well it was hers. Hers, hers, *hers!* It was her hand in everything we did at that time!"

"More's the pity," Sr Enuda said under her breath — and to me, I was surprised to realize.

"I heard that!" Lady W snapped. "Anyway, what difference does it make — whether or not you knew it at the time? You know it now — thanks to this young ... person. Your bishop can make up his mind now as well as he could then, I suppose?"

Sr Enuda shook her head. "It makes the entire adoption null and void, Lady Wilkinson. Suppression of material facts, whether wilful or not, nullifies the process. It no longer matters whether your *Deputy Assistant"* — she laid scornful stress on the words — "Advocate-General disagrees with Sir Digby Crawshay, one of the most eminent QCs of our day. It is now beside the point, which is that there never was a valid adoption for either gentleman to pass his opinion upon. I shall be writing to the bishop to let him know of this. I must ask, meanwhile, for your solemn word that you will not remove Teresa from our jurisdiction — the episcopal see of Truro?"

A second apoplexy threatened. Lady W looked wildly about her and, chancing to see my cheque on the desk, snatched it up and said,

"What's this, anyway?" Her eyes scanned it rapidly and, if it had been possible for skin that had never once felt the direct touch of the Indian sun to turn paler than pure white, she would have turned paler. "Pshaw!" she exclaimed scornfully. "Forty guineas — is that all? I'll let you have twice that."

"Forty guineas is what I have asked you for several times, Lady Wilkinson — as tactfully as I knew how."

Lady W tore my piece of paper to shreds and tossed them in the waste basket. "Three times, then," she said. "You shall have a hundred and twenty guineas tomorrow, or ... soon."

Triumphantly she challenged me to match it.

But the triumph faded when Sr Enuda, God bless her, said, "Teresa never was for sale."

"My carriage!" She rose and spoke as if ordering it from an unseen footman. Habit, I suppose. She unlocked the door and opened it.

"Lady Wilkinson!" Sr Enuda called out as the old woman went into the hall.

But I held up my hand and pleaded with my eyes for her to say no more. I knew she was going to repeat her demand for an assurance Teresa would not be kidnapped a second time — but the woman would refuse, as she had done before, and those were not the last words I wished her to carry from this meeting. I ran out after her and took her elbow as if I believed she needed assistance to walk. "I wouldn't dream of taking Teresa back if she preferred to stay with you," I said earnestly.

She stopped in her tracks and stared at me, convinced that this was some new trick, I think — and so it was, in a way, but only a trick to stop her from being foolish and doing something that would get all our names plastered over the vulgar newspapers. "I beg your pardon?" she asked. Her tone was not gentle but it was the nearest she had come to it so far.

"If Teresa prefers to return to India with you, and if she tells me so to my face — with no one there to browbeat her — then I personally will ask the bishop to bless and sanction the adoption. I give you my solemn undertaking on that, with Sister Enuda here as witness. Now may I have *your* undertaking not to take Teresa away until I have seen her and spoken to her?"

She hesitated.

"Perhaps you don't trust her?" I suggested.

"I don't trust *you,*" she said coldly.

"Well, trust has to start somewhere — and in your case, it has to start with me."

"Oh, very well!" Her wattles rattled again. I felt that bits of bark or woodlice or something ought to be falling out of the folds. "You have my word."

Sr Enuda was going to see her to the carriage but the old woman slammed the door behind her, right in the nun's face.

She sprang back in time to avoid trapping part of her habit. Then she looked at me with incredulity. "Such a hostage to fortune, Mrs Collett! Why on earth did you make such a foolish concession?"

"To lull her suspicions," I said. "Listen — this is urgent! She has no intention of keeping that bargain. She will ..."

"But she has given her word!" Sr Enuda was aghast at my suggestion.

"Even so, she will not keep it. Trust me — I know. If she can get Teresa out of ..."

"But she is a member of the aristocracy!"

I have this awful tendency to riot after hares and lose the fox. A baronet is a member of the peerage, of course, but *not* of the aristocracy — a useless bit of knowledge I had somehow retained from the period when Susan had hoped to become a lady. So help me, I *almost* pointed out the fact to Sr Enuda then! And a fine old argument that might have started! Fortunately the business was so desperate that I was able to get back on the right scent without too much loss of time.

"No matter," I said. "I saw her eyes when she spoke. You did not. Just take it from me, if she can get Teresa beyond the reach of the English law tonight — never mind the see of Truro — she will. Our efforts have become *that* desperate." I looked her in the eye and added, "It is *our* efforts now, I trust?"

She smiled sheepishly and nodded.

"How free are you?" I asked. "Can you go up to Bastian and Tregilgas now?" I had seen the name of their solicitors among the papers scattered on her desk.

"What ever for?" she asked.

"To arrange for Teresa to be made a ... what is it?" I snapped my fingers in vexation. "To protect children?"

"Ward of court? I don't think I could do that."

"I'll pay the cost. I'll write another cheque before I go, by the way. But I'll pay all the costs, no matter what — barrister, court fees ... everything."

Still she hesitated.

"D'you want your names in the papers?" I asked. "Saint Breaca's, the bishop's ... Fleet Street would have a carnival!"

"That's just what I'm afraid of, my dear."

"They're not going to make much of a little ward-of-court case. But if Teresa is kidnapped for the second time, I'll fight to get her back and I'll fight through every court in the land — right up to the House of Lords, if need be. Don't doubt it for a moment."

"I don't!" she exclaimed heavily.

"Any inaction on your part now would not look well."

"I know," she said in anguish. "You're not telling me anything new!"

It was no moment to relent. "The present bishop has hopes of following his predecessor, Bishop Benson, to Canterbury, I think. It would do little to increase his chances!"

"Oh, very well!" She tore out imaginary hair, whose real counterpart the church had long since shorn, and looked at me for mercy. "If only we hadn't thrown away *all* Sister Berrion's whisky!"

On an inspiration I went back into her study, to the *Dictionary of The Bible,* behind which Sr Berrion had hidden a bottle. It was still there!

I produced it with a flourish.

Sr Enuda sat in her chair and began to laugh — feebly, not hysterically. "The world is at long last about to discover what happens when the irresistible force meets the immovable object!" she murmured as she accepted the glass I had poured out.

I went with her to Bastian & Tregilgas and asked them to send the bill to me. They said that, 'on the basis of information laid and furnished,' Teresa could be made a ward of court by tomorrow afternoon, after which, the police would be obliged to intervene to prevent any attempt to remove her from English jurisdiction. I was sure Lady W knew as much, too. Even if she did not know we were making this application, she would assume the worst and act accordingly — that is, remove Teresa tonight.

Falmouth!

She'd find a ship in Falmouth, 'for orders.' If not she'd surely find some sea-going craft with a complaisant skipper who would get her over the Channel to France.

I ran all the way from St Breaca's to the Police Station, up by the Town Hall and laid information (and furnished it, too, for all I know) that Lady Wilkinson had abducted my sister and, I believed, intended carrying her abroad tonight, before she could be made a ward of court.

The sergeant, a big tub of lard, laid his pen down at that point and advised me to do just that — make her a ward of court. He took it up again when I told him I had already done so. He put it down again when I explained that Lady W was my aunt (I thought too many 'greats' would make her sound harmless and sweet).

"This is a family squabble," he said.

There it was again — family!

"Therefore?" I asked.

"We stay clear of family squabbles," he explained patiently.

"Including family murders?" I asked.

"Murder's a hanging offence," he replied pompously — until he realized that so was kidnapping still — technically, anyway.

"The very least you could do," I told him, "is cable the Falmouth Docks police, who could then alert all the masters of seagoing vessels about this business — so that they know if they carry her and the little girl abroad, they'll be in trouble. She'll be easy to spot as she has an Indian page-boy with her."

As I left, for I could spare no more time to argue, I said, "If you sit back and do nothing, it's not going to look very good when it all comes out in court."

Then, fortunately, I got a passing cab back to Mulberry.

It was teatime by now. Jim and Cass had finished down on the beach and I was astonished to find the pair of them — and Mark — toasting each other in champagne. Naturally I assumed Susan had had her baby while I was out. But no!

"Why didn't you *tell* me?" Jim asked, just on the tipsy side of merry.

"Tell you what?"

They were all bubbling over with repressed mirth.

"That Cass Potter is the greatest salesman the world has ever known," Jim replied. "A hundred and twenty-seven people on the beach — I know because I counted them — and how many orders d'you think he's taken? Not sales down at the kiosk — actual firm orders in advance."

I shrugged and picked an impossibly high figure. "Thirty?"

They howled with laughter. "Fifty-eight!"

Cass toasted me with his champagne. "You never told me neither," he said, "that it's about as difficult as teaching cows to evacuate."

They all had hysterics at that. Of course, I was delighted, too, but I don't think Jim understood why I didn't join in the celebrations as wholeheartedly as he had expected me to.

My 'gardening angel,' as Marian had put it, must have been working double tides that day. If I had not been delayed, first by that obtuse police sergeant, then by the celebrations of Cass Potter's genius, I should have missed the telegram from Aunt Eph — the first she had ever sent in her life, she told me afterwards. It informed me that 'the parties' were going to Plymouth on the seven-thirty from Redruth.

That telegram arrived at four-twenty. The next up-train was the four-fifty, which reached Truro just before six. The seven-thirty from Redruth (which originated as the six-forty from Penzance) stopped at Truro a minute or so before eight. I knew all these times by heart, thank heavens, because they were for trains we took when we had been travelling daily between Falmouth and Penzance. (Sometimes we missed them, of course — which is when they *really* get engraved on your heart.) I also knew that the second of these trains — the one 'the parties' were taking — was the last train out of Cornwall each night and arrived at Plymouth some time after ten.

So all I needed to do was take the first up-train as far as Truro, where I would enjoy the luxury of two whole hours in which to find Marian — who had not yet sent me her address, of course — and persuade her to come to Plymouth with me on the second train — taking care not to be seen by Lady W, who would be on it. In Plymouth we would immediately execute my brilliant plan (of which I hadn't the foggiest notion as yet) and bring darling Teresa back home with us — and the little Indian page-boy, too, if he wanted to come. I thought he would add a distinctive tone to the studio-portrait side of our business when we started it in September or thereabout.

"Simple enough, really!" as Jim said when I told them why there'd be one less for supper that night. He also insisted on coming with me, of course. And, but for the fact that I insisted even more that he shouldn't, he would have, too. It was not arrogance on my part, nor a vainglorious desire to go it alone. It is a sad truth that, while the courts take a lenient view of 'silly, hysterical women' who break the law for the sake of their families, men are not allowed the excuse of *crime-passionelle*. Besides, I thought that if I went alone — or with only Marian to help me — I might manage it without breaking the law at all. Men turn to violence so readily — especially Cornish men, for whom the act of heaving a brick through somebody's window is almost a meek apology.

Jim was quite wonderful, though. He said he'd go on the eight-ten, which terminated at Truro, and change there for Falmouth — just in case Lady W had meanwhile heard of a convenient ship there and changed her mind. I don't think there are many husbands who'd have had so much confidence in their wives that they'd let her do the main part of the business alone.

Actually, it wasn't true to say I had *absolutely* no plan. I had prepared for a number of general situations — such as having to move in a hurry after the banks had closed ... or making sure Teresa would recognize me by keeping the battered old bonnet I always used to wear around Porthleven — things like that. Also keeping my gladstone bag packed with toothbrush, change of underwear, spare shoes, railway timetable, and so on.

The brief champagne celebrations ended downstairs while I was assembling these things — and trying to assemble my thoughts, as well. Jim and Mark went into the darkroom to make all the prints that Genius had geniussed people into ordering. Genius himself, having nothing to do for the moment, blocked the doorway and watched me getting everything together.

"Shall I run out for a cab?" he asked.

"It'll be quicker to run downhill myself. I'm in good time, anyway."

"How long have you had all this stuff ready?"

"Over a year. Now if you don't mind ..."

"'Struth! I hope *we* never cross swords, you and me!"

"We will if you don't shut up and let me think! Go down and count me out thirty quid from the safe — banknotes for preference."

He whistled. "Ain't that enough for yer?" He pointed at the wallet lying beside my handbag. "How much have you got there?" At the same time he took out a wad of his own money and began counting, otherwise I should have exploded. "Fifty," I said. "It ought to be enough but I'd hate to run out."

He counted out a hundred and five pounds, which he added to my own hoard. "You may have to break the law, my old darling," he said. "In which case you can't have too much of the old spondulicks. Did you ever notice that? The kid who lifts a pocket-wipe gets sent to nick. But the man who swindles millions gets a seat in the House of Lords. Go on — take it!"

I was overwhelmed with gratitude — or almost. But, such is the nature of an all-consuming obsession like mine, part of me saw that he kept back a fair little wad of notes for himself and, God forgive, I resented it!

I went to the darkroom door and tapped gently.

"Can't come in!" Jim shouted in alarm. As if I would!

"Come to the door," I said.

"What now?" he grumbled, but he came.

"Can you see the knot in the panel on the side nearest the hinge?"

"Just about. Why?"

"Kiss it. I'm kissing it now, out here." These last words were barely intelligible, to prove it.

"Silly sausage!" he said affectionately. Then there were mumbled words to prove it on his side, too.

Then Cass dragged me away, saying now we'd be late. We made it just in time, and in all honesty I must also confess to resentment that he just stood on the platform and waved me off — so much so that I didn't poke my head out of the window and wave and wave him out of sight, the way I usually do. I was grateful for the loan of the money — genuinely — but I thought that after all his fine sentiments about losing his own family and wanting to help me bring ours back together … well, he might at least have offered to come with me. I should have refused, of course, for reasons already given. But he might have offered.

However, by the time we were gathering pace through the shunting yards, I had put Cass Potter and The Shilling Picture Co. out of my mind entirely, turning instead to plans for preventing Lady W from taking Teresa abroad. Before we even reached Redruth they had ranged from the brute-simple (hire a plug-ugly down at the docks and pay him to murder the odious woman in her bed) to the absurdly elaborate (drag the postmaster from the bosom of his family to concoct and deliver a fake cable from the General, forbidding her to hazard his career by openly flouting the law). The only category of plan that was missing was the one labelled 'sensible and practical.'

At Redruth I took the risk of stepping out briefly onto the platform to keep an eye on all who got into the First Class. I thought that if Lady W had changed her plans and caught this train instead, it would be better to be observed than to miss them altogether. For this one arrived in Plymouth shortly after eight, which might just give them time to arrange a departure tonight.

I inspected the platform from end to end before the train halted. No sign of them. I got out and stood behind a laden luggage trolley, keeping my eye on the platform entrance. Imagine my surprise when, only seconds after I began my vigil, I saw Felicity striding down the platform, peering intently into each carriage as she passed.

My instinct was to hide from her but I could not do that without losing sight of the entrance and the First Class carriages. Even so, she was about to rush past me, so eager was she to see if I was on the train. And it was *me* she was seeking. In the light of that day's events there could be no doubt of it. For my part I never once took my eyes off the entrance but, as she drew near, it occurred to me that if she did not see me on her way down the platform, she was bound to do so on her return. So when, out of the corner of my eye, I saw her about to go past, I said quietly, "Looking for me?"

"Ah!" She almost collapsed with relief. "I *knew* you'd be on this train. I just knew it."

"I can't think how," I said, offering her my cheek but still keeping my eye on the entrance.

"Never mind." She kissed me there. "It'd take too long to explain. And you needn't bother to look out for her just yet. She's catching the seven-thirty up-train."

I almost blurted out, 'I know — to Plymouth,' but that caution which is never far from me when Felicity is around made me hold my tongue. "I knew she'd try to get away tonight," was all I said.

"You've really set the cat among the pigeons!" she exclaimed. "It's lucky for you that Cousin Stella is visiting Nancekuke House at the moment. You got our telegram?"

I shook my head.

"Then I don't understand. Why are you on this train if …?"

"Instinct," I replied. "The moment she stormed out of St Breaca's I knew she'd do a bolt. They think they own the earth. They imagine they're above the law, people like her."

"You must have left just before it got to you." Felicity ignored my little provocations. "Her Ladyship's making for Falmouth, of course. I looked at today's *Lloyd's Register* in the library. There are two vessels sailing tonight. I've written them down."

I gave the list a perfunctory glance and saw that the *Madeleine* was leaving for Liverpool at ten and the *Excalibur* was bound off for France at midnight.

"Her train will get to Falmouth just after nine," Felicity added. "So she could catch either."

The guard blew his whistle and twitched the hand holding his green flag. My quarry was not on this train, of that I was sure. Therefore I was ahead of them. "Thank you, *dear* Felicity," I said as I stepped back aboard. "You've made it absurdly easy now. I'll thank you properly when it's all over."

As I settled back into my seat, a great surge of relief filled me, for I now knew, beyond any shadow of a doubt, that Lady Wilkinson was intending to escape by way of Plymouth. For all her seeming wayward-ness, dear Felicity had proved to be wonderfully predictable!

Even so, I did not drop my guard. When we arrived at Truro I risked peering in at all eight First Class compartments, just to make sure they hadn't got on at Camborne or Grampound Road, which would also have been within reach of Nancekuke House. Again I drew a blank — along with a wonderful assortment of affronted First Class stares. You'd have thought I was taking their photographs or something insulting like that! But now I was double-copper-fastened sure I had my quarry cornered on the eight-three to Plymouth.

By now, too, I had laid the foundations of the first sensible and practical plan. We — Marian and I — with our lack of heavy luggage, would nip out of Plymouth North Road, bag a hansom, and then wait for her ladyship, more encumbered than us, to emerge. She'd probably take a growler, or two hansoms. Either way, we'd just tell our driver to follow them. It was very unlikely that anyone arriving at half-past ten at night could drive straight down to the docks and walk onto a boat to France, but if she did, Marian and I could kick up enough fuss between us to worry the docks police and make the ship's master realize it wasn't worth his while to carry her. They do hate it so when people walk aboard and nail bits of legal paper to the mast! However, the most likely thing was that she'd stop at some hôtel overnight and try for a boat first thing tomorrow morning. She'd feel safe enough to do that — and a lady seeking a passage by day would be far less remarkable than one who turned up at dead of night.

My grandmother had once referred to the Drake as 'my family's favourite hôtel' in Plymouth. I just prayed that by 'family' she had meant the Wilkinsons rather than the Trevartons.

I put my gladstone bag in the left-luggage but carried my handbag (and money!) with me down the hill into Truro. Roche's haberdashery in Boscawen Street was easy enough to find and, the hour being only six, they were still open. I asked one of the young assistants there if she knew of a Mr Colin Pearce and could she direct me to his house in the town? I was aware of a certain tension in her — almost an unease — at the mention of the name Pearce. She glanced uncertainly over her right shoulder. The gesture attracted the attention of an older woman — the supervisor, I presumed — who came gliding along behind the glass-top counter as if on castors.

Her rapid movement, in turn, attracted the attention of Colin Pearce himself, who must have been standing almost next to the woman, but around the corner and out of sight from where I was. He arrived among us before the assistant was even half way through explaining my request to her superior.

"Oh, Mister Pearce, sir," she simpered in the most servile manner — also with a tinge of fear. "If it please you, sir, this young lady here is inquiring after you, sir."

"Mister Pearce?" I held out my hand and gave him my warmest smile. "I'm Mrs Cristobel Collett, Marian Moore's sister. I'm sure she's mentioned me? I was hoping …"

"You!" he said brusquely. "Yes, I've heard all about you."

I already knew about love-at-first-sight. Now I learned that hate-at-first-sight exists, too. He certainly was not 'the most handsome man in the world,' as Marian had put it. In fact, if 'handsome is as handsome does,' he was pretty close to being the ugliest. His face was thin and pinched — and spotty with blackheads — but from his neck down he swelled like an exaggerated pear to an aggressively large paunch, as in a caricature by Daumier. He absolutely refused to tell me where I could find Marian and ordered me to clear off out of 'his' premises before he called the police.

Having nothing to lose, except precious minutes, I sat down and said, "Please do so. I shall wait."

Like all bullies he did not know what to do when one of his threats failed. "We'll soon see about that!" he said. But, instead of going to the door and blowing his whistle, he went back round the corner — to his office, I presumed. It occurred to me that the shop might be connected to the telephone company but it seemed most unlikely for such a small business. I smiled at the two ladies. The older one turned her back on me and resumed her earlier station. The younger one whispered, "Buy something, quick! Ribbon, buttons, anything!"

I thought this was some legal advice — like, I couldn't be ejected from the shop if I could show a bona-fide receipt or something — and gratefully complied. But after she had written out the receipt I noticed she tore my copy off the carbon paper and added another couple of lines. Then she folded it and handed it to me, saying out of the side of her mouth, "Don't look till you get outside again."

Shortly after that Pearce returned. "I've telephoned for the police," he said with a triumphant sneer. "They should arrive at any minute."

I could tell from the supervisor's startled reaction that he could have done no such thing, but I pretended to be alarmed. "All right," I said anxiously. "I don't want to cause any trouble." And I scuttled for the door. There, however, I turned defiantly and said, "But I'll come back next week and I'll find her then. You shan't keep her from me for ever!"

That was to stop him from putting on his hat and coat and following me out, for it would surely occur to him that I might inquire elsewhere.

So much for my cleverness, though — it didn't work on Mr Colin Pearce. I went back toward Victoria Place and then hid myself in a shallow doorway to a solicitor's office, closed at that hour, of course. There I deciphered the address — in Lemon Street, the posh part of Truro — and was just about to set off when I saw the man himself emerge from 'his' shop and step out briskly in the same direction. Now it was a question of rescuing not one sister but two!

I saw I could do the young assistant a favour by pretending I'd followed him directly, instead of her directions. So I tore the receipt up and threw it in a waste-basket as I set out after him. He looked about him several times but failed to notice me — mainly because I had been wearing rather a striking hat in the shop but had now put up that battered old thing I had brought for Teresa to recognize me by. Also, I knew where he was going and so could hang back much farther than I would have been obliged to do had I not known. All the same, I didn't want him to arrive too far ahead, so that he'd have time to get Marian out of the way.

He did his best, though, and if I'd hung back another minute, he'd have succeeded. It was still two hours before sunset, so, even though his house was near the top of Lemon Street, just before the bend, and I was still near the bottom, I saw her come out with a letter in her hand and turn away from me, continuing on up the hill. He must have given her some particular reason to post it in the pillar-box up on the Falmouth road — and he had probably sent her on a further errand from there.

That's what I'd have done in his shoes, anyway.

Now I really had to hurry. I didn't know my way around Truro at all well, apart from two or three main streets that I'd explored between trains. But a little way up the hill I saw an entrance to a side street — Tabernacle Row, as it turned out — which looked as if it ran parallel to Lemon Street — and so, taking a chance on it, was able to cut round the back of Pearce's house that way. I took an even greater chance on the network of streets above that and, more by luck than anything, came out onto the Falmouth road just in time to see Marian climbing a stile into a field on the eastern side of the highway.

I called out and she stopped, unable to believe it was really me, even when, utterly out of breath, I reached her and hugged her half to death.

"I can't stop," she warned me. "I'm on a most urgent errand. See that house over there?"

"Never mind," I told her. "You're not on any sort of errand at all — at least not for Mister Colin Pearce. He's sent you on a wild goose chase just to get you out of my way." And I explained what had happened down in the shop.

"But they haven't got a telephone," she objected.

"I know!" I said in exasperation. "He's all piss and wind!"

"Crissy!" she almost screamed. "What are you saying!" I don't think I ever saw her so shocked.

"I'm not feeling in the least bit ladylike tonight. Tonight I'm ready to sell my soul to the Devil!"

"Really?" she asked, excitement quickly replacing the shock. "Can I stand near by and watch?"

Sobriety returned when I told her what had passed between me and Lady W that afternoon, the fears it had aroused in me, and the confirmation provided by Aunt Eph's telegram. All the same she said she couldn't come and help me. "Colin would never forgive me."

"And if you don't help me, Marian," I said, "*I* shall never forgive you. Nor will Tom, nor Gerald, nor Arthur. To say nothing of Teresa herself. So you just make your mind up."

"Oh, *please!*" she begged. "Don't put it like that. You're asking me to make an impossible choice."

"Take your time," I said. "No hurry. I'll give you thirty seconds."

She began to cry, until I said, "Twenty!" Then she stamped her foot and argued angrily, until I said, "Ten!" Then she walked away a few paces, turned, and walked back again, fixing me with a baleful stare.

"Time," I said.

"I'm not coming. I can't. You can't ask anything so cruel."

I turned away before she finished, mainly so that she should not see the tears in *my* eyes now. "That's it, then, Marian," I shouted over my shoulder as I walked away.

"You're a beast and I hate you for *ever!*" she screamed after me.

I did not hesitate, much less look back.

The next forty-five minutes, until precisely two minutes to eight, when the train pulled out of Truro, were the most melancholy I had ever known — worse even than the time after our mother's death. For this was a species of death, too — a living death in which she and I would be twenty miles — and twenty *million* miles — apart, at one and the same time.

The train waited six minutes at Truro, so, after I had reclaimed my bag, I hung back on the footbridge until a porter with a laden luggage trolley gave me the chance to slip past the First Class without being noticed. (This stratgem also let me watch the way out, just in case Felicity had, for once, been telling the truth. She hadn't, of course.) Shielded by the trolley, I went as far down the Second Class as I could, to be well away from the First when I got out at Plymouth. I was just in time, too, for, as I climbed aboard, the guard was hefting his watch and spanking his leg impatiently with the green flag. I sank into my seat, feeling more lonely and dispirited than ever.

But then something — I don't know what — made me let the window down half way and poke my head out. And who should I see walking down the train, peering anxiously into all the Second Class compartments, but Marian — in alpine hat and cape, and carrying a much smarter bag than mine!

I glanced behind and saw the guard put his watch away and start fumbling for his whistle. I began to panic. I didn't want to shout her name, much less did I want her to holler out mine. I stepped out of the compartment and, holding the door open, began to jump up and down on the platform, frantically waving my arms.

She saw me and began running in the same moment as the guard blew his whistle. I leaped aboard and held the door open for her. She threw her bag in first, almost bowling me over, and then leaped in to join me just as the train began to pick up speed.

"Last-minute Marian — as always!" I said in exasperation, before we threw our arms around each other again and hugged for dear life.

We went through St Austell just after sunset, but with the long summer evening there was still plenty of light in which to point out Tywardreath to Marian. It was a rather eerie feeling as we passed it to think that, what with Teresa only yards away and Tom across the valley there, we were physically closer as a family than we had been at any time during the past sixteen months. It was an omen, I felt sure. And the nearer we drew to Plymouth, the closer we should get to Gerald and Arthur, too.

"We can't bring Teresa back from Plymouth and leave the boys there," Marian said. She was right — and not for sentimental reasons, either. Felicity would never forgive me for ignoring her advice this night.

But how we'd get them away was something I could not even begin to consider just then.

Between there and Plymouth we discussed the tentative plan I had formed on the way to Truro. Marian came up with the most likely explanation for the one thing that had puzzled me — why, when there was at least one ship bound for France waiting in Falmouth, Lady W had chosen to go to Plymouth, instead.

"Because of the little Indian page," she said. "Falmouth is the most obvious port to watch, and a boy like that would stick out a mile there. But in Plymouth there'd be blackamoors, lascars, Chinese — people from all over the Empire."

Foreign breeds were fairly common in Falmouth, too, of course, but her general point was right. An Indian boy of nine or ten would be pretty unusual there.

What we were going to do, once we had discovered their hôtel, was still a blank. Should we allow them to retire and take rooms there, too — and then try to kidnap Teresa back during the night? Or inform the police? Or try to discover their ship and threaten her master with dire consequences if he carried them? Or bribe a cab-driver to take them to the wrong quay — for Plymouth had a tidal harbour and ships could not afford to wait too long, especially in such slack winds as we had been enjoying lately. And if all else failed, would the Royal Navy go after them if we reported a kidnapping directly to them?

There were just too many questions without answers, but at least in discussing them we were sort of *half* getting ready to meet each difficulty if and when it hit us. We both agreed it would be heaven-sent if they stayed at the Drake — especially if Milly was still in service there.

After a while I dared to ask her about Colin Pearce.

She said, "I've burned my boats there," and made it clear she did not wish to discuss it further.

"And the baby?" I asked.

"Greedy, ungrateful little thing!" she said.

So, after all that, it was another of Marian's typical skyrockets. Whizz, bang … darkness!

The first part of our plan went like clockwork. I got out of the station as quickly as I could and nabbed a hansom. Marian, whom Lady W would not recognize and whom Teresa would hardly know in those elegant clothes, lingered awhile and then joined me, cock-a-whoop. "A big, pale dame with gills and a tired little brown boy with teeth like pearls …" she began — and then her voice caught.

"And Teresa?" I asked eagerly.

She nodded and sniffed and smiled and swallowed heavily. "Yes," she whispered. Then, brighter, she added, "She hardly limps at all now."

Our cabbie, who was studiously not eavesdropping on us, said, "Is that them now?"

Marian looked back. "Yes," she said.

I risked a little peep, too, and my heart almost broke. It was Teresa, all right — and such a little lady! But, limping or not, she looked dead on her feet, poor mite, and so did the little page. It was all I could do to stop myself from leaping out and snatching her back, then and there. I only managed it by promising I would kill Lady W rather than let her succeed again.

"Do 'ee want to know where they're goin'?" our man asked. "Is that the general idea?"

We told him it was. The Devon accent always sounds strange to me — like people trying to talk Cornish and not quite succeeding. No doubt the Devonians have reciprocal feelings about us.

Lady W took a growler, as I had imagined she would.

"Bert!" our driver called out to theirs as he set off. "Where you bound off, then?"

"Drake Hôtel," Bert called back. Marian and I hugged each other in glee. "No good to me," our man said mysteriously — though no doubt the exchange had carried some meaning among the two drivers.

And thus we were spared the dangerous necessity of trailing them closely. In fact, we gave them a good fifteen minutes head start so as to be sure they were well retired for the night by the time we arrived. I asked the cabbie to go by way of Ebrington Street, to point out the Sutton Orphanage to Marian. On our way back from this detour we drove up part of Union Road, where all the ladies of the town were to be found, and I told Marian about Milly's strange fascination with the business. It started Marian off on one of her 'isn't life funny when you think of it' rambles, because she herself had once been accused of leading an immoral life, but for which she'd never have gone to Little Sinns, nor Hampstead, nor Colin Pearce's place in Lemon Street ... and thus wouldn't be here tonight!

I didn't see the logic of the final link. I mean, if my grandmother had taken us both in at Fenton Lodge, we could still both be here tonight. But when I said as much, her scatterbrains leaped immediately onto some quite different track and she asked why I thought our grandmother had, in fact, taken me in at all. And I was just too tired — and otherwise exercised — to follow her down that path. Who can possibly say why that old woman did anything at all, especially now she's no longer here to speak for herself?

Marian said I was doing my usual trick — claiming I needed her and couldn't live without her, and then getting bored with her after an hour or two and refusing to talk to her any more.

I was just about to make a real effort to be nice and follow her down whatever butterfly path she wished, when her eye was caught by an especially flashy young woman in the roadway up ahead, who had lifted her skirts right up to her knees and was parading up and down in a most defiant manner. A swelling crowd of sailors and other idlers laughed and shouted encouragement. She looked drunk, or drugged — or both. Just before we reached them, one of the sailors dashed out of the mob and, picking her up in his arms, carried her off into a dark alleyway to our left. As we swept past they were briefly silhouetted *in flagrante,* as the *crim-con* reports in the papers put it.

Marian whistled in amazement. The cabbie, feeling some comment was required, said, "You did ask to be brung this way, ma'am."

When we arrived at the Drake, Marian went in and scouted the ground. She returned swiftly and said all was well. I asked the cabbie to wait, for I had an idea we might go down to the docks and see what news we could pick up of vessels bound for France.

The hôtel manageress didn't recall me at sight and I didn't remind her. I just asked, as she showed us to our room, if Milly was still with her.

"No!" she snapped, making it plain that Milly was *out.*

When she'd gone, however, the porter who had brought up our bags cleared his throat and asked what our interest in Milly might be.

I told him I had news of a bereavement for her — a second-cousin — no one close, but the deceased's mother would be glad of a letter. If I'd hit on any other tale, he might not have told me, but bereavements, even remote ones, somehow release the brakes of moral scruple.

"She's ... er, down Union Road — if you follow, ma'am," he said.

"Ah!" My tone implied that I was not entirely surprised — which, now that he said it, I was not. "You wouldn't know where, I suppose?"

"I'm not going down there," he said at once.

"I think it's news we ought to break to her in person."

That alarmed him even more. "But you can't venture down there neither," he assured me.

I tipped him sixpence and patted his arm reassuringly, saying, "My sister and I are no strangers to rescue-mission work" — just in case he should get any ideas that we were interested in joining young Milly in her new profession! I realized then that I had never heard her surname, or, had forgotten it, perhaps. "You don't know what name she might be using these days, I suppose?" I asked him.

"Milly Scott, I should think," he replied. "Same as when she was here — she couldn't blacken it no more than what she done then!"

From which I presumed she had begun her new life even before she left her old employment. "And where might we find her?" I added.

He shrugged and shook his head. I fiddled with my purse and took out another sixpence. "It's a bow at a venture," he warned me, "but you could do worse than try the upper-circle gallery at the Palace Theatre. Someone there is bound to know her."

Worth sixpence, I thought, especially when he threw in for nothing the information that Lady W was in the room at the end of our corridor — the room my grandmother had occupied on our last visit here.

Once again it was very hard for Marian and me to turn our backs on the door to that room, knowing the dear little bundle who was, we hoped, fast asleep behind it, but we did so by superhuman effort. I remember seeing prisoners in the Helston lockup, standing at the barred windows and staring out at all that freedom. It brought home to me what a huge difference a little three-foot jump would make — if only they were able to make it! Being so close to the door to Teresa's room had the same chilling effect on Marian and me.

"Why are we going down to see this Milly Scott?" she asked as we descended to the ground floor.

"Stay here if you'd rather," I told her.

"Catch me!" She laughed. "All the king's horses wouldn't keep me away — as long as I'm with you. You didn't answer."

"I'll tell you when we're on the way," I promised.

I put all but ten sovereigns in the hôtel safe. It was quite a ritual, with sealing wax and double envelopes and signatures across all sealed flaps. I was impressed. Then we got back in the cab and I asked the fellow to take us to the Palace Theatre. "Haven't seen enough, eh?" he asked sarcastically. "Talk about slumming!"

"Now!" Marian said, rubbing her hands like a child about to be told a promised fairy tale.

"We're interested in ship movements, yes?" I said. "And who better to tell us about that at this time of night, if it's not the sailors who man them? And where's the best place to find sailors at this time of night?"

"Where there's lots of the company they've been missing for months," she said with a self-deprecating sigh. "You're so *clever,* Crissy. It sounds obvious when you explain it but I'd never have thought all that out."

"Keep your eye peeled for a Salvation Army uniform," I said. "I noticed a couple on the way here."

"Why? Are we going to clonk them on the head and steal their clothes as a disguise?"

She was teasing me, of course, but I was getting wiser to her ways by now. "Unless you can think of something more sensible," I replied.

I spotted a pair of them half way along Union Road and I told the driver to stop a mo. They were rather astonished when I asked for a couple of dozen copies of *War Cry,* but they were happy enough to take five shillings for them.

"Clever!" Marian said admiringly as I returned to the cab. "Have you thought of absolutely *everything?*"

"It just came to me when the porter was so horrified — that's why I said that about mission work. I saw a Salvation Army lady going in and out of low dives in Penzance once, and I must have remembered it."

She nudged my arm and grinned. "Sly boots! What were you doing going in and out of low dives in Penzance, eh?"

"Please, Marian," I said wearily. "It isn't the night for teasing."

"You're as fascinated by low life as …" I'm sure she was going to say, 'as I am' but she changed it to "… as you say Milly Scott was. I'll bet it was *you* dragged *her* down here that evening — go on, admit it!"

" 'Or so her *sister* says, her *married* sister says,' " I responded — quoting one of Cass Potter's bawdy songs and leaving a puzzled Marian to try to work it out.

Luckily we drew up outside the Palace just then. Again I asked the cabbie to wait.

"You do surprise me!" he said.

I tried to slip into the theatre for free by waving copies of *War Cry* and saying I only wanted to sell them, but the man at the desk said he wasn't born in Cornwall and I'd have to come up with something better than that. So there went another shilling.

And another, because Milly wasn't in the upper-circle gallery. She had *graduated* to the dress circle, as one of her erstwhile sisters informed me with a sneer. I must have looked blank for she added, "She goes with *gentlemen* down there for five shillings a time. Up here it's riff-raff for three-and-six!"

We weren't dressed for the dress circle but the Cerberus on the door *was* born in Cornwall and our copies of *War Cry* — and that other shilling — got us through.

Milly didn't recall me at first. When the penny finally dropped she was overcome by a curious mixture of embarrassment and bravado. However, when it became clear that I wasn't there to say, 'Tut-tut!' — despite the Salvation Army literature — she relaxed and became her old ebullient self.

I explained our predicament then and asked her how we could find out — both reliably and within the next hour — what ships were sailing for nearby foreign ports, or even for India itself, on the morning tide.

She said she knew just the man — a clerk who thought himself no end of a swell, but he worked in the harbourmaster's office. And he was either here or at the Judy, the other theatre, most nights. She slipped away to the bar at the end of the gallery to find out.

She returned a moment later and said, "You'll never guess what he wants in exchange!"

I was about to say I'd gladly pay the five shillings when she went on: "Is it worth a quid to you, love?"

I gave it her without a word, because, of course, it was information without price.

"Only I *never* give it away," she said fiercely as she returned to the bar.

It was another ten minutes before she left the dress circle, clinging to his arm and looking up into his eyes as if he were the most fascinating young man she'd ever met. He was darkly handsome, too, which somehow made me uneasy. I thought it odd that I could contemplate what they were about to do much more readily if he were old and bald and fat. I don't know why.

When he went to collect his hat and cane, Milly sidled over to us and said, "Follow us up the street — it's only a hundred yards — you'll see where I go indoors. I'm on the first floor. Give us a minute or two and then come on up. I'll leave the door unlocked. You can sit in the parlour. I won't be more than twenty minutes, but you shouldn't hang about the street. Not Union Road, anyway!"

"But he'll see us when he comes out," I said, because she seemed very eager for us *not* to be seen with her now.

She laughed. "It won't matter *then!*"

She didn't know I'd kept the cab, and by the time she saw us getting into it, she couldn't come back to say in that case not to bother. Besides, Marian was bursting with curiosity to see the inside of a fallen woman's boudoir, and I … well, yes, I too was mildly curious, I must allow.

It was a depressingly commonplace little parlour — and so, I suspected, was the little transaction taking place in the next room. There was nothing personal here, no prints that I felt only Milly could have chosen — just *The Broken Pitcher* by Greuze and *Les Baigneuses* by Ingres — rather obvious examples of restrained, sentimental, but high-class wantonness. The only book was called *This Age of Marvels* and was all about the electric telegraph, the Great Eastern, the Britannia Bridge, and — a small concession to the French — the daguerreotype.

I was so engrossed in this last chapter that I did not see Marian go tiptoe over to the bedroom door and place her ear to one of its panels. I only noticed her when she flashed me a giggly grin and placed her hands in an attitude of prayer — except that they were horizontal — and began moving the top one up and down on the other — presumably in time with whatever sounds she was hearing from inside.

I had to tiptoe over there myself and pull her away. If the keep on that door had been the least bit yielding, she could have gone bursting into the room and spoiled everything.

She resumed her seat very grumpily but, fortunately, we had not long to wait. We had hardly sat down before we heard the sound of two people reaching the peak of their ecstasy. We humans really are far closer to animals than we like to admit. Then silence. Then ordinary conversation and laughter. Then the door opened and the young man came out, rather red in the face.

I thought he'd go even redder when he saw us sitting there but, to my horror, he assumed we were fallen women, too, and made a tasteless suggestion — at which Marian, I'm sorry to say, giggled.

However, Milly sent him on his way — rather indelicately — and then she collapsed on the sofa beside Marian and said, "What a day!"

I thought it would seem rather brusque if I just asked her for the information and left, so I tried to make a little conversation. "Aren't men fools!" I began.

She looked at me in surprise. "Why?"

"To pay you a pound in order to do something that gives you that much pleasure anyway."

She stared at me in consternation and then burst into laughter. "I've never taken pleasure with *them* in my life," she said in disgust. "Vermin, they are. Lower than vermin. The very idea!"

"Not even when they're handsome like that?" Marian asked.

"Especially not with them!" She stared from one to the other of us as if across an unbridgeable divide. "Listen, darlings — you don't want to know what it's really like. You may think you do, but you don't — believe me! Here's your information — just take it and escape!" She thrust a piece of paper into my hand. "You're in luck," she added. "There's only one out for France tomorrow morning."

I saw its name, *Wagram,* on the paper.

"She's a shallow-draught steamer so she can cast off anytime. He thinks it'll be about eleven, though. And the other boat, the *Fair Maid,* she's Liverpool-registered, a coastal lugger, really, with no passenger accommodation — bound for some godforsaken little port in Spain. Not very likely. Well, dears!" She rose and held her arms apart like a wilting scarecrow to usher us out. "Got to earn a living, somehow! If I sit too long, I shan't want to get up again, and that'd never do, would it!"

Her tone was so deliberately jolly that, as we started back down the stair I turned and said to her, "Are you happy now, Milly? Happier than at the Drake?"

"Happy?" she echoed and laughed again. "Of course I'm happy, love. You heard me upstairs, didn't you? Happy as the night is long — that's me!"

I f I learned anything during the few hectic hours we spent in Plymouth, it is that there's a world of difference between preparing for something and planning for it. Preparing is essential, planning is a waste of time. How could anyone have planned what actually happened? How, for instance, could I have planned to obey a call of nature at precisely the same moment as Nimrod, the little Indian page-boy? (He has a proper Indian name but 'Nimrod' was the nearest the Wilkinsons could manage, and he was proud of it when they told him it means Mighty Hunter.)

The closet was at the other end of the passage from Lady W's room. We were only three or four days short of a full moon so there was light enough for him to recognize me by — but not enough for me to see whether those huge whites of his eyes represented fear, happiness, or just plain surprise.

"You know me?" I whispered.

"Yes, Memsahib."

"Don't call me that. Call me Crissy. You know why I'm here?"

"Yes, Mm... Crissy." He giggled at the shocking familiarity.

"Will you tell Lady Wilkinson you've seen me?"

"No!" He was so emphatic I had to put a finger to his lips to shush him. Then he did an extraordinary thing — he grabbed my hand and kissed it. "Me, too," he said. "Please?"

"What d'you mean?"

"Take me, too. I protect Miss Teresa."

"How old are you? What's your name?"

"Nimrod — Mighty Hunter." He swelled with pride.

I realized then that the gleam in his eyes, which was still there, was neither fear nor surprise. "You're not surprised to see me," I said.

"I see you at the railway station."

"Have you said anything about it to Teresa?"

"No. I wait."

I smiled. "You are a very thoughtful young boy, Nimrod. May I ask how old you are?"

"Twelve."

I corrected myself. "You are a very thoughtful young *man*. Will you wait for me out here? I won't be two minutes."

I took him back to our room and woke Marian. Between us we concocted a plan whereby he would go back to Lady W's room, wake Teresa as quietly as possible, grab an armful of her clothes, and bring her back to us.

"If the Memsahib wakes up ..." I began.

He moved quick as lightning and suddenly there was a knife in his hand — the wavy kind they call a kris.

Marian and I just managed to stifle a scream. "Where did you get that?" she asked.

He stretched his leg out from under his nightshirt and there was a scabbard strapped around his calf, but neither of us had seen him snatch it from there.

"You'd better leave that with us," I told him. "Or we'll all end up on the gallows. If she wakes up, just start shouting 'Fire!' Act a little hysterical. Shake her. Pull her out of bed."

He giggled at the picture.

"We'll be dressed, ready. We'll all get away in the pandemonium."

"And I come with you?"

"Of course. Give me the knife, now." I was starting to shake from the delayed shock.

I'm sure I've never dressed and packed as quickly as I did then — and I *know* Marian never has, either. "No corsets!" I said to her. "Your favourite fashion!"

She waved a weary hand as people do when you remind them of long-dead fads and enthusiasms.

"The money!" she said in horror. "All our money's in the safe."

I grinned and showed it to her, all back in my wallet. She had gone to sleep at once last night but some sixth sense — or just plain avarice — had made me uneasy at being parted from all those lovely spondulicks, so near and yet so far. So I had gone downstairs again and, fortunately, caught the manageress just as she was locking up for the night. I gave Marian half of it again, for safety's sake, as before.

And then we sat and waited what seemed three lifetimes, though by the clock it was no more than a few minutes. I put a fiver in an envelope and wrote on it, 'For the room.' The room was actually only fifteen shillings a night but I thought the extra would stifle any complaint about the damage we might have to do in breaking *out* of the place. It would be just too absurd to get away with a kidnapping but be chased for a broken window!

When we heard some creaking out in the passage our hearts almost jumped out of our bodies, for it sounded like the knell of doom and we felt sure the entire hôtel would wake at it. I tiptoed to the door and pulled it slowly open but I didn't dare show my face in case it made Teresa forget herself and come running.

Marian rose and joined me. I could hear my own heart thumping away, of course — like a piledriver behind my ears — but, in that nerve-shattering silence, I realized I could also hear *hers,* galloping beat-for-beat with mine.

And then there she was — our little darling sister! A plump bundle, half-asleep still, yawning and simultaneously gasping with astonishment that what Nimrod had whispered to her was actually true and not some Indian fairy tale. Marian and I stooped as one and swept her up into our arms, pressing her to us, me whispering, "Ssh!" into her right ear and Marian whispering the same into her left, and both of us trying not to give way to tears because the need for action was so urgent now. We did not entirely succeed but it was enough to be proud of.

The two youngsters dressed in even quicker time than Marian and I had managed and soon we were creeping downstairs, placing our feet at the very edges of the treads to avoid the creaks and groans, and tiptoeing to the front door.

It was open!

And yet I could swear I'd seen the manageress herself lock and bolt it.

The curious thing about 'a piece of luck' like that is that you don't think it's a piece of luck at the time. My suspicions were immediately aroused. This was surely a trap! Never mind the absurdity of it — for how could anyone know in advance that Nimrod and I were going to meet out there in the corridor? — someone had clearly plotted all our moves and was just playing cat-and-mouse with us.

It had one good effect, though — it killed any impulse we might have felt to pick up our skirts and run the moment we were out in the street. We crept along the front of the building, hugging the wall, cursing the near-full moon, darting past the darkened windows, and did not even walk fast until we were well away.

It was three in the morning — almost two hours before sunrise — and Plymouth was like a ghost town. The gaslamps danced for no one's benefit. Shrubs poured their scent into the gardens and only the moths noticed. Cats slunk away at our approach. Somewhere, streets away, a dog barked and was answered by others from even farther off. But around us a brittle silence reigned. Teresa kept catching my eye and grinning. Such an adventure! In between she did the same with Marian.

At the corner of the street, opposite the Orphan Asylum, stood a growler! Again I did not believe this 'luck.' I pressed the other three back against a nearby garden wall and went forward as quietly as I could, ready to turn and run on an instant.

It must have been standing there some time, for both the horse and driver were asleep — the horse on his feet but with head bowed low in his nosebag, looking like something carved in anthracite. They both woke up, though, when a gravelly cockney voice said from inside the vehicle, "You took your time, gel. I almost gave you up."

Cass Potter!

I was in such a state of nerves by now that I could do nothing but stand there, rooted to the spot, stricken with lockjaw and rigor mortis and catalepsy and everything else that was going around that part of Plymouth at that hour of night. I just stared in disbelief — until he showed his grinning monkey-face at the carriage window. "Going my way by any chance?" he asked, enjoying the moment hugely.

I went forward to him then but I still had to touch his cheek before I could really, actually, finally believe it. "How long have you been there?" I asked him.

He opened the door and stepped out, stretching himself. "Too long," he replied. "Like this government." He stooped and picked up Teresa, holding her almost at arm's length above him. "So this is the little lady all the fuss is about, eh? Are you happy now, my darling? Glad to be back with your two big sisters?"

Teresa nodded shyly, biting her lip, wary of his effusiveness.

"Love her!" he said and put her in the carriage. "Come on, then! No time to waste. We've got more kidnapping to do before sun-up."

Marian and I looked at each other, then at him.

"You're surely not leaving Gerald and Arthur behind?" he asked.

"No," I said. "But ... kidnapping! I mean, we can't just go in and take them — can we?" A wild hope was springing up within me that he would now lay out a plan to do just that.

He merely chuckled and bent to pick up Nimrod, who was much too heavy to hold at arm's length. Instead he hefted him on his hip. "Taking little Blackie, too, are we?"

"His name's not Blackie, it's Nimrod," I said. "And he's tonight's real hero — he got Teresa out of their room without waking Lady W."

"And," Marian said, "he's got a knife sharp enough to cut the head off your body without you even feeling it."

We hadn't actually given it back to him yet, but I wasn't going to spoil her story.

Cass looked at the boy askance. "I shall have to start treating you with respect, Nimrod — shan't I?"

"Yes, Sahib!" Nimrod grinned at him.

"In you go then — welcome aboard!" He swung the boy in through the door and turned to us. "Now ladies, may I ... er ... *assist* you into my ekki-paahge?" He held out a gallànt hand — which I pushed aside, assuring him we were perfectly capable of mounting two steps unaided, but he might 'assist' our bags if he would be so kind.

He let me go in unmolested but he managed to get a hand on Marian — 'where it wouldn't blind her,' as the saying goes — as she followed me. "Miss Marian Moore, I presume?" he said.

"You presume too much, Mister Potter," she replied, laughing as she peeled his hand away.

The driver, who had meanwhile warmed himself liberally from a hipflask and removed the nag's nosebag, leaned over and said, "The Sutton's next is it, Mister?"

"The Sutton," Cass replied as he finally joined us and we set off.

At last it was safe to indulge in a small orgy of hugs and kisses. Marian and I took turns to smother Teresa, who now broke down and wept for joy — as did we all. Nimrod held back at first but then, when it was Marian's turn for Teresa, he flung his arms about me and took his share of the general goodwill and joy. In fact I, who had earlier imagined he could be no more than ten, now began to wonder if he had told the truth in saying he was only twelve — for his idea of kissing was extremely grown-up. He giggled like a boy, though, so I didn't make a fuss.

When euphoria had run its course I left Teresa in Marian's lap and turned at last to Cass. We were by then in Union Road again, eerily deserted at last, and about half way to our next port of call.

"The first train back to Penzance is at four-forty from North Road," I said to him.

"That's right," he replied.

"Well, shouldn't Marian take these two and be sure of catching it — just in case we're delayed? That'll be after sunrise. Lady W will surely be awake by then. There's bound to be a hue and cry."

He just chuckled.

"In fact, I wonder if she shouldn't take them and go east rather than west? To throw them off the scent. Take the six o'clock to Bristol and find passage on a boat from there back to Penzance or Falmouth ...?"

His chuckling continued until, at length, he reached forward and tapped me on the knee, saying, "Peace, be still! Her ladyship isn't going to wake up until nine or ten o'clock."

"How d'you know?"

He fumbled in his pocket and produced a little bottle which he passed to me. It was too dark for me to read the label but the cork was half in, half out, and I could feel by shaking it that it was empty. "Ten at the earliest," he repeated. "We'll all be back in Penzance, gobbling our breakfasts by then."

After all the melodrama and skulduggery of Teresa's rescue — what with knives and sleeping potions and tiptoeing around the place at dead of night — the recovery of Gerald and Arthur proved refreshingly dull and mundane. At the Sutton they rose with the sun and slept with it, too, to save tapers and candles. So the Rogerses were already stirring, if not quite up, when we arrived.

I thought Cass would go in and use his genius-charm to get the boys away, but he said I'd done all right so far and I should try to think of him as the man who followed the elephants with a bucket and shovel — adding, "Nothing personal, of course!"

At first the master and his wife, the matron, absolutely refused to countenance the idea of releasing my brothers into the care of their married sister. Even when I showed them my marriage lines, which I had brought with me in case there had been an argument over Teresa, they remained obdurate.

In that case, I wondered, why were they still bothering to talk to me? They showed no inclination to end our discussion. It was almost as if they were waiting for me to say, 'Abracadabra' or 'Open sesame!' or some such magic incantation.

Talk about naïve! I suppose I was just too tired for the penny to drop at once. I went off all around the houses, trying to discover the proper, official way to arrange things — which was, of course, through the Camborne — Redruth Union and the Sutton guardians ... and Arthur would be shaving by the time I'd finished.

Then Mr Rogers, growing impatient at my obtuseness, said, as if he were just tossing out a bit of general information, "The only way a boy here can be released on the spot is to an apprentice-master. Or," he added helpfully, "an apprentice-mistress, of course."

I knew nothing about all that, except what I'd read in *Oliver Twist* — that bit where Mr Bumble puts up a notice offering five pounds to anyone who'll take Oliver on as an apprentice, and Mr Sowerby, the undertaker, comes along and Bumble says, "Liberal terms, Mister Sowerby! Liberal terms!"

But I didn't imagine that an evil which Dickens had campaigned against so hard in that novel could still be rampant. And then the penny dropped! The Rogerses weren't suggesting they should *give* me five pounds a head to take my brothers away on the spot. But if a certain amount of crisp paper — or 'the oil of angels,' as it is sometimes called — were to change hands in the *other* direction ...

"Apprentice them to *me,* then," I said brightly.

If they had both been wearing extra-tight corsets and the strings had suddenly snapped, they could not have relaxed more swiftly.

"Now *that,*" Rogers said, "is a horse of a different colour!"

"They'd be worth a lot to you, Mrs Collett," his wife added helpfully. "More than to anyone else, I shouldn't wonder?"

It was on the tip of my tongue to offer the Oliver-Twist sum of a fiver each but then I thought why use my fingers when there was a sledge-hammer near by? "Twenty-five pounds apiece," I said.

They almost fell out of their chairs in disbelief. I realized that five pounds apiece would have done the trick after all!

"Liberal terms, Mister Rogers," I said, keeping a straight face. "Liberal terms!"

"Indeed, Mrs Collett," he hastened to reply. He was now in terror I might change my mind. "Indeed they are!"

And fifteen minutes later, fifty pounds the poorer in pocket but richer in all other ways, I was ushering a still slightly bewildered pair of boys out to be reunited with their sisters in the carriage.

Boys! I don't think I'll ever really understand them, though I'd quite like half a dozen of my own. They were delighted to be back with us — at least they said they were — but they were far more interested in Nimrod, especially when Teresa, in a slightly desperate bid for their attention, told them about his amazing knife. And when Marian and I tried to hug them, they just giggled and squirmed. Arthur put his arm around me when I got them a cup of tea and a stale bun at the early-morning café by the station, and Gerald sheepishly did the same with Marian. It was cupboard-love, to be sure, but we had to content ourselves with that.

And at four-forty precisely, with the risen sun behind us, and not only risen but twenty-five minutes up into a clear blue sky, we steamed out of North Road with one of the most rousing cheers that station has ever heard, I'm sure.

An hour later we were toiling on foot up the hill to Tywardreath — for, of course, the logic that had prevented us from leaving Plymouth without bringing the two younger boys also prevented us from passing through St Austell without doing the same for the eldest.

The young men of the farm school were all out in the fields by then, working up a sweat for a plunge in the sea, which they enjoyed before breakfast every morning in summer (and which also saved on baths and laundry). Even I barely recognized Tom. The others failed completely. With only a month to go until he turned fourteen, he had shot up a good four inches over the past year. And talk about muscle! His bare torso was almost a triangle from his huge, broad shoulders down to a tiny, wasplike waist. In fact, if he had not been our brother, both Marian and I would have flirted with him quite shamelessly. And even as it was, she flirted with him quite shame-*fully*, there in the farm lane.

He had seen us coming up the hill, recognized me, guessed the rest. Then he came bounding across the field toward us like a young percheron, specks of clay flying behind him.

I had forgotten Mr Vingoe's promise to do what he could to discover Teresa's whereabouts for me. So much had happened since then. But Vingoe himself clearly hadn't.

"I see you managed to find your little sister without any help from me, Miss Moore," he said apologetically.

I showed him my wedding ring and told him I was Mrs Collett now.

However, the fact that he remembered his unkept promise was a sign of some guilt, however small. Working on that, it took little persuasion for him to let Tom have the rest of the week off and come away with us.

In all England there was no happier band of brothers and sisters than ours as we caught the nine-four from St Austell, which would terminate at Penzance at eleven o'clock. How we chattered! Teresa most of all, for she had led the most interesting life of the six of us during the past fifteen months. But Arthur and Gerald vied to describe the fleet, dressed overall, as they had seen it in Plymouth Sound at last month's review. And Tom, not to be outdone, told us all the wonders of the Royal Cornwall Show, which the whole school at Tywardreath had been taken to see — including a Guernsey cow that had yielded eighteen hundred gallons last lactation. When he started on the veterinary wonders, though — especially a new, bloodless, gelding pliers — Marian interrupted, and made such a romance of life in Hampstead that even Cass blushed at the whoppers she told.

From Truro onward it was my turn. I pointed out the line to Falmouth, and the distant prospect of Little Sinns, and a brief glimpse of Nancekuke House — or the grove of trees surrounding it — and the general area where Aunt Eph and Uncle Jim lived and so was able (when Teresa's interruptions permitted) to tell them something of my own rather humdrum year.

Between Camborne and Gwinear Road, though, it occurred to me that, now we were all together again for the first time since our mother's death, there was one small ceremony we could not, in all conscience, avoid. When I mentioned it to Cass, he said he quite understood and he'd take Nimrod on with him to Penzance. But Nimrod protested that he was Missy Teresa's servant and could not leave her side. He'd taken quite a liking to Cass by then — well, all of them had — but still he did not want to part from us. I was slightly annoyed at his insistence, because I wanted it to be only family, but he pleaded so earnestly that I hadn't the purist heart to refuse him.

However, we were a much more solemn little group on the little chug-chug branch-line train, which terminated in Helston at half-past eleven. It was rather a beautiful time, actually. Quite spontaneously we began recalling our happiest memories of our mother. Marian recalled a day when she had locked our father out of the house — not because he was drunk or anything, just for a lark. She was very giddy, like Marian, in many ways. Then she took us children upstairs — her, me, and Tom, because she was still carrying Gerald then — and started bathing us by the nursery fire. And our father shinned up a launder pipe and scared the wits out of us by leaping in through the window.

And I had forgotten it until that day, though I can see him now, leaping in with a grin like a bear!

And Tom remembered one day when she took us to Harvest Fair to go on the swing boats, and we passed the stall that sold dead people's false teeth for twopence a set and she bought us a set each and we had gone round trying to frighten people and couldn't understand why they had simply thought it disgusting.

Gerald said what about that time when the Loe threatened to flood St John's and the men had gone out to cut a channel in Loe Bar, to drain it out to sea, and she'd taken us to watch. And when it was over we'd all gathered wave-polished flints in the channel the water had left. And we pretended they were gemstones and made royal cloaks for ourselves out of old flour sacks and studded them with the pebbles.

Arthur reminded us of all the tricks she'd taught us with cats-cradles and he and Gerald then showed us some of them. Nimrod was fascinated for he'd never seen anything like it.

Teresa tried to remember some especially happy time but, alas, for most of her young life, our father was the drunken despot of our household and our mother was but a fading shadow of what she once had been. In the end, all the little giglet said was, "I remember her hair. She had lovely hair."

After that, there seemed nothing more to be said.

We walked down over the fields at the back end of the town, through Gwealfolds and Belmont, to the churchyard. On the way Marian said, "You didn't tell us your memory of our mother, Crissy. Tell us now, before we get there."

"Yes," Tom added, "and we don't want to hear about ghostly voices telling you to go to her old people in Falmouth!"

The younger ones sniggered.

"You may mock," I said. "And anyway it wasn't *ghostly* voices, it was *her* voice in my own head. And if she hadn't told me to go there, none of you would be here today. They'd have split us up and we'd never have seen each other again until we were all reunited in heaven."

"Anyway, tell us, tell us!" Teresa begged.

"I'll tell you a memory of *hers*," I said. "Not my memory of her but one of hers about herself. I'd forgotten she told it me until after she was dead and I went to work at Fenton Lodge. I was standing at the back window one day, looking down into the stable yard, and I suddenly realized I was standing where she used to stand — I mean, *exactly* where she used to stand, when she first fell in love with a dashing young groom called Barry Moore. She used to stand there for hours, she said, either hoping for a glimpse of him or feasting her eyes on the most handsome, the most adorable, the most wonderful young fellow in all the world. And I remembered what she said to me when she told me all this —

which was not long before she died — and you know what our father was like *then!*"

They all nodded solemnly but no one spoke.

" 'He's still there, Crissy,' she said to me. 'Don't just think of him the way *you* see him, because I can see that other darling man, too. He's still *there!*' That's what she said, and that's what I remember now. And that's why I'm glad they're buried side by side in here."

In silence we went through the churchyard gate and in silence walked down over the uneven sward to the incongruously grand memorial our grandmother had erected to our parents' memory. We ranged ourselves haphazardly along the kerbstones at the foot of the grave and I gave them time to read the inscription, including the recarved one I had commissioned, giving our father's proper dates: 16th January 1848 to 5th March 1890. Then I called out, "Look!"

They all turned and stared at me.

"No," I said, "not you. Them! I'm telling them to look — because we've done it! Against all odds, we've won! We're all here together again — with them! A *family* again!"

I bent to pick up Teresa and give her yet another special hug, but Tom beat me to it. The two younger boys slipped their arms round Marian. I was about to put an arm each around Tom and Marian, so that we would be one living tableau, when I caught sight of poor little Nimrod hanging back a little, two or three grave-plots away. I smiled and opened my arms to him instead, and he came flying into them, almost bowling me over backwards upon our parents' grave.

"Me, family?" he said.

I kissed his cheek — dodging one of his grown-up kisses in return. "You, family," I assured him.

No one cried!

Perhaps we were beyond it or perhaps we were just too happy at the way everything had all turned out.

Then Teresa wriggled and said, "I'm starving!" And then we all agreed we were starving, too, so we trooped up to The Angel in one raucous band, and there we took a private room and gorged on beefsteak-and-kidney pie and summer pudding and lemonade. And Marian had a glass of claret while the rest of us looked on in disapproval because we knew, better than most, where That Sort Of Thing can lead.

We were just in time to catch Wearne's bus to Penzance, which left at half-past two. At three o'clock it rolled through Porthleven, and it was a sore temptation to get out and flaunt ourselves before Harry Angell and his wife. I managed to curb their eagerness however by promising to hire the grandest phæton in the livery at Stable Hobba, outside Penzance, and come back in *real* style. At the corner of the harbour, where the road to Penzance turns inland again, I caught sight of Phyllis Hoad, the constable's wife, and called out to her.

She looked at us, looked again, and at last believed what she was seeing. Then she came running after us, shouting, "Oh, my gidge! Oh my dear life! Just wait till I tell Hoad 'bout this!"

"See you again!" I called back to her as the bus gathered pace.

Up the hill to Breage we laboured, and then onward to the summit at Ashton, where we changed horses and set off again at a spanking pace, down to Praa, up again to Perranuthnoe, down again to Marazion, and then more or less level into Penzance. And all the way I could see my brothers' and sisters' eyes filling with the light of joyous reminiscence as half-remembered scenes and long-forgotten occasions came back to them. And every yard of the way said *Home!*

We alighted from the bus at Chyandour Cliff and started to walk the last hundred yards up the hill to home. There was no hope of keeping our approach a secret from Jim and the others for we are not one of those quiet, well-behaved, orderly families. Indeed, Jim must have heard us as soon as we started up the hill. We were still twenty paces off when he came running out into the road.

"Oh, so you've come at last!" he cried sarcastically. "Where *have* you been, you silly people? Susan's had twins this morning. You've gone and missed *all* the excitement!"

And that is where I thought my tale would end. I had written it all down, as frankly as I knew how — sometimes on the very day it happened, sometimes a week or more afterwards — so that my family could catch up, so to speak, with that part of my life which they had not shared. I hoped, by my example, to encourage them to do something of the same. And perhaps they will, too. It's early days yet.

But something happened just this morning which has made me reopen this little memoir for one final note. 'This morning,' by the way, is Wednesday the fifth of August, 1891 — just to keep the record straight. Exactly a month after that exciting night in Plymouth.

We have moved into Devoran, the house next door to Mulberry — as I always promised myself we would. We have renamed it 'The Moorings,' of course. And though we have eaten and slept here for some time, we are still in the process of moving this and that across.

The Trevartons and their two little treasures, twin boys called William and John (who are *just* beginning to grow on me), now live in isolated splendour — give or take the odd studio, waiting room, and darkroom.

Cass has decided it's time he settled down and is to become our chief (that is, only) salesman, with a view to partnership if he likes it enough. Mark and Jim already like him enough to agree at once, but he's wise to be a little cautious, I think.

However, all of that is just ordinary life going on. And on and on and on — the way it always has. If I reopened these pages to record such matters, I'd be at it every month. No, the thing that has spurred me to do so now is a little bit of the leftover past — something I don't know whether to bring out into the open or just let lie and quietly fade back into memory.

I was over in Mulberry this morning, moving a few more things over to The Moorings. I was packing some of Jim's clothes, folding them neatly into a big basket for a couple of porters we had hired to pass over the garden wall, and, as a matter of routine, I was clearing out his pockets. Well, what should I come across but a *Plymouth* bus ticket punched with the date 7—7 — the seventh of July — the very day Marian and I went there to rescue Teresa! And it was also the day — or the evening, rather — when he told me he'd go to Falmouth to head Lady W off if she tried to flee abroad that way.

So what am I to make of it? It can't be from a year ago. I'm not as good a housekeeper as people imagine but I'm not as lazy and careless as that! Did Jim come to Plymouth with Cass that evening — Cass was travelling Third, which is why we failed to notice him though he was on the same train as Marian and me. Had Jim been there, too?

It would be the easiest thing in the world to ask him, of course. But I get a glorious, warm-bath feeling running right through me just to think that he *might* have been there, ready to step in and save the day if I had made a mess of it — but ready also not even to admit he was there when (thanks to Cass) Marian and I carried it off. Something would be spoiled if that doubt was replaced by certainty.

Within a family, some things are better left unsaid, and even better left unknown — especially, I sometimes think, *in my family.*